Look to the West

Volume I
Diverge and Conquer

Tom Anderson

SEA LION PRESS

First published by Sea Lion Press, 2016
Copyright © 2016 Tom Anderson
All rights reserved.
ISBN: 1533404305
ISBN-13: 978-1533404305

Acknowledgements

Many people have contributed towards making this book a reality. As always I must thank Tom Black of Sea Lion Press for getting the publication project off the ground, Jack Tindale for another excellent cover, and my family for their support. Over several years I have also enjoyed the support of countless forum beta readers, some of whom have contributed with graphics and occasionally text (Nick Bieter, "SimonBP", "Nugax", "Umbric Man", and more). A special thanks must go out to Alex Richards, who has worked tirelessly to produce four excellent new maps to accompany this volume. My readers have also contributed constructive criticism over the years and some of them show a particular talent for pointing out when I have killed off the same General or Pope twice, sometimes in the same chapter ("Grand Prince Paul II", "Finn", "Admiral Matt" to name a few). And far too many readers to list have offered praise and encouragement to keep me going over the years, when far less ambitious projects might have been abandoned. Some of them have cameos in the timeline. You know who you are.

Many writers of histories and historical fiction gave me inspiration for particular parts of the timeline: Frank McLynn, Gunther Rothenburg, Bernard Cornwell, William Hague, Patrick O'Brian, Jeremy Black to name a few. A final thanks must go to to both Tony Jones (of *Monarchy World, Cliveless World*, etc.) and Jared Kavanagh (of *Decades of Darkness* and *Lands of Red and Gold*), who both proved that an alternate history work of this scale was possible and set the gold standard of both quality and formatting.

Foreword

I first began working on *Look to the West* in 2006 and it finally makes its published debut one decade on. In that time it has grown from an idle attempt to produce an alternate history setting to a work that has now stretched to five volumes—of which is this only the first—and has a word count exceeding Leo Tolstoy's *War and Peace*. "The tale grew in the telling" to quote J.R.R. Tolkien (some years after commenting that he expected his planned sequel to *The Hobbit*, *The Lord of the Rings*, to be *shorter* than it...)

You may wish to know what inspired this project. At my school, the history curriculum rather oddly skipped almost directly from the English Civil War to the Victorian age and never discussed the intervening two centuries from around 1666 to 1866 or so. It was only years later that I learned that this was arguably the most influential age in history for building the world we see around us today. This may seem a strange claim considering the impact of later events such as the World Wars and the advent of electronics. Nonetheless, this period saw 'the Second Hundred Years' War', over a century of on-again off-again conflict between Britain and France which ultimately determined the fact that the modern world speaks English rather than French; an ideological cold war between enlightened absolutism and parliamentary government quite as bitter as the twentieth-century one between communism and capitalism; breakthroughs in science and technology as diverse as the steam engine, the battery and the rifle; and a cultural flowering of art, music and literature that continues to enrich our world to this day. This was the age in which Europe began to see itself as not merely a collection of inadequate successor states to the Roman Empire but as the centre of global trade and civilisation—for better and for worse. It was a time both of the horrors of the slave trade and of enlightened writers who fought against it, a time of fortunes made in manufacturing which upset the established social order and of revolutions that bathed the streets in blood. It is not a time one would think advisable to pass over in any historical treatment attempting to explain the world in which we live today.

It was also, of course, the age in which the American Revolution gave birth to a new power, causing shockwaves that continue to reverberate around the glove to this day. Not only was the United States of America a republic in an age mostly of kingdoms, it was the first power to be predominantly European descended yet based outside Europe; arguably the first major nation not to see its language as defining its identity (speaking English without being English); and the first country to attempt to govern such a huge but then-sparsely populated area by the means of constitutional federalism. This event was so significant that it has naturally been an area of much counterfactual speculation in history, if perhaps less well known to the general public than 'the Nazis win'. What if the Revolution failed? What if it never happened in the first place?

The American Revolution arouses such strong feelings that it is tricky to address such a scenario, however, with American depictions usually portraying any modern-day British America as 'oppressed' and just yearning to break free at any moment (for example, in *Sliders*); meanwhile the precise opposite is shown in Turtledove and Dreyfuss' *The Two Georges*, which presents a British America that it not only positively utopian in many ways but also incongruously using modern British terms like lorry for truck, as though such differences in terminology did not abound in our own world's later British colonies. Others have tackled the problem over the years with variations such as Sobel's *For Want of a Nail*, describing a world including both a continuing British America and a breakaway United States founded by defeated revolutionaries.

My own personal view is that by the time the American Revolutionary War broke out, the situation was already fundamentally unsalvageable. Britain could have won militarily, but it is doubtful whether the colonies could ever have been meaningfully governable again without a cost in military commitments holding the rebels down that Parliament would have been reluctant to countenance. While nothing is impossible, I therefore decided that it was more interesting to explore a world where the Revolution had been averted before it began. I see the major cause of the Revolution as being that the American Colonies had simply become used to being left alone and managing their own affairs for years, and it was when Westminster tried to take more of a direct hand in governance there from the end of the Seven Years' War that the resentment began. Specific policies, the so-called Intolerable Acts, were certainly unpopular—but it was more the principle that Westminster was interfering at all. Yet it is absurd to posit a world where Westminster is simply not allowed to govern colonial America—then it might as well be independent in the first place. Therefore, any movement bringing Britain and America closer together must begin in the colonies. And I began to think about a certain prince, neglected by history, who lived in this time before his untimely death by a cricket ball...

Look to the West begins with American affairs, but it does not end there. The world is a complex place and I have tried not to neglect any corner of it as the tale has grown. The eighteenth century was a melting pot of ideas, many of which could have developed any number of different ways in This Timeline (TTL) to Our Timeline (OTL). I trust that you will find this work not only to be an entertaining work of fiction, but also one that both informs you about peculiar and improbable corners of world history and one which makes you think about how things could have gone differently.

"As it's only Fred who was alive and is dead, why, there's no more to be said." Or is there?

Dr Tom Anderson
Doncaster, United Kingdom
January 2016

Here lies Fred,
Who was alive and is dead.
If it had been his father,
I would much rather;
If it had been his brother,
Still better than another;
If it had been his sister,
No one would have missed her;
If it had been the whole generation,
So much the better for the nation.
But as it's only Fred,
Who was alive and is dead,
Why there's no more to be said!

– Epigram of Prince Frederick Lewis of Wales (1707-1751),
OTL

Prologue: Across the Multiverse

18/04/2019. Temporary headquarters of TimeLine L Preliminary Exploration Team, location classified. Captain Christopher G. Nuttall, seconded from British SAS, commanding officer. Addressed to Director Stephen Rogers of the Thande Institute for Crosstime Exploration, Cambridge, United Kingdom.

Director Rogers:

My team has completed the preliminary one-month survey of the alternate Earth that the Institute has designated 'TimeLine L'. We are, of course, aware that this report will be the primary basis for the International Oversight Committee for Crosstime Exploration's decision on whether TimeLine L is worthy of further expeditions being dispatched. As of now, sir, I must confess that my own opinions are still divided on this issue.

Perhaps, as I and my team set down what we have learned, we will make our own decisions, just as you will. The information we have obtained from TimeLine L is primarily in the form of extracts taken from history books, and we have tried to gain these from several different sources to avoid making mistakes based on national bias. As you will see, sir, this has not always been easy. Wherever possible, we have annotated the extracts with the titles of the books in question, their authors, and the dates published. We have also used those basic information gathering techniques as recommended by the Institute, attempting to casually question the contemporary populace in a manner that does not provoke undue suspicion.

Identifying the point at which another history diverged from our own—the so-called Point of Divergence—is often not so easy as the training films would have us believe. Even chaos theory cannot be relied upon: individuals may be born after the PoD with a different combination of genes due to effects of random chance, but they are nonetheless born to the same parents as their 'counterparts' from our timeline. Therefore, their names, temperaments and even destinies may still seem hauntingly familiar to that of the history we are familiar with. Or they may have subtle, unexpected differences. It is only another generation after the PoD, when those people grow up to marry different spouses and have children, that unambiguous and radical differences are typically seen.

A note on terminology. Our own world's history, also sometimes called "TimeLine A", shall in this report be contracted to 'Our TimeLine' or OTL for short, as is the Institute policy. Comparisons to OTL are inevitable as we study TimeLine L (henceforth referred to as This TimeLine, TTL) but it is my opinion that they should not be taken too far.

Let me use an example from the history of my own country. A Scot from a timeline where Scotland remained independent might well look upon the United Kingdom of OTL as being an English Empire in Scotland. But an Englishman from a history without a United Kingdom might not consider OTL to be an improvement, because change always goes both ways and many of the things he considers emblematic of the England he knows will also be gone. This 'grass is always greener' paradigm is all over TTL, as you will soon see.

Enough beating about the bush. The jury is still out on the PoD, but Dr Lombardi has the strongest theory so far.

It all begins in the year 1727, at an event that Dr Pylos insists on referring to as the Coronation of the Hun, when the axis of history began to spin the world towards a different fate altogether...

Chapter #1: The Coronation of the Hun

From: "Nasty, Brutish, and Short—the Reign of King George II of the Kingdom of Great Britain" by Peter Daniels (1985)—

On the eleventh day of June in the Year of Our Lord 1727, a man of sixty-seven years suffered a stroke and died. And, ninety-nine times out of a hundred, the world would not have marked such an event. But when the man was the King of Great Britain, the King of Ireland and the Elector of Hanover, things were different indeed.

King George I's reign had been important both for symbolic and practical reasons. The accession of a foreign monarch by virtue of his Protestantism and by the will of Parliament had firmly established the anti-absolutist values of the Glorious Revolution of 1688 and the ensuing British Constitution, as well as the triumph of the Whig Party over their Tory rivals. Furthermore, George's reign—with his limited command of English and disinterest in British affairs—had allowed Parliament to grow in supremacy. The South Sea Bubble economic scandal of 1720 had resulted in the resignation of most of the Cabinet, allowing the untainted Sir Robert Walpole to assume more power than any individual Minister had ever had before. Later generations would call him the first true Prime Minister, though in his lifetime it remained a disparaging term. In 1727, Walpole sought to continue a policy of steering the Kingdom of Great Britain through peaceful economic prosperity, avoiding entanglement in European wars. But now this policy was called into question.

Three days after the death of King George I, the Accession Council convened to proclaim George's only son, also named George, as King George II. Many had anticipated this event with some degree of dread. As had become well known among the

English, the Hanoverians had a tradition of violent disagreements between father and son. While he had been Prince of Wales, the younger George had done everything he could to undermine the rule and policies of his father. It was no secret that he wished to replace the popular and skilful Walpole with Sir Spencer Compton, a nonentity. This would be George's revenge for the treachery of Walpole, who had formerly been part of the Prince of Wales' faction before abandoning to joint a government loyal to the King.

In the event, and probably better for the sake of England, George was persuaded by his wife, Queen Caroline, that Walpole must stay. This guaranteed the continuing rise of the Whig Party, to the extent that they would dominate Parliament for the foreseeable future. The old divisions between Whig and Tory were largely abandoned, as the Tories became a useless rump unable to win power: from now on, the true contest would merely be between different factions of the Whigs.

It was no secret that George II disliked England, with its meddling politicans interfering with the divine right of Kings, and like his father always considered himself a German first. This was an advantage in some ways for Walpole, as it let him draw more of the King's powers to himself and Parliament, but also alarmed him: Walpole intended to continue to keep the Kingdom out of damaging European wars, and George felt quite the opposite.

All of these issues would eventually return throughout George's short reign, but none of them would ever eclipse the one which plagued him all his life, for his best efforts. The curse of the Hanoverians reared its head once more: just as George had detested his father, so his son, Prince Frederick Lewis, detested him.

For all the accusations that have been levelled at him in latter ages, and as he has been darkened by the shadows of some of his more illustrious descendants, George II was not stupid. Reckless, yes, and careless of privilege, but not stupid. He did not want to repeat the mistakes of history. He would not let his son gather political support against him and be the same thorn in his side that he had been to his own father. So George II had an idea.

Prince Frederick would go, not back to Hanover (which in George's mind, if perhaps not Frederick's, would be a blessing) but to the godforsaken ends of the Earth.

To England's Colonies...

His wife, Queen Caroline, dissuaded him of this reckless course also, and in the end George went to be coronated in Westminster Abbey, on October 4th 1727, with his son Frederick by his side.[1]

The coronation would, perhaps, have been well remembered in any case, for the noted Hanoverian composer Handel had been brought in to write numerous new pieces of music. Perhaps the best known is 'Zadok the Priest', which remains performed at many coronations throughout the English-speaking world today. But the music of Handel, and indeed all else, would be overshadowed by the events that meant this date would live in infamy.

A confusion over arrangements meant that Handel's superb pieces were nonetheless played in the wrong order, which led to many of the churchmen becoming panicked and flustered. It was, in fact, a particularly loud and unexpected note in Handel's "Grand Instrumental Procession", coupled with perhaps a rumple in the blue carpet, which led to the King, on the way to his throne beside the Queen, to stumble and fall before the great dignitaries there to pay homage to him.[2]

A deathly silence descended, and indeed it might have ended there, for the assembled Lords Spiritual and Temporal knew better than to incur any royal wrath at this injuncture. The incident, they thought, as the king picked himself up with as much dignity as possible, would never be mentioned again.

The young Prince Frederick, twenty years old and retaining much of his teenage precociousness to go with the traditional Hanoverian inter-generational hatred, did not show so such restraint. He let out a single 'Ha!' of delighted laughter, and with

---

[1] Everything up to now is as in Our TimeLine (OTL); George really did have such a plan, but nothing came of it in the history we know and love. But what if things had been just *slightly* different...?

[2] This is the Point Of Divergence (POD) from our history. A minor thing in the grand scheme of things. 'For want of a nail...'

it, changed the world forever.

The embarrassed George was furious. Seldom had an Archbishop of Canterbury had to place a crown on a head so reddened with suppressed fury. An apocryphal rumour suggested that the sacramental oil sizzled on George's forehead when Archbishop Wake anointed him. Immediately after the coronation was complete, the new King told the Queen that he had elected to return to his original plan. Caroline reluctantly agreed, almost equally upset at the Prince's behaviour.

The paperwork caused by the incident was immense, as Walpole complained in his memoirs. Prince Frederick was, as the eldest son of the King of England, rightfully the Duke of Cornwall, a title that could not be attainted. George did everything else he could, though. Frederick was banished to the American Colonies, to Virginia, indeed to the newly founded town that had been named for him: Fredericksburg. A title was invented for him as a sinecure, that of Lord Deputy of the Colonies. It is strange to reflect that what was at the time the work of a few arbitrary strokes of a clerk's pen before he departed to the pub for lunch would one day shake the foundations of the globe...

King George, meanwhile, calmly foisted the title of Prince of Wales on his younger son William Augustus, already the Duke of Cumberland at the age of six. No secret was made of the fact that William was now George's heir, and upon George's death would be coronated William IV. Some kingdoms might have blanched at such a move, but Britain had the precedent of the Glorious Revolution and the Georgian succession, casually throwing out countless closer claimants in order to get a King she liked. Few suspected that George's plan would face much opposition.

And as for Frederick? As the disconsolate Duke stood on the prow of HMS *Lancaster* and turned away from the islands receding into the distance behind him...Frederick looked to the west.

Frederick looked to the future.

Chapter 2: A Town Fit For A King

From: "Yankee Fred: The Story of the First Emperor of North America", by Professor Randolph Thorpe (1979)—

The Royal Colony of Virginia already possessed a rich and long history by colonial standards, and despite the long and often treacherous sea voyage from England, had remained surprisingly closely affected by home affairs since its inception (as a Company) in 1607. When Prince Frederick finally arrived there in 1728, having been delayed by just one of those long sea voyages as well as a series of futile attempts to change his father's mind before being forced to depart, he found the colony a mass of contradictions. On the one hand, the Virginians were proud of their land's status as the "Old Dominion", the land where the faithful Royalist supporters of the Stuarts had fled during Oliver Cromwell's tyranny, and this had been recognised by Charles II upon the Restoration. On the other, Virginia's equally proud tradition of limited self-rule, through the House of Burgesses, owed a lot to Cromwell's dispatching of more independent-minded governors during his brief rule.

It was the latter, based in the new colonial capital of Williamsburg,[3] that was the greatest surprise to Frederick. His father, as is well known, cared little for England and less for her colonies, and had left their governance to his ministers. What

---

[3] Williamsburg was the capital of Virginia between 1699 and 1776 in OTL, upon which it was abandoned for Richmond as British and Loyalist forces controlled much of the coastline and its cities—for a similar reason many other American colonies moved their capitals inland, and it is likely this is the origin of the American tradition of the capital of a state rarely being its largest and most important city. In OTL, Williamsburg is today a preserved/reconstructed colonial town and living museum.

would his reaction have been, the Prince must have thought, had he known that England's "perfidious parliament" had spawned another, across thousands of miles of ocean? Perhaps the thought of his father's expression cheered the Prince. Certainly, he seemed to recover fairly quickly from his initial gloom at being exiled.

Williamsburg was the first city in Britain's North American colonies, having received a royal charter in 1722. A far more pleasant place than the older, mosquito-infested Jamestown, the House of Burgesses had decamped there with some relief several years before. The House was subordinated to the Governor's Council, an upper house loosely analogous to the British House of Lords, and ultimately to the Royal Governor himself. The powers of the Governor over the House had been increased by James I and Charles I, but then decreased again by Cromwell's envoys. As was then common in the North American colonies, the appointed Governor (then George Hamilton, the first Earl of Orkney) never visited his constituents, any more than the Chancellor of the Duchy of Lancaster was actually expected to be a Lancastrian anymore. The British political establishment saw no contradiction in this. Therefore, the real power lay in the hands of the Royal Lieutenant Governor, then known simply as William Gooch.

Gooch had taken over from his predecessor, Robert "King" Carter, only a year before, but was already making a name for himself with his energetic policies of promoting trade and encouraging westward settlement. Like his absentee superior Lord Orkney, Gooch was a veteran of the First War of Supremacy, but he would eventually go on to fight in the Second.[4] People were already beginning to call him a worthy successor to the now

---

[4] The terms used in TTL to refer to what we would call the War of the Spanish Succession/Queen Anne's war, and the War of the Austrian Succession/War of Jenkins' Ear/King George's War, respectively. Note that although the War of the Spanish Succession predates the POD, naming wars is usually a matter of after-the-fact *historiography* and often varies between countries and times: in OTL, the English-speaking world used the term 'Great War' to describe the French Revolutionary and Napleonic Wars in the nineteenth century, before it was then displaced for that title by World War I.

retired Alexander Spotswood, unlike those lacklustre Lieutenant Governors that had filled the post since.

Williamsburg would have been the obvious place for the exiled Prince to hold his court. After all, it was the home of the House of Burgesses and the capital of the Colony, and it was over these people—together with all the others in the Colonies—that Frederick was supposed to exercise his highly theoretical powers as the first Lord Deputy of the Colonies. It is surprising, therefore, that he instead elected to purchase an estate in the much newer town of Fredericksburg with the pension funds that his father had grudgingly allowed him.

To say Fredericksburg was new is an understatement. It had, in fact, only just been founded when the Prince groggily stepped off the deck of HMS *Lancaster* at Williamsburg harbour (to be met by a puzzled crowd of local dignitaries). As noted above, travel between Britain and the Colonies was fraught with difficulties at the best of times and could take months, with the result that the stories of Frederick's disgrace had reached Virginia only in confused and incomplete forms. This was not helped by the fact that even the best-informed travellers from England had set off at a time when it still seemed as though King George might change his mind. Reports of the exile and attainder from the position of heir apparent were dismissed as wild exaggerations. A possible future King of Great Britain and King of Ireland, here in Virginia? Surely not!

So it was that the new town on the Rappahannock River, though founded months after George's coronation and Frederick's disgrace, was still named for him as its fathers confidently believed he was still the Prince of Wales. It has borne that name ever since, for better and for worse, through good times and ill. Frederick built himself a modest house with his pension on the new land. Of course, his choice of such humble accommodations may well have been influenced by his father's stinginess and the fact that he needed permanent lodgings as soon as possible, and it is true that the house was much extended and grandified in later years. Nonetheless it endeared him, perhaps accidentally, to the locals. The Virginians had grumbled for years about the overly extragavant Governor's House in Williamsburg, and Spotswood's own home in Germanna was nicknamed the 'Enchanted Castle'. They took great delight in discovering that a potential heir to the throne was living in humbler circumstances, making the self-righteous Governors seem stuffy by comparison. Frederick's house would eventually be nicknamed 'Little St James', an epithet given by his supporters, who believed that he would one day reside in the real St James' Palace in London as King of Great Britain and Ireland.[5]

Frederick had other advantages. Though he had left Hanover at the age of seven, and did not identify with the German homeland as his father and grandfather did, German was nonetheless his birth tongue and he remained fluent in it. This was remarked upon by the colonists in general, who jokingly referred to him as the 'Third Wave of Germanna'—a reference to the fact that, not far from Fredericksburg, two groups of German religious refugees from the Rhineland and Palatinate had been allowed to settle in 1714 and 1717. The Germans were tolerated by the Virginians providing that they did not leave the boundaries of Spotsylvania County, named after Spotswood who had masterminded their settlement. But most English-speaking Virginians had little to do with their neighbours to the north, often seeing them merely as a useful barrier between them and the still-persistent Indian raids. Everyone remembered the massacre at the frontier town of Henricus many years before, and there was some resentment among the Germans.

Frederick changed all that. He was one of the few notables in Virginia who spoke both English and German fluently, and though the Germanna settlers were mostly poor peasants (even by Virginian standards), he had quietly resolved to do anything

---

[5] St James' Palace was the primary royal residence of the British monarch at this point in history, which is preserved in the fact that the British royal court is still referred to as the Court of St. James' in OTL. (In OTL the building itself was damaged by fire in 1809 and this, together with it being too cramped for an increasingly large Royal Family, meant that they spent more time at Buckingham Palace—Queen Victoria finally making the move official in 1837; her descendants have remained there ever since).

he had to, fall in with any folk he must, to gain a shot at regaining his rightful place. So it was that it was Frederick, and a growing circle of admirers that included many of Virginia's notables, who began to break down the barriers between the Germanna and the English.

And he had no shortage of admirers. Many colonial towns were named for royals, but few could boast that said royals actually lives there. Little St James was always busy with visitors, and Frederick's servants—mostly hired Germanna, eager to escape their often wretched agrarian Spotsylvanian existence—were called upon to produce many parties and banquets of state. For that was what they truly were. Frederick was holding court, more like a king of old, and it is in this only, perhaps, that taints of Hanoverian absolutist thinking crept in. Nonetheless, the Prince was perfectly aware that his position was tenuous and he could not afford to assume too many of his royal prerogatives. More by luck than judgement, he had begun to win the hearts of the people of Virginia, both common and noble. It opened a tiny window of hope that he could build a power base strong enough that he would one day to return to England in his rightful position as Prince of Wales, and then King.

Frederick's supporters thought that there was a better than even chance of him achieving this aim—if Prince William died without issue, then the succession would automatically revert to Frederick, for George II had no other male heirs and was not expected to produce any more. So it was that ingratiating oneself with a man who was currently living humbly and wanting of favours, but might one day be one of the most powerful and wealthy men in the world, seemed a very attractive proposition.

Before Frederick's exile, a number of North American colonials had been knighted and given titles by the monarchy, but most of them immediately decamped to England in order to exercise their new influence in the Court of St James. The Colonies lacked a true native aristocracy, save perhaps Virginia with its old Company holdovers and its Planters. Just as Lord Orkney never visited Virginia, many Governors treated their occupation as merely another courtesy title to go alongside their knighthoods and marquessates and earldoms. Once more, Frederick changed that.

London was still the place where a North American title-holder could exert the most influence and gather the most wealth, but many realised that they could gain favour with Frederick for future rewards with far less effort than they could gain favour with George for current ones—and facing far less competition. It was almost like a financial investment, literally so in some cases. Frederick was soon involved with Lieutenant Governor Gooch, and with the members of the House of Burgesses—including the by now venerable James Blair, the clergyman who had founded Williamsburg's William and Mary College, the second-oldest university in America.[6] Frederick pledged, perhaps glibly at the time, to patronise the College if he ever became King. It was considered a wonder that the Prince could get on both with Blair and with the retired Spotswood (through his work with the Germanna), as in the prime of their careers they had been bitter political enemies.

Of course, Frederick did not lead a charmed life. He came close to losing everything he had built up more than once. Perhaps his greatest problem was also his greatest advantage: the fact that all but the titled Virginians were unaccustomed to meeting royalty. After he had made a few moves that were popular with the commoners, they began to see him as a paragon of idealised kingly virtue, a story come to life, a man worth following. But this image came very close to being shattered in 1732, when he had at last began to feel that he was making progress towards building a strong position for himself.

As well as mutual paternal dislike, Frederick inherited another of the Hanoverians' infamous habits—womanising. He was not such a terrible offender as his father, but nonetheless enjoyed a mistress or two. The problem was that the Virginian commoners, unlike their English contemporaries, had never experienced such royal depredations and, to put it mildly, did not recognise his *droit*

---

[6] Unlike many colonial-era universities, the College of William and Mary still retains its old name in the modern USA, and it is indeed the second oldest American university after Harvard.

de seigneur.

Things came to a head with a scandal in 1732 when Frederick was allegedly caught in bed with one Mildred Gregory by none other than Gooch himself, after the Governor had unwisely dashed into Little St James' with an urgent political matter on which he thought Frederick's patronage would be of help. Here Frederick's at first accidental and then carefully cultivated informal style worked against him: his servants did not think to announce Gooch.

The Governor himself was persuaded to keep the matter secret—after all, Frederick's ruination would also destroy all the investments in pseudo-royal favour made by Gooch and his fellow politicians—but it nonetheless leaked out. "They who have ears, let them hear," the Prince is thought to have ruefully quoted from Scripture (in German). Mostly the story was dismissed as an attempt to blacken the Prince's name by those who retained a strong allegiance to George and thus Prince William. Only a few knew the truth of it. Unfortunately for Frederick, one of those few who found out was Augustine Washington, Mildred's brother. At the age of thirty-five, ten years older than Frederick, she had already outlived two husbands and had three daughters from her second marriage. As Gooch is reported to have remarked, "God only knows what he saw in her." Certainly, Frederick at first intended her to be merely another mistress. Augustine had other ideas.

The Washingtons were not rich, nor were they especially poor. Augustine owned a plantation at Popes Creek and was looking to expand. Royal patronage, even by the disgraced prince, would be useful, and he was persuaded by his new second wife Mary to cool down from his initial anger. Blackmail would be a more useful tool than simple revenge. However, he was still determined to see his little sister right, for Mildred had quietly informed him that she was pregnant.

With misgivings, Frederick agreed to meet the Washingtons at Little St James' and was informed of Augustine's demands. Augustine was the son of Lawrence Washington, a former burgess and sheriff who had come to Virginia after having his family's lands confiscated by Oliver Cromwell and failing to have them returned by the restored King Charles II. A great injustice, did the Prince not agree? The Prince did. Something that should surely be rectified, or at least compensated, if a more...reasonable Person should occupy the throne of England? Why, naturally.

It was the second part of Augustine's demands that appalled Frederick. It would be wrong to call the Washingtons simple, but they were stubborn colonial folk with a strong sense of Anglican morality. Frederick would have to do something about Mildred's pregnancy. Compensate her, leave her to raise an illegitimate royal son as so many Englishwomen had on his funds? No. Frederick was relieved, for despite his invieglement with the Virginian notables, his own funds remained limited. This relief did not last. No, he would not compensate Mildred. He would *marry* her.

Nothing the Prince could do could make Augustine budge. As well as fulfilling his sense of the correct restribution, he knew that this would be the ultimate way of forcing Frederick not to go back on any promises if he became King. Kings couldn't divorce, not without a host of scandals and potentially even wars. Frederick protested that Mildred was an inappropriate wife, a widow with children from a previous marriage. That would not have been a problem if she had been titled, of course. Frederick had expected to be married off to a German princess, as George was already planning to do to Prince William. Well, Augustine pointed out, if he kept his promises, Mildred—and the rest of the family—*would* be titled. Problem solved.

Frederick was forced to bow to his logic, knowing that the Washingtons had connections and could easily ensure that the truth of the scandal reached prominent ears. That would finish him, unless he wanted to flee and try to start again somewhere else. He rejected that. After all, he had expected a loveless marriage anyway, and did it truly matter if it was to a colonist commoner rather than a German princess? The latter would ultimately have been for political advantage, and so would this. All that mattered was that he would one day wear the crown, and who cared who sat beside him?

It is thus rather surprising that Frederick apparently did grow to possess some feelings for Mildred as the years went on, and in March 1733 she bore him a son, Prince George Augustine of Cornwall (called George FitzFrederick, in the illegitimate style, by the Williamite detractors who did not recognise the morganatic marriage). Nothing could have been calculated to make Frederick decide his marriage was, on balance, a good thing. It is thought that his choice of George for the name may even have been a deliberate swipe at his father's condemnation. On the other hand, some historians have argued that it has a rather different derivation. For, a year before the young prince's birth, Augustine Washington too had chosen to bestow the name upon his newborn son...

Chapter 3: A Cornish Nasty for German George

From: "A Political History of the Anglo-Saxon and Celtic Peoples",
Volume III (various authors), 1971—

There had never been any question of Prince Frederick simply lying down and accepting his exile. It is debatable whether even George II truly thought that merely sending his elder son several thousand miles away would stop him interfering in British politics. Certainly, Frederick's *spiritual* absence from the British political scene lasted only a few years. Though his body might remain in Fredericksburg, his political will, through his supporters, continued to stretch all the way across the Atlantic to Westminster.

In this, Frederick had several advantages. Firstly, his acquaintance with Lieutenant Governor Gooch meant that he was well aware of the latter's new policies towards Virginia's vitally important tobacco crop, long before the London-based investors. The Tobacco Inspection Act of 1730 required Virginian tobacco planters to bring their crops to public warehouses, where it was inspected and stored. This reduced fraud and improved the quality of the overall crop, and within a few years, 'Virginian tobacco' was renowned throughout Europe as a superior blend, coming into great demand.

Frederick had gambled on Gooch's scheme succeeding, and had invested a large part of his still quite meagre funds in the tobacco business. In this he was later helped by his connections with the Washingtons, and some believe that he first encountered Mildred Washington Lewis Gregory due to his inquiries into the important tobacco planting families. Frederick borrowed money from the richer burgesses he had become acquainted with, as well.

He was able to pay it back within a few years, as his investments more than matured thanks to Gooch's policies. Frederick is thus almost unique in British history as a royal who made his own fortune. This too may arguably have endeared him to the colonists' frontier spirit.

By March 1734, Frederick felt his position—both financial and political—was now secure enough to return to his major mission in life: regaining his rightful heirship. It had been more than six years since his exile began, and he was determined that his father would not rest on his laurels for much longer. Firstly, he would need more influence, and he found a good excuse to go searching for it. He had been given the invented post of Lord Deputy of the Colonies when he had been exiled, a post which technically gave him theoretical powers over all the Colonial Governors. Frederick had never used this power, though, recognising that he would not be taken seriously and it would damage him politically if he gave an order to a Governor only to be politely brushed off. He had instead relied upon suggestion and persuasion to inviegle himself with Gooch and the House of Burgesses. But Virginia, though one of the most populous and important of the British colonies in North America, was not the only one. It was time for Frederick to spread his wings.

In March, Mildred was pregnant again (with a daughter, the future Queen of Denmark, also named Mildred) and Frederick took the opportunity to leave her behind in Fredericksburg with young George and most of the servants. He embarked on what he called his 'American Grand Tour', spending slightly more than a year travelling around the Colonies and trying to make at least one appearance in each colonial capital. Stories of him had, of course, already spread throughout North America, and some of the dignitaries of the other Colonies had already come to visit him in Fredericksburg. These men included Lieutenant Governor Patrick Gordon of Pennsylvania, who was not merely a political supporter but had become a genuine friend to Frederick on his rare visits. Regardless of the reasons the far-flung colonial dignitaries had aligned themselves with Frederick, they agreed to find the Prince accommodations for his stay in return for his patronage.

Much has been written about Frederick's tour, not least by Frederick himself, though he restricted himself to short pamphlets. Most of these at first seemed innocuous, with titles such as *Travels in the Woods of Penn's Land (With Accurate Illustrations)* or *American Ingenuity, OR, Instructive Innovations of Our Colonial Cousins*. However, they always had a hidden meaning that attacked King George's policies and person. It has been suggested by many historians that Frederick's works were mostly ghost-written by North American writers, given that he had no history of authorship before his exile and the fact that the writings are almost universally pro-colonial. Frederick did develop a general liking for the land of his exile, but not the love of a native that the pamphlets profess.

It is instructive to contrast Frederick's two longest stays in his tour, in Pennsylvania (May—June 1734) and New York (July—August). In the first province, he was already friendly with the Lieutenant Governor, Patrick Gordon, and appeared at events in Philadelphia supporting him. It was in Pennsylvania that Frederick was first introduced to the Indians as anything more than a vague threat on the horizon—Pennsylvania was looking to expand at the expense of its Lenape Indian neighbours, potentially ruining the relatively good relationship the colonists had had with them in previous years. Frederick also met with representatives of Pennsylvania's German population, much larger than that of Virginia, and once again forged new connections with them due to his own ancestry.

New York was different in almost every way. The Governor was William Cosby, a new and oppressive ruler who disliked Frederick and was fiercely loyal to George II.[7] Thus it was that in New York, it was with Cosby's political enemies, the so-called Morrisite Party, that Frederick met, so enjoyed popularity with the people of New York. When Cosby had arrived two years earlier, he had demanded half the pay of the acting governor, Rip Van Dam, and

---

[7] Unlike many of the other colonies, New York's colonial Governor did actually travel there and fulfil his duties rather than handing it off to a Lieutenant Governor.

had then fired Chief Justice Lewis Morris when he had declared the demand illegal. Frederick promised the Morrisites that he would have Cosby thrown out and replaced with one of their own, perhaps Morris himself, if he ever became King. So it was that he achieved more influence with those peers who identified with the Morrisite cause.

It was also whilst in New York that Frederick became involved with John Peter Zenger, a German immigrant who printed the Morrisites' political paper, the *New York Weekly Journal.* Cosby had attempted to close the paper down several times, as it attacked his policies—his failure to defend against Iroquois raids, his suspected rigging of elections, and his permission for French ships to illegally dock in New York harbour. Frederick had made it a policy of his own to use his German language skills to become friendly with important or powerful German-speakers in the Colonies. Zenger was not rich, but his role as mouthpiece of the Morrisites meant that he could be very useful to Frederick indeed. The Prince later embarrassed Cosby on his way back to Virginia in winter 1734—the Governor had attempted to have the Journal burned and Zenger arrested for sedition. Frederick used his influence to have the case thrown out[8] and a frustrated Cosby died just one year later. However, this was not the end of New York's problems, as his successor George Clarke was also a member of the 'Court' or Tory Party and continued to interfere with Van Dam's policies.

Though Frederick had glimpsed Indians in Pennsylvania, he actually met them face to face for the first time in New York. The exiled Prince took tea with a delegation from the Iroquois Confederacy (or Six Nations as it was then known) along with several senior Morrisites. Although the Morrisites had attacked Cosby for failing to respond effectively to Iroquois raids, they also acknowledged that at least some of those raids had been the result of Cosby's clumsy attempts to appropriate lawful Iroquois land.

Frederick's chief contribution to the meeting was when he

---

[8] Thus, unlike OTL, there is no extended 'Zenger Case'. One consequence of that is that there is no precedent set on the matter of libel law, i.e. that a statement is not libellous if it is true, as was the case in OTL.

noticed that the Indians seemed to dislike being referred to as Iroquois. Via an interpreter, he asked them about this. The Iroquois replied that the name was, in fact, an insulting epithet given to them by their Huron enemies, and meant Black Snakes. Few Englishmen had ever bothered to learn their true name, which was Haudenosaunee.

Frederick, to everyone's surprise, seemed delighted at this and even clapped his hands when the words were translated for him. He explained to the puzzled Iroquois about his own people, the Deutsche, who had resigned themselves to being referred to as 'Germans' by the English, who in turn gave the name Dutch inaccurately to the Nederlanders.[9] "Perhaps it is too late to undo that injustice," the Prince commented, "but I, for one, shall call you by your true name." In fact, Frederick's German accent meant that he had trouble pronouncing the word Haudenosaunee, but the Indians seemed to appreciate him making the effort. Their meeting would have much more important consequences in years to come, but Frederick is believed to have started a fashion for referring to the Iroquois as Haudenosaunee or just Hauden, anglicised to Howden, for short. The choice of which name to use would take on political overtones a century later.

The rest of Frederick's tours in North America are less important to history, although it is said that he came away with the firm belief that there was no significant difference between any of the feuding New England states. The story of his meeting the young Benjamin Franklin in Boston is almost certainly apocryphal, although the two of them did work together in later years. Frederick more or less managed to fulfil his own target of speaking in every Colonial capital.

Frederick also visited the territory of Nova Scotia, recently (re-) conquered by British and colonial forces during the First War of Supremacy and still occupied by French Acadian settlers who had been forced to swear an oath to the crown, but with the proviso that they would not be called upon to fight either French or Indian

---

[9] This rather anachronistic statement—many Englishmen of the time referred to all Germans as Dutch—has persuaded some historians in TTL that this story may be a fabrication.

forces. It is not known precisely what first gave Frederick a dislike of the Acadians—possibly simply that their oath made them loyal to George—but one of his pamphlets, entitled *The Horse of Troy*, stated that "What advantage do we gain by possessing a land whose men have no obligation to serve the same duties as our true colonists? Nova Scotia is a British colony in the same sense that the wearer of our Crown is the King of France." This was a jab at the British King's absurd holdover claim from the Hundred Years' War to be the King of France, which George II had not abolished.[10] The Prince's low opinion of the Acadians' loyalty would also have serious repercussions in years to come.

Frederick returned home to Virginia in early 1735, having missed the birth of his daughter Mildred Dorothea. He remained there for six months, continuing to build up his position, and then toured the southern colonies in a much shorter trip. In the Carolinas, an intrigued Frederick also met with representatives of the Cherokee Indians, who had just concluded a treaty in which they agreed to be a protectorate of George II and to halt their raids on Carolina.[11] Frederick promised to respect this treaty if he ever became King. He also met with Governor Robert Johnson and Carolina's own band of German settlers. Like the Virginians, the Carolinians saw these Calvinist refugees as a useful first line of defence against Indian raids, but unlike the Virginians there were serious accusations of the religious differences with the Anglican Carolinians causing potential civil problems. It was a complex situation that Frederick realised could one day go up like a powder keg. Ultimately though it would be other issues that would dominate the future of Carolina, and indeed it is perhaps

---

[10] And which in OTL would not be abolished until the turn of the nineteenth century.

[11] At this time, North Carolina had just been split off as a separate colony and the remainder was referred to simply as 'Carolina', as it was the part most Europeans thought of when they heard the name. It eventually became known as South Carolina. Carolina had been a royal colony for some years at this point, but North Carolina had only just finished its period of proprietory (Company) rule and still retained huge swathes of land owned privately by one of the Company's Lords Proprietors—the Granville District.

the need for common cause between Anglicans and Calvinists in the face of these that eventually led to the region becoming known for its religious toleration in general.

Frederick also briefly visited the newly created Proprietory Colony of Georgia, only just split off from Carolina. Georgia also had its Indian problems, in this case with the Creeks. It is thought that Frederick took a dislike to Georgia simply because it was named for his father, although his later actions towards the colony were certainly much more a direct response to events and not due to his holding a grudge.

The exiled Prince returned to Virginia in late 1735 and remained in Fredericksburg until the Second War of Supremacy. However, he was already being informed of the havoc his work was wreaking for his father back in England.

The political system in Frederick's time was quite different to that today. By the British Constitution of 1688—a document that was referred to almost as holy writ by all politicians—each county elected two MPs, albeit with a very limited franchise dependent on property ownership. The Universities of Oxford and Cambridge also elected two MPs each, with any matriculated Members of the University being able to vote. In addition to this, though, there were plenty of so-called 'rotten boroughs', meaning tiny villages which could elect more MPs than great towns. The most infamous example was Old Sarum, under the control of the Pitt family, which in the recent 1728 election had elected the candidate Colonel Harrison by a four to one margin—literally four votes to one. It would continue to return two MPs until the nineteenth century, at one point ceasing to have any voters at all. At the same time, no new parliamentary seats had been created since the 1670s due to procedural deadlock, which eventually simply became 'the way things were' and some MPs claimed the current situation was perfect, even as growing industrial towns chafed without representation.

There was also the House of Lords, of course, which was to some extent under the influence of the King as he was responsible for creating peerages. However, he also had to cope with the existing Lords created by his father or inherited from their predecessors, whose titles could only be attainted in extraordinary circumstances.

Political parties meant little then. The old labels of Whig and Tory were still in use, but the official Tory party was a shattered rump at this point after supporting the Jacobite Rebellion of 1715. Governments were not formed of exclusively Whigs or Tories, but generally of Whigs and perhaps one or two Tories *who happened to support the King*. The opposition was made up of the majority of the Tories and plenty of rebel Whigs. Also, precisely how the labels Tory and Whig were applied was often a matter of opinion. This situation did not significantly change until the nineteenth century, although additional party labels were often used to describe particular factions within the Whigs.

These more informal factional groupings and coalitions fulfilled the roles of true parties. The loyalist Whigs of Robert Walpole continued to dominate the Commons, although their majority was reduced in the 1734 General Election after Walpole's attempt to introduce an unpopular customs and excise tax. A far more serious threat to Walpole and George II materialised soon after. Walpole had many enemies in Parliament, including William Pulteney and the young, up-and-coming MPs William Pitt and George Grenville. Previously they had not worked together as a united opposition, but Prince Frederick's influence from across the waves began to consolidate them into a single movement which he called the Patriot Boys.[12] As their name suggested, one of the Patriot Boys' tactics was attacking Walpole's policy of avoiding wars in the interests of trade. Though European wars were indeed unpopular, and Walpole had been praised for preventing George II intervening in the War of the Polish Succession (1733), Frederick knew that colonial interests would be served by them.

As well as North American-born and economically influenced peers and MPs—of which there were a few—Frederick had the advantage of being Duke of Cornwall. Cornwall was an oddity, possessing many historical anachronisms as a result of the 1688 Constitution. It elected no fewer than 22 MPs, largely due to

---

[12] This group existed in OTL but was a purely British phenomenon as Frederick was still in Britain.

Elizabeth I packing the House with her supporters a century and a half before. This was only slightly fewer than the whole of Scotland, and more than any other English county despite being one of the smallest and least populous. Crucially, most of these constituencies were under the direct control of the Duke of Cornwall—either directly through patronage or indirectly through his authority over the Stannary Parliament, a sort of early trade union for the tin miners who formed the primary basis of Cornwall's economy. Frederick also controlled some seats in Wales that still saw him, not William, as their rightful Prince, and he had achieved some level of support from Scottish peers such as Lord Orkney (the nominal Governor of Virginia) and the Earl of Bute. It was this coalition that led to one of Walpole's loyalists, the Earl of Godolphin, sourly labelling the Patriot Boys as "A band of Scotch, Welch, Dutchmen and Colonials who think they can rule England." Godolphin's peerage was Cornish in origin, he had served as High Steward of the Duchy in the past, and he appeared nervous about the level of popular support that the exilic Prince was gathering in the county.

Indeed, Frederick clawed back a surprising level of support in general, but the Patriot Boys (led by the rebel Whig Pulteney) never came close to unseating Walpole's Government. Nonetheless, they caused headaches for his father and ensured that the people of England could not forget their absentee Prince.

Frederick's plan was going as well as could be expected, but everyone's plans were thrown out when an unthinkable event happened: Walpole supported a war.

And it was a war that began in America...

Chapter 4: The "Yes, but we've changed our minds now" War

"European wars do not have to have causes or explanations. It is the rare European peaces which must be explained and annotated to show why they came about."

- Philip Bulkeley, 1840

From: "A Guide to the Second War of Supremacy" by Dr James Foster (1950)—

Robert Walpole had made a career of keeping Britain out of damaging wars, but both that policy and, latterly, his career were coming to an end. Lord Cobham is known to have remarked that Walpole was 'destroyed by the two Fredericks', an apt observation. The exiled Prince Frederick's Patriot Boys had been assailing Walpole's Whigs for years, but what sent him on the final path to ruin were the whims of another Frederick. Frederick II, King in Prussia.[13]

The legal cause for the war had its roots in events of decades earlier. After the First War of Supremacy, Spain had come under a Bourbon dynasty and the Austrian Hapsburg empire had benefited from sweeping up several former Spanish possessions. These included the formerly Spanish and now Austrian Netherlands,[14] greatly desired by France. More importantly, Charles VI, the Holy Roman Emperor and Archduke of Austria, had no male heirs.

---

[13] Between 1701 and 1772 in OTL, the Prince-Electors of Brandenburg were allowed to call themselves "King *in* Prussia" by the Holy Roman Emperors, but it only after the successes of the Silesian Wars and the First Partition of Poland did they feel strong enough to proclaim themselves "King *of* Prussia". In TTL, things will end up a little differently...

[14] OTL modern Belgium, more or less.

He possessed only a daughter, Maria Theresa. On his death, she would become Queen of Hungary and Bohemia, Archduchess of Austria, and Duchess of Parma, Piacenza, and Guastalla. The elective position of Holy Roman Emperor was separated from the Hapsburgs for the first time in centuries and awarded to her husband, Francis I the Duke of Lorraine.

Charles VI had been well aware that this would cause complications, and so he had made all the great powers agree to his Pragmatic Sanction of 1713, recognising Maria Theresa's inheritance. Unfortunately, Charles did not perhaps take enough lessons from history. The First War of Supremacy had technically been unnecessary, as the fate of Spain's royal succession had already been agreed some years earlier, but that had failed to stop the European powers fighting over it anyway. The Second War was much the same. As soon as Charles died in 1740, Maria Theresa ascended her thrones and most of the great powers decided that they had collectively had their fingers crossed behind their backs. More to the point, Frederick II of Prussia pointed out that he had never been consulted on the Sanction in the first place, and suited actions to words by invading Austrian Silesia. France and Bavaria also decided to rescind their recognition of Maria Theresa's claim. By the attitudes of the time, it was thought that a mere woman would soon crumble beneath the pressure and the vast Hapsburg empire would be the allies' to dismember. The end result of this confident assertion is the reason why Maria Theresa is today something of a Cytherean[15] icon.

Great Britain might never have got involved if the war had occurred in isolation: Walpole had already managed to dissuade George II from entering the War of the Polish Succession some years before. However, Britain was already engaged in a war from 1739 that eventually blended into the wider European war. This was originally called the War of Jenkins' Ear, and stemmed from the fact that, according to the 1729 Treaty of Seville, Britain was forbidden from trading with the Spanish colonies in America. The Spaniards were allowed by the Treaty to board and search British vessels in Spanish waters in case of such trade violations,

---

[15] TTL term for feminist, approximately.

but in 1731 a British captain, Robert Jenkins, claimed that a brutish Spanish officer had cut off his ear while performing the inspection on his brig *Rebecca*. The rumour became reality when Jenkins exhibited his preserved and pickled ear to the House of Commons in 1738, and not even Walpole could restrain the outrage of the House. To much cheering, he finally gave in and declared war on Spain.

Britain's naval task force was commanded by Admiral Edward Vernon, known to his men as 'Old Grog'. Vernon's men and troops were often drawn from the Colonies, and included Lawrence Washington, Augustine Washington's eldest son by his first wife, as his Captain of Marines on his flagship. Vernon himself, though persuaded of Prince Frederick's qualities by Washington, remained personally loyal to George II.

Vernon's first victory was in the first year of the war, when he captured the Spanish port of Porto Bello in Darien.[16] His victory was so decisive and absolute that the Spanish changed their trading practices, no longer using a few very large and rich ports with enormous treasure fleets, instead splitting them between many smaller ports. Vernon briefly returned to England and was acclaimed by the English people for his victories, including the first ever performance of *God Save King George* (later *God Save The King*). However, his performance in the rest of the war went badly, with Vernon's attempted descent[17] of Cartagena-des-Indes in New Granada in 1741 being embarrassingly repulsed by greatly outnumbered Spanish defenders under Sebastian de Eslava. 1742 saw Vernon occupy Guantanamo Bay in Cuba, temporarily renaming it Prince William's Bay,[18] before being driven from Cuba by Spanish irregulars. For now, at least, Cuba would remain Spanish.

The Spanish did not fight a wholly defensive war, either. A Spanish attack on Georgia in 1742 was repulsed at the Battle of Bloody Marsh, and the colonials attempted equally futile attacks

---

[16] Today in OTL this is the town of Portobelo in Colón Province, Panama.

[17] A contemporary term for amphibious assault.

[18] In OTL he named it Cumberland Bay, for the same person.

on Spanish Florida at the same time. It was an indecisive war, one in which Vernon's early victory was eclipsed by his later defeats. Historically he is more remembered for the introduction of watered rum into the Royal Navy, affectionately nicknamed 'grog' in his memory. Lawrence Washington nevertheless remained an admirer of Vernon, and managed to persuade Prince Frederick not to launch savage attacks on him as a means of targeting his father.

It has been suggested that this otherwise desultory war was an awakening of national consciousness, for it was at this time that the term *American* began to dominate over *Colonial* as a word to describe the British settlers in the Americas.

After 1742 the war merged into the greater European conflict when France joined Spain. It was at this time that Walpole's government first began exacting increased taxes on the Americans in order to pay for the war, a highly unpopular policy and one which Frederick, of course, capitalised upon. Frederick also witnessed one of the failed American attacks on San Agustín, Florida,[19] although he did not participate, and it was here that he began to realise that these almost entirely colonial-based military ventures were creating a distinct American identity. This was a fact almost entirely missed by the British government.

In Europe, the war had spiralled out of control. France and Sweden had joined Prussia after Frederick's victory at Mollwitz in 1741, with France supporting Charles Albert of Bavaria's claims to Maria Theresa's titles. The alliance suffered a defeat when Russia knocked Sweden out of the war by 1743 and annexed most of Finland, though Russia withdrew from the war after this.

The Franco-Bavarian forces, commanded by Marshal de Broglie and supported by the Electorate of Saxony, did not work at all well together. By the end of 1742 they had a tenuous grip on Bohemia, while Prussia controlled Silesia. The Peace of Breslau temporarily ended the Austrian-Prussian war, with Prussian control of Silesia acknowledged by Austria. Prince Charles of Lorraine's army was released by this peace and was able to mostly eject de Broglie's forces from Bohemia. King Louis XV's ministers, realising they

---

[19] OTL modern St Augustine, Florida.

had an inadequate army in place, stripped more French forces from where they had been guarding the potentially hostile Hanover and threw them into the fight.

Britain's initial contributions to the European war were in the Mediterranean, where a British squadron forced French-allied Naples to keep its troops at home, and, due to some peculiarities of the war declarations, Spain sent troops through France to fight Piedmont-Sardinia without Piedmont-Sardinia actually being at war with France.

1743 saw even greater losses for the French. Charles Albert had crowned himself Holy Roman Emperor in Prague, but then the Franco-Bavarians lost not only Prague but were also forced back through Bavaria as well, the Austrians augmented by enthusiastic Hungarian levies who supported Maria Theresa. The role of the Hungarians in the victory would eventually result in a more privileged position for them within the Hapsburg empire. It was at this point, with the Franco-Bavarians losing the initiative in Germany, that George II personally went to the Continent with Prince William and raised an army in Hanover. This would be a fateful decision for the future of Britain.

The Anglo-Hanoverian army, supported by the Austrians, met the French at the Battle of Dettingen on June 27th (by the Julian calendar which Britain still used). George, delegating his command to William, was outmanoeuvred by his superior French counterpart, the Duc de Noailles. However, the British still won the day, but at a terrible cost.

As George personally led his troops into battle on horseback, he was wounded in the shoulder by a French musket ball. The wound was not great, and George completed the battle with his shoulder bound up and Noailles forced to concede the field, withdrawing his army. It was at this point that Prince William became an admirer of Scotch troops, as the Royal Scotch Fusiliers had played an important role in the victory.

But George's wound became infected. Stricken by a fever, he died in Hanover on August 12th. Britain and the Colonies mourned when they heard the news, although Prince Frederick saw it as the first step towards his return and is rumoured to have thrown a tasteless party.[20]

The transition was surprisingly orderly. The new King William IV had always been George's favourite son and the two thought much alike. William returned to Britain after being defeated by Marshal Saxe at Fontenoy in 1745, a victory which according to some was spectacular enough that it bought the French *ancien régime* another thirty years of life in the face of growing dissatisfaction among the common people.[21] William put down Charles Edward Stuart's Jacobite rebellion in 1745 with the Scotch troops he admired, committing acts in the process that were accused of being atrocities by many—the image of 'Butcher Billy' would be a useful propaganda tool for Frederick. George II's body was returned to England and buried in Westminster Abbey. The British army in Europe was delegated to the Earl of Stair and continued to fight on alongside Charles of Austria. France entered the war directly, while fighting between Prussia and Austria over Silesia broke out once more. France abandoned Prussia and focused on the conquest of the Austrian Netherlands, which under Saxe's brilliant leadership was successfully accomplished. A complex conflict in Italy eventually left Austria as the dominant power in that theatre.

The war dragged on until October 1748. In India, it was known as the First Carnatic War, and French East India Company forces under Joseph François Dupleix took Madras from their British counterparts. In the Colonies, though, American forces from New England successfully conquered the French fortress of Louisbourg on Cape Breton Island in 1745, a seemingly impossible task. And this time Frederick was there in person, fighting as a cavalryman and honourary lieutenant colonel. He did not seem to be put off by the fact that his father had died in a similar role, rather noting with annoyance that he and William had won glory as a result of it. The operation was commanded by William Shirley, Governor

---

[20] In OTL George also fought at Dettingen—indeed he was the last British monarch to personally command troops in battle—but he was not wounded in the process.

[21] This observation was made by Napoleon Bonaparte in OTL.

of Massachusetts and another acquaintance of Frederick's. After fifty days of a land siege and far more of a naval blockade, the French surrendered. "This is a great Yankee victory," Frederick said, upon standing in the Catholic chapel of the fortress. The American operation had taken on the air of a crusade, and the troops took great delight on stripping the island of 'popery', particularly if said popery was composed of gold and easy to carry.

The glory turned to disgust in 1748. The Treaty of Aix-la-Chapelle was signed to end the war. It was almost a treaty of *status quo ante bellum*,[22] save that Prussia retained Silesia—France withdrew from the Austrian Netherlands in an astonishingly unpopular move (a common saying at the time in France was that something was 'as stupid as the peace') and King William IV agreed to return Louisbourg to the French in return for Madras. The move was just as unpopular with the Yankees who had bled and died to take Louisbourg as it was with the French who had bled and died to take the southern Netherlands. But the difference was that the Colonies were thousands of miles away across the ocean. And they had a leader.

For Prince Frederick saw that this was his moment. The order to return Louisbourg to the French, though felt most painfully in New England, had been condemned by all throughout the Colonies. Frederick was on good terms with most of the colonial governors and legislatures. For those he did not, several of them technically owed their allegiance to the deceased George II, not having sworn oaths directly to William. So it was that at Fredericksburg, on February 4th 1748, the twelve governors and many other important dignitaries met with Frederick and signed the Declaration of Right, recognising Frederick as the rightful heir to the throne and proclaiming William's claim void. The Prince had come into his element.

And the War of the British Succession had begun.

---

[22] A diplomatic term meaning 'put everything back the way it was before the war'.

Chapter 5: How I Killed My Brother

Yankee Doodle won his war
By treachery and trick'ry
Pushed over a Frog's nest
And called it a great vict'ry
Yankee Doodle, run and fly,
Yankee Doodle yellow,
Go back to your golden fields
And grow your baccy mellow.

- Song of the Williamite troops in the War of the British Succession, to the tune of "Lucky Locket"; author unknown[23]

From: "The War of the British Succession", by Dr Colin FitzGeorge (1987)—

The War is one of the greatest 'what if's of history, oft quoted by the writers of speculative romances as they consider the knife edge on which our world has walked since the beginning of time.[24] It was viewed with delight by Great Britain's continental enemies, who were willing to jump on any chance to take the hated islanders down a peg or two. However, no great invasion

---

[23] "Yankee Doodle" may have been around as early as the 1740s in OTL, though its history is disputed. What is certain is that it began as a British army song disparaging American colonial troops as rustic and reluctant to fight, but in OTL was reclaimed by the Americans as a bit of calculated irony after several American Revolutionary War victories over the British. Note the last line of this version is a reference to the now universal praise for Virginia tobacco thanks to William Gooch's policies.
[24] Speculative romance is the term used in TTL for what we would call alternate history or counterfactual history (though the division of genres is slightly different in any case). It is a somewhat more mainstream genre there.

materialised. Most of the European powers were busy rebuilding for the next war, for the Peace of Aix-la-Chapelle had solved no-one's grievances—though Britain was the only power to actually fight a civil war over it. France, Austria, Prussia and Russia were caught up in an arms race for when the peace inevitably failed, while Spain was focusing on rebuilding its fleet and improving its methods of trade after its losses at Edward Vernon's hand.

Britain was divided in its loyalties, America much less so. Generally speaking, those in Britain who were on top now owed it to the patronage of George II or William, and so inevitably supported William, while those who had much to gain supported Frederick. Few in the Colonies, save some of the colonial officials, owed much to George and still less to William. After a few arrests and a handful of Williamite loyalists fleeing the colonies, America stood squarely behind Frederick, 'our prince'.

Frederick's bid to gain the crown would have been impossible without America's support, but would inevitably fail if that was all he had. Fortunately, Britain had many supporters of Frederick as well. The Cornish and many of the Welsh, of course, were under his control through the rotten boroughs and the Stannary Parliament. England was the most fiercely divided, with the Patriot Boys and their allies supporting Frederick and the current Whig government supporting George. The distribution of MPs meant that Northumbria and Yorkshire had the greatest overall number of Patriots outside the Home Counties, whose stance could not be so readily divided on geographic grounds. London above all often had loyalties divided even within its families.

The political situation in Britain had changed little after George's death at Dettingen. Walpole had already finally been forced to step down in 1742 and had by now passed away. He had been replaced by his old rivals the Earl of Wilmington (titular Prime Minister) and John Carteret (*éminence grise*). Wilmington, by then old and ill, had died soon after taking office, and had in turn been succeeded by the pro-peace Henry Pelham, who had misgivings (to say the least) about this new conflict following on the tails of the old.

The Opposition was led by the Patriots under William

Pulteney, after the death of Lord Cobham earlier that year. Although still not having achieved anything near a majority, they were a thorn in the side of Pelham and William IV. Perhaps their most significant asset was the silver tongue of William Pitt, who made several highly calculated attacks on William and praising Frederick, without ever technically denying William's right to the throne. That would open him to prosecution under the Treason Act of 1702, for which the penalty if found guilty was death. Pitt and the other Patriots merely argued that the legality of George II's disowning of Frederick ought to be examined, "in view of the extraordinary circumstances in Parliament at the time". This was still enough for William to become nervous, though, and he forced a reluctant Pelham to arrest and imprison several prominent Patriot MPs. Pitt, Grenville and Pulteney were all imprisoned in the Tower of London, albeit in relatively luxurious conditions, just as Robert Walpole had been thirty years earlier.

Nothing could have been better calculated to stir the British people's sense of injustice, of course, and popular feeling began to turn against William and therefore towards Frederick. The worst part for William and Pelham was that the imprisonment didn't even have that much effect—by some means, perhaps a sympathiser in the guards, the three Patriot prisoners managed to continue getting their writings and pamphlets out into London.

Both Frederick and William realised that the war and dispute could be ended at a single stroke: one of them had to die. William had not yet married, negotiations with various German princesses having been interrupted by the Second War of Supremacy, and had no blood heir. Frederick did have children, but by Mildred, claimant Duchess of Cornwall, and the Williamites did not recognise the morganatic marriage and hence the legitimacy of their three children. Realistically, either Frederick or William being killed would end the problem, because their supporters would then have the unpalatable choice of either cleaving to the other or trying to find another claimant, possibly from Europe, and having the headaches of George I all over again.

William was always the more martial of the two, courageous if somewhat lacking in tact, and decided that the best way to settle the dispute quickly was to simply sail a grand fleet to America and give battle. The provisions of the Treaty of Aix-la-Chapelle were still up in the air thanks to Frederick's forces refusal to withdraw from Louisbourg, and so the French had in turn refused to return Madras to the British East India Company. William realised that if his fleet could take Louisbourg quickly, then it could be immediately handed back to France and settle the disputes. Frederick could then be tackled later, assuming that his Yankee forces did not break and shatter immediately; the British soldiers of the period had a poor opinion of colonial American fighting strength.

The King needed an Admiral, of course. He is reported to have inquired into the disgraced and retired Vernon returning to duty, but Vernon refused and is thought to have issued a warning that the Americans might be tougher than was believed. (This is often considered by historians to be a direct reference to Lawrence Washington). If Vernon did give a warning, it was unheeded. The fleet was placed under the command of Vice-Admiral John Byng,[25] who had previously served as Governor of Newfoundland and thus knew the waters William's forces would be travelling through. Perhaps William also thought Byng might be able to rally the relatively few permanent residents of Newfoundland to the Williamite cause. If so, it was an unfounded hope; Byng had only served as Governor for less than a year in 1742.

The fleet sailed in April 1749. Frederick, meanwhile, had divined his brother's purpose and had repaired and reinforced the fortifications of Louisbourg. He issued orders (conveyed by the Governors or Lieutenant Governors-in-residence) that if colonial forces met William's, they were first to appeal to their reason and not to fire first. This was looked on by contemporary commentators as a benevolent gesture, but may have been more calculating: Frederick was willing to do anything that might blacken William's image by forcing him to resort to violence first.

---

[25] In OTL Byng is best known for being controversially court-martialled and executed by firing squad for his actions at the Battle of Malta, leading to Voltaire's satirical phrase in *Candide:* "The English occasionally feel the need to execute an admiral, to encourage the others."

By standing on the defensive, he had already made William paint himself as the aggressor.

It is at this point that the speculative romantics become most excited, pointing out that if the war had dragged on, Frederick might have been reduced to merely leader of some rebel confederation of the Colonies, or William's forces might have come into direct conflict with the Yankees and driven a wedge between the Colonies and the homeland. In practice, fortune smiled upon the fate of England. Helped along a little by Frederick's lack of scruples.

On his grand tour a few years earlier, Frederick had been most impressed by the use of rifles in America, a weapon still scorned by most British and all European troops as being ungentlemanly. Longarms were almost always used by common soldiers, they argued. It was fine for them to blast away in musket line, where no-one could tell whose ball hit what, but to use an accurate weapon like a rifle, where a target—which might be an officer on horseback—was deliberately lined up and shot? Unthinkably vulgar!

If Frederick had ever had any appreciation for this kind of view—and this is debatable—it was ground out of him by his exile. Both his relentless mission to return, and perhaps also the frontier pragmatism of the Americans around him, convinced him to resort to almost any means to get his throne back. This did not extend to actual assassination by any means that might paint him as a blackguard, though. It had to look like an accident.

So, the would-be King decided on a grand gamble. He knew, or at least had was fairly certain, that Frederick would make an attack on Louisbourg, perhaps after watering in Newfoundland. He set things into motion.

Frederick assembled a fleet of his own. It was made up largely of converted fishing boats, with one or two sympathetic Royal Navy ships with largely American crews. It would be no match for Admiral Byng's force, but it didn't have to be. Frederick also chose one particular ship, a Nantucket whaler commanded by Captain Samuel Starbuck, for his task.[26] Fortunately for him,

---

[26] The Starbuck family, originally from Derbyshire, emigrated to Nan-

Captain Starbuck and his crew volunteered for what could easily have been a suicide mission, and he promised to reward them if they succeeded. As whalers, they were used to high risks for rich rewards. They took with them ten men, mostly New England huntsmen, whom had been the winners of a grand tournament organised by Frederick a few months before. The competition had been to find the best and most accurate riflemen in the Colonies.

It is thought that Frederick vetoed Major (promoted unofficially to Colonel by Frederick) Washington's volunteering to join the mission. Augustine Washington had died five years earlier, leaving Lawrence as his heir, and Frederick did not want Lawrence's death to provoke the remaining Washingtons to release their blackmail information. Not at the moment of his triumph.

Frederick sent out many other whalers and fishermen, their presence not unusual at all at a time when the fine fishing waters off Newfoundland were actually contested in war between Britain and France no less viciously than the land itself. These boats were assigned to search for the Williamite fleet. Byng's force was first sighted on August 14th, 1749 by Captain William Folger, a fellow Nantucket whaler, who was later knighted by Frederick. Under orders, Frederick's fishermen in turn allowed themselves to be boarded by Byng's ships, and Folger even had an audience with Byng himself. The admiral wanted intelligence on Frederick's movements, and the men fed him mostly accurate reports about Frederick's reinforcement of Louisbourg. However, this only redoubled William's determination to take the fortress.

Byng's fleet arrived at Louisbourg on August 28th and his bomb-ships[27] immediately began shelling the fort from a safe

tucket in the 1630s and soon became synonymous with whaling. Several members of the family discovered Pacific islands in OTL. The Starbucks coffee chain is indirectly named after them, taking its name from the first mate of the *Pequod* in *Moby Dick*, who was so named by Herman Melville as he knew of the family's whaling connections.

[27] Short for 'bombardment ships', bomb-ships were a type of warship used in this era designed for amphibious siege operations. Rather than conventional cannon firing solid cannonballs at short range, they were armed with mortars firing explosive shells on a ballistic trajectory that could arc over defensive walls and detonate, destroying whatever was

distance. Louisbourg's guns, which had been brought back into action by American smiths, kept up a halfhearted return fire, and it seemed that the stories of American cowardice were true.

But the fort nonetheless raised two great flags, flags which had been sewn for Frederick by Boston weavers just weeks before. One was a great Union Jack, while the second was a new flag, a flag that had been designed by a committee of Frederick, the Washingtons and some of his others allies. It was based on the Blue Ensign, but had a great red cross like the White En sign— the red cross on blue being derived from the Royal Colonial Arms of Virginia—and in its lower right quadrant bore the symbol of the Dukes of Cornwall, fifteen golden bezants in an inverted triangle. Frederick had calculated that carefully and, just as he expected, William was roused to see this vulgar spectacle. His brother came out on deck, visible at a distance by other 'innocent fishing boats', which signalled with flags. Now Frederick's plan went into gear.

Another fishing boat appeared, a swift sailor, from out of the open ocean. In fact it had taken a looping course. The ship flew a flag with a white cross on blue, the French merchant colours. Once more, this was no surprise, for the French fishermen contested these waters often, and France and Britain were now at a (provisional) peace. The ship sailed very close to Byng's fleet, not altering its course, and Byng questioned William whether he wanted it stopped and searched. William's thoughts were entirely on retaking Louisbourg and, hence, forcing the French to cleave to the Treaty. Anything they could use as an excuse to continue to dither had to be avoided. He told Byng to ignore it. The admiral complied, for after all, it was obvious that the ship carried no cannon.

So it was, at a distance of perhaps a hundred and fifty yards from Byng's 80-gun flagship HMS *Devonshire*, that Frederick's

---

behind them. They are remembered in the line from *The Star-Spangled Banner*, 'and the rockets' red glare / *bombs bursting in air*', the bomb-ship HMS *Meteor* being largely responsible for the latter in its bombardment of Fort McHenry, Maryland in 1814. As for the rockets, those would take a little longer...

crack Riflemen emerged from under cover, took careful aim on William in his prominent marshal's uniform, and fired.

Of the twelve shots fired, Byng's steward records in the log book that four hit the King—three in the torso and one to the head—and this fourth one meant he died instantly. The other eight embedded themselves in masts, wounded two midshipmen, and pierced a hole through Byng's hat without him even noticing until much later.

All attention aboard the *Devonshire* was on the prone figure of the king, blood and brain splashed everywhere "in a most vulgar spectacle", as Byng recorded in his diary. Other ships in the fleet attempted to give chase to the fisherman, but Frederick had chosen a fast ship and the Williamites were unprepared. Given enough time, of course, they would have caught up, but to the bemusement of Byng and his captains, two frigates also flying Royal Navy ensigns appeared seemingly out of nowhere and raked the fishermen with cannon fire, then boarded her and set her alight.

The field of battle was in total confusion, with Byng, not the most commanding of Britain's admirals, uncertain of what to do. As Frederick had planned, this gave him an opening. One of the frigates—the other quietly evacuating the "prisoners" to shore where they would blend in with Frederick's army—approached the *Devonshire* and flew the flag of truce. Not having any other options, Byng took it, and he met with Frederick, Colonel Washington and Governors Gooch and Van Dam of Virginia and New York, the latter promoted to full Governorship by Frederick after he had unilaterally sacked George Clinton.

Between them, they hammered out a deal. Having witnessed a dastardly French attack on the person of the King, it fell to Frederick to take the crown and avenge his brother. Such was only proper, just as William himself had for King George on the fields of Dettingen. Of course William had been the true King, 'had been' being the operative word. Frederick had never truly been in rebellion, his position had been...*misrepresented*. But now William had unaccountably died without leaving an heir...

History was carefully rewritten in the admiral's cabin of HMS

Devonshire, and Byng acknowledged King Frederick I of Great Britain and Ireland. After watering at less forbidding American ports, the fleet would return to England with Frederick and his senior allies at their head, and the King would be coronated. This was only proper. And of course there would be no question of returning Louisbourg to the enemy, not after an act of treachery against the laws of war like this, no? No.

Some commentators record that Frederick was a changed man after the meeting, for he came upon the body of his dead brother, mutilated by the accurate rifle fire of the Americans. The last time he had seen William had been in 1728, when his brother was merely seven. Ever since then, Frederick had always painted him as a small-scale copy of his father, and due as much hatred. But it is said that when he saw him like this, he saw the little boy he vaguely remembered, and broke down. Many say that his coldblooded acts of deception in gaining the throne haunted him for the rest of his life, a latter day Richard III, or perhaps Henry VII is a less damning comparison.

The fleet wintered in America, the tensions between the British and colonials evaporating as William's former sailors and soldiers revelled with their colonial cousins, celebrating the warmest Christmas that most of them had ever known. Something else spread throughout the Colonies, as well: the flag that Frederick had commissioned. Known then as the Patriotic Banner of the Colonies, it would eventually become known as the Jack and George (Union Jack and St. George's Cross), symbol of the sons of Britannia in America forevermore.

When the fleet finally sailed in March 1750, though, together with Frederick, his important allies and his family, his trials were not over. He had won the throne back from William, but there was still another contender in the ring. In Ireland, and the Highlands of Scotland, choosing between William and Frederick had never been a question worth asking. For there was a third option.

The Jacobites were rising once again...

Chapter 6: The Second Glorious Revolution

O'er the seas our merry band,
To Ireland, Cornwall and England,
King Fred commands, and we obey,
Over the seas and far away...

- Colonial marching song from the War of the British
Succession[28]

From "The Prodigal Son: King Frederick I" by Arthur Yeo (1959)—

When William left Britain in 1748, the Jacobites had only recently suffered a catastrophic defeat in Scotland at his own hands. Bonnie Prince Charlie's Highland rebellion, which had at first seemed so close to success, had been crushed by William's forces. Nonetheless, Charles Edward Stuart remained undaunted by the humiliating manner of his escape (disguised as a lady's maid) and plotted a new rebellion whenever the time was ripe. Not even he, though, had expected that that time would come so soon.

Charles was the charismatic son of James Francis Edward Stuart, son of James II and claimant King James VII and III of England, Scotland and Ireland.[29] James had remained in France after the failure of his own attempted rebellion in 1709—at the hands, incidentally, of Admiral Sir George Byng, father of the

---

[28] The original *Over the Hills and Far Away* comes from the War of the Spanish Succession, aka the First War of Supremacy in OTL, and it has undergone many permutations for later wars in OTL, just as it has here in TTL.

[29] The Jacobite Stuart claimants denied the legitimacy of the Act of Union, which had been passed after James II had been deposed, and thus continued to claim the thrones of England, Scotland and Ireland separately rather than Great Britain and Ireland.

man who led William's fleet. The '45 had also failed, but its initial successes convinced Charles that victory would eventually be his. The Stuarts all continued to ignore the fact that they had almost zero support in England, even from Catholics, and what little sympathy they had from the Episcopalian movement in '45 would have been quenched by the failure of that rebellion. There remained a Jacobite circle in London which had contact with Charles at this time, but they were adamant that Charles would only be accepted by them if he converted to Anglicanism.

The Kingdom of France continued to give the Stuarts asylum, but treated their ambitions as, at best, a minor distraction to their English enemy which might benefit France a little, and at worse merely a quixotic fancy to add colour to the French court. Notably Louis XIV had even permitted James to be crowned King of England at his court in the traditional way, including the defunct claim to be King of France. The fact that the real King of France permitted a pretender to be crowned King of France in his presence demonstrates how seriously (or otherwise) the French took the Stuarts.

However, the French had also discovered that Charles had a strong will as well as the charismatic presence that had let him rally so many Highlanders to his doomed cause. Notably, he maintained to the French that he would have the crowns of all three kingdoms (England, Scotland and Ireland) or none. He would not merely be a French puppet in Scotland or Ireland.[30]

When William left, Charles immediately began making more plans for another rising, despite some misgivings among his supporters. The French Foreign Minister, the Vicomte de Puisieulx, warned Charles that no French troops would be guaranteed, as Louis XV was concentrating on his domestic affairs and reworking his army for the next round of battle in Europe. Charles famously remarked with some venom: "Odds fish! Three times I have been promised armies of France and three times none have come! Now that the Viscount has told me in no

---

[30] In OTL Charles made this claim in 1759 after the Duc de Choiseul approached him with a proposal to make him King of Ireland alone, backed by a French invasion.

uncertain terms that no men can come, it will not surprise me if a vast legion appears to support our cause!" (Some French troops did support the '45, but they turned up late and in much smaller numbers than had been promised).

Although Charles was not willing merely for his father to become King of Ireland, he was persuaded by his supporters that an Irish rebellion might be a more successful way of starting, as Scotland was still locked down quite tightly by what remained of William's army. Accordingly, the Stuarts chartered a fleet that sailed from Nantes in April 1749 (just as they had five years earlier) and landed troops at Limerick. Charles' ragbag army numbered about 20,000, including a number of exilic Scottish and Irish troops in service with the French Army whom Louis XV had reluctantly, unofficially, released. These included portions of the French Royal Scots and Irish Brigades, some of whom had fought in the '45.

Limerick was chosen for a variety of reasons. It was an important city, it was isolated from the major British garrisons in Ireland, it remained poorly fortified, and most importantly, it had a special place in the hearts of Jacobites and especially their Irish supporters. It was at the Siege of Limerick in 1691 that James II had finally fled, beginning the Jacobite exile, and the ensuing Treaty of Limerick had guaranteed civil rights for Irish Catholics—which had then been ignored by successive hostile British Parliaments. Not for nothing was the Irish Brigades' battle cry *"Remember Limerick and Saxon Perfidy!"* Now, almost sixty years later, the Jacobites sought their revenge.

Despite Charles' somewhat disorganised army, Limerick was taken in a week-long siege from its complacent British defenders. The city retained a large Protestant Irish minority, many of whom suffered revenge attacks either by the Jacobites or by their Catholic neighbours.

News of Limerick's capture spread like wildfire through Ireland and, in a somewhat slower and more confused manner, to Britain. By the time that Prime Minister Henry Pelham was certain that the reports were more than rumours, the Jacobites had already sailed a part of their force to take Cork as well, and the Catholic interior of the isle was beginning to rise in support.

Pelham had been chosen as Prime Minister specifically because he was almost a nonentity, able to smooth things over in the fiercely divided Parliament of the late 1740s by being all things to all people. Admirable a peacetime leader as he might be, he was sorely unsuited to this crisis. By January 1750, the Patriot opposition (those who had not been locked up by William) were trying hard to topple the government with speeches in the House. They failed, primarily because the Whigs remained fiercely divided and no-one could agree on a non-Patriot replacement. The Whigs therefore continued to support Pelham and his brother, the Duke of Newcastle, who unofficially shared his power.

The news out of Ireland continued to be discouraging. Though the British troops marching to meet Charles' forces were generally superior in training and equipment, most of the Irish countryside was against them and they found they had to live off the (poor) land—which only provoked more resentment when they confiscated food and shelter from the locals.

A Jacobite army under the ageing Lord George Murray comprehensively defeated a Government army under Sir Robert Rich when some of Rich's own Royal Irish defected, or at least refused to fight. The scandal almost brought down the Government, but Pelham continued to cling onto power, while somewhat exaggerated rumours of the Jacobites storming Dublin circulated. Ulster dissolved into vicious partisan warfare between Irish Catholics and Protestants (both Anglicans and Dissenters), and the remaining Government forces were pulled back to Dublin. It seemed, just as it had in ages past, that English power in Ireland was about to be reduced to the 'Pale' around Dublin once more.

More seriously, scattered but nonetheless existent Jacobite risings began to occur in the Highlands, though most were immediately crushed by the large number of British troops still stationed there. The only persistent and organised rising was that of Lord Cosmo Gordon. London was in a panic, just as it had been in 1745, and there were demands that troops be pulled back to defend the capital in case the Jacobites appeared from nowhere.

Most historians today believe that Charles' mission, despite its surprising early successes, was ultimately doomed, just as the '45 had been. However, what response from Pelham's tepid Government might have eventually materialised was as nothing to the spectacular events which actually occurred.

With a sense of timing that would be considered outlandish even in a work of literature, the fleet of King Frederick returned from the American colonies on June 4th, 1750, and landed in Ireland. Frederick had heard from the occasional Atlantic fisherman of the troubles and he sensed an opportunity for glory. The former Williamite army, combined with the American forces, landed at Cork and quickly overran the Jacobites, who lacked sufficient troops to defend every town they took. An initial attack by an army under Colonel Washington failed to take Limerick, though the town was later abandoned by the Jacobites anyway. The conflict had the result, whether intentional or not on Frederick's part, of welding together the mutually suspicious Williamites and Americans into a single force united against a common foe—a model for what would occur later on with Britain and America themselves.

Some historians and alienists[31] have speculated that Frederick may have wanted a decisive Jacobite battle just to have another opportunity to match his brother's achievements… "his Culloden". He certainly had that. Frederick's force met up with one of the shattered Government armies at Wexford and then crushed Charles Edward Stuart's force near Kilkenny on September 1st, 1750. The *"Remember Kilkenny!"* would in the future be as much of a rallying cry for Irish Catholics as *"Remember Limerick!"* had been in this war.

There would be no escape for Charles Edward Stuart this time, ignoble or otherwise. He was hit by a musket ball at the moment when the battle turned to rout, just as he had been on the verge of rallying his troops with his famous charisma. His last words are reported to be "Now and forever, my Father is King!" The body was witnessed by Frederick and several of his generals, but vanished some time after the King ordered it to be taken back to London.

---

[31] An older term for psychologist in OTL, still in current usage in TTL.

It is thought that it was stolen by Irish Jacobites, and there remain legends today of a secret shrine in a cave somewhere near the battlefield at Kilkenny, although none of the many adventurers who have gone looking have ever found it.

James Francis Edward remained in France as the titular James III and VIII, but the death of Bonnie Prince Charlie effectively ended the Jacobite cause. James' second son Henry Benedict Stuart was a cardinal in the Catholic Church, and thus would both never produce an heir and would never be recognised as King by almost everyone in England and indeed Scotland. Also, France, Spain and the Papal States ceased their charade and did not recognise Henry as Henry IX on James' sorrowful death three years later. Within a decade or two, Jacobitism was just a romantic legend.

After his triumph in Ireland, Frederick withdrew his army—Irish Catholic partisan warfare would continue for some years—and sailed for Penzance. His army marched through Cornwall, and Frederick was greeted with cheers by men and women who had always held fast to their Duke throughout the hard years of George and William. He bestowed many more favours and promises, his army picked up a number of new recruits, camp followers and wives, and they marched eastward.

On November 15th, 1750, Frederick's army entered London. There was talk from his remaining opponents of forming a civil militia to repel them, but by now Pelham's government was as paralysed as it could be. Just as Frederick had hoped, instead his homecoming was as a second Glorious Revolution (as indeed it would be named in the history books), with people in the street cheering his victorious troops and the Irish victory still fresh in everyone's minds. The Jack and George was flown, and remarked upon, and the image of Lawrence Washington and his volunteers marching on horseback through the streets of London, bearing the new flag, was immortalised in Gainsborough's *Stout Colonials*.

Frederick entered the House of Commons whilst it was still in session, as no King had since Charles I, and waited patiently with his troops while Pelham blustered. Meanwhile, Washington's volunteers freed Pitt, Grenville and Pulteney from the Tower, as well as less prominent Patriots from house arrest, and these MPs converged on the Palace of Westminster. When all were assembled, Frederick spoke:

"I find the Government of these islands has suffered somewhat drastically in the absence of a strong guiding hand. Therefore, I present my own. *Honi soit qui mal y pense!*"

It is probably apocryphal that both Pelhams fainted at this... probably.

Frederick was crowned on Christmas Day, 1750, at Westminster Abbey, evoking the coronation of William the Conqueror almost seven centuries earlier. His disgrace had begun with a coronation, that of his father, and now it ended with one. And Frederick took note of the debts he owed, though in his own words he knew he could never repay them all. So it was that, after taking the coronation oath, he adopted a new title:

Frederick the First, by the Grace of God King of Great Britain, France and Ireland, **Emperor of North America**, *Defender of the Faith, etc.*

Frederick's first act as crowned King was to dissolve Parliament and call a general election, which the Patriots unsurprisingly won handily. In February 1751, William Pulteney became First Lord of the Treasury, with William Pitt as Secretary of State for the Southern Department and George Grenville as Secretary of State for the Northern Department. Among first bills to be passed by the new 'Patriotic Parliament' were the infamous Act of Suppression, detailing new measures by which Ireland and the Scottish Highlands would be secured against further risings; the Act of Succession (1751) in which William was recognised as King William IV reigning 1743-1749, as Frederick had promised; and, perhaps most importantly for future generations, the Colonial Act (1751), in which the first seeds of true self-government in Britain's North American colonies were laid, with the declaration of the Empire of North America.

Part of this Act was probably a calculated insult at the French and Spanish, as while the British colonies were very populous, they still only occupied the Cisappalachian region of the North American continent, whereas the French and Spanish claimed far more. Yet, as well as simply adding another title to that of the British monarch, the Act both increased the local powers of the elected American colonial assemblies—abolishing the Lieutenant Governors and forcing Governors to remain resident at their posts—and paved the way for wider Parliamentary reform later on. Notably, with Frederick as King, the post of Lord Deputy of the Colonies was now vacant. Renamed Lord Deputy of North America, Frederick bestowed the post upon Lord Thomas Fairfax, the only British peer who had preferred to dwell in the Colonies even during William's reign, and an old acquaintance of the King's from his Virginian exile days.

The new King was not swift to punish members of the former regime for supporting his brother: after all, had he not retroactively acknowledged William as King? However, many members of the later Walpole and Pelham governments found themselves unaccountably shunned by society and Parliamentary appointments, several Establishment families taking multiple generations to regain their former status, and some never achieving it. One area in which there was decisive action concerned the Colonies, with for example the Carteret family being heavily pressured to cede the Granville District lands to the North Carolinian colonial government (though they retained many possessions and interests within it). Colonial towns named after men such as the Earl of Wilmington were also renamed: North Carolina's Wilmington reverted to its old name of Newton and Delaware's was renamed after William Pulteney.

Frederick meanwhile liberally showered his American friends and supporters with peerages and positions in thanks for their help returning him to his rightful place, and Lawrence Washington in particular was rewarded with the Washingtons' ancestral English home, Sulgrave Manor, and a newly created peerage. It is said that Lawrence may have rejected Frederick's original choice of peerage, the Marquessate of Northampton, stating that, after all this time they had spent together, the King should understand his people more. There was a dead silence, among which Frederick's courtiers held their breath, and then the King grinned and agreed. So it was that Lawrence Washington was the first man to receive a hereditary peerage credited to a town outside England, Scotland or Ireland: he was made Sir Lawrence Washington, First Marquess of Fredericksburg.

The War of the British Succession was over. But the Age of Supremacy had just begun...

MAP OF THE EMPIRE OF NORTH AMERICA IN 1751

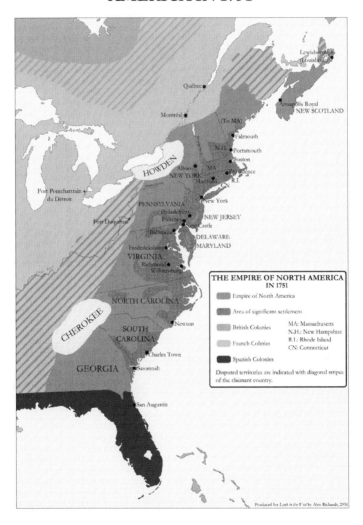

THE EMPIRE OF NORTH AMERICA
IN 1751

- Empire of North America
- Area of significant settlement
- British Colonies
- French Colonies
- Spanish Colonies

MA: Massachusetts
N.H.: New Hampshire
R.I.: Rhode Island
CN: Connecticut

Disputed territories are indicated with diagonal stripes of the claimant country.

Produced for *Look to the West* by Alex Richards, 2016.

Interlude #1: The Age of Supremacy

INSTITUTE MISSION TAPE TRANSCRIPT 07/06/2019: CLASSIFIED LEVEL EIGHT

Captain Christopher Nuttall: Director, you may take issue with the means that this report has been constructed. I have been assured by Dr Pylos and Dr Lombardi that any other approach would be overly confusing. For clarification, I present their recommendations.

Dr Bruno Lombardi: Hello? Yes? Is this thing on? Thank you, Captain. Yes, indeed, it has been our understanding that-

Dr Theodoros Pylos: -that the political and cultural landscape of the *present day* of TimeLine L is too alien, too different from our own world for a ready understanding, and that-

Lombardi: -that incorrect snap judgements may be made if the mind is not prepared by tracing the changes in this world from their very beginning, and-

Nuttall: Gentlemen, could we get to the point?

Lombardi: Of course.

Pylos: Mm.

(Pause)

Lombardi: Director, you may have been confused by the use of local terminology in a few cases.

Pylos: To that end, we present this short excerpt from a book that I, personally, risked life and limb to get my hands on, for such works would appear to be restricted in the vicinity of-

Lombardi: Yes, yes. I'm not convinced by that, I think you've misinterpeted—anyway. The point is that the book is written from a different perspective to the British Whig histories we have previously drawn upon and thus may present a more balanced perspective.

Pylos: I wouldn't say that—more imbalanced in a different direction...

Nuttall: Gentlemen?

Lombardi (muttering): Roll the tape.

> *"History is written by the victors."*
>
> - George Spencer-Churchill the Younger, *On Empire* (1947)

From: "Historiography: Overcoming a Barrier to Societal Unity" by Paolo Rodriguez of the Instituto Sanchez (originally published 1962—unauthorised English translation 1974)—

Wars of Supremacy. A concept developed by the English/West Indian[32] Whig historian Thomas Macclesfield as an underlying theme for the eighteenth century. Macclesfield sought to place the largely meaningless clashes of that time into an ideological context, and emphasises the idea that the eighteenth century was effectively one long war with short breaks for regrouping. He did not class every eighteenth-century conflict as a War of Supremacy, however. Most notably, although Macclesfield dates the start of his Age of Supremacy to 1688 with the flight of the

---

[32] *(Dr. Pylos' note):* The introduction to this book mentions that this unauthorised translation has reintroduced the more usual terms for countries and geographic regions in place of the original, which used terms like "Zone 14 Island Groups 16-25" for the British Isles.

Stuart dynasty from England, he does not consider the War of the Grand Alliance, of which that flight was a part, to be a War of Supremacy. Some successors in the same tradition, notably George Spencer-Churchill the Younger, have retroactively dubbed that conflict the 'Zeroth War of Supremacy'.

Macclesfield and his successors defined a War of Supremacy as a *global* conflict, in which significant fighting occurred in at least three widely separated theatres. These are usually considered to be "Europe, the Americas, and India", although the latter is more negotiable. Supposedly the War of the Grand Alliance did not count, as while it had European and North American theatres, there was no conflict in India or another third area.

The term is often misunderstood. The 'Supremacy' does not refer to military but cultural domination. It was a central thesis of Macclesfield's that purely European conflicts usually had no long-standing impact, although his own narrow cultural background prevented him from following this through to its logical conclusion that the only solution was correct Societal Unity. Macclesfield argued that only wider, colonial, Wars of Supremacy had long-term consequences. Many colonies trading around the world, their inhabitants speaking the language of their mother country and following their practices, would result in a very slow but sure cultural domination of the world by that country—in Macclesfield's conception, which was contrary to the ineluctable principles of Sanchez.

Similarly, the term 'Age of Supremacy' is misleading, as it refers to not a period in which one culture dominates the world, but a period in which the various cultures are contesting that domination. Age of *War for* Supremacy would be a more appropriate term.

Engaging in Wars of Supremacy might not bring gains in the short term, but looked at from the perspective of a historian, the victors in such wars would define not just what the future would look like, but how the inhabitants of that future would look back on their own history. George Spencer-Churchill the Younger has characterised this by the phrase "He who controls the present, defines the past."

From Macclesfield's point of view, the victors of the Wars of Supremacy were England and to a lesser extent Spain, while the losers were France and Austria. Of course, any short-term impact of such wars will be negated in the long-run by the ineluctable march to Societal Unity.

Macclesfield's definitions of the Wars of Supremacy and accompanying conflicts follow, with annotations for changes made by his successors.

1688-1697: The War of the Grand Alliance.

England, United Provinces of the Netherlands, the First German Empire,[33] Spain, Sweden and the Duchy of Savoy **versus** *the First Kingdom of France and allied Scottish and Irish Jacobites. Indecisive result. Failed attempt by English colonists in North America to take French Quebec. Not considered to be a War of Supremacy by Macclesfield but dubbed the 'Zeroth' by George Spencer-Churchill the Younger.*

1701-1714: The War of the Spanish Succession: <u>The First War of Supremacy.</u>

(Incorporating the Great Northern War between Sweden and the Ottoman Empire versus Russia, Saxony, Denmark-Norway and the Commonwealth of Poland-Lithuania, plus other German allies.)

Portugal, England/Great Britain, the German Empire, the United Provinces of the Netherlands and Spanish and Catalan Austriacistes versus Spain, the First Kingdom of France, and Wittelsbach Bavaria. Indecisive result in Europe, but Britain was ceded several parts of French Canada. It is this that appears to cause Macclesfield to consider this a War of Supremacy, as there was no significant Indian theatre.

1733-1738: The War of the Polish Succession. Not a War of Supremacy, although it might well have been if George II's Britain had entered.

1740-1748: The War of the Austrian Succession: <u>The Second War of Supremacy</u>

---

[33] There is a historiographic reason why a twentieth century Societist writer does not refer to these two as the Dutch Republic and Holy Roman Empire respectively.

Kingdom of Great Britain and Kingdom of Ireland, German Empire or Austria, United Provinces of the Netherlands, Saxony, Piedmont-Sardinia and Russia versus First Kingdom of France, Spain, Prussia, Wittelsbach Bavaria and the Kingdom of Naples and Sicily.

This is indisputably a War of Supremacy as it incorporated both a North American theatre (Britain occupied, among other places, Fort Louisbourg) and an Indian one (the French East India Company took Fort St George). According to Macclesfield's notions, this resulted in a supremacist cultural victory of Britain in part of North America, and France in the Carnatic region of India. However, as with most other Wars of Supremacy, the European result was indecisive.

1748-51: The War of the British Succession. Not a War of Supremacy .Britons were divided between the claims of claimant Kings William IV, Frederick IV and James III. No other powers officially entered the conflict, although there was some unofficial French support of the Jacobites.

1755-1759: The War of the Diplomatic Revolution: The Third War of Supremacy.[34]

Great Britain, Ireland, the Empire of North America, Hanover, Prussia and minor German states versus the First Kingdom of France, Austria, Russia, Spain, Sweden, Saxony, Piedmont-Sardinia, Naples and Sicily.

Note that these are the dates used by Macclesfield, and in Continental Europe the war is usually considered to end in 1761.

Result: Decisive British *cultural supremacist* victory in North America, minor French victory in India, dismemberment of Prussia and Poland in Europe.

Note that only these first three Wars of Supremacy have had this name accepted as their predominant or defining label in those parts of the Unliberated Zones that currently use English as their primary dialect. The remaining wars Macclesfield labelled are

---

[34] Note that in OTL the corresponding war is known as the Seven Years' War, but in TTL it did not last seven years. We are now starting to see more global divergences from OTL in terms of historical events, as well as merely relabelling older ones due to down-the-line shifts in attitudes.

more debated by other historians and are certainly not *primarily* known by that name.

1760-63: *The First Platinean War*: *Not a War of Supremacy, but set the stage for one.*

Spain fought Portugal and Britain. Result: Spanish victory in South America but defeat in Europe.

1778-1785: The Second Platinean War : **<u>The Fourth War of Supremacy</u>**: Britain, Portugal and the UPSA fought Spain and France. UPSA victory in South America. Indecisive results in Europe. British victory in India.

1794-1809: The Jacobin Wars : **<u>The Fifth War of Supremacy</u>**. Macclesfield did *not* consider the Jacobin Wars to be Wars of Supremacy; these have been added by later historians due to the revisionism of the period by the British government in order to justify the return of hostilities, and which merely typifies their futile struggle to delay the inevitable march of Societal Unity with the false promises of nationalism.

Lombardi: Now that the stage has been set, we can move on. We have established how things begun to change in TimeLine L.

Pylos: The start was in North America, and in Britain. The ends... the ends would affect everything and everyone.

Chapter 7: And They Call It Peace

From: "The Reign of King Frederick I" by Dr Daniel Clarke (1975)—

Frederick had won back his throne by a combination of valour and base cunning. But, as Shakespeare had said so many years before, *uneasy lies the head that wears a crown.* Having returned to his position partially by treachery, Frederick remained somewhat paranoid towards usurpers for the rest of his life. Of course, not all of this was delusion. From a modern perspective looking back, we can see that after 1751 the Jacobites were shattered and would never threaten the House of Hanover again. But Frederick and his ministers were always wary of another attempt, and took steps in order to guard against it.

More steps were taken to reinforce the guard on the Scottish Highlands, with a new road network being built specifically in order to move troops around easily, building upon similar provisions enacted by Marshal Wade after the earlier '15 rising. Colonel Edward Braddock, a Scot who had previously fought with King William IV's army in the Netherlands during the Second War of Supremacy, was promoted to major-general and given extraordinary powers over the portions of Scotland that possessed Jacobite sympathies. He became known as *The Tanner* by the Jacobites, a reference to the fact that they had called William IV *The Butcher*—they claimed that William had slaughtered the Scots and now Braddock was turning their skin into clothes, i.e. turning Scotsmen into little Englishmen. Later historiographers have repeatedly attempted to draw a direct line of descent between Scottish resentment over this regime and the SPP movement of Donald Black a century later, but this remains controversial.

Ireland was arguably a more difficult problem. Perhaps

fortunately for Frederick, the Lord Lieutenant at the time of the Jacobite rising—his enemy Lord Carteret—had died in the struggle. Frederick was persuaded by his ministers not to appoint a hardliner who would only encourage further rebellions. Instead, the Duke of Dorset—a man who had previously served as Lord Lieutenant before falling afoul of the Pelhams' government—was reappointed to the post. Frederick was content with stationing increased numbers of British, American and German troops there. Mostly Protestants, of course, and this too increased resentment against the mainly Catholic Irish population. Under the laws passed in 1716, the Catholics had been disenfranchised from voting for the Irish Parliament, so while that institution was elected, the majority of the population was not eligible to vote. The Irish Protestants, of course, were themselves seeking vengeance after the Jacobite depredations, and continued to elect hardliners.

Frederick was a more dynamic and active monarch than his father or brother had been, but for the most part continued to let Parliament run things, acknowledging the established system of government. He only directly intervened when Parliament attempted to pass laws on subjects close to his heart, primarily the American colonies, and though he had left them behind forever, the Americans esteemed his name once more when he shot down or watered down several unpopular Bills. Almost alone among the British establishment, Frederick had something of an understanding of the American mind—and he was at the top.

It was his long period of exile in Virginia, along with his friendship with slaveholding families such as the Washingtons, which has resulted in his often-attacked—then and now—relaxed attitude to slavery. His son George, actually born and raised in Virginia, was even worse. It did not help that both of them had lived through the New York slave rebellion of 1741, which had been put down by Governor George Clarke—ancestor of Matthew Clarke, a prominent figure in the Great American War. Abolitionists were not censured in Frederick's day, but nor were they taken seriously. Though America and the West Indies remained the most common destination for black African slaves, it was a fashion among British ladies of the day to have black slave manservants, raising them from children. For the vast majority of the voting population, slavery was such an integral part of their lives that they could not conceive why anyone would want to abolish it. Few save the most foresighted dreamed that the slavery question would one day tear nations apart. For the present, abolitionism remained merely another high-minded dream of the intelligentsia, along with political reform and freedom of religion.

Frederick had made some progress on the latter issue, at least in some ways. Knowing the bad blood between the German Calvinists and English Anglicans in Carolina, he supported laws passed by Pulteney's Parliament which, while acknowledging the supremacy of the established Anglican Church, began to return rights to other Protestants. This was not controversial in the Colonies, where the Anglican Church continued to have little temporal power and had no state authority, but was considered very radical in Britain. Frederick and his government thus enjoyed strong support from German Calvinists and Lutherans as well as French Huguenots, most of them exiles from oppression on the continent. The Acts of Toleration (1752 and 1757) enacted these provisions.

A more complex question approached with the rise of the Wesleyan Revival, which had come onto the scene while Frederick was in America.[35] The Wesleyans were evangelical, frightening the staid Anglican establishment with their fervour, and they were also supporters of abolitionism. It is thus unsurprising that Frederick compromised with the Church on this issue, and Wesleyans remained subject to relatively mild repression well into the nineteenth century. Of course, this only made the movement more popular, as the Church always thrives under persecution.

The one area in which Frederick was certainly not going to increase religious freedoms was the Catholic Question. Catholic emancipation remained a romantic cause among intellectuals (and, obviously, Catholics), but was deeply unpopular elsewhere.

---

[35] The Wesleyans are more often known in OTL as Methodists, originally an insulting name. For one reason and another, that disparaging term did not catch on in TTL.

Popery continued to be seen as an insidious threat to the country that would take over if the merest concessions were made to it, much like many popular views towards Societism today. In Ireland, Scotland, England and America as well (most obviously Acadia), Catholics remained disenfranchised, were not permitted to become officers in the Army or Navy,[36] and were technically forbidden from possessing weapons, although this was rarely enforced.

The continued hostile approach to popery was not merely a reaction to the Jacobites, but also related to Frederick's icy foreign policy towards France and Spain, which was reciprocated in full by Louis XV and Ferdinand VI. Spain at this time was recovering from the Second War of Supremacy using internal reforms enacted by the chief minister, Zenón de Somodevilla y Bengoechea, Marquis of Ensenada. Ensenada also softened Spain's policy of Bourbon absolutism, giving the state more of a paternal attitude towards the Spanish people.

France, on the other hand, remained true to the original interpretation of Bourbon absolutism, and indeed Louis XV even lacked anything analogous to a chief minister after Cardinal de Fleury died in 1743. Perhaps the closest thing to to a head of the French government in this period was the King's mistress, the Marquise de Pompadour. Louis was a relatively peaceful man, and would have preferred to reform his existing 'perfect hexagonal kingdom' than to try and win more territory through war, but nonetheless events conspired to lead France to war again and again. Reform, too, was a lost cause; with the help of Pompadour, Louis unsuccessfully tried to impose taxes on France's privileged classes from the provincial estates. The aristocratic *Parlement de Paris* spoke out against these reforms, labelling itself the defender of the fundamental laws of the kingdom against the arbitrary whims of a monarch. Louis had remained popular with the common people for these failed attempts at taking the nobility in hand, until he had handed back the Austrian Netherlands at the

---

[36] Technically, they had to take an oath against the Pope. In practice there were a fair number of secretly Catholic officers who lied through their teeth.

'Stupid' Peace of Aix-la-Chapelle after so much bloodshed. This was probably the moment when the French *ancien régime* sealed its own fate.

One piece of territory France had taken had not been returned, however. Quite understandably, after Frederick's Britain refused to ratify the Treaty of Aix-la-Chapelle (due to the requirement of returning Fort Louisbourg), the French had in turn refused to withdraw from Fort St George in the city of Madras in India.[37] This meant that the French East India Company would dominate the Carnatic, at the expense of their British rivals. The British East India Company were therefore one of the relatively few groups of powerful people in England to absolutely and nigh-openly detest Frederick.[38] Under the able leadership of their Governor-General, Joseph François Dupleix, the French continued to extend their influence throughout southern India.

The French had taken many Britons prisoner when they had taken Fort St George, and they were not released for many years later. Technically, as Frederick had refused to sign the Treaty of Aix-la-Chapelle, Britain and France were still at war, although during the period between the Second and Third Wars of Supremacy, this was typically reduced to scattered skirmishes in India and on the frontiers of the Colonies. The war did not begin again in earnest until the Diplomatic Revolution of 1756. As the British prisoners languished in French captivity, many died—some from disease, some shot while escaping, and one actually committed suicide, having suffered from lifelong depression. His name was Robert Clive, and this obscure young soldier is only remembered by history because of the famous lament *Clive of India*, penned by his fellow prisoner James Boot. Boot used Clive's tragic death as a symbol of the Company's greater failure, hence the poem's title: Clive's death matched the death of the

---

[37] Madras is generally known as Chennai today in OTL, although the older name continues to be used for a style of curry.
[38] In OTL the Honourable East India Company did not formally have a 'British' adjective, in the same way the Royal Navy is simply the Royal Navy. It unofficially acquires one in TTL because it does not have such a pre-eminent position that 'the' East India Company automatically means the British one.

Company's ambitions for total domination of India.[39]

The British East India Company remained in power further north, in their Presidencies of Bengal and Calcutta, though relations with the Nawab of Bengal, Ali Vardi Khan, were sometimes strained. On the other hand, the French had equal problems. Dupleix's attempt to capture the British Fort St David at Cuddalore in 1747 had failed due to an attack by the British-allied Nawab of Arcot (also called the Nawab of the Carnatic), Anwarooddin Mohammed Khan. The French had eventually patched over relations with the Nawab, but a second attempt to take Cuddalore before the Second War of Supremacy ended also failed. Dupleix held a grudge against the Nawab ever since, and the Nawab continued to favour the British after the war officially ended—thanks to the fact that they now had less influence in the area, and were thus less likely to usurp him if he aided them. Thus, from 1749 to 1754—in the period between the wars—Dupleix aided the usurper Chanda Sahib against first Anwarooddin Mohammed Khan, and then his son Mohammed Ali, supported by the British. Chanda Sahib and the French won a great victory at the Battle of Arcot.[40] After this, British influence in the Carnatic remained patchy, and then almost nonexistent after Fort St David was finally taken by the French in 1757. The BEIC resorted to building up a new army in Bengal and Calcutta, which only alarmed their patron, the Nawab of Bengal...

...back in Europe, things were moving apace. Lawrence Washington returned to the Colonies in 1754, despite being a member of the Privy Council and now possessing lands in Britain and the right to sit in the House of Lords. At the age of 36, he was promoted to Major-General and effectively headed all the

---

[39] Robert Clive indeed suffered from depression in OTL and twice attempted suicide before finally succeeding aged 49. However, this came after presiding over Plassey and other huge victories for the East India Company. In TTL Britain's colonial ventures in India will therefore have to manage without Clive's leadership...

[40] Due to the absence of Robert Clive. Yes, no matter how 'Great Man Theory of History' it might sound, the battle was won by the British in OTL because the young Ensign Clive led a diversionary attack of 300 men that drew part of Chanda Sahib's army away from the battlefield.

colonial militias of Virginia.[41] He left his younger brother and protégé, George Augustine Washington, in Britain to be educated by the same royal tutors as his one year younger namesake and lifelong friend, George Augustine, Prince of Wales: the future King George III.

The European situation was changing. Austria and Britain had mutually decided that their alliance was unprofitable—Maria Theresa had been furious at having to withdraw from Italian territories due to William IV's demands to meet the Treaty of Aix-la-Chapelle, and then after she had done so, the fact that Frederick's Britain had then gone on to ignore the treaty itself was merely the icing on the cake. Equally, Prussia was becoming a more receptive potential ally for Britain. An agreement signed in 1754 by '*Les Deux Frédérics*', as the French called them,[42] stated that in exchange for Prussian defence of Hanover, the British would not assist Austria in regaining Silesia. This was a notion of Pulteney's government; Frederick was unpopular in Hanover for not having a particular fondness for the land where he had been born. He only visited it once, in 1753. Voltaire aptly remarked that Frederick was 'an Englishman to the Germans, an American to the English, and a German to the Americans'.

Another war was not merely likely, but a certainty. Europe had only paused to gather its strength again for yet another struggle. Despite the shifting alliances, though, few would have suspected that things would change so radically. The Third War of Supremacy would be no futile, deadlocked European war. It would have consequences that echo around the world...

Any number of causes could be named—skirmishes in the Colonies or India, incidents between British and French ships at sea—but what clinched it was the 'Diplomatic Revolution', in which France and Austria matched the Anglo-Prussian

---

[41] In OTL Lawrence Washington died young of tuberculosis in 1752 at the age of 34. In TTL he has managed to avoid picking up the disease.

[42] This is probably an error on the part of the author of the book quoted here. Frederick of Prussia spoke French as his first and preferred language and diplomacy was still predominantly conducted in French, so the term might as easily have originated with the Prussian or British governments as with the French.

agreement by burying their differences and forming an alliance of their own. At the signing of the Treaty of Versailles in 1756—which formalised the Franco-Austrian alliance—King Frederick I declared war on France, and King Frederick II invaded Saxony.

Once more, the world was flung into the fire, and who would have predicted what would result?

Chapter #8: To Add Something More To This Wonderful Year

Come cheer up my lads, 'tis to glory we steer
To add something more to this wonderful year!
To honour we call you, as freemen not slaves –
For who are so free as the sons of the waves?
Heart of oak are our ships, jolly tars are our men –
We always are ready—steady, boys, steady!
We'll fight and we'll conquer again and again!

- "Heart of Oak", words by David Garrick,
music by William Boyce

From: "The War of the Diplomatic Revolution", by Arnold Claythorn (1987)—

At first, the war appeared to be nothing more than another of the largely futile struggles that the European powers had engaged in throughout the eighteenth century, and indeed the seventeenth before it. But the War of the Diplomatic Revolution, as it was called at the time, was truly a War of Supremacy greater than any before or, perhaps, even since. Earlier and later conflicts would also have fronts outside Europe, but none would match the Third War. In Macclesfield's terms, it had a greater impact on whose culture, whose language would grow to dominate the world than any other.

The war formally started upon the signing of the Treaty of Versailles by Louis XV's France and Maria Theresa's Austria in May 1756. Frederick of Prussia's forces crossed into Saxony, and the state of quiet war[43] that had existed between Britain and

---

[43] The term used in TTL for what we in OTL would call a cold war.

France since 1751 was ignited into a full-blown conflict.

In this struggle, King Frederick I remained a dynamic leader, but suffered the loss of his wife Mildred in December 1756 and never truly recovered. Despite the fact that the marriage had initially been forced on him, Frederick had grown to genuinely love his American bride and refused to listen to timid proposals from Parliament about the possibility of him remarrying to a German princess for a dynastic alliance. At the same time, and possibly for that reason, Frederick drifted apart from his eldest son, George Augustine, Prince of Wales. George was the first Hanoverian firstborn not to hate his father's guts, a fact which many ascribe to the infusion of American blood from his mother, but he nonetheless had many disagreements with his father. The most significant was the fact that he wanted to fight in the war, and in America, the land of his birth. Frederick refused him permission, and this at a time when George's friend George Washington was also returning to serve under his uncle Lawrence as a captain of the Virginia militia.

With a mule-headedness that he could only have inherited from his father, Prince George vanished in early 1757 and, despite the best efforts of Frederick's agents, could not be found. Of course, he had gone to the Colonies, and once there he too bought himself a captain's commission under the name of Ralph Robinson.[44]

George was not the only child that Mildred had borne Frederick; there was also the second son, Frederick William, the young Duke of York, and his elder sister Princess Mildred—an object of controversy among the princes of Europe, who couldn't work out whether marrying into the royal line of powerful Britain was worth overcoming their revulsion to her half-commoner background. (King Christian VII of Denmark eventually decided on the former, and married off his son to Mildred in 1765). Still, George was Frederick's favourite, and his disappearance on top of Mildred the elder's death pushed the King into a depression.

However, Frederick was fortunate enough to have extremely

---

[44] The OTL version of George III used this as an alias for publishing pamphlets about agriculture and environmentalism.

capable ministers. William Pulteney remained Prime Minister, while William Pitt effectively managed most of the conduct of the war from his position as Secretary of the State for the Southern Department—which gave him authority for dealings with France, the Mediterranean, India, and the North American colonies. Grenville moved up to become Chancellor of the Exchequer, leaving the less important Northern Department to Henry Fox.[45] The latter had been in government under George II and William IV, and thus it took a lot for Frederick to let him return. However, Fox was a skilled speaker, able to hold his own against even Pitt. Unfortunately, the reason everyone knew this was because he had been a great enemy of Pitt in the days of George II. Thus, there was some chilly friction in the Cabinet, but at least Frederick had the ablest of ministers on all sides.

The fact that Fox, as Secretary of State for the Northern Department, had anything at all to do in the war reflected the number of enemies lining up to take a potshot at Britain and Prussia—both of which had acquitted themselves well in the Second War of Supremacy, and thus needed taking down a peg or two. As well as the Franco-Austrian alliance and their chief German ally Saxony, the usual enemies Sweden and Russia entered the war *on the same side* against Prussia. The Commonwealth of Poland-Lithuania, although neutral, was by this point suffering bureaucratic deadlock from its elective monarchy and recent wars, and allowed Russian troops to pass through its territory and attack the Prussians.

Against this mighty alliance stood only Britain, Prussia, and their dependencies—Ireland, Hanover, the new Empire of North

---

[45] The slightly strange government setup in eighteenth-century Great Britain divided matters between the Secretary of State for the Northern Department, whose responsibility was domestic policy for northern England and Scotland and foreign relations with the Protestant northern states of Europe, and the Secretary of State for the Southern Department, whose responsibility was domestic policy for southern England and Ireland and foreign relations with the entire rest of the world. It would not be for some decades in both OTL and TTL until these were reorganised into the more sensible positions of Foreign Secretary and Home Secretary.

America, and two minor German states, the Landgraviate of Hesse-Kassel and the Duchy of Brunswick. However, the Anglo-Prussian alliance embodied the two states with the greatest navy and army, respectively, in Europe. Britain had the advantage of being an island, and thus was only vulnerable to invasion if the inferior French navy managed to gain control of the Channel—quite unlikely. Prussia had no such protection, but nevertheless fought off simultaneous French, Austrian, Swedish and Russian invasions under the dynamic generalship of Frederick II. As Voltaire remarked, Prussia was an army that happened to possess a country, not the other way around.

Valour, revolutionary army drills and Frederick's leadership could not win the war alone for Prussia. The country was kept afloat by subsidies of five million pounds a year from Britain,[46] jealously guarded by the thrifty Grenville and Pitt. Britain herself avoided continental conflict as much as possible thanks to the tactical doctrines of Pulteney and Pitt, which confined British land attacks to a series of descents on the French coast, intending to tie up French troops without actually trying to seize or hold any territory. The one exception was the descent on the Isle d'Aix in September 1757, but the British rapidly found it was impossible to reinforce their occupying troops thanks to the shallow seas preventing any of their larger ships from approaching. The operation was an embarrassing washout, with Pitt being furious over the loss of a million pounds with nothing to show for it.

Frederick II, King in Prussia, continued to astound the world by defeating an Austrian army at Leuthen and a French one at Rossbach. Despite the fact that Maria Theresa had attempted to reform the Austrian army on Prussian lines, Frederick's forces continued to excel. However, the Austrians did manage to break Frederick's Siege of Prague in 1757.

The Mediterranean struggle focused on a French attack on Minorca (British since the First War of Supremacy) early in the war, in the year 1756. A British attempt under Admiral Edward

---

[46] In OTL it was seven million. This version of Britain, lacking as many rich Indian possessions thanks to the French retaining Madras and therefore having a smaller share of the Indian trade, has less to spare.

Boscawen—a hero of Vernon's attack on Cartagena in the previous war—failed with a shocking defeat of the Royal Navy by the French fleet. Boscawen was disgraced, though he escaped a court-martial on the grounds that witnesses swore he had fought as hard as any man could be expected, and was sent off with a ragtag fleet to try and take the French sugar islands in the West Indies. Meanwhile, the British occupied France's African colony of Dakar in 1758.[47]

The North American theatre was astonishing in its activity. From the farthest north of Canada to the balmy sugar islands of the West Indies, Briton and American fought Frenchman, while the Indians were divided, some owing allegiance to one side, the rest to another. The French ostensibly laid claim to a vast territory called New France, from 'Québec' in Canada—one area which did have a large number of French settlers—throughout the entire Mississippi river region, enforced by scattered fortresses, and down to Nouvelle-Orléans at the swampy mouth of the river. The French Governors-General since 1749 had repeatedly tried to gain influence with the independent-minded Indian tribes of the Ohio Country, most of whom preferred to trade with the British. Despite the general lack of French success, this alarmed the Iroquois. Their leader, who went by the anglicised name 'Chief Hendrick', met with the then Governor of the Province of New York, the Duke of Portland (an appointment by Frederick), and appealed to the British to help block French expansion. Portland provisionally agreed to start trying to foil the French missions, though warned that for the moment the war must remain shadowy and unproveable. Frederick later concurred with his judgement when the matter came up.[48]

---

[47] Dakar was also captured by British forces in the OTL Seven Years' War, but was returned at the Treaty of Paris in 1763. In OTL it went on to become the capital of French West Africa, and then the modern Republic of Senegal.

[48] In OTL the Governor of New York was George Clinton, who as an ally of the Pelhams had been sacked by Frederick and excluded from power. In OTL Clinton failed to sufficiently reassure Hendrick and so the Covenant Chain between Britain and the Iroquois Confederacy was broken. In TTL the Anglo-Iroquois alliance remains fairly firm, and the

The Governor of Virginia, Robert Dinwiddie,[49] concurred and also worked to try and stop French expansion in the Ohio Country. American militiamen clashed with the French, and Indian allies on both sides. The French built forts in the land of Vandalia, claimed by Virginia, Fort Presque Isle and Fort Duquesne (named after the new Governor-General of New France, the Marquis de Duquesne). Dinwiddie attempted to take these forts in 1754, while Britain and France were technically at peace (although even *more* technically at war),[50] but his attacks were repulsed.[51] The Ohio Company, later merged with several other ventures into the Grand Ohio Company, continued to thwart French ambitions in the region up until the outbreak of war.

British, American, German and Iroquois troops fought together against French, Hurons (the hereditary enemies of the Iroquois) and Algonquins. There were also some attacks from opportunistic members of the more independently-minded tribes, including the Lenape and the Susquehanna. As the British controlled Fort Louisbourg, the French would have found it very hard to reinforce their troops by sending ships down the St Lawrence. This was an entirely hypothetical question because the government of Louis XV, led by the Duc de Choiseul and the Marquise de Pompadour, did not consider colonial conflicts to be that important and reserved troops for the European war. The French only did as well as they did in North America and India because they had some very able commanders capable of making a little go a long way. In North America, this was Louis-Joseph de Montcalm, while in India, Dupleix's star once again rose.

Iroquois do not become divided in their allegiances.

[49] Dinwiddie also held this post in OTL, and unlike Clinton lacks any political connections of the type that would get him blacklisted in TTL.

[50] As Frederick's Britain threw out the Treaty of Aix-la-Chapelle, technically Britain and France had been in a state of resumed war ever since, but only in the same way that North and South Korea today are still technically at war.

[51] George Washington is still in Britain in 1754 in TTL and is therefore not involved (unlike OTL, where his presence at these battles helped make his name).

Montcalm's warfare in America was in some ways not unlike that of Frederick II in Europe; hopelessly outnumbered, he nonetheless astounded his foes by several early aggressive victories, but in the end the sheer numbers of his enemies wore him down. The French took several forts in New York in 1757, most notably Fort Frederick William, which eventually peacefully surrendered to Montcalm after its relief column failed to materialise. Montcalm was castigated for a 'massacre' of Britain's troops, which was in fact perpetrated by his Indian allies, whose own rules of war required plunder and slaves from defeated enemies and did not recognise the European rules of warfare. It is probable in reality that Montcalm attempted to stop the massacre, but failed.

The massacre did galvanise American public opinion against the French. Prior to this, New England in particular had been lukewarm towards the war. Notably, the Bostonian writer Ben Franklin—already famous for his Almanac—had created a political cartoon "UNITE, OR DIE", featuring a cut-up snake with the names of the colonies on each piece. At the time it was believed that a cut-up snake could come back to life if the pieces were rejoined. The cartoon captured the public imagination and Franklin is credited for the Empire of North America's eventual national symbol being a rattlesnake. Another interesting point is that in his cartoon, the New England colonies are represented as 'New England', not separately as Massachusetts, Connecticut, Rhode Island and New Hampshire, reflecting Franklin's political beliefs that would become very important after the war.

The war in America was of course close to King Frederick's heart, and Pitt too thought it an important theatre. When Pulteney died in 1758, Pitt became Prime Minister (Fox taking over the Southern Department) and moved the American front up to top priority. Despite Montcalm's genius, Anglo-American and Iroquois armies, led by General James Wolfe ("*he huffed and he puffed and he blew the French down*"—Philip Bulkeley) drove the French from vital strategic points such as Fort Niagara, and soon the French were fighting on their own soil, in Québec. The cities of Québec and Montreal fell in 1759, the Americans' *annus mirabilis*, and Montcalm was killed. British casualties in the operation were heavy, although Wolfe survived: wounded in the leg, he was carried from the battlefield by a number of impromtu stretcher-bearers. The scene is captured in Boudinot's seminal painting "The Wolf Lies Down with the Lambs" (1811) which incorporates a story whose historical fact is disputed: that among the stretcher-bearers was a young Royal Navy surveyor called James Cook, who was shot at long range by a French rifleman and killed when the stretcher party was almost back to the Anglo-American lines. The story is considered romantic because Cook effectively inadvertently took the bullet for Wolfe and allowed the general to recover from his minor wound, and it is certainly true that a surveyor named James Cook was present at the battlefield and died there, but there is no direct evidence for this story. Of course this is irrelevant: the popularity of Boudinot's painting means there is no question in the minds of the general public that the story happened.[52]

Most astonishingly of all, a Major Washington—the brother of General Lawrence Washington who commanded the American army now successfully driving the French from their Appalachian forts—came off the battlefield with a wounded comrade named Ralph Robinson, hit in the shoulder by a French musket ball. The world was astounded when this turned out to be none other than the Prince of Wales. Both Washington and the Prince had previously fought against the Hurons before being redeployed to Wolfe's army.

It was also at this time that the New Englanders perpetrated what later generations would call a racial purge[53] against the Acadians in Nova Scotia. Refusing to fight the French and possibly even hindering the British forces stationed there, they were considered a threat. The British deported some of them back to France, but many of them—along with the Canadians later on—were deported to, or fled to, the remaining French holdouts on the southern Mississippi, swelling the population of Nouvelle-

---

[52] A major divergence from OTL, where Wolfe died at his moment of triumph and James Cook survived, famously going on to discover Australia (or rather New South Wales).

[53] Equivalent to the term 'ethnic cleansing' in OTL.

Orléans and its environs.[54]

In India, the British East India Company had been building up a vast army in Calcutta with which to finally retake Madras from the French. This might have worked, had it not been the fact that the Nawab of Bengal became convinced that the BEIC was plotting to seize his throne. Bengali forces took the British Fort William and the Nawab infamously locked hundreds of British troops in a tiny room, the 'Black Hole of Calcutta', in which most of them perished. Throughout the rest of the war, the British were forced to focus on fighting their former ally and reclaiming the territory they had already had. By 1759, the Nawab was dead and the BEIC had directly taken over Bengal through a half-dozen minor princes as their proxies, at the cost of the lives of many British (and Indian sepoy) troops. By contrast, the French under Dupleix had finally taken Cuddalore and Fort St David, and were beginning to expand their influence over the whole of South India—to the extent that it began to alarm Haidar Ali, effective King of Mysore. As well as grabbing back power in Bengal, the BEIC reverted to a more conservative policy, returning its focus to Bombay on the western coast and expanding power into the Peshwa-ruled hinterland. There were also suggestions that the BEIC ought to try once more to take the East Indies from the Dutch, which would cause friction later on.

Things began to turn against the Prussians in Europe in 1758 as the massive numerical advantage of Prussia's foes began to turn against Frederick. No financial injection from Pitt could change that. The Austrians captured much of Prussia's artillery corps at the Battle of Hochkirk, and the next year—while it brought some miracles for the British, with the fall of Quebec, Montreal, Calcutta, Guadaloupe and the naval victory at Quiberon in just twelve months—was a disaster for the Prussians. Count Saltykov of Russia defeated one of Frederick's generals at Paltzig, while the Austrian General Daun forced an entire Prussian corps to surrender at Maxen. Furthermore, Hanover—whose army had

---

[54] This happened in OTL as well, and is the origin of the 'Cajun' group in Louisiana, being a corruption of 'Acadian'. However, in TTL they will not be the last francophones to make the journey...

been neglected by the policies of Frederick of Great Britain—failed to defeat a French invasion at Minden.

Even Pitt was beginning to consider a continental strategy at this point, as it seemed the only way to save Britain's European interests. At the Battle of Kunersdorf on 12th August, Frederick of Prussia stood his ground against a superior Austro-Russian force and watched as his army was annihilated. No longer caring for life, the King drew his epée and stood on a hill, determined to hold the line against the enemy all by himself or die trying. In the event, he died trying, although it is recorded that he slew an absurd number of Austrians and Russians before succumbing.[55]

Prussia literally collapsed without Frederick's leadership. The heir to the throne, Frederick William II, was only 15 years old and his father's brother and old sparring partner, Prince Henry, took over as regent. Henry was also a great general, but he believed the war was lost and Prussia would face total annihilation if it continued fighting. He made one direct plea to Pitt to send British forces directly to Prussia to fight, which was refused due to Swedish control of the Baltic and the French contesting Hanover. Henry therefore approached the Franco-Austrians in November 1759 and sued for peace.

The peace was harsh, as might be expected. Silesia was returned to Austria, but also the southern half of the old Ducal Prussia was awarded to Poland-Lithuania (now firmly in the pocket of Tsaritsa Elizabeth's Russia) and the northern half to Sweden. Saxony received the Prussian enclave of Cottbus, plus the town of Liegnitz and the surrounding area. Even more punishingly, the Hohenzollern possessions scattered throughout the rest of the Holy Roman Empire were stripped from Prussian control. Though the Hapsburgs would have liked to annex them directly, they recognised that this was not politically feasible and would anger too many potential allies, so Emperor Francis I instead had the idea of transferring these minor states to Saxony. Saxony was a reliable ally of the Hapsburgs, always under threat of invasion

---

[55] OTL Frederick was persuaded to retreat by a Captain Prittwitz and his cavalry squad, which failed to get through in TTL. Mind you, he considered suicide even after being rescued OTL as well.

by Prussia, meaning this was almost as good as direct Hapsburg control over those German states. What could possibly go wrong?

Prussia, in fact, was no longer worthy of the name, and Austria began to officially refer to it as the Electorate of Brandenburg again—though the Kings in Prussia, obviously, rejected this. France had been promised the Austrian Netherlands in exchange for her help, but in the event this failed to materialise (angering the people of France against Louis XV once again). Prussia had been reduced from a major to a minor power again, while Russian influence in Poland was now contested only by Austria. And the Austrians were more concerned with exerting their will over a Holy Roman Empire that, with the dismemberment of Prussia, was now a lot easier to bring back under some semblance of centralised imperial control. For a time at least, the Empire had meaning once more, and Francis I and his successors attempted to pursue the idea of a powerful Germany under Austrian leadership, no longer divided and subject to infighting. The Hapsburgs' efforts, though weak and lukewarm, would go on to inspire the German unificationists of almost a century later.

Britain's own position was now divided. King Frederick had fallen ill with a lung infection[56] and now rarely left St. James' Palace, leaving Pitt to make the decision. The Prime Minister had already been on the verge of abandoning Prussia even before Frederick II's death. Now the only question was whether to continue with the war with France, given that it appeared that Portugal and Spain might enter the war sooner or later. Pitt decided to approach the French for a peace, and Choiseul was receptive.

The major provisions of the Treaty of Amsterdam (signed in the neutral Dutch Republic) were as follows:

India: French control of Madras and Cuddalore to be recognised by Britain.

North America: British control of Nova Scotia, Louisbourg, Quebec, Montreal and the Ohio Country to be recognised by France. The borders of the remaining French Louisiana to be

---

[56] In OTL he died of this, years earlier in 1751, in combination with being hit on the head by a cricket ball of all things.

defined and agreed upon.

West Indies: Guadaloupe to be returned to France.

Africa: British control of Dakar to be recognised by France.

Europe: Hanover to be evacuated by France and its pre-war status restored.

Generally: France recognises Frederick as legitimate King of Great Britain, and the status of the Empire of North America.

Britain concluded a separate peace with Austria, Russia and Sweden, against whom she had barely fought. The peace was honourable, and relatively amicable, though tensions remained over the French massacre at Fort Frederick William and the Acadian Expulsion by the Americans.

Frederick had demanded that Prince George return to answer for his crimes. The young prince did indeed return, along with Washington, in 1760—by which time his father was on his deathbed with the infection. In a reportedly tearful scene (and certainly presented that way by countless historical films), the King made up with his son before passing away. King Frederick I, King of Great Britain, King of Ireland, Elector of Hanover and first Emperor of North America, passed away on February 19th 1760. The nations mourned, the Colonies more than any other.

George Augustine became King George III. For the most part, he retained his father's ministers, but he nonetheless alarmed many British Parliamentarians. Far more so than his father had been, he was obsessed with American affairs, almost considered a colonial rustic (hence his nickname 'Frontier George'[14]) and, while it would increase Parliament's powers to once more have a monarch disinterested in British affairs, George was no less dynamic and active a king than his father.

This would lead to some problems later on. For while the British dominions settled down to a period of peace, a new war, an invisible war had been declared. A war not of flesh and blood and iron and steel, but of something far harder to destroy than mere human lives.

Interlude #2: A War of Ideas

TimeLine L Expedition Mission Log

Dr Bruno Lombardi: However, it would be a mistake to assume that the eighteenth century of TimeLine L consists solely of one long unrelenting series of wars.

Dr Theodoros Pylos: How so?

Lombardi: Er... *(long pause)* What I meant was...other things happened as well.

Pylos: Well, of course.

(Pause)

Captain Christopher Nuttall: Gentlemen, need I remind you that time is of the essence? Even with the new compression algorithm, our transmission bursts can only carry limited data.

Pylos: (coughs) Err, yes, sir.

Lombardi: Sorry, sir. *(Ahem)* The eighteenth century was also noted for the rise of two closely related concepts, scientific Linnaeanism and ideological Racialism.

Pylos: Because of the part these played in the eventual global ideological makeup of this world, we have once again chosen to obtain a work published by one of the Societist writers of the Instituto Sanchez...

It is not pleasing to me that I must place humans among the primates, but man is intimately familiar with himself. Let's not quibble over words. It will be the same to me whatever name is applied. But I desperately seek from you and from the whole world a general difference between men and simians from the principles of Natural History. I certainly know of none. If only someone might tell me one! If I called man a simian or vice versa I would bring together all the theologians against me. But perhaps I ought to, in accordance with the law of the discipline of Natural History.

- Karl von Linné, letter to Johann Georg Gmelin, dated February 1747

Carolus Linnaeus—a great man of the sciences, and incidentally also the creator of the second most destructive political ideology that has ever darkened the world. A fine example of why scientists should be on tap, not on top.

- George Spencer-Churchill the Younger, 1941[57]

From: "A Life in Life—the Biography of Carolus Linnaeus", by JoSe Vivaro of the Instituto Sanchez (originally published in Novalatina 1971—unauthorised English translation 1977)—

The man known to posterity as Karl von Linné or Carolus Linnaeus was born in 1707 into a farming family in the area of Zone 15 known to the nationalistically blinded as southern Sweden. It was an era in which self-identified Swedes did not commonly use surnames, and the surname Linnaeus was chosen by Carl's father when he went to university, being a Latinised form of the Swedish for 'lime-tree'. It would be an appropriate name for a man who would spend most of his life applying more concise names to every living thing in existence.

Linnaeus attended the University of Uppsala, and in 1732

---

[57] Both the Linnaeus quote and the second part of the Churchill quote are from OTL, though the latter was made in OTL by *Winston* Churchill.

received funding for a long-term botanical visit to Lapland in the frozen north. At this point, Sweden's economy was suffering, and one policy idea to remedy this concerned finding valuable plants that would grow in cold Sweden, as the country lacked an East Indies trading company. Some wondered if strains of spice plants could be found that would grow in colder climes than their native ones. To do so, Swedes needed both to survey what currently grew in Lapland and also to make examinations of the economically valuable plants that grew elsewhere. Linnaeus, as it turned out, achieved both in his lifetime.

His major early achievement was the creation of a new classification system that permitted plants to be classified by their flowers, and more specifically by the precise shapes of their stamens and pistils. In this he was influenced by Sebastien Vaillant's *Sermo de Structura Florum*, which he read in 1718. Linnaeus' approach was new in that it focused on sexual characteristics as a means of classification. This would have been vulgar enough in the eyes of society, but Linnaeus had a cheerfully dirty mind and commonly applied Latin words for sexual organs to plants that bore the most passing resemblance to them.[58]

Linnaeaus spent the years 1735-38 in the Netherlands, printing his seminal *Systema Naturae*, the first form of his system of classification. Linnaeus' approach was controversial as it ignored the Great Chain of Being[59] and, almost as significantly, the approaches established by the Greek writers, who had based their groupings of organisms solely on gross external appearance. Linnaeus' approach focused more on shared ancestry (sex, again) and included data from dissections, comparing internal organs of animals as well as their outer appearance.

During this time, Linnaeus visited Britain, specifically Oxford University. In 1737 Linnaeus was introduced to George Clifford,

---

[58] Just as true in OTL.
[59] The Great Chain of Being is a concept popular in the Middle Ages and Early Modern period but ultimately derived from the writings of Plato and Aristotle. It is based on the idea that everything falls into a stable hierarchy, with God at the top, then angels, astronomical objects, people (kings, aristocracy, then commoners), then animals, plants, and minerals. For obvious reasons, this view was popular with the ruling classes.

a wealthy Amsterdam banker who possessed a famous garden that included plants collected from all over the world, primarily via the Dutch trade from the East and West Indies. Linnaeus published the treatise *Hortus Cliffortianus*, a description of the plants in Clifford's garden. He also wrote a more general work, *Classes Plantorum*, which was published in Leiden in 1738. After that he returned to Sweden, marrying Sara Morea and helping to found the Royal Swedish Academy of the Sciences.

Linnaeus went on other field-trips around Sweden, helped inspire a younger generation of natural historians who made similarly extravagant trips around the world, and briefly returned to London in 1754, being presented to the returned King Frederick I. He met the by now ageing Stephen Hales, a great pioneer of plant and human physiology, and they discussed such matters as they applied to taxonomy. Perhaps his most significant meeting was with a young man, an English Dissenter named Joseph Priestley, who thanks to Frederick relaxing the restrictions on Anglican supremacy was now able to study natural history at the University of Cambridge.[60] Although Priestley was still a student, the two of them meetomg after he had attended a visiting lecture by Linnaeus, the young man nonetheless had a profound effect on the old Swede and persuaded him that his controversial ideas about humans being closely related to apes should not be silenced. Priestley cited the examples of Galileo, Copernicus and Paracelsus fighting for their ideas, and that the free thought of natural philosophy should not be constrained by the attitudes of the day.

It is perhaps the example of Copernicus that most appealed to Linnaeus, for just like that pioneer he was careful to only publish his seminal *Taxonomy of Man* posthumously, in 1780. His work on humanity's possible relations with the animal world were taken up by later writers, including Priestley himself and Jean-Baptiste Lamarck, a French Enlightenment philosopher and anti-

---

[60] In OTL Priestley trained as a dissenting clergyman and only later became primarily a natural philosopher, although he had always had that inclination. Frederick's reforms make it possible for him to pursue that path earlier on.

clericalist who went to play a part in the Jacobin state. For the moment, Linnaeus' human studies focused on less controversial subjects, and it was from this that the ideology known variously as Racialism or 'Linnaean Racism' sprung.

Linnaeus was the first to give humans a Latin name, *Homo sapiens* ("Thinking Man"). However, he also added four lower-level taxae to divide humanity into subspecies, influenced by the old mediaeval theory of the four humours. These consisted of *Americanus rubenscens*, Red Americans (American Indians), who were said to be stubborn and angered easily; *Asiaticus fucus*, Sallow Asians (Chinese), who were said to be avaricious and easily distracted; *Africanus negreus*, Black Africans, who were said to be lazy and negligent; and *Europeus albescens*, White Europeans, who were said to be gentle and inventive. Obviously, the principles of Societal Unity enlighten us that this was merely an artificial division imposed to prevent humanity reaching its destiny of togetherness, and furthermore that Linnaeus' classifications were clearly biased in favour of Europeans.

The system was attacked in his own lifetime for failing to provide a classification for East Indians, Turks and Semites. There was also a debate as to whether Slavs were European or some other group. This ultimately spawned the far narrower and more chauvinistic theory Nationalist Racism *[as dubbed by Societists]*,[61] which is a tool that has been used by the ruling elites in many nations, enemies of Societal Unity, to keep their peoples apart. Nationalist Racism began in France, and stemmed from the ideas of Voltaire and other Enlightenment writers[62] who refined Linnaeus' ideas to impose divisions within the European Race, broadly defined as Latins, Germanics and Celts (and also sometimes Slavs).

The movement was approved of by the French court and the mostly ethnically 'Latin' Roman Catholic Church (ironically in

---

[61] (Dr. Pylos' note: This is an annotation from the translation, with the footnote that most people in this world would call this ideology simply 'Linnaean Racism' or more imprecisely 'Jacobinism' and the term used here is part of Societist jargon).

[62] In OTL Voltaire was a slave owner and notably contemptuous of black Africans in his writings; this has not changed here.

retrospect), which made it harder later for the clergy to go against Linnaeus' ideas of humans being related to apes: they had already committed themselves to at least giving a fair hearing to anything with Linnaeus' name on. The French Nationalist Racists considered the Latin subrace to be superior, citing the Roman Empire as an example of Latin civilisation when Celts and Germanics had still been barbarians, and the idea that the Latins had held true to the Catholic Church while the Germanics had fallen into Protestant heresy. Of course one objection was that the Roman Empire had fallen to Germanic invasions, but the French argued that modern European states—most obviously their own—were the result of Germanic peoples becoming 'Latinised' in their thought patterns and thus civilised. After all, did not the confederacy of *German* states call itself after the *Latin* Roman Empire?

The movement was ridiculed in the 'Germanic' Protestant countries, not least pointing out the hypocrisy that Linnaeus, the man who had started it all, was a Swede and therefore one of the French's inferior 'Germanics'! In Britain and many other places, a rival movement sprang up. It was led by a number of British intellectuals, including the Earl of Chesterfield, ironically a man who was on speaking terms with Voltaire and, instructively, the two of them seemed to treat the whole nationalistic fervour whipped up by their words as a kind of private joke. Chesterfield also funded Dr. Samuel Johnson's *Dictionary of the English Language*,[63] and as a condition of such, asked him to choose a form of English spelling that was more 'Germanicised' and to take out French-sounding spellings. Johnson himself disliked the Nationalist Racist movement, but was willing to accommodate Chesterfield's whims if his Dictionary could be published (although he added some whimsical definitions mocking the movement throughout the Dictionary). The anti-French spelling movement was not very successful, the English language historically being quite resistant to prescription, but did manage to make some long-lasting changes – *picquet* and *racquet* became *picket* and *racket*, for

---

[63] Samuel Johnson failed to gain Chesterfield's patronage for his dictionary in OTL and had to look elsewhere.

example.[64] These misguided and halfhearted efforts in the service of a Contrasanchezista cause only highlight the importance of forward planning and full focus required for the true linguistic harmonisation demanded by Societal Unity.

Linnaeus' controversial ideas about humanity's relationship with the animal world would not become public knowledge until 1780, after his death, when they sparked an enormous debate. One consequence of this was that, as there were almost pseudo-Biblical arguments about the veracity of translatioons of Linnaeus' work, many were desperate to get hold of Linnaeus' writings in the original Swedish and learn enough of the language to interpret them. This unexpectedly resulted in a temporary boom for other Swedish writers, who had previously languished from writing in a language which few non-Swedes understood. One of the more famous was an apothecary named Carl Wilhelm Scheele, who was able to alert the world of natural philosophy to his discovery of several new chemicals in the late 1770s. He developed the notion that the atmosphere was composed of a mixture of the lufts [gases] elluftium and illuftium, which was an important foundation for the later work of Priestley and Lavoisier, as well as making several more important discoveries.[65]

---

[64] There was a minor anti-French, anti-Latin spelling "Back to Anglo-Saxon" movement in this time of OTL, which is somewhat more influential in TTL (though the words used as examples here also had their spellings changed in OTL). One impact is that in TTL's English, spellings like *almanack* and *physick* remain in use to the present day. One will notice that that means all the excerpts of the books in this report have been changed into modern OTL English spelling by Nuttall's team.

[65] These are oxygen and nitrogen respectively, worn down from the Swedish *eldluft* and *illaluktandeluft*, 'fire air' and 'foul air'. Scheele made all these discoveries in OTL, as well as an early means of pasteurisation, an easy way of making phosphorus matches, chlorine, barium, tungsten, manganese, molybdenum, citric acid, glycerol, prussic acid, hydrogen fluoride *AND* hydrogen sulfide! And yet he received credit for little of it in OTL due to his works being published in Swedish, a language which few non-Swedes spoke. Thanks to the Linnaean controversy in TTL, though, Swedish-speaking British and French intellectuals learn of his discoveries and they are not lost. Note that the term 'luft' is that used for gas in TTL—our word gas is a peculiar spelling of the Flemish word for chaos, and before the nineteenth century gases were referred to as 'airs' in

The controversy raged on throughout the wars of the latter eighteenth century, and in particular, the war with which it ended. The conflict in which the ideas of Linnaeus would mutate into one of the most influential and destructive ideologies the world has ever seen.

The Jacobin Wars.

OTL—but here it has been 'translated' into gas by Nuttall's team. This is not the only translation they have made, but they are not very consistent about it.

Chapter 9: Sowing The Seeds

"When considering the systems of government prevalent in the eighteenth century, Bourbon France and Romanov Russia are often compared on the basis of their absolutism. This is a gross mistake. The Bourbons had sat down and decided that what France most needed was an absolute monarchy. To the Romanovs, on the other hand, it had simply never occurred that there could be any other state of affairs."

- George Spencer-Churchill the Younger, "A Century of War" (1941)

From: "The Storm Before The Storm—Conflicts of the 1760s" by Daniel Harkness (1938)—

It might be expected that, after the global violence of the Third War of Supremacy (1756-9), the nations of Europe would take the opportunity to rest in a few years of peace, or at least take the time to lick their wounds. No such luck for the people, the soldiers, or even the nobles and politicians, many of whom would have preferred to avoid such conflicts. Events conspired against them. Cultures and ambitions continued to clash, fuelled by jockeying for trade and influence.

If war had been predicted, few would have forecast that it would involve no clash between Britain and France. Relations between Louis XV and the new George III remained cold, but both had their own reasons to avoid another war. George was attempting to come to terms with a duty that he had previously only thought of in a vague, theoretical way, and tried to master the British Parliamentary system without becoming a slave to it. Meanwhile, Louis XV was aware of the alarming state of

France's finances,[66] and knew that another great naval war with Britain would only make things worse. He appointed Étienne de Silhouette as Comptroller-General of Finances, a skilful Basque economist inspired by English mercantilism. His attempts to raise more funds by taxing the rich were not a success, for the same reasons as Louis' more personal approach had failed earlier, but Silhouette did manage to cut corruption in the French East India Company and ensure that more of the funds raised from the rich East India trade went into the French national purse. Although this made him somewhat popular at home, Joseph François Dupleix famously sourly remarked that the 'Shadow of Silhouette' (*L'ombre de Silhouette*) was hanging over everything he did in India, and this phrase entered the French vocabulary.

As it turned out, Britain and France both became involved in wars, but in a peripheral capacity, and in separate conflicts which did not significantly affect the other. The first of these wars had been brewing for a long time, and stemmed from the failure of the old Spanish-Portuguese Treaty of Tordesillas (1494) to define reasonable spheres of influence and colonisation in the New World. It had rapidly become obvious that the original meridian, based on incomplete information at the time, allotted far too little territory to Portugal. In 1748, the Spanish and Portuguese governments took advantage of the temporary environment of peace to sign the Treaty of Madrid (1750).

This, also known as the Treaty of Limits, acknowledged Tordesillas and all other former border treaties to be null and void. It defined the new 'line in the sand' to be the 46th Meridian. It also attempted to resolve a dispute over Colonia del Sacramento (Sacramento Colony), a Portuguese town on the northern bank of the Rio de la Plata (variously translated as the River Plate or River of Silver) which had been founded almost a century before and had been contested by the Spanish ever since. The Treaty held that Portugal should cede Sacramento to Spain, and in return Spain would give up the lands of seven Jesuit missions known as San Miguel, Santos Angeles, San Lorenzo Martir, San Nicolas,

---

[66] Though not quite as bad as OTL due to the increased French East India trade from French-dominated southern India.

San Juan Bautista, San Luis Gonzaga, and San Francisco de Borja.[67] These were all located on the east side of the Uruguay River, which according to the treaty was now Portuguese territory.

Although the Treaty had been formed with the best of intentions to preventing further Spanish-Portuguese wars, it did not pay much attention to the facts on the ground, and required both the costly movement of the missions to the Spanish side, and also the forced relocation of several thousand Guaraní Indians, who did not see eye to eye with the proposal (to put it mildly). The Jesuits themselves agreed to move by 1754, but the Guaraní refused and this sparked an unusual, quixotic war in which Spanish and Portuguese forces fought on the same side against the Indians. The Guaraní were defeated, but it was a hollow victory, as the whole affair cast a shadow over the Spanish-Portuguese deals and relations were beginning to break down for other reasons.

King Joseph I of Portugal had helped initiate the Treaty negotiations in the first place when he succeeded to the throne in 1750, but his capable chief minister, Sebastião José de Carvalho e Melo[68] was now beginning to have second thoughts. This had been sparked by the fact that Spain's King Ferdinand VI had died in the interval and been replaced by the drastically different Charles III in 1761.[69] Charles brought back the disgraced Zenón de Somodevilla y Bengoechea, Marquis of Ensenada, as chief minister, and his highly francophilic and anglophobic attitudes clashed with Portugal's priorities. Also, Charles was very much an enthusiast of Bourbon enlightened absolutism, while in Portugal Carvalho had spent much of his ministry crushing the power of

---

[67] The territory in question is around where the borders of the modern OTL states of Brazil, Argentina and Paraguay come together.

[68] Note that in TTL he doesn't become Marquis of Pombal, so he is referred to as 'Carvalho' rather than 'Pombal'.

[69] This happened in 1759 OTL. Butterflies from the POD are taking effect: in OTL Ferdinand VI lost the will to live after the death of his beloved wife Barbara of Portugal from asthma in 1758 and he died the following year. In TTL she manages a few more years, and hence so does he. The primary impact of this is that the Spanish-Portuguese falling-out is delayed to the point that it does not become a part of an existing global conflict as it did OTL.

the Portuguese ruling classes and adopting relatively egalitarian policies, including the abolition of slavery in the Portuguese colonies in India. He had also been praised for his handling of the devastating Lisbon earthquake of 1755, the recovery from which would define Portuguese foreign and domestic policy for generations.

With George III's Britain publicly declaring its condemnation of the Seven Missions conflict and racial purging (a somewhat ironic complaint given its own guilt in shifting the Acadians just a few years before), Hispano-Portuguese relations soured and, in 1763, another border incident resulted in the outbreak of war.

The First Platinean War (1763-7) was for the most part desultory in itself, but had several important ramifications. The Spanish Army in South America performed admirably, not only quickly taking back the territory of the former missions, but pushing forward and occupying the entire Rio Grande do Sul[70] region by summer 1765. An attempted Spanish descent on Santa Catarina Island in Portuguese Brazil in 1766, though, was defeated by an Anglo-Portuguese squadron under Admiral Augustus Keppel. Overall, though, things at first went well for the Spanish in South America.

The same was not true in other theatres. American troops invaded Florida in 1764 and took the last holdouts, in San Agustín, at the end of 1766—a far cry from their failure a generation before. More worryingly, after two Spanish invasions of Portugal failed in 1763 and 1764, a British descent on A Coruña was combined with a successful Portuguese occupation of Galicia. The best of Spain's army was engaged in South America and, while what remained in Spain managed to defeat Anglo-Portuguese siege attempts of Ciudad Rodrigo and Badajoz (1765 and 1766), the Portuguese could not be dislodged from Galicia. Charles III had counted on French support, which had not materialised for a variety of reasons: firstly because Louis XV was attempting to stay out of all but the most essential wars due to the state of France's finances, and secondly because Spain was not the only ally pestering him for support. So the Bourbon Family Compact

---

[70] OTL modern Uruguay.

was not honoured, with Charles III even having to briefly flee to France in 1766 when Madrid was consumed with food riots. Following his return, Spain proposed peace terms on March 17th, 1767.

One apparently inconsequential footnote to the war was the British occupation of Buenos Aires, in Spanish Rio de la Plata, from 1765 to 67. The Spanish national armies were still engaged in Rio Grande de Sul, and no reinforcements came from an increasingly desperate Spain. However, the local colonial peoples formed militias and—despite the regulations against *criollos*[71] bearing weapons—successfully inflicted an embarrassing defeat on the British forces, mostly Royal Marines, at the city of Rosario in summer 1766. Although the ill-prepared British were not entirely dislodged by the time peace was signed, it was a great embarrassment for the Royal Navy (for the British Army had not been involved) and necessitated the court-martial and then, controversially, execution by firing squad of Admiral Marriott Arbuthnot, the commanding officer.

Nonetheless, the war was overall an Anglo-Portuguese victory. Spain was forced to accept *status quo ante bellum* borders, minus Florida which was annexed to the Empire of North America, and also to open up its colonies to British trade—a highly unpopular move among businessmen in the colonies. The Marquis of Ensenada, guilty of the terrible crime of being right about France's policy priorities, was exiled to Spanish America. He eventually gravitated to Buenos Aires, where the people were furious about their great victory being ignored by Spain, by the fact that they had to return the conquered mission lands in Rio Grande de Sul to Portugal, and that the new British trade would undercut their livelihoods. Ensenada was good at working with discontent, and he of course had the recent example of Prince Frederick when it

---

[71] Related to 'Creole' in English, a term used in Spanish America to describe people of wholly Iberian blood but born in the Americas rather than in Iberia—those who were born in Iberia being known as *peninsulares*. The *Casta* (caste) system meant that the *peninsulares* had all the power and influence in the colonies, with the *criollos* as second-class citizens followed by a complex hierarchy of mixed-race people based on different racial combinations, then the native Indians, and with blacks at the bottom.

came to engineering an exile backfire with colonial help...

After the war, Spain focused on internal reform under the restored chief minister Richard Wall (AKA Ricardo Wall), an Irish exile, while Carvalho remained chief minister of Portugal until the death of Joseph in 1769,[72] upon which the King's daughter Queen Maria I sent him too into American exile. Carvalho had brought Portugal kicking and screaming into the modern world, curbing the powers of the nobility, suppressing the Jesuits and bringing in greater religious freedoms. And, inevitably, the people hated him for it—although perhaps more so for the 'reign of terror' he had imposed in response to the attempts on the King's life.

Carvalho went to Rio de Janeiro, and it is perhaps inevitable that he eventually met up with his old enemy Ensenada in Buenos Aires. But it should have been known by now that if two such keen political minds could be persuaded to work for the same cause, then the foundations of the world would tremble...

---

[72] He died in 1779 OTL. He long suffered from the wound of a failed assassination attempt in 1758 which could have killed him at any time, In TTL the failed attempt still occurs, and the wound happens to kill him ten years earlier than OTL.

Chapter 10: Pole to Pole (and Lithuanian)

From: "Born Under A Squandering Tsar: Monarchy in 18th Century Russia" by Dr Andrew Sanderson (1948)—

Many in Europe had viewed with relief the aftermath of the Third War of Supremacy, in which Prussia had been reduced from a budding European Great Power down to a mere regional power. It was true that the Prussian army was still one of the best, if not the best, trained in Europe—but the losses of the war, both in men and land, coupled to the death of the charismatic Frederick II, meant that any Prussian revival would be a long hard road. Unless the Franco-Austrian alliance broke down, many commentators opined, it would be impossible.

Events intervened, though, as they often do. In 1762, Empress Elizabeth of Russia died and was succeeded by her nephew as Peter III, Emperor and Autocrat of All the Russias. Peter was a quixotic figure, which was somewhat worrying considering he occupied a position that still maintained absolute power over the country. Having been born in the Germanies himself, he was an unashamed Germanophile and had particularly admired Frederick II before his death. Some Prussian commentators even sourly remarked that, if his aunt had had the decent to die a few years earlier, he would have made Russia switch sides in the Third War.[73]

---

[73] The Prussian wits are not being that serious in TTL, but in fact this actually happened in OTL—at least, Russia pulled out of the war, although it didn't formally switch sides, when Peter came to the throne. This move made Peter very unpopular in Russia OTL as Russian troops had been occupying Berlin itself, and yet after the war Russia was not even invited to the negotiating table. Because these events are averted in TTL, Peter's position and authority are a bit more secure than in OTL.

Frederick had also been succeeded by his own nephew, who how reigned as Frederick William II, King in Prussia. Young and inexperienced, he relied heavily on advisors, most of whom were the surviving generals who had served under his father. Some counselled that attempting to regain Silesia from Austria or her minor possessions from Saxony should be Prussia's first priority, but the Franco-Austrian alliance—coupled with the fact that George III's Britain currently had problems of its own to deal with and would not be too receptive to an alliance anyway— meant that for the forseeable future, it remained an impossible dream.

Poland had been ruled since the War of the Polish Succession (in the 1730s) by Augustus III, better known as Frederick Augustus II of Saxony. Augustus cared little for Poland proper, seeing it merely as conferring a royal dignity and providing a way of gathering more power to himself in Saxony. Geographically isolated, the vast Commonwealth became paralysed with an indifferent elected king and a vast nobility (*szlachta*) unwilling to part with any of its power.

Augustus died in 1765, leaving Saxony to his son Frederick Christian, but Augustus' unpopularity in Poland meant that Frederick Christian was not the natural successor for the Sejm to elect as king.[74] Stanisław Leszczyński, a Swedish-imposed king who had ruled for two periods in the 1710s and 1730s and had eventually become Duke of Lorraine, died mere months after Augustus. The Polish system was not based on heredity, and even if it had been, he had left only two daughters—the younger of whom was Louis XV's queen consort, Maria Leszczyńska. The throne remained empty and the opposing factions deadlocked despite the efforts of the Interrex, the Archbishop of Gniezno

---

[74]The Polish-Lithuanian Commonwealth was an elective monarchy, with a king being elected for life by the Election Sejm, a special session of the Polish Sejm (parliament). Although only nobility (*szlachta*) could vote, the definition of what constituted noble blood was very broad and incorporated many poor farmers, meaning that over ten percent of the population could vote for the king—a bigger proportion than could vote for parliamentary representation in Great Britain due to the restrictive property franchise there.

and Primate of Poland.[75] Months passed and no king was elected. Civil war openly broke out in July 1766, and it became obvious that the great powers neighbouring Poland would intervene.

Austria produced the Archduke Joseph Ferdinand, second son of Maria Theresa, as their candidate for King of Poland. (Later he would generally become known as 'Archduke Ferdinand' after his elder brother Ferdinand Francis became Holy Roman Emperor as Ferdinand IV and confusion could be avoided). Maria Theresa's armies occupied the Kraków region, preparing to take Warsaw and attempt to impose Austrian-backed rule on the country, just as Sweden had fifty years earlier. However, a deal between Frederick William of Prussia and Peter of Russia emerged in 1767, with both states declaring war on Austria—though mysteriously they did not produce a candidate of their own for the Polish kingship.

Commentators who had expected the Prussians to drive mulishly for Silesia again were left gaping as Frederick William's forces invaded Polish Royal Prussia and then retook the Polish-occupied southern half of Ducal Prussia that they had lost in the Third War of Supremacy. The Swedish-occupied northern half was left untouched; it later emerged that Peter had, somewhat controversially, bought Sweden's neutrality by promising them Courland. The Prussians met up with the Russians and, in a crushing series of victories at Warsaw, Poznan and Breslau (finally entering Silesia), the Austrians were driven from Poland. The Poles themselves typically fought on both sides, as well as some *szlachta* factions maintaining private armies manoeuvring for the establishment of some other candidate as king. There was no unified resistance until it was too late. The conflict would be recorded in the history books not as the Polish Civil War, but as the War of the Polish Partition...

The major provisions of the Treaty of Stockholm (1771):

Austria to retain Silesia and the vicinity of Kraków (though

---

[75] The Interrex is a temporary position appointed by the Sejm to oversee the transitional period between monarchs, modelled on a similar office used in the classical Roman Republic. The office was usually given to the Archbishop of Gniezno and Primate of Poland, the most senior Catholic clergyman in the Commonwealth, who at this point was Władysław Aleksander Łubieński.

not all of Galicia), but renounce any and all claims to the Polish throne.

Royal Prussia and the formerly Polish Ducal Prussia to be annexed to Prussia.

Sweden to retain northern Ducal Prussia and be awarded Courland as well.

Some eastern vojvodships[76] of Poland (those with a Ruthenian majority) to be directly annexed to Russia.

The Grand Duchy of Lithuania separated from the Commonwealth as an independent state, with a Russian-imposed Grand Duke.

The remainder of Poland to be reorganised into a rump Kingdom of Poland in personal union with Prussia.

The territorial integrities of the resulting Polish and Lithuanian successor states to be guaranteed.

Peter appointed his son Paul, the Tsarevich (crown prince), as Grand Duke of Lithuania. This position rapidly became accepted as the Russian equivalent to Britain's Prince of Wales or Spain's Prince of Asturias, always occupied by the crown prince. There remained periodic uprisings in the former Commonwealth against foreign occupiers, especially in the southeastern vojvodships where Polish lands had been directly annexed to Russia and the Orthodox religion imposed, but in the rump Poland proper the situation eventually subsided to something not unlike the apathy during the reign of Augustus III. However, Frederick William was far more interested in his new (reduced) Polish domain than Augustus had been—not something his new Polish subjects became very pleased about. This was true to the extent that within a few years people spoke of 'Prussia-Poland' or even 'Brandenburg-Poland' as though 'Prussia' now described the combined area of both states.

Prussia had bounced back admirably from its humiliation, with Peter's alliance sometimes being called the 'Miracle of the House of Brandenburg' before that term would later be applied

---

[76] Vojvodship, also spelled voivodeship, is an anglicised term for the word used in Poland (and many neighbouring countries) for province or sub-division (województwo in Polish).

to even more unlikely events in the nineteenth century involving Frederick William's grandson.[77] The Tsar's position was steadied at home, but a coup plot involving his strong-minded German wife Catherine emerged in 1772.[78] Peter purged the Leib Guards, who had collaborated against him, and had Catherine exiled to the appropriately named Yekaterinburg, on the other side of the Urals.

Meanwhile, on the other side of the world, a crisis of quite a different kind was taking shape...

---

[77] In OTL, this described Peter's aforementioned act of withdrawing Russia from the Seven Years' War.
[78] In OTL of course she succeeded and became Catherine the Great.

Chapter 11: Don't Tread On Me

JOHN STUART, 3RD EARL OF BUTE (TORY, OPPOSITION): Can the noble lord deny that the colonials enjoy the same comforts, the same benefits as true Englishmen? Can he deny that they have been defended against the rapacities of the French and protected from piracy by the Navy? Then why can he not see that it is only just that they pay their fair share of tax?
CHARLES WATSON-WENTWORTH, 2ND MARQUESS OF ROCKINGHAM (WHIG-PATRIOT, FIRST LORD OF THE TREASURY): Indeed, sir, I cannot. But why, then, I ask the noble lord, must his reasoning proceed in only one direction? The colonials—the Americans—have not stood idly by while our valiant forces defend them. They have bled and died alongside what the noble lord calls true Englishmen. Why, then, are they denied the liberties that we all agree are the birthright of every trueborn Englishman? Can the noble lord answer me that?

- Exchange in the House of Lords, 5th October 1767, as reported in *The London Gazette*

From: "The Making of a Nation", by Peter Arnold (1987)—

Many scholars have debated just when the awakening of a national consciousness can be said to have taken place in Britain's colonies on the North American continent. To be sure, there was some semblance of independence from the motherland almost since the colonies were founded: the isolation from England, the separation across a vast ocean, meant that this was unavoidable. When contact with the King was typically limited to him occasionally sending a new governor every few years and ultimately initiating some of the wars in which the colonials fought, the colonies were independent in name if not in fact. And they developed as such, creating their own means of governance, indeed effectively trialling many new constitutional ideas in different colonies. Many colonies had local assemblies elected on varying means, and, for reasons of historical accident, lacked an established Church. Any attempt to impose Anglicanism on the colonies now would run into the problems of the numerous German Calvinists and Lutherans, to say nothing of the Presbyterian Scots and the (few) Catholics who had settled there. Thus, America had always been a little different.

Prince Frederick's exile was an epiphany. The vast majority of the colonial Americans had never seen their monarch, even their future monarch, on anything except a coin or a print, much less in the flesh. When he was travelling up and down Cisappalachia, politicking with governors and occasionally solving disputes, suddenly the King was not just some vague figure over the horizon, but a man of flesh and blood who was at work in the world. It was, as the nineteenth-century commentator Philip Bulkeley remarked dryly, as though America's Judaean concepts of monarchy had suddenly become those of Christendom.

Even after Frederick himself departed, the plans and promises he had set in motion meant that there were serious political upheavals. Tyrannical governors were no longer tolerated, and Frederick appointed more native-born Americans—for so they were now called—as governors. He was the first monarch to elevate significant numbers of Americans to the peerage, and many (including Lawrence Washington) elected not to take up their seats in the House of Lords, but to remain at home in the colonies where their titles at present meant little. It was an important message: Americans were not simply Englishmen who happened to be born abroad, and returned home when they became important and influential men. They identified more with their birthplace, the thin line of civilisation bordering the vast tracts of unexplored wilderness, than with the green fields and pleasant hills of England.

This awakening took some years in America, beginning in the 1730s and coming to a climax some thirty or forty years later. It took rather longer for the British public consciousness to become aware of it, hence the relative surprise with which the Troubled Sixties and the Crisis of 1765 were held in many quarters.

It is impossible to cover here all the causes leading up to the situation, but the Crisis ultimately stemmed from the fact that the Third War of Supremacy had cost Britain dearly and, given that a great part of the war expenditure had been devoted to forcing the French from Québec, many British politicians considered it only appropriate that the Americans should pay their fair share of the taxes levied to cover it. Furthermore, the colonies had always had extremely lenient tax regimes compared to the home country. That was one reason why the British settler colonies had grown in population so rapidly, while their French counterparts had floundered—French law was the same everywhere, so there was less reason for a Frenchman to move to a wild colony if he would have to pay the same taxes when he got there. When the British government of the 1760s now tried to alter this comfortable status quo, it resulted in tax protests such as the Pittsburgh Whisky Riots of 1768.

Nonetheless, it was clear that the situation was unsustainable. The Americans regardless were defiant on the subject, and a committee of their peers was formed to negotiate directly with the newly formed Department for Home and Colonial Affairs.[79] The committee was headed by Sir Benjamin Franklin, the celebrated natural philosopher and political writer who was respected on both sides of the Atlantic.[80] Franklin had, in

---

[79] In OTL the Northern and Southern Departments were eventually turned into the Department for Home Affairs and the Department for Foreign and Colonial Affairs, i.e. colonial affairs were attached to the Foreign rather than Home Ministry. In TTL the colonies are a little nearer to the government's heart, and furthermore the change happened rather later in OTL, *after* the American colonies had broken away, so the remaining colonies at that point were viewed as less important and integral.

[80] Unlike OTL, Ben Franklin is *not* the first American to be really notable in Europe in TTL, and does not rise to prominence until after the War of the British Succession with its martial figures like Lawrence Washington. Hence he is accepted more readily by European educated society and there are no silly disputes over the best shape for a lightning conductor 'because colonials are rustic idiots so they must be wrong' as in OTL.

recent years, provoked a stir in his native Massachusetts with the publication of a short volume entitled *Unite or Die: The Case For A New England Confederation.* The title was a reference to his famous political cartoon representing the colonies as the parts of a snake that would have to come together to vanquish the French. Previously, the fiercely independent New England colonies had voiced much opposition to any sort of unified confederation, in particular King James II's short-lived Dominion of New England that had also attempted to include New York. In the end, of course, that particular project had been voided by James' overthrow in the First Glorious Revolution, and few had dared reopen that particular can of worms.

But now the situation had changed. In particular, there was a growing division between the colonies as a whole. The colonies had originally been founded when the British believed that North America was much narrower than it is, and had envisaged there being only ten days' march between the Atlantic and Pacific coasts. Based on that assumption, the colonies' charters stated that their territory would go from the east coast westward until it reached the Pacific. As North America turned out to be rather wider than expected, this meant that if this was implemented, a map of the British lands would look like a series of long stretched-out stripes stacked one on top of the other.

All fine and good in theory; but, for the first time, the Third War of Supremacy meant that at least part of the dream could be realised, and now it ran into the problems of reality. The French had been driven both from Québec, and more importantly from the point of view of the colonies, the Ohio Country, which was claimed under the old charters by Pennsylvania and Virginia. Similar claims were made by colonies further north and south, extending their theoretical borders westward into the wilderness that was now nominal British territory, though inhabited by many Indian nations. The problem was firstly that many of the colonial claims clashed with each other, particularly those of the New England colonies, and secondly that some of the colonies were now surrounded on all sides by others, and simply had no westward frontier on the wilderness into which they could expand.

Maryland was one of these, but the New England colonies were the worst. Rhode Island was unambiguously cut off, and some claims by New York might also cut off Masachusetts (except in their separated northern Maine territory) and Connecticut. The latter continued to insist on claims to a disconnected strip of land *beyond* New York, but few took this seriously—particularly after the widely condemned 'Hartford Tea Revolt' over tea taxes in 1767. Regardless of how much the New Englanders might dislike the idea of confederation, they began to realise that the alternative might be being reduced to small, plaintive, ignored voices in an Empire of North America that included vastly expanded colonies of Virginia, New York and Pennsylvania.

These were two of the problems. There were othersWhat to do with the Catholic French in Québec, currently under the effective military dictatorship of James Wolfe, and certainly not an appropriate land for many of the principles of British government. What the rights of the Indians, both as individuals and as nations, should be (the Americans and some British armchair imperialists disagreed strongly on this). And, of course, the fact that 'representation' had become a clear, if vague, call in the colonies. If Americans were to pay taxes like Britons, then they ought to be able to vote like them, too.

The American cause might well have been doomed, had it not had the man at the top on their side. King George III had grown up in Virginia, indeed spoke with a rather strange hybrid German/Planter accent that was much ridiculed in continental Europe, and continued to defend the colonies' interests at court. Having said that, his quote "Born and raised in this country, I glory in the name of *American*" is most probably apocryphal.[81]

The situation was not helped by the fact that, after the retirement of Fairfax in 1764, King George had appointed the young but politically vigorous Lord William North as Lord Deputy of North America.[82] North had encouraged political debate on the

---

[81] OTL's version of George III famously said "Born and raised in this country, I glory in the name of *Briton*."

[82] More or less the same as OTL's Frederick North, except that being born in 1732, in TTL he was named after the new Prince of Wales (the

subject and, in 1768, accepted a joint call from several significant American figures to call a new Albany Congress. The first, thirteen years before, had been called in the spirit of unity against the French and Indian enemies during the Third War of Supremacy. Even back then, Franklin had drafted an early plan of unifying the colonies under a strong executive, which had been largely ignored at the time, but had provoked further discussion.

Despite the long sea journey between Britain and America, some common interests began to emerge. George was helped in that, after Pitt died in 1766, he was replaced by the Marquess of Rockingham, a singularly capable manager of interests in the House and a steady hand at Government. Rockingham was, in particular, responsible for bringing Charles James Fox, third son of Henry Fox and technically too young to be an MP according to law, into the core of the Whigs. Fox was something of an enigma, being a political radical in almost every conceivable way, although he drew the line in some areas and criticised the more extreme John Wilkes. Fox was a defender of colonial rights from the start, although he did not get on with the King due to his staunch abolitionist views and the King's relaxed attitude towards slavery. This would cause problems later on.

By 1771, the North Commission, having exchanged members and had one or two die and be replaced, had settled on a rough arrangement that would eventually become the American Constitution of 1788 when ratified by all the colonies' assemblies. Ironically enough, any objections from the British people over 'special treatment' of the Americans may have been masked by a common cause in 1772 when the British government decided to switch over to the Gregorian calendar after centuries continuing to use the Julian, henceforth known as 'Old Style' or O.S. The people's chant—on both sides of the Atlantic—of 'give us back our eleven days' is often today portrayed as a pure act of ignorance

---

later William IV) and not Prince Frederick like OTL. It may be news to some OTL Americans that North was actually a fairly astute and capable politician, though one who consistently put local interests above the whole. This is still true in OTL, only this time, being Lord Deputy of the Colonies, he's being narrow-minded and provincial *on America's side.*

by peasantry who believed they had literally had their lifetimes shortened. However, the riots were often provoked by the more prosaic reason that the eleven days in question which the crafty government had 'abolished' in order to synchronise the calendars just happened to be ones which included a pre-existing public holiday. Though the demanded compensation was never obtained, mutual annoyance by ordinary people in Britain and America may have smoothed over any transatlantic disagreements over the North Commission.[83]

The North Plan, as it was known, modified Franklin's original scheme to take into account recent developments. Franklin had already acknowledged at the time that Delaware would have to be subsumed into Pennsylvania, as it was already for most intents and purposes, and he had not counted Georgia as a colony. This proved prophetic, as the young colonial administration faltered in the late 1760s after its capital was sacked by a Chickasaw Indian attack, its territory reabsorbed back into South Carolina. However, the North Commission considerably expanded these tentative consolidation ideas, and eventually developed the concept that became known as *Five Confederations and One Empire*.

Under this new and quite radical proposition, the original colonial charters would be modified and combined to produce five new units with elected 'Confederate' assemblies, all of which would have suitable outlets to the west for expansion into the new territories. The first of these was the Confederation of New England, formally formed in 1776 and incorporating Massachusetts, Connecticut, Rhode Island, Nova Scotia (ostensibly including Newfoundland) and New Hampshire. A unitary national or 'Imperial' government over the Confederations was also created. The North System was based on North America receiving a parliamentary voting system like Britain's, but due to the wildly varying sizes and populations of the colonies—far more

---

[83] This is largely as OTL, except in OTL the whole calendar conversion and resulting arguments happened in 1751, twenty years earlier. In TTL the War of the British Succession and the Second Glorious Revolution meant that things were a little too hectic to consider matters as prosaic as the calendar at that point.

so even than Britain's counties—standardised voting 'provinces' were created. Typically, small colonies like Rhode Island consisted of one province, while larger and more populous ones were divided into several. Members of the hypothetical American parliament would be elected based on these provinces for country representation and on certain cities given borough status for urban representation. The old colonial borders were sometimes retained for other administrative and traditional purposes, though. (It is notable that many of these ideas were built on proposals by Pro-Reform groups at home in Britain who saw America as a suitable testbed; Britain's own unreformed electoral system after all had the equivalent of Rhode Island having over ten times as many representatives as Virginia).

Other Confederations were more typically dominated by one state: the Confederation of Pennsylvania (including Delaware and half of New Jersey), the Confederation of New York (including the other half of New Jersey), the Confederation of Virginia (including Maryland), and the Confederation of Carolina (including both Carolinas and the former Georgia). A sixth Confederation, Canada (Québec), was also posited, although never implemented: the magic number of five would not be altered until the mid-nineteenth century.

The new reorganisation was not exactly universally popular throughout the colonies, many of whom had populations proud of their histories and distinctive identities, but it did provide for equitable opportunities for westward settlement. Furthermore, King George had taken a relatively hard line towards the Indians. Over the next few years, Indian nations were either asked to formally become British protectorates or else remove to the west. Some of the larger Indian nations, including the Cherokee and the Iroquois (Howden), agreed to the protectorate status, while some of the others fought, including the Creek and the Lapute. After some vicious fighting, the American colonial troops won, somewhat reassessing British home opinions of how seriously they needed to treat the Indian nations. The Cherokee agreed to sell some of their current lands for Carolinian settlement in return for taking over the lands currently held by the defeated

Creek and assimilating them into their nation.

Taxes in America remained generally lower than those at home, though no longer by an enormous margin.[84] The first elected 'Yankee Parliament' (officially known as the Continental Parliament) met at 1788 in Fredericksburg, perhaps an inevitable choice for the national capital given both its central location and its history. It was opened by George III himself, on a state visit, and it was also in this year that the Constitution was finally ratified by the last of the Confederations, Carolina. The date had been chosen purposefully, one hundred years to the day after the Glorious Revolution had created Britain's own constitution, which had provided much of the groundwork for the American version.

Taken from George III's Opening of the First American Parliament, 1788:

"Let this new dominion, this great Empire, show itself to the world and stand proud beside the home nations! Let it fulfil its clear purpose and destiny in spreading the Protestant religion and the liberty of England from sea to shining sea! And let it be the home to my people, and my heirs, from now until the ending of the world."

From: "The Making of a Nation", by Peter Arnold (1987)—

But while the American crisis had been neatly averted, the politics of Sir Benjamin Franklin, Lord North and King George III were scarcely the only reason. Something came about in the intervening years, something which both reminded the Americans why they still needed defending, and reminded the British why it was imperative that they should hold fast to their colonial cousins.

In the year 1779, a Peruvian shot a Spanish governor and set the world down a track that would lead to wrack and ruin for centuries to come...

---

[84] In OTL American taxes rocketed after independence, but by that point rights matched demands...the same is true here.

Chapter 12: Southern Sunrise

"Ideology, the most insidious of evils to afflict our world. Those masses who yearn for freedom and liberty will soon find themselves enslaved by Freedom and Liberty."

—George Spencer-Churchill the Younger

From: "Rise of a Nation" by William Rogers (1928)—

The causes of the Andean Revolts are too complex to be completely considered in such a brief summary, even if they were entirely known. Primary sources remain scanty in many areas, particularly those dealing with the rural rebel groups that played the key role in the initial stages of the crisis. However, certain broad strokes can be discerned...

Spain's approach to colonialism had always been quite different to that of Britain and France. Partly, of course, this was because Spain had been a colonial power for far longer, indeed it may not be an exaggeration to say that she was the first true colonial power in history. Thus, the government of the Spanish colonies in the Americas could be said to still be firmly rooted in the feudal institutions of the Middle Ages. A carefully designed racial hierarchy was in place by which the *peninsulares*, or white Europeans born in the Iberian homeland, were ranked above those pure-blood Europeans born in the colonies, *criollos*, who were in turn ranked above the half-white/half-native *mestizos*, and so on for the native *amerindians* and with the African *negros* at the bottom. People with parents from different castes were slotted into one of several intricately constructed half-way stages, each with its own unique name and place in society.

This system, which now seems so alien to modern mainstream thinking, was aided and abetted by the growing popularity of the Linnaean Racist philosophy in the mid to late eighteenth century. Existing convention was thus backed up with scientific (or 'natural-philosophical') justification, and many Spanish and *peninsulare* writers of the period expounded on the natural virtues of the Casta system. Perhaps as a result of this, this same period coincided with a national awakening among the *criollos* of Spanish America, particularly in the south where the system was most rigid. Pamphlets arguing against the system were widely distributed, despite official attempts to crack down. It is quite probable that this movement was quietly masterminded by the exiled Marquis of Ensenada, from his estate in Buenos Aires where he periodically met with his old Portuguese foe Carvalho. The two former ministers were certainly involved with the development of their ideological philosophy at some point, at least. Ensenada and Carvalho may have seen the Criollistas as merely a King Frederick-inspired means to an end that would lead to their return to power in the Peninsula (ironically), but if so, events escaped their control.

The *criollos* were arguably primed for rebellion by the 1770s, as the excesses of the Casta system were combined with punishing new taxes from Spain's government under Charles III and his new Italian-born chief minister, Bernardo Tanucci, who had formerly headed affairs in the dynastically tied Kingdom of Naples. Tanucci was also a fervent anti-clericalist and his government had masterminded the crackdown on the Jesuits in Spain. Despite Ensenada's own anti-clericalist streak, the Criollista movement was generally quite pro-Jesuit, and in defiance of the official pronouncements of the Jesuit missions in New Spain being dissolved in the late 1760s, the 'black-robes' continued to operate fairly openly in the Viceroyalty of Peru and the Captaincy-General of Chile.[85] The Jesuits' 'Reductions', settlements intended

---

[85] In OTL Spain established a separate Viceroyalty of Rio de la Plata in 1776. In TTL this was butterflied away by the different events of the First Platinean War compared to OTL, in which the Spanish/Portuguese dispute over the Missions was part of the wider Seven Years' War. The lands that became the Viceroyalty of Rio de la Plata in OTL are therefore still part of the Viceroyalty of Peru and ruled from Lima in TTL. This has sparked some resentment considering how far away Lima

to Christianise and 'civilise' the natives and protect them from overt colonial encroachment, had played a large part in expanding Spanish control in South America. Now they were seen by many colonials in Spanish America as being an integral part of the colonies' cultural identity. However, while the people remained broadly in favour of the Society of Jesus itself, they were quick to settle the now vacated Jesuit lands. For example, in the Viceroyalty of New Spain, the city of Las Estrellas in Upper California was founded at this time.[86]

However, the initial spark of rebellion came not from the Criollistas, but from the Indians. José Gabriel Condorcanqui was the great-grandson of Tupac Amaru, the last Sapa Inca (emperor) of the Tahuantinsuyo, the native civilisation known (inaccurately) to most Europeans as 'the Incas'. He was also vice-governor of the province of Cusco. In this capacity he repeatedly petitioned the authorities in Lima to improve the lot of the native peoples— in particular conditions in the mines and textile mills. However, indifference on the part of the *peninsulare* authorities, combined with the fact that Criollistas from as far away as Buenos Aires were also continually making petititons at Lima at this time, served to ensure that Condorcanqui was repeatedly rebuffed.

In response, Condorcanqui returned to his native roots and took the name Tupac Amaru II, organising the first serious rebellion against the Spanish colonial authorities in two centuries. With the execution of the tyrannical Governor Antonio de Arriaga in 1779, the Great Andean Rebellion began.

The colonial authorities hastily organised a militia under Tiburcio Landa, which was sent out to fortify the town of Sangara. However, Tupac Amaru's forces caught the few hundred volunteers on the road to the town[87] and decimated them, despite the rebels having a shortage of muskets and powder and relying

---

is from the Plate.

[86] Las Estrellas is the city known in OTL as Los Angeles.

[87] OTL, Tupac Amaru won a similarly crushing victory, but in Sangara itself. This required burning Landa's forces out of a fortified church, which was successfully spun by Spanish colonial propagandists into painting Tupac Amaru's rebellion as anti-Christian, turning the majority of the people against him. In TTL this doesn't happen.

largely on more archaic weapons such as slingshots. Furthermore, Tupac Amaru had access to a number of Indians and a few sympathetic *criollos* who had served with the Spanish Army in the First Platinean War in the 1760s, and thus arguably possessed more trained veterans than the authorities in Cusco.

On the advice of Tupac Amaru's wife and fellow commander, Micaela Bastidas, the rebel army successfully captured Cusco on Christmas Day 1780. Another militia force, this time sent by the government in Lima, suffered losses due to poor logistical planning and failed to retake the town in February 1781. It was at this time that news of the rebellion truly began to reach Spanish and other European ears, as well as those within Britain's Empire of North America.

The rebellion also inspired others. In Upper Peru,[88] the Aymara rebellion of Tomas Katari had actually begun slightly before Tupac Amaru's, but it was Tupac Amaru's successes that whipped Katari's into a real fervour. However, the native Indian forces failed to take La Paz in 1781 and Katari's army retreated to Cusco, combining with Tupac Amaru's. Parts of Upper Peru remained under Spanish control throughout the war, although often reduced to the fortifiable cities.

The loss of face to Spain was tremendous and so in 1781 a force sent from the homeland was united with colonial armies in New Granada. The war did not go entirely the rebels' way, but the Spanish were nonetheless unable to achieve a decisive victory. However, it is likely that the rebellions would have eventually been crushed, had it not been for the interference of other states.

For more than a century, one of France's chief foreign policy ambitions was that Spain's rich empire in the Americas should be transferred to French control. This could take place via the kind of Bourbon union that the outcome of the First War of Supremacy had prevented, but might eventually become more feasible as

---

[88] Approximately OTL modern Bolivia. Lower Peru is what we now simply call Peru. The Aymara are the main native people of Bolivia/Upper Peru, just as the Tahuantinsuya (AKA the Incas) are the largest native people of Peru/Lower Peru.

Spain waned and France waxed. Now the young King Louis XVI,[89] having inherited a state that was shaky but recovering, buoyed by the riches brought in from the Indian trading empire of Dupleix (now under the rule of Governor-General Rochambeau),[90] saw that chance slipping through his fingers. Despite warnings from his Swiss-born Comptroller-General of Finances, Jacques Necker, that France's treasury could not sustain another great war, Louis thought war the only option.

However, he had two possible approaches to consider that might deliver French hegemony over Spanish America. Firstly, renew the Bourbon Family Compact, help Spain quell the rebellion, and use this as a foothold towards drawing the Spanish Empire towards France. Secondly, support the rebels against Spain and gain influence over any succeeding rebel state. Both of these involved sending French troops to Spanish America, and so the order to do so was proclaimed long before the indecisive Louis had made any clear decision on which option was to be taken—or, for that matter, informed the Spaniards.

It is hopeful but possibly incorrect to believe that the resulting comedy of errors can no longer take place in our time, with our Photel[91] and other innovations in the area of communications. In any case, in 1782 a French fleet under the Duc de Noailles and Admiral de Grasse was sent out from Quiberon, with the intention of landing troops "in the Viceroyalty of Peru, and

---

[89] *Not* OTL's Louis XVI, but his father Louis-Ferdinand, known in OTL only as "Louis, Dauphin of France", who never came to the throne as he died of consumption in 1765, predeceasing his father Louis XV who died in 1774. In TTL he lives longer and succeds his father as king. *OTL's* Louis XVI is thus the Dauphin (crown prince) at this point rather than king, and will presumably succeed his father as Louis *XVII*. The French Bourbons' rather limited choice of names for their princes can result in some confusion...

[90] Jean-Baptiste Donatien de Vimeur, comte de Rochambeau. A veteran of the Second War of Supremacy/War of the Austrian Succession, in OTL he is best known for commanding the French expeditionary force that intervened in the American Revolutionary War. In TTL, with no American Revolution, Rochambeau has instead been assigned to India and has risen to replace Dupleix as Governor-General.

[91] The term used in TTL for radio, derived from 'photonic telegraphy'.

linking up with our allies", orders which were understandably ambiguous in just who those allies would be, but were rather less excusably ambiguous in just *where* in the vast Viceroyalty this was supposed to happen.

This meant that in August 1782, owing to what we nowadays would call crossed wires, the French expeditionary force was under the impression that Spain was the enemy and the native Indian rebels should be supported—this being the favoured option before the fleet left. Meanwhile the King had changed his mind and his ministers had concluded a new Family Compact with Charles III, with the Spanish Government believing that the French were their allies. The results were predictable. Repeating the British attempt of a generation earlier, Admiral de Grasse's fleet sailed up the River Plate and took Buenos Aires as a blow against Spain— at the same time that the propagandists of the Spanish colonial authorities in the region were trumpeting the invented successes of their French allies against Tupac Amaru II. Rumours of the French ravaging Buenos Aires, inflated from a few scattered incidents, served to unite the entire Criollista movement against France and in alliance with the Indians, who otherwise they might have seen as enemies: after all, many Criollistas had liked the idea of confiscating Indian lands and moving into them. But the French blunder had unified what otherwise might have been disparate groups prone to infighting into a coherent resistance outraged by the 'betrayal'. The whole of the Plate region, supported by the Captaincy-General of Chile from early 1783, rose in revolt. The Second Platinean War had begun.

The great rebellion could perhaps still have been contained, but Britain and Portugal entered the war on the side of the rebels. Portuguese support was largely clandestine, with war being undeclared on the Iberian frontier, and was secured in return for the rebels promising to make several border adjustments favourable to Portuguese Brazil. An Anglo-American force under Admiral Howe defeated de Grasse's fleet at the mouth of the River Plate, then landed an army commanded by the American General George Augustine Washington. While the people of the Plate were still suspicious of the British from their experiences in the last war, after the British participated in the rebel capture of Córdoba, they were accepted and Washington was treated to a parade through the streets of that city. This event, a great irony considering the events of the next century, was captured in oil on canvas by Antonio Vilca. Vilca was a former apprentice of Marcos Zapata, the last great artist of the hybrid 'Cuzco School' in which native South American Indians painted (largely) religious works according to Spanish instruction, but added their own cultural influences. These paintings were characterised by the recurring figure of the *ángel arcabucero*, a warrior angel depicted in then modern clothing and wielding an arquebus as his weapon. Vilca portrayed Washington and his men in a style clearly influenced by these long-established figures and neatly expressed his own sympathies that the Americans, no matter their own Protestant faith, were fighting on the cause of God. The original painting *Los Libertadores* was later acquired by the Washington family and now hangs in the Fredericksburg Museum of Art. Vilca was far from alone, however, and his sudden fame overseas meant he somewhat unintentionally founded a new school of art which would come to symbolise the distinct artistic heritage of the rebels and their eventual nation: the *Escuela Cordobés* or Córdoban School.

Although the French remained in control of the city of Buenos Aires until the end of the war, they were unable to break out of their initial pockets of control. A joint Franco-Spanish fleet was assembled at Cadiz in late 1783, with the intention of punching through the Royal Navy blockade of South America and landing reinforcements to support the Duc de Noailles' army. However, another British fleet under Admiral Augustus Keppel met them off Cape Trafalgar. The combat was a shock defeat for the British; although the Franco-Spanish fleet slightly outnumbered the Royal Navy ships, the British were accustomed to being able to fight above their weight at sea. The combat exposed serious flaws in how the Royal Navy had been handled after the Third War of Supremacy, eventually leading to a great shipbuilding programme under the latter half of the Marquess of Rockingham's first term as Prime Minister, but for the moment tempers were salved with the court-martial and disgrace of Keppel.

While Trafalgar was a British defeat, Keppel's forces had managed to sink several Franco-Spanish transport ships and the fleet was forced to return to Cadiz. Also, the shock victory had convinced the overly impressionable Louis XVI that now was the time to seize control of the English Channel and invade Britain herself, something which France's strained treasury was simply not capable of funding. The French forces were still pointlessly moving into position in Normandy for the hypothetical, impossible invasion at the time of the Treaty of London in 1785. Meanwhile, the Royal Navy licked its wounds and was desperate to mend its reputation with a victory, facing strong criticism in Parliament. The bold Captain Philip Anson, son of the politically disgraced Admiral George Anson,[92] acted on intelligence reports suggesting that the Franco-Spanish were preparing to pre-emptively occupy Malta, at the time still under the somnambulant rule of the ancient Order of the Knights of St John. Whether there was any truth to these reports remains unclear even to this day, but Anson decided to strike first and took control of the strategically valuable island in March 1784, with barely a shot being fired in the process. The act proved controversial across Europe and, while Malta remained British at the Treaty of London, Anson the younger had not chosen a good way to try to repair his father's mistakes: he would die a decade later after being reassigned to the death sentence of the Fever Islands in the West Indies.

Back in South America, the Spanish had finally achieved a decisive victory over Tupac Amaru at the recapture of Lima in 1784, but by now Criollista rebel control over Platinea[93] and Chile was virtually uncontested. A relief army from the Criollistas prevented the Spanish from pressing further into the lands held by the Indian rebels. The surrender of La Paz and Havana in 1785

---

[92] In TTL Admiral George Anson was unable to recover his position of power after the Second Glorious Revolution as he was seen as too close to the Williamite governments he had served. A knock-on effect of this is that Anson's voyages of discovery in the 1740s were not followed up on to the same extent as OTL. In OTL Anson had no children, but in TTL his wife Elizabeth bore a son.

[93] I.e. OTL Argentina – both Argentina and Platinea ultimately mean Land of Silver.

marked the end of the war and the punishing Treaty of London, whose provisions were as follows:

Spain to acknowledge the loss of Cuba to Britain, to recognise Britain's claims to Gibraltar and Falkland's Islands, and to accept the independence of the entire Viceroyalty of Peru and Captaincy-General of Chile under the rebel provisional government (as yet unnamed).

France to cede the northern hinterlands of Louisiana to the Empire of North America. An Anglo-American siege of New Orleans in 1784 was successfully resisted by the French, meaning that the French kept the more densely populated southern heartland. The dividing line was intended to approximately conform to the thirty-fifth parallel north, although this was never hard and fast and would later be subject to change.

Some lands in Upper Peru and Platinea to be ceded to Portuguese Brazil by the rebel provisional government, a government which would eventually become the United Provinces of South America (not established until the Convention of Córdoba in 1790).

Thanks to a Québecois rebellion in support of France (1784-5), a second Great Expulsion would see all the remaining French colonials in British North America deported to French Louisiana or France itself, at least on paper; in practice many remained in Canada by paying lip service to Anglicanism and speaking English. The former laws giving limited protection to the French Canadians and protecting them from English colonisation were torn up. Canada was opened to settlement from the Confederation of New England; protests from the other Confederations saw the eventual Act of Settlement (1794), by which New England ceded its claimed westward territories back to the imperial government in return for Canada being formally added to New England as a new series of provinces and territories. Disputes over legal ambiguities concerning the New England western cession would cause headaches in Fredericksburg for decades afterwards.

The Treaty would lead to trouble for *all* its participants later on, but for the present, to say it was a shock to Spanish society was an understatement. The lands of the Spanish Empire, it was said, had been granted by God, and if He were to take them away, what did that say about the state of Spain and her governance?

Charles III had already been forced to flee the country once thanks to food riots in 1766. Now he fled again, as street riots ruled Madrid and Bernardo Tanucci was killed by a mob. Controversially, Britain supported Charles' return to Spain, believing that the alternative might be Louis achieving his Franco-Spanish Union after all. However, Charles was forced to adopt far more liberal methods of government under chief minister José Moñino y Redondo, conde de Floridablanca, who had previously been known for assisting with the expulsion of the Jesuits and reform of the Spanish education system. Under his ministry, the powers of the Spanish Cortes were somewhat extended and the Audiencias in New Spain and New Granada[94] were reformed, giving them more independence and authority to respond to rebellions, lest Spain lose the rest of its American empire.

The young United Provinces of South America was characterised from the start by radical ideas, although they expressed themselves in odd ways. Possessing a population that was almost entirely strongly Catholic, the country nonetheless made a break with Rome, beginning rather unofficially in the 1790s thanks to Spanish domination of the Papacy meaning that the Pope condemned the UPSA and refused to appoint new bishops for its sees. The UPSA's religious position was formalised after the passing of the Dissolution Act of 1802, which disestablished the Roman Catholic Church in the country. Jansenist ideals, popular with many European Catholic dissenters in the eighteenth century, were embraced and became associated with the intellectual classes. Many radicals from other nations whose ideas were suppressed at home moved to the UPSA to take advantage of its religious and social freedoms, including the British republicans Thomas Paine and Joseph Priestley.

The UPSA's population was also boosted by deserters from Noailles' army, including Noailles' own son, who had fled after his father's disgrace and suicide, and a young captain named

---

[94] Approximately modern Mexico+Central America and Colombia+Venezuela+Ecuador, respectively.

Jean-Charles Pichegru, who eventually became Marshal-General of the UPSA's military, the *Fuerzas Armadas de las Provincias Unidas*. From the very beginning, the UPSA was known to be a place where the usual European laws did not apply, and a place where oppressed groups might be able to settle in piece. The Casta system was abolished, and certain areas were set aside for native Indian or other non-European settlement, while others were reorganised and exploited. Radical positions were staked out on abolishing slavery and giving rights to the Africans who had been at the bottom of the Casta system: however, in the short term, what improvements actually materialised were rather limited and half-hearted. This issue would return to affect the politics of the UPSA many times.

From the beginning, the government was republican, its *Cortes Nacionales* modelled on the Dutch *Staten-Generaal*; it was the Dutch United Provinces, and their rebellion against Spain two centuries earlier, from which the country's name had taken its inspiration. One thing the name 'United Provinces of South America' did not readily allow was a short demonym to describe the identity of the citizens of the new country; 'Sudamericano' and 'Provinciaunidense', two early suggestions, hardly rolled off the tongue. The name that eventually stuck was 'Meridian', derived from how maps of the time (still largely labelled in Latin) called South America '*America Meridionalis*'.

In addition to the Cortes Nacionales, a directly elected head of state, the President-General, was created. At the time the role was poorly defined in the Constitution, something that would also cause political difficulties later on.

The symbols of the new nation were visible from the beginning. The Silver Torch of Liberty, present on the final form of the national flag, referenced the irregulars who had stormed colonial forts by night bearing such torches. The Golden Sun of Córdoba, borrowed from the symbolism of the Tahuantinsuya and other natives, referred to the sun coming out from behind the clouds when the delegates stepped out of Córdoba's town hall to announce the final form of the Constitution. More metaphorically, it also stood for the UPSA's example shining out on and enlightening the world. The Torch would become a significant enough symbol that it would eventually find a place on the national flag. However, the flag adopted by the UPSA in the immediate aftermath of its revolution instead drew upon two more simplistic predecessors from the conflict. In the early years of the war, some Platineans had sought to express loyalty to the Spanish colonial cause while standing against the actions of the present government. They had taken the red 'ragged cross' of Burgundy on a white background, the colonial flag used throughout the Spanish Empire, and simply reversed the colours. Later, other groups had chosen a more radical golden banner with '¡LIBERTAD!' (their battle cry, 'Freedom!') written across it in red. The first flag of the UPSA simply combined these two, the inverted cross of Burgundy in the canton and the golden field with its proud battle cry. Later, the flag would evolve as the legacy of the Spanish colonial past disappeared altogether and the battle cry of the past was expanded to the more orderly motto *Libertad e Independencia* ('Freedom and Independence'). The Torch was added, and though the Sun was not, the golden colour of the flag's field remained in an oblique hint of that alternative symbol, the two shining upon the world together.

In days to come, the UPSA would change the world by its own direct efforts, but for now, that enlightening republican example alone—that, and the expenses suffered in a failed attempt to halt its birth—would have decidedly dark consequences for the Kingdom of France...

EXCERPTED FROM "THE REGISTER ATLAS OF THE WORLD, 2nd EDITION"

Flag plate #4

3. Flag of the Platinean Revolt (early period). Lacking much in the way of unifying symbols—and in part deriving from colonial forces opposing a French attack—the early Platinean rebels simply took the Cross of Burgundy used in Spain's colonies and inverted the colours, producing a banner of a white 'ragged' cross on a red field.

4. Flag of the Platinean Revolt (later period). Plain yellow (or golden) flags were used by more radical rebel groups; these were married to the earlier inverted cross and bore the battle cry of '¡LIBERTAD!'

5. Flag of the United Provinces of South America (adopted 1792). The 'ragged' look of the inverted Cross of Burgundy is preserved but the Cross itself is converted to two lines bearing the name of the country. The Torch of Liberty is added to the yellow field in red together with the motto *Libertad e Independencia*.

3. Platinean revolt flag (early)

4. Platinean revolt flag (late)

5. United Provinces of South America

Chapter 13: Before the Storm

From: "Exploration and Discovery in the Later 18th Century" by Francois Laforce (originally published in French 1961, authorised English translation 1968)—

The modern student of history, his views being unavoidably coloured by ideological matters in these trying times, must feel the temptation to regard the second half of the eighteenth century as merely a time in which two radical revolutions occurred that would change the world—that of the UPSA and that of France. To do so is both disingenuous and misleading. Many other important breakthroughs and changes occurred in this period which have certainly had a significant effect on shaping the modern world in their own right. The case of the often overlooked[95] constitutional foundations of the Empire of North America is by now well publicised, but what of the voyages of exploration and discovery that opened up the world to new vistas, scarcely less than in earlier ages did the journeys of Columbus and Magellan?

The official 'discovery' of the sixth continent in 1788 is a case in point. In fact the land then known to English speakers as 'New Holland' was already well known on maps of the period, its barren northern coast having been mapped by the Dutch more than a century earlier, but dismissed as holding no interest. It took a Frenchman, though, Jean-François de Galaup, comte de La Pérouse, to discover the parts of 'New Holland' that were actually worth possessing. A remarkable Frenchman indeed...

La Pérouse was already a respected naval war hero, which in pre-Bonaparte France were few and far between. He had defeated a British frigate in the West Indies during the Second Austrian

---

[95] Often overlooked by scholars outside the English-speaking world, that is.

War[96] and then gone on to play a role in the Second Platinean War. At the celebrated Franco-Spanish naval victory over Augustus Keppel's fleet at Cape Trafalgar in 1783, La Pérouse was captain of the ship of the line *Saint-Esprit*.[97] Having received a minor wound at that battle, La Pérouse did not take part in the rest of the conflict, though some writers of speculative romance have argued that he might have turned the tide at later battles. It is debatable as to whether this is anything more than hero worship.

After the Treaty of London in 1785 and the end of the war, the chief issue at hand was the strain on the French treasury and the need for reform. Despite the apparent need for restraint on spending, La Pérouse nonethele4ss succeeded in obtaining royal funding from Louis XVI for a voyage of discovery, which set out late in the year 1785. This consisted of his former task force from the war, four frigates plus a single supply ship. The force would be led by his new flagship *Amiral d'Estaing*, named after the hero of Trafalgar— Jean Baptiste Charles Henri Hector, comte d'Estaing.

The intent of La Pérouse's voyage was to expand French knowledge of the Pacific, particularly the rich Asian markets, and perhaps to lay down new trade connections. It certainly succeeded in all three aspects, though the final consequences of these actions could not have been predicted at the time.

The fleet initially sailed to Buenos Aires, in which La Pérouse famously smoothed over relations between the newly independent republic (not yet having taken the name UPSA) and France by throwing a grand banquet for the leaders now drawing up their new constitution. Having made reports on the radical thoughts now sweeping the country amid these constitutional arguments— not dreaming of what effects these reports would ultimately have on his own mother country—La Pérouse proceeded to sail around Cape Horn. He journeyed to the Columbus Islands and Easter Island in 1786, making recommendations that they be suitable

---

[96] The French term for what English speakers in TTL name the Third War of Supremacy.

[97] This ship, built in 1763, existed in OTL as well, and played a part in the Battle of Chesapeake Bay during the American Revolutionary War.

for whaling bases.[98]

The *Amiral d'Estaing*'s crew complement included one Pierre-Simon Laplace, a respected common-born natural philosopher who had elected to accompany this voyage in order to escape his angry peers at home, as well as the Roman Catholic Church due to his controversial views. An astronomer, Laplace used the voyage to make the famous Laplacian Austral Catalogue of the stars of the southern night sky. He also collaborated with Jean-Baptiste Lamarck, a former soldier who had recently published several works on the flora of France and accompanied the mission due to its opportunities for research. Lamarck and Laplace's *Observations on the Fauna of the Îles de Colomb*[99] was a seminal work in the history of evolutionary theory and is credited with bringing back the evolution debate in France, whereas previously Voltaire and other writers had mainly focused on the related Racialism movement brought about by Linnaeus' works on humans.

La Pérouse was rebuffed from Japan thanks to the latter's isolationist policies. His expedition to China was also a failure, with the Qing Dynasty government being paralysed at the time, the Daguo Emperor being on his deathbed and concerns over the succession abounding. Fortunately, these fears turned out to be unfounded…this time. However, La Pérouse's voyages through the East Indies nonetheless resulted in long-lasting changes for both France and the world.

He rediscovered the islands then called New Zealand by the Dutch, who had dismissed them as inhabited by savage natives. La Pérouse, though, was able to establish mostly peaceful relations with the Mauré natives, and went on to popularise *Autiaraux*, the

---

[98] The 'Columbus Islands' is the name used in TTL for the Galapagos Islands (a translation of the name used by Spanish-speakers in OTL, *Archipiélago de Colón*. In fact the name Galapagos Islands was in use *at this point of history* in TTL, but as historians generally do, the writer has updated it to modern terminology. Easter Island was named in 1722, before the PoD, and this name is also used in TTL.

[99] This is therefore an 'updated' version of the title of the book, altered by the historian: the actual original publication would have used the name Galapagos.

native name for the islands, as the definitive one.[100] La Pérouse's voyage was responsible for an increased interest in the outside world by the Mauré, in particular because La Pérouse had introduced them to gunpowder. Though the French left behind only a few muskets with the Mauré *iwis* (tribes) they had had contact with, those *iwis* were swift to realise their usefulness. They initially lacked the industrial base to make their own weapons, but were able to duplicate the gunpowder. They both used this to keep their small number of muskets in use, and also to make crude bombs capable of breaking through the palisades of the *pa* forts of rival *iwis*. This dramatically changed the balance of power of the islands, with those *iwis* being first to adopt gunpowder weapons achieving an early dominance, and many longstanding powerful *iwis* being cast down and assimilated or enslaved by the powder users. A complex series of events followed over the next few decades (q.v.) ultimately ending in the national unification of the islands as a single Mauré state. This meant that the Mauré were one of the few classically 'native' peoples well prepared to resist any European or American attempts at colonialism later on.

La Pérouse famously mapped the southern coast of 'New Holland', discovering the more fertile lands there and planting the settlement of (Nouvelle) Albi, named after his birthplace.[101] He returned to France in 1789, a France by that time seething with the birth pangs of unrest, but was nonetheless able to obtain more funding and ships to expand the budding colony. La Pérouse left again for Nouvelle Holland, increasingly now called 'Terre de la Pérouse', mere months before the flames of revolution would ignite in 1794...

---

[100] The OTL names 'Maori' and 'Aotearoa' are spelled *Mauré* and *Auti-araux* in TTL, showing more French influence in their transliteration.
[101] Founded near the site of OTL Sydney. The settlement is originally named Nouvelle Albi, with the adjective eventually being dropped as it outstrips its prototype in size and cultural significance.

Chapter #14: A Man, a Plan, a Han—Japan!

"Writers of speculative romances seem, to my mind, overly enamoured with the Yapontsi islands. To presuppose that this cultural backwater could ever produce a great imperialistic power, as they fancifully see it, I believe speaks for itself in its absurdity."

- From a 1970 speech by Dr Sanjaï Mathieu, Université de Trivandrum (English translation)

From: "A History of Russian Expansionism in the East, Volume II" (various authors, 1987):

After the Treaty of Stockholm in 1771, a new paradigm for the political spheres of influence in Central and Eastern Europe had emerged. Austria had been excluded from Polish affairs, save Galicia and the city of Kraków (then usually known by its German name of Krakau). The old Polish-Lithuanian Commonwealth, noted for its unique governmental structure but having become sluggish and a puppet for outside powers, finally came to its end. Poland was brought into personal union with Prussia, while the Grand Duke of Lithuania became an ally of Russia, its Grand Duke being a hereditary post occupied by the current Russian Tsarevich. Sweden had been neutralised during the war by being promised Courland and the retention of northern Ducal Prussia, including the city of Königsburg, and this was confirmed by the Treaty.

Some commentators had predicted that this state of affairs was shaky and would only last a few years, inevitably leading to a second war. But events conspired against such forecasts. The Poles were certainly suspicious of their new Prussian rulers, given the two states' history, and there were several uprisings in following years, mainly over the privileges of the Polish nobility (*szlachta*).

A temporary settlement was soon reached with the most senior members of the *szlachta* being given the same rights as Prussian nobility. However, the unusual system of nobility in pre-partition Poland had meant that many even relatively poor people had *szlachta* status: fully ten percent of the population, in fact. The vast majority of these were excluded by necessity from the upper classes of the combined Prussian-Polish union, and remained a disenfranchised and restless minority for years to come.

If anything, the Grand Duchy of Lithuania seemed an even more volatile proposition. Contemporary commentators' general position was that the Lithuanians would sweat under Russian bull-in-a-china-shop demands for a few years, rise up, be crushed and the country finally be directly annexed to Russia. This was not an unreasonable suggestion, based on previous historical examples, but it failed to take into account just how seriously the Russian Tsarevich Paul (Pavel) took his new job as Grand Duke Povilas of Lithuania.[102] Although his relationship with his father Tsar Peter III remained relatively good, he continued to defend independent Lithuanian interests in the face of attempts by the court in St Petersburg to subordinate them to those of Russia and her own political factions.

Paul's motivations in this seem to have been to carve out his own position of power not directly dependent on his father, for which he needed the support of the Lithuanians—d rather than it being the product of a genuine belief in the ideals of a fully independent Lithuania. His successors would differ in this respect, but years would pass before this became apparent. Paul promoted the Lithuanian language against the formerly prevalent Polish without trying to impose the Russian language as anything other than an equal alternative. He also limited the activities of the Orthodox Church, only giving it equal status alongside the Catholic Church rather than trying to impose Russian Orthodox practices on the population. The Lithuanian people were pleasantly surprised with this unexpectedly light-handed rule. There were still some uprisings, of course, but on the whole

---

[102] 'Povilas' being the Lithuanian form of the name Paul (Pavel in Russian).

it seemed that against all the odds, a Russian ruler gave Lithuania more freedom to be Lithuanian than a Polish (or German, in the last few years) ruler had. At the same time, the new positions of the Orthodox Church and Russian language were gratefully received by the White Russian (or Belarusian) component of the Grand Duchy, effectively ensuring Paul enjoyed a broad range of support.

Paul instigated several national prestige projects during the 1780s to help feed the idea of the new Lithuania standing on its own two feet. One of the most important of these projects was the construction of a Lithuanian navy, known as the Patriotic Fleet. The Polish-Lithuanian Commonwealth had previously been too consumed by its own internal strife to construct much in the way of a Baltic navy of late, and had thus suffered somewhat in the wars for being unable to intercept raids from Sweden or other Baltic naval powers. Although Russia and Prussia had successfully bought off Sweden in the War of the Polish Partition, both governments, and particularly the Russians, were quite certain that this state of affairs was not sustainable. In particular, the Russians still had ambitions to conquer Finland, which would eventually require another war with Sweden. Sweden already had one of the largest and most powerful Baltic fleets, and the Swedish possession of the shipyards at Königsburg and Libau would only make this worse. Unless the Russians wanted to attempt to fight a war with Swedish troops able to land near St Petersburg with impunity, it was time to rectify the situation.

While Tsar Peter's own shipyards were simply expanded and the existing Russian Baltic fleet renovated, the situation was more difficult for Grand Duke Paul. Lithuania had not had a history of shipbuilding for some years, although the territorial revisions at the Treaty of Stockholm had awarded her the valuable port of Memel, now known by its Lithuanian name of Klaipeda. While the city was vulnerable to Swedish attack from both north and south, Paul decided to build up Klaipeda into a major shipbuilding centre in order to give Lithuania a Baltic fleet of her own. This was both to supplement the Russian force in the event of war, and to be a patriotic project (hence the name) that would create jobs for Lithuanian workers and reinforce the idea that Lithuania was an independent ally of Russia, not merely a puppet.

Just as Peter the Great had when Russia had built her first navy, Paul decided to look to a more established nation of shipbuilders, the Dutch. Rather than going to the Netherlands himself as his great-grandfather had, Paul simply brought in Dutch (and other European) shipwrights, builders and sailors to expand Klaipeda and train his Lithuanian volunteers in shipbuilding and naval affairs. This ambitious project was surprisingly successful, though it is questionable whether the Dutch would have been so ready to help if they had known the long-term consequences of Lithuania gaining such naval power.

In the event, the much-anticipated Baltic war was postponed. In Sweden, the Cap party was enjoying a long period of dominance at the Riksdag, with the Hats' policy of anti-Russian alignment and war largely discredited.[103] Austria suffered financial crises in the 1770s and 80s and, when she finally recovered a few years before the French Revolution, now had a government (led by Emperor Ferdinand IV) more interested in centralising the Holy Roman Empire and expanding Hapsburg influence in Italy than having another stab at Poland. Prussia remained too weak and too consumed with holding down Poland to make another attempt at recovering Silesia from Austria. Tsar Peter opposed, in the short term at least, a war with the Ottomans or trying to conquer the Crimean Khanate.[104] So, the potential catalysts of war lay largely silent for many years, and Russia and Lithuania were left with

---

[103] Eighteenth-century Swedish politics was dominated by two loosely defined parties known as the Caps and the Hats. The Hats were associated with martial tricorn hats because they were a gung-ho, pro-war party that advocated alliance with France against Russia. The Caps were associated with night-caps due to accusations of timidity, being anti-war and favouring alignment with Russia against France.

[104] In OTL, Catherine the Great succeeded in her coup against Peter III in 1762 and led Russia into the Russo-Turkish War of 1768-1774. This led to the formerly Ottoman-allied Crimean Khanate being neutralised by the Treaty of Kuchuk-Kainarji. Catherine then broke the treaty in 1783, taking advantage of a civil war in the Khanate to directly conquer and annex it to Russia. With Peter III still on the throne, none of this has happened in TTL.

shiny new fleets and nothing to do with them.

Being Baltic forces, these navies consisted of a large number of oar-driven galleys, though these were finally starting to become obsolete, and a smaller number of sail-driven high seas vessels. From around 1784, the Patriotic Fleet adopted a policy of sending the latter oceanic navy on voyages around European ports, both to give their sailors more high seas experience and to 'fly the flag' for Lithuania abroad. These voyages succeeded in broadly changing former foreign impressions that Lithuania was nothing more than a puppet state of Russia, but they were also expensive propositions. One mission in 1788 even reached the Empire of North America, and carried a Lithuanian ambassador to attend the opening of the first Continental Parliament by George III.

That ambassador was born Benyovszky Móric, but has gone down in history by the Russified form of his name, Moritz Benyovsky.[105] His actual ethnic background is fiercely debated, with everyone from Germans to Poles to Slovaks trying to claim him, but scholarly opinion suggests he identified primarily as a Hungarian. This enigmatic character is one of the most colourful in Russian, or indeed world, history. Initially fighting for the Polish-Lithuanian Commonwealth against the Prussians during the War of the Polish Partition—commanding one of the few Commonwealth forces to achieve any coherent success during that conflict—he escaped from the Prussians and settled in Lithuania in 1772. He joined the new Lithuanian army and rose rapidly to the rank of colonel thanks to both the ramshackle nature of the makeshift army and his educated background. Possibly he initially intended to use this position of power to turn the army against the Russians in an uprising, but he caught the eye of Grand Duke Paul. Benyovsky entered the Lithuanian government, going from acting Minister for War to Foreign Minister and then leading the

---

[105] In OTL he is known mainly as Maurice Benyovszky in English, but the multitude of ethnic groups fighting over his identity mean that his name can be found spelled any number of ways. Note that in Hungarian naming format, the family name comes first. However one spells his name, Benyovszky certainly had a colourful career in OTL as well, leading Polish rebels, escaping from a Russian prisoner-of-war camp in Kamchatka and eventually becoming the first King of a united Madagascar.

1788 expedition to the Empire of North America.

However, Benyovsky's greatest achievements were yet to come. Since the 1770s, Tsar Peter had become paranoid about equalling the achievements of his namesake, Peter the Great, and had decided that, like his grandfather, he must expand Russian power and control in the Far East. He balked at an ambitious invasion of Outer Manchuria drawn up by his generals: at the time, Qing China, though leaning towards a path of isolationism and decay, was still a formidable military power. Furthermore, such a plan would destroy the careful trade system with China that Russia had set up a century earlier at the Treaty of Nerchinsk. China was notoriously hard to open up to trade and it was foolish to risk the Russians' earlier unusual success with this treaty. Even a victory and the conquest of Outer Manchuria could only lead to a loss of trade wealth from the rest of China. Peter instead decided on a course of action probably just as ambitious—to attempt to open up the land then known as Japan, closed to trade for a hundred and fifty years under the Tokugawa Shogunate.

An expedition from Yakutsk led by Pavel Lebedev-Lastoschkin had already failed to establish trade links with Japan in 1774. The Japanese feudal fiefdom in Edzo,[106] the Matsumae Han, had received him favourably but simply stated that they did not have the authority from the Shogun to trade. Japanese trade was restricted to two southern ports, Kanagawa which traded with China and Nagasaki which traded with the Netherlands—both of which were inconveniently far away from any Russian holdings.

Lebedev's disappointing report spurred the Russian government to consider other approaches. Grand Duke Paul agreed to contribute three Lithuanian ships, his best crews, to add to four Russian vessels. These would set out from the Baltic to sail around the Old World with the supplies needed to expand the port at Okhotsk, and then would carry diplomats from both countries to attempt to establish trade links both at Matsumae-

---

[106] This is the Russian name for Hokkaido, then called Ezo(chi) in Japanese, and it is the name by which the island is commonly known to international audiences in TTL. In OTL in this period English sources often used other transliterations such as 'Jesso' or 'Yesso'.

town in Edzo and, if necessary, in Nagasaki or in the capital Edo itself. As a logical progression from the Lithuanian flag-flying missions around Europe, the ships carried a fair number of elite troops with the intention of impressing the Japanese authorities. Peter took the opportunity to get rid of numerous Leib Guards whose competence was unquestioned but whom he thought, quite possibly accurately, still supported his exiled wife Catherine.

The Russian side of the mission was placed under the command of Adam Laxman, a Finnish-born officer who had formerly served in the Swedish navy; using foreign-born emissaries was a common practice in eighteenth-century Russia. The Lithuanian portion could have no other leader but Benyovsky, and Paul was quietly relieved to have the man safely a long way away. He was supremely capable but also ambitious and volatile. As the Japanese would learn...

The missions set sail in 1792 and, with the assistance of hired Dutch navigators, made the first recorded Russian and Lithuanian rounding of the Cape of Good Hope and passage of the Malacca straits.[107] This was a new approach to the previous overland attempts at establishing trade with the East, although scarcely less inconvenient. After observing Nagasaki from a distance in late 1794, the joint fleet proceeded to Okhotsk and began building up the port as ordered. By this point, the Jacobin Wars had broken out in Europe, but in faraway Okhotsk, this was not learned until almost five years later.

Laxman was dutiful, but the bombastic Benyovsky became impatient with the preliminaries and sailed directly to Edzo in 1795 in an attempt to establish a trade mission. Blown off course and with his men unfamiliar with the waters, they failed to find Matsumae-town and ended up making landfall elsewhere in Edzo. This meant that Benyovsky, exploring as usual, soon ran into a group of the indigenous Aynyu[108] people of the island. Viewing the experience as an opportunity to practice his negotiating skills with an alien people, he did manage to establish trade with

---

[107] In OTL this would not happen until 1803-1806 with Adam Johann von Krusenstern's mission.
[108] Spelled 'Ainu' in OTL; this is a Russified form.

them, mainly raw materials and food in exchange for Russian manufactured goods.

Including firearms…

Interlude #3: Sometimes, All I Need Is The Air That I Breathe

THANDE INSTITUTE MISSION TAPE TRANSCRIPT
12/06/2019: CLASSIFIED LEVEL SIX

Dr Theodoros Pylos: It is at this point that we find it instructive to once again turn away from the general political upheavals of this period-

Dr Bruno Lombardi: -to concentrate on the scientific developments at hand.

Pylos: Strictly speaking, shouldn't you say 'natural philosophical' developments?

Lombardi: No, Thermo. The term 'scientist is anachronous at this time, but not 'scientific'.

Pylos: How curious! I had assumed-

Captain Christopher Nuttall: Gentlemen?

Pylos/Lombardi: Sorry sir.

Man now stands like the worker in the mill who begins to realise how his work, his machine, relates to and fits in with the whole process of manufacture, in that case. Our understanding of how the universe is made—and for what purpose—is for ever increasing. We can only hope that the Creator is happier to see us do so than the mill owners.

- Joseph Priestley, 1807

From: "Air: A History" by Daniel Johnson (1966)

The discovery of elluftium [oxygen] by Carl Wilhelm Scheele in 1778 was enormously influential in how chemical theories developed from thereon. For some years, natural philosophers struggled with how to incorporate this new concept into the established phlogiston theory. As it was then seen, a burning object gave off the substance known as phlogiston, which was visible as the flames themselves. Phlogiston's exact nature was imprecise and we should not confuse it with the modern conception of a substance with defined mass: that idea would have to wait for a few more years. Phlogiston was seen as more of a 'principle', like light and heat.

It fell to Joseph Priestley, a noted English Dissenting clergyman and political radical, to link the two ideas. Priestley drew heavily on the mid-century works of Stephen Hales, who published detailed accounts of the circulatory systems of plants and animals. As part of his conception of the 'Aerial Economy',[109] Priestley developed the notion that air could be phlogisticated (by an item burning within it) or dephlogisticated. Dephlogisticated or 'fixed' air was vivifying when breathed. Priestley thus explained Hales' earlier observation that it was dangerous to breathe stale air: it was phlogisticated.

Scheele had made similar observations, and Priestley—who

---

[109] In OTL this is an archaic term specific to Priestle's conception of the *moral* qualities of fresh air and the need to provide trees and parks in cities, lest otherwise the moral character of a city be degraded by its citizens breathing stale air. In TTL it is still in general use and has eventually come to mean something like the OTL term 'carbon cycle'.

had learned Swedish due to youthful arguments about Linnaean Racialism—read his original works. Elluftium was identified with dephlogisticated air. But how did this relate directly to phlogiston?

Priestley made numerous experiments with sealed glass vessels. A mouse sealed alone inside one would run out of air and die, but when a plant was also added, the mouse would live for much longer. Therefore, the plant was 'fixing' the stale air into the form that the mouse could breathe. But was the plant producing elluftium or absorbing phlogiston? It took Priestley some years, and several accidental observations, to realise that the answer was 'both'.

His work *On the Nature of Phlogiston* (1785) was controversial as it suggested that phlogiston, or phlogisticated air, was deadly to animal life—going against the largely philosophical arguments at the time, "rudely interrupting them with empiricism" as Philip Bulkeley would put it in his biography of Priestley. Priestley rapidly expanded the paradigm of the mouse and plant to envisage a great cycle of the world, with animals taking up illuftium and breathing out phlogiston, and plants taking up phlogiston and expelling illuftium. This, his 'Aerial Economy' (inspired in its terminology by eighteenth-century Britain's obsession with the stock market) purported to see a 'Necessary and Natural Union' between the different forms of life.

Priestley's major breakthrough at this stage was to use a burning glass, then a new lab instrument, on a sample of calx of mercury.[110] He was able to reverse the combustion, leaving metallic mercury, and he proceeded to repeat this experiment with other calxes. Around the same time, Priestley's lab assistant Anna Barbauld inadvertently performed the mouse-in-jar experiment after the jar in question was contaminated with a mixture of limestone powder and the caustic soda[111] that Priestley used to clean his

---

[110] A burning glass is a magnifying glass used to focus sunlight into a burning beam, a commonly used scientific instrument of the time. "Calx of" is essentially eighteenth century terminology for "oxide" and in TTL this older terminology is still in use in a modified form. A calx or oxide essentially describes the remaining residue (ashes) after a substance is burnt.

[111] Now known under the scientific name sodium hydroxide, though the

equipment. She discovered that the mouse lived for much longer than it should have done. After more experiments, Priestley eliminated the possibility that the chemical (soda lime) was giving off elluftium, and therefore it must instead be absorbing phlogiston. This was the first indication that the two processes could be decoupled, whereas before there was the possibility that phlogiston going from A to B was simply an artificial mathematical negative of illuftium going from B to A.

Priestley's discoveries were celebrated and debated both in Britain and on the Continent, but it was at this time that the French natural philosopher Charles-Augustin Coulomb threw a spanner in the works. Coulomb's major work was on quantifying things which had thought to be unquantifiable, for example human labour (based on improving the economic production of plantation slaves in the West Indies). To do this, he developed new means of measurement, such as very precise torsion balances that let the tiny charge repulsion between two charged surfaces be measured in the form of a change in weight. While using this balance, Priestley's French rival Antoine Lavoisier discovered that after a substance was burned, the combined calxes actually *GAINED* weight, when they should have lost phlogiston.

Most of the contemporaries attempted to explain this by philosophical means, claiming that phlogiston was an abstract principle with negative or sub-air weight, but Priestley instead used his new theories to argue that phlogiston was simply lighter than elluftium, and the phlogiston given out by the burning substance was more than balanced by elluftium being absorbed. This was, in fact, inaccurate—phlogiston is heavier than elluftium, but there is less given out than illuftium absorbed. Priestley did not think in terms of such defined quantities and it fell to Lavoisier, with his Coulomb methods, to discover this later on. Between them, largely via a series of half-friendly, half-hostile letters, Priestley and Lavoisier developed the idea that animal life is fuelled by a very slow, controlled version of combustion, thus linking these new ideas to Priestley's earlier discovery of the Aerial Economy. This was not explicitly confirmed until the

older name 'caustic soda' is still used by many non-scientists.

1820s, when new techniques were developed.

Lavoisier and Priestley are both hotly debated by modern British and French scientists as the 'Father of Modern Chemistry'. It took, however, Priestley's successor Humphry Davy to work out the precise relationship between elluftium and phlogiston—that the act of burning incorporates elluftium into the substance that burnt, producing both the calx and phlogiston. Priestley did not need to know the exact nature of phlogiston in order to create a treatise on the Aerial Economy which found favour with King George III, a man who had grown up in rural Virginia and was choked by the smokes of industrial London.[112] Priestley argued that living in cities with their dephlogisticated air was bad for the human body and might even lead to a moral decline as the brains of men ceased to be fuelled correctly. He advocated the construction of many arboreal parks throughout towns in order to balance this out, and this was adopted by many British cities, most obviously London. As well as being chemically sensible, this was clearly also aesthetically pleasing. Arguably this was part of an international phenomenon in reaction to dawning industrialism, sharing a century with the first incarnation of the Physiocracy movement in France.

Despite his good relationship with the King, Priestley's anarchist/republican leanings led to him being chased out of the country in 1791 by an angry mob, stoked by business interests Priestley had offended. He and his family emigrated to the United Provinces of South America, which was experimenting with political liberalism, and Priestley took his final discovery with him: soda water, water impregnated with phlogiston. Though the phlogiston itself might be harmful, water impregnated with the substance bubbled most delightfully and had medical applications. Thanks to Priestley, for the century to come it would be UPSA businesses that dominated the world soda water market, and all those that would be derived from it...

---

[112] In this respect TTL's George III is like OTL's; although OTL's George III did not grow up in America, he was a fervent environmentalist. He favoured Priestley's theories for this reason, ironically given Priestley's own republican views.

Lombardi: We may take this opportunity to notice the interesting ways in which the aforementioned events different from OTL and how this shaped a different path for science—something which these books naturally must leave out.

Pylos: Indeed. This process illustrates what the scientific historian Thomas Kuhn describes as 'incommensurability'—scientific theories can never be directly compared, because what Newton called 'gravity', for example, is a different concept from what Einstein called 'gravity', using different units and underlying concepts.

Lombardi: Quite so. In OTL some theories are still, in the abstract, thought of as 'correct'…

Pylos: Such as Galileo's heliocentric solar system.

Lombardi: Yes, even though these 'correct' theories have very little in common with current theories.

Pylos: To follow up my example, Galileo had perfectly circular orbits, and still had the fixed stars with the sun at the centre of the universe. We now know these ideas are wrong, yet schools teach 'Galileo was right' as though it is an absolute, because we think of it as being purely a debate between him and the geocentrists.

Lombardi: Similarly, modern evolutionary theory is described as 'Darwinian', even though it has as little to do with Darwin as it has to do with Paley.

Pylos: Perhaps not the best comparison to make, given events in TTL…

Lombardi: Shh, spoilers.

Pylos: Oh right, sorry.

Lombardi: Anyway. In OTL, phlogiston theory is described as an 'obsolete theory' but in TTL it has survived by the Kuhnian method—simply by changing what it *means* by phlogiston.

Pylos: Instead of an abstract concept or 'principle', phlogiston has become a real substance—that which we call carbon dioxide.

Lombardi: Yes. If this sounds unlikely, you may be surprised to learn that exactly the same thing happened in OTL; Scheele's work never spread, Lavoisier discovered oxygen, and regarded oxygen as an abstract principle, never identifying it with a specific element with weight and other defined properties.

Pylos: Quite, it was only his successors who changed the meaning of the term 'oxygen' so that it now means what it does today...so Lavoisier was 'right' in OTL and Priestley, with his phlogiston, was 'wrong'. If we just used the term phlogiston instead in OTL, then Priestley would be 'right' and Lavoisier would be 'wrong'.

Lombardi: Such is how science works.

(Background noise)

Nuttall: Ah, gentlemen, are you still digitising that segment on those scientist chaps? I need you to come and start putting that global history roundup into order.

Lombardi (muttering): Oy vey…

Chapter 15: Two Great Men

"A disturbing number of the greatest Englishmen who ever lived were foreigners."

- John Spencer KS (Alliance Party, Oxfordshire); speech to the Combined House, 1921

From: "England's Captain, France's Saviour" by Albert Harrison (1940)—

Having spent oceans of blood and failed to gain an inch of new territory in Europe in the 1740s and 50s—largely thanks to Louis XV's unpopular policies—it is ironic that in the 1760s France gained considerable new lands with the death of only one man. When the Duke of Lorraine died without male heirs in 1765, his lands defaulted to France and were annexed to the Kingdom. These were the last remnants of the once-great state of Lotharingia, now reduced to a few scattered enclaves throughout the region. By assuming control over Lorraine, France completed the expansionist path that Louis XIV had instigated, and now unquestionably dominated that region.

The impact upon history of the end of Lorraine seemed, at the time, slight. Its only direct effect was to remove the Duke, a former King of Poland, from any consideration of restoration. This served to quicken the Russo-Prussian ambitions to divide the Polish-Lithuanian Commonwealth, and the rest is—well—history.

An arguably far more significant acquisition by France was that of Corsica. The island was theoretically ruled by the Republic of Genoa, as it had been for centuries, but in practice rebels had held the island since 1755. Corsica had become an independent republic in all but name, with the Virgin Mary as titular monarch of the 'kingdom'. Unlike the venerable oligarchic republics of Genoa, Venice and the Netherlands, the new republic in Corsica was constructed on modern Enlightenment principles—famously being the first nation to routinely allow women to vote and stand for election.[113] Its leader was Filippo Antonio Pasquale de Paoli, who had served in the Neapolitan army and now commanded the rebel military forces as well as being effective head of state of the republic.

During the thirteen-year existence of the First Republic, an Enlightenment-inspired constitution was drafted and the state received praise from contemporary thinkers such as Voltaire and Rousseau. James Boswell, a companion of Samuel Johnson, wrote an account of the Republic which made Paoli and the constitution famous (or notorious, depending on whom one asked) throughout Europe in the 1760s. It was this account which was one of the inspirations for the revolution in Platinea twenty years later that would give birth to the UPSA, and indeed the original Meridian Constitution owed much to Corsica's.

In 1767 the Genoese lost the island of Capraia to the Corsican Republic and decided that this was the last straw; the old Italian republic now had little chance of ever subduing the rebels. Furthermore, the Genoese treasury was almost exhausted. Recognising this, the Genoese cut their losses and signed the island over to the Kingdom of France in exchange for financial reparations. The vast and experienced French army invaded in 1768. Paoli's republicans fought hard before being finally (as it seems) defeated in 1769. Paoli and numerous other republican leaders and soldiers fled to Britain, which was at the time thought of as the most liberal country in Europe. In the 1760s, radical republicans were treated as amusing and entertaining curiosities by the British government, which did not see them as a serious threat until later on, and the Corsican refugees formed an exilic community in London not unlike the Huguenots before them.[114]

---

[113] This is as OTL. The Corsican Revolution was an influence upon America's OTL one in some respects, which is remembered in place names such as Paoli, Pennsylvania.

[114] All this is more or less as OTL, but there are more Corsican refu-

Among the Corsicans was Carlo Buonaparte, a young supporter of Paoli.[115] A law student prior to fleeing the island with his wife and two-year-old son Napoleone,[116] he decided to complete his studies, switching to English Common Law. Buonaparte converted to Anglicanism to escape the anti-Catholic laws and changed his name to the anglicised 'Charles Bone'.[117] He received his law doctorate from the University of Cambridge in 1774 and eventually became well-known for his skilful seeking out of loopholes in the anti-Catholic laws, freeing many English Catholics from legal trouble. Bone had mastered unaccented, idiomatic English and covered his tracks well; very few knew that he was himself Catholic (and foreign) in origin, though many made accusations (without evidence).

If Bone became an enemy of the ultra-Tory faction opposed to Catholic rights, this almost automatically made him popular with radicals who supported Catholic emancipation, including Charles James Fox, who became a close friend. Bone would eventually become an MP towards the end of the century.[118]

---

gees than OTL. This is because the French forces in Corsica were led by the Marquis de Contades rather than the Comte de Vaux as in OTL, and he elected to use harsher measures against members of the Corsican populace suspected of collaboration with the rebels. In OTL Contades was disgraced after leading the French forces to defeat at Minden in the Seven Years' War: TTL's Third War of Supremacy, with its more luke-warm British involvement in the Continental theatre of the war, had no exactly analogous battle to Minden and Contades has escaped disgrace, remaining a plausible choice of commander.

[115] In OTL Buonaparte verbally attacked the French invasion early on but later switched sides; here he stayed with the rebels, again because the French invaders were seen as more ruthless compared to OTL.

[116] This is *not* OTL Napoleone Buonaparte (known to history as Napoleon Bonaparte), but his elder brother, Carlo's first child. In OTL this brother died young and 'our' Napoleone, born a few years later, was named for him. In TTL he survives, and is in some ways similar to 'our' Napoleone, but is not identical.

[117] Immigrants seeking to enter British society in this period often an-glicised or even translated their names; an example of the latter is the gentleman's club White's, which was founded by an Italian named Fran-cesco Bianco, AKA Francis White.

[118] In OTL Carlo Buonaparte died in his early forties, but in TTL he avoids disease, has a better quality of life from his lucrative legal job, and

Though an interesting character in and of himself, Charles Bone is necessarily overshadowed by his eldest son, Napoleone, known to English ears as the 'less foreign sounding' Leo. Charles enrolled his son as a midshipman in the Royal Navy at the age of thirteen, as was customary at the time, and he served on HMS *Ardent* from 1777 onwards.[119] Mister Midshipman Bone passed his lieutenant's examination at the RN school in Malta, 'Anson's Folly', in 1783. He was transferred to HMS *Raisonnable*, during which time he served alongside the slightly senior Lieutenant Horatio Nelson, and the two young men became fast friends.

The *Raisonnable* scored several victories against French and Spanish ships in the Second Platinean War, and the British losses at the Battle of Trafalgar meant that several new captaincies were left open: thus first Nelson and then Bone were made master and commander, with Nelson inheriting the *Raisonnable* and Bone taking over the almost obsolete 28-gun frigate HMS *Coventry* in 1786. He was noted for a concentration on rapid gunnery and weight of fire, a strategy that he had developed in connexion with Nelson,[120] and grew to command a great loyalty from his men. Boswell met him in 1788 and Bone makes a then-overlooked, but today well known, brief appearance in one of his accounts. Boswell described him as being the epitome of the Royal Navy commander whose men would follow him into the jaws of hell rather than face the shame of being left behind.

Bone was made post[121] in 1791, taking command of the newly

---

lives longer.

[119] Interestingly, in OTL even 'our' Carlo Buonaparte who stayed in Corsica wanted to enrol the (younger brother) Napoleon in the Royal Navy at one point. In OTL HMS *Ardent* was captured by the French in 1779 during the American Revolutionary War, which did not happen in TTL and so the ship is still in service by the Royal Navy at this point.

[120] It has been noted by some OTL historians that Nelson's tactics at sea were ironically quite similar to those of Napoleon on land: emphasis on artillery, using concentrated, well-trained forces driven by personal charisma to overcome much larger but poorly motivated enemies, and the like.

[121] Being 'made post' means a promotion to the rank of (post) captain, which is particularly important both because it gives an officer a higher pay grade when not at sea, and also as it means they are entered on the

built frigate HMS *Diamond*—bringing a great deal of his former crew with him, as the now outdated *Coventry* was paid off—and immediately making a name for himself with an action against Algerine pirates off Malta in 1793. But it would be with the coming of the Jacobin Wars in 1795 that Bone's story becomes one not merely of history, but of legend...

From: "John Company: The Life of Pitt of India" by James Rawlings (1974)—

By 1760, the situation in India looked bleak for Britain. The great French victories of the 1740s had been built on in the 1750s, with the British East India Company failing to retake any of their former strongholds in the Carnatic, and finally losing Cuddalore. A betrayal by the Nawab of Bengal had resulted in much of the BEIC's effort being focused on fighting the rebellious Bengalis and installing a more pliable series of six puppet princes in the Nawab's place. This was eventually achieved, and Britain kept the rich trading post of Bombay on India's western coast, but the south and much of the interior became closed to British influence.

In the successive Mysore-Haidarabad Wars of the 1770s and 80s, it was clear that the British had far less influence with Haidarabad, the side they backed, than the French did with Mysore. These wars did, however, result in the Nizam of Haidarabad withdrawing the Northern Circars region from French control due to overt French support of his Mysorean enemies. The BEIC moved in to defend the Circars from any FEIC attempt to retake them. A French siege of Masoolipatam, the chief town in the region, failed in 1786.

It is worth noting that the conflicts between the FEIC and BEIC often had little or nothing to do with the wider wars between Britain and France in Europe and the New World, and when Britain and France were supposedly at peace with each other, fighting continued in India.

The FEIC remained under the able leadership of Joseph

Admiralty list and will inevitably be promoted to Admiral at some point if they survive long enough.

François Dupleix until his death in 1770. The post of *gouverneur général* was taken up by Jean-Baptiste Donatien de Vimeur, comte de Rochambeau, who lacked Dupleix's unique mercurial genius but was nonetheless a competent commander and administrator, and dutifully became versed in Indian matters.[122] The BEIC struggled to find one equally capable who could lead them back to a position of power. They would not find him for some years.

William Pitt had been an able Prime Minister to King Frederick I for many years and had led Britain through the Third War of Supremacy, but he had never managed his finances very well and when he died, he left his family in debt. Furthermore, in order to retain his image as the Great Commoner, he had never taken a title, limiting the income of his eldest son John.[123] John decided that in order to restore the family finances, he would have to imitate his great-grandfather, Thomas "Diamond" Pitt, who had made his fortune (initially quite illegally) from the diamond trade in India. The elder Pitt had eventually become Governor-General of Madras, now lost to the French, and had once saved it by buying out the Nawab of the Carnatic...

John Pitt enlisted in the East India Company in 1773 and travelled to India. He became a cornet of cavalry, just as his father had started, but saw rather more frontline combat. He achieved a colonelcy by 1786 and fought at the Siege of Masoolipatam

---

[122] In OTL, Rochambeau's chief opponent in the American Revolutionary War, Lord Cornwallis, became Governor-General of (British) India: in TTL the situation is therefore something of a reversal.

[123] In OTL William Pitt (the Elder)'s eldest son was also called John, but TTL's John Pitt was born a few years earlier and is therefore a different person. He has some characteristics of 'our' William Pitt the Younger. We now see direct changes from the Point Of Divergence: in OTL, Pitt the Elder spent many years working with Prince Frederick and so, as Frederick was in America all those years in TTL, his life is one of those most immediately changed by the POD. Therefore, his children are also different. One particularly significant change is that Pitt the Elder chose not to take a peerage in TTL, whereas in OTL he eventually accepted the earldom of Chatham—for which he was ridiculed by many who previously had respected his reputation as 'the Great Commoner'. Note that TTL historians do not call him 'William Pitt *the Elder*' because there is no William Pitt the Younger to contrast him with.

against the French, as well as in many earlier conflicts with native states. Pitt received a wound to the leg at the siege from a French musket ball, ending his career on the front line as it forced him to walk with a cane, but by this time, at the age of 30, he had already made his fortune and paid off his family's debts. Nonetheless, Pitt had developed a love of India and chose to remain. He became Governor-General of the Presidency of Calcutta in 1790, and so was the pre-eminent British official in India at the time of its greatest, most unpredictable upheaval since the fall of the Mughal Empire...

Chapter 16: The Last Roundup

From:"In The Eleventh Hour: The 1780s" by Professor Andrew Colquhoun (1971)—

Bavarian Question (18th Century) [See also: Bavarian Question (19th Century)]

A diplomatic triumph for the then-Archduchy of Austria towards the end of the eighteenth century, which in other circumstances might have spiralled out of control into yet another general European war.

In 1783, the last Wittelsbach Elector of Bavaria, Maximilian III, died without issue.[124] The important Duchy of Bavaria defaulted to the Sulzbach line, specifically Charles Theodore (then known as 'Charles IV Theodore'), Elector of the Rhine Palatinate. Charles Theodore was uninterested in ruling Bavaria and negotiated a deal with Holy Roman Emperor Ferdinand IV, who by this time had also succeeded his mother Maria Theresa to become Archduke of Austria and ruler of the associated Hapsburg lands.[125] Adding

---

[124] In OTL Maximilian died in 1777. This led to the brief War of the Bavarian Succession, in which Austria cut a deal with the heir Charles Theodore to acquire part of the Bavarian territory in exchange for the Austrian Netherlands, but this was disputed by a Prussian-Saxon alliance because it did not take into account the fact that Charles Theodore had no heirs and after his death the territory would pass to Charles II August, Duke of Zweibrücken, who opposed the deal. In OTL the short and rather farcical war ended with Charles Theodore keeping all of Bavaria an the Austrians keeping the Austrian Netherlands. In TTL, with no strong Prussia to object and Charles Theodore possessing an heir (due to marrying a different wife), the plan goes through smoothly.

[125] In an example of the butterfly effect on events following the POD, Maria Theresa's eldest surviving son is named Ferdinand rather than Joseph like OTL: an older brother Joseph died in infancy, but even had he survived he would have been rather different to OTL's Joseph II.

Bavaria to the Hapsburg domains would firmly establish Austrian supremacy in the Empire and put an end to any ideas of Prussian revival after the downfall of Frederick II's ambitions. While Prussia had not made further attempts to displace Austria as supreme power within the German states since the Third War of Supremacy, the Austrian defeat by the Prusso-Russian alliance in the War of the Polish Partition had been an embarrassment.

Ironically enough, it was this very victory that hamstrung any Prussian attempt to respond to the Bavarian crisis. Prussia was bogged down in suppressing a rebellion by disenfranchised Polish *szlachta* and King Frederick William II was unwilling to risk the Prussian army to try and dissuade the Austrians by force. Ultimately this rebellion would have another negative effect on Prussia's fortunes, for Prince Henry was killed by Polish partisans on the way to command the army based in Warsaw, and so the inexperienced Frederick William II was left without his chief advisor. Prussian retribution for the partisan attack was savage, further poisoning relations with their supposedly equal co-kingdom, and further distracting the Prussians from any attempt at a coherent foreign policy within the Empire.

The late Maximilian III's consort, Maria Anna Sophia of Saxony, having failed to receive Prussian backing, next attempted to use her influence in her native Saxony to bring that state into opposition with Austria's plans. Predictably the Elector of Saxony, Frederick Augustus III, refused. Saxony had grown considerably in power thanks to reaping the spoils of the Third War of Supremacy, but as of yet was in no state to face Austria alone. Furthermore—just as the negotiators who had ended the Third War of Supremacy had foreseen—many of Saxony's new territories existed purely at the sufferance of Austria, and the gains made in that war would rapidly be reversed if Saxony opposed Austria.

It is possible, of course, that France, Britain and Russia might also have seen fit to oppose the Austrian move, but all three were busy with their own conflicts—France and Britain with the Second Platinean War, Russia with preparations for the Baltic war with Sweden (which, in the event, never materialised). Therefore, Charles Theodore's deal went through with no attempts from the other powers to prevent it. As the rightful heir to the Duchy of Bavaria, he ceded it to the Austrian crown in exchange for the Austrian Netherlands, which were incorporated as the new independent Duchy of Flanders.[126]

Flanders was in personal union with Charles Theodore's original lands of the Rhine Palatinate, far separated from it by the territory of countless other German states, and Flanders herself was split in half by the prince-bishopric of Liége.[127] Thus, the state could only function within the bounds of the Holy Roman Empire and on the Emperor's say-so, which suited Ferdinand IV down to the ground. Austria had had little real interest in the southern Netherlands since acquiring them from Spain in the War of the Spanish Succession, unable to fully exploit their economic potential as the Dutch jealously closed the Scheldt to Flemish trade whenever it looked as though they might be getting somewhere. Providing the southern Netherlands were denied to France, the Austrians were thus indifferent to their fate. The old Austro-Dutch treaties were renewed by the Duchy of Flanders, ensuring that the fortresses along the Flemish-French border would be manned by Dutch troops.

Charles Theodore's new subjects had mixed feelings about him. Nearly all of them were happier to have a less distant ruler than Ferdinand IV, whose policies to centralise the Holy Roman Empire around Austria had left the southern Netherlands neglected and forgotten. Furthermore, Charles Theodore established a new academy of the sciences in the capital, Brussels, just as he had in the Palatinate years before. He was also a patron of the arts, promoting the works of Flemish artists, sculptors and composers

---

[126] Of course the state also includes modern OTL Wallonia, but 'Flanders' was at the time often used to mean all of what we now call Belgium. Note that in OTL, the (aborted) plan was that Charles Theodore was only to cede some parts of Bavaria to Austria, but in TTL it is the entire Duchy—illustrating the stronger diplomatic and military position Austria is in due to Prussia's decline relative to OTL.

[127] The city of Liége in Belgium is now spelled 'Liège', with a grave rather than acute accent, but this was a change made as late as the 20th century and does not apply in TTL, for reasons that will eventually become clear...

in the fashionable circles of European nobility. However, some Flemings feared that, without the assured might of Austria directly behind them, the new state would be easy pickings for the next time France decided to attempt a conquest, and who knew if the next Marshal Saxe would have a Louis XV as king to so meekly trade it back again?

As for Bavaria itself, the Bavarian people rapidly grew to dislike Ferdinand IV's policies of centralisation and integration, with Bavaria increasingly being treated as just another Austrian province. Some voices at the Emperor's court argued that the Bavarian army should be dismantled and incorporated directly into the Imperial forces, both to make matters more efficient and to make it more difficult for Bavaria to be detached again following a future Austrian defeat. In the event, though, these plans were not implemented, at least not in time to make any difference.

For a new power was arising in Europe. Unpredictably, inexorably, it would topple all the grand schemes and new orders of the continent's nobility, leaving them to crash in flames and threatening to take their progenitors with it. Everything this new power touched turned to dust.

In France, the Revolution had begun...

Interlude #4: Nation Building

Dr Theodoros Pylos: But before we depart for the first great tragedy of this world's history-

Dr Bruno Lombardi: -that term is debatable, but yes, we should cover one more area. Namely-

Pylos: -the constitutional makeup and the national symbols of the Empire of North America-

Lombardi: -lest these come as a surprise when we cover the entry of Imperial troops into the-

Captain Christopher Nuttall: Gentlemen? Brevity, if you please.

Pylos: Er—yes, sir.

Lombardi: The national symbols of the Empire of North America.

From: "The History of the Empire of North America: An Introduction" by Dr Paul Daycliffe (1964)—

The national symbols that we take for granted were not always with us, of course. It is probably true that the turkey would have come to symbolise North America even without its endorsement by Sir Benjamin Franklin, as it was thought of as a sign of the exotic and promising land of America in Europe long before that. Other symbols, however, could easily have been different if history had turned a different way.

There were many previous tunes associated with America long before an official national anthem was considered appropriate.

"Hail, America" served as a unifying national song for many years, though now it is forgotten save by patriotic orchestras. Each Confederation, and even many individual provinces, also had their own songs, and regiments called from these Confederations brought their music all over the world in the wars of the nineteenth century. It would not be until the latter half of the nineteenth century that "The Cross and Stars Forever" would be recognised as the official national anthem—as should be obvious from the fact that the events depicted by the song did not occur until the midpoint of that century.

Furthermore, the old Jack and George itself was not always been universally beloved by the people over whom it waved, even before the Flag Debates of the nineteenth century. Many in the northern Confederations objected to the clear Virginian influence behind the design, at least until the events of the 1840s and 50s altered the balance of power within the Empire. After that unfortunate period, the Jack and George was, on the contrary, clung to by some nostalgics as a memory of the national unity which now seemed to be slipping through Americans' fingers. It is perhaps no surprise that the supposedly radical departure of a new flag following the Reform period ended up in reality quite closely resembling its predecessor. The older Jack and George forms are still, of course, very popular to signify both historical sites and as a political statement, and remain in current use by some military and civic organisations.

The maple tree remains a universally acknowledged symbol of North America, though this was and is sometimes objected to by those parts of some Confederations where that tree does not grow. However, the maple is now inextricably linked with America in the minds of Europeans, and any attempts by those objectors to add southern trees such as the dogwood or palmetto were always doomed to failure even before the tides of history made the question irrelevant. Ironically the one southern candidate that might have a large enough geographic range to catch on, the magnolia, had become irrevocably associated with a narrow political identity by the point in time that this debate emerged, and thus was never an option.

It is anachronistic, though, to claim that an American national identity existed before the end of the eighteenth century—just as it is anachronistic, in many ways, to claim a British one existed. It was in the crucible of a great war that the self-image of the two nations was fixed, a self-image that would persist long after the reality had drifted from the myth. The Jacobin Wars might have had a more immediately apparent effect on France and continental Europe, but they also had profound consequences for Britain and the Empire of North America...

Excerpts from the Constitutional Acts of 1788:

An Act Declaring the Rights and Liberties of the Subjects of the Empire of North America, and the Manner of Government thereof.

WHEREAS in pursuance of His Majesty's most gracious recommendation to the two Houses of Parliament in Great Britain, to consider of such measures as might best tend to strengthen and consolidate the connection between H.M.'s domains, the two Houses of the Parliament of Great Britain and the assembled delegates of the Provisional United American Assembly have severally agreed and resolved that, in order to promote and secure the essential interests of Great Britain and America, and to promote the Protestant religion and the liberties of England throughout the corners of H.M.'s domains, it will be advisable to concur in such measures as may best tend to allow H.M.'s subject within the Empire of North America coëval rights and liberties to those of his cousin residing in Great Britain, and on such terms and conditions, as may be established by the Acts of the respective Parliaments of Great Britain and of the Empire of North America.

And whereas, in furtherance of the said Resolution, both Houses of Parliament and the Assembly have likewise agreed upon certain Articles for effectuating and establishing the said purposes, in the tenor following:

Article First. That the said Empire of North America shall, upon the 1st day of January which shall be in the year of our Lord one thousand seven hundred eighty-eight (N.S.), be recognised in law as a Dominion to which is granted the same Parliamentary rights and powers as of Great Britain, or of Ireland, pursuant to the following terms and conditions…

Here follows the opening paragraphs of the American Constitution of 1788, whose creation was commissioned by the above Act of the Westminster Parliament:

Constitution of the Empire of North America (1788)

We the appointed Representatives of the Subjects of His Imperial Majesty's Empire of North America, in Order to form a more perfect Union, protect our Rights, defend our Religion, insure domestic Tranquility, provide for the common defence, promote the general Welfare, and secure the Blessings of Liberty to ourselves and our Posterity, do propose this Constitution for the Empire of North America.

Article First
   That a Continental Parliament be called, under the Acknowledged Precepts of the Westminster Parliament as Established in the Constitution of 1688, Suitably Amended for the Differing Conditions of Colonial Existence;

Article Second
   That this aforesaid Continental Parliament shall consist of two Houses, of Lords Spiritual and Temporal and of Commons, and that the Former shall be appointed by His Majesty the King-Emperor or his invested Lord Deputy, and that the Latter shall be Elected subject to the following Terms and Conditions;

Article Third
   That the Commoners, styled Members of the Continental Parliament, shall be elected by the Free Vote of all Protestant Freeholders with residence in the Empire of North America, that One Member shall be elected by each Province, and further, that Additional Members be elected by those Towns and Cities granted the status of Borough by His Majesty the King-Emperor…

13 further Articles are included in the original Constitution, for a total of 20. Notably absent in this Constitution is much in the way of detail about the internal workings of the Confederations and their specified powers in relation to the imperial Continental Parliament. The former deficit would be interpreted as leaving this up to the Confederations themselves, leading to much in the way of diverse forms of government, while the latter would provoke much argument and amendment in the nineteenth century.

The original 20 Articles of the Constitution have since been largely obscured by successive amendments and replacements, but the original Bill of Rights (though itself much amended) is better known to the popular imagination and can be quoted by many American schoolchildren:

American Bill of Rights (1788)

The following Declarations of the Rights and Liberties of all Imperial subjects are made:

That the pretended power of suspending the laws, dispensing with laws, or the execution of laws by regal authority without consent of the Continental Parliament is illegal;

That levying money for or to the use of the Crown or by the Westminster Parliament by pretence of prerogative, without grant of the Continental Parliament, for longer time, or in other manner than the same is or shall be granted, is illegal;

That it is the right of the American subjects to petition the Emperor, and all commitments and prosecutions for such petitioning are illegal;

That the raising or keeping a standing army within the Empire in time of peace, unless it be with consent of the Continental Parliament, is illegal;

That the subjects which are Protestants may have arms for their defence suitable to their conditions and as allowed by law;

That election of members of the Continental Parliament ought to be free to all Protestant freeholders;

That the freedom of speech and debates or proceedings in the Continental Parliament ought not to be impeached or questioned in any court or place out of the Continental Parliament;

That excessive bail ought not to be required, nor excessive fines imposed, nor cruel and unusual punishments inflicted;

That jurors ought to be duly impanelled and returned, and jurors which pass upon men in trials for high treason ought to be freeholders;

That all grants and promises of fines and forfeitures of particular persons before conviction are illegal and void;

And that for redress of all grievances, and for the amending, strengthening and preserving of the laws, Continental Parliaments ought to be held not less than every three years.

From: "A Constitutional History of the World" by J. G. Flamboise (1987)—

The American Constitution of 1788 is notable for being a 'test bed' for many policies advocated by British Radicals for adoption within the Westminster Parliament; for example, the holding of Parliaments every three years rather than seven and the implicit lack of rotten boroughs (which, of course, had never existed in the first place in America). As the more conservative Whigs and Tories initially ignored the nitty-gritty of the American project, this meant they were unable to effectively respond some years later when the successful public trials of these policies in America resulted in the British Radicals, led by Charles James Fox, incorporating elements of them into the British Constitution in the opening years of the nineteenth century...

Pylos: That should suffice for a brief overview of the background of the early Empire of North America.

Nuttall: Good. In that case, can we move o-

Lombardi: Of course, we should do the same for the United Provinces of South America, a country which in many ways is even more influential on this world's history than the ENA.

Nuttall (sighs): Why am I not surprised. All right, go on...

From: "A Constitutional History of the World" by J. G. Flamboise (1987)—

Although the Constitution of the United Provinces of South America in its original form was highly influential on the early French Revolution and other radical attempts at constitutionalism in the perioid, it was also a rather vague document and one in many ways rooted in a kind of soft patriarchal conservatism that did not gel well with the overall radical tone of the new state. It would take considerable rewriting and amendments over the course of the next fifty years before the constitution would settle into a form we would recognise. Some historians have criticised the founding fathers of the UPSA for their 'slapdash job', but we must recognise that the early UPSA—before it even had that name—represented a coming together of disparate regions of the former Viceroyalty of Peru and Captaincy-General of Chile that formerly had had little contact with each other, and had often been liberated by completely unconnected rebel groups with divergent aims. From this point of view, it is admirable—no matter what might have come later—that the founders were able to weld any kind of functional federation together at all.

Even the name of the new state was unsettled at the time of the Constitutional Convention in Córdoba in 1790, and Córdoba's own status as the capital was notional and considered temporary. During the war the city had been chosen as the *de facto* capital of rebel Platinea because it was a long way from the coastline, and the French had conquered Buenos Aires while the Spanish raided places like Valvidia and Santiago de Chile. Later it remained the capital by default, just because the Platineans would veto Santiago while the Chileans would veto Buenos Aires, and Lima was hated by everyone else, so Córdoba represented the least bad compromise.

The name United Provinces of South America may seem obvious in retrospect, but also represented a slightly awkward compromise. Some delegates to the Convention favoured Federation, others Confederation, representing a disagreement over how much power the central government should have relative to the provinces. United Provinces was chosen as a deliberately vague term allowing both sides to claim victory, pushing that argument to a later date—where it would gradually be won, over a period of years, by the federalists. 'South America' was also a slightly ambiguous term to use, as the UPSA controlled less than half of the continent and it might be perceived as implicitly holding ambitions of conquest towards the Spanish Viceroyalty of New Granada and Portuguese Brazil. Once again, though, this term ended up being set into the constitution by default due to disagreements between those who wanted to use a pre-existing name for part of the new state ('Chile', 'Peru', etc.), those who wanted to use a native Indian name to distance themselves from Spain, and those who wanted to invent a new name out of whole cloth or name it after one of the heroes of the revolutionary war. 'South America' was chosen despite its ambiguity, and in any case the potentially misleading demonym was soon displaced by 'Meridian'.

Given these kinds of arguments, it is remarkable that the Constitutional Convention achieved as much as it did. Despite the Sun of Córdoba ultimately being derived from a native symbol,[128] one can understand the story of it coming from the delegates finally walking out of the town hall to announce the final form of the constitution and the clouds parting, the sun shining dramatically upon them.

The *Cortes Nacionales* (literally National Court, but in practice meaning parliament) was the first and chief institution of government created by the original constitution. Members of the Cortes, referred to as deputies, were elected on a provincial basis, but the constitution importantly enshrined the right to universal householder suffrage—which would eventually be expanded even more radically to universal male suffrage. This clause would overrule any attempt by the provinces to decide how their deputies were elected, unlike the very different balance of federalism seen in the ENA. The Cortes was always intended as the primary organ of government, with the President-General

---

[128] As can be seen in the flags of OTL Argentina and Uruguay for example.

initially being seen as effectively a republican stand-in for a ceremonial monarch, right down to serving for life. The original plan would even have had the President-General elected by the Cortes itself. At the last moment, however, this was changed to a national popular vote, and this measure would go on to give the President-General an unintended authority stemming from this popular mandate. The President-General's executive power would grow over time: when the constitution was first drawn up, executive power was intended to rest collectively in the Cortes. Of course in practice, with the growth of factionalism, a 'first among equals' arose in the Cortes, known as the President of the Cortes (often translated as Prime Minister in English) but this position would not be formally recognised in the constitution until a later series of amendments—by which time he had become secondary to the President-General in any case.

The first President-General was, of course, Simón Riquelme de la Barrera Goycochea. Riquelme was the perfect choice: a hero from the war, but a decidedly backseat one, not the sort to be able to command the army to launch a coup if he felt like it; someone whose family had lived in South America since the 1600s, therefore being a statement against the *peninsulares*; and a Chilean, when most of the first government was of a Platinean background, thus balancing the government. He was also the only President-General ever to actually serve purely in the ceremonial, pseudomonarchical way that the constitution-writers envisaged.

Given the slant towards federalism from the start, provincial government was rudimentary, consisting of Intendants appointed by the Cortes (later, appointed by the President-General and confirmed by vote of the Cortes) and councils appointed by the Intendants. Elected Intendants and provincial audiencias would not come until many years later. The power of individual Intendants tended to depend on the size and coherency of their provinces: the Province of Chile, the largest and wealthiest, tended to have a powerful Indendant, while some of the smaller and more arbitrary provinces did not.

This federalist-slanted form of government was in part intended to curb the ambitions of Lower Peru and Lima in particular. Lima was conservative and Spanish-loyalist in character, and more importantly furious at losing its formerly pre-eminent position as capital of the Viceroyalty of Peru, which had taken in most of what became the UPSA. It was in part a spiteful desire to stamp down on Lima and Lower Peru that led the delegates to decide to entertain the desires of Tupac Amaru II and Tomas Katari (now calling himself Tupac Katari) to establish autonomous states for the Tahuantinsuya and Aymara peoples under their traditional monarchies. This would carve territory out of Lower (and Upper) Peru and reduce its voting power in the Cortes, and so men who cared nothing for the romantic self-determination ambitions of the Indians eagerly voted for a policy that would let them realise their dreams…at least to a certain extent. The bad blood this stored up with Lower Peru would, of course, haunt the UPSA for years to come.

For now, though, the early UPSA's rudimentary constitutional arrangements seemed to serve it fairly well, with none of the rebellions, fragmentations or coups that many had predicted for the young nation. The flaws in the constitution would not become apparent until European events, events which the UPSA itself had inspired, would start to intrude upon its politics…

MAP OF THE EMPIRE OF NORTH AMERICA IN 1788

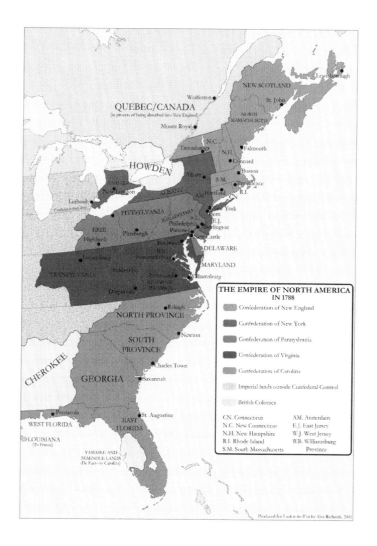

THE EMPIRE OF NORTH AMERICA IN 1788

- Confederation of New England
- Confederation of New York
- Confederation of Pennsylvania
- Confederation of Virginia
- Confederation of Carolina
- Imperial lands outside Confederal Control
- British Colonies

C.N. Connecticut	A.M. Amsterdam
N.C. New Connecticut	E.J. East Jersey
N.H. New Hampshire	W.J. West Jersey
R.I. Rhode Island	W.B. Williamsburg
S.M. South Massachusetts	Province

Produced for *Look to the West* by Alex Richards, 2016

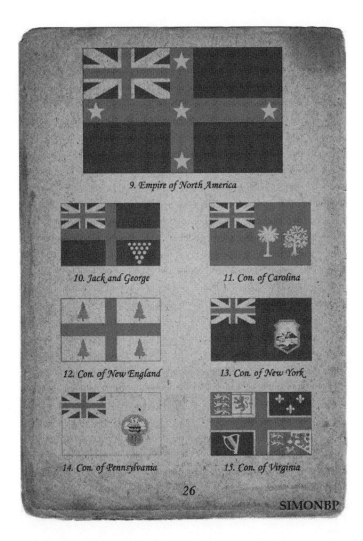

9. *Empire of North America*

10. *Jack and George*

11. *Con. of Carolina*

12. *Con. of New England*

13. *Con. of New York*

14. *Con. of Pennsylvania*

15. *Con. of Virginia*

26

SIMONBP

EXCERPTED FROM "THE NEW AMERICAN WORLD
ATLAS, 3rd EDITION" (1839)

Flag Plate #26 by Simon Beauchamp-Prince

9. National Flag of the Empire of North America (adopted
1788). Five stars stand for the five Confederations comprising
the Empire.

10. The original 'Jack and George' flag preceding the one

currently in use. The fifteen bezants (gold coins) are taken from the arms of the Duchy of Cornwall, Emperor Frederick I's possession in exile.

11. Flag of the Confederation of Carolina. The Oak of England stands alongside the Palmetto of Carolina on a Red Ensign. Here the trees are depicted as white, but some versions of the flag colour them yellow instead. The Confederal General Assembly recently voted to use the latter as the standard.

12. Flag of the Confederation of New England. The pine tree was used on Massachusetts and New England flags as early as the seventeenth century, often together with the St George's Cross of England. Along with Virginia, one of two Confederal flags not to feature the Union Jack.

13. Flag of the Confederation of New York. One of the less memorable designs, featuring the Confederal coat of arms (in which the sun rises over the Hudson River) against a Blue Ensign.

14. Flag of the Confederation of Pennsylvania. Much like New York's, this design depicts the Confederal coat of arms (showing Pennsylvania's agricultural wealth and shipping connections) against a modified White Ensign with no St George's Cross. The original version of the flag used a Blue Ensign but it was officially altered by the Pennsylvania Council and General Assembly in 1798 due to persistent confusion with the similar New York flag.

15. Flag of the Confederation of Virginia. The most complex of all the American flags, this represents an attempt to depict the Virginian coat of arms in vexillogical form. It incorporates royal heraldic representations of England, Scotland, France, Ireland and Hanover (reflecting the possessions and claimed possessions of the House of Hanover at the time the coat of arms was made).

Chapter 17: *Beaucoup de bruit et de chaleur, et qui ne signifie rien*

From: "FRANCE'S TRAGEDY: A History of the Revolution" by A.J. Galtier (originally published 1973, English translation 1984)—

Many have tried to describe the causes of the Revolution in France (for so we must append it, the oft-quoted, blame-shifting title of 'Jacobin Revolution' applying properly only to the latter stages). Many, too, have attempted to provide a conclusive linear chronology of events leading up to the fateful incidents.

In truth, none of these attempts can end in anything other than failure, for the simple reason that no-one alive knows everything. Nor, indeed, did any one man in 1794. What records were made in those heady days were frequently destroyed almost immediately by the next phase of the Revolution as it acquired its own momentum and sought to dissociate itself with all that had gone before in a bonfire of memories. Indeed, what we do know is often derived more from contemporary visitors to France than from French writers. Those visitors, of course, can only have presented biased accounts thanks to the very reasons they were in France: either pro-Revolutionary accounts from sympathisers such as Thomas Paine, or anti-Revolutionary accounts from the more numerous visitors whose business and contacts depended on the *ancien régime.*

So one appreciates that it presents a challenge to any historian to recount any sort of coherent record of those days of infamy, much less attempt to explain *why* they came about. The fact that so many writers have not let ignorance of the facts stand in the way of their theories is doubtless all to their credit, but here stands an account that tries to be as neutral as possible given the nature of the world in which we live.

Many have noted the fact that France, historically, was particularly prone to peasant revolts of all stripes. The Jacquerie of the fourteenth century is an exemplar, and one which—for reasons that will become clear—was often compared to the early phase of the Revolution. Many other similar revolts followed throughout the history of France. It is true that no European state entirely escaped such struggles, but France seemed particularly unlucky, whether by chance or design. Some of these periods of strife took the form of religious wars, resulting in the fateful flight of many Huguenots to Britain, but the majority were simple peasant revolts precipitated by famine and heavy taxation. The policies of the King and the nobility-dominated Estates-General were blamed, whether by creating wars that resulted in the suffering of the people, or else simply drawing more riches to themselves at the expense of the peasantry.

The centralisation of power and Bourbon Absolutist policies of the seventeenth and eighteenth century, modelled on the ideals of the Enlightenment, can in part be considered an attempt to prevent further such revolts. The original Jacquerie had been precipitated by the fact that the Estates-General was paralysed between different interests. By effectively eliminating the Estates-General by simply never calling it, and centralising power in the hands of themselves and their chief ministers, the French monarchs hoped to achieve a more coherent and equitable national policy. The former goal was achieved, at least to some extent; the latter, however, only became harder to reach.

Louis XV's reign was one of paradoxes. The King was known to be a something of a friend to his poorer subjects, but his attempts at reform were continually blocked by the nobility and clergy who had the most to lose. While the Estates-General no longer met, the Estates-Provincial and the local Parlements conspired to provide the very roadblock to reform that the Absolutist thinkers had hoped to remove. In particular, the Parlement of Paris, which in the absence of the Estates-General often acted as though it was the national legislature, acted as a voice for the whole establishment, and it was a voice raised in warning against the

King's attempts at reform.[129] Louis XV had to submit. This failure, coupled with his ill-judged return of the Austrian Netherlands after the Second War of Supremacy, served to make the once-loved king a highly unpopular man at his death in 1772.

His successor, Louis XVI,[130] at first seemed like an improvement. He was cultured, educated and modernist, disliking the usual 'kingly' pursuits of hunting and balls, and was also keenly interested in military affairs. He had previously fallen out with his father after making a rash charge at a battle during the Second War of Supremacy, and while he had been kept out of the front line since then, he had remained interested in the theory of war. When he became King of France and Navarre in 1772, the new Louis gave patronage to several writers advocating radical reforms to the army. He also revived the work on Nicholas-Joseph Cugnot's *Fardier à vapeur*, an early steam-tractor, which had previously been cancelled due to several accidents. In this way, then, all modern motor vehicles ultimately owe a debt to Louis (and, of course, Cugnot).[131]

The reforms of the French army typically focused on the artillery, using newer breakthroughs in mathematics to improve accuracy. The primary conceptual use of Cugnot's *fardier* was

---

[129] This was true in OTL as well, with many people acting as though the Parlement of Paris was an equivalent institution to Britain's Parliament, despite only representing the establishment of the city of Paris. This is indicative of the centralisation and emphasis on the capital that characterised the Bourbon Enlightenment period, and still arguably defines French political culture to some extent today.

[130] Recall that this is not 'our' Louis XVI, but Louis XV's son Louis-Ferdinand (the father of OTL's Louis XVI) who in OTL died before his father.

[131] Cugnot's steam tractor existed in OTL as well. It accidentally ran into a wall of the Arsenal and knocked it down in 1771, 'the world's first car accident', which is sometimes cited as being the reason the French Army decided the project was a failure. The reality, as is usual, is more complex—it was simply that the Army considered the trials to be an interesting experiment but that Cugnot's prototype vehicle was not of practical military use. They were correct, of course, but if the investment and support had been provided for Cugnot to continue improving his design, things might have been different a few years down the line. And in TTL, Cugnot has just received personal backing from the new King…

also as an alternative means of towing artillery, though this did not become practical until some of the more refined designs produced by Cugnot's team in the 1780s. While steam tractors were generally more troublesome than using horses—particularly since the army's logistics were already in place to support horses, not feed steam engines with coal— some improvements in overall speed were noted when towing artillery on flat ground and good roads over long distances. As well as their use on the battlefield, *fardiers* were later commonly used in triumphal displays by the Republic, towing huge siege guns through the wider streets of the new Paris.

The French infantry benefited rather less from Louis' reforms, although Louis was persuaded to adopt the rifle on an experimental basis. Unlike Britain and the Empire of North America, no dedicated Rifle regiments were formed, but some elite skirmishers of conventional musket regiments were trained in the longer-ranged, more accurate weapon. This would be considered both a blessing and a curse by many in Europe, later on.

Unfortunately for Louis, the one war into which he led France into was something of a disaster. The Second Platinean War was, necessarily, fought mainly at sea, and he had neglected the French Navy. Nonetheless, thanks to some excellent officers, mistakes by the British and the assistance of the Spanish fleet, victories were won at sea, most notably Trafalgar. However, the French army in Platinea was cut off from resupply and eventually was forced into a humiliating surrender. Many French soldiers deserted and joined the new Platinean republic, later to become the UPSA, while others brought back new radical ideas, sowing the seeds for what was to follow.

Another contributor to this atmosphere of radical thinking was the acquisition of Corsica in the last years of Louis XV's reign. France might have obtained a strategically important island and gained more influence over Genoa, but the revolutionary ideas of the Corsican republic also filtered back to France.

There was no *coherent* popular response to Bourbon Enlightenment absolutism, despite what many historians like to pretend. History is rarely so neat. Cartier (1959) has described the undercurrent of popular feeling in the early stages of the Revolution as a simple, unanimous, animalistic *"NON!"* The key difference to the former revolts, all the way back to the Jacquerie, was that political ideology was finally beginning to make itself known, albeit in a disjointed fashion. The Enlightenment ideals of Voltaire and the 'scientific Racialism' of Linnaeus' imitators were intermixed with more radical republican notions from Platinea and, especially, Corsica. Great Britain was viewed variously, and sometimes *simultaneously*, as an inspirational liberal democracy and a perfidious reactionary tyranny. The same was true of the Empire of North America, though even revolutionary France suffered a certain chauvinism that suggested that any ideas from the New World were inferior, notwithstanding the clear influence of the Platinean revolt on French thinking.

Some Diversitarian philosophers of the Vitebsk school have described the notion that an initial, pure, proletarian rebellion must inevitably fall prey to what they describe as 'ideological poisoning'. The starving man in the street wants only to gorge himself, take back what he believes to be rightfully his, punish those who took it from him, and perhaps destroy the signs of the former state of affairs, taking delight in the animalistic notion of pure destruction. However, the inevitable question must be asked: "then what?" The rule, throughout history, is that the rebellion peters out into confusion and disarray and the *ancien régime* returns to power, savagely extinguishing any signs of the rebels. But the introduction of the printing press and rising popular literacy slowly began to change this pattern over the centuries, and the Enlightenment sealed the shift. Suddenly there were educated men who did not identify with the royal establishment, and wanted more. Men who could ride the crest of a rebellion and steer it into a true revolution, remaking an entire state in their own image.

The most dangerous men in the world.

There is a question often asked of the schoolroom tutor, to the extent that he stereotypically finds it rather tiresome. "Why did the French people support a revolution that would end up producing a state far more cruel to them than the *ancien régime* it replaced?" The tutor might be tempted simply to point out that such comments are easy to make with the benefit of hindsight, and the French people had no such notion of what the future would hold, indeed how could they possibly have had one? The truth is, of course, somewhat more complex. The Revolution in France, more so than any of the great revolts to shake the world since that time, is a clear example of a series of transformative phases. Each phase seemed reasonable enough at the time, and yet when our schoolroom pupil considers making the leap from the first to the last, it seems inconceivable that any sane man would choose to do so.

A humorous exercise in logic from England is illustrative. *A piece of paper is an ink-lined plane; an inclined plane is a slope up; a slow pup is a lazy dog; Therefore: a piece of paper is a lazy dog.* A deliberately absurd leap, yet each step makes logical sense. So too the Revolution.

Early Revolutionary leaders were idealists, the exemplar being the man who gave the early Revolution its other name of the Second Jacquerie: Jacques Tisserant, known reverentially as "Le Diamant" (The Diamond) for his image of incorruptibility. Tisserant was a labourer who worked variously for Parisian opticians and Flemish cartographers, but he gained an education of sorts and worked his way into a position of power. The skills he had learned resulted in the publication of the most celebrated document of the Revolution, though original copies are now very rare thanks to the later phases ordering them to be burnt or carefully edited. This was *La Carte de la France.*

Despite what the name suggests, it was not simply a map of France, not in a strict geographic sense. Rather, it was a symbolic map, not unlike the humorous maps popular in the eighteenth century—the "Drunkard's Atlas", containing only those countries producing wine, and the "Map of Matrimony", describing the journey of man and woman through the lands of Happiness while avoiding the dark vistas of Loneliness.[132] It was the latter that most inspired Tisserant. Instead of the paths of lovers through

---

[132] Both of these humorous maps were published in OTL as well.

time, he showed the path of France, describing that France under the *ancien régime* would eventually, inevitably, decline to the shadowy countries of Irrelevance and Tyranny. He presented a second path, a path of Reform and of Equity, which would restore France to its place as a proud nation and a happy people.

La Carte was banned by Louis XVI's ministers, probably their first wrongfooted step. Matters were not assisted by the Great Famine of 1789 and the rumours that a comet would strike France in 1791, which threw the peasantry into a panic. The Royal French East India Company continued to bring riches to the home country from its trading possessions in southern India, but these inevitably failed to trickle down to the lower classes. Revolution was in the air.

Le Diamant created a proletarian movement known as the *Sans-Culottes*, the 'Men Without Trousers', so called because they scorned the use of the fashionable knee-breeches of the upper classes. Sans-Culottes wore long pants instead, but Le Diamant was supposedly rumoured to give speeches wearing nothing below the waist at all, allegedly due to his commitment to equal treatment for all classes rather than simple revenge on the aristocrats. In truth, of course, this may be a piece of vulgar slander by his political enemies: with the aforementioned issues we face with the destruction of records, we cannot be certain. Such a move, though it may seem vulgar to us, was not out of character for the kinds of behaviour seen in the heady days of the early Revolution. And, after all, *Equity!* was always the battle cry of the Sans-Culottes.

Things came to a head in February 1794. Having had their petitions continuously rejected by the Estates-Provincial and the Parlements, the Sans-Culottes marched on the Palais de Versailles and demanded the restoration of the Estates-General, with a dramatic expansion of both the Estates' powers and the size of the Third Estate, making it more representative of the population of a whole of France.[133] The march caught the palace guard by surprise,

---

[133] The Estates-General consisted of three estates of equal size and (theoretically) voting power, representing the aristocracy, the clergy and the common people respectively.

and many of the lower-born infantry sympathised with the Sans-Culottes. Le Diamant famously walked forward, alone, into their midst, and made a speech of which no full record survives, but is believed to contain the phrase "Will one man who grew up in a gutter shoot another on the whim of a man who cares not one jot for either of them?" According to more spurious sources, it may also have featured the phrase "You wouldn't shoot a man not wearing pants, would you?"

It was not, as many feared across the capitals of Europe, a bloody revolt. Louis XVI had been, deliberately to some extent, isolated by his ministers from the news of the tide of popular feeling sweeping France. He was shocked at what he saw, and willingly heard Le Diamant's grievances, agreeing to recall the Estates-General.

That was the beginning. It seemed so hopeful, and that is what the tutors must tell their schoolboys with their awkward question. It was the dashing of that hope that makes the whole story so poignant, so terrible, so tragic.

The Tragedy of France.

Chapter 18: The Betrayal of the Revolution

From: "FRANCE'S TRAGEDY: A History of the Revolution" by A.J. Galtier (originally published 1973, English translation 1984)—

How often has the question been asked! Who would have thought that such an auspicious beginning of the Reform of France—as it was, at first, so innocuously dubbed—could have ended in our history books being written in blood?

In a tragic irony, the Revolution could never have got as far as it did without its charismatic, popular leader Jacques Tisserant, *Le Diamant*, and yet it was that popular support that was used to destroy everything Le Diamant stood for.

Le Diamant had persuaded King Louis XVI to recall, for the first time in centuries, the Estates-General in February 1794. It was also at this time that, recognising the vast gulf between the portion of society the Third Estate represented (around 25 million peasants and bourgeoisie) and the few hundred clergy and nobles represented by the Second and First, the number of representatives of the Third Estate were tripled. However, the Second and First Estates used every political trick they could find to reduce the impact of this.

Louis wished the Estates-General to focus on the tax reforms that his father had always failed to implement, but this turned out to be a forlorn hope. The Third Estate, revelling in its newfound power, sought to reorganise and strictly define its powers, a Constitutionalist group growing as the factions in the Estates began to form the nuclei of true political parties. The British Houses of Parliament—and often their more modernised counterpart in the Empire of North America—were initial inspirations in this period, and the Third Estate renamed itself the *Communes* (House of Commons).

While the Second and First Estates looked upon this development with some alarm, they nonetheless generally participated in and encouraged the Communes' internal debates, not least because it meant that Louis' tax plans were shelved, and it was the members of the Second and First Estates that would have the most to lose from those.

By July 1794, a consensus was reached that the existing system of government was inadequate, still in many ways stuck in the Middle Ages. France had changed, and its governance would have to change with it. Louis XVI had some misgivings about this strident proclamation by the Estates, but Le Diamant's moderating influence again resulted in a compromise. The National Constitutional Convention of August-December 1794, somewhat inspired by that of the United Provinces of South America a few years earlier, abolished the Estates-General and created a new National Legislative Assembly to replace it. This was a unicameral chamber in which the First and Second Estate representatives were appointed, as were one-third of the Third Estate (Communes), but the other two-thirds would be elected by universal householder suffrage. Louis XVI's title was altered from "King of France and Navarre" to "King of the French People of the Latin Race". This was an early sign of the Linnaean Racialist policies, long ideologically debated by the French bourgeois intelligentsia, which would later characterise the Revolutionary state.

The Constitution was unpopular with both supporters of Bourbon absolutism and with those in some of the regional Estates-Provincial (most notably Brittany, but also in *généralities*[134] to the southeast such as Burgundy). The new centralised state took away a lot of the autonomy that these so-called *Pays d'État* had formerly enjoyed, and laid the foundations for many of the the later counter-revolutionary insurrections.

---

[134] A *géneralité* is an administrative subdivision of France used by the *ancien régime* chiefly to organise taxation, and growing in importance in the 18th century after Louis XIV's dissolution of the Estates-General. Each *géneralité* was administered by an *intendant* appointed by the King's Comptroller-General of Finances. At the time of the French Revolution (in both OTL and TTL) there were 36 *géneralité*s.

Nevertheless, the Constitution was implemented, with the first elections to the NLA due to take place in 1799 and further elections held on a five-year term basis. At this point, it is worth examining foreign reactions to the Revolution thus far. Britain, North America and the UPSA all saw nothing but positive events—Charles James Fox went so far as to openly praise the Revolution as a repeat of Britain's Glorious Revolution of a century before. In fact, what criticism did exist in Britain was largely that of those who combined patriotism with intellectual musings on political systems—if constitutional parliamentary monarchy was really the motor that had driven Britain to successes in America and, to a much lesser extent, India—then the last thing they wanted was the French getting hold of it!

The more reactionary nations of Europe, on the other hand—in particular absolutist and Catholic Austria and Spain—viewed these events with alarm. Spain, after all, also had a Bourbon king, and the last thing Philip VI[135] wanted was for his own "mob" to get any funny ideas—particularly considering that his predecessor, Charles III, had already been forced to temporarily flee into exile by popular uprisings twice, and the third time might prove to be permanent. It turned out that this worry was largely unfounded: the Spanish people remained reasonably francophobic and this would only intensify as time went on. An imaginary Spanish imitation of the Revolution would turn out to be the least of Philip's worries.

Back in Paris, the Comte de Mirabeau, a moderate member of the First Estate, became chief minister and struggled to implement the new constitutional monarchy amid sniping from all sides. Reactionary absolutists, allied to the provincial interests, attacked the constitution, while on the other side a new radical force was

---

[135] In OTL, Charles III's first son Philip was born mentally handicapped and epileptic, and was thus disqualified from the throne in favour of his younger brother Charles, who ascended to the throne as Charles IV on his father's death in 1788. Charles had previously been effective governor of Naples and Sicily, two junior Spanish Bourbon possessions, under the title 'Prince of Taranto'. In TTL, butterflies mean that Philip is born healthy and succeeds his father as King of Spain in 1788, while his brother Charles continues as ruler of Naples and Sicily.

growing. Aside and apart from Le Diamant's Sans-Culottes, a new faction was created. They would eventually be known as the Jacobins, after the name of the Paris club in which they held their meetings. These men were on the whole not proletarians with legitimate grievances as the Sans-Culottes were; for the most part, they were members of the bourgeois intelligentsia more interested in applying abstract idealistic Enlightenment concepts to the government of the state than they were in solving any of the real immediate problems that faced France and its poor. In that respect, they were no different from any of the great Enlightenment statesmen who had served in Iberia and indeed France itself throughout the past century—but now that the old system of royal power had been overturned, there were nothing to prevent them gaining absolute power in turn.

Things came to a head on April 2nd 1795, when the death of Mirabeau of natural causes paralysed the NLA and allowed the Jacobin faction, putting out the loudest and most coherent message to the people, to gain momentum. The moderates, led by the Marquis de Condorcet, advocated that Louis XVI's Swiss-born finance minister Jacques Necker should replace Mirabeau as chief minister, while the Jacobins put forward the relatively unknown lawyer Jean-Baptiste Robespierre, of the *Généralite* of Lille.[136] This was accompanied by savage propaganda attacks on Necker by the Linnaean Racialist political faction that would soon become synonymous with the Jacobins. The Jacobins had begun to combine the existing French Enlightenment view of the superiority of the Latin race with a narrower sense of French nationalism as embodied in the French language. Either way, foreign-born officials were suspect. This was backed by an undercurrent of feeling in the more proletarian Sans-Culotte faction, though there are no surviving records that Le Diamant ever definitively spoke on the subject—and thus his admirers have argued over it ever since. It was particularly ironic given that one of the Jacobins' own leaders, Jean-Paul Marat, was also Swiss-

---

[136] As can be seen by his different first name, this is not the same person as OTL's Maximilien Robespierre, but shares his parents and upbringing and is similar in many ways.

born, though he took some pains to conceal this.

As the legitimate political debate degenerated into ever more savage verbal—and not just verbal—attacks, with rival political gangs fighting in the streets of Paris, a nervous Louis XVI ordered regiments to be recalled from the frontiers to Paris in an attempt to keep the peace. In practice this only resulted in the regiments being seen as tools of the king against the people and resulted in numerous attacks on soldiers by the fierier political radicals. This rarely succeeded in accomplishing any immediate goal, but in the longer term significantly reduced the popularity of both the king and the army as reprisals were mounted and often misfired, with innocents being caught in the crossfire.

The atmosphere in Paris, indeed throughout much of France, was tense. Everyone knew that, metaphorically speaking, one dropped matchstick could ignite the smouldering country into the inferno of full-blown civil war. Even Charles James Fox began to moderate his praise of the revolution as reports of intense political violence in the cities of France crept out.

Despite being somewhat insulated from the events on the streets by what remained of the royal trappings, Louis XVI decided something must be done to relieve the tensions. A figure that everyone could agree on must be made chief minister...a man who had become the national hero of France.

Jacques Tisserant.

It was after a month of unrest that, on the May 3rd 1795, Louis XVI summoned Le Diamant into his presence to discuss the possibility. Precisely what happened next remains unclear due to the lack of surviving records, many of them deliberately destroyed by the later regime for revisionist reasons. Attempts at establishing a historical record from eyewitness accounts years after the fact must inevitably be flawed, but this is what most historians accept as the rough sequence of events:

It would seem that the King was still just insulated enough from events for one fatal mistake to be made. Le Diamant arrived with four loyal Sans-Culottes armed with muskets as bodyguards, a common sight by now and a sensible precaution on the wartorn streets of Paris. The captain of the royal guard asked Louis if he wanted Le Diamant's guards to be disarmed, and Louis, not realising how dangerous his capital had become and how social norms had changed in response, replied "Of course!"

But the Royal soldiers on the ground were nervous, after so many attacks, and demanded that Le Diamant's guards give up their weapons while they were still more than half a mile from the gates of the Palais de Versailles. The bodyguards refused, on the reasonable grounds that there was too much of a risk of an attack from one of the political gangs stalking the streets. The captain replied that they would protect Le Diamant themselves. The bodyguards replied that frankly, they did not trust the royal soldiers with Le Diamant's life.

Le Diamant himself attempted to smooth things over, but it was already too late. As he and his bodyguards faced off with the soldiers and the procession came to a halt, a crowd began to gather around them, a crowd mostly made up of Jacobin sympathisers. The crowd chanted anti-Royal slogans, jeered at the royal guards and, infamously, one voice suggested that Le Diamant was being taken away to be executed.

That ignited the tension. The bodyguards refused to leave Le Diamant's side or give up their weapons, the soldiers insisted, someone fired the first shot—quite possibly someone in the crowd—and all hell broke loose.

A few minutes later, seventeen men were dead. Among them was Le Diamant himself, the man who had led France's Revolution thus far, the man who had given it the momentum that would now be seized upon by others for their own ends. It is not even certain that it was the soldiers who killed him, in the confusion of the brawl and the blurring of the historical record. Indeed, some modern Adamantians have argued that Le Diamant was deliberately killed by the Jacobins, having planned for what would happen next. Whether this is literally true or not, the Jacobins certainly proceeded to *metaphorically* murder everything Le Diamant had stood for. For enough Jacobins had been present in that crowd, enough had escaped, for the "true" story to become official: Le Diamant had been murdered, on the King's orders, by Royal troops. And France destroyed itself.

MAP OF EUROPE IN 1794

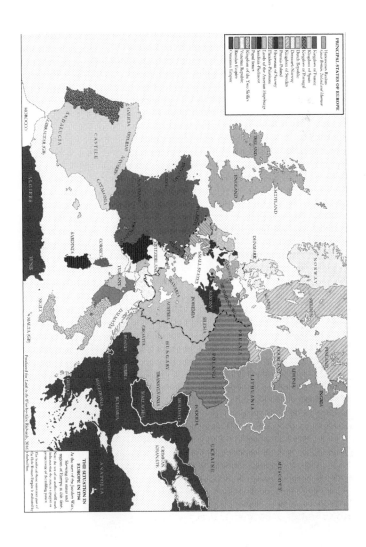

Chapter 19: Choke Point

From: "FRANCE'S TRAGEDY: A History of the Revolution" by A.J. Galtier (originally published 1973, English translation 1984)—

It has often been suggested that the death of Le Diamant was the ultimate catalyst for the darkest phase of the Revolution and the rise of the Jacobins. While there is certainly some truth to this assertion, it is disingenuous to assume that these developments were inevitable. Indeed, to do so (in the fashion of the Montevideo school of Societist thought) leads to the dangerous intellectual fallacy of absolving those who committed atrocities of their crimes, as they were simply "fulfilling a historical inevitability". Small comfort to the thousands who died with their lungs phlogisticated or their heads rolling on the ground.

It is quite possible that, if the National Legislative Assembly had possessed more moderate and pragmatic members, the incident could have been smoothed over, even worked to a liberal advantage by using it as an excuse to reduce royal powers further, towards a "British-style" (as it would have then been termed) constitutional monarchy.

But cooler heads did not prevail. Once more those of the Montevideo school would argue that the lack of such cooler heads is another historical inevitability, that Louis XVI paid for the fact that he and his predecessors had allowed absolutism to continue so mercilessly for so long, putting off reform until it was required to avert economic collapse. If the Bourbons had reformed more gradually, the Societists argue, they might have eventually had a more moderate National Legislative Assembly and not suffered such terrible losses and tragedies. But to make such an argument is to abrogate the NLA of its crimes, and that is a mistake.

Riding a wave of public anger at the death of Le Diamant,

the Jacobins—already the largest faction within the NLA as a whole, if barely—seized the instruments of power. Their former candidate for chief minister, Jean-Baptiste Robespierre, began issuing orders as though he had indeed been approved by the King for the position. Louis XVI was not a stupid man, but once more he paid for being so insulated from real events. The King did not hear of the Jacobins' actions until fully two days after Le Diamant's body had hit the cobbles, and then waited three hours before issuing orders to the troops to keep the peace, agonising about whether it would inflame the situation. By then, it was too late.

A large percentage of the royal troops simply deserted, often defecting straight to the Jacobins. Many of them were Parisians who could not stand the shame of the people of Paris jeering and hurling stones at them, accusing them of murdering the popular Le Diamant. Thus the majority of the *Gardes Françaises* were lost. Others, those from the *Gardes Suisses* and regiments brought in from other provinces and generalities, simply retreated in the face of public anger, not having clear orders from royal authority as to whether they were supposed to fire on civilians or not. The civic government of the city disintegrated. Paris was ruled by the mob, and the mob was controlled by Robespierre.

Yet many troops remained fiercely loyal to the King, even in the absence of coherent orders from His Most Christian Majesty. Several loyal companies of the *Gardes Françaises* were rallied together with outside troops by Phillipe Henri, the Marquis de Ségur, one of the Marshals of France and the only one present in Paris during the crisis of Le Diamant's death. Ségur believed that the chaos, along with the revolution as a whole, was a transient fad and could be weathered if the military would hunker down in carefully chosen strongpoints and stand fast as the waves of disorganised public opposition beat uselessly against them like water on cliffs. "What the shopkeeper or the farmer or the peasant wants more than anything is not liberty or rights or even riches, but simply the knowledge that tomorrow he will be in much the same state as he is today, his belly full and his family secure," he wrote. "All we have to do is wait for the revolutionaries to prove to the people that the chaos they promise is more likely to end their lives than enrich them, and then the whole mass of traitors will collapse".

Unfortunately for Ségur, there were two fatal flaws to his plan. Firstly, since the logistics and communications apparatus had broken down along with the rest of military discipline across much of Paris, he was simply unaware that the vast majority of the forces stationed in Paris had deserted or defected. Either that, or else he dismissed such reports as Jacobin propaganda. Secondly, the mob he faced was not as disorganised as he imagined, but ideologically fed and led by the Jacobins. And, in a moment of irony, it was Ségur himself who would unintentionally give the Jacobins the mythic image they needed to cement their hold on France.

Ségur realised that the most important point to be held in Paris, except the Palais de Versailles itself, was the Bastille Saint-Antoine. Originally built as a defensive fort, much like England's Tower of London it had gradually become both a prison and an arsenal. Thus, it was both a defensive position and an endless store of ammunition and supplies for any army that sought to hold it. In addition to this, the Bastille was seen in the popular imagination as a symbol of royal power, and so if Ségur's forces could hold the fort against Jacobin attacks, it would be a potent symbol that the monarchy would withstand the Revolution.

All of which was true, but it also meant that the reverse result— that of the revolutionaries taking the Bastille—would create an equally potent symbol for the opposite cause. And this was in fact what occurred.

Ségur's forces first moved into the the Bastille on the evening of May 4th1795, quickly turning it back into a fortress. While military discipline held sway in the Bastille, at the same time most of the rest of the military forces in Paris were disintegrating, unbeknownst to Ségur. It was not until the afternoon of the 5th that Ségur heard that Versailles was threatened and considered sending forces to escort the King to the Bastille, where he could be protected. By that point, the Jacobin-inspired mob had already managed to overwhelm the royal guard and seize the palace. What resulted was what Goethe described as "the New Barbarism", even though it would rapidly be overshadowed by later developments. The palace was ransacked, with countless valuable paintings and tapestries looted or destroyed, and soon the furniture of kings could be found in common houses and hovels scattered all over Paris.

The royal family themselves were not harmed. At this point the majority of the mob still had an inbuilt fear and respect for the royals, a relic of the *ancien régime* they had been raised under. The King in his person, as opposed to as a symbol of royal power, attracted more curiosity than hostility from the common people. They had captured the King and Queen, the Comte de Provence, the Duc d'Orleans and Maria Antonia of Austria (Marie-Antoinette), the wife of the Dauphin.[137] The Dauphin himself was not present, though; Louis, technically re-titled "Prince of the Royal Blood of Latin France" by the NLA's early reforms, had been sent to Navarre for discussions as to whether Navarre would be directly incorporated into the new French state or would become a separate kingdom, perhaps with himself as its king. He, and his entourage, therefore escaped the coup.

The royal family was swiftly placed under arrest by Robespierre and the Jacobin-dominated NLA. At the same time, Robespierre's fiery lieutenant Georges Hébert ordered the expected attack on the Bastille by the mob, supported by those troops who had defected to the Jacobin side. Because they still wore the same uniforms as the loyalist troops on the other side, to avoid friendly-fire confusion those rebel troops discarded their shakoes and instead marched bare-headed or with red cloth caps designed to represent the Phrygian Cap of liberty.[138] On this day,

---

[137] Recall that this is the person known to OTL as Louis XVI, or his ATL "brother" equivalent at least: he was born a considerable number of years after the POD, after all. Franco-Austrian geopolitics being similar in both timelines, however, he is still married to an Austrian princess and she happens to have the same name as her OTL counterpart, though she is a different person. Her brother, the Archduke of Austria and Holy Roman Emperor, is Ferdinand IV.

[138] Phrygian caps were worn by early French Revolutionary troops in OTL and it remains a symbol of republicanism today.

May 7th 1795 (or 18th Flóreal of the year Minus 1 as it would later be known to some), the soon-to-be dreaded uniform of the Revolutionary soldier would start to come into being. Before the week (or decimalised *décade* for that matter) was out, it would be completed.

The first attack on the Bastille was, predictably, bloodily repulsed by Ségur's professional troops. Grapeshot ripped the still largely undisciplined mob to shreds. It is no exaggeration to say that the streets ran with blood like water, perhaps even that they were flooded with it as the gutters blocked and overflowed. After the first two frontal attacks were both reduced to bloody rags filling the streets around the Bastille, Ségur ordered his troops to hoist the royal flag, a white banner with the countless golden fleur-de-lys of *France ancient*, to mock the Jacobins.[139] *Give up your futile struggle!* was the message he wished to send.

But the Jacobins did not give up. Just like Ségur, their commanders knew that the revolutionary fervour of the people would eventually run out and they would hesitate, no longer willing to charge into a hail of bullets for the sake of an idea. To that end, on the 6th of May, yet another frontal attack was launched, with no further success, while defecting sappers concealed themselves in the mess of bodies on the streets and used the distraction to plant gunpowder explosives beneath weak points of the Bastille wall. At midnight, when the majority of Ségur's garrison was asleep, the fuses were lit and the old fortifications were blasted apart by the modern techniques devised by Vauban and his successors.

Ségur's troops were still disciplined and immediately attempted to plug the gap, before being hit by grapeshot from cannons that the Revolutionaries had brought up in the night. The mob cheered as the troops got a taste of their own medicine, and then charged through the breach.

Despite most of the troops being hastily awakened and the rest being killed by the grapeshot, the Revolutionaries still suffered

---

[139] A field with many fleur-de-lys is heraldically known as *France ancient*, while three large fleur-de-lys is known as *France modern*. Both types were used on French flags in this period, and with either a blue or white background; the *ancien régime* did not have a single consistent national flag.

heavy casualties. But by the time Ségur was apprised of the events, it was already too late to do anything about it. The old Marshal went down fighting, both of his pistols being fired mere seconds before the butcher's knife of a Sans-Culotte sliced through his heart. In later times, Ségur would become a hero, a martyr, of French Royalism. For now, he would be used for the Jacobins' own purposes.

As the crowd cheered and looted the Bastille, releasing the few prisoners from the dark fort—the Jacobins would claim that it was this act of liberty that had motivated the attack, not getting hold of the arsenal there—one man, a soldier who had gone over to the Jacobins, came to the fore. His name is not recorded in history. Like Le Diamant, he became a legend, *L'Épurateur*, the Purifier, a name given to him by Robespierre. He had only defected the day before, but in that time his ears had been filled with the revolutionary message the Jacobins preached. There is no fierier zealot than a new convert still half trying to convince himself of the truth of his new way.

L'Épurateur was already covered in blood from the battle, like most of his fellow survivors. Now, he took out his sabre and cut the head from Ségur's corpse, working meticulously. He took the head to the largest flagpole, where his fellow Jacobins had brought down the Royal flag and had been about to tear it to pieces, but L'Épurateur shook his head. "*Non.*" It was not enough for the flag simply to fall. The people must see what that flag had stood for.

He took the flag and smeared it all over with Ségur's blood, dying the pristine noble white with the shed blood of the people. Then he turned it upside down and it was raised once more, the fleur-de-lys turned over, the monarchy overthrown by the blood that had been shed by the revolutionary fighters.

And thus the symbols of the Revolution were complete. The crowds saw L'Épurateur standing on the battlements of the Bastille in the moonlight, the white parts of his blue uniform stained red by the blood of the battle, wearing the Phrygian cap, his white Bourbon cockade dyed bloodred, and the red flag flying above him.

Vive la Révolution!

Et mort au roi!

Chapter 20: Cette obscurité glorieuse

From: "FRANCE'S TRAGEDY: A History of the Revolution" by A.J. Galtier (Université Royale de Nantes, 1973)—

It all happened so rapidly. Indeed in many ways, for many years to come, in France everything would seem to come in a rush. The new powerful men of France knew that their position was tenuous. They did not have the luxury of the Bourbon kings who had come before them, when it had taken centuries for discontent to coalesce into an organised and intellectual-backed revolution instead of ineffective peasant revolts. No; the Revolutionary genie was out of the bottle, and they risked it turning against them. The solution was to keep the people so occupied that they did not have the chance to do so.

Even as the royal family were placed in a mean common jail by the Jacobins, the NLA began to issue "reforms" at a bewildering rate. It was not merely a case that a man could wake up in a different state to the one that he had fallen asleep in; France changed by the hour. This also meant that foreign commentators in Madrid, London and Vienna barely had a chance to absorb the information of the earlier, more benign stages of the Revolution before the news of Le Diamant's death and what came after fell upon them. When moderate figures there were being assailed by the confusing shift of the Revolution, only two groups held firm—ultraroyalists who would always condemn anything associated with the Revolution no matter how reasonable, and radicals who would praise any such thing no matter how horrific. As a consequence, the partisan divide sharpened and narrowed, with few willing to embrace a position of qualified approval or disapproval. The Revolution was not merely the death of moderation in France, but elsewhere also.

The unknown soldier known as *l'Épurateur* was never seen again after that fateful night, when he raised the Bloody Flag above the Bastille. What happened to him has been the subject of many theories then and since. The most likely possibility is that he was simply killed later that night in the fighting still raging throughout Paris between the Jacobins and Sans-Culottes and the royalists. However, some have suggested that L'Épurateur simply faded into obscurity and died in a later battle. Most controversially the Royalist historian Pierre Beauchamp has claimed that l'Épurateur disowned his "drunken" antics on the Bastille and later returned to the Royalist side.

No-one will ever truly know, but Hébert, who had witnessed the event, was swift to capitalise on it. L'Épurateur became a mythic figure, emblematic of the new France and thence a martyr, stabbed in the back by a Royalist assassin for his act of courage. A large number of French people, even some historians, still believe that l'Épurateur was purely an invention of Hébert and there was never such a living, breathing person. Whatever the truth, the Jacobins and their Sans-Culotte allies were driven to new strengths by the great symbol they had been gifted with.

By the hour and the day, the NLA was "reformed". Moderate 'Mirabeauistes'[140] still in favour of a constitutional monarchy were shouted down and even attacked in the street. Those genuine royalists among the Third Estate's deputies fled, or claimed a conversion to Jacobinism—L'Épurateur's own late switch made this sufficiently plausible that a number of royalists either fearful of their lives, or believing that their cause was lost, were able to switch sides.

The deputies of the First and Second Estates were sidelined as those Estates were effectively disenfranchised, all in the name of liberty. In less than one week, all titles of the nobility were abolished, the Catholic Church was effectively "nationalised" and turned into an arm of the government, with priests having to swear allegiance to the Revolution, and land ownership was revoked. The Revolutionaries sought to usurp the Great Chain of

---

[140] More or less like OTL's Girondist faction but they're not so associated with the deputies of one region, hence the alternative name.

Being itself, so that all men would be equal—and death to those that disagreed.

In those early, heady days, the revolution was pure, if nonetheless horrific. Slavery was abolished and women were emancipated, as defenders of Revolutionary thought have cited ever since (particularly those of the Monterey school). Freedom of religion was guaranteed, which in Britain both intrigued the large Huguenot-descended population and was used by the Radical Party as an argument for Catholic emancipation at home.

Robespierre, still acting as de facto chief minister in a government that had imprisoned its own king, argued for "*la rupture tranquille*" (a clean break) with the past, adding "In ten years' time, we should not be able to recognise France". These two innocuous sentences would come to drip with blood in years to come...

The policy was implemented in numerous ways. Initially, the NLA severed all links with the Estates-General that had preceded it, incorporating or ejecting all the members of the First and Second Estates. The democratic constitution adopted the previous year was reformed entirely: democracy remained the central pillar of the constitution, although a quiet provision for the suspension of elections "in times of emergency" would cause troubles in years to come. In addition, the English-born radical Thomas Paine co-authored his "Declaration of the Rights of Man" which would be the French constitution's answer to the English Bill of Rights. The Declaration embodied the rights to representation, to be tried by a jury of peers, and to freedom of worship.

At the same time, Jacobin thinkers were devising new ways of measuring the world, known as the Rational System.[141] Decimalisation was applied to measurements of length, weight, even time. A new calendar with purely descriptive titles of months was implemented. This is illustrative of another feature of the Revolution: while initially there was some identification with

---

[141] This is a bit like the OTL metric system, but is combined with other initiatives such as the republican calendar—it's more organised top-down than OTL and is seen as an all-or-nothing affair.

the Athenian democracy of the ancient world and therefore other classical culture, this was swiftly rejected by mainstream Jacobin opinion as characteristic of the aristocratic culture they sought to abolish.[142]

The NLA rejected a presidential system like that of the United Provinces, which was otherwise regarded as the only halfway pure republican influence in the world, with the Dutch, Genoese and Venetians being merely merchant oligarchies. The French people remained wary of concentrating all power in one man after their experiences with Bourbon absolutism. What emerged was closer to the British parliamentary system but perhaps also showed some influence from Rome, despite the supposed rejection of classicism. A three-man Consulate was elected by the NLA, which would collectively possess presidential powers but all three members must agree in order for decisions to take place. This was widely referred to as the Triumvirate, especially in the English-speaking world.

Although the Consulate was intended to moderate and provide checks and balances on power, in practice the large radical Jacobin majority meant that Robespierre was able to manipulate the NLA into electing those of his choice: himself, of course, plus Hébert and Jean Marat. Other radical Jacobins remained in positions of power, such as Georges Danton and the then relatively obscure Jean de Lisieux. Moderate voices were shouted down. A Revolutionary Tribunal was established to try 'enemies of the revolution', a category which seemed to swell day by day in an attempt to implement Robespierre's "clean break"—and his paranoia at the revolutionary genie turning against him.

At the same time, voices in the NLA who supported Paine's Rights of Man advocated that a more humane means of execution be devised, arguing that capital punishment should be seen mainly as a means of removing criminals from society rather than actually inflicting pain. Accordingly, breaking on the wheel and

---

[142] A major difference to the OTL revolution which retained more neo-classicist admirers in positions of power. This perhaps indicates a greater sense of continuing populist input by Le Diamant's supporters in TTL's revolution.

execution by axe and sword were both abolished. The invention of "Le Chirurgien" has never been accurately credited to any one man, although it clearly showed influence from existing 'humane gibbets' such as the Scottish Maiden and Halifax Gibbet. While similar devices had existed for a long time, they had never been used so extensively before. Le Chirurgien's first patients were minor nobility and royal ministers who had been unable to flee or convincingly convert to the revolutionary cause. On trumped-up charges, the king's own surgeon, Antoine Louis, was ironically among them.

However, another range of opinion in the NLA argued instead that there should be a more "Scientific" method of execution. Hébert approved the creation of the "Chambre Phlogistique" (later "Phlogisticateur"), in which the corruption of the criminal would be visited back unto him by means of phlogisticated air. Thus the humanitarian work of Joseph Priestley on the Aerial Economy was turned to darkness, and the Revolution forced Antoine Lavoisier and his assistants to build the machine. It took the form of a large glass bell-jar, entirely airtight. Whereas Priestley's experiments on airs had used mice in jars, this one was large enough for a human to stand inside. And then? A powerful air-pump could be applied to remove all the air, but that was so "seventeenth-century". Better for burning glasses to be directed on the Chambre. They could be used either to attempt to ignite the clothes of the victim, or merely to burn fuels placed inside, creating phlogiston with no need for a naked flame. Thus the hands-off means of execution was created, in which the sun itself made the killing blow instead of any human.

The first "criminal" to be subject to the Chambre was Citoyen Louis Capet, as the revolutionaries mockingly titled their former King. Louis XVI's quiet defence, self-delivered, remained a rallying cry to French Royalists ever afterwards. In its most momentous exchange, the fiery Danton accused "Capet" of treason against the state, and Louis simply quoted his great-great-grandfather in response: "I *am* the state."

It made no difference, of course. Louis XVI was led out to the first Chambre, in Paris' Place du Louis XV, recently renamed

Place de la Révolution. In a grim irony, the Chambre stood on a stage not far from where nobles and bourgeoisie had once watched convicted criminals being dismembered alive. The Revolutionaries were fortunate in that the 15th of May was a hot, sunny day. "Citoyen Capet" gave his last words, clearly inspired by those of Charles Stuart one and a half centuries earlier. "Remember this day," he said. "One day, not too long from now, you will look back on the darkest and hardest days of my reign with envy."

Prophetic words, but they made no impression on a crowd that was baying for blood. "Capet" was sealed inside the Chambre and the great burning glasses were directed against the sawdust piled on the floor of the glass room. The sun set the dust alight and smoke began to rise. Unlike later victims, "Capet" did not try to beat out the flames or otherwise prolong his death. Ten agonising minutes later, he succumbed to asphyxiation from the phlogisticated air.

And as the crowd cheered, the Chambre was opened, the smoke billowed out over the Place, and the glasses began to burn the corpse also, in its simple prisoner's garments. Royalists have claimed ever since that a white dove rose with that smoke, taking the king's blameless soul to heaven where he would look down on what became of his nation, and wept.

That night, Antoine Lavoisier took his own life, swallowing a fatal dose of an arsenic compound he was studying. But the Revolutionaries had enough clever artisans to duplicate the design now it had been built once.

The blades of the Chiurgiens hissed and the belljars of the Phlogisticateurs burned, and war rumbled on the horizon.

Chapter 21: L'Étrangerie

From: "Foreign Reactions to the Jacobin Revolution" (Dr Jacques Desaix, Université de Toulon; published 1974 in the original French, authorised English translation 1986)–

The Revolution in France can always only be truly understood in a wider European, even global, context. In the most obvious instance, the Revolution took much of its inspiration from other foreign republics derived partially from Enlightenment principles, such as Paoli's Corsica and the United Provinces of South America. Both of these had had French troops serving against them at some point, and it is unsurprising that ideas were paradoxically brought back to France by those same soldiers. However, most writers focus on the intellectuals among the troops, primarily the officers, who wrote those ideas down and went on to organise the Armée de la République. While their influence is unchallenged, we cannot ignore the enlisted soldiers, either—had they not been exposed to an actual Enlightenment republic while serving in Corsica and South America, it is unlikely that there would have been such support for the Revolution in the Royal Army.

The Navy had always been less keen—after all, the French Navy's conduct in the Second Platinean War had firstly been at sea, away from the South American revolutionaries, and secondly the Navy had enjoyed several victories over the British under de Grasse and Picquet de la Motte. Unlike the Royal Army, humiliated by the surrender on the River Plate to U.P. and British forces, the Navy had little reason to resent the *ancien régime* and what it stood for. This would have important consequences a little later on, but for now, let us return to the subject of foreign reactions to the Revolution.

At first, perhaps unsurprisingly, the import of the Revolution was not completely understood in other European countries. The British in particular tended to view the Revolution as a logical consequence of the failure of Bourbon absolutism, and according to the Whig interpretation of history, France would now slide towards a constitutional monarchy of the British model. Indeed, much British opposition to the Revolution in its earliest form was simply an alarmed national chauvinism that the French might acquire the same 'state of perfect government' as Britain was thought to enjoy under the 1688 settlement, with a comparable boost in military fortunes. In particular, Britain's large Huguenot-descended population wondered if the Revolution, with its attacks on Catholicism, would finally begin using the resource of French Protestants rather than condemning them. The drastically different character of *this* Revolution would not become apparent to the British until mid-1795.

Spain, which accepted Louis the Dauphin into asylum after the execution of the French royal family, initially viewed the Revolution as just another peasant revolt. Spain herself had suffered similar outpourings of the popular will, mainly rooted in francophobia, against the attempts by her own Bourbon kings to introduce reforms or fashions perceived as French. Given that the French Revolution incorporated a certain element of ultra-Linnaean xenophobia and Racist nationalism, this was perhaps an understandable assumption. The Spanish government, led by Floridablanca (who had continued to serve under Charles III's successor Philip VI) believed the revolutionaries to be absent a guiding ideology and that the "revolt" would soon be crushed. Floridablanca publicly condemned the violence; as a great supporter of liberal ideas himself, he argued that the Revolutionaries had squandered their capital and missed the chance to institute a stable constitutional monarchy by instead reverting to barbarism. In this, the official Spanish response was ironically not unlike that of the British, though approached from the other direction.

Austria was the greatest source of opposition to the Revolution from the start. This opposition stemmed from many roots: Ferdinand IV ruled over a massive, multi-ethnic empire and

Linnaean Racist nationalism of the type growing in France could only undermine that; Marie-Antoinette, the Dauphin's consort, was Ferdinand IV's sister Maria Antonia of Austria; and the Revolution's nationalisation of and attacks on the Catholic Church also sent shockwaves throughout the Holy Roman Empire. Great swathes of land were still under ecclesiastical authority, and the French idea of the Church becoming subordinate to the State would lead to chaos if it spread to the Empire, with every prince and duke and landgrave squabbling to carve up those Church lands. In summary, it was obvious from the start that it was in Austrian interests to oppose the Jacobin Revolution at every turn.

Speculative romantics have suggested that, had Louis XVI called for Austrian military assistance at an earlier stage, the Revolution could have been crushed—though doubtless the resentment of a king kept in power by foreign forces would have continued to simmer. In any case the question is academic: insulated from current affairs by his entourage of sycophants and the Palais de Versailles, Louis had been unaware of the scale of the situation until it was too late. Therefore Ferdinand IV, though gathering an army, was unable to act until a suitable casus belli—the death by phlogistication of Marie-Antoinette on August 12th 1795. Then, an imperial proclamation was issued 'in support of the rightful King of France'—Austrian refusal to recognise the Revolutionary government meant that no declaration of war could be legally possible—and Austrian troops began to move into France from Baden and the Duchy of Flanders, first crossing the Rubicon (as latter historians would put it) on the 3rd of September.

As for the Dauphin's reaction, a rather inaccurate picture of the situation has been (deliberately) engendered in the years since by the proliferation of prints of the painting *Who Hath Unleashed The Hounds?* by Joseph Ducreux, Louis XVII's favourite painter, showing the young exilic king pointing dramatically at the unseen Jacobin hordes with an accusing look on his face and one hand on his sword. Though the painting depicts Louis in Navarre, supposedly hearing the news of the latest Jacobin outrage, it was in fact painted several years later in 1801, shortly before Ducreux's death and when the character of the Revolution had become undeniable.[143]

Further abroad the French Revolution as yet had little effect. Russia would not hear of the full import of the Revolution until the end of that year, although by then it would lend a distinctive character to the Russian Civil War, already rumbling on the horizon as the aged Peter III, having survived innumerable assassination attempts, finally fell into a terminal decline.

Just as the UPSA had inspired the Jacobins, so the reverse now took place, with Jacobin ideas driving more radical notions in the UPSA. Egalitarian notions, which had originally mainly focused on equality between *peninsulares* and *criollos*, now began to spread to questioning the basis of the blood caste system as a whole. One import of much broader character was an increase in calls for the abolition of the slave trade and slavery itself, everywhere from the UPSA to the Empire of North America to Portugal to Britain. In practice, though, this probably harmed the abolitionist cause in the long run—as the greater excesses of the Revolutionaries became known, it was easy for those with vested interests in the slave trade to tar their opponents with the brush of Jacobinism.

And what of France herself? As the Jacobin-dominated NLA meeting in the old Palais de Tuileries continued to make ever more radical reforms and changes, these spread out across France in waves. Before people in Lyon or Bordeaux had even heard of Le Diamant's death, Louis XVI had gone to the *chambre phlogistique*, and many similar situations prevailed in this age before rapid communication. France could have so easily slipped into utter anarchy, and yet in an ultimate irony, the Jacobins were assisted by the very Bourbon absolutism they had overthrown. The centralisation of the French state, proceeding in several stages since the end of the Hundred Years' War and most prominently under Louis XIV, had focused power in Paris as much as the person of the king. Thus, what came out of Paris was generally accepted, no matter how shrill its tone. The exception was in those provinces which retained feudal privileges of autonomy, had held onto them stubbornly throughout centuries of centralisation,

---

[143] Joseph Ducreux was 'First Painter to the Queen' at the OTL Louis XVI's court and painted the last picture of Louis alive.

and were not about to let go of them now. Brittany would be the exemplar, but it far from alone.

Realising the import of the Austrian invasion (together with some Spanish inroads, possibly aimed at trying to reclaim Navarre with the tacit consent of the Dauphin), the NLA immediately shifted to a war footing. The Consulate understood that an external war would give them carte blanche to push through further reforms and it would provide a rallying call for the French people. Though the Jacobins were still busy purging or attainting aristocrats from the Royal Army, vast numbers of Sans-Culottes (the so-called Légion du Diamant) volunteered as recruits. Thus the character of the Revolutionary Army, possessing overwhelming numbers but of poorly trained soldiers, came to pass.

Initially the old royal regimental flags were simply turned upside down. However, realising that the men needed a truly Revolutionary symbol to fight for (and finding an excuse for another attack on the symbols of the Church, as the old flags bore white crosses), Hébert designed a new series of regimental flags, based on squares of white cloth that were dyed reddish-brown. The legend was that the 'dye' was in fact the blood of executed nobles from the *chirurgien* and/or the blood of the martyrs before the Bastille, although historians have continued to debate whether this was really the case. The new flags bore simple designs, usually either one or more inverted fleur-de-lys to symbolise the downfall of the ancien régime, or else rerpresentations of Le Diamant or L'Épurateur. They also always bore words, usually illegible in battle, which spelled out Revolutionary slogans. Finally, a new finial, based on a representation of a Phrygian cap in bronze, was added.

The new colours were 'blessed' by NLA vote rather than Church sacrament, and the Revolutionary armies marched forth to meet the Austrians for the first time. They wore the same uniform that L'Épurateur had 'created', albeit for the moment somewhat haphazardly and inconsistently adopted: the same blue and white uniforms as their Royal predecessors, but with all the white parts dyed red, and their shakoes replaced with a standardised Phrygian cap. They bore the white cockade of the Bourbons also dyed revolutionary red. It was not surprising that they soon received the nickname of *Les bleus et les rouges* (which became a nostalgic phrase after the blue parts of the uniform were changed to black under the later Administration).

Meanwhile, quite a different situation was occuring with the French Navy in Toulon, as a certain British captain named Leo Bone would soon discover...

Chapter 22: The Making of a Legend

"...always be wary of telling lies, especially when they turn out to be the truth."

- Leo Bone, Captain, RN

From: "The Man With Three Names—The Life and Times of Napoleone Buonaparte" (Dr Henri Pelletier, University of Nantes Press, 1962)—

The Toulon incident was at first overlooked in the broader chaos of the dawning wars of the Revolutionary Age, but from our perspective, with the benefit of sitting comfortably atop more than a century of distance from these events, it was as important as the Battle of Saint-Quentin or the Flight from Fleurus. It sealed the fate of naval affairs in Revolutionary France, leading to some obvious consequences and some that were anything but.

By October 3rd 1795, when a small Royal Navy force under Captain Leo Bone ventured into the Rade d'Hyeres, several of those northern battles had already been won and lost. News of this filtered very sporadically down to Provence, though, which by now had broken with Paris. Ostensibly this break was a Mirabeauiste project due to the Jacobins' perversion of the Revolutionary sentiment—but if there had ever been any truth to this, in any case the Royalists soon seized power from the Mirabeauistes and Provence became a straightforward counter-revolutionary stronghold. The bulk of the French Mediterranean fleet—which until the mid 18th century had been an entirely separate force from the oceanic[144] navy—was in harbour at Toulon, and this gave whoever held Toulon a major bargaining chip.

The fleet in question was under the command of the Comte

---

[144] Oceanic navy is the equivalent term to 'blue-water navy' in TTL.

d'Estaing, Jean-Baptiste Charles Henri Hector. While d'Estaing had scored a rather filmish[145] if minor victory over the British at the Battle of Bermuda, during the Second Platinean War, he was an indecisive commander. In particular, at the present the Revolution presented a dilemma to him. He had supported the reforms of the Diamant period, but had remained loyal to the Royal Family and was unable to countenance their executions. But, without any orders from above, he could not decide what course to take in this new, ugly era. His best hope was that the Dauphin would return from Spain with new orders.

At the same time, the Jacobins in Paris had heard of the breakaway of Provence and Robespierre flew into a rage, ordering the raising of another new regiment, and its immediate dispatch to "purge" the province and in particular the city of Toulon. This was not the wisest choice considering the rumours coming out of Flanders and Picardy of a general Austrian victory on that front, but nonetheless the orders were obeyed. This reflects the centralisation of power in the Consulate even by this early stage, in which the allegedly free men of the NLA were dragged along. It was also the first use of conscription in the Revolutionary army, the *levée en masse*—the army had previously relied on the existing large Royalist armies (suitably 'purified' of 'traitors'), augmented by the new volunteers of the Legion du Diamant.

Unsurprisingly, the resulting force was less than professional, but as usual with Revolutionary armies in this period, its overwhelming quantity was a quality of its own kind. The army was under the command of the attainted Comte de Custine, Adam Philippe, who had escaped the *chirurgien* or *chambre phlogistique* because Robespierre had taken a liking to him. More importantly, unlike the vast majority of the overpromoted Revolutionary generals at this point, Custine had genuine military experience, having served in the Platinean conflict. It was there, after Noailles' army had surrendered to the Platineans, that Custine had first become familiar with the revolutionary ideals that would soon sweep over his own country.

Thus, in Custine the army had a competent commander, but in

---

[145] A term equivalent to 'cinematic' in TTL.

practice his task was not unakin to herding cats. The vast number of Sans-Culotte volunteers and the new conscripts simply overwhelmed the existing logistical system, with the result that the army turned to "foraging" across the countryside—*la maraude*, as it was later infamously called. Custine's army was scarcely unique in this, and the resulting resentment by the French peasantry only served to justify Robespierre's paranoia that 'there is an enemy of the Revolution behind every door!'

The army reached Toulon on September 17th and Custine called a truce, meeting with the Comte d'Estaing on his flagship *Améthyste*. Custine defended the latest depradations of the Consulate and argued that d'Estaing's oaths were to France, not the royal family, and that France now needed his ships to safeguard the ideals of the Revolution.

If Custine had got there a week earlier, it is quite likely that the dithering Comte d'Estaing would have been persuaded, but by now he had become emotionally invested in the defences of Toulon that he and the few royal officers in the town had been putting together. The town was quite a defensible position from the land, providing that the besieged town could be resupplied by sea. D'Estaing proceeded to do just that, sending Custine back to his army with a degree of icy-cold chivalry as though he were an enemy general which, d'Estaing slowly began to realise, was in fact the case.

D'Estaing ordered that elements of the fleet make a voyage to Corsica and return with powder, shot, food and preferably some of the troops still stationed there. Those ships reappeared on the 1st of October, or some of them did: news of the Revolution was spreading throughout the lower decks, and some crews had successfully risen up in mutiny. D'Estaing was appalled to learn that some of his frigates had apparently taken up 'democratic piracy', while others had simply beached their vessels on Corsica and fled there. This is likely the means by which the news of the Revolution in turn spread to Corsica so rapidly.

While d'Estaing's gamble did little to relieve the Siege of Toulon, it did serve to intrigue a British captain named Leo Bone and his small force of HMS *Diamond* and two smaller frigates.

Since being assigned to the Mediterranean, Bone had already unofficially visited Corsica several times, curious about the land of his birth he barely remembered. He justified these to the Board of the Admiralty as 'exploratory operations'.[146]

While there under an alias, he learned of d'Estaing's ships being present and even witnessed a shootout in Aiacciu[147] between the officers and men of one of those ships, as Revolutionary sentiment grew too strong. Bone had of course heard of the Revolution by this point, but as with practically all Britons his information was sketchy and incomplete. Intrigued, he bought drinks for one of the less wounded Revolutionary crewmen and got a clearer account (at least, at first). He then supplemented this with an account from one of the officers of another ship, over a game of Vingt-et-un in an inn in Bastia.

By the time the remaining ships of d'Estaing returned, Bone had as clear a picture of the Revolution as anyone in Toulon, and this gave him an idea. An audacious, unimaginably brash idea, but one that suited the highly ambitious captain down to the ground. His father Charles Bone had passed on some of his political ideas, and the younger Bone wondered whether, on the back of triumphs at sea, he could enter Parliament and eventually become Prime Minister. The minister who finally presided over the passing of Catholic emancipation...that would be the way to make Charles proud.

So it was on 3rd October that Bone's trio of ships shadowed d'Estaing's back into the Rade d'Hyeres. By this point d'Estaing was despairing and barely acknowledged the foreign, possibly hostile ships. Custine's army had begun to overwhelm the fewer and scarcely more disciplined defenders of Toulon. However, the heart of the city was still held by the Royalists with resupply by d'Estaing's ships. Realising this, Custine found several good sites for his heavy artillery and, using the new Cugnot *fardiers*, towed them into position.

Bone claimed in later accounts to be unflustered by the guns apparently moving by themselves, though his subordinates at

---

[146] An 18th century euphemism for spying.
[147] Known in OTL English as Ajaccio.

the time recorded that he was anything but. In any case, slowly but steadily the guns rose to the summits of the hills and ridges that Custine and his artillery commander had chosen. Briefly they were hidden by clouds of steam, but then the Cugnot steam engines were dampened and the guns rotated. Then Custine spelt out a simple message on the ridge of l'Evescat in white shirts held down by stones, visible to everyone on the French ships who could read: SURRENDER OR DIE.

Not a minute later, the first guns began to fire, tearing through the ships at close range and wreaking horrible casualties. Custine had sited his guns well and d'Estaing's attempt to silence the guns by counterbattery fire failed. Soon there were more mutinies on nearby ships, with revolutionary (or opportunistic) crewmen hastily raising the red flag in a bid to escape. Other ships began to retreat and flee, abandoning Toulon. And, inevitably, d'Estaing was indecisive.

That indecision could have killed him, and perhaps France, but for the audacity of Leo Bone. He himself spoke fair French, his father having told him to 'know the enemy' and, inevitably in the national mix that was the average Royal Navy crew, he had several more fluent speakers. Bone seized the day and brought a boat out to the *Améthyste*, even while Custine's roundshot was splashing huge waterspouts up all around him. D'Estaing was startled out of his funk by the appearance of this rowing boat, flying a flag of truce, calmly appearing amid the destruction. He quickly received the energetic British captain, who told him in schoolboy French that the Dauphin had made a treaty on behalf of 'true France' with the British, and that the loyal French forces here were to retreat to a safe British port and await further orders.

D'Estaing must have realised that Bone's supposed "envoys from the Dauphin" (his French-speaking crewmen in makeshift costume) were anything but, but at this stage he was willing to cling to any straw. Quickly, essentially just repeating what Bone 'advised' him to do, he ordered that the remaining ships were to rescue as many royalist fighters from Toulon as possible and then follow the *Diamond* into retreat. The coincidental name of the British ship resonated throughout the French crews, and soon there was the rumour that the Dauphin had accepted Le Diamant's reforms but continued to oppose the Consulate. This largely prevented any further mutinies. Two more ships were lost while evacuating men from Toulon—not least because women and civilians tried to pile on board—but a significant number of royalist troops, irregulars and ammunition were saved.

As the 3rd of October 1795 drew to a close, the remains of the Toulon Fleet followed HMS *Diamond* to Malta, even as the Revolutionary army of Custine finally fell upon the city as a whole and subjected it to what became a legendarily infamous night of rape and pillage. Custine's own attempts to hold back his disorganised army were ineffectual.

When news of the incident got back to Paris, some deputies wanted Custine's head, but Robespierre defended him once more. A large part of the fleet had been destroyed or captured, after all, and more importantly in Robespierre's estimation, Toulon had certainly been 'purified'.

Current historians put the figures at eight ships destroyed by Custine's artillery, six lost to mutiny between Corsica and Toulon (some of whom became 'democratic pirates'), eleven captured by the Revolutionaries...but twenty-two, including four first-rate ships of the line, were brought out of Toulon and followed Bone to the promised land.

But there was an unpleasant surprise for Leo Bone when they reached Malta. He had planned to keep up his audacious subterfuge and con d'Estaing into turning his ships over to the Royal Navy one at a time, resulting in the most bloodless addition to the fleet by capture in history. But now, he was learning, his lie had become the truth...

Chapter 23: History Repeats Itself

"Can it truly be conceived that this nation would take up arms against this new beacon of liberty, born of the tongue which gave us, via the bequest of de Montfort, our parlement*?"*
"I understand that the honourable gentleman has apparently failed to understand that the present unpleasantness in France has been an undermining of the aforesaid parlements*. We should not seek to compare the acts of barbarism in the south to our own revolution, whereby we received our perfect Constitution by approval of the sitting Parliament. We should not imply any continuity between the lawful Estates of the King of France and this self-appointed ministry of murder."*

– Charles James Fox and Edmund Burke, debate in the British House of Commons on 'Response to the Revolution in France', July 30th 1795

From: "The Jacobin Wars" by E.G. Christie (1926) –

The response of Great Britain and her Hanoverian[148] sister nations to the Jacobin Revolution was always confused and divided, even from the start. The political landscape had by this point settled into a more or less stable pattern compared to the unrest of the mid-eighteenth century. The Parliament elected in 1791 reflected this. Political parties at the time were far more fluxional and notional than nowadays, but broad divisions can be discerned.

Officially, the party labels remained Whig and Tory, though the relevance of those names had ceased with the decisive final

---

[148] In TTL the term 'Hanoverian' has come to mean something like 'Anglosphere', as all the English-speaking countries were ruled by the House of Hanover at this point. (Paradoxically, this excludes the German region of Hanover itself).

defeat of the Jacobites in the aftermath of the War of the British Succession. Only a small rump of declared Tories remained in Parliament, largely from Scottish constituencies. The vast majority of MPs claimed to be Whigs of some stripe or another, but it is a mistake to assume any kind of unity from this. Labels overlapped, but a continuity can be traced from the ministry of Pitt (1758-1766) and the first Rockingham ministry (1766-1782) through to the government party of 1795, who were most commonly termed Liberal Whigs (or simply Liberals). Although competent and reasonably popular, Rockingham had been forced to resign in 1782 due to the Africa Bubble scandal.[149] His government had, however, survived almost intact and the inoffensive Duke of Portland was appointed titular Prime Minister while Edmund Burke, Secretary of State for Foreign Affairs, became the real power behind the throne.[150]

The largest opposition party was that of Charles James Fox, usually referred to as the Radical Whigs or simply Radicals (although there were also unaffiliated, more extreme groups describing themselves as Radicals, who had little to no Parliamentary representation). The Radicals advocated the abolition of the slave trade, Catholic relief and Parliamentary reform; the third course was by far the most popular among

---

[149] In OTL the Royal Africa Company (aka the African Company and the Royal African Company) was a chartered company that traded with West Africa, mainly in slaves, and repeatedly went bankrupt and had to be reformed. In TTL rather than several minor crashes and reforms, the Company's stock inflated alarmingly in 1781 on rumours of a profitable reform and the resulting losses were comparable to the South Sea Bubble of sixty years before. The Marquess of Rockingham, as Prime Minister, was the effective scapegoat for the recriminations following this and was forced to resign. The Company itself was rebuilt from the groundwork up and turned over to two former BEIC directors, Arthur Filling and Thomas Space, of which more q.v.

[150] This is William Cavendish-Bentinck, 3rd Duke of Portland. At this point the title Prime Minister is still unofficial and largely mocking. Portland's official title was First Lord of the Treasury. Typically in this era those Prime Ministers with real power also held the post of Chancellor of the Exchequer, effectively making them Lord High Treasurer; the fact that Portland does not is a sign that he is only the titular head of the government and Burke has the real power.

other groups in Parliament and the general public. Prior to the Jacobin Revolution, the Radicals had pointed to the new system of parliamentary governance in the Empire of North America as a model for reform in Great Britain, as well as expressing admiration for the republican Cortes Nacionales of the UPSA. However, Fox's support for the Jacobins typically broke any link in the British public imagination between the Radicals and the Americans, who were later more identified with the Liberal Whigs of the government.

As well as these broad divisions, there was also the inevitable lasting trace of a distinction between the Court and Country parties, the latter being MPs from rural constituencies and Lords from rural estate who would typically vote against any given ministry unless placated, usually by bribery. MPs elected from rotten boroughs were common, even among the Radicals who advocated the abolition of such boroughs. This perceived hypocrisy did nothing to help their cause.

The Revolutionary sentiment in France initially drew broad approval from the Parliament of Great Britain (in that of Ireland, as we shall see later, the situation was somewhat more complex). As news of Revolutionary atrocities filtered down, however, Parliamentary support fell away until only the core of Foxite Radical Whigs was left, continuing to argue that any unfortunate incidents in Republican France were excusable compared to the centuries of royalist repression that had precipitated them.

The Liberal Whig government, however, turned against the Revolution. Edmund Burke drew a sharp distrinction between the Whiggish conception of the gradual progressive growth of liberty across history and the Jacobins' abrupt, violent revolutions. He also rejected comparisons of republican France with republican South America, arguing that while both were born of war, the UPSA had never turned on its own people with such viciousness, not even those who had been Spanish loyalists.

Nonetheless, even the government was divided on the question of what the response of the Department for Foreign Affairs should be. The situation was not without precedent: when England had briefly become a republic in the previous century, several European powers had continued to recognise the Kingdom of England, even when it was reduced to merely the Isles of Scilly. The more reactionary Whigs and most Tories argued that Britain should recognise the Dauphin as King Louis XVII and that any French government formed without his approval should be considered illegal and to have no authority. Burke was leaning towards this view and it was likely that an Act to that effect would have been passed even in the absence of provocation from Republican France. In practice, however, the decision was made for him.

The Revolution had been accompanied by a general campaign of anti-foreigner violence on the part of the mob. This has been common to most proletarian revolutions throughout history (for example, the Peasants' Revolt in England in 1381 was accompanied by attacks on Flemish weavers in London) but the Jacobin Revolution was the first to explicitly place such violence within a coherent ideological framework. This was prior to the publishing of de Lisieux's seminal work *Les Races*, however, and thus cannot be understood through the usual prism which modern commentators associate with the Linnaean-Racialism of Revolutionary France. This is however beside the point. As well as attacks on foreign-born soldiers and merchants, an admixture of the anti-establishment tone of the Revolution meant that foreign dignitaries were not spared. Most ambassadors to France managed to escape the tides of violence, having seen what was coming, but the rose-tinted vision of the Revolution early on in the British Parliament had evidently spread to its representatives in Paris, and it was not until the phlogistication of Louis XVI that the British and American ambassadors attempted to leave.

(It should be noted at this juncture the remarkable nature of the presence of an American ambassador. This was a notion that had only arisen a few years previously, in 1790, as one of the earliest acts of the Parliament of North America. It had been a point of argument by the autonomist and relatively radical Constitutionalist Party there that America should have equal representation overseas. In practice, both the American and British parliaments watered down the proposals sufficiently that only those nations with colonies bordering North America were given American representatives – primarily France and Spain – and that these were officially referred to merely as consuls, although in practice they were commonly termed ambassadors. The American 'ambassador' in Paris at the time was Thomas Jefferson, a prominent member of the Constitutionalist Party whose appointment there had largely been a way that Lord Hamilton's moderate ministry could keep this brilliant orator safely a long way away.[151] At the time there was debate, as part of the Irish parliamentary reform argument, that the Kingdom of Ireland should also appoint its own ambassadors, and it is interesting to speculate how different the Parliament of Ireland's response might have been if a hypothetical ambassador had been present alongside Frederick Grenville and Thomas Jefferson).

It remains a sore point of debate even today whether the attack on Grenville and Jefferson was officially directed by any order from the NLA or whether it was a simple act of mob violence. In any case, even if the records had survived the de Lisieux era, it is not a distinction that is readily made. By this stage, and particularly later on, fear of the Consulate was such that any confident con man in France could gain anything he wanted by claiming authority from Robespierre. The new and frequently contradictory pronouncements coming out of the Tuileries daily only served to reinforce such an idea. In the end it is perhaps enough that the NLA did not denounce the attacks on the ambassadors, or even acknowledge them.

Grenville escaped with a severe bullet wound to his right arm, forcing its amputation while he lay in a fever, hiding out in Calais. However, he survived to give a moving if chilling testimony of events to the British Parliament in September. Jefferson was not so lucky: his own personal sympathies to the Revolutionary sentiment meant nothing to the mob, and his body was never found. When Thomas Paine attacked this monstrous act in the

---

[151] Alexander Hamilton was made First Baron Hamilton by George III in 1785 during his tenure as Governor of the then-Province of New York, and by 1795 had become Lord President of the Imperial American Privy Council, the approximate equivalent post of Prime Minister in the Empire.

NLA, he was removed by the Consulate, imprisoned and then given the chirurgien's deadly kiss early in the following year. The Reign of Terror had begun in earnest: no-one was safe.

These atrocities, accompanied by reports of several more minor attacks on British and American sailors in French ports fallen to the Revolutionaries, served to turn most of Parliamentary and public opinion in Great Britain against the Revolution. By mid-August the reactionary option had won out, and Parliament officially recognised King Louis XVII and declared the Consulate and NLA illegal. On September 2nd, 1795, the British Parliament voted 385 to 164 in favour of a declaration of war on the Republic of the French People of the Latin Race—only just beating the NLA's own pre-emptive declaration of war on Britain. By the time the news reached America in November, the story had if anything grown to more mythic proportions, and the Parliament of North America voted almost unanimously in favour of the war.

It would not be for many more months that the news reached other potential theatres of conflict, some of which would become highly important: India, the West Indies and La Pérouse's Land. But for the Consulate and the people of Republican France, Britain remained nothing more than a distant noise. Though Spanish troops moved into Navarre, it was Austria that was the greatest threat to the Republic, and even now the ramshackle Revolutionary armies were moving to face the forces of Emperor Ferdinand IV...

Chapter 24: A Revolutionary War

Wars are always good for science, and science is always good for wars.

- John Farman (OTL)

From – "A Societist Study of Revolutions, Volume III" by JuAn Lopez of the Instituto Sanchez (originally published in Novalatina 1959— unauthorised English translation 1968):

Thinkers throughout the world, both Societist and nationalistically blinded, have debated the import of the Revolution in France almost since the day Le Diamant was killed. One particular topic of interest is the spread of the revolution, and what consequences the character of the revolution had on that spread.

It is unsurprising that it was the immediate neighbours of what was then only vaguely considered "France" who were first to experience Revolutionary ideals. The notions of the revolution spread by a variety of means, and depending on whether the speaker was a true believer or a person fleeing the perceived oppression of the revolution, would necessarily determine the character of the revolution envisaged by those who listened.

Furthermore, it is impossible to ignore, however much we might want to, the effects of the vile poison of Linnaean Racialism within the Revolution, here taking the form of Panlatinism. This variant, unlike many others, is now universally condemned even within the nationalistically blinded geographic regions. The Panlatinist character of the Revolution – or perhaps simply Latinist is a more accurate term in its early days, before the revolutionaries' twisted notion of unionism took hold – further determined which states would be primarily exposed to revolutionary ideas.

Notably the Italies, Spain and Portugal were strongly evangelised to in the early days of the Revolution. The latter two regions of considered statehood easily cracked down on the scattered outbreaks of revolution within their own borders, aided by the fact that the strongly anti-Catholic character of the revolution turned large portions of their own devout populations against it. The Italies arguably had the same advantage but their own regions of considered statehood were too small and ineffective to present such a strong response. Thus, we may see the vindication of two Societist teachings: that the larger and more unified the state, the stronger it is – to infinity; and that an avowedly atheist universal movement will indeed successfully unite the world, but only against itself.

These teachings are arguably further supported by the eventual fates of the small republics in the Italies, notably the Latin Republic of Liguria (formerly Genoa) and the Latin Republic of Lucca (formerly Tuscany, after forcing Grand Duke Charles to flee into exile). However, that is not a matter for this early history.

At this point we should consider the views of the Noveltist school of Reactivist thought among the Tory interpretation of history, no matter how repugnant we may find them for other reasons. The Noveltists argue from the results of the 'revolutionary halo', as they term it, that ultimately what many of the people of France and other revolutionary areas wanted was a sense of newness, toppling the old order, rather than any specific change.

The Noveltist writer Sir George Smith-Stanley pointed out that this may explain some of the otherwise inexplicable and nihilistic aspects of the revolution, changing not only those aspects of society which were objectively in need of reform (such as royal France using at least six different systems of measurement), but also petty and unimportant items simply for the sake of change. Smith-Stanley argues that the fossilised Italies, like France itself, were ripe for the spirit of this revolution. Flanders, by contrast, had had a major change in its constitution and rule only recently and that this, together with the fact that Charles Theodore I was reasonably popular,[152] explains why the revolution never got very

---

[152] Recall that the Hapsburgs managed, in TTL, to switch Bavaria for Flanders and Charles Theodore rules Flanders and the Palatinate. He is considerably more popular there than in Bavaria OTL, which he never

far in Flanders. The Prince-Bishopric of Liége, however, saw what turned out to be a strategically important outbreak of revolution after the initial indecisive battles of late 1795, when revolutionary ideas had had a chance to leak in from France. The fact that Liége was francophone must also be considered.

Of course, we need not consider the alarming conclusions that Noveltist writers draw from their arguments, and the lavishing praise they and their Whig counterparts place upon the British parliamentary system as supposedly the most resistant to revolution—despite all the evidence of the history books in front of them.

Ultimately, however, the spread of the revolution cannot be fully understood, alas, without considering the vulgar results of the concomitant military action…

From: "Revolutionary Ideas in Warfare" by Peter William Courtenay, 4th Baron Congleton (Vandalia Province, Virginia), 1925—

While it should be obvious to any gentleman, I am forced to issue the disclaimer that an admiration for any Jacobin idea in warfare does, clearly, not constitute an endorsement or admiration for Jacobin ideas in general.

…

The Flemish War (1795-7) was indecisive in its early stages, but is notable for the use of several revolutionary tactics and weapons by the then-ramshackle French Republican Army. It can be argued that it was these novelties that allowed the French to hold off the more disciplined Austrians for long enough to ensure the eventual reorganisation of the army into a more effective fighting force.

The Austrian Army of Flanders was under the command of General Johannes Mozart,[153] who understood that he was fighting

---

really wanted to rule.

[153] "But just try to imagine, my dear sir, that Wolfgang Amadeus was born…into the family of a rough military man, he would have become a mediocre officer with a love of military marches" – *Azazel/The Winter Queen* by Boris Akunin (published in the original Russia 1998, English translation 2003).

an *idea* and that decisive tactical victories, to sap enemy morale, would be more important than attempting to destroy altogether the vast armies he was facing. This also meant it was rather difficult to predict the fighting strength of any given French force, as whether they were veterans or new recruits was often hard to discern until battle was joined. The new recruits, particularly the Legion du Diamant, were notoriously erratic and tended to fight quite acceptably when morale was high but otherwise were prone to desertion when they saw what war was truly like. Mozart's strategy exploited this.

The situation in Lorraine was quite different, in which Austrian troops were often welcomed as liberators by the population. Much like the people of Brittany and Navarre, the Lotharingians – whose former ducal lands had been added to the French crown only a few years before – did not like the sound of the rhetoric coming out of Paris, about one state, one racially and linguistically French state. However, the Lorraine front was relatively unimportant for the war as a whole and was fought almost exclusively with conventional methods. While the defence of the Col de Saverne by Colonel Ney may have been undoubtedly filmish its tactics and weaponry were not revolutionary.

The French generals in the Flanders theatre were a motley crew of former royal officers and those who had risen to the top under the revolutionary reforms. Some of the latter were exceptional soldiers, while the vast majority were anything but. The most famous of the exceptional soldiers was Pierre Boulanger, who requires no introduction. It was Boulanger who was the first to realise the value of the revolutionary weapons already within the army's arsenal, and to halt Mozart's slow and steady advance through northern France.

Most French generals were sceptical of the Cugnot steam tractors (*fardiers*) that their artillery had been equipped with, back at the tail end of the royalist era. Many simply used them as they would horses, while complaining that finding coal was much more difficult than allowing horses to forage. Boulanger quickly saw, however, that when operated by well-trained crews, the *fardiers* could be started and stopped more rapidly than horses could be unlimbered and hitched up again to field pieces. The *fardiers* could also typically tow pieces that would have required a full team of horses, although they needed time to build up a sufficient head of steam. Finally, the *fardiers* were eerily almost silent, save for the occasional whistle of escaping steam. Boulanger used all of these factors to his advantage at the decisive Battle of Lille (actually taking place some distance from the city).

Boulanger, along with other French generals, swiftly saw that the best thing to do with a large number of nervous but willing recruits was to make them attack in column. This exploited the fact that few needed to have good performance with a musket, as only those around the outside could actually fire, and the compact mass of men meant that none could flee in the heat of battle. Furthermore, it lent courage to them. It was not the attack of the column itself, but the psychological power of the vast mass of men heading towards the thin enemy lines, that lent the formation its usefulness. Furthermore, after a column had driven back the enemy a few times, its men had gained sufficiently in courage and morale that they could be trusted to deploy in line.

A column could be smashed easily enough by either enemy artillery or sufficiently well-trained and disciplined troops fighting in line. After a few reverses, Mozart was able to use these tactics to destroy most of a French army at Laon. Those Sans-Culottes who survived the artillery bombardment decided to stage their own little revolution, execute their own general, elect a new one from among themselves, and flee. This story has been repeatedly told and exaggerated over the years, notably after being lampooned in several Gillray caricatures.

Boulanger finally met Mozart's main force at Lille on November 4th, 1795, near the end of the campaigning season. So far, things had gone badly for the French. An attempted attack on the Dutch-manned forts on the Flemish border had been repulsed, and the Austrians had managed to win three of Mozart's desired decisive battles, Laon being the crowning glory. Another part of Mozart's army was besieging nearby Maubeuge, demonstrating that its Vauban-era fortifications were now somewhat outdated, and unless Boulanger won this battle, the town would be forced to surrender.

Understanding the danger of a French relief of Maubeuge, Mozart took the greater part of his army to meet Boulanger's some way east of Maubeuge, along the course of the Sambre and closer to Lille (hence the name of the battle). The Austrian army, which was in fact slightly numerically inferior to the French force, but had a larger percentage of veterans, encamped in a strong position and blocked Boulanger's route, forcing him to make the attack.

Boulanger rapidly concocted a plan based on the fact that the battlefield was typically Low-Countries flat, and the Sambre was forded a short distance behind the Austrian lines. Guns placed on the far bank would be able to keep up a withering enfilading fire on the Austrian lines, and if the ford were defended by a force of veterans, it would be very difficult for the Austrians to attack the guns. The problem was that the ford was of course behind the enemy lines. But Boulanger had a way around that…

Both armies encamped for the night, and as was common had sentries out. Attacks at night were not unknown. But before the sun dipped below the horizon, Boulanger's exploring officers told him that there was a small gap in the Austrian lines. There was no way that a regular artillery team could be sneaked through there, even under cover of darkness – but a *fardier* team, as quiet as the grave…?

The plan was audaciously risky in retrospect, and we can only wonder whether the then notoriously unreliable Cugnot *fardiers à vapeur* let off whistles of escaping steam. We can only conclude that the Austrian sentries had no notion what these sounds were, never having heard them before on a battlefield, and must have considered them to be the call of a strange bird or somesuch. Nonetheless, by dawn the French guns were assembled on the far bank, the veterans were arrayed on the ford, and the main force of Boulanger's army attacked in column. Mozart arrayed his own troops in line to meet them, but then Boulanger played his trump card: unlike most Revolutionary French generals at the time, he had successfully scraped together a cavalry force. While his cavalry was undeniably inferior to the Austrians', it fulfilled its requirement: the Austrian troops, seeing French cavalry about to attack, formed square. The dense formation made them invulnerable to cavalry attack, but sitting ducks for artillery bombardment. Which now commenced.

The battle lasted perhaps three hours, with Mozart soon realising the source of the round shot murdering his men, and making two unsuccessful attempts to break the French veterans on the ford before giving up. The Austrian troops milled desperately between a line formation to escape the artillery and a square to defend against the French cavalry, with the result that all discipline was lost. Rather than see his army slaughtered, Mozart ordered a withdrawal, with his own cavalry covering the retreat and preventing the French cavalry from attacking. He lost perhaps a fifth of his troops, but knew that the real loss was far worse. The French could relieve Maubeuge, and more importantly they had a legend: a legend of victory.

And Joseph Cugnot himself, who had found himself locked up by the Revolutionaries along with most other scientists and engineers known to have worked for the *ancien régime*, was suddenly released and ordered to work with a much larger budget...

Chapter 25: The Baltic Crisis

*"Our victory is ultimately assured: though the nationalistically
blinded powers may form temporary alliances and coalitions against
us, history teaches us that all we have to do is survive, and they will
eventually turn on and destroy each other for us."*

– EnRiq Salvador Lopez, speech to the Global Assembly, 1957

From: "A History of Scandinavia" by Adolf Ohlmarks (1984)—

The revival of Danish power in the late 18th century is a topic
much debated among historians, both of the Baltic and elsewhere;
but some elementary conclusions may be drawn here.

Certainly, one turning point is most beloved of those speculative
romantics (most often hailing from across the Øresund) who
yearn for a different path for Denmark in the eighteenth
century. This is of course the death of Crown Prince Frederik,
who would have succeeded King Christian VI as Frederik V, in
a riding accident in 1743. Frederik was widely considered to be
his father in miniature and his death resulted in the quickening
of Christian VI's own demise in 1745. This plunged Denmark
into something of a governmental crisis in the middle of the
Second War of Supremacy, but this was not a great problem, as
policy under Christian VI's capable chief minister Adam Moltke
was to carefully steer Denmark out of European wars. Although
Sweden, Prussia and Russia were by that point engaged in war in
Poland, Denmark remained in a state of careful armed neutrality.

Christian's second son, of the same name, could not have
been more different. Rejecting his father's unpopular pietism
and conservatism, Christian VII would go down in history
as a dynamic and effective, if impulsive, ruler. He shocked the
Christiansborg Palace court by summarily dismissing Moltke

and several more of his father's experienced ministers, bringing in his own untested favourites. There was method in his madness, however: he wished to bring about a radical shift in Danish foreign policy, and significant changes in domestic policy – and quite correctly suspected that Moltke would block him at every turn.

As a populist measure, Christian reversed his father's introduction of adscription—a new form of serfdom by any other name. He then reconvened the Danish Diet, which had lain dormant for over a century since absolutism had come into fashion. Most biographers believe that Christian himself was, in fact, a reflexive believer in absolutism and he did not bring back the Diet for altruistic purposes but rather as a pragmatic divide-and-rule strategy. The Diet's powers were severely limited and it was intended mainly as a foil for the powerful Danish aristocracy, which had to be curbed at every step for the King to remain an effective ruler. The fate of Poland-Lithuania was a damning example of what happened when this failed.

Christian VII's other great early move was one which surprised commentators throughout Europe. Since the War of the British Succession and Great Britain's Prince Frederick successfully retaking his throne from an American base, a new interest in the Americas had been sparked throughout many European courts. This encouraged the existing colonial powers to take more interest in their colonies – ultimately fatally so in Spain's case – and those without colonies to consider founding some, for prestige if no other reason. In practice, most of these schemes came to nothing, as the economically useful parts of the eastern seaboard of the Americas was by now almost completely settled by the Spanish, British and French. Nonetheless, eyebrows were raised when Christian VII decided to balk the trend by selling Denmark's own colonial possessions.

Denmark and her trading companies retained their profitable trading outposts in India, but the slave depots on the Gold Coast of Africa, along with the Virgin Islands in the West Indies with their plantations, were sold on to the United Netherlands for a considerable sum. Christian and his ministers also previously considered Courland, which was interested in regaining West Indian possessions after the loss of Tobago, but the somewhat impoverished Duchy was unable to match the Dutch bid. Abolitionists then and now praised Christian for this move, even though it was born purely of pragmatic calculation and it is doubtful whether Christian gave two figs for the fate of the slaves in question—who after all probably cared little whether they were suffering on a Dutch slave ship or a Danish one.

Denmark's North Atlantic possessions – Greenland, Iceland, and the Faeroes – were sold to Great Britain. Iceland had declined over the past few centuries since its mother country Norway had gone to the Danish crown, for the Icelandic exports of fish and wool were far less valuable to Denmark than they had been to Norway. Danish policy on protectionist trade and absolutism, removing the Icelanders' cherished right to elect their own assembly, had also contributed to this decline. Britain, under King Frederick I and Prime Minister William Pulteney, annexed the Faeroes to the kingdom (being retroactively considered part of the Scottish islands) while the status of Iceland and Greenland remained constitutionally unclear for some years.

Despite its small population, Iceland was eventually granted the status of a full kingdom, like Ireland and Hanover (the latter's royal dignity not being recognised by any other European state thus far). Iceland's ancient parliament or 'Thing' was also restored. The Icelandic economy somewhat recovered thanks to the free-trade policies of the British Patriot and Liberal Whig governments, with Icelandic fish particularly being in demand in Ireland, though Iceland had problems with the North American market thanks to New England's vast fleet of fishing boats. Greenland was the odd one out: under Christian VI it had been re-explored for the first time in an attempt to find the original lost settlements and convert the natives to Lutheranism. With the decline of Christian VI's Pietism, this fell in priority and few in Denmark resisted the sale of Greenland to Britain. The British eventually transferred it to the Confederation of New England, which established a few settlements. It was a Nantucketer explorer, George Folger, who gave the natives their modern name of 'Enwickers'.[154]

These moves on Christian VII's part were part of a grander strategy to refocus Danish power in Europe and, more specifically, the Baltic. A Russo-Danish alliance against Sweden was his major goal, but this was not realised in Christian's lifetime. The major problem with the plan was that Peter III of Russia was also one of the dukes of Holstein-Gottorp, a traditional Danish enemy and Swedish ally. However, it was apparent to many eyes that the current Prusso-Russian policy of buying Swedish neutrality with land was purely a stopgap measure and would have to be reversed eventually. Christian prepared Denmark to take advantage of that eventuality, building up and modernising a Baltic fleet of both galleys and line ships, while retaining his father's policy of scrupulous neutrality with mainland European wars.

Christian was also Duke of Oldenburg, though much like his father's the German state was low down on his list of priorities. Nonetheless, the greater focus on Denmark as a European power naturally meant that Oldenburg made a slightly larger intrusion on royal policy, which would be significant later on.

Christian VII died at the age of sixty-three in 1787, leaving behind a heavily armed state in which challengers to royal authority had been carefully twisted back onto themselves, with the Diet and the aristocracy squabbling among themselves. He had also restored some of the faith of the Danish peasantry in the monarchy, which had slipped under Christian VI's adscription and Pietism. He was succeeded by his son, Johannes II, breaking the chain of alternating Frederiks and Christians, and named for the last Danish monarch to rule the Union of Kalmar...

---

[154] The singular of Inuit is Inuk, which an Englishman or Nantucketer might spell Enwick, which sounds more like the name of a place, and so the mistaken belief arose that Enwick was a chief native town in Greenland and its inhabitants were called Enwickers – which was then generalised as the names of all Greenland natives.

"My people, before the new century is upon us, I shall make my namesake no more than a forgotten oriental soldier, we shall eclipse all his triumphs!"

– Aleksandr Grigorovich Potemkin, speech in Moscow's Red Square, February 15th 1796[155]

From: "War on the Steppes" by Henry Abikoff (published by Royal Bostonian House, 1948)–

The Russian Civil War was arguably preordained by Emperor Peter III's decision in 1772 simply to exile his Empress Consort Catherine for masterminding an attempt on his life, rather than executing her. In retrospect this may have seemed a poor idea, but in practice it was unlikely that Peter would have been able to get away with such a deed. At this stage, Catherine was still very popular with elements of the Russian public and it was all Peter dared to execute Grigory Orlov and those Leib Guards implicated in the conspiracy. Later, Catherine's exile in Yekaterinburg meant that the fickle Muscovites and Petersburgers may have forgotten her, but Peter still did not act. It fit with his decision to release the deposed Emperor Ivan VI from prison, considering that this poor man who had been locked up and isolated since childhood was no threat. In that case, he turned out to be right, but in Catherine's was anything but.

Peter was fortunate enough to outlive Catherine, who died in 1792, but she had put her twenty years of exile to good use. Catherine brought with her numerous favourites, and other Russian potentates found excuses to travel through the region. Ironically, Peter's own interest in the colonisation of Siberia, and the Yakutsk-bound missions of Lebedev and Benyovsky, helped disguise the suspiciously increased traffic going eastward from European Russia. Catherine, who remained a powerful presence,

---

[155] Note that the name Red Square has nothing to do with Communism and is far older, predating the POD of this timeline—it allegedly comes from the fact that part of the area in question was once used for public executions.

took many lovers from among the Russian nobility and plotted a new way to unseat Peter. Several more assassination attempts failed, Peter having replaced the Leib Guards with new forces largely recruited from Prussia, but none were ever traced back to Catherine.

Catherine's longest dalliance was with Grigory Aleksandrovich Potemkin, a Leib Guard who had escaped Peter's purge and had been in on her coup attempt from the start. Potemkin, descended from a family of Muscovite diplomats, followed Catherine into exile and soon became the effective prime minister of Catherine's Uralic domain. Potemkin played a double game, working his way back into St Petersburg under an assumed name and securing the responsibility for one of Peter's colonisation projects. He proceeded to ensure that numerous settlers bound for Siberia were redirected to the environs of Yekaterinburg. Towards the end of Peter III's life, it was questionable whether he truly ruled any of the Russian domains east of the Urals, such was Potemkin's skill.

Potemkin himself died in 1791. He was far from Catherine's only lover, as she had used her incomparable charms to secure the general Sergei Vasilievich Saltykov and many others also, but he was the only man to father children by her (a category including, some tongues wagged, Peter himself). Potemkin's two sons by Catherine were Aleksandr, born 1773, and Ivan, born 1775. The point that she gave birth in her forties was questioned by some who argued that the boys were not genuinely her sons; historians will doubtless debate this point *ad infinitum*. Though still in their teens throughout the 1780s and 90s, the boys proved to have inherited much of their parents' ability – Aleksandr, Catherine's ruthless ambition, and Ivan, Potemkin's talent for organisation. After their parents' deaths, Aleksandr effectively inherited Catherine's position of authority over many older men: Uralic Russia had truly become its own shadowy state within a state.

Many people have pondered whether Peter III's slow death from illness and old age in 1795 was, in fact, the result of a poison plot finally going right for Catherine's forces. In truth this is probably unlikely – the Potemkin brothers were only twenty-two and twenty years old respectively, and it is likely they would have wanted to wait longer and build up more support, Aleksandr wanting to appear a more realistic contender for the crown. However, events forced their hands. Their father had set up an elaborate spy network, with the result that they learned of Peter's death only days after Peter's heir Paul, who was at this point Grand Duke of Lithuania.

The Lithuanian people and *szlachta*, on the most part fairly content with the status quo, were alarmed by this development and hushed discussions took place across the Grand Duchy. There was the possibility that Paul would continue as Grand Duke as he took the throne of Russia, neglecting Lithuania as so many other rulers with other domains had, or even create a Russo-Lithuanian union. While the *szlachta* believed this might be tolerable under Paul and his son Peter the younger (Petras), who had grown up in Lithuania, Peter's own heir would presumably be raised in Russia and it was probable that, a few decades down the line, a Russian Emperor would try to impose Orthodoxy and Russian law on Lithuania. To avoid this eventuality, the Lithuanians entered into secret talks with the Poles, who were plotting a revolt of their own as soon as Frederick William II of Prussia died. There was talk of restoring the Polish-Lithuanian Commonwealth, but there was always the nagging question "Then what?" A shaky, hastily restored Commonwealth could not resist counter-invasions by Prussia and Russia. The Poles argued for an alliance with Austria, but the Lithuanians were dubious about the prospect, and besides, Austria had had no compunctions about annexing Kraków after the War of the Polish Partition.

In the end, the talks broke down when Paul announced that he was stepping down as Grand Duke Povilas I, in favour of his eighteen-year-old son Peter as Grand Duke Petras I. This was met with much relief throughout Lithuania, as Petras had grown up there, spoke fluent Lithuanian and could be *relied* upon to defend the Grand Duchy's interests against those of Russia. The Lithuanian szlachta quietly withdrew their support from the planning of the Polish rebellion, and historians have cited this as the moment when the idea of the Polish-Lithuanian Commonwealth truly breathed its last.

Paul immediately left for St Petersburg and on January 1st 1796 (Russian calendar) was crowned Pavel I, Emperor of All the Russias and Duke of Holstein-Gottorp. His coronation celebrations, however, were interrupted by shocking reports from the east. The Potemkin brothers had assembled an army under General Saltykov and had marched on Moscow, taking the city and declaring it capital of Russia once more. Aleksandr was crowned Alexander I in St Basil's Cathedral, and made the claim that Paul was illegitimate. In truth Paul's own claim to the throne was somewhat shaky thanks to the meandering of the Romanov dynasty throughout the previous century. Despite Aleksandr and Ivan sharing a (German) mother with Paul, it was the boys who first founded the idea of Slavicism in Russia. They used as propaganda the fact that there was not one drop of Slavic blood in Paul, and portrayed his supporters as a German conspiracy – a thread always guaranteed to resonate with the resentful Russian peasantry.

Of course, Paul was not willing to give up without a fight. He assembled his army, ironically under General Nikolai Saltykov, a distant relative of his opposite number, and marched to meet the Potemkin brothers' forces at Smolensk.

The Russian Civil War had begun…

Chapter 26: Devil's Bargain

From: "A New History of the Low Countries" by Dr Jan van der Proost (1977), English translation (1982)—

The winter of 1795 was a decisive moment in the history of the Jacobin Revolution and what it held for Europe as a whole. Many pro-Austrian commentators have presented the opening stages of the Flemish campaign as a series of victories for Ferdinand IV and reactionary forces, but the truth is far from that rosy image. While the professional Austrian armies had indeed usually defeated the inexperienced and untried French conscripts at most engagements, they had failed to achieve a decisive battle of the type Mozart knew he needed for purposes of morale. General Boulanger's victory at Lille put paid to even a vague Austrian advance, and as the armies retired to winter quarters, the Austrians were left holding only scraps of northern France.

The Holy Roman Empire, more unified and effective an organisation than it had been for years, had nonetheless lost its opportunity to strangle the revolution in its cradle. During that fateful winter, Pierre Boulanger was fêted through the streets of Paris in recognition of his decisive victory – the first major one of any Revolutionary force, and now irretrievably linked with Cugnot's steam technology in the public imagination – and the ideals of the Republic were consolidated. Failed generals were forced to resign, sometimes even executed, more often pensioned off or demoted. The conscript armies were ruthlessly reorganised and trained according to Boulanger's recommendations. The general was a new Revolutionary hero, an icon who joined Le Diamant and L'Épurateur in the pantheon (literally, under Hébert's quasi-atheistic new pagan religion) as a symbol. The difference was, he was still alive and talking – and this presented a problem to the paranoid Robespierre, who saw everything as an attempt to undermine him. Not even an assassination of Boulanger and blaming it on the Austrians was politically possible at this stage.

In truth, Boulanger may actually have caused damage to the French war effort in some areas. He was, after all, of little military experience himself, being one of the Revolution's children, a baker's son risen to high command. He had a talent for warfare which, as many Revolutionary apologists have pointed out, would doubtless have never been allowed to surface under the *ancien régime* – but it was a savant's talent, instinctive rather than learned, difficult or impossible to teach to others. French tactics and infantry training techniques took on an almost artistic air that bought the Revolution some of its intellectual admirers abroad, but may have not been the best use of an inexperienced conscript army.

It is believed by some historians that Jean de Lisieux first met Boulanger on the direct orders of Robespierre. Lisieux was seen by Robespierre as his natural lieutenant, one of the few as 'Incorruptible' as he, one who would send his own brother to the *phlogisticateur* if the purity of the Revolution demanded it. He was one of very few men who Robespierre never saw as a threat to himself, ironically as it turned out.

Lisieux and Boulanger first met with Cugnot himself in the Café Procope, away from the usual sounding boards of the Jacobin Club, and the three discussed their ideas for the use of Cugnot's steam technologies. Lisieux realised how great a propaganda tool they could be if handled correctly, while Boulanger was interested in further military applications. Later they were joined by Robert Surcouf, one of France's more brilliant sailors and a man who specialised in privateering. Surcouf recognised that France's navy would always be a secondary force to its army, second in all considerations of training and funding whether under the *ancien régime* or the new Republic, and could thus never have much hope of defeating Britain's Royal Navy even before the losses of the Marseilles and Quiberon mutinies. Therefore, he advocated the development of new tactics with small ships, and in discussion with the Boulanger-Cugnot-Lisieux triad, realised that the Cugnot steam technology could also be a new and unpredictable force at sea…

Much of the fate of the world was arguably decided in those few, brief meetings. Boulanger was called away to his winter quarters in Saint-Quentin (soon to be renamed the more Revolutionarily proper Diamantville), a move welcomed by Robespierre. It emerged that Revolutionary ideas had been flowing across the border with Flanders even in the winter, brought by travellers, merchants and some French deserters. While the Flemings themselves remained fairly well-off, the Prince-Bishop of Liége played second fiddle to Charles Theodore, and francophone Liége was also more susceptible to French ideas straight from the horse's mouth. Liége had also been a centre of French Enlightenment ideas in the decades preceding the Revolution, and so could be said to be 'primed' to follow France down the red path.

During the coldest and most deprived January days of the winter, Revolutionary sentiment was ignited and the people rose up, overthrowing the Prince-Bishop. A hastily-elected popular council requested entry to the French Republic. This naturally provoked alarm in the Holy Roman Empire, and Mozart promptly reacted by giving siege to Liége. The city held, but was already low on supplies and had been weakened by the damages of its private revolution. Boulanger's deputy in Saint-Quentin, Thibault Leroux, immediately brought part of the French army out of winter quarters and marched to relieve the siege. The army was joined by Boulanger midway, the general abandoning his cosy meetings in Paris cafés.

Jean de Lisieux had not forgotten those discussions, though. It was at this time that he published *La Vapeur est Républicaine* ("Steam is Republican"), a pamphlet which used the Revolutionary ideology to promote Cugnot's steam engines as being fundamentally Revolutionary in character. "The aristocrat…possesses a horse, and thus must possess the land and feed and servants to maintain that horse, and so the people know that he wishes to be known as rich and…superior…however, a Cugnot wagon cares not whether the man at the wheel was born in Versailles or the slums?" Thus, steam was ideologically correct, and steam became The Thing. In addition to Cugnot receiving additional funding, intrigued French and even foreign artisans and inventors begged apprenticeship, and soon many applications for steam engines were developed. Some of this got back, belatedly, to Britain and the Germanies, where steam engines already existed but were still mainly used for stationary applications, such as pumping water out of mines. In Britain, the new applications were masterminded by James Watt and John Wilkinson, while the young Richard Trevithick remained in the mines, but began to wonder if the Cugnot wagon concept could also be applied to a minecart on rails…

But steam technology played little part in Boulanger's relief of the Siege of Liége. In the end, the Austrian army, having outrun its supply lines, was forced to withdraw. Boulanger had scraped together some cavalry while in Paris – riding, of course, those very improper horses – and overcame his earlier problem, harrying Mozart as he retreated. The frustrated Austrian and Imperial forces, who had been hoping for plunder, pillaged the hinterland of the Prince-Bishopric as they withdrew, and continued doing so even after crossing into Flanders proper. Mozart may have been a fine general in many ways but he could not control his men's marauding. It is ironic that at this stage such behaviour actually worked in favour of Revolutionary France.

Flanders began to seethe with resentment at the Imperial presence. Duke Charles Theodore and his chief minister, Emmanuel Grosch, were sensitive to these undercurrents and knew that their position was tenuous. Charles Theodore had only gained Flanders a few years before thanks to the Austrian land exchange, and while he was fairly well liked, the murmured incidents of Austrian pillaging and other destructive incidents served to remind people of his origins – installed by the Holy Roman Emperor. Ferdinand IV's name was openly defamed in the street.

And yet the Flemings were not receptive to the Revolutionary ideals pouring over the border, at least not save a few francophones. Perhaps it was simply the notion that one France is as bad as another, and memories of Marshal Saxe. Perhaps, as the Noveltist Reactivists in Britain argue, that Charles Theodore's very sense of newness saved him from the Revolution, in contrast to the never-ending line of Louises in France. Certainly it seems a far cry of our modern picture of the Route des Larmes and the Malraux Doctrine, but in 1795 André Malraux was but a child of two years.

But Charles Theodore knew he and his fragile young country were being squeezed in a vise. If the French won the spring campaign, all was lost. And if they lost, then Flanders would be forced to supply the vast Austrian army, which might spark public feeling into an attempted coup. The example of Liége was there, though its specific sentiments perhaps not widely shared.

Grosch had visited the battlefield of Liége and knew that Boulanger was honourable, whatever his proletarian origins. He advised Charles Theodore that here was a man they could negotiate with. Boulanger, for his part, was nervous. He was confident that his newly reformed French armies could blunt the spearhead of the Austrian advance, but for once the Austrians had managed to pull most of the powerful states within the Empire into the war. Counter-revolutionism had finally, shakily united Saxony and what was left of Brandenburg with the Austrians, who now also commanded the former Bavarian army. Separately, Badenese and Württemberger forces were marching into Lorraine, despite now-General Ney's best efforts. With the Austrians also allied with the Kingdom of Sardinia whose armies were poised to strike at Provence and the Dauphiné, France was fighting a war on too many fronts. The French were fortunate only in that the abortive Spanish advance had glided to an unenthusiastic halt after the seizing of Navarre. Not unconnectedly, the disconsolate Dauphin would switch his exile to Britain soon afterwards. Boulanger knew what was needed was to reduce the number of contact points with the enemy, to give France to expand its army and concentrate it where it was needed best. So Grosch's proposal came heaven-sent to him, or whatever proper Revolutionaries were supposed to believe in this week.

Indeed, the winter of 1795 also saw the development of many more classically Revolutionary ideas, such as the decimalised calendar and Thouret's departmental system, but the outrageous compromise of the Boulanger-Grosch agreement was perhaps the most significant. Strangely, at first glance at least, Robespierre approved the deal. It might seem contradictory with his own ideas about spreading the Revolution and defiance against the idea of compromise, but he saw it as a way of undermining Boulanger – which, *in the short term*, it did…

The spring 1796 campaign included the deployment of a small number of British troops to Flanders under Prince Frederick George the Prince of Wales (grandson of his namesake), while both Britain and the Empire of North America continued to raise and train new regiments for the coming war. Ironically perhaps, it was the Americans who had a greater number of skilled troops on hand, if not for this kind of warfare. Since 1759, America had fought several wars of expansion with the Indians on its borders: the Iroquois/Howden and the Cherokee had remained allied with the Empire, but the Lenapa, Creek and many others had been driven westward or even wiped out. Notably, the French-backed Huron were decisively smashed by an American army and only two remnant groups survived. One petitioned for entry into their old enemies the Howden Confederacy as a Seventh Nation, and was eventually accepted with reduced rights compared to the older members. The second fled westward, but remained a more coherent group than most, and would eventually play a part in the genesis of Superia. But that is another aside.

In spring 1796, Mozart decided to leave a small besieging force at Liége and press on into France itself, trying once more for his elusive decisive battle. The French remained dispersed, forcing Mozart's armies to match their positioning, but Boulanger implemented a new strategy of pinprick raids by Cugnot artillery supported by cavalry. Mozart brought his army back together in reaction and was faced by a far larger French army under Boulanger at Cambrai. Mozart won a pyrrhic victory, proving that the old-fashioned Austrian deep line tactics could still triumph against the conscript columns and Cugnot artillery. However, the Austrian-Imperial army had lost sufficient numbers and supplies that the cautious Mozart decided to retreat back to Flanders in order to bring up the numbers from newly arrived Bavarian levies. And this was when Grosch's plan came into play.

Duke Charles Theodore, speaking in Brussels' Grand Place to the people in the Revolutionary manner, made a public declaration of independence from the Holy Roman Empire. "The destiny of the Low Countries lies not with the Empire, nor with the Republic, but with our own path." The Duke proclaimed neutrality and barred the entry of armed forces loyal to either the Consulate or the Emperor to Flemish territory. Those forces already there were asked to leave. It was a ridiculous boast in the abstract, for Flanders' own army remained small, but Grosch's trump card was a shock declaration of support for Charles Theodore from the Flemings' traditional enemy—the Stadtholder-General of the United Netherlands, William V of Orange. William knew that, to the Jacobins, oligarchic republics like his own were just as objectionable as absolute monarchies. The fate of Genoa would be a telling example. There was a strong undercurrent of Revolutionary sentiment among the Dutch, who typically did not equate such sentiment with French conquest as the Flemings did, and William was aware his position was tenuous.[156]

Despite rivalries between the two halves of the Low Countries since the conclusion of the Eighty Years' War in 1648, the Dutch already had some agreements with the Flemings, such as using their troops to man the forts on the Franco-Flemish border. It was primarily Dutchmen who fired the warning shots to repel Mozart's army when he attempted to retreat into Flanders. Likewise, the Dutch Navy – second in Europe only to Britain's – offered to transport Prince Frederick's untried little army back to Britain free of charge, and warned that any attempt to prosecute the war further would result in naval clashes. This was shamefacedly accepted by the Duke of Portland's government,

---

[156] The lack of an American Revolutionary War means that there has also been no Fourth Anglo-Dutch War, which has slowed the progress of the Patriot movement in the United Netherlands and means that there was no abortive revolution in 1787—which was crushed by Prussian troops OTL. This therefore changes the character of the internal pro-democratic opposition William faces compared to OTL, but it is all the more persistent for the fact that it has not yet faced a setback in TTL.

and this humiliation was one reason behind that government's fall in July 1796.

The more important reason was that Edmund Burke had died the week before, and without his presence as an éminence grise, Portland had no hope of retaining the House's confidence. Portland resigned, but George III asked the Marquess of Rockingham to form a new Liberal Whig government with court party support. Rockingham was still unpopular over the Africa Bubble scandal, but he was known to have experience as a wartime Prime Minister during the Second Platinean War, and was therefore broadly welcomed. The new Rockinghamite government advocated the prosecution of a naval war and supported rapproachment with the Dauphin's exilic Royalist government. However, it would shed supporters as the war went on with little progress in sight. One of them was Richard Burke, Edmund's son,[157] who rejected the pragmatic Rockinghamite approach ("how can this situation benefit Britain?") and essentially argued that an ideological problem (the French Revolution) required an ideological solution. It is notable that Burke, though considered too young to be a minister at the time, was commonly to be seen in Blanche's, a new London club opened for exiled French royalists to congregate, speaking with the Dauphin himself…

As for Mozart's army, after failing to force the Dutch-manned border forts and being repulsed by French-held Liége, it was led on a long southern retreat down to the border of Trier, where the remnants of the army could finally cross back into the Empire. All along the way the Austrian-Imperial was harried by French Cugnot-artillery, cavalry and even peasant partisans. Though Mozart had won a victory, by the time his tired army glimpsed the towers of Trier's cathedral, it was a shadow of its former self. Meanwhile, the Bavarian army in Flanders had been decisively defeated by the Dutch and turncoat Flemish and had also retreated into the Empire. Bavaria was still unenthusiastic about

---

[157] In OTL Richard Burke failed to live up to his father's talents, though he remained beloved and it was his early death that drove the elder Burke to his grave. In TTL genetic butterflies mean that this version of Richard Burke is more his father's son.

Austrian rule and its troops remained low on morale in such a conflict, in which their homeland was clearly not threatened (yet).

So it was that Grosch's and Charles Theodore's shocking gamble paid off, astonishing the world. By the Treaty of Liége, the Republic of France kept that city but Flanders took the northern hinterland of the former archbishopric, helping to join up Charles Theodore's scattered territories. The Netherlands signed a formal treaty with Flanders on August 4th 1796, the treaty that became the Maastricht Pact. Some minor territorial exchanges were carried out for similar reasons, and the Dutch recognised the Flemish claim to Trier, which Charles Theodore could use to combine Flanders and his Palatinate into a single functioning state. In turn, Flemish forces helped crush an attempted Dutch revolution in Amsterdam and Den Haag around October 1796, with the result that William V kept his position as Stadtholder, and his head. The Dutch Navy continued to be enough warning to prevent Britain from intervening, while the Austrians soon had too much on their plate to pay back the Flemings for their betrayal…just as Boulanger had planned.

This was, therefore, the first step down the path that would one day lead to the Kingdom of Belgium. But for now, few would have guessed how the twists and turns of history would have led to the sequence of events that would one day see the Low Countries united. For now, all that was important was that Boulanger had closed off one of France's vulnerable fronts. He had bought the Republic time, precious time—and that would change the world.

Interlude #5: World News Roundup

Dr Bruno Lombardi: We now come to a stage where it is perhaps worth examining those divergences from our own timeline outside the Western world and those areas immediately affected by it.

Dr Theodoros Pylos: You will understand that many of these changes may not be referenced in source material –

Dr Bruno Lombardi: A historian limited to his own timeline cannot write that a civil war *hasn't* happened, for example.

Dr Theodoros Pylos: Quite so.

Dr Bruno Lombardi: Therefore, though it is not a method which I personally favour, being open to misinterpretation and subjectional colouring –

Captain Christopher Nuttall: Gentlemen, please just get on with it.

Dr Theodoros Pylos: Very well. Let us begin with the Middle East…

Captain Christopher Nuttall: Excellent!

Dr Bruno Lombardi: Pardon?

Captain Christopher Nuttall: Nothing. I didn't say anything.

Summary of Divergences, notes by Dr Bruno Lombardi:

Oman: As in OTL, Persia was driven from Oman in 1744 and Ahmed ibn Sayyid As-Sayyid was elected Imam. However, unlike OTL, the Qais branch of the As-Sayyid family was essentially strangled at birth…it remains unclear as to whether this was due to the deaths of important figures or simply historical 'butterflies' in schemes during the period of Ahmed As-Sayyid's rule… however, what is clear is that the entire nation passed peacefully into the hands of Ahmed's son Sayyid ibn Ahmed As-Sayyid and there was no division as OTL into Muscat and Oman. Two important consequences of this are firstly that united Oman further cultivated its East African trading colonies relative to OTL, and secondly that the port of Gwadar in Baluchistan was not ceded by the Khan of Kalat. This reduced Omani interest and influence in India relative to OTL…

Persia: Unlike OTL, Abol Fath Khan was a worthy successor to his father Karim Khan, and led Zand Persia in a successful crushing of the Qajar rebellion in Mazanderan – with the death of the Qajar leader Agha Mohammed Khan. The Zand dynasty continued to rule over an expanded but largely peaceful domain. The later eighteenth and early nineteenth centuries were largely a golden age for Persia, as the Ottomans remained focused on Europe and Europeans penetrated far more slowly into the neighbouring Indian states relative to OTL. Abol Fath Khan maintained his father's title of *Vakilol Ro'aya*, Advocate of the People, rather than Shah, although that remained in informal use.

As with Mysore (q.v.), Persia was one of the few non-European states to take an interest in the development of the French Revolution, and some Revolutionary ideas were experimented with. Mohammed ar-Ramadi, a merchant and natural philosopher at the royal court in Shiraz, developed a new decimalised system of measurements that managed to incorporate the customary units mentioned in the Koran, but fitted them into a more rational framework.[158]

Under the Zands, Persia retained greater territories in, and influence over the remainder of, Mesopotamia than the Ottomans relative to OTL. Some new European-inspired weapons and tactics were incorporated into the Persian army, though to a lesser

---

[158] Similar to the system used in the OTL People's Republic of China, in which traditional names for units are used but they correspond to new metric lengths.

extent than occurred in some of the states of India (who were witnessing the importance of those tactics themselves). Portugal remained Persia's major European trading partner, and Portugal's unofficial alignment with the United Provinces of South American meant that Meridian ships were soon commonly seen trading in Persian ports also. It was a Meridian navigator, José Rodriguez-Decampo, who made the first scientific survey and sounding of the Shatt al-Arab in 1803, under commission by Governor Sadiq Khan of Arabistan Province.[159]

Japan: Is difficult to judge, as few unbiased records of the relevant period survive for comparison with OTL, for reasons that will become clear…Dr Pylos and I intend to devote a fuller update to this when time permits so that we may do the subject justice.

Corea: The spelling in TTL remains the older OTL one, with C rather than K. Corea under the Joseon dynasty remained isolationist until events in China meant that the status quo was no longer tenable – once more, records of the relevant period are sketchy. There appear to have been no significant changes in rulers or policy relative to OTL throughout much of the eighteenth century. This changed, however, in 1770… (q.v.)

China and Burma: During the reign of the Yongzheng Emperor, his favourite son, Hongli, the Prince Bao (who in OTL became the Qianlong Emperor) seems to have drowned in a river in 1733. This was a dramatic shock to both Yongzheng and Chinese political culture in general, as everyone had expected Hongli to become Emperor and he had been beloved of both Yongzheng and his predecessor, the illustrious Kangxi Emperor. Foul play by siblings was suspected, as Yongzheng had himself risen to his position by defeating his brothers and been frustrated in his ambitions ever since. Yongzheng fell into a long fevered illness as a result, but recovered and, unlike OTL, lived until 1754 rather than 1735. Possibly he realised that he needed to create a clear new line of succession before his death, else China fall back

---

[159] This Sadiq Khan is Abol Fath Khan's son, named for Karim Khan's brother, who does not become Shah in TTL. Note that at this point southern Khuzestan was generally known as Arabistan in Persia.

into a warlord period with no obvious candidate for Emperor.

Although suspicious that he had, in fact, been responsible for Hongli's death, Yongzheng eventually settled on his elder brother Hongshi, favoured by Yongzheng's minister Yinsi the Prince Lian. Hongshi adopted the name Prince Zhong, which evoked the idea that he would be a bridge between a glorious past and a glorious future. When Yongzheng did die, Hongshi/Zhong ascended to the Dragon Throne in a fairly peaceable manner, with only desultory attempts from other candidates. He took the era name Daguo or Great Nation, with overtones of a strong fortress. This reflected his policies as Son of Heaven: due to his father's own lack of success in combating the Dzungars on the steppes, he decided that it was not possible for the Chinese army to beat the nomads on their own turf—inaccurately, as Qianlong managed it OTL—and instead adopted a more conservative, defensive policy. Daguo created what was known poetically as Xin Chengchang, the New Great Wall, on China's eastern frontier with the Dzungars – in practice this was more of a series of fortified towns and military outposts than a 'wall' in the literal sense of the original. While Dzungaria proper was not brought under Chinese rule, the Dzungars were defeated twice during attempted invasions and eventually paid at least token homage to the Daguo Emperor.

During Daguo's reign, the Dzungars seemed a decidedly minor threat compared to expansionist Burma under the Konbaung dynasty, which successfully conquered the Mon kingdom of Pegu and the Siamese kingdom of Ayutthaya. Burmese power and influence was beginning to extend into Chinese areas, which was unacceptable to the Emperor. In the 1760s, Burmese General Myat Htun seized the capital Ava and attempted to establish a renewed Toungoo Dynasty, overthrowing King Naungdawgyi of the Konbaung. However, Naungdawgyi assembled his own army and gave siege. It was at this point that the British East India Company offered to support the royal forces in return for greater trading rights, and Naungdawgyi accepted. (In OTL the Burmese massacred some Britons in 1759 and the EIC, after briefly attempting to secure reparations and an apology and then continue trade, decided it wasn't worth it, as they were no longer competing with the French for Burmese trade anyway. In TTL French power in India was anything but crushed, there was no massacre and the EIC greatly desired the superior trading position with Burma).

Myat Htun fled with his army when he heard of the British deal, having learned of the power that the BEIC could call upon during one of his western campaigns, and sought exile in China. The Daguo Emperor's ministers realised that this could be used as a weapon against expansionist Burma, and sent Myat Htun back with a Qing army to "restore the native dynasty" – this being a little hypocritical considering the Qing's own origins as Manchu invaders of China.

Naungdawgyi had ruled Burma unopposed, with extensive trade with the BEIC, from 1760 to 1768, when the Chinese invaded. By this point, only token BEIC forces remained in Burma, and Naungdawgyi was defeated by the Qing. In OTL Naungdawgyi died young and was succeeded by his brother Hsingbyushin, who successfully defeated several Chinese invasions with some able generals – as Naungdawgyi did not exactly inspire loyalty in OTL, with many more rebellions and breakaway generals than Hsingbyushin, I gather that the Burmese response to the Chinese invasion in TTL was much less coherent and decisive.

The Kingdom crumbled after the Chinese took Ava and Myat Htun installed Mahadammayaza as restored Tougou Dynasty King. The new state, which extended little beyond Ava, was firmly in China's pocket and closed to British trade, as were the "freed" states of Pegu and Ayutthaya. Naungdawgyi's brother Minhkaung Nawrahta, the Viceroy of Tougou (the city, no present connection to the dynasty) established his own state, which continued trade with Britain and requested EIC assistance against further Chinese expansion. In truth, though, Daguo was content to have smashed any semblance of a united, powerful Burmese state, and did not seek further control among the remnants.

More importantly in the long run, Hsinbyushin, another brother of Naungdawgyi, fled south and west with much of what remained of the Burmese army, abandoning Ava. A charismatic leader, Hsinbyushin managed to inspire even this dispirited remnant to overrun and seize the kingdom of Arakan, which had already been weakened by several Burmese attempts in recent years. After defeating the Arakanese army, Hsinbyushin established his seat of power in the Arakanese capital Mraukou and continued to exercise control over the south and west of what had been the Burmese kingdom. During his reign the Arakanese language was suppressed in favour of Burman, and direct contact with the British in Bengal was made. Hsinbyushin's minor empire is generally referred to in later histories as "Burmese-Arakan".

Having secured a position of power in the south and defended against the Dzungars in the east, it appears that the Chinese government remained oblivious of what was happening on its northern frontier until 1799...

Chapter 27: New Worlds

"...there is no better example than America, when one considers the notion that our actions have consequences far removed from the present. Groups have gone into that wilderness and been swallowed like a black star,[160] only to re-emerge as strange tribes or nations centuries later. It is a furnace and a forge, which takes up raw material and spits it out against as strange tools indeed..."

– private journal of President Henry Starling, on the election of Andrew Everett as President of Superia (1994)

From: "Annum Septentrium: A History of North America", by Paul Withers (1978)—

Although the Continental Parliament of the Empire of North America was not truly instated until 1788, it had been widely recognised that this step was inevitable since the (oftsince exaggerated) protests of the 'Troubled Sixties'. The Pitt Ministry in London had begun the constitutional processes to set the new Parliament in motion, despite opposition from the Tories. Indeed, it was Pitt's position which had brought a large number of Radical Whigs into the succeeding First Rockingham Ministry, when (as a study of his second ministry will show) Rockingham was hardly a man to attract men of such political persuasion in the abstract.

The British Radicals approved of the Continental Parliament, both on principle and because it allowed them to 'test' more revolutionary political ideas which would never be accepted at home, at least not yet. In fact some British Radicals took the opportunity in the 1760s to move across the Atlantic and gain residency in American provinces so they might stand

---

[160] An alternative term for 'black hole' from OTL, used as the primary one in TTL.

as MCPs. This did not meet with much success, however. The American people had been used to more minor parliamentary institutions, such as the Virginian House of Burgesses, for many years, and typically had a stronger preference for electing local men than the British, who were willing to tolerate absentee MPs providing they defended local interests. Only three of the hopeful Radical statesmen were elected, all of them in borough constituencies,[161] and the vast majority eventually returned home and re-engaged with British politics. It is interesting to speculate on the consequences if more of them had been elected, as the late eighteenth and early nineteenth century was largely a time of reactionary thought in America and radicalism in Britain – it could easily have been reversed.

It is also, then, not a surprise that the Continental Parliament began business almost immediately, and outstanding issues considered universal by the Confederations were dealt with first. While there was a general disagreement on how much power the federal Continental Parliament should have vis-à-vis the Confederal assemblies (broadly speaking, even at this point the sentiment became less federal and more confederal as one moved south), some areas were considered important enough by all the confederacies to move on regardless of constitutional questions. Arguably, this set the scene for the general federal consensus that persisted for some decades, as this became 'the way things are done, the way that we know works'. It is generally considered

---

[161] The American electoral system is based on the contemporary British one, with some refinements as it has been implemented from scratch rather than slowly developing over time. Each province or 'shire' within the confederations elects one or two MPs, like the counties of Great Britain (two for each English county, one for each Scottish or Welsh county). In addition to this, any city recognised as a Borough by royal charter elects one or two MPs, loosely depending on population (unlike Great Britain, which at this point infamously lacked any connexion between population and representation). So, for example, the Confederation of New England as of 1788 elects 8 MPs: one each for the provinces of Connecticut, Rhode Island, New Hampshire, New Connecticut, South Massachusetts, North Massachusetts and New Scotland, and one more for the city of Boston, which is the only one with Borough status at that time.

that the Constitutionalist Party would have instituted a more Confederal consensus stance if they had had a majority in the first parliament, but by the time they achieved power, moderate Imperial federalism had become the accepted status quo.

Some of the areas in which the Continental Parliament was most active in the early days included: transfer of control of all taxation from Westminster to Fredericksburg save military-related taxes; agreement on the settlement lines for the different Confederations and the territories assigned to the allied Indian nations (only the Howden were actually consulted on this); the issue of American stamps and the establishment of an Imperial Mint so that the American economy would not rely chiefly on Spanish dollars (the first gold 'Imperials', equivalent to Britain's Sovereign, were minted in 1794) and, most significantly perhaps in the long run, the closing of all Confederate lands to transportation.

Britain had been using the American colonies as a dumping ground for convicts for decades, a policy that was (understandably) rather unpopular with the colonists who had settled there by choice. In 1789 the Continental Parliament passed the Anti-Transportation Act, signed into law by Lord Deputy William North, which made transportation to the Empire illegal unless specific permission was granted by Confederal legislatures (a sop to the more Confederal-supremacy sympathies in the Constitutionalist Party). The bill had been passed overwhelmingly, and North advised the King-Emperor in a letter that American public feeling on the issue was too strong to ignore. In this he was supported by Prince Frederick George, the Prince of Wales, who was touring the colonies at the time. George III and Edmund Burke (the real power behind the nominal Prime Minister Lord Portland) took this advice seriously and, despite strong protests from some established interests at Westminster, an accompanying Anti-Transportation (North America) Act was passed—far more narrowly—by the Liberal Whig government. Transportation to Imperial lands became illegal, although it still continued to a lesser extent by privateering transporters who sold out their services to corrupt magistrates, usually in British seaports.

This in turn arguably led to the creation of the American Preventive Cutter Service[162] in 1796 to take action against illegal transportation and smuggling, one of the two geneses of the Imperial Navy (see also: HMS *Enterprize*). The British had no intention of ceasing transportation with all the advantages it seemed to offer as a means of disposing of criminals, so a new location for a penal colony was required. In reality several were used, and it is simply that Susan-Mary was the largest and most infamous.

Initially, it appeared Newfoundland would be the new choice. It was easily accessible from the Atlantic, was isolated and an island, thus making escape difficult, and the British interests who supported its use believed the existing population was too small to matter. However, this proved an incorrect assumption when, in 1803, the Newfoundland colonists petitioned to join the Confederation of New England as a province, disliking the establishment of the Cloudborough penal colony on the island's northwest coast. Although arms were twisted and only the free-settled half of the island was actually accepted as a province, this soon tied up the penal colony in red tape and meant it never became the primary solution to the transportation problem that its instigators had hoped it would be.

Some convicts were sent to West Africa, playing a role in the early projects of Filling and Space, of which more shall be found in the Bibliography. The American West Indies, then jointly controlled through the Imperial government, also accepted a few convicts, often finding it difficult to obtain volunteers for some of the more infamous and fever-prone islands.

However, even compared to such places, the most infamous penal colony was that of Susan-Mary. At first its location may seem rather nonsensical, even paradoxical, and some have theorised that its choice was deliberately forced by idealistic parliamentary

---

[162] In OTL His Majesty's Coast Guard was implemented under the name Preventive Water Guard in 1809, while the U.S. Coast Guard was created under the name Revenue Cutter Service in 1790. The name of this body is a hybrid of the two, particularly as the primary objective here is the prevention of smuggling and illegal transportation rather than enforcing tariff revenue as with the OTL United States version.

Radicals who wanted to discourage the practice of transportation by making it more difficult. In practice, however, it appears that it was primarily a Wolfean colonisation policy.[163] As a result of the Treaty of London (1785) which ended the Second Platinean War, Britain and latterly the Empire had gained control over much of the northern hinterland of the former French Louisiana territory, though France had retained New Orleans and some of the surrounding lands. While the newly-won Louisiana territory was mostly unsettled, the lands around Lake Michigan had possessed a small but significant French presence dating back to the seventeenth century. This was considered dangerous by both London and Fredericksburg; few doubted that yet another war with France was shortly around the corner (although few could have predicted the form it would take) and there was always the possibility that the French colonists centred around Fort Pontchartrain du Détroit might be able to stab the Empire in the back, particularly if they could threaten the Confederation of New York's traffic on the Great Lakes.

An agreement signed in 1794 killed two birds with one stone. The British would create a new penal colony out of the lands around the north of Lake Michigan—ceded by New England to Imperial control in return for taking possession of Canada. The penal colony would represent the enaction of Wolfean policies there to 'dilute out', as it was euphemistically put, the French population. At the same time, New York and New England would create a Great Lakes Patrol which, though far less ambitious in scope than the later, Atlantic coastal American Preventive Cutter

---

[163] A term based on the policies of the first Governor-General of Canada, James Wolfe, who in TTL did not die in the hour of his triumph. Wolfe oversaw the de-francisation of Québec (generally just called Canada in TTL), a policy which met with mixed feelings in British circles, outrage in France of course and approval in the Empire. By the 1790s, Québec City had been renamed Wolfeston, while Montréal had been anglicised to Mount Royal. The remaining French colonial population was outnumbered by immigrants from New England, it having been agreed that the territory would eventually become a series of New Englander provinces. Many *canadiens* emigrated from Canada to Louisiana, the last French possession in continental North America, where they became the source of its 'Canajun' subculture.

Service, would serve to prevent prisoner escape (at least by a water route) and guard against any attempt by the French colonists to build a fleet. In truth these ideas were largely borne of American paranoia, the remaining French being too few and in no position to threaten anyone, but it sold the idea to the American public.

The first survey of the region was conducted in 1796 by HMS *Marlborough*, whose crew included the naturalist Erasmus Darwin (jr.), who published a series of articles on the flora and fauna of the Great Lakes. The *Marlborough*'s Captain Paul Wilkinson recommended the use of the small French city of Sault-Ste-Marie as the centre of the new colony, rather than Fort Pontchartrain as had been initially assumed. Wilkinson argued that Pontchartrain was unsuitable for a variety of reasons and that the fort would have to be demolished or re-manned for safety (today it is the modern city of Lerhoult). By contrast, Sault-Ste-Marie was a major French population centre by Michigan Country standards and most urgently required a 'Wolfean Dilution'.

The First Fleet of convicts left Britain on May 15th, 1801. After a brief stop at Mount Royal, the fleet sailed up the remainder of the St Lawrence and its living cargo was transferred overland from Lake Ontario to an American counterpart fleet on Lake Erie. This, it must be remembered, was a time before any of the later canal bypasses, and Niagara Falls was not merely a wonder of nature but a huge problem in transferring ships between the Atlantic and the Great Lakes' interior. The American fleet arrived at its destination on November 12th of the same year.

The early history of the colony has much been attested to in its harshness, of cruel treatment of both the British convicts and French colonists by the military regime in place there. The colony swiftly became a dumping ground for incompetent and cruel British military officers as much as it was for the convicts themselves: the coming war and the successor to Rockingham's government would ensure there were plenty of those being demobbed. The official name of Marlborough Colony was soon forgotten, and it was a crude convict anglicisation of the French name…*Sault-Ste-Marie* becoming *Soo San Maree* and then *Susan-Mary*. That would be the name the colony would be known

254

by in the eyes of history.

A history on which it would have far more impact than anyone would have dreamed, a history written in letters of blood, one which would begin to play out while the eyes of the world, even the eyes of North America, were turned elsewhere...

Chapter 28: The Trident

La terreur n'est autre chose que la justice du Peuple.
Terror is nothing more than the People's justice.

–Jean-Baptiste Robespierre

From: "France Under the Consulate" by Étienne Jacquard (1925)—

Scholars debate upon defining when Robespierre's Reign of Terror truly began. Some date it from the start of the Consulate, when Robespierre became First Consul and cowed the National Legislative Assembly. However, though the *chirurgien* and the *phlogisticateur* were both in bloody action from that day, it is possible to argue that in the early days of Robespierre's reign, such measures were at least aimed at men and women who had been privileged under the *ancien régime*, sometimes even having committed directly attributable crimes.

As 1795 wore on, though, and all such people were either executed or fled the country, any hope that the killing machines would slow proved a vain one. Robespierre believed first and foremost in the 'purity' of the Revolutionary French state. Though he supported the idea of exporting the revolution eventually, this would have to wait until France herself was free from any reactionary elements. 'Reactionary elements', it rapidly became clear, were essentially defined as those who did not agree with Robespierre.

March 1796 saw the events from which many historians draw the start of the Terror. A group of Parisian counter-revolutionaries, their cell having been discovered, were attacked by Sans-Culotte irregulars led by Georges Hébert himself, who took delight in personally supervising the destruction of churches and other symbols of the *ancien régime* by the mob. Notre Dame herself had been reduced to merely a warehouse for storing power and shot. Thus, when the counter-revolutionaries took refuge in the Église Saint-Sulpice,[164] apparently one of Paris' few major surviving church buildings, Hébert was determined to see their defeat with his own eyes. He ordered them to be burned out. A mistake.

As soon as the first Sans-Culotte had dropped his smoking carcass[165] through the church window, it exploded. Hébert had been wrong –unbeknownst to him, his men had already converted this church just as they had Notre Dame, and the counter-revolutionaries had known it. They sacrificed their own lives to take the others with them, detonating the huge powder store that the Revolutionaries had kept here for dealing with just this sort of incident.

The explosion was sufficiently powerful to devastate a large chunk of the surrounding streets south of the Seine, with hurled fragments of statue and gargoyle landing in a rain of fire as far as the Île de la Cité—a dramatic scene captured by François-André Vincent in *Le feu de ciel* (Fire From Heaven), his last painting and often considered his greatest. Vincent was in hiding at the time, his name having been added to Robespierre's ever-expanding list, and it was only by chance fortune (if that word can be used) that he was a witness to the dramatic scene of burning debris raining down around Notre Dame—perilously, given its current purpose.

The fire spread and destroyed perhaps one-sixth of the city before it was put out. Hébert himself, of course, and all the Sans-Culottes were virtually vaporised. No remains were ever found, and when there is no body and no confirmation of death, any man can claim to be acting in the name of he who has vanished. That was as true under the Consulate, with its power concentrated in three men, as it had been under any decadent kingdom with pretenders to the throne— a point which many Royalist writers

---

[164] During the OTL French Revolution, this church was converted into a 'Temple of the Supreme Being' (traces of the ensuing redecoration remain visible today if one visits it) and the remaining Christian believers in the area secretly decamped for a chapel which is now part of Saint-François Xavier des Missions étrangères.

[165] A term meaning a burning sack of straw etc. used by sappers, not as in a corpse.

made at the time and continue to do so today.

It never took much for Paris to erupt into mob violence, and the church explosion was a particularly potent trigger, being easy to portray as the wrath of God against the Revolution. Counter-revolutionaries fought the new Garde Nationale, commanded by Jean de Lisieux, which absorbed or destroyed all remaining Parisian Sans-Culotte militias in the process. Lisieux was aided by his contacts in the "Boulangerie" or "Steam Circle", as the group of technological and military thinkers working on Cugnot's technology were known. Lisieux, who at that point was known for his grandstanding, used some of the new Cugnot applications to the full. One of Cugnot's latest works was a huge armoured steam-wagon with holes in the sides for musketeers within to shoot out. He called it "*La Tortue*", the Tortoise. Experiments had shown it was too slow and cumbersome to be of much use in the field, but it worked well enough on the wider of Paris' streets. After the Tortues had cleared the mob from the Champs-Élysées, Lisieux stood atop the flat roof of one of the Tortues and waved the Bloody Flag, accompanied by cheers from his followers. This may seem peculiar given the man's later reclusive behaviour, but these were the days when he was making his name.

The counter-revolutionary rising was short and Lisieux's rapid crackdown was effective at suppressing it, but it had two important consequences. One was that Robespierre, having lost his chief lieutenant Hébert, degenerated further into paranoia. Of course, the fact that the counter-revolutionaries had come seemingly from nowhere only fed his belief that 'impurity' was always lurking behind the next corner. The second consequence was that Jean de Lisieux was catapulted into a new position of power, effectively having assimilated the Paris mob into his Garde Nationale. He who controlled the mob ruled Paris, and both Lisieux Robespierre knew it.

Hébert was quickly declared dead by the National Legislative Assembly, although it did not stop some impostors making further comeback attempts – the most celebrated of which was the case of Josué Dechardin, who fooled the people of distant Gascony that he was Hébert sent on a special mission. He extracted money, women and privileges from the terrified Gascon locals for a full year, until the fate of the real Hébert was published and he high-tailed it out of town with the more portable parts of Bordeaux's treasury. This case too is often quoted by Royalist writers.

In the aftermath of the rising, Robespierre unilaterally chose Lisieux as the new Consul, realising that he had no real choice lest he provoke the Paris mob. However, this enraged both the remaining Mirabeauiste faction of the NLA—which still believed that the Revolution should be a force for democracy—and Danton's splinter faction of the majority Jacobins, as Danton had saw himself as next in line to be Consul. Robespierre reacted predictably, hauling off about a third of the NLA to be summarily executed as enemies of the People, including Danton, and then reducing the suffrage to Sans-Culottes only.[166] Lisieux's power grew, eclipsing the resentful third consul Jean Marat, and Robespierre continued to personally sign so many death warrants that he barely had enough time to consider any other state business. This upsurge of the Terror was partly an attempt to undermine Lisieux's support, as Robespierre saw how powerful he was becoming, but this largely failed – not least because it was men loyal to Lisieux who actually ran the *chirurgiens* and *phlogisticateurs*. And while Robespierre was consumed with organising the Terror, Lisieux was quietly taking over much of the day-to-day business of the state...

From: "The Jacobin Wars – the Italo-German Front" by Joshua H. Calhoun (University of New York Press, 1946)—

The early stages of the Franco-Austrian war had been indecisive, with Boulanger stopping the Austrian thrust through Flanders through first battle and then diplomacy. 1796 ended with no real change from 1794, with France holding a few towns in Savoy and Austria a few in Lorraine, but none of the decisive, dramatic shifts that people had expected from one side or the other. That now changed. Both sides had built up their forces and prepared for a war-winning stroke.

---

[166] May sound mad but also happened in OTL, all in the name of liberty.

Ferdinand IV's Austria focused on calling more German states to their side: the loss of Flanders had been a bitter betrayal, particularly considering that it had been Hapsburg machinations which had originally placed Charles Theodore on his throne. Saxony, the most powerful German state after Austria itself, ceased to sit on the fence and finally entered the war when Flemish troops occupied the Archbishopric of Trier in what was called 'Charles Theodore's Road', connecting Flanders with the Palatinate so that both could be held against attack. Trier's Archbishop was a younger son of the Wettin ruling family of Saxony, making the incident a personal one for the fading Elector Frederick Christian II.

The Kingdom of Piedmont-Sardinia on the other hand was already at war with France, but had suffered losses in the 1796 campaigning season as the people of Genoa overthrew their ancient Republic and were occupied by French forces under General Lazare Hoche, handing France a dagger pointed at the heart of Piedmont.

The French, meanwhile, focused on training their existing troops according to Boulanger's ideas and in recruiting more men for the army and the Garde Nationale, whose secondary role was to repulse foreign invasions and organise resistance against occupiers. Ironically, Robespierre's Terror actually helped recruitment, as many young Frenchmen decided that they were less likely to be killed if they went to a foreign field and were shot at by Germans, as opposed to staying at home quietly and waiting for their name to eventually, inevitably come up on Robespierre's list of enemies of the people. Technically conscription was already in force, but at this stage it was difficult to enforce outside the Île-de-France where the Revolutionaries exerted absolute power. As before, their looser control over wider France was essentially a relic of the Bourbons' centralising policies, in which it was customary to do whatever Paris said and thus control appeared to be easily obtained without direct enforcement. The exception to this was western France, but most Revolutionaries did not realise that their power over those regions was only theoretical until later on...

During the winter of 1796, the "Boulangerie" became effectively France's high command in all but name. Far from being disgraced as Robespierre had planned, Boulanger was now drawing up strategic war plans for all France's armies. His eventual plan for the 1797 campaigning season was called *Poséidon*. The code name was chosen to confuse British agents into thinking it was a naval plan, perhaps making them believe that Britain was in danger of being invaded (which, as over half the French fleet had been destroyed or gone over to the exiled Dauphin, was simply not the case). In truth the plan was so-named because of Poseidon's trident: it was a three-bladed stroke.

Although modern writers think of Poséidon as being a great triumph of strategic thinking, in fact it was largely a compromise between conflicting interests. General Ney favoured a head-on blow against the Austrians in Lorraine, arguing that they had no other choice lest the Austrians break through, take Nancy and be in a position to march on Paris. General Hoche argued that they should build on his successes in Piedmont and attack the Austrians through Northern Italy and the Alps. In the end Boulanger, taking advantage of his army's great numbers, decided to do both. The central stroke, at Switzerland, was a hasty late addition once French agents there reported the populace were ready to rise in the name of the Republic. This was, in fact, a gross exaggeration (possibly at Robespierre's orders as he tried to undermine Lisieux's plans) but Switzerland was unable to put up much resistance in the event.

Of course, the plan incorporated some of Cugnot's new inventions, primarily improved steam *fardier*s for artillery: most of the more ambitious ones remained on the drawing board. However, in April 1797 Surcouf demonstrated his first steam-powered ship, an ugly-looking tug that wallowed drunkenly, low in the water. Its great strength was that it could tow larger ships far more effectively than the existing methods of letting down the small rowboats to tow or, on smaller frigates, using the emergency oars. Surcouf successfully towed the frigate *Cap-de-Mort* from Toulon Harbour out into the Mediterranean and back on a calm day when no British ships were able to come near, demonstrating the fact that steam could free a ship from its reliance on the winds and tides. The *Vápeur-Remorqueur* saw a great deal of work in Cugnot's secondary workshops around Toulon, with Surcouf and his engineers improving on the design, trying to make it suitable at first for the Mediterranean and then for the high seas. Surcouf also envisaged a *Vápeur-Galère*, a steam-galley which would have the same advantages as an ordinary war galley (freedom from the wind), but lacking oars would not have its fragility, and would be able to fight on the rough Atlantic seas…like *La Manche* for example.

For the moment, though, steam remained largely a tool of the artillery and occasionally self-propelled carriages for the Revolutionary elite and some generals in the field. They were far from stealthy, though, as the steam plumes were visible from miles away, especially on a cold day.

Another important innovation in the field of battle was the war-balloon, invented by Jean-Pierre Blanchard—his own work a refinement of early experiments by the Montgolfier brothers. France had already led the world in aeronautical experiments under the *ancien régime*, and this was continued under the Revolution – despite their pedigree they undoubtedly evoked the same revolutionary novelty as steam engines. Balloons were thus far subject to the whim of the wind—although after Blanchard joined the 'Boulangerie' and after drinking most of a dead aristocrat's confiscated wine-cellar, the innovators briefly planned to try and mount a steam engine on there. Such ideas were well ahead of their time, and so for now balloons were typically fixed to the ground by ropes, observers being sent up before a battle to survey the land. Between battles the deflated balloons were often transported on yet more Cugnot steam carriages. Some generals, including Boulanger's deputy Thibault Leroux, tried keeping the balloon up there throughout the battle and having the observers signal down with flags, but the limited nature of what signals could be sent meant that this was not as useful as it might have been. Nonetheless, this attempt also illustrates the interest in new communication methods in the Republic, which would come to fruition a few years later.

General Leroux was given command of the thrust into Switzerland, the middle prong of Poséidon, while Ney took command of the left wing into Lorraine and Hoche into Savoy. 1797 was the year of breakthrough for the French. Mozart could have stopped them, perhaps, but he had been disgraced after Boulanger's diplomatic coup and was cooling his heels from Vienna at the time, his command given to the less imaginative Count Joseph Kinsky.

Ney's task was the most difficult, as the Austrians had concentrated their own forces, the Saxons and the Hessians on the Lorraine front. Despite the French still possessing a slight numerical superiority, the Austrians defeated Ney at the Battle of Saint-Dié and went on to occupy Nancy, as Ney had feared. However, France was saved when a messenger brought the word that Saxony had a new Elector who had changed policies, withdrawing from the war with France due to a war breaking out with Brandenburg (q.v.). The Saxon army returned to Saxony, leaving the Austrians outnumbered. The Austrian General, a native Lorrainer named Dagobert Sigmund von Wurmser who had fought for France in his youth, still might have had a reasonable chance at shattering the Republic if he marched on Paris. Yet he was cautious, and remained entrenched at Nancy, penetrating no further and waiting for reinforcements that did not come. The Hapsburgs were too busy fighting on other fronts.

General Leroux, meanwhile, successfully smashed the Swiss militias and occupied the whole Confederation by the end of 1797. A political plan by Robespierre and Lisieux meant that a new Swiss Republic was established under the leadership of an exiled Jean Marat, who had been sidelined by the other two Consuls. He was replaced by newly promoted Marshal Boulanger, revealing firstly how the Constitution was now worth less than the paper it was written on – Boulanger was not even an elected deputy – and secondly how much influence Lisieux now wielded over Robespierre, who hated and feared Boulanger.

Hoche, displaying a brilliance that made him perhaps the finest of France's generals, fought a celebrated campaign through Piedmont, at one point successfully dividing his own force to take on two different – and superior – Austrian armies closing on him at Vercelli from north and south. Hoche's risky gamble blunted the nose of the two armies sufficiently for the northern one under the Hungarian General József Alvinczi to pause at Omegna, expecting Hoche's small thrust to be the vanguard of his full army. Alvinczi prepared to give battle, while Hoche wheeled, recombined all his forces and then smashed the southern Austrian army of Paul Davidovich. Two months later, he finally met Alvinczi east of Milan and won a less dramatic but no less convincing victory. By the end of the 1797 campaign season, Hoche had driven the Hapsburgs from much of Northern Italy. The autumn of 1797 saw a small thrust against Parma, successfully capturing the Spanish possession and striking a blow against a power that, so far, Revolutionary France had been forced to give ground to.

1797 ended with Austria having an army in a precarious but potentially useful position in Nancy that could form the core for a march on Paris. Many speculative romantics have argued that if the Austrians had reinforced that army and attacked Paris, the Revolution would have crumbled, its centralised power base removed in a *coup de main*. Who can say? As it was, Ferdinand IV was too concerned about the French gains in Switzerland and Italy, which put them uncomfortably close to the Hapsburgs' core territories. The Holy Roman Emperor withdrew Wurmser's army from Nancy and prepared to move against French-occupied Switzerland and Piedmont in 1798.

But 1798 was also the year in which any attempt by Ferdinand IV at a united Imperial front crumbled irreparably…for it was the year when the Russian Civil War expanded to encompass all the Baltic states.

Chapter 29: Furore Normannorum

From George Spencer-Churchill the Younger's 'A History of Modern Warfare, Vol. III' (1953)—

What is generally termed 'the Baltic War' of the late 1790s and early 1800s was in fact a convergence of several overlapping conflicts, even as the Baltic War itself overlapped with the wider Jacobin Wars by its effects on the Germanies. Most scholars would state that the core of the Baltic War was the Russian Civil War between Paul Romanov of Lithuania and the brothers Potemkin. It was the entry of other nations into the war that changed the makeup of the conflict from Russian Civil War to the War of the Russian Succession, and that intervention had its own deep roots, going back to the War of the Polish Partition or even earlier.

The international situation agreed by the Treaty of Stockholm (1771) had envisaged peace kept by a Russo-Prussian alliance that would dominate Eastern Europe. Lithuania was dynastically linked to Russia and Poland dismembered, with some parts annexed to Prussia, others to Russia, and the the remainder a rump kingdom placed in personal union with it. Swedish neutrality in the war had been bought by the cession of Courland to the Swedish monarchy and the guarantee of existing Swedish possessions in Northeast Prussia, Finland and Pomerania. However, at the time, most had imagined that a renewed war would come soon enough between the Russo-Prussian alliance and Sweden for control of the Baltic. Many speculative romantics have considered the possibility, but in fact what occurred was far from it. The predicted *casus belli* persistently failed to materialise, as Sweden enjoyed a period of peaceful and prosperous rule under King Charles XIII[167] and the

---

[167] In TTL Adolf Frederick named his eldest surviving son Charles; he

Cap Party. Prussia continued to look northward to the Baltic, but Russia was increasingly distracted by eastward expansion and the occasional skirmish with the Ottomans in Moldavia and the Crimean Khanate. For more than twenty years, the precarious situation set up by the Treaty held, longer than most of its own writers had thought possible.

It was in April 1796 (O.S. Russian calendar) that this status quo began to crumble. Though the eyes of the world were on Revolutionary France as it degenerated into a charnelhouse, not a few of those eyes kept flicking nervous glances back to Russia. Whether the Romanovs or Potemkins triumphed in the civil war would decide many nations' policy towards Russia. Paul was known to favour a Baltic focus and was not particularly aggressive internationally, while the Potemkins advocated the outright annexation of Lithuania as part of their Slavicist propaganda against Paul. As if there could have been any more pressure upon the armies of both Generals Saltykov...

The armies of the two Russias met at Smolensk on April 14th. Paul had beaten the Potemkins to the strategically important city and now held it against their siege. However, the Potemkinite army had been reinforced by fresh troops raised in Moscow, and outnumbered the Romanovians by three to two. The Potemkins gave siege and, by using hot-shot artillery to set parts of the mostly wooden city on fire, forced Paul's army to retreat. While the retreat was in good order, this was a huge blow to the Romanov army's morale, and the news ricocheted around Europe. Statesmen began to plan for a Potemkin victory. This would not be not good news for Lithuania or the Ottoman Empire, but it was known that the Potemkins would probably have less of a focus on the Baltic than Peter and Paul had embraced.

The Swedes knew that here was an opportunity to be seized, lest it slip by. Though Charles XIII was a well-liked and decent ruler, he had failed to produce an heir. Sweden had already gone through one unhappy period not long ago under a foreign (Hessian) king brought in to resolve a similar crisis, and any possible claimants

---

therefore takes the place of OTL's Gustav III in the succession.

after Charles' death enjoyed claims so tenuous that they would almost certainly result in a civil war – a civil war that the Danes and the Russians would doubtless intervene in and so weaken the Swedish state.

Therefore, to buy time to sort out their own dynastic crisis, the Swedish Riksdag moved to intervene in the Russian Civil War before the Russians could return the compliment. The aggressive Hat Party was returned to power for the first time since the 1760s, and the long-prepared Swedish Baltic fleet was assembled, both sailships and Baltic galleys.

Meanwhile, Paul's retreating army was attacked by a secondary Potemkinite force led by General Suvorov[168] on May 14th, near Vitebsk. Suvorov employed aggressive and ground-breaking tactics which divided Paul's force in three and then proceeded to virtually destroy one-third of the army while holding off the rest. It is possible that Suvorov could have broken Paul's army altogether, but for the fact that he was killed at the height of the battle by a stray roundshot and his lieutenants were unable to maintain his intricate battleplan. The majority of Paul's army escaped, and Nikolai Saltykov rallied sufficient forces to rout what remained of Suvorov's smaller force, but the overall effect was once again a triumph for the Potemkinites. The armchair generals in their pubs and coffee houses across Europe were quite certain. As far as most people were concerned – including ordinary Russians – the Potemkins had won. St Petersburg remained in Romanov hands, but for how long?

The remainder of Paul's army retreated to Vilnius, while the Potemkins set about consolidating their power. Alexander secured what remained of Smolensk with Sergei Saltykov and prepared a march on St Petersburg, while his brother Ivan returned to Moscow and began a purge of the existing civil service, reversing many of Peter III's reforms. It was at this point that he was contacted by the Swedish consul, Ingvar Horn, who

---

[168] As there have been fewer Russo-Turkish and –Polish wars than OTL to distinguish himself in, Suvorov is not such a legendary figure as OTL, regarded as merely a competent general now approaching the end of his career.

had a proposal…

To surprise from some quarters, the Potemkinite attack on St Petersburg, in August, failed. A Romanov army led by Mikhail Kamenski defeated Saltykov's force near Novgorod; though it was not a dramatic battlefield victory, the pragmatic Kamenski attacked the Potemkinites' siege train and successfully captured or spiked much of their siege artillery. Deprived of these weapons, there was no prospect of Saltykov forcing the well-defended city. After a brief, half-hearted siege, the Potemkinites retreated. By autumn 1796, the situation still seemed to be going the way of the Potemkinites, with them holding almost all Russia by default – but the repulse from St Petersburg revealed that the Romanovs were still in the game.

The overall impression from observers abroad was now that Russia was tearing itself apart, and showed no sign of stopping anytime soon. Policy in neighbouring countries was adjusted accordingly. The Ottoman Empire, under the rule of the cautious and philosophical Sultan Abdulhamid II[169] did not directly take a position on the war, but took the opportunity of a distracted and fragmented Russia to quietly re-exert more direct control over neighbouring provinces. Bessarabia, which had been unofficially going back and forth between Turkey and Russia for decades, was now brought fully back under the rule of the Sublime Porte via its puppets in the Danubian Principalities. Turkish troops were stationed in the Khanate of the Crimea to 'discourage' the state's current alignment with Russia, and both the Ottomans and Zand Persia were able to expand their influence considerably into the Caucasus, with the Persians extending a protectorate over all Azerbaijan and the Ottomans to the border of Georgia.

Though the Potemkinite-Swedish treaty was secretly signed in November 1796 (after news of the defeat at St Petersburg had reached Moscow) it was not publicly announced until April 1797, when campaigning began in earnest again. The Kingdom of

---

[169] A son of Abdulhamid I. Ottoman succession was based on the eldest male family member as heir, i.e. often passing from brother to brother rather than father to son; however, all Mustafa III's sons predeceased Abdulhamid I so Abdulhamid's own son inherited the sultanate.

Sweden officially recognised Alexander Potemkin as legitimate Emperor of all the Russias, and Alexander, in turn, ceded various territories in Finland and Estonia to the Swedes. Alexander also proclaimed the annexation of Lithuania to the Russian crown and then immediately turned it over to Sweden, a legal fiction effectively allowing Sweden free reign to attack the Romanovs there.

Europe watched to see if Prussia would honour her unofficial alliance with Russia made by Peter III and Frederick William II by declaring war on Sweden. However, it was at about this time that Frederick William II himself died after a long illness, and even as his young son succeeded the throne as Frederick William III, the Poles took this as a signal to revolt. A rebellion led by the professional soldier Kazimierz Pulaski[170] seized control of Warsaw and successfully defeated the first token attempt by Prussia to put down the revolt – which was far more serious than previous outbreaks had been. This encouraged the Poles to rise up in several other cities, with much of the interior of the rump Kingdom of Poland soon under patriotic rebel control. Prussia was far from defeated, but with Frederick William III's hands full, it was clear that there was no way the Prussians would be directly intervening in the Baltic war anytime soon.

Denmark, though, was another matter. Christian VII had spent much of his life rebuilding Danish power in Europe, and now it was time for his son Johannes II to put that power to use. The Swedes could not be allowed to gain supremacy over the Baltic, as they doubtless would if Lithuania and Estonia indeed passed to Swedish rule. Denmark declared war on Sweden and the Potemkins in May 1797, and it was at this point that the Russian Civil War became the Great Baltic War...

---

[170] Who in OTL famously played a significant role in the American Revolutionary War.

Chapter 30: Indian Summer

You say that you are our father and I am your son...
...We will not be like Father and Son, but like Brothers.

– from the Iroquois-American Covenant Chain, signed in 1692
between the Iroquois Grand Council and representatives of the
Province of New York

*From: Annum Septentrium: A History of North America, by Paul
Withers (1978) –*

Long before the founding of the Continental Parliament of North
America, or even the Empire itself, what was generally known
as the Indian Question had been hanging over the heads of its
inhabitants. The Americas were known to have produced great
indigenous civilisations: no map of the New World was complete
without illustrations of the great cities of Tenochtitlan and Cusco.
But the British and German settlers who became Americans were
not there to spread the Catholic faith and hunt for treasure as the
Spanish *conquistadores* had been, those same Spaniards who now
ruled in Tenochtitlan, renamed Ciudad Mejico—even if Cusco
was now, at the sufferance of the UPSA, back in Tahuantinsuya
hands.

No, the Americans had come to the New World to grow
tobacco, to escape religious persecution and, ultimately, to spread
a belt of colonies across the continent to reach the Pacific and the
rich trade that went with it. That goal had become increasingly
harder as it emerged that the North American continent was
much wider than it had at first been thought – when the colonies
had first been laid down in the seventeenth century, most
mapmakers had thought that the Pacific coast was only about a
dozen days' march to the west of the Atlantic coast. One relic of

that belief was the fact that the colonies were entitled to strips of land going westward from their settlements on the east coast, which had intended to be neat rectangles but swiftly became ridiculous narrow stripes going across the larger continent. In the words of one contemporary historian, the colonies – and then the Confederations—had become like medieval villeins ploughing their little strips of private land. The solution was the same as it had been to that situation, too: land reform and common holdings. And, to continue the metaphor further, it would be a far more troublesome and drawn-out process than its naive proponents might have guessed.

The first move of the game began with New England giving up its westward claims to joint Imperial control—incidentally leading to the creation of Susan-Mary—in exchange for Canada being opened up to New Englander settlement. The other Confederations, though, were forced to face the Indian Question. How were they to continue westward settlements when there were Indian tribes in the way, some of them quite advanced and allied to Britain, entirely capable of opposing that settlement with force?

The solutions adopted were different in different Confederations. Generally speaking, Carolina and New York were considered the most enlightened in their dealings with the Indians, probably because said Indians were among the most powerful of all those in North America – the Cherokee Nation and the Six Nations, the Iroquois or Haudenosaunee (Howden) Confederacy, respectively. In both cases, dealings with the Indians were made on a discreet and quite respectful basis. The Confederal parliament of New York (still known as the Provincial Assembly for historical reasons) appointed a Special Commissioner for Indian Affairs, Albert Gallatin,[171] who handled all direct negotiations with the Howden Grand Council. Gallatin was able to negotiate a relatively equitable settlement with the Howden, although he constantly butted heads with the Speaker of New York, Aaron Burr, a confirmed Constitutionalist and political enemy of Lord

---

[171] In OTL Gallatin, a Swiss-American, pursued the study of the Cherokee people after his retirement from politics.

Hamilton.[172] The Constitutionalist Party generally favoured a more hawkish attitude to the Indians, as much of their support came from the 'pro-settler vote', while the ruling Patriots advocated a more measured response.

The 'Gallatin Accord', as it was known among Anglophones (otherwise, the 'Renewal of the Covenant Chain', after the original treaty signed between colonial New York and the Howden in 1692[173]), secured a path for westward expansion for New York, removing a strip of land from the south of the Confederation in exchange for new Iroquois lands granted on the north side of the St Lawrence, in Niagara.[174] This was supported by five of the six nations, the dissenters being the Seneca, who lost the most land, but were voted down at the Grand Council. The new lands were allocated between the Six accordingly, with the settlement being judged by the relatively neutral Gallatin. The Confederation of New York kept the rest of Niagara and was now capable of expanding into the Ohio Country, frustrating the ambitions of Pennsylvanians who wanted to establish ports on the shores of Lake Michigan—at first...

Carolina had a more mixed history of Indian relations than New York's century-old alliance with the Howden. The Carolinians had previously allied with the Yamasee tribe against the Tuscoara, successfully expelling the latter from the Carolinian hinterland in the 1710s—the Tuscoara then migrated north and became the Sixth Nation of the Howden Confederacy. The Cherokee entered the war on the side of Carolina in 1714, at the urging of two Carolinians who had no real backing from the

---

[172] Like the United States' state legislatures of OTL, 'speaker' in ENA Confederal parliamentary procedure signifies a role similar to prime minister or premier, the leader of the largest party in the assembly, rather than the neutral oversight figure of the modern OTL Westminster system. Note that the Governors of the Confederations remain appointed offices and at this point they are growing increasingly ceremonial and less powerful than the assemblies they answer to.

[173] Recall that Prince Frederick stopped George Clinton becoming Governor of New York, the Covenant Chain wasn't broken back in the 1750s like OTL, the Iroquois/Howden Confederacy didn't fragment and all six nations remain firm allies of New York in TTL.

[174] A term used in TTL to mean the area of OTL southern Ontario.

colonial government to conduct negotiations, and helped defeat first the Tuscoara and then the Yuchi. When the Yamasee turned on the Carolinians afterwards, the Cherokee hedged their bets, theoretically remaining part of the pan-Indian alliance against the colonists, but deciding that the Carolinian militia was too strong to be worth challenging. The Cherokee were divided on whether to pursue an active alliance with the Carolinians against their traditional Creek enemies, but any doubts as to the power of Carolina were dismissed when the Carolinians defeated their former Yamasee allies and forced them to relocate to then-Spanish Florida, proceeding to settle their former lands.[175] In a further humiliation, the Yamasee would themselves later face absorption by the Seminoles.[176]

In the 1730s the Cherokee politically unified, with the pro-British Chief of Tellico, Moytoy II, becoming Emperor of the Cherokee Empire, recognising King George II as his Protector. British representation to the Cherokee was provided by Sir Alexander Cuming and then, after the War of the British Succession restored Prince Frederick to the throne, by his political ally Sir Michael McAllister. Carolinian treaties with the Cherokee for land were typically lower-scale than those conducted by New York with the Howden, largely because the Empire was at first a fairly ceremonial government, with many affairs still conducted on the township basis. Over time, though, this began to change.[177] Many Cherokee political leaders visited England, Moytoy's envoys having signed the Treaty of Westminster with the British Government in 1730, and this was far from the last time they would make the trip. The state visits are thought to have impressed upon the Cherokee both the importance of an effective

---

[175] All of this is OTL history (before the POD in 1727).

[176] Which is still a better fate than OTL, where the Yamasee virtually vanished from history altogether and only a few survivors joined the Seminoles and the Hitchiti.

[177] In OTL centralisation stalled, British interest lapsed after Cuming's mission, and the Cherokee fell out with the treaty-breaking governors of the Carolinas by the 1760s. TTL, Frederick's American focus keeps the alliance strong and the Cherokee are more influenced by British and American ideas.

273

central executive, and the fact that a war with the Carolinian settlers might not stay restricted to America, as the colonies could call upon their distant motherland for more hardened soldiers if necessary.

During the Third War of Supremacy, the Creek and Choctaw allied with the French in Louisiana against the Cherokee, their Chickasaw allies and the British/Americans. After the French were driven from all lands east of the Mississippi in 1759, the Creek and Choctaw alone were destroyed in a long and bitter war that lasted well into the 1760s. Eventually the power of those two nations was broken as the Cherokee focused their warriors into cohesive armies, and the Carolinian militia was backed up by both British regulars and new regiments raised in America for the late war. The Tennessee War, as it was known (after the river and the Cherokee town of Tanasi on it) was the greatest shift in the Indian nations since the Tuscoara and Yamasee had been expelled a half-century before. Once again, it had been the combined power of the Carolinians and the Cherokee which had accomplished this.

The shattered remnants of the Creek fled westward and south into Florida, while almost nothing remained of the smaller Choctaw nation. The newly vacated lands were divided between the Cherokee (who had by this point practically absorbed the Chickasaw as a protectorate) and the Carolinian settlers in an equitable treaty signed by McAllister in 1766. As with the Howden, some existing Cherokee land was transferred to Carolinian in return for greater concessions elsewhere, allowing for Carolinian control of the future Province of Franklin[178] and the Gulf of Mexico coast. The Carolinians also claimed Florida, which had been won mainly by their troops during the campaign of 1766 against Spain in the First Platinean War, but the precise status of Florida as an Imperial or Carolinian possession remained up in the air for some years afterwards.

It was this feat of conquest, fighting alongside British soldiers from the homeland and allied Indians alike, which earned Carolina its Confederal motto after 1788: FIDELIS ET VERAX, *Faithful*

---

[178] OTL eastern Tennessee.

and True. When the American colonies were suffused by the 'Summer of Discontent' in the late 1760s and 1770s, when greater representation and less meddling from London were demanded, the Carolinas were the colonies who remained the most peaceful and loyal, with little of the radical mutterings that briefly emerged in New England and New York. This—and the motto—was rather ironic, considering the latter history of Carolina...

The other British colonies, and then the Confederations they became, typically took a less enlightened view of Indian relations. Often 'their' Indian nations were less powerful, and also more prone to breaking treaties and raiding settled land, not least because they tended not to be politically unified and thus a treaty signed by one chief might not be upheld by another. The Pennsylvanian militia, backed up eventually by the Royal Pennsylvania Rifles and the King's Own Philadelphian Dragoons, all but destroyed the Lenape people. At the same time, the Virginians bulldozed the Shawnee through both warfare and persistent settlement, just as they had to the Powhatan years before – the same 'Wolfean dilution' policy that was pursued on an official level by the Empire against French colonists in Canada.

It soon became obvious to all well-informed Indians that the Empire was now powerful and populous enough to defeat any single Indian nation, even ones as great as the Howden and the Cherokee, and that began to inform Indian ideas of, for want of a better word, foreign policy...

Roots have spread out from the Tree of the Great Peace, one to the north, one to the east, one to the south and one to the west. The name of these roots is The Great White Roots and their nature is Peace and Strength. If any man or any nation outside the Five Nations shall obey the laws of the Great Peace and make known their disposition to the Lords of the Confederacy, they may trace the Roots to the Tree, and if their minds are clean and they are obedient and promise to obey the wishes of the Confederate Council, they shall be welcomed to take shelter beneath the Tree of the Long Leaves.

– from the *Gayanashagowa*, the Great Law of Peace which formed the original basis of the Constitution of the Howden Confederacy

The Indians of America were much like the Indians of India in one way: both peoples conducted wars in alliance with France or Britain regardless of whether Britain and France themselves were at war at the time. President-Governor John Pitt of Calcutta once commented 'I have fought more French soldiers while our countries were at peace than I have when we were at war!' Those soldiers were, legally, in the service of the Tippoo of Mysore. In America a similar legal fiction meant they were formally independent warriors allied to the Indian nations that the French supported there, such as the Ojibwa and the Algonquins.

So it was that, while the Tennessee War overlapped with the wider First Platinean War in the 1760s, the Ohio War overlapped with both the Second Platinean War in the 1780s and then the Jacobin Wars in the 1790s. The Ohio War was fought between an alliance of the Howden Confederacy on one side, backed up by New York and Pennsylvania, and the tribes who had formerly received French support – and still occupied the Ohio Country and the lands around the Great Lakes – on the other. The war was instrumental in establishing American control of the Great Lakes, allowing the formation of the Susan-Mary penal colony a few years later. The Ottawa tribe north of the St Lawrence survived but were forced to migrate westward, to the lands north of Lake Huron. The powerful Hurons, on the other hand, allied to the Lenape, were finally broken by their longstanding Howden enemies.[179]

The Hurons had dominated both the Ohio Country and parts of Canada for so long that their defeat and fragmentation was another major shift in Indian politics. Pennsylvania and New York expanded and settled westward into the Ohio Country, while New York, the Howden and New England occupied the lands conquered in Canada. The Hurons lost their political unity (formerly being a confederacy like the Howden) and fragmented back into their constituent nations. What was left of the Arendarhonon and Attigneenongnahac nations moved westward

---

[179] Note that the Huron and Lenape are also called the Wyandot and Delaware, respectively – the same peoples but given different names by English and French explorers.

and northward, where they would eventually join the Lakota Confederation of Seven Fires.[180] The Attignawantan nation migrated more to the west and south, eventually reaching the northern border of the rump French Louisiana. The possibility of the Attignawantan settling within French territory was rejected, as the displaced Canajuns from former French America were already hungry for the best land; however, the Attignawantan were permitted to settle north of the border and received French colonial assistance in return for providing a buffer state against other Indians. The Attignawantan were technically occupying British/Imperial land, but as almost no-one had even explored it yet, they had years in which to recover and rebuild their strength before any prospective Virginian colonists arrived.

It was the final Huron nation, the Tahontaenrat, who were destined to make history, when under the visionary chief Rontondee (War Pole), they approached the Howden with a view to being accepted into the Confederacy. The Tahontaenrat had not been at the forefront of the recent fighting, but their lands were now subject to being swallowed up to Pennsylvanian settlement. The situation was not unprecedented. The Howden had previously absorbed a Huron people, the neutral and separated Attawandaron, some years before − however, the Attawandaron were not acknowledged as a distinct nation in the Confederacy. However, after the Tuscoara had been expelled from Carolina, the Howden had accepted them as the Sixth Nation, increased from the ancestral five, though the Tuscoara had fewer voting rights than those five.

After much consideration, the Howden Grand Council agreed to accept the Tahontaenrat and their lands into the Confederacy. Anything that would stave off the day when the Confederacy was surrounded by densely settled American country, a day when they might be forced back into the relationship of father and son rather than brothers…

---

[180] The easternmost of the Sioux groups. Note that there is some debate in OTL about whether the names of the Huron nations were still in meaningful use as separate entities by this point, but the assumption here is that they were.

THE SEVEN NATIONS OF THE HOWDEN CONFEDERACY

(as of 1800)

SENECA or ONONDOWAHGAH, the People of the Great Hill

CAYUGA or GUYOHKOHNYOH, the People of the Great Swamp

ONONDAGA or ONUNDAGAONO, the People of the Hills

ONEIDA or ONAYOTEKAONO, the People of Upright Stone

MOHAWK or KANIENKEHAKA, the People of the Flint

TUSCOARA or SKARUHREH, the Shirt-wearing People

TAHONTAENRAT or SCAHENTOARRHONON, the People of the Deer

Interlude #6: State of the Empire

A summary of the Continental Parliament of North America as of 1800, including the number of MPs elected by each Confederation.

Confederation of New England
  Province of Connecticut: 2 MCPs
  Province of Rhode Island: 1 MCP
  Province of South Massachusetts: 2 MCPs
  Province of North Massachusetts: 1 MCP
  Province of New HaMCPshire: 1 MCP
  Province of New Connecticut: 1 MCP
  Province of New Scotland: 2 MCPs
  Province of Wolfe: 1 MCP
  Province of Mount Royal: 1 MCP
  Province of Newfoundland: 1 MCP
  Borough of Boston: 2 MCPs
  Total: 15 MCPs

Confederation of New York
  Province of Amsterdam: 2 MCPs
  Province of Albany: 2 MCPs
  Province of East Jersey: 1 MCP
  Province of Niagara: 1 MCP
  Province of Portland: 1 MCP
  Borough of New York: 2 MCPs
  Total: 9 MCPs

Confederation of Pennsylvania
  Province of Philadelphia: 2 MCPs
  Province of West Jersey: 1 MCP
  Province of Delaware: 1 MCP

Province of Pittsylvania: 1 MCP
Province of Ohio: 1 MCP
Province of Chichago: 1 MCP[181]
Borough of Philadelphia: 2 MCPs
Total: 9 MCPs

Confederation of Virginia
Province of Richmond: 2 MCPs
Province of Williamsburg: 2 MCPs
Province of Maryland: 2 MCPs
Province of Vandalia: 1 MCP
Province of Transylvania: 1 MCP
Province of Washington: 1 MCP
Borough of Richmond: 1 MCP
Borough of Williamsburg: 1 MCP
Total: 11 MCPs

Confederation of Carolina
Province of North Carolina: 2 MCPs
Province of South Carolina: 2 MCPs
Province of Georgia: 2 MCPs
Province of West Florida: 1 MCP
Province of East Florida: 1 MCP
Province of Franklin: 1 MCP
Province of Tennessee: 1 MCP
Borough of Charleston: 1 MCP
Total: 11 MCPs

Total number of MCPs in the Continental Parliament as of 1800 = 55

---

[181] Not a typo: the spelling of "Chicago" was highly variable at first (e.g. "Checagou") and TTL happens to settle on a slightly different variation than OTL. Note that at this point Chichago is a small fort and unpopulated hinterland hardly warranting parliamentary representation, but this is effectively a subtler way of packing the Commons than traditional rotten boroughs: if you coMCPlain, you're being unpatriotic and anti-settler for saying Chichago isn't going to be a thriving city one day soon...

Breakdown:

   33 Patriots (governing party, majority of 5)

   18 Constitutionalists

   4 Radicals

The American House of Lords has 26 members as of 1800, the majority of whom are either Patriots or crossbenchers.

Chapter 31: Enter the Bald Impostor

From George Spencer-Churchill's 'A History of Modern Warfare, Vol. III' (1953)—

The Great Baltic War was a milestone in many ways. It was the last war at sea to be fought primarily with oar- galleys. It decided the fate of the governance of Russia. It decided who would dominate Scandinavia out of Sweden and Denmark, both having risen from low points in the early 18th century to new relative zeniths of power at its end. And ultimately, perhaps, it decided the fate of the Ottoman Empire. The speculative romantics have often pointed out how different our world would be today if Emperor Peter III had simply executed Catherine on her coup attempt, rather than allowing her to plot and produce heirs (allegedly, at least) in Yekaterinburg. But the truth was that this would have been politically impossible. Throughout Peter's reign, Catherine retained many supporters, indeed otherwise the brothers Potemkin, with their decidedly flimsy claim to the throne, would have got nowhere when they launched their bid.

Our tale so far stands at May 1797, when all the players in the war – save one – were committed. The brothers Potemkin had defeated Paul Romanov, though hardly decisively, at Smolensk and Vitebsk, and the Romanovians had retreated into Lithuania, which Paul had ruled as Grand Duke Povilas I for years and was now under the rule of his son Peter as Petras I. The Potemkinites held Moscow, Vitebsk and everything in between, though they had failed to take St Petersburg after their siege train was torn up by General Mikhail Kamenski. The Russian possessions in former Polish Ruthenia had yet to be decided one way or the other, though it was assumed that they would eventually fall in line with whichever house could convincingly claim victory.

Sweden, seeing the Potemkinites on the up but not yet in place to win a decisive victory, declared war on the Romanovians and Lithuania. The Hat Party hoped to expand Sweden's Baltic power and to subordinate or at least seriously weaken Russia, avoiding the nightmare of a war with both Russia and Denmark at the same time. However, this hope was dashed when Denmark proceeded to declare war in May. Prussia was busy putting down a Polish revolt which soon expanded into a wider war, and so was not directly involved with the Great Baltic War – contrary to all the Prusso-Russian friendship treaties of the mid-18th century.

So in May 1797 things looked bleak, though not yet hopeless, for the Romanovians. Peter and Paul raised a new army in Lithuania under General Michael Andreas Barclay de Tolly, a Scottish-Lithuanian who had previously taken Russian service and fought the Turks. European commentators – or, at least, those not consumed with covering the far more urgent Jacobin Wars – compared the act to that of Maria Theresa raising Hungarian levies during the Second War of Supremacy, which had perhaps prevented Austria from collapse in that war.

The naval war for control of the Baltic was now met in earnest. The vast bulk of the Royal Swedish Navy had been dispatched to defeat the smaller Lithuanian Patriotic Fleet and seize control of the Baltic port—which left Sweden herself with only secondary forces when Denmark unexpectedly declared war. The first victory in the naval war, therefore, was an easy one for the Romanovian allies, as the Danes defeated the Swedes at the Battle of Anholt (in reality taking place in the sea fairly distant from the island) and seizing control of the Kattegat. A second Swedish fleet remained in port at Malmö, Admiral Johan Cronstedt[182] being too canny to risk his small force in direct combat with the full power of the Royal Danish Navy. By being able to sortie at any time, however, he created headaches for the Danes' plans to land troops in Scania across the Oresund. Despite their early dramatic victory at Anholt, the Danes' war plans stalled.

Meanwhile, on June 7th 1797 the Swedes made a descent upon Klaipeda in an attempt to seize the port and burn the Ducal

---

[182] An ATL 'brother' of OTL's Carl-Olof Cronstedt.

Lithuanian Navy's fleet in harbour. The Swedes' descent in itself was remarkably successful, with Klaipeda being crushed between the marines from the north and the regular Swedish army moving in from Swedish Prussia to the south. The town was immediately renamed once more, to Karlsborg (after King Charles XIII). However, the Lithuanian fleet sortied under Admiral Vatsunyas Radziwiłł and escaped the ship-burners. The main Swedish fleet, led by Admiral Carl August Ehrensvärd in his flagship HMS *Kristersson*, were blockading the port, so it seemed as though the Lithuanians would be trapped.

Admiral Radziwiłł, however, proceeded to create a tactic which has been debated by naval historians ever since, and would come to greater prominence with the invention of the steam-galley by Surcouf and Cugnot a few years later in France. The admiral made the decision to sacrifice his slow-moving galleys that made up perhaps a quarter of the fleet, as they would be unable to keep up with the sailships anyway. The galleys, capable of moving independently without the wind, were used to hammer a gap in the Swedish line along a specific angle. This would allow the Lithuanians, sailing to the east away from Klaipeda, to have the wind abaft the beam, while the Swedes would be forced to tack. Ehrensvärd had of course anticipated this and made his blockade strongest in that area, but Radziwiłł's sacrifice of his galleys – which went to the bottom of the Baltic but took a number of Swedish men-o'-war with them – meant that the bulk of the Lithuanian Patriotic Fleet was able to escape.

Radziwiłł led the remainder of hus fleet to St Petersburg. Paul by now had heard of the heroic defence of the capital by Kamenski and had both promoted him and made Prince Alexander Kurakin, a long-held Petersburger ally and correspondent of his, the new Governor of the city. Paul's emissaries, along with Kamenski and Kurakin, had succeeded in achieving total control over the Russian Navy in port there, purging all suspected Potemkin sympathisers. In truth the Petersburgers were quite disposed to be loyal to Paul in any case, having had the city's importance increase further under Paul's father Peter, who – like his namesake Peter the Great – wanted Russia to have a European face, and that face was St Petersburg. For much the same reason, the former capital Moscow tended to support the Potemkins even before they marched into the city.

The outcomes of the initial Baltic engagements were therefore somewhat misleading. The Danes had beaten the Swedes in home waters, but were unable to capitalise on that victory, while the Swedes had failed their objective of actually destroying the Lithuanian fleet, yet still had the immediate naval dominance they required to shift armies into their Baltic possessions. Troops flowed into Lithuania from Courland and Swedish Prussia, but rather than aiming straight for Vilnius, the Swedes instead turned northward in an attempt to regain Livonia, which they had lost to the Russians after the Treaty of Nystad in 1721. This more than anything illustrated how the Swedes did not so much favour the Potemkins (or oppose the Romanovs) as simply desire to regain as much power over Russia as they could—by whatever means necessary.

The focus on Livonia was also a strategic error, giving the Lithuanians enough time to organise their new levies under Barclay and integrate them with the loyalist Russian remnant army led by Nikolai Saltykov. The Russo-Lithuanians defeated three Swedish armies in quick succession at Seinai, Alytus and Trakai, expelling the Swedes from the Trakų Vaivadija (Vojvodship of Trakai) but leaving them in undisputed control of Žemaičių seniūnija (the Eldership of Samogita), which lay between the Swedes' holdings of Courland and Swedish Prussia. Nonetheless, this repulsion of the too-thinly-spread Swedish forces encouraged the Swedish army to focus on regaining Livonia rather than attacking Lithuania. The Swedes were unable to commit as many troops as they would have liked, as a large part of the army was either slowly pushing east from Finland or holding the frontier in the west against any Danish attack from Norway.

By August 1797 the war had almost stagnated, with the Romanovians having built up a new army but, with the Swedes hanging over their heads, unwilling to commit it to regaining Russian cities from the Potemkinites. Meanwhile, the Potemkinites were unwilling to move against Lithuania until they had taken St Petersburg, and were gearing up for another attempt. The war still hung in the balance, but what tilted it came not from any of the current players, but quite another source…

One interesting feature of Peter III's reign was that, given his Germanophilia, he had encouraged the settlement of Germans in Russian territory. In some ways this was akin to how the British American colonists worked, accepting German refugees fleeing religious persecution but then promptly putting them down on a frontier between British (or in this case Russian) colonists and some dangerous natives. The Caucasus was a particularly common area for Germans, often Prussians, to migrate to; another common area was the Volga, where German farmers were used as a buffer against the eastern khanates.[183]

The story of the Bald Impostor has been told and retold so many times after the event that, by now, it has become confused by legend and myth. Nonetheless, the story goes that one of the German families who made the decision to move to the northern Caucasus were a certain Herr and Frau Kautzman. The Kautzmans made the journey early in Peter's reign, in 1764. They had a child, a son, only months after settling on a farm near Stavropol. However, barely three years later, the farm was attacked by (as they thought at the time) nomads, and their son Heinrich vanished, presumably lost. The Kautzmans grieved for many years, but went on to have other children and vanished from history.

However, the attack on the farm had in fact been the work of rogue Don Cossacks, who supplemented their official employment with the Tsar with the occasional raid, particularly on the German settlers who often had no way to report the attacks to the Russian authorities. Peter III's reign had been a relatively peaceful one, something that was positive for many Russians but not for the Cossack mercenaries. Heinrich had not been killed, but carried away by a Cossack who thought that the little boy 'had spirit' when he protested loudly in broken Russian about the Cossacks'

---

[183] OTL Catherine the Great also did this, but Peter III's well-recorded Germanophilia has led to an even greater scale of German immigration in TTL.

attack on the house and attempted to bite the Cossack in the ankle. That Cossack was named Yemelyan Ivanovich Pugachev, and he adopted the young Heinrich Kautzman.[184]

Though the boy initially sulked and tried to escape, he was raised in the Cossack fashion, taking the second name Ivan after Pugachev's father, and eventually fought beside them in wars against the Turks and (undeclared) conflicts with the Crimeans. Ivan née Heinrich became a huge, powerful figure who shaved his head in the Cossack fashion. He thus did not stand out from his Cossack fellows due to hair colour, but his German blood still showed in his bright blue eye—for which he was nicknamed 'the Bald Impostor'. Under Peter III, Pugachev rose to become leader of the Don Cossacks and Heinrich continued to follow his would-be foster father.

When the Civil War broke out, the people of southern Russia elected to hedge their bets, waiting to see which side would come out on top before backing it. Heinrich, however, advocated supporting Paul from the start, arguing that the Potemkins would do to the Don and Caucasus just what they had to Yekaterinburg, filling it full of their favourites and ending the (relative) peace between the peoples there. Pugachev agreed, but was unwilling to commit his forces just yet. Heinrich stormed off and journeyed south, perhaps in search of his real parents at last, though if so it is thought he never found them.

What he found instead was a man of fine Georgian dress, who despite his two bodyguards was being overpowered by a gang of Russian bandits. Heinrich went into action and sabred down three of the bandits in the Cossack fashion before the rest could even react. Startled by the assault, the remaining bandits fled. One of the Georgian bodyguards died of his wounds, but the other survived—as did his master. The Georgian nobleman introduced himself as Prince Piotr Bagration, a scion of the Georgians' ancient and sprawling royal family. He had been sent to the north from King George XII, who had signed a treaty placing Georgia

---

[184] Pugachev is of course (in)famous in OTL for his revolt against Catherine the Great in which he claimed to be Peter III, allegedly merely deposed rather than murdered, and acted as a pretender to the throne.

under Russian protection back in the 1780s, but yet now Georgia was threatened by Ottoman encroachment[185] and the Russians had done nothing. Bagration had not even heard that Russia was deep in a civil war until a few days before.

His words gave Heinrich a wild idea, and he brought Bagration back to Pugachev. Together they hatched a plan, a plan not unlike the one that had been concocted in the court of King Charles XIII in Stockholm. They would assist one of the two sides, and be in a position to make their diverse demands at the end of the conflict. The Ottomans were beginning to make threatening moves towards Georgia, but Abdulhamid II remained a cautious ruler and would not commit to a direct invasion. On Prince Bagration's advice, George XII thus agreed to all the Turks' demands for vassalage at the time, committing the Georgian army to the north instead. The Georgians wintered in Rostov-on-Don, where they met up with Pugachev's Cossack forces and Russian peasant levies who supported Paul. The new army was powerful, yet fragmented, and the Georgians would not submit to any general other than Bagration, while the Cossacks said the same for Pugachev. In the end, then the compromise solution was simple. The young Heinrich, the Bald Impostor, respected by all and yet not of any of the kindreds, led the army into battle.

In March 1798, Kiev fell to the new Romanovian army, followed by Voronezh and then Kazan in July, as Pugachev bit deeply into the heart of the Potemkinites' natural territory.[186] At the same time, the Russo-Lithuanian fleet met the Swedes at the Battle of the Irbe Strait. Admiral Radziwiłł won a Pyrrhic victory, defeating Ehrensvärd at the cost of most of his own ships. Nonetheless, this was the signal for the Danes to step up their own efforts. With no further need to watch the Baltic for the return of the Swedes' main force, the Danes left a squadron to bottle up Cronstedt's remaining Swedish naval forces in Malmö and then deployed the rest of their fleet to a descent on Swedish

---

[185] OTL Qajar Persia was the main threat to Georgia in this era, but TTL Persia is still under the control of the Zands who have different priorities.
[186] Ironically in OTL Kazan was largely destroyed by Pugachev during his revolt in the 1770s.

Pomerania, conquering the German province and adding it to the Danish crown. The Swedes successfully defeated the small Danish force in Norway and besieged Christiania,[187] but at this point the Danes finally made a landing in Scania. King Johannes II and the Danish Diet proclaimed the return of the lands lost to Sweden in 1690 to Denmark, and the Swedes withdrew forces from Norway and Finland to prevent a further Danish breakout.

The Swedes continued to control Livonia, but their discomfiture elsewhere persuaded Paul to risk his Russo-Lithuanian army further east. Vitebsk was retaken in August against only a token Potemkinite force, but it was once more near the ruins of Smolensk that the main Potemkinite army met the Romanovians. The battle lasted three days, and was fiercer and bloodier than any other in that war. Finally, on the third day, the Potemkinites broke the Romanovian line in two and a cavalry charge led by Alexander Potemkin himself encircled Barclay's command staff. At this perilous moment, rumours came from the rear that the forces of the mysterious Bald Impostor had taken, and were sacking, Moscow. The rumours were exaggerated, though indeed the Cossack and Georgian forces were moving into the region around September. The rumours spread through the Potemkinite army and morale collapsed. Many of the Potemkins' soldiers were Muscovites recruited there after their initial triumphant entry, and the knowledge that their city and families were under threat caused the whole of the Potemkins' Muscovite-manned left wing to crumble. Barclay escaped, and the Lithuanians swept around in a decisive pincer movement. It was the turn of Alexander to be trapped. Ivan Potemkin and Sergei Saltykov escaped with the bulk of their army, but the brash young claimant emperor was in enemy hands.

Paul's following decision has been cited by many as questionable, and perhaps not unlike his father's to exile Catherine to Yekaterinburg. Rather than summarily executing Alexander Potemkin for treason, he offered him possession of the Duchy of Courland if he would call off his forces and reocgnise Paul as Emperor. This was a rather ambitious offer, given that Courland

---

[187] The name of the city now called Oslo in OTL.

had been Swedish before the war and was now deep in Swedish-controlled territory. Alexander Potemkin accepted, giving up his claim to the throne. It is very possible that at the time he viewed this as his only choice, and intended to go back on his word later, but events rendered any such assumption irrelevant.

By the early months of 1799, the Potemkinite army was shattered. Rumour belatedly became fact as Moscow indeed was taken by the Bald Impostor's forces, while Kamenski and Kurakin successfully held off the Swedes and then threw their weakened army back into Finland, forces being stripped from it to hold back the Danes in Scania. Ivan Potemkin, dithering over whether he should try to fall back to Yekaterinburg and try again, was captured along with Sergei Saltykov near Nizhny Novgorod. The civil war was over—both far more abruptly than anyone would have guessed, and with an outcome that would have seemed starkly not so many months before. Paul was restored to his throne.

The newly restored Emperor realised that the great strength of the Potemkins was in their partnership, and so separated the two. Paul exiled Ivan and Sergei Saltykov to Yakutsk with orders for them to develop the area as they had Yekaterinburg. Saltykov was originally planned to be executed, but the sentence was reduced to exile after his relative Nikolai Saltykov spoke in his defence to the Emperor. It is difficult to judge in retrospect whether the choice of Yakutsk was driven by a deliberate policy judgement to support the efforts of men like Benyovsky and Lebedev in their Far Eastern trade missions, or whether it was simply Paul finding a map of his empire and pointing at the most inhospitable-looking part of it he could find.

Paul returned to Moscow in May 1799 and met with the Bald Impostor, who gave him certain demands: liberty for the Cossacks, support for the Georgians against the Turks, and the emancipation of the serfs. Paul argued and negotiated for days, but in the end a settlement was hammered out. Otherwise, as was unspoken but well known, the Bald Impostor would have held the city and fought Paul for it.

It was the end of 1799 before Sweden left the war, the Russo-Lithuanians not only having retaken Livonia but now had begun to invade Courland and Swedish Prussia. In truth Sweden was still in a relatively strong position, having held back the Danes in Scania and almost flung them back into the Baltic, but Stockholm was now paralysed by a constitutional crisis. Charles XIII was assassinated by a madman on October 30th and he left no heir, threatening to plunge Sweden into a civil war or a war of succession. The Danish Diet entered into hurried, secret negotiations with the Swedish Riksdag, and a treaty was quickly agreed. The Swedes would accept Johannes II of Denmark as King, re-creating the Union of Kalmar. In exchange, the Danes would only annex the western half of Scania which was still the most culturally Danish, and would ensure that the Swedes retained Finland (which the Russians were not yet in a position to invade). The Swedes had already lost Pomerania, Swedish Prussia and Courland, but it was clear that this was best settlement Sweden would get while in such a weak constitutional position. The Riksdag grudgingly agreed.

The Danes thus made peace with Sweden on December 4th, and warned the Russians that Sweden, and hence Finland, was now a direct possession of King Johannes II (as John IV of Sweden). The Russians were in no position to dispute this, and so the Treaty of Klaipeda (restored, of course, to Lithuania) ended the war on the last day of the 18th century, December 31st 1799 (O.S. Russian calendar) –

Courland to become an independent Duchy once more, under Alexander Potemkin as Duke.

Swedish Prussia to be transferred to Lithuania (the Kingdom of Prussia protested at this, seeing the territory as rightfully its own, but was in no position to enforce this protest with arms).

Livonia to remain an integral part of Russia.

Paul is Emperor Paul I of Russia.

Peter son of Paul is Grand Duke Petras I of Lithuania.

Johannes II of Denmark is also John IV of Sweden, including Finland.

Swedish Pomerania transferred to Denmark.

Emancipation of Russia's serfs, initially in the southern

governorates only (later expanded in 1805 to include the provinces east of the Urals, to encourage settlement of the 'Eastern Road')

Liberty for Cossacks, and the protectorate status of Georgia to be enforced by military action against the Turks.

So the Great Baltic War ended, and like all wars, sowed the seeds for the next.

Chapter 32: Three Lions and One Tiger

"Folly awaits the man who seeks to conquer the heart of India. Indeed, he should consider himself fortunate if India does not conquer his heart."

– John Pitt, Governor-General of British India

From: "India in the Age of Revolution" by Dr Anders Ohlmarks (1974, authorised English translation 1980)—

Ever since the start of penetration by European trading companies in the sixteenth century, India had been considered 'elsewhere' by European powers, more so even than the Americas. A war might be declared in Europe yet its participants amiably work alongside one another other in India, or – more commonly – the reverse. Certainly, it was difficult to tell what constituted a war between Europeans in India, as the wars in question were usually, at least on some level, a conflict between rival Indian nations each backed by a trading company.

Initially the Portuguese and Dutch had dominated the India trade, but by the eighteenth century they had been sidelined by the British and French. Just as they had in America, the two great powers of the century fought their Wars of Supremacy (as the English have it) in India, with the French generally allied to the Marathas and the Keralan states, and the British to the Nizam of Haidarabad, the Nawab of the Carnatic and the Nawab of Bengal. This volatile situation shifted as the dynamic century rolled on. First the French took Madras in the War of the Austrian Succession and proceeded to conquer British Cuddalore as well, reducing the Nawab of the Carnatic to a French puppet.

The French East India Company, under Dupleix and then Rochambeau, moved its headquarters from the old French trading post of Pondicherry to the far better equipped former British Fort St George at Madras. The British withdrew from southern India altogether, save for the Northern Circars (which they ran on behalf of the Nizam of Haidarabad) and fought a war against the treacherous Nawab of Bengal, eventually unseating him and replacing him with six invented principalities in the pocket of the Company. Aside from capturing French Chandranagore in the process (and thus ejecting French influence from Bengal) this had so consumed British efforts in India that the French had crept further ahead, despite the FEIC's relative dearth of funding from Paris compared to the BEIC's from London. Dupleix in particular was a genius at running colonies and trade agreements with no help whatsoever from home, and the systems he set up would go on to serve French India well.

By the 1780s, the Maratha Empire had collapsed following defeat by the Afghans and allied Indian Muslims in the 1760s, after the Marathas' Rajasthani allies deserted them at the last minute at the Third Battle of Panipat. The Empire had been reorganised as a looser Confederacy, with the Peshwas losing their former power. French influence declined among the Marathas as their previously universal treaties and trade agreements were vetoed by the new local rulers. Instead, the French under Rochambeau focused on expanding their influence into southern India, cementing an alliance with the Kingdoms of Mysore, and Travancore. Travancore's coastal neighbour Cochin allied with the British during the War of the Austrian Succession, and in the aftermath of the British defeat was largely absorbed by French-backed Mysore.

Mysore at that time was under the rule of the Hindoo Wodeyar dynasty, but during the 1760s a Muslim soldier, Haidar Ali, rose to prominence after heroic deeds during the Mysorean invasion and conquest of Bangalore. Haidar Ali became effective chief minister of the King and soon usurped most of his power. He formed a strategic alliance with the French against British-backed Haidarabad, and went on to mostly win the Mysore-Haidarabad Wars of the 1770s and 80s. Mysore had become the most powerful state in India, with the Marathas decaying into ineffectiveness and Haidarabad on the back foot. Haidar Ali's son Tippoo Sultan, who first rose to prominence as a general of the Mysorean army, was a remarkable visionary. Noting Travancore's successful expulsion of the Dutch East India Company, he foresaw a time when India could be entirely freed from the European trading companies – under Mysorean leadership, naturally. But the Tippoo ably understood the problems of ruling over Mysore's new empire in southern India, with the mish-mash of peoples, languages and religions. Kerala alone included Portuguese Catholics, Jews, Thomasite Syrian Orthodox Christians and some Protestants in addition to the more common religions of southern India such as Sunni Islam, Hindooism and Jainism. To that end, the Tippoo (though a devout Muslim himself) allowed the building of churches and Hindoo shrines in Mysorean cities.

The Tippoo was a realistic thinker and decided that the path to being free of European interference was to first assist the French in ejecting the British from southern India, and then to turn on them. It was hardly a remarkable event in India, which had weathered and absorbed countless waves of invaders since before the time of Ashoka, successively turning each group against one another. By 1790, the Tippoo judged, the British had ceased to be a serious threat south of Masoolipatam, and all that remained was to wait until the French became vulnerable. He did not have long to wait…

News of the French Revolution was slow to travel around the world, even by the standards of the day—despite the obvious importance of the event. The reason for this was chiefly that, thanks to Leo Bone's trickery at Toulon and mutinies in Quiberon and Marseilles, most of the former Royal French Navy was out of the Revolutionary government's hands. The government of the Marquess of Rockingham in Britain allowed this relatively large number of ships to dock in British ports, resulting in riots in Portsmouth and Chatham due to fights between British and French sailors who had been shooting at each other only about eight years previously. Thereafter, the Rockingham ministry removed the French ships from the major English ports and instead commissioned the Royal Engineers to expand secondary ports, such as Liverpool, Kingston-upon-Hull and Lowestoft. This was a significant event in those towns' histories, paving the way for their later importance as trading ports in the nineteenth century, and traces of this history remain in the French names of some of the streets laid down at the time. A portion of the French Royal Navy eventually removed to Louisiana, but the majority remained under the direct control of the Dauphin in London, who hoped that it might be used for a seaborne invasion to support a rising of royalists in France.

In any case, this meant that the Revolutionaries had few ships to spare and the British, with their great naval numerical superiority, were capable of blockading Republican French ports. The Jacobins did send ships out to bring news of the Revolution to the French colonies, but few of these got through the blockade. Those which did manage the feat typically only did so after several years of unsuccessful attempts, leaving while inclement weather disabled the British blockade. So it was that by the time *L'Épurateur*, a second-rate ship of the line of seventy guns (formerly the *Bordeaux*) reached Madras in May 1798, confused reports of the French Revolution had already been filtering through India for years. Some of these came from Zand Persia, which retained extensive trading links with much of India, and had enthusiastically embraced discussion of Revolutionary principles and adoption of some of them in a milder form. Other reports, usually rather biased, came from East Indiamen and Royal Naval ships calling in to Indian ports after hearing the news from Britain.

Therefore, when the Revolutionary envoy René Leclerc presented himself to Governor-General Rochambeau and demanded his oath to the Revolutionary government and to attaint himself of his countship, the Governor-General already knew something of what he spoke of. Enough, though it might come from British sources, to know that he wanted no truck with any of it. Quite apart from loyalty to the Crown and his own Catholicism, Rochambeau saw that Linnaean Racist ideas unleashed on India would make the storm of the old Goanese Inquisition look like an overcast evening. To that end, Rochambeau politely rejected

Leclerc and had the frothing envoy dragged from his presence by Arcotian bodyguards.

Rochambeau, though, being a gentleman and not considering them a threat, did not impound Leclerc or *L'Épurateur*—a decision which he would later regret. Whilst plotting how to have his revenge for the 'infringement of his rights of man', as he termed it in his journal, Leclerc was approached by a messenger from Tippoo Sultan. The Tippoo had become intrigued by the tales of the French Revolution and wanted to know more, inviting *L'Épurateur*'s crew to Mysore. Leclerc agreed and the ship docked at the great port of Cochin, now controlled by Mysore.

Leclerc and his assistants were received at the court of the Tippoo in Mysore city by a salute of twenty rockets, which startled and astonished the French. Rockets were largely unknown as weapons in Europe at the time, but had been introduced to India by the Nawab of the Carnatic, and Tippoo Sultan had become enamoured of them while serving as a soldier. Therefore, just as Haidarabad was famous for its great artillery – the 'Nizam's Beautiful Daughters' – Mysore had become legendary for its rocket brigades, or *cushoon*s. The rockets were greatly inaccurate, but fired in large numbers they could be murderously effective. They were often equipped with either exploding tips or long knives attached to the head, which would scythe in a deadly fashion among massed infantry as the rocket spun drunkenly around in midair. Another use for rockets was to drop them in a confined space filled by the enemy, such as a breach in a wall, and they would bounce around off the walls trailing fire, burning and panicking the enemy defensive troops.

René Leclerc, a man who enthusiastically embraced the view of Lisieux—that Revolutionary political thought must go hand in hand with Revolutionary innovations in military technology and tactics—was greatly impressed by the rockets. In turn, he instructed the Tippoo in the political and administrative details of the Revolution, and the Tippoo proved to already be better informed than most in India, having questioned traders and obtained copies of Revolutionary texts from Persia. The Tippoo's family were of Persian blood and he still read Farsi as well as the

Arabic which a devout Muslim must.

The Tippoo, like the Zand Shahs, embraced some Revolutionary ideas, partly for genuinely idealistic reasons and partly to fit his own ends. Leclerc gave the Tippoo plenty of information about the FEIC which the Revolutionaries had derived from the archives in Paris, allowing the Mysoreans to exploit Rochambeau's weaknesses, and also gave the Tippoo some Revolutionary innovations. These included Gribeauval artillery (actually invented some years before the Revolution, but associated with it in the public mind), the Cugnot steam wagon (an early model was carried along on *L'Épurateur*) and the standardised Moiselle Rifle that had been adopted by elite Tirailleur skirmishers under the late *ancien régime* and was now being revived thanks to Boulanger's reforms de-emphasising that the army should be republican to the extent that all soldiers should be equipped identically.[188]

Though the Tippoo preferred his rockets to even the efficient Gribeauval system, he enthusiastically adopted the steam wagon and the *chirurgien*, and had already been using rifles (of the more bespoke variety made in India, used mainly for hunting) for years. The Tippoo organised a sharpshooting competition among his *cushoon*s (regiments) and picked 'those men with the Eye of the Tiger' to form the core of his own Tirailleurs. The Tippoo had an obsession with the Tiger as a symbol of Mysorean power, India and himself. Leclerc made him an official Citizen of the French Republic.[189]

Leclerc stayed with the Tippoo for a year and a half. Then, in October 1799, the chance came that he had been waiting for. The King of Travancore, Dharma Raja Karthika Thirunal Rama Varma (known as Dharma Raja) died after a long reign and his seventeen-year-old son, Balarama Varma, became King. The

---

[188] OTL the French did not much use the rifle and Napoleon in particular was opposed to it. TTL, thanks to the Americans using rifles so much and American troops serving in British armies elsewhere in the world, the French and the rest of Europe have decided that rifles may be the way forward after all.

[189] This actually happened in OTL. People's Republics run by absolute monarchs were not an invention of the Soviets.

Tippoo, who by this point had sidelined the Wodeyar dynasty of Mysore and claimed royal power for himself, declared that Balarama Varma was too young and also illegitimate, claiming that Dharma Raja had been too old at the time to truly sire him. Flimsy though this claim was, it was largely just a *casus belli*. Travancore, alone, could not hope to resist Mysorean annexation, and then the Tippoo would rule unopposed over all of Kerala, as well as Bangalore and Mysore proper. Of course, Travancore had a treaty with the FEIC, who would be obliged to either turn on their former ally Mysore, or back down and demonstrate that the Tippoo was the real power there.

Which was exactly the confrontation that the Tippoo wanted. Leclerc would sign up to anything that would hurt Rochambeau and the royalist FEIC, even if privately he worried what the Linnaean policies of the Revolutionary government towards a situation like this would be. Still, Robespierre was far away, and he wanted revenge on Rochambeau for his humiliation.

The plan of Leclerc and the Tippoo was put into place. It was an excellent plan, and by rights should have worked. The FEIC was not powerful enough, without support from Paris that would now never come, to directly challenge Mysore. Rochambeau would have to back down before a power that was aligned with the Revolutionary government, which would be the start of an inevitably slide towards the Royalist Carnatic shifting to the Republicans as well. For the FEIC to triumph, it would have to be aided by other Indian great powers, and the only ones capable of doing so – now the Marathas were no longer an option – were the FEIC's deadliest foes. It seemed an impossibility.

Unfortunately for the Tippoo, though, in Calcutta's Fort William was a man who would one day be immortalised by his quote "Impossible is only a word…"

Chapter 33: Alea iacta est

"The tactical doctrine of the Yapontsi[190]…a much neglected subject in western military schools…states that wars might be won by a Kantai Kessen, a single decisive engagement. In the real world, of course, the majority of conflicts do not work that way…but there is the well-known counter-example of Pierre Boulanger and the Rubicon Offensive…"

- Excerpted from a 1930 lecture by Peter William Courtenay, 4th Baron Congleton

From: "The Jacobin Wars – the Italo-German Front" by Joshua H. Calhoun (University of New York Press, 1946)—

The 1797 campaigning season had seen the launch of the Poséidon Offensive, the first real success by French Jacobin troops in not only holding back their Austrian foe, but in putting the Austrians on the defensive. After the withdrawal of Wurmser's army from Nancy, the Austrians held no French territory and were on the back foot in Italy and Switzerland. However, Wurmser's dynamic thrust into Lorraine had blunted the left-hand prong of Poséidon. The French were much more successful in the centre, with Switzerland falling to Leroux's army in days and Hoche's brilliant outmanoeuvring of Alvinczi, no mean general himself, in the Italian campaign. As the troops retired to their winter quarters at Christmas 1797 (not that it strictly existed in France anymore thanks to Hébert's promotion of deistic-atheism), the Republic was left in a better position than most of its generals had dared hope a year earlier.

---

[190] The Russian word for 'Japanese'. While the term 'Japanese' exists in TTL, by the twentieth century it is considered outdated, not unlike referring to Thais as Siamese in OTL.

However, a successful defence, even a proactive one, was not the same as a true victory. In this Boulanger, Lisieux and Robespierre were, for once, in full agreement. The three Consuls agreed to continue to make the war against Austria the top priority, though Robespierre feared an invasion by Britain in the west. "Without a respectable fleet to shield us," he allegedly wrote in a private journal, "we run the risk of presenting our proud Republican face to the quailing Germans, while the mongrel shopkeepers stab us in our proud Republican arse."

Nonetheless, even with the conscription of the *levée en masse*, French troops were too few to spare any reasonable number of serious soldiers for the west, not without impairing the war effort against Austria. Instead, Boulanger suggested that raw recruits be paraded through the western lands (as yet not yet reorganised into *départements*) and this show display hopefully worry any British spies, while also giving the troops some experience at battle-marching. Robespierre agreed, and thus signed up to a plan that, though sensible-sounding at the time, would eventually prove to be his downfall…

The Austrians were in even worse straits, however. Ever since Prussia had been damaged so badly in the Third War of Supremacy, the Holy Roman Emperors had become accustomed to resuming a fraction of their old authority within the boundaries of the Empire. There had been few wars between German states since the 1760s, and for this war against Revolutionary France – which had united Europe against it, at least in theory – the Austrians had marched to battle with the armies of the two most powerful German states, Brandenburg and Saxony, at their side.

But this did not last. Events spilling over from the Russian Civil War in the East served to break up the unity of the pan-German force, incidentally creating an exemplar that Sanchez—at this point merely a child—would get so much mileage out of, years later. Frederick William II of Prussia died merely two months before Frederick Christian II of Saxony,[191] but they were

---

[191] In TTL Frederick Christian I is succeeded by Frederick Christian II, an entirely different character to OTL's Frederick Augustus III, and he dies notably younger, from disease, without issue.

two extremely eventful months. The death of the King in Prussia was the signal for a long planned for Polish uprising to begin, calling itself the Confederation of Lublin.[192] This was far better organised than the previous chaotic attempts at revolts which had been easily put down, even by a Prussian army that had found itself limited by treaties and the loss of land (and therefore soldier-producing families) to Austria and Sweden. The Polish rebels seized control of Lublin, Warsaw and Bielsk within the first week of the rebellion and declared a restored Commonwealth of Poland. The absence of the Poland-*Lithuania* modifier was significant, as the Lithuanian *szlachta* had refused to join with their former comrades in rebellion—although they certainly did not do anything to hinder them, either.

After some consultation among themselves, the Polish *szlachta* decided that electing a king from among their own number would not be a winning strategy. The Prussians were disorganised at present from their shift in kingship and the suddenness of the rebellion, but there were enough cool heads at the top of the Confederation to realise that, given time to reorganise and withdraw their troops from the pan-German anti-French force, they would easily crush the ragtag Polish soldiers. Therefore, the nascent new Poland required allies, and the best way to guarantee such allies was to offer them the kingship—which was not the position of absolute power it might be in other monarchies, so trading it away did not represent giving up on Polish independence before it began.

There were some suggestions of appealing to Emperor Ferdinand IV to either become King of Poland himself, in addition to his other titles, or send someone from one of the Hapsburg cadet lines. However, this seemed a questionable strategy, given that Ferdinand IV was determined to hold the pan-German alliance together and would not move against the Prussians. In any case,

---

[192] TTL the Hohenzollerns haven't felt confident enough about their position since the 1760s to claim the title 'King *of* Prussia', as they did OTL. Note that the fortress town of Bar, which gave its name to the earlier OTL Polish rebellion the Confederation of Bar, is now in Russia, as the Russians annexed the more Ruthenian vojvodships of the Polish-Lithuanian Commonwealth after the War of the Polish Partition.

it was voted down when a far more attractive option presented itself. Frederick Christian I of Saxony had failed to be elected King of Poland on the death of his father, Frederick Augustus II, who had also been Augustus III of Poland. His own son Frederick Christian II had been an even less likely candidate for King of Poland had Poland still existed: he was concerned mainly with expanding Saxon power throughout all the Germanies, investing heavily in developing the western enclaves Saxony had acquired from Prussia after the Third War of Supremacy. This policy would prove to be of questionable value in the years immediately following.

Two months after the death of Frederick William II of Prussia, Frederick Christian II of Saxony died of an illness and without issue. The throne passed to his brother, who became Elector John George V. A more contrasting sibling it is hard to imagine. John George was both more dynamic than his brother and concerned with establishing Saxony as a power full stop, not merely one within the Holy Roman Empire. After all, Prussia had risen to such heights (before crashing down again) by building power in Poland, outside the borders of the Empire. When the newly-summoned Polish Sejm offered him the crown of Poland, not long after he had succeeded to that of Saxony he immediately accepted with the tendency for audacious gambling that would characterise him in later life.

The Saxon army was withdrawn from the front against France at almost at the same time as the Prussian messengers (who had had further to go) got through and recalled their own army to help put down the Polish rebellion. Ironically, the Saxons did not know *why* they had been recalled, and the Prussians had not yet heard that Saxony had declared war on Prussia, so the two armies infrequently camped together on the way back east before returning to their homeland and learning they were to fight each other. This rather surreal affair has unsurprisingly also been quoted by the disciples of Sanchez as support for their ideologies.

Losing one of their biggest allies at such a critical time would have been bad for Austria; losing both was a disaster. Furthermore, the image of pan-German cooperation shattered along with it, and the more minor German states began to hesitate and pull back their own armies, alarmed at the prospect of a Prusso-Saxon war spilling over their own borders (as such wars invariably did). The withdrawal of the Hessian and Thuringian states began a domino effect, with each statelet worrying about the armies of their neighbours being at home when their own were still abroad. Soon, only the Austrian army and those of other Hapsburg-ruled and vassalised states were in play – as well as those of the states directly threatened by the encroaching French. The Hanoverian army remained in place, on the direct orders of Britain's King George III, but fought rather half-heartedly—more concerned about reports of Dutch and Danish activity worryingly close to their home electorate.

Thus, the Rubicon Offensive can be thought of as not merely a triumph for Revolutionary France but also a disaster for Austria—a disaster that was already unfolding before the first Sans-Culotte walked out of his barracks in Spring 1798. The problem was exacerbated by the fact that, as with Poséidon (which the Allies had thought was a sea operation, presumably aimed at Britain), the code name fooled the Austrians' spies, who thought that it must literally refer to a further French offensive in northern Italy, as Caesar's prototype had been. However, Boulanger (or more likely one of his subordinates, as he did not have a classical education) was simply referring to the idea of a single decisive throw. Rubicon was certainly that.

Aside from garrison troops, French forces were steadily withdrawn from Switzerland over the winter of 1797. Robespierre ordered the burning of the Habichtsburg, the ancestral Hapsburg castle in Aargau, as a symbolic spite to Ferdinand IV. The French were able to hold down the rebellious Swiss effectively enough, but gave ground to the Austrians when they attacked in the spring of 1798. However, even a small number of troops could slow down an enemy offensive in Switzerland's Alpine terrain, and the Austrian advance was itself half-hearted. Hoping to match Wurmser's success the previous year, the Austrians focused on Italy, believing it would be where the French massed their army. This miscalculation would cost them dearly.

The Austrian army in Italy was placed under the command of Archduke Ferdinand, a younger brother of Ferdinand IV's who was also the Duke of Krakau (and hence the most likely candidate to be suggested as King of Poland if the Poles *had* succeeded in getting Austrian support for their rebellion). Ferdinand had not received his position purely through family connections; he was genuinely one of Austria's best generals. He demonstrated this throughout the 1798 campaigning season as he fought Hoche's mercurial brilliance with a more stolid, logistically-based but no less effective style. When Ferdinand led his army from Hapsburg Tyrol, through the Venetian Terraferma and into French-occupied Mantua and Milan, Hoche struggled to repel him. The French general had not expected such a large Austrian army so soon, and a third of his own force was away south, pacifying the former Spanish Parma.

Hoche, for one of the few times in his career, hesitated. There was the possibility of withdrawing his own forces to Parma in order to then give the Austrians battle with his full force, but that would put the French army in a sticky position. Hapsburg Tuscany lay to the south, a potential threat, and the Austrians could easily bottle him up in Parma and cut off the French army from its supply chain. Hoche therefore decided against such a strategy. He sent messengers to his forces in Parma, telling them to regroup and then cause as much trouble for the Austrians as possible, then led his men on a retreat westward, back into French-occupied Piedmont. Hoche intended to resupply his army and hopefully rest his men in the newly set up Revolutionary depots at Turin, before the tired Austrians would then attack him on a battlefield of his own choosing – and lose.

All but the most disciplined armies find it difficult to sustain morale on a retreat, seeing the places they have already seen before, heading back the way they came. Hoche's charisma helped to some extent, but his men almost mutinied nonetheless when his plan was scuppered. A second Austrian army under Wurmser came down over the Alps through Graubünden and blocked his retreat. Once more Hoche hesitated. Wurmser's army could, in his estimation, be defeated, but to give battle would give Ferdinand enough time to catch up.

Hoche then considered turning south and heading for Genoa, but Ferdinand anticipated this and divided his army into two parts, the larger blocking the road south. Hoche seized even this tiny opportunity, though, wheeled about and attacked the smaller portion of Ferdinand's army, the one that remained in pursuit. Despite the French army's troubled situation, Hoche's audacious attack stunned the Austrians and Hoche managed to win a victory at Pavia, at the cost of a fifth of his army and half his artillery. The other half was abandoned days later to speed up the pace of the march, as Hoche's wounded and tired men fled the other two Austrian armies.

Hoche found there was only one realistic destination his men could make while avoiding Hapsburg forces: Venice. Even the tired and wounded French easily defeated the inexperienced army of the Republic at Padua and then fell upon Venice the city. Such was the Violation of Venice, as is lamented in song. The relief of Hoche's men at the end of the great race, at escaping their captors, was such that they gave themselves over to a spree of looting, rape and arson. It is certainly true that we only know what the original St Mark's Square looked like from old illustrations…

The end of the Republic of Venice's thousand-year history, significant though it was, was ultimately overshadowed by events further to the north. Ferdinand was preparing to besiege Hoche in Venice when an urgent recall came to him from Tyrol. Rubicon had not been aimed at Italy, after all, but through Lorraine.

The hammer blow that Boulanger assembled consisted of two great armies under Ney and Leroux, intended to sweep around to the north and south and pocket any Austrian defenders between them. The free city of Strassburg was taken in March and annexed to the French Latin Republic as Strasbourg; the Austrians were ejected from Haguenau mere days later. The rapidity of the French advance outdid even Hoche's stunning manoeuvres in Italy, and illustrated two important innovations by the French Revolutionary Army: the Cugnot steam wagons for transport of artillery and important supplies, and also a slimmed-down supply chain, with troops encouraged to live off the land (*la maraude*).

This did not endear them to the locals, but meant they could move further and faster, not having to worry about outrunning their own rations.

On April 1st 1798, the northern army under Ney took Karlsruhe, capital of the Margraviate of Baden. The French advance had been so rapid that the Badenese army had literally been overtaken and the people of the city were unaware they were in danger until the first Bloody Flags were seen on the horizon. The Margrave and his family were captured by the French and, on Robespierre's orders, publicly executed by *chirurgien* in the market square. The Schloss was then taken over by French troops and a military administration imposed. However, the bulk of the army was still moving forward. The staggered Germans named it *Blitzkrieg*, the War of Lightning. The name was so apt that the French soldiers soon adopted it themselves in translation, naming Boulanger's mode of warfare the *Guerre d'éclair*.

Ney's forces were in Stuttgart a month later, though the Duke of Württemberg had the sense to flee before their advance. It was not a case of the French necessarily defeating the Austrian and local Swabian armies sent against them, but simply manoeuvring around them and threatening to isolate and surround them. The Austrians were forced to keep withdrawing as cities ever deeper into the Germanies were threatened. In the few set-piece battles that took place, the Austrians were generally disorganised enough to suffer defeat. Also, as they were now out of the mountainous regions of Lorraine, the Cugnot steam-wagons could be used to full effect. The Austrian tactics of fighting in line collapsed when hit with the French columns and the steam artillery trundling along beside them, moving into positions where they could enfilade the thick Austrian lines. Battle after battle was lost for the Austrians as France focused her full might on this new breakthrough. The Austrian armies continued to reconquer France's previous gains in Italy and Switzerland, but what was that compared to the double-edged sword driving straight for the heart of Germany?

As Ney's army reached Franconia and brushed up against the territory of the neutral Palatinate, Boulanger ordered that the forces be divided. Leroux continued eastward and Ney's army spread out to hold down the vast swathe of territory that had been gained. An Austrian army was pocketed near Hechingen but managed to fight its way through Ney's thinly spread forces to rejoin the rest of the Austrian force regrouping in Bavaria. This illustrated the effect of panic that made *Guerre d'éclair* so effective – if the Austrians had continued fighting instead of retreating, Ney's forces were too thinly spread to stop them, and all of the Republic's gains could have collapsed. But they did not, for the speed of the French advance meant that no-one would have been surprised to learn that Leroux was in Warsaw by next Sunday. Captured printing presses industriously turned out Jacobin propaganda in Fraktur text to aid such an impression.

In truth, the French invasion slowed. Even with Boulanger's ruthless approach to supply trains, Leroux was outrunning his essential supplies and ammunition, and also was away from the coal depots that had been set up to fuel his Cugnot-wagons. Germany's own coal supplies mainly lay to the north, out of French reach for the moment, and so Leroux paused lest his army reach Vienna only to be without artillery. This was the moment in which the French invasion could have faltered, had the Austrians had delivered a decisive hammer blow to the French flank— now that there was only one French spear rather than two driving eastward. But the only Austrian general with the skill and temperament for that was Archduke Ferdinand, and he was still obliviously chasing Hoche around Italy.

After the fall of Ulm in July, Ferdinand IV desperately reinstated the formerly disgraced General Mozart as head of Austria's armies, but by that point not even Mozart could entirely salvage the situation. Having stared at a map for an hour, Mozart simply told the Emperor pointedly that Vienna, perhaps, could be defended againstthe French onslaught – but only if they pulled everything back now.

Ferdinand IV was appalled by this pessimism on behalf of his Salzburger general, but a few days later was forced to agree. Davidovich had scraped an army together and attempted to blunt Leroux's march at Burgau. The battle, fought on 2nd August, saw the almost total annihilation of the Austrian forces as Leroux used his Cugnot-artillery in Boulanger's patent style, positioning them on flat ridges adjoining the battlefield and moving them around so as to direct plunging fire down onto Davidovich's lines. Mozart warned that now the magnitude of the task he faced was even greater. With a heavy heart, Ferdinand IV gave the order and then left for Regensburg, calling what would be the last Reichstag of the Holy Roman Empire…

Chapter 34: Eire and Water

"Just because a man is born in a stable does not make him the Lord."

– Richard Wesley, 2nd Earl of Mornington

From: "The Jacobin Wars" by E.G. Christie (Hetherington Publishing House, 1926)–

Ireland. The Emerald Isle, Hibernia, the nation that had saved the English from the Vikings in the year 873 and had regretted it ever since. Though scenic, it had never been a particularly good place to live even before the First anything-but-Glorious Revolution disenfranchised most of its population: wet, swampy, unable to support many people before the introduction of the potato changed everything. Ireland might be poetically green, but only because of all the rain. And since 1689, thunder and lightning had been added to that rain. Oh, the English had sought to expand power in Ireland ever sincec the Norman Conquest, but the rules of the game had changed since William III had become King of England. Once upon a time, to the English, Ireland had been that wild island full of cannibal barbarians, but now it was that desolate island full of priest-ridden traitors.

The intervening century had only served to deepen the divisions in Ireland between the relatively prosperous Protestants – concentrated in the old Plantations in Ulster – and the Catholics, who had been poor enough to begin with and suffered under a great deal of discriminatory laws. With each rising the situation got worse: Ireland had been a front in both the First Glorious Revolution and the Third Jacobite Rebellion that had formed part of the Second. Even when reform-minded Englishmen sought to end Catholic suffering in Ireland, they were angrily opposed by the Protestant Ascendancy Irish, who feared the fact that they were in a minority and jealously guarded their power.

It was fairly obvious to any objective commentator what had to happen. The Catholic Irish would rise again at some point. The last Jacobite rebellion had been cut down in 1750, almost fifty years ago, allowing plenty of time for angry young men to grow up and for old men to forget the sorrows of what had followed the past risings. All they required was something to distract the British, and that something was the Jacobin Wars with France.

Except. And it was a big except. Many historians today believe that the Catholics *would* have risen in their old manner, given a few more years as their organisations planned patiently...

Except the Protestants rebelled first.

On the face of it this was madness. Irish Protestants had a uniquely privileged position under the order imposed after the Williamite War and the following conflicts. They could both vote and serve in Parliament, enjoyed a disproportionate fraction of the island's scant wealth, and could go off to Britain and have more distinguished political careers there – as many did, not least Edmund Burke. To do anything to jeopardise that, to bite the hand that fed them, was inconceivable. But then so were many things that spun off the jagged wheel of Revolution.

Many Protestant Irish, especially the most politically active Presbyterians in Ulster, resented the fact that their parliament had little power compared to the one in London, which could go head-to-head with the King and win (and often did). By contrast, the Lords Lieutenant in Dublin, though often quite competent men, remained in an old-boy's-club network with the Irish parliamentarians and little ever really got accomplished. Those Protestants seeking reform initially cast themselves as Liberals, aping the moderate path that Burke had carved out in England. (Burke himself had spoken of the miserable situation of Irish politics, but not done a great deal himself about it). Many of these reformers hesitated at the question of Catholic emancipation, though. Even the most open-minded Irish Protestants were concerned at the thought of being out-voted by at least three to one, by men they considered to be ill-educated, superstitious and priest-ridden. Clearly, they could not be expected to understand modern enlightened politics.

The Revolution changed all that. France was undeniably a Catholic country and yet had launched the most radical political force ever witnessed in Europe. Revolutionary principles were far more popular in discussion in political circles in Scotland and Protestant Ireland than they were in England, not least because of the influence of Burke's bald condemnation: there was a paradoxical urge to see what all the fuss what about. Scotland had also suffered in the Jacobite Rebellions and had had a new road network built in King Frederick I's reign specifically to move British troops around more easily, putting down any future rebellions. However, these roads also meant that trade between Scottish cities picked up throughout the latter half of the eighteenth century, and by the late 1790s, Edinburgh and the newly industrialising Glasgow had as much of a trading class as London. And the men composing such a class both have the money to exert a sizeable political influence as a whole, and are singularly hostile to anything that constitutes a change in policy, much less a revolution. It might endanger their profits, after all. So in Scotland French Revolutionary ideas remained just idle talk—for now.

Not so in Ireland. Despite the Third Jacobite Rebellion, British attempts to build a new road network there had stalled, partly because of the more difficult terrain and partly because of the intricate land-ownership laws that meant getting permission from fifty landlords to build a mile's worth of road. Ireland remained a backwater relative to Britain, sleepy, impoverished, and with more longstanding grudges than you could shake the proverbial stick at. Ireland was ripe for revolution.

And yet among the Catholics who had the most grudges to hold, French ideas took little root. Partly it was simply that Protestant propaganda was not entirely a lie: many Catholics were illiterate and poorly-informed, and only heard about the Revolution through their village priests, who naturally took the Pope's orders and condemned the Revolution. However, there were also plenty of Catholics well-informed enough to make their own decision, and the vast majority rejected the Revolution.

No-one with anything more than the most desultory belief in his own religious identity would be anything but horrified by the treatment of Catholicism under Hébert and Robespierre. The vast majority of Catholics who *would* ignore such things in favour of Revolutionary fervour were typically those who had already converted to Anglicanism in order to gain greater powers and freedoms. Those that were left mostly held their faith sufficiently paramount to reject such compromises, much less endorse the ruthlessness of the Jacobins.

So it was that while the nascent United Society of Equals was theoretically a joint Catholic, Presbyterian and Anglican organisation, its membership was made up almost entirely of Presbyterians and Anglicans. A few unorthodox Catholic priests and others did join up, but more for symbolic reasons than anything. The Society was led by Tom Russell,[193] who notably said that "Religion has led to so many divisions, so many wars, on our island this last century…the only solution for peace is to do away with it." And as Sanchez later observed, they fulfilled the historical imperative common to most atheist movements, successfully achieving their goal of uniting the isle – *against themselves*.

Although rumours of the USE's existence were flying as early as 1795, the scale of the organisation did not become apparent until the summer of 1798. By this point, Robespierre in Paris was becoming increasingly paranoid about the possibility of a British invasion on the western coast of France, attacking the poorly defended lands while most of France's armies were committed to the invasion of Germany and Italy. As well as fatefully suggesting his strategy of marching raw recruits up and down the coast to persuade the British that there *were* troops stationed there, Boulanger stated that the best way to avoid a British intervention would be to give *les rosbifs* something to chew on closer to home. A naval attack, even a feint, was simply impossible for what was left of the Republican French Navy, which would be annihilated in combat with the Royal Navy even if the Royal French Navy

---

[193] Note the absence of Theobald Wolfe Tone, who has already left Ireland by this point in TTL…

stood aside rather than fighting their former comrades. With such a direct option off the table, that left a more subtle stirring up of trouble.

Lisieux had been using the 'Boulangerie' to build an intelligence network separate to Robespierre's (and superior to it, as it did not rely on flaming ideologues). He now learned of the activity of the Society, and how they desired a united republican Ireland without state religion and fully independent of Britain, with a powerful parliament. Robespierre signed up readily enough to the notion of spreading the revolution, his particular ambition, and was enthusiastic enough not to think to question where his information had come from.

Privately, though, Lisieux and Boulanger were certain that any rebellion launched by the Society would fail and they had no intention of supporting them any more than they had to. The important thing was that such a revolt would alarm the British and force them to divert troops to Ireland to subdue it, discouraging or delaying any planned offensive moves. Token support for the USE could be given with just a few smuggled shipments of weapons and printing presses for the production of propaganda pamphlets. Lisieux consulted the Boulangerie, and after patiently rejecting a helpful suggestion by Jean-Pierre Blanchard that they fly the supplies to Ireland in a fleet of balloons, secured the contacts they needed to effect the plan. It was almost impossible for French ships to sneak past the British blockade, at least in any numbers (isolated ships, as with *L'Épurateur* and *Le Rédacteur*, did manage to make it through on missions to the colonies).

Therefore, Lisieux co-opted Breton smugglers, little realising the import of his own actions at the time. But then how was he to know that one crate of pamphlets would be mistakenly left behind, opened by the Bretons' curious relatives, and then taken to Nantes for translation as few of them spoke good French?

The Society was contacted and, in October 1798, an already-planned rebellion was accelerated and amplified in scope by the French assistance. The French also sent some elite troops as token help along with General O'Neill, a politically suspect *ancien régime* Irish-exile general who had previously fought in Ireland during the Third Jacobite Rebellion.[194] What the British later referred to as the Great Ulster Scare exploded into existence with the USE seizing control of much of Ulster and parts of Leinster in the early days of its actions. The French supplies had helpfully included disassembled *chirurgiens* and they were soon reassembled and put to work, executing British- and Irish Parliament-appointed officials all across the province. Belfast was made the temporary capital of the new Revolutionary Irish Republic, but already USE forces were moving on Dublin. The relative speed of their offensive (and the fact that communications in Ireland rarely moved much faster than an army) meant that a large number of Irish MPs and Lords were in session in Parliament when the city fell to the USE and the building was burned down – with the lawmakers still inside it.

The British garrisons in Dublin and Belfast both fought hard, but had been cut back severely in recent years as Whitehall had moved more troops back to the South Coast in fear of an invasion—the Admiralty's estimates of Republican fleet strength were considerably exaggerated. Despite their valour, the remaining troops eventually succumbed to the USE fighters. Worst of all, and widely reported by Liberal Whig newspapers in England, was the fact that the USE fought harder and more skilfully than previous Irish rebellions. Why? Because so many of its members were veterans of Britain's wars in India and America. Protestant Irish could serve in the British Army, after all. This was no longer peasants with pitchforks territory: anyone could be under suspicion, even the titled gentleman with the whimsical accent in the corner of your club's bar.

The problem for Britain was that news of the rebellion did not reach London until it had already exploded out of any ability to be contained. Naturally rumours also amplified the often sketchy reports. Before long men were seriously telling the ailing Marquess of Rockingham that Dublin had been entirely burnt to the ground. Confused reports inevitably led to anti-Catholic

---

[194] In OTL it was Hoche was sent to support a similar Irish rebellion and he died in the process, prematurely ending the career of a man who some say had the ambition and skill to match Napoleon.

riots in London.

The British government was in a quandary. By the time it became clear that the USE rebellion was too serious to ignore, the rebels already held much of Ulster and Leinster, including most of the island's east coast. The old British strategy of working with the Protestant Ascendancy and raising local militias could not succeed, partly because it was clear the Protestants could not longer be trusted, and partly because the main Protestant lands were already under USE control. Reports of the burning of churches of all denominations by the more radical wing of the USE served to inflame political passions in London. It was intolerable that Britain could allow French ideas to run riot over Ireland. Something had to be done, but what?

Rockingham's government had been considering an invasion of northwest France since 1796, and when the tide of war turned against Austria, preparations were stepped up so that the invasion could be launched in time to relieve the pressure on Austria before it was too late. Robespierre's paranoia of a British invasion had not been entirely unjustified. Now, though, Britain could hardly send those troops to France and ignore the rebels in Ireland, but sending a big part of the army over the Irish Sea would inevitably end up delaying the operation against France – possibly fatally for the anti-republican alliance, given Austria's rapidly deteriorating situation.

It was not an easy decision, but in the end Rockingham's mind was made up by reports coming out of Galway. One of the relatively few Irish parliamentarians who had not been present at the Battle of Dublin – and thus remained in the land of the living – was Richard Wesley, the second Earl of Mornington.[195] The Earl had fought in Bengal against Burmese-Arakan and in Haidarabad against Mysore, before returning to Ireland in 1793 on the death of his father and assuming the Earldom. Wesley was

---

[195] The Wellesley family was called Wesley before changing it to sound more English, which hasn't happened in TTL. In character the Richard Wesley of TTL is essentially an amalgam of OTL's brothers Arthur and Richard Wellesley, the Duke of Wellington and Earl of Mornington respectively.

a hard-headed Anglican and ultra-reactionary, who nonetheless grudgingly accepted for purely pragmatic reasons that Catholics should have equal rights. He fiercely rejected anything that smacked of French republicanism, though, even if the USE had not prominently listed his name on their ever-growing list of planned *chirurgien* patients.

Wesley is widely credited with diffusing the situation in Limerick, always the city that had been most resentful under Protestant rule, and whose Catholic population was ready to take advantage of the USE in order to rise up, even if they did not agree with the rebels' aims. Wesley donned his old East India Company colonel's uniform and ordered the British garrison to stand down and come out of their fortified buildings, then successfully bribed the city's innkeepers into providing a week-long 'celebration' with cheap drink. By the end of it, the British soldiers and the Protestant and Catholic townspeople were, if not quite old friends, close enough when faced with a common foe. Wesley used similar tactics elsewhere and by the end of the year was effectively king of Munster, also providing a rallying point for the people of Galway. The half of Ireland not occupied by the USE looked to one of their last surviving Parliamentarians for leadership, and Wesley had already proved himself to be more than the usual corrupt old landowners who had dominated the Dublin Parliament before going up in smoke.

He was also a soldier, and a soldier of India no less, used to the idea that Whitehall ever sending British regulars to a trouble spot in time to make a difference would be helpful but rather unlikely. Therefore, and in direct violation of the British Bill of Rights (which banned Catholics from owning firearms), Wesley raised an army from the strange, ramshackle realm he effectively ruled, using members of his own family as lieutenants. The British regulars already there, cut off from orders, were used as the core of his force and assigned to train new recruits. Often, both the Catholic and Protestant Irish grew to equally despise their British taskmasters, and shared hatred is always only one step away from comradeship. Perhaps Wesley even planned it that way.

So it was that when the USE went on the offensive again in

early 1799, Wesley successfully held them back at Roscommon and the historically important Kilkenny, where Prince Frederick had defeated Bonnie Prince Charlie. He requested assistance from London, and Rockingham decided he could spare three regiments from the planned invasion of France – whose implementation had become unavoidable due to the impending Austrian collapse. As the Seigneur Offensive left Chatham, Portsmouth, Plymouth and Lowestoft, then, those Royal Navy ships which remained were transporting those three regiments (the 23rd, the Royal Welch Fusiliers; the 58th (West Essex) Regiment of Foot,[196] and the 79th (New York) Regiment of Foot). Ironically, no loyalist Irish units abroad could be spared as they were all assigned to either the West Indies or the Maltese garrison at that time.

The Welsh, Essexmen and New Yorkers all landed at Limerick in March 1799 after a particularly choppy crossing, just as Prince Frederick had almost exactly fifty years earlier. By that point, Wesley's forces were confident enough with their string of victories and fighting retreats against the USE that they were able to view the pale, seasick redcoats with an air of superiority and contempt. Yet they were soon grateful enough for their arrival. The British and Americans had also brought food supplies, desperately needed given Wesley's strategy of not living off the land in order to gain the favour of the people who lived there— effectively a prototypical version of the later *guerre de tonnere* strategy. The new troops had also brought artillery companies. Most of the Royal Irish Artillery, based in Dublin, had been captured by the USE when they took the city, and though the USE had few trained artillerymen to use the guns, Wesley's army had formerly had little choice but to retreat whenever they were confronted by artillery they could not reply to.

Wesley's army met the USE's fighters in their first truly decisive engagement near Carlow in May. They were both heterogenous

---

[196] In OTL all the regimental numbers moved down two places after the British disbanded the two American regiments, the 50th and 51st, after the Seven Years' War, i.e. the 58th became the 56th. In TTL the American regiments were not disbanded and therefore the old numbers are retained.

forces, and both had some men in red uniforms (the USE's former soldiers had kept theirs) and some in civilian clothes. Therefore, they both adopted the old Civil War-era measure of wearing some brightly coloured token to identify them to their friends: the USE used an orange ribbon and Wesley's army a blue. The use by the USE of orange illustrates the Protestant majority that affected their thinking and traditions without them even realising it. This was also reflected in the rebels' flag, based on the French Bloody Flag but in orange rather than red and with an inverted Leinster harp rather than a fleur-de-lys.

The USE forces fought hard, but Wesley's new superiority in artillery was telling. The loyalist forces were not, perhaps, as effective as they might have been, however. The British and American colonels of the three new regiments were all sceptical about treating Wesley – a former East India colonel, not even a 'proper' one – as their general, and failed to respond to orders quite as rapidly as they might have. This perhaps contributed to the fact that a large part of the USE army was able to make a successful retreat under O'Neill. Still, the battle was remembered for the poetic way that the Royal Welch's grenadier company marched stolidly into the face of withering USE fire, flanked by Wesley's Irishmen, to the strains of 'British Grenadiers'.[197]

Though the Battle of Carlow was not as great a victory for the loyalists as it could have been, it effectively ended the USE's winning streak and their increasingly uncertain supporters began to melt back into the woodwork as Wesley took Kildare and the West Essex, supported by Irish recruits under Wesley's younger brother George, secured Wicklow. In doing so they bypassed a small USE army in the south of Leinster, which congregated on Wexford and then dissolved in panic from the news from the north, some of its members eventually escaping to France or the UPSA.

The USE's armies regrouped to defend Dublin, which was bloodily fought over throughout September as Wesley laid siege. In the end, the city's walls were successfully escaladed by the

---

[197] In OTL the Royal Welch did this during the American Revolutionary War.

New Yorkers, as is told in Robert Tekakwitha's epic *True Liberty*, with so many good men being shot down from their ladders by USE sharpshooters. Yet the New Yorkers did it, and one of their number – a certain James Roosevelt – had his revenge by gunning down General O'Neill with his Ferguson rifle.[198] This feat already made him something of a household name, but, of course, there would be even greater things in store for the young man.

Wesley's army was initially consumed by the usual rapine fervour for looting and burning that flows freely when an army finally takes a fiercely defended city. After all, even his Irish troops were mostly recruited from distant Munster and Connaught and might not always have shared a sense of comradeship with the people of Dublin. Nonetheless they sobered when they saw the burned-out wreck that was all that remained of the Irish Parliament. Some men even swore that the horrible roast-pork smell of burnt human flesh clung to it forever.

The final defeat of the USE did not come until Christmas, though Belfast was the last city they truly fought to defend. Wesley's army was not so restrained this time and angry reports of rape and murder against the locals circulated throughout Britain and Ireland. Russell took poison rather than fall into British hands and face executed for treason, naturally—and perhaps intentionally—creating a legend that he had survived to escape and/or would return in Ireland's hour of need. Many men of the USE escaped or faded back into Irish society as a whole. Being 'accused of Equalitarian leanings' was for time a witch-hunt accusation in Ireland, levelled against many inoffensive men and women against whom their accuser had a grudge.

The situation in Ireland did not stabilise for a long time. Whitehall, busy with the war with France, did not have much time to consider what to do next, and full order and communications were not restored until mid-1800. By that point, of course, Wesley

---

[198] The Ferguson breech-loading rifle has still been invented in TTL's 1770s. Much like OTL, the British military establishment is still dubious about it, but it has enjoyed much popularity as a hunting weapon in the Empire of North America, and New York regiments in particular have adopted it as the weapon of choice for their Rifle skirmisher companies.

was firmly ensconced in an informal position of power, and he had his own ideas about the island's future course…

Chapter 35: The Empire Spreads Her Wings

"In 1751, we won our independence as the Empire. In 1788, we won the right to elect our own representatives to our own Parliament. But it was in 1796 that North America, her own house put in order, first began to reach out to the world…"

– introduction to a North American school history textbook, 1892

From: "A History of North America" by Dr Paul Daycliffe (William and Mary, 1964)—

In reaction to the mob attacks on the British and American ministers in Paris, on September 2nd, 1795, the British House of Commons voted 385 to 164 in favour of a declaration of war against Revolutionary France. This was matched in November 14th by a vote of 46-9 in the Continental Parliament, which was particularly outraged by the treatment of Thomas Jefferson, and this swung over many Constitutionalists who would otherwise have sympathised with the motives of the Revolution.

Almost immediately thereafter, commentators in both countries began to consider by what mode the war against France would take. The Admiralty and Horse Guards had, of course, made considerable plans for a future war with France, as this seemed to be a rather predictable occurrence every two decades or so during the Age of Supremacy. However, such plans revolved around the geopolitical situation remaining more or less as it had been since the First War of Supremacy. British Continental policy was largely aimed at attacking France via continental proxies such as Austria or Prussia, paid off with British funds and backed by British-controlled Hanover and British-influenced Brunswick. The main thrust of Britain's own war effort would be outside

Europe, taking more colonies from France (with the assistance of the Empire of North America) and undermining French influence in independent states such as Ayutthaya.

These plans all went up in smoke when the Burke Strategy, as it was later called, was implemented in 1795. Against the views of opportunists, who initially included the Prime Minister Lord Rockingham himself, Parliament voted not to take advantage of the French Revolution in order to sweep up French colonies around the world, but on the contrary to make sure as many of them as possible *stayed* French and declared loyalty to the Dauphin, now King Louis XVII in British eyes. This ideologically-based rather than opportunistic approach shocked the British public establishment and reflected the brief but intense feeling of outrage that the attacks on Jefferson and Grenville had caused. The French Republic was too dangerous to allow to exist, even if it had led to the downfall of Britain's old enemy, the Bourbon monarchy. "Better the devil you know than the Jacobin you also know all too well," as the Marquess of Bute[199] said in his famously mangled quote.

The new war plan resulted in much head-scratching at the Admiralty and Horse Guards, and not merely from the crusty oldtimers who were unable to contemplate an alliance with any kind of French on principle. Britain's war strategies had always been primarily naval, and various mutinies and Leo Bone's trick at Toulon meant that Revolutionary France was unlikely to attempt a naval invasion of Britain or any major sea operations at all. Additionally, with the Royal French Navy loyal to the Dauphin (Louis XVII), the combined forces easily had enough ships to blockade all the French ports *and* sweep the seas for any Revolutionary ships that did get out. This overwhelming superiority was, paradoxically, met with a sense of depression from the Royal Navy, whose captains disliked the prospect of a war filled with dull blockade and convoy duty and with little chance of taking prizes.

---

[199] John Stuart, 4th Earl of Bute, 2nd Marquess of Bute (in TTL the 3rd Earl was made Marquess as he remained in opposition and never became the unpopular Prime Minister he was in OTL).

The British Army, on the other hand, faced the opposite problem. It had always been small by continental standards and rarely fought alone, always backed up by big forces from allies among the German states –which ones were allies and which were enemies changed regularly in the 'stately quadrille'. The Army was professional enough but lacked the European armies' experience of fighting on modern battlefields – it was more used to lending a regiment or two to a skirmish in America, India or elsewhere, participating with local forces. And given the *Armée républicaine françaises*'s gradually increasing successes in the war with Austria, it looked as though the British Army would eventually have to send forces to assist the Austrians or even (as the war wore on) to prevent Hanover and the current allied German states from falling to French invasion.

The solution was to increase recruitment, which always caused headaches at Horse Guards. The British people remained violently opposed to the idea of a large standing army: memories of Cromwell's military coup ran deep. The creation of any standing army, except by the express consent of Parliament, was specifically forbidden in the British Constitution. Even considering the current situation, Horse Guards had to tread very carefully in a call for increased recruitment. It was true that the country was ripe to give up a larger number of suitable recruits than the past, though. Britain's Army had always recruited a disproportionate number of down-on-their-luck commoners, including petty criminals, and the burgeoning Industrial Revolution was producing plenty of those—as people moved from the countryside to the industrialising cities to find jobs and often found poverty and starvation instead. Also, the Navy's lack of need for recruitment above peace levels meant that the Naval press-gangs were not operating, freeing up more men of the right age for army service instead. The recruiting sergeants spun tales of rich plunder to be had in the Germanies, and the young men signed up, apparently not wondering why that if those sergeants had seen such plunder, they remained sergeants.

Yet the numbers raised still did not come close to Horse Guards' estimates for a force required to defend Hanover and support Austria. Reports of both Boulanger's new tactics and the superiority of French artillery (both in the Gribeauval system and the Cugnot steam tractors) were at first exaggerated in Britain, and Horse Guards generally considered that the only immediate response would be to try to achieve numerical superiority over any French army faced in the field. Given the vastness of Boulanger's conscript armies, this seemed futile, but of course instituting conscription in Britain would be seen as utter madness and would doubtless lead to the Government falling.

Therefore, Horse Guards turned to rather unorthodox solutions. The organisation, originally very old-fashioned (even compared to the Navy) had been severely purged by King Frederick I after the Second Glorious Revolution to weed out anyone who might 1) disagree with his right to the throne and 2) have the influence to raise an army to support that disagreement. An unintended consequence of this was that Horse Guards had become far more open to new ideas, particularly since Frederick had introduced a number of loyal American military veterans to positions of power. Even after Frederick's reign, this had continued, particularly since there were now a reasonable number of American regiments on the lists contributing worthy officers.

The Commander-in-Chief of the British Army at that point was Jeffrey Amherst, 1st Viscount Amherst.[200] Although a Kentish Man born and bred, he had served for most of his career in North America, fighting the French in the Third War of Supremacy under Wolfe, and had served as military governor of the Lake Michigan region immediately after the war.[201] Amherst's own detailed notes and explorations of the region were used extensively by the Michigan Commission, the body which planted what would become the Susan-Mary Penal Colony some years after Amherst's death. Amherst was considered 'more than half a Jonathon' by some of the more fossilised parts of the Army bureaucracy (even though he himself was in his eighties), and

---

[200] As in OTL, although OTL he was only a Baron.
[201] OTL Amherst was governor of Canada and then of Virginia – TTL Wolfe is governor of Canada and Virginia now gets native-born Americans appointed as governors.

had overseen several appointments of senior American officers to Horse Guards posts.

One of these was General Sir Fairfax Washington, second son of the by now deceased Lawrence Washington and brother of James Washington, 2nd Marquess of Fredericksburg.[202] Sir Fairfax had cut his military teeth as a young lieutenant of the Virginia militia in the Indian wars, then had served as a captain of the newly created 63rd (Virginia) Regiment of Foot, which had fought under his uncle General George Washington in the Plate during the Second Platinean War. He had risen to become colonel of the regiment, then had in 1791 become Master General of the Ordnance. Sir Fairfax's tenure was noted for his support for Henry Shrapnel and Douglas Philips' development of a hail shot, a hollow cannonball filled with musket balls and gunpowder, which exploded in midair (in theory) and had the same bloody effect as canister on close-packed enemy troops, but at a much greater range. The hail shot was later one of the British Army's best weapons against the close-packed French columns they faced.[203]

However, Sir Fairfax is best remembered for his participation in the recruitment crisis of 1795 and 1796. He suggested to Amherst that they increase recruitment in the Empire of North America, to which Amherst was sceptical: he pointed out that America's open expanses of new land to be settled meant that there was less chance of producing the down-on-their-luck young men that the British Army relied on for its recruitment. Sir Fairfax countered that settlement had presently largely stalled in some of the Confederations, such as Carolina and New York, and even in those still opened up to settlement, not all young men could afford to buy their own land. The promise of plunder in a European war to finance their plans might be very attractive...

---

[202] OTL, before his death from tuberculosis at a young age, Lawrence Washington had four children, none of which survived beyond youth. He both lives longer himself and has surviving children in TTL, who naturally share some names with those from OTL.

[203] In OTL Shrapnel worked alone and his weapon was known as case shot (though today it is often referred to eponymously as a Shrapnel shell).

Amherst agreed and put the proposal to King George, who accepted readily. Parliament was less enthusiastic, though a slim majority favoured the proposals. However, Sir Fairfax realised that the practice of having to appeal to Parliament to raise each new regiment would hamstring and slow down the programme too much. Together with Amherst, and with Royal backing from the King, they launched the American Regiments Bill, which sought to transfer the responsibility for raising American regiments from Westminster to Fredericksburg. This was considered greatly controversial in the British political scene, but happily for Sir Fairfax, coincided with the reports of Boulanger's shock defeat of Mozart in November. As usual a week is a long time in politics, and for that week the chattering classes were consumed with the certainty that the French Jacobin forces would carry all before them and that the Hanoverian Dominions needed all the regiments they could get. It did not matter that in a week or two, when reports of Ney's retreat from Lorraine emerged, they became equally certain that the French Jacobin armies were doomed—because it was during that week that the American Regiments Act (1795) was passed.

The Act was somewhat watered down by the House of Lords, but passed in its original spirit. It was joined in February 1796 by the Shipping Act (1796) which, among other things, increased the authority of American dockyards to build ships to a Royal Naval standard. However, the Admiralty remained unified and based in London, it being assumed at this point that any American contribution to the naval war effort would be minor and superfluous, given British and Royal French overwhelming numerical superiority.

The grandly named Commission for Continental Regiments was created by an act of the Continental Parliament in April 1796 and took up office in the Cornubia Palace, a building originally intended for King Frederick's royal residency in America but in practice usually empty, as when the royals visited America they usually travelled between the colonies and stayed as the guests of the local nobles. The Palace was large enough to be filled out with several other newly created Continental Commissions (essentially the early American version of departments of State) as the war wore on. In order that Westminster might be able to demand accountability of American actions, a further Act was passed in 1797 which saw a Special Commissioner for Home Affairs appointed, essentially an American minister to Britain in all but name, mirroring the Lord Deputy. The first of these was Albert Gallatin of New York, appointed by his key political ally Lord Hamilton the Lord President. As Gallatin's and Hamilton's great political enemy, Governor Aaron Burr of New York (and a noted anglophobe) remarked sourly, 'Well, he has managed to gain profitable relations with the savages of the forests and rivers to the west; now let him attempt it with those on the foggy island to the east.'

At the founding of the CCR, only eight American regiments actually existed: the 80th Royal Pennsylvania Rifles, the 14th King's Own Philadelphian Dragoons, the 63rd (Virginia) Foot, the 79th (New York) Foot, the Royal American Company of Artillery (not numbered, and recruited from across the Empire), the 84th (Carolina) Foot, the 78th New England Rifles, and the 83rd (New England) Foot. The first new regiment to be formed was the 99th (Pennsylvania) Foot, that Confederation originally having preferred to rely on its own militia than form a regiment of the Line, but the lessons learned from the Lenape War showing the folly of that approach. Five new regiments were formed between May 1796 and September 1798, when the 'Seigneur Offensive', the invasion of the western coast of France, was launched. The vast majority of their men were still considered green by that point, despite having been drilled by veteran American sergeants from the Second Platinean War. However, even those that were not fit to fight in France were still useful: assigned to the frontier forts, they filled the boots of the more competent troops who had originally been stuck there, freeing them up for France while still warning off Indian raids. Ironically, this was the same tactic, on Robespierre's part, which was responsible for the immediate success of 'Seigneur'…

The American regiments taking part in the invasion of France were the 80th, the 84th and the 78th Rifles, while the 79th

New Yorkers were busy assisting Lord Mornington in quelling the USE rebellion in Ireland. Generally speaking, however, throughout the course of the war, the greatest contributions to the army came from New York and Carolina. These were the two Confederations least concerned with westward settlement, Carolina's way mostly blocked by the Cherokee and Royal-French Louisiana, New York's by the Great Lakes and the Iroquois. Pennsylvania was also a fairly large contributor but remained concerned with securing its newly won western lands from the Indians. Virginia and New England did contribute forces, but not in proportion to their population, and the reason for this was that they (specifically Boston and Norfolk) were centres for the new American shipbuilding programme permitted by the Shipping Act. Although the captains acceded through the usual precedence on the post-lists, the crews were often drawn locally, and thus fewer recruits were available for the Army regiments.

And of course it was one of the Boston dockyards that built the most famous American ship of them all, HIMS *Enterprize...*

Chapter 36: Cross of Fire, Heart of Blood

"Dieu, et mon droit."

– Louis XVII's first words upon setting foot on the soil of
Brittany

*From: "The Jacobin Wars" by E.G. Christie (Hetherington Publishing
House, 1926)–*

Looking back on the issue, many historians have found it
rather strange that the French Republican government under
Robespierre had not foreseen the fact that Brittany and the
Vendée would be trouble spots for the Revolution. Both areas
had benefited under the same quirks of the *ancien régime* that the
urbanite supporters of the Revolution had hated. In the words of
Arthur Spencer, "no farmer has ever complained about a law that
makes it more difficult for him to pay taxes to the government".
As a Duchy, Brittany continued to enjoy special privileges and
autonomy under the Kingdom of France, including its own
relatively powerful *parlement*.

The Vendée, though having no such special constitutional
status, possessed a nobility that was more down-to-earth and less
divided from commoners than that in Paris, and the excesses of
the Revolution against the First Estate shocked Vendean public
opinion. But it was those against the Second Estate that really
clinched it. Perhaps because it had been a battleground between
Protestant Huguenots and Catholics two centuries before, the
Vendeans were some of the more fiercely devout Catholics in all
France. Anti-clerical measures on the part of the Revolution –
both relatively passive ones such as stopping clerical privileges,
and active ones such as Hébert's pogroms – served to further align
Vendean feeling against the Republican government.

The strange part was that there was no open rebellion for the first three years of the Republic's existence. This was simply because, to oversimplify somewhat, no-one had ever been sent from Paris to check that the western provinces remained loyal to Paris. The idea that *to possess the capital city is to possess the state* (or more coloquially, 'to hold the heart is to hold the nation') was a cornerstone of Revolutionary thinking. The Republicans' possession of Paris did serve to turn much undecided French public opinion to their side in the early days. However, Brittany in particular had been largely unaffected even by the trend towards centralisation during the days of Bourbon absolutism. It was not a case of rebellion in the years between the King's phlogistication and 1798: simply that Vendean and Breton officials ignored any pronouncements coming out of Paris. Even though Robespierre feared a British invasion of the western coast of France, the Republican government did not try to enforce its authority there simply because it was focused entirely on defeating Austria.

This changed in 1798. At a meeting between the three Consuls (Jean-Baptiste Robespierre, Pierre Boulanger and Jean de Lisieux) in Christmas 1797 (a.k.a. Chien Nivôse de l'an Deux), Robespierre voiced his fear of a British invasion, noting that no real troops could be spared from the planned invasion of Germany, the Rubicon Offensive. Boulanger had suggested that the *Armée républicaine françaises* (ARF) instead use the western coastlands as training ground for raw recruits, marching them up and down to provide a convincing military presence for any British spies. Robespierre had agreed, noting that this would also help extend governmental control into an area that had been reported (vaguely) to be…difficult.

Ironically, it was this move that first sparked rebellion in the west. The first French recruits left their barracks in March 1798, at around the same time as the launching of Rubicon in the east. Initially Boulanger's plan worked, with overly nervous British agents reporting that the French were moving troops in to secure the west, and that the British government's planned Seigneur Offensive would have to be cancelled. However, even as the doddering Marquess of Rockingham hesitated, things came to a head. The recruits were drawn from all over France, practically foreigners to many of the locals, and they were led by drill sergeants often considered too undisciplined to be serving against Austria. And one of the things the troops practised was Boulanger's strategy of living off the land. The result was a reign of terror against the local people, with looting and 'confiscation' rife. The troops were used to a world, by now, where one could get away with anything if one could bluff the other person into thinking one had sanction from Robespierre. The Vendeans did not dwell in that world.

Historians are divided on what incident first sparked off the Chouannerie, just as they are on the causes of the Jacobin Revolution. Many people have drawn attention to a particular crime, the rape of a mother superior, the burning down of a noble's house with his family still inside, the desecration of a church. It is quite probable that we will never know for sure. What *is* known that, in an action similar to that of the Polish rebellion raging at the same time in Eastern Europe, many quietly organised rebel groups sprang into life on the same day: October 9th, the day of St Denis, patron saint of France. That day, Sarrasin Vendémiaire de l'an Trois, was also a day of celebration for the Republicans, at least before they heard about what was happening in the west. It was on this day that the French armies took Regensburg and the Holy Roman Empire breathed its last (q.v.)

Yet victory in the east came together with crisis in the west. The rebels, who called themselves *chouan*s after their owl-call recognition signal, conducted a surprisingly organised counter-revolutionary campaign in the first few days of their existence. Drunken recruits, fat from eating off the backs of the Vendean people, had their throats cut. Captured Republican officers were executed by the same *chirurgiens* they had unleashed on the local nobles. Bloody Flags were burned, hastily erected Temples of Reason blown up before their mortar could dry. The white flag of the monarchy came up, and with it was another: a red cross and heart on a white field, accompanied with the words *Dieu le Roi*, God the King – the Sacred Heart of the Vendée. The people had issued a challenge to the Revolution, the first serious one it had faced from within since Toulon.

The Vendeans were joined by the Bretons, who raised an army under Charles Armand Tuffin, the Marquis of Rouërie (or Rogery, as it was literally and amusingly translated by English journalists). Rouërie was a veteran of the Second Platinean War[204] and was generally liked by the Breton people, who saw him as one of them. The Bretons added the Vendean heart to their own ermine flag and joined the Vendeans in their campaign against the terrorising troops. By November, the Jacobin presence in the two provinces had been virtually wiped out. Royal France was no longer merely an *outre-mer* idea, a government in exile with some colonies. The King effectively once again held territory in France itself.

The Chouannerie consumed the attention of both the British and Republican French press in the winter of 1798, despite Robespierre's attempts to gag the latter. Equally, both nations' politicians began to demand intervention. In Parliament, when Charles James Fox naively attempted to condemn the Chouans for 'backsliding against the cause of liberty', he was booed down. It was at this point that Richard Burke, the still youthful son of Edmund, tabled his first Parliamentary motion by asking for British intervention on the side of the Chouans. Meanwhile in Paris, even the cowed rubber-stamp that Robespierre had reduced the National Legislative Assembly to nonetheless managed to pluck up the courage to insist on action.

It was not as though Robespierre himself disagreed, though. He had always considered Britain to be a dangerous enemy to have at one's back, and here was a blatant opportunity for the British to attack. The Consuls recognised that this would obviously have to be some sort of seaborne invasion, so one mode of action would be to attempt to intercept the British forces in the Channel (*La Manche*). However, when Lisieux asked Surcouf to consider a plan for such an eventuality, the pioneering sailor simply stared incredulously at him for half a minute before replying that it would be nothing more than a waste of lives. Republican France had only perhaps a third of the navy that pre-Revolutionary France

---

[204] In OTL he fought in the American Revolutionary War, usually referred to as 'Armand' in American sources.

had possessed, and that of often suspect loyalty and training. Too many good sailors had left with Leo Bone and joined the Dauphin in Britain. Surcouf suggested that either the Dutch or Spanish Navies could at least give the Royal Navy pause, though, if there were some way that they could be drawn into the war diplomatically.

This exchange is often used to illustrate the difference between Lisieux and Robespierre. Upon hearing this, and informing Surcouf that it was extremely unlikely that the services of the Dutch or Spanish could be acquired, Lisieux rejected the idea that the Republic could mount a serious challenge to Britain's forces enroute. They would simply have to find a way to defeat them on land. Robespierre, however, dismissed this opinion (and indeed Lisieux had to talk him out of sentencing Surcouf to a summary trial and execution for faint-heartedness). Having been told by one sailor that it was impossible, Robespierre simply asked another and another until he got the right answer. This came from Charles Villeneuve, a character who was afterwards considered a lunatic by both French sides, but bizarrely was quite popular among the British, who have always appreciated a really dramatic futile gesture, and he was sometimes referred to respectfully in the British press as 'Monsieur Newton', the direct translation of his name.

Villeneuve argued that much of the Royal Navy was dispersed around the world and that the home fleet would lack experience (apparently not being aware of the Royal Navy's practice of rotating ships between fleets fairly frequently). More sensibly, he pointed out the example of the Battle of Trafalgar in 1783: the British had lost to the Franco-Spanish forces, but had nonetheless achieved much of their objective (to stop the allies resupplying their forces in South America) as they had sunk many of the troop transport ships and forced others to turn back. Villeneuve suggested that the small French Republican Navy could force a similar Pyrrhic victory on the British invasion force now.

Aside from the questionable wisdom of a course of action that was assumed to end in the near-destruction of the Republican French fleet even if it succeeded, Villeneuve's plan fell short in other ways. Seigneur, as the British operation to cross the Channel and support the Chouans was called, was a far cry from the Second Platinean War operation Villeneuve had compared it to. The Franco-Spanish in that conflict had been trying to support troops thousands of miles away, across a vast ocean. The Channel, no matter how much some among the British might wish it was, was hardly an enormous gulf separating Britain from France. The French would have a very narrow window of opportunity to attack the British fleet, and furthermore if a British troopship was damaged, it might well be able to return to port, be repaired and out again within a day or two.

Nonetheless, Robespierre seized on the plan and approved it. Lisieux reluctantly consented, but he and Boulanger privately assumed that it was unlikely to work, and began secretly withdrawing forces from Germany to build up new armies to use against the Chouans. This is sometimes cited by historians as being the reason behind Mozart's victory at the Siege of Vienna in March 1799, but in truth the effects of the shift of troops did not really emerge until midsummer of that year. It was simply that Leroux's army had finally outrun its supply lines, despite Ney's efforts, and that the Jacobin armies' tactic of living off the land did not work very well when it came to besieging a city for months.

The British launched Seigneur in February. The political side of the plan was the brainchild of Richard Burke and the Dauphin, who had cooperated while the latter had been staying in London and raising support among French exiles there. Their political alliance and friendship meant that Louis XVII was exposed to the political system of the British Parliament, and recorded in his diary that it was: "…certainly not without its flaws…but, much like the table they keep, the constitution the British maintain is devoted to a solid, stodgy sense of stability…and in the aftermath of what we have witnessed, perhaps France needs such a monastic Diet for some time…" It is perhaps a blessing that the Dauphin had been born a prince rather than a journalist if he enjoyed puns of that type.

Seigneur was deployed from the four ports of Chatham, Portsmouth, Plymouth and Lowestoft. The first three contributed mainly British troopships carrying British or American troops and supported by British warships, while the Lowestoft fleet was a motley collection of borrowed troopships (some of them converted former slave-ships, a fact which Jacobin propagandists had much fun with), carrying the Most Catholic and Christian Royal Army of the King[205] and supported by the French Royal Navy ships that Leo Bone had 'rescued' from Toulon. The French force was commanded by the indecisive Admiral the Comte d'Estaing and his more competent subordinate Captain Etienne Lucas. The British Channel Squadron was under the overall command of Admiral Sir William Byng, the son of John Byng the hero of the Second Glorious Revolution. Under Byn's authority, the Plymouth fleet was commanded by Commodore Horatio Nelson, the Portsmouth fleet by Commodore Leo Bone, and the Chatham fleet by Rear-Admiral Adam Duncan, a senior veteran. Each force consisted of about a dozen ships of the line and twenty frigates, protecting around fifteen transports of various sizes carrying infantry, cavalry and artillery.

Against these four forces – which themselves only represented part of Britain's worldwide naval strength – Villeneuve had twenty ships of the line and eighteen frigates; most of the Republic's frigates had already been sent off by Surcouf on raiding or messenger missions. The British were aware, via their spy network (augmented by the fact that the Dauphin could call upon secret loyalists in France) that Villeneuve was concentrating his forces in Dieppe in order to raid any Channel-crossing force. However, British opinions of Villeneuve's capabilities were low. "The French spend more time repainting their ships than they do rolling out their guns," sneered Commodore Nelson in his diary, a reference to the new red-and-black Revolutionary chequer pattern that the Republican Navy had adopted.[206] The British made no serious attempts to harry Villeneuve's ships as they gathered from other French ports.

---

[205] This may sound parodically redundant but some actual French Loyalist forces in OTL had similar names.

[206] Ironically, as in OTL it was Nelson who popularised a (yellow and black) chequer pattern on Royal Navy ships.

Seigneur was launched on 14th February, St Valentine's Day—perhaps appropriate given the Sacred Heart symbol of the rebellion it sought to support. Villeneuve was kept well informed by his own intelligence network, a series of disguised fishing boats that communicated over the horizon using signal flags, and was informed of the launch bare hours later. He had more time to prepare because the British did not go straight across the Channel, instead forming up the four fleets to swing around Finisterre to the west and launch a concerted descent on Quiberon. Villeneuve launched his own forces on short notice: despite Nelson's scepticism, he had drilled his men well and they fought as well as could be expected considering the disadvantages they faced. Villeneuve was determined to intercept one of the British fleets before they combined: like Hoche on land in Italy, he believed that success might be grasped if he could divide the enemy and hit each portion with his whole force.

The wind was with Villeneuve and one of his ships, the *Égalité*, sighted the Chatham fleet before Admiral Duncan had joined the others. It was just as possible that Villeneuve could have found the Royal French fleet that was travelling through the same waters, and some speculative romantics have considered the consequences of what might have happened if Villeneuve had managed to sink the Dauphin's ship.

But no: Villeneuve attacked Duncan with the divide-and-conquer strategy he had developed. The French ships of the line formed the usual line against their British counterparts, tying them down, while the frigates ignored their British counterparts and engaged the transports directly, suffering damage as their did so. Villeneuve's aggressive action was surprisingly successful in the short term: though the French lost eight ships of the line and ten frigates (against ten and three British, respectively), the French frigates managed to sink half the British transports before the others' captains, deciding that their own escorts were not doing their job, gybed and returned to port. Villeneuve, his objective completed, ordered a withdrawal and regrouping. This required leaving some damaged French ships behind, but Duncan was unable to pursue. French gunnery tactics focused on attacking the masts, sails and rigging, with the result that many British ships were left only lightly damaged but disabled. Duncan's remaining movement-capable forces, mostly frigates, were not enough to challenge even Villeneuve's wounded fleet. Two frigates tried and were hulled at long range by French stern chasers before they could reply.

Villeneuve's attack had been remarkably successful, though he had lost a significant part of his own force in the process. Deciding that today was his day of luck, he decided to find another British force, but soon his scouts reported that the two remaining British fleets and the Royal French had successfully amalgamated off Portland and, having waited for a day for Duncan, had given up and set sail for Finisterre.

The French Admiral pursued, setting a course for destiny…

Chapter 37: And Charlemagne Wept

"The Holy Roman Empire is neither holy,
nor Roman, nor an Empire"

– Voltaire

From: "The Jacobin Wars – the Italo-German Front" by Joshua H. Calhoun (University of New York Press, 1946)—

Not since the Third War of Supremacy had Austrian forces been so outclassed. Forty years later, history repeated itself as battle after battle went the way of the enemy. Thibault Leroux was no Frederick II of Prussia,[207] but he did not need to be. Unlike the Prussians of their grandfathers' day, the French were not fighting with outnumbered forces against two or three powerful foes at once. With the increasing dispersion of the German states' armies to defend their own frontiers, the forces that Vienna could bring to bear were sloughing off thousands daily without ever meeting the enemy.

The chaos of the unilateral withdrawals also served to more directly hurt the Austrian war effort, as Ferdinand IV's ministers would assume a town defended by loyal Hessian or Saxon troops, only to learn days later that they had abandoned it to the French. Sometimes an Austrian army under a good commander would make a stand and hold back one of Leroux's armies, only to have to withdraw anyway, as the French had almost surrounded them by occupying areas that had been abandoned by Austrian allies. Such was the terrible beauty of the War of Lightning strategy: the French's rapid advance had been the cause of the withdrawals in the first place, as the German states looked nervously at the

---

[207] NB in TTL he is not remembered as Frederick the Great, because Prussia lost the war badly in the end, despite his early victories.

fate of Baden and Württemburg; and now those withdrawals only aided the speed of the French drive to the east. It was a vicious circle, ever decreasing in diameter, and Austria's survival sat at its heart.

Only Brunswicker and Hanoverian troops, backed by token British forces, continued to fight on, but they were too small in number to provide much help to the Austrians. Matters worsened as the Second War of the Polish Succession heated up, threatening to spill over into states bordering Saxony and Prussia, and states such as Mecklenburg – which had previously left their armies in place, considering their home territories not threatened by the French – joined the general withdrawal. The pan-German alliance, the attempt to rebuild the Holy Empire in spirit as well as name, had crumbled long before the French reached Regensburg.

The total defeat of Davidovich at Burgau in August 1798 resounded throughout all of Germany. Davidovich's army had been Austria's last hope of stopping the French advance before it entered Bavaria – which was now considered part of Austria's core territory by the Hapsburgs since the land exchange in 1783. The Bavarian army was as yet not integrated with its Austrian counterpart, and many Bavarians were unenthusiastic about being part of Austria. Ferdinand IV feared that the French might find willing collaborators in the country, which would be both a disaster for Austria in general and sound the death knell for his attempts to reunite Germany. The current withdrawals were helping the French indirectly, but if Germans openly embraced Revolution and fought other Germans, then all was lost.

Leroux's advance stalled somewhat throughout September. The War of Lightning was not about taking and holding territory; that was the task of follow-up operations, such as those that Ney was now pursuing in Swabia, having made his base of operations at Stuttgart. No, the goal for Leroux was simply to remain on the offensive, aggressively attacking along a narrow axis of advance aimed at Regensburg, and then Vienna. The Revolutionary doctrine of *to hold the heart is to hold the nation* was about to be tested.[208]

---

[208] This is before it was exploded the Chouannerie, which begins in Oc-

But Leroux realised that the Austrians would fight tooth and nail here, and if they remained on the defensive, the French could easily expend their strength and achieve nothing. Things were fragile. French victory rested on, not solid military power, but an *idea*, the idea among the Germans that their invincible armies could be anywhere, everywhere, and were backed up by a horde who devastated the lands in their wake. If Leroux was routed at Regensburg, that image of invincibility would collapse. Ney's position was still delicate, and if the Badenese and Württembergers rose up in combination with a renewed Austrian offensive, the French position in Germany could yet collapse. Determined to avoid that nightmare scenario, Leroux allowed the advance to slow while he built up his forces, waiting for the ammunition wagons to catch up (some pulled by horses, others by steam *fardiers*) and for Ney to send reinforcements through.

This gave the Hapsburgs a few weeks to prepare. Mozart had been placed in command once again by Ferdinand IV, and he withdrew the majority of the Austrian armies to Lower Austria itself. Mozart, an insightful general, had discerned the French strategy of aiming at possession of the capital. Therefore, he reasoned, if the French could be defeated at Vienna then their whole plan would come apart and Austria might be saved. He knew that they would first aim for Regensburg, but believed that there was simply not enough time to reinforce the Holy Roman capital, and that to do so would only fruitlessly throw away men that woul be needed to defend Vienna. He authorised only a single army under Alvinczi as a delaying force, then began to bring in troops from all across the Hapsburg dominions.

Archduke Ferdinand's army came up through the Brenner Pass, leaving a small guard to prevent Hoche's force from following. Using the Alpine terrain against the French just as Marat's Swiss Republic forces had against them the previous year, the Austrians were able to wear down Hoche's already depleted forces sufficiently that even that dynamic general gave up and retreated to Venice. Officials and garrison troops sent from Paris were already converting Venetia into an integral part of Hoche's

tober 1798.

341

invented Italian Republic, which also encompassed Piedmont, Modena, Parma, and Milan.

Also, echoing Maria Theresa's efforts of fifty years before, Mozart called up levies from the Hapsburg possessions in the east: Hungarians, Croats, Transylvanians. An attempt to levy troops from Krakau failed, with the city practically in revolt due to the war in Poland next door. However, these forces served to bolster the Austrians massing in Lower Austria. Mozart ordered the building of new defensive fortifications, mostly makeshift, knowing that he had little time. Vienna had resisted two sieges from the Turks, from the east, but could it survive this outbreak of new barbarism from the west?

Meanwhile, Ferdinand IV arrived in Regensburg to address the Reichstag. The Emperor, it was universally agreed by eye-witnesses, was not a well man. He had spent the past three years pacing up and down the Schönbrunn Palace, being fed gradually worsening news from messengers from the front. Perhaps even more damaging to him than the stories of defeats and reversals were those that told him that he was betrayed, that his great dream to recreate a Holy Roman Empire worthy of the name was dead forever. He first began to visibly sicken upon hearing of Charles Theodore of Flanders' betrayal and non-aggression treaty with France, and had rapidly worsened after the successes of the Poséidon and Rubicon offensives.

Now, on October 9th, he addressed the Reichstag in the city hall of Regensburg, where it had been meeting permanently for the last century and a half. Representatives of all the German states were there, though most of those states had practically withdrawn unto themselves and now remained in isolation, hoping that the French would pass over them like the angel of death if they made no aggressive moves. The Reichstag was a strange organisation. Ever since it had settled down in Regensburg, it had become gradually more and more divorced from real events in wider Germany, and had produced an elite ruling class of politicians and civil servants who had more in common with each other than either had with the states they were supposed to be representing. Even now, the Saxon and Brandenburger (Prussian) representatives discussed matters cordially, while their homelands fought a vicious, bloody war over the fate of Poland. It had an air of unreality, otherworldliness, as though concerns of the outside world could never come here.

But that was a lie. Even as Ferdinand IV stood up to address the Reichstag, the first distant rumbles began to sound on the horizon. Not thunder, something far worse. Leroux was on the move, his Cugnot-propelled heavy artillery in the lead, blasting a path through Alvinczi's lines west of the city.

Despite this distraction, Ferdinand IV commanded the whole attention of the Reichstag. His eyes wild and staring, dead with hopelessness, the Emperor gave his infamous Dissolution Speech, culminating in:

"We are betrayed. The Empire is no more. I have failed as Emperor, and let that name die with me. The French are coming, and you must look to yourselves...as you already have. No more shall come from Vienna. I am the new Romulus Augustulus, and behold, my Odoacer comes out of Gallia! It is finished. Go! Take your fools' baubles, and beg the Lord for mercy!"

By the end of his speech, the Emperor was having to shout, both over the words of outrage from the Reichstag and the thunder of the French guns from outside, as Alvinczi's army was crushed. Ferdinand IV became red in the face with the effort, after he had remained in the Schönbrunn Palace and weakened for so long, and bare seconds after getting out the word 'mercy', he collapsed. The Reichstag descended into chaos, and it did not take long for the rumour to emerge – the rumour that was the truth. Emperor Ferdinand IV, Ferdinand the Last, had died from a heart attack.

The Holy Roman Empire was unique in its own way. Though the Empire had been made hereditary centuries ago, Joseph's heir the young Archduke Francis would only become King of the Romans on his death. It was required that the Council of Electors confirm him before he become Emperor Francis II, and now the Council of Electors fled from the Regensburg city hall, followed by the Council of Princes and the Council of Cities. Legend says, though it has not been backed up by any historian, that the first one out of the door was the representative of Charles Theodore of Flanders and the Palatinate, the first Prince-Elector to betray Ferdinand, and he was followed by those of the Margrave of Brandenburg and the Duke of Saxony. But in the end they all fled the city. They had all heard of the rumours from the west, of how the wild Sans-Culottes troops would lock all the nobles of a town in the city hall and then burn it down, capering and whooping as the sick stink of burning flesh wafted over the countryside.

Once the Reichstag had fled, the collapse at Regensburg was swiftly precipitated. Although Alvinczi himself escaped with a portion of his army, the French rolled over the city and burned down the city hall, even though no-one remained within. Both the Protestant mayor of Regensburg and the Roman Catholic archbishop – Regensburg was technically five states in the Reichstag, with the Protestant Imperial City and the Catholic archbishopric and three monasteries – attempted to surrender the city to the French, only to be cut down by the raging Sans-Culottes. Despite Leroux's efforts to moderate the slaughter, the French armies were out of control and the sack of the city culminated in a fire that destroyed large portions of it. The monasteries were 'requisitioned', with the monks thrown out and the buildings used as arsenals.

Leroux was furious, both because the sack had destroyed much of the supplies he had hoped to obtain from the city, and because he had lost much of his chance for gaining support from the people of Bavaria. He pressed on regardless, reassembling the army, bringing it back under control. Regensburg was possessed by the forces of Revolutionary France. All that remained now was to take Vienna.

And yet, on the same day, the Vendeans and Bretons rose up in the Chouannerie, and in the darkest hour of Germany, a faint hope began to bloom that the Revolution's hellish triumphs would one day come to an end…

Chapter 38: Confrontations

"The great Chinese writer Sun Tsuy[209] writes that if you know your enemies and know yourself, you will not be imperilled in a hundred battles; whereas if you do not know your enemies but do know yourself, you will win only half the time. This is unsurprising, as any politicially aware individual will know that half the real enemies lie within..."

– General Pavel Alexandrovich Andreyev, 1924

From: "The Sons of George III and I", by Philip Hittle, University of Philadelphia Press (1948)–

After his father's unconventional marriage, the British establishment was desperate to return to a policy of dynastic alliances with George III. British attempts to form alliances with the royal houses of Germany – marrying off daughters and granddaughters of George I to the rulers of Denmark, Prussia, the Netherlands and many more – had stalled with the Second Glorious Revolution, for Frederick I had become estranged from most of his sisters and aunts. British influence in the Germanies waned, and was only slightly restored when Frederick's only daughter Princess Mildred was married to King Johannes II of Denmark.

From the perspective of the establishment, it would be better to walk before one could run. Hanover itself had grown gradually more distant from Britain over the years, the branches of the

---

[209] Russified transliteration of Sun Tzu. To avoid confusion, there has not been a consistent attempt to use the Russian-influenced form of Chinese transliteration most commonly used in TTL, but occasionally names of prominent figures whose names are often left in older transliterations in OTL, e.g. Confucius, have been depicted in this way.

House of Hanover still living there mostly having preferred William IV to Frederick and being suspicious about the manner of his death. The governments of Rockingham and Portland (*de facto*, Burke) were determined to rebuild the bridge between Britain and Hanover with ties of blood. To that end, George III married his cousin Princess Sophia of Hanover, the daughter of Frederick's sister Princess Amelia Sophia.[210]

The marriage, though not as violent perhaps as that of his grandfather George II, was certainly loveless and it is generally acknowledged that George III maintained an American mistress. However, as it often paradoxically the case, it produced a large issue, whereas Frederick's had only led to three surviving children – George III, Frederick William the Duke of York, and Princess Mildred, who became Queen of Denmark. George III, by contrast, was father to Prince Frederick George the Prince of Wales, his heir (born in 1765), Princess Carolina (born 1767), who became the Landgravine of Hesse-Kassel; then a gap due to two sons dying in infancy; then Princess Amelia (born 1770), who became the Duchess of Brunswick after marrying her cousin the Duke, sealing one of the rifts Frederick I had opened up; then Prince Henry William, the Duke of Cambridge (born 1771) and finally Princess Augusta (born 1772), who never married.

Prince Frederick George was a dashing and popular heir, generally agreed to embody many of the best traits of his namesake grandfather. He became an officer in the British Army, serving in America against the Indians and then leading an army to Flanders during the early stages of the Jacobin Wars. Although that incident ended with an embarrassing withdrawal due to Charles Theodore's declaration of neutrality, most men believed that Frederick William was a decent commander, and not so arrogant that he did not delegate to more experienced lieutenants. When he was placed in command of the Seigneur Offensive, the invasion of western France to support the Chouannerie in February 1799, these experienced men included General Sir Ralph Abercromby, Colonel Sir Thomas Græme and Colonel Sir John Moore, resulting in the *Register*'s well-known cartoon

---

[210] Who in OTL died without issue, but in TTL married within Hanover.

depicting the French Revolutionaries fleeing from an army of men in full mediaeval battle-armour from the waist up, but kilts from the waist down, i.e., an Army of Scottish Knights.[211]

His younger brother Prince Henry William could not have been more of a contrast. An intellectual, he preferred discussing art over the dinner table to the foxhunt, and took a proactive part in political debates, somewhat alarming the establishment, which felt that royals doing so was in violation of the British Constitution. Like most of the descendants of Frederick I, he travelled extensively to the Empire of North America and liked the country – mainly for its fauna and flora, possessing such a larger scale and wilder character than those of Europe. Henry William sponsored the further expeditions of Erasmus Darwin II to the Susan-Mary region, and patronised the creation of the Royal and Imperial Museum of Natural History when it was separated from the British Museum in 1793. But, unlike his father and grandfather, Henry William was horrified by what he saw of the institution of slavery in the American colonies, writing extensive pamphlets on the subject—which irritated many established business interests who thought that royalty should be above such things. It was inevitable that Henry William should become attached to the Radical-leaning Whig movement led by Charles James Fox, which sought extensive political reforms.

The majority of Britons, therefore, were considerably relieved when Prince Frederick's wife Princess Charlotte of Ansbach conceived in the winter of 1798, just before Frederick left for France. Anything to avoid such a dangerous individual as Henry William sitting on the throne of Great Britain…

From : "The Jacobin Wars" by E.G. Christie (Hetherington Publishing House, 1926) –

After Admiral Villeneuve's effective if Pyrrhic victory at the Battle of Wight[212] the Frenchman was unsatisfied. He knew that

---

[211] In OTL the *Daily Universal Register* soon renamed itself *The Times*, which is what it remains to this day. In TTL it's just been shortened to *The Register*.

[212] The name given to his engagement with Admiral Duncan, the Isle of Wight being the nearest point of land.

he had to inflict as much damage as possible on the combined fleet, to sink as many troopships as he could: each would make the job of the overstretched French land armies just a little easier, and the Republic could afford to lose ships more than she could afford to lose soldiers, for the war would be won or lost on land. Villeneuve had a cold appreciation of all this, and was willing to give his life—and all those of his men, of course—to ensure it.

To that end, Villeneuve paused only to make cursory repairs, to run up new sails and to swab out all of his guns. It was at this point that his ships of the line successfully sunk two pursuing frigates of Duncan at extreme range with their stern chasers, providing a boost of morale to the Republican sailors. Villeneuve seized the moment and sent out his famous message in flags: "*Allons, enfants de la patrie! Qu'un sang impur colore la Manche du rouge républicain!*" [213]

Possibly the message would have been more effective if the Revolutionary naval ministry had not changed the flag codes eight times in the past month in an attempt to find the most 'rational' one; as it was, only about half of Villeneuve's ships worked it out, but it was nonetheless an historic moment. The Republican fleet pressed on westwards, but their damaged sails and hulls meant that they only slowly closed the distance with the combined Allied fleet, even though the latter was hampered by their sluggish transports.

The Allied fleet had formed up off Portsmouth the day before. It was organised to place the Royal French forces in the centre, with Nelson's forces taking the van and Bone's guarding the rear. The British were determined to protect the Royal French at all costs, recognising that they were a valuable propaganda tool that turned this war ideological – liberal monarchists united against violent republicans – rather than being yet another futile round of Anglo-French war. The latter would be useless, as France had no possessions left that Britain wanted, save in India, and the

---

[213] "Onward, children of the Fatherland! May their impure blood turn the Channel a Republican red!" Of course, this evokes the *Marseillaise*, which was written in a modified form in TTL but has remained only a popular marching song, not an official anthem.

results of wars in Europe had little impact on what happened in India. The French retained Louisiana and Haiti in the New World, but both possessed so many French colonists – Louisiana had been a sinkhole for all those the British had ejected from Acadia, Canada, the Ohio Country and Susan-Mary – that trying to assimilate them would be futile. In order for Britain to be able to achieve a continental victory, they had to have support from some of the people of France, and to do that they needed the King of France.

Villeneuve realised all this as much as the British. He received good intelligence from co-opted fishing boats that spied on the Allied fleet as it moved slowly around Finisterre. He correctly guessed that they were aiming at Quiberon – though it was still possessed fortifications held by besieged Republican troops, the British had previously fought there in 1759 and many of their older commanders would remember the layout of the bay from their service there as young midshipmen or lieutenants. So, for that matter, would the Royal French, many of whom had fought in the same battle on the opposite side. An advantage like that in intelligence could be significant.

The Republican Admiral decided, then, that the only target worth going for was the Dauphin's ship, the Royal flagship – the *Améthyste*. Sacrificing all his ships in a quixotic attack would be worth it, because the death of the Dauphin should result in a collapse of morale among the Chouans and Britain losing the ideological character of its war. To that end, Villeneuve drew up an attack of startling aggressiveness, which featured a feint on Bone's guarded transports followed by a rapid push through to attack the *Améthyste* when Bone broke away from the main fleet to form his line of battle. It would almost certainly result in the destruction of the Republican fleet, but if Louis XVII was cut in half by a cannonball then nothing else would matter. Villeneuve issued the orders. Blood would turn the Channel red indeed…

From: "The Man With Three Names—A Life and Times of Napoleone Buonaparte" (Dr Henri Pelletier, University of Nantes Press, 1962) –

Commodore Leo Bone had served in several actions after his great coup of 'seizing' the French fleet from Toulon. The Admiralty had moved him out of the Mediterranean, perhaps fearing the man's burning ambition following the publication of slightly self-aggrandising papers describing his adventure; if he could convince an entire fleet to leave the Republicans by sheer brazen force of will, what more might his charisma do? Bone was therefore assigned to dull blockade and convoy escort duty for years, but had nonetheless successfully taken two Republican prizes that had been attempting to reach the West Indies, and the prize-money served to grease the rails of his ascent to commodore. He had left the *Diamond*, not without a moment of sorrow to say goodbye to the tough little frigate that had been the scene of his greatest act of tactical audacity—so far. Now he had been given the second-rate ship of the line HMS *Lewisborough*.[214]

Command of the rearguard of the Seigneur Offensive was his greatest responsibility yet. Like his friend Nelson (now in command of the first-rate HMS *Mirabilis*[215]), he had been chosen over the heads of many senior commanders because of his youth, vigour, and unorthodox tactical ideas. The strategy that Admiral Charles Villeneuve adopted against him at the Battle of Penmarc'h might have worked on one of the crusty, conservative British Admirals mostly now consigned to blockade and convoy escort duties, though it would still have cost him most of his ships. It would not work on Leo Bone.

When Villeneuve attacked Bone's transports with his fleet's bow chasers as a challenge, Bone did not form the conventional line of battle as Villeneuve had expected. Instead, Bone told off his frigates and arranged them into lines of *attack*, a strategy which he had developed together with Nelson. Villeneuve initially assumed that the frigates were going to engage that part of his fleet attacking the transports, and thus ordered the rest to push

---

[214] Named for Prince Frederick's victory over the French in 1759. Not the most politic name when escorting a fleet of allied French, of course...
[215] This is the ATL equivalent of HMS *Victory*, laid down in 1760. Both were named after 1759, the *Annus Mirabilis*, the Wonderful Year of Victories.

through the remainder of Bone's force and advance towards the Royal French.

However, when the Republicans (who had the wind gauge) advanced, Bone's frigates snapped into their lines and drove a three-pronged thrust through the mass of Republican ships, blasting away with their broadsides almost below the waterline of Villeneuve's first-rate monsters. The French guns were, as usual, elevated to target the masts and rigging of other ships of the line, and so the Republican response was largely ineffective against Bone's smaller ships. Only a few of Villeneuve's ships reacted fast enough, and Bone lost just three frigates. The others turned, tacked and began attacking Villeneuve's rear.

Villeneuve recognised Bone's strategy too late, and saw that all he could do was to push through the enemy as rapidly as possible. However, he also realised that Bone was the most dangerous man on the waterborne field of battle in the immediate tactical sense, even if the Dauphin's death was his strategic goal. Thus while the bulk of Villeneuve's fleet was sent through to attack the Royal French, Villeneuve's own flagship *Egalité* and one other first-rate, the *Jacobin*, targeted the *Lewisborough* and attempted to pound the smaller British ship to smithereens before Bone could react. The Lewisborough was trapped in a crossfire between the two larger, superior French warships.

Bone, however, trusted his captains to act independently, having drilled them thoroughly beforehand. He saw he could therefore use Villeneuve's move against him. The *Lewisborough* hoisted her royals and her skys'ls and fled, using the southerly wind to cut around the main fleet and make for the French coast. Villeneuve presumed that a man like Bone could not simply be making cowardly flight, and thus became convinced that it must be part of some grand strategy. As his frigates were now fully engaged with Bone's remaining ships of the line and the Royal French – who were putting up a harder fight than Villeneuve had hoped – all Villeneuve had to pursue the *Lewisborough* with was the *Egalité* and the *Jacobin* themselves. Making a snap decision, he ordered that the *Jacobin* pursue the *Lewisborough* alone. Meanwhile, he brought the *Egalité* deeper into the battle and, even as his masts crumbled before the terrific hammering of both British and French gunnery, gave the order to engage the *Améthyste* at point-blank range. A boarding party was prepared to finally bring the fight to the would-be King of France, and if Revolutionary justice would be imparted by the blade of a cutlass rather than a *chirurgien*, Villeneuve cared not.

Leo Bone's quixotic strategy had failed to be quite as successful as he had hoped, but he had drawn off one Republican ship and given the Dauphin a fighting chance. In order to maintain the pursuit and keep the *Jacobin*'s attention, he ordered that sails be hauled down in time with the *Jacobin*'s volleys, as though they were being shot down. The *Jacobin* finally caught up with the *Lewisborough* off the Île de Yeu, a full day later—ensuring the Republican ship had been entirely taken off the scales of the battle off the Pointe de Penmarc'h.

The *Lewisborough* and the *Jacobin* now engaged in a terrific battle. The *Jacobin*'s captain, François Barral, was a disciple of Surcouf and used an unorthodox strategy by French naval standard. Scorning the usual tactics of attacking the masts and rigging, he instead hit the *Lewisborough* with plunging shell fire from howitzers, a weapon rarely carried aboard ship. Bone's carronades returned fire and smashed a hole in the side of the *Jacobin* at point-blank range. The Republican ship sank soon afterwards, though Barral and his officers escaped by boat.

Nonetheless, the damage to Bone's ship was done. One of the *Jacobin*'s shells had blasted the poop deck of the *Lewisborough*, and as well as killing twenty sailors and smashing all the windows in the officers' cabins, the resulting shockwave caused the planks of the hull to part near the keel. The *Lewisborough* began taking on water faster than her pumps could expel it. Bone ordered that they drive for the French coast, hoping to swiftly take some little-defended harbour and then lay up there and repair the damage. He considered throwing his guns overboard to save weight and thus buy them more time, as was standard Royal Navy practice; however, in the end he decided that they were not too far from the coast and that the guns might be needed later. Thus Leo Bone was saved from not only sinking into the English Channel, but into the obscurity of a historical footnote. As her hull gradually slid ever deeper into the water, the wallowing *Lewisborough* sailed for Saint-Hilaire, and destiny...

But what of the Battle of Penmarc'h? Villeneuve himself led the boarding party onto the *Améthyste*, shouting down his second-in-command: "This is where we succeed for the glory of the Republic or fail utterly! If we win it shall be by my hand, and if we fail then what savour shall there be in life?"[216]

Villeneuve himself shot Admiral d'Estaing as his opposite number rallied his sailors, but was then knocked unconscious by a blow to the head from Captain Lucas. When he awoke, it was in the *Améthyste*'s brig. He did not learn until later that his fleet had lost half its remaining strength before surrendering, and though several troopships had been sunk and Leo Bone had vanished, Villeneuve had failed in his mission. The Dauphin lived; indeed, he came to visit him at one point, and Villeneuve's later memoirs record his shock at the incident. Louis XVII was quite unlike what he had expected. The exilic prince had been influenced by Richard Burke's ideas and had already been fairly liberal by the standards of the House of Bourbon even before the Revolution. "Must Frenchman slay Frenchman in the name of liberty, while the genuine tyrants of all classes profit from our division?" the Dauphin asked Villeneuve. The admiral had no answer.

The Allied fleet attacked Quiberon, as had been planned. The Republicans still held the fortifications that the French had built on the peninsula after the British victory in 1759, and barrages of hot shot ripped through the Allied fleet, sinking ten British and French ships. But a swift action by British and American Marines, spearheaded by Lieutenant Alexander Cochrane, seized the fortress from the land side and the great guns fell silent. Cochrane was promoted to captain, as he had personally led the Forlorn Hope that escaladed the walls of the Quiberon fort.[217]

---

[216] As has doubtless already become clear, this Villeneuve is a wee bit different in character to his allohistorical "brother" from OTL who commanded the French fleet at Trafalgar...

[217] A Forlorn Hope, from the Dutch *verloren hoop*, is the name given to a group of soldiers spearheading a very dangerous attack (such as through a newly breached fortress wall) on the assumption that they are likely to

The British and Royal French finally fell on the city, the transports disgorging their troops and the Breton locals mostly welcoming them as liberators, at least before they drunk all the taverns dry. Louis XVII took his first steps on the soil of France for more than three years, and standing beside the Prince of Wales, spoke his famous words: "By God and my right, I reclaim my birthright."

The war had entered quite a different phase...

---

lose their lives—but if they do not, they receive immediate unconditional promotions and other kudos.

Chapter 39: O Vienna

DREI HELDER; DREI RETTER; DREI MÄRTYRER.

- inscription on triple monument to Niklas Salm, Johann Sobieski and Wolfgang Mozart, Stephansplatz, Vienna[218]

From: "The Jacobin Wars – the Italo-German Front" by Joshua H. Calhoun (University of New York Press, 1946)—

Some contemporary commentators attributed the stalling of the French advance into Germany (following the battle of Regensburg in October 1798) to the fact that Robespierre ordered the withdrawal of forces from the German front in order to repel the Anglo-Royal French Seigneur offensive in February 1799. The disparity in dates should immediately suggest the unlikelihood of this oft-repeated lazy assumption. While it is true that the French armies in Italy and Germany did not receive many reinforcements after February – all new troops being diverted to the Vendean front – this did not take effect until the start of Spring 1799.

It is more accurate to say that the French armies in Germany had simply reached their limits. Leroux's *Guerre d'éclair* strategy had arguably been self-defeating by its very successes. The Jacobin forces had, like Britain's Duke of Marlborough and Frederick II of Prussia before them, proved capable of moving faster into Germany than the Austrians had thought possible. Yet, though their '*la maraude*' practices meant they could live off the land effectively without much of a supply train – at the expense of stirring up resentment among the locals against them – the

---

[218] "Three heroes, three saviours, three martyrs." Count Niklas Salm and Johan Sobieski (King John III of Poland) were the most prominent commanders in the repulsions of the Turks from Vienna in 1529 and 1683 respectively.

French still needed a ready supply of powder, shot and cartridges to fight battles, and these could not be so easily stripped from occupied country. Ironically, the superiority of French Gribeauval artillery—coming mostly from *ancien régime* programmes originally, but the popular eye has always associated them with the Revolution—caused problems when *les maraudeurs* tried to use captured Austrian ammunition to restock their supplies. The new French cannon had been built to a slightly different calibre to their Austrian counterparts, with the result that the Austrian roundshot were too large. Leroux found himself being forced to order the drilling out of several cannon in order to use the captured shot, and such thinned weapons had a tendency to burst after prolongued use, killing their crews.

Also, while the conscripted French armies were larger than the forces the Austrians could bring to bear against them, they were of course greatly outnumbered by the increasingly resentful civilian population. There was a limit to how much territory the French could hold down with the number of men they had, especially when Leroux needed to retain a large enough fighting force to meaningfully continue the offensive. While Ney successfully built his authority in Swabia, creating the puppet state *La République Germanique Souabe* (the Swabian Germanic Republic), Leroux was plagued continuously by bandits attacking his supply train even before the instigation of the formal *Kleinkrieg* which gave its name to an entire genre of warfare in years to come. Leroux was placed in a difficult quandary: if he stripped more troops from his van to guard his rear, he lessened his chances of victory in any engagement, but if he did nothing, then his larger van might not get the supplies it needed to fight at all.

The spring of 1799 arguably marks the start of a breakdown between the various Republics, though this was of course not formalised until the Double Revolution. Ney refused to send more forces out of Swabia to guard Leroux's supply lines, claiming that his dispersed troops were already hard-pressed in preventing a rising by Württemberger irregulars (almost certainly an exaggeration). Away to the south in Italy, Hoche reacted unfavourably upon hearing that Robespierre had diverted his precious reinforcements away to the Vendean front. This meant that Hoche's Army of Italy could not try to force the Brenner Pass against Archduke Ferdinand's rearguard, and it also meant that a pre-emptive expedition against the Hapsburg forces in Tuscany would be too much of an overstretch. Hoche was often impulsive enough to order offensives against the odds, but even he could recognise the realities of the situation. Without reinforcements, he only had sufficient forces to hold down the existing arc of territory he had conquered from Savoy to Venice. The Italian Latin Republic, which was largely synonymous with the person of Lazare Hoche, began to collectively realise that it was on its own. Only the Swiss Republic remained fully linked to Paris—or at least the French army holding it down and the effectively exiled Jean-Paul Marat were.

This background serves to explain why Leroux's advance after the Sack of Regensburg began to stumble. The French took far longer to advance the two hundred and fifty miles from Regensburg to Vienna than they had in their lightning push over the similar distance from Haguenau to Regensburg. Despite Leroux's difficulties, General Mozart – now in supreme command of Austria's armies, marshal in all but name – held firm and refused to authorise an attack on the Jacobin army as it slowly ground closer to the capital. The separate Army of Bohemia pushed down from the north under Quosdanovich and gave battle at Linz, joined by local militia forces who feared the same fate as their neighbours to the east. Despite holding a strongly defensive position, the Austrians were decisively defeated by Leroux's force, which was comparable in number. Mozart's caution, previously derided as cowardice by many armchair generals, suddenly seemed like the only course distinct from suicide.

The young Archduke Francis, now King of the Romans and unelected claimant Holy Roman Emperor Francis II, supported Mozart wholeheartedly. Francis believed the general to be Austria's best hope at weathering the French attack and surviving: undoubtedly the fact that this tense wait for the Jacobin hordes was his baptism of fire as monarch coloured his perceptions in later life and helps explain many of his odder views in subsequent years.

Francis' support meant that many of Mozart's more unusual proposals were pushed through in time to do some good. Despite the many conflicts in Germany during the eighteenth century, Vienna itself had not been threatened since the Ottoman siege of 1683, and the two situations, more than a century apart, were painfully similar in many respects. Vienna's fortifications were once again by now outdated and the city sprawled comfortably beyond them, safe in the knowledge that it lay at the core of a vast and powerful Empire. The main city wall, the *Linienwall*, was almost a hundred years old and unsuited to face modern artillery.

But Vienna was now again faced by a war far more earnest and vicious than the usual territorial conflicts between the German states. In 1683 that had been a holy war between Catholic Christianity and Islam; in 1799 many Hapsburg loyalists saw it as one between Christianity and the French's deistic-atheism. Others regarded it more conventionally as one between monarchism and republicanism, the latter term still being synonymous with the bloody reigns of terror that later generations would more specifically call Jacobinism. Either way, both political ideology and religion lent a sharper edge to the conflict. The horror stories coming out of Swabia and Bavaria reinforced the idea that this was all or nothing. If Mozart lost, if Vienna fell, the whole world as German-speakers knew it might fall with it, future generations reduced to nothing but hewers of wood and drawers of water for the 'superior Latin race'. French propaganda drew parallels between the Romans' attempts to conquer 'barbarian' Germany and their present attack: the Austrians retaliated with woodcuts comparing Mozart and Francis to Arminius, a Germanic chieftain who had defeated one such Roman attack in AD 9.

Now Mozart's ruthless ideas took shape. Taking inspiration from 1683, he had all the houses built outside the *Linienwall* razed, providing a plain suitable for an artillery killing field. New temporary forts with modern Vauban-type star bastions were constructed around the *Linienwall*. The hastily-built nature of these meant that they would probably not be as durable as Mozart would like, but he believed the important thing was to delay the French, rather than attempt to defeat them. "A siege can break the most invincible army," he wrote. "Not merely roundshot and canister from our walls, but also sickness and starvation; they hurt the besiegers as much as, if not more, than the besieged. And all of this saps their morale. A Turkish army outnumbering the defenders twenty to one failed to take this city by siege. The French are far fewer in number. Let us hope and pray that the same strategy will be successful".

Francis, meanwhile, made several public speeches to rally the people of Vienna. Our stereotyped picture of him today makes it easy to forget that he was a skilled orator, more so than his father, and made the firm link in their minds between the Turkish sieges of 1529 and 1683 and the present invasion. "This is the third time the forces of barbarism have tried to topple civilisation," he said. "This time, the barbarians come from the west rather than the east; but they shall be no more successful this time."

Those confident words were not backed up by events, not until March 1799. Leroux's army besieged the city starting from the third of that month, successfully repulsing attempts by Hungarian and Croatian cavalry to harry them as they dug in. Leroux was, like Boulanger, from a fairly humble background (the son of a cobbler) and though a gifted amateur at military affairs, he lacked much previous experience before this campaign. He therefore invested direct command of the operation in the experienced General Lucien Cougnon, an artilley officer who had previously been reognised as a master of siege warfare under the *ancien régime*. It bespoke of Cougnon's value that he had managed to retain his position through the worst of Robespierre's purges.

Cougnon's approach was fairly straightforward; he sought to demolish five of Mozart's new forts, opening a gap large enough to bring the whole army through without its flanks being enfiladed, and then to make a frontal assault on the outdated *Linienwall*. He was confident that the modern French artillery could make sufficient breaches in the wall that the Austrians would be unable to effectively defend them all. Leroux endorsed the plan and the French's steam *fardier*-towed artillery began pounding Mozart's forts from March 17th. The fragility of the hastily built fortifications swiftly proved itself, with two of the forts being battered down after only two days of bombardment. They were then taken by small forces of elite grenadiers without many losses on the French side. The mood in Vienna was 'a gloom of inevitability' in the words of the artist Ferdinand Bauer, who was living in the city at the time.[219] Just as the Revolutionaries had defeated every general sent to stop them since Wurmser withdrew from Nancy, now Mozart too could not stop them.

Vienna was arguably saved by a night attack led by Kováts Istvan[220] on the 21st. The Hungarian cavalry under Kováts were this time able to break through the complacent French sentries and raid the artillery positioned against the three other forts which Cougnon sought to destroy. The Hungarians wrought havoc before a counter-attack led personally by Leroux forced them to withdraw. Kováts had specifically equipped his men for sabotaging guns, and when the light of day dawned, Leroux found that – as well as a large number of his artillerymen being sabred down, some in their sleep – the vast majority of the guns had been spiked. Most of the damage was not irreparable, as Kováts' forces had had limited time and had wanted to remain stealthy, so could not try something more permanent and spectacular like forcing the guns to burst. Nonetheless it would take time to repair – and those trained artillerymen could not be so easily replaced. In one stroke, the Hapsburg forces had made their foe's job significantly harder.

The two French artillery companies directed against the now-destroyed forts had survived, and Cougnon redirected them against the remaining forts, while Leroux ordered repair

---

[219] OTL's version of Bauer is famous for his botanical drawings of Australian plant life as part of Matthew Flinders' expeditions. While he was born long after the Point Of Divergence of this timeline, he was the son of an artist and followed his father in his craft, so it seems likely his allohistorical 'brother' would in TTL as well.

[220] The grandson of Kováts Mihály (Michael de Kovats), who in OTL founded the United States Cavalry during the ARW. In TTL he remained loyal to the Hapsburgs all his life and his son and grandson (not born OTL) have followed him into the cavalry. Note that in Hungarian the family name comes first.

work to commence on the damaged guns. However, perhaps emboldened by the French setback, those three Austrian forts fought considerably harder and inflicted bloody casualties when they were stormed by Leroux's grenadiers. The French lost several grenadier companies, significantly blunting what Cougnon had wanted to use as the vanguard for assaulting the breaches he planned to make in the *Linienwall*.

The last of the forts was finally secured on April 2nd. Leroux ordered his long-awaited advance and the remaining French guns began pounding the *Linienwall* on April 6th. Cougnon's prediction about the wall's ineffectiveness proved accurate, and several breaches were rapidly made. Mozart quickly made a decision. Just as Cougnon had thought, the breaches were too many to be defensible by the Hapsburg defenders. Mozart gave the order that he had long dreaded: the bulk of the armies focused in Vienna were to sortie forth and engage Leroux's army on the killing field cleared of houses, hopefully keeping the French in place where the guns on the *Linienwall* could continue to inflict casualties on them. Only a skeleton force was left defending the breaches. It was a desperate gamble, and a sign that Hapsburg Austria had truly reached the end of its tether.

The Battle of Vienna was epic, a defining moment in the history of Europe. The Austrians outnumbered the French by a little more than three to two, but Mozart had still yet to find an effective defence against the Revolutionary tactics introduced by Boulanger. Leroux, taking over command again from Cougnon as the siege shifted to a field battle, hammered Mozart's deep lines with his columns again and again. Meanwhile the steam-towed Cugnot artillery trundled left and right across the treacherously flat killing field, enfilading the Austrian lines as quickly as they redeployed. Twenty-pound roundshot continued to plunge from the walls and every shot killed dozens of Frenchmen in their compact columns, but many of the huge Austrian guns were unseated by return fire from Leroux's own siege guns. If Kováts' ploy had not succeeded, the French would have been even more successful, perhaps making a crucial difference. As it was, Leroux was forced to divide his remaining artillery between enfilading the Austrian troops and unseating the guns on the *Linienwall*, with the result that neither task received as much focused bombardment as he would have liked.

Still, it seems clear that Mozart would have been defeated, had it not been for the Miracle on the Danube. As the sixth of April drew closer to night, with Mozart's forces close to breaking point, the people of Vienna heard the sound of a distant trumpet. Archduke Ferdinand and General Wurmser had returned from Italy, bringing their armies with them. Though the body of the Hapsburg armies were spread out along the road for miles behind, having made forced marches to return in time, Wurmser's large force of Croatian cavalry trotted in the vanguard of his army. Seeing the situation, the general immediately ordered that they charge the flank of the compact French army aimed at the *Linienwall*.

On the brink of victory, the French were nonetheless vulnerable. Mozart's defence had been effective enough that Leroux had been forced to send forward some of the reserves guarding his flanks in order to keep up the pressure on the Austrian lines. He had gambled that the Austrians had already committed all their forces and they had no reserves with which to take advantage of this weakness. This had been an accurate guess…until now.

The Croats hit the French rear with such suddenness that the Revolutionaries – made up mostly of Sans-Culottes, enthusiastic but inexperienced about fighting in any manner beyond that which they had been hastily drilled in – had no time to form square. Leroux hesitated, considering if there was any way the Croats could be repulsed without giving Mozart the breathing space to regroup. As he paused, a roundshot from the walls removed his head.

Without their commander, French morale crumbled. Cougnon took command and ordered a fighting retreat. He aimed the small force of Revolutionary cavalry straight at the centre of Mozart's lines in an attempt to hold back the main Austrian army, then shifted his most experienced troops – *ancien régime* veterans – to face the Croats in square. The Sans-Culottes Revolutionary rabble were evacuated swiftly westward. A fire-breathing Jacobin,

Colonel Fabien Lascelles, effectively seized command of those troops, the bulk of the French army in numerical terms if not fighting capability.

Cougnon successfully repulsed the Croats and retreated after the Sans-Culottes. His quixotic cavalry attack, though of course demolished by the overwhelming numbers of the Austrian troops, was more successful than he had hoped; the cavalrymen, armed with rifles,[221] managed to target and shoot down several Austrian officers in their prominent uniforms – including Wolfgang Mozart. The general sustained a wound in his shoulder which immediately took him out of the battle. This meant that the Austrians held steady under cautious lieutenants, rather than pursuing – when they might have routed the disorganised French.

Vienna had repulsed its third epic siege, and the bulk of Ferdinand and Wurmser's armies paraded through the Graben to cheers and fanfares when they arrived a week later. However, Mozart's wound became gangrenous, and he died on the 21st. His last words, spoken to Francis, were reportedly (on speaking of his great public acclaim among the people for his victory) 'It means nothing to me, O Vienna'. There is some evidence that Mozart believed he had only snatched victory from the jaws of defeat by an act of Providence, and went to his grave still believing he had somehow failed the Austria and the House of Hapsburg. This belief was not shared by the Hapsburgs and their people, who erected many statues to the general over the years. A symphony by Beethoven, *Vittoria*, was dedicated to Mozart and largely drew on his actions in the Battle of Vienna, focusing on martial, clashing harmonies.

It was a turning point. Vienna marked the most eastward advance of French Revolutionary armies. The army formerly belonging to Leroux retreated to Linz, at which point a brief civil war was fought between its commanders. The fanatical Lascelles (who despised all associated with the *ancien régime*), had Cougnon assassinated. Cougnon's distraught veteran troops

---

[221] Recall that the assassination of William IV by Frederick's Americans sparked a new interest in the rifle as a weapon of war in Europe, and it is much more common in armies of the period in TTL than it was in OTL.

fled rather than serve Lascelles. Lascelles then further organised a retreat to Regensburg, his intention being to set up a Bavarian Germanic Republic.

Cougnon's troops, meanwhile, remained as a coherent force under Major Phillipe Saint-Julien. This smaller force turned northward, seizing the Bohemian town of Budweis[222] and establishing it as a minor military fiefdom, with only a token nod to Jacobin Republican ideology. The Austrian failure to respond to this occupation is often cited as the reason behind the growth of the Bohemian national consciousness in the first part of the nineteenth century, just as the Spanish failure to respond to the British occupation of Buenos Aires in the First Platinean War had contributed to the idea of a Platinean national consciousness. In days to come, the Austrians would have similar cause to regret this oversight, though Francis II would not live to see it.

Austria had been set back on its heels, but the time was now ripe for a counterattack. The country retained able generals such as Archduke Ferdinand, Wurmser and Alvinczi. Austria still had plenty of armies and could call upon more levies from Hungary or Croatia. The French occupation of Swabia was new and shaky, that of Bavaria even more so. A decisive attack could shatter it and undo all the gains of the Rubicon Offensive.

But fate did not smile upon Vienna a second time. Since Hoche had sacked and occupied Venice, ending the ancient mercantile republic, the fate of the Venetian possessions in Dalmatia had been up in the air. The land was ethnically mostly Croatian, suggesting a possible Austrian claim based on flimsy historical justifications, but this was opposed by the Ottoman Empire. November 1798 had seen the death of Sultan Abdulhamid II and he was succeeded by a dynamic nephew, who became Murad V. Murad and his vizier, Mehmed Ali Pasha, saw the fall of Venice as a significant opportunity. The Ottomans had focused on internal reorganisation under the cautious Abdulhamid's reign, and their response to the Russian Civil War had chiefly been the soft expansion of power. Ottoman influence had increased

---

[222] The German name; České Budějovice in the modern OTL Czech Republic.

in the Khanate of the Crimea, the Caucasus and the Danubian principalities,[223] sometimes displacing existing Russian puppets in those states' governments. However, now Murad discerned that the Russians' internal struggle meant that a war over Dalmatia would be restricted to conflict with the already weakened Austria. The Austrian ambassador to the Sublime Porte was summoned on 15th May 1799 and informed that a state of war now existed between Constantinople and Vienna. An Ottoman army under Damat Melek Pasha, a Bosniak, crossed over into the formerly Venetian Dalmatia on the 26th of May.

Francis was in an unenviable position. Without the legitimacy of confirmation by the Prince-Electors, he had diminished authority in his claim to act as Holy Roman Emperor. Having defeated one great invasion, Austria now apparently faced a second – though the Ottomans' declaration of war was largely a simple consequence of their desired annexation of Dalmatia. There were little signs that the Sublime Porte wished to attempt another wholesale invasion of the Hapsburg dominions themselves, but nonetheless Austria could hardly pursue an offensive war against the French occupying Swabia and Bavaria with the Turks sweeping up through the Balkans.

Thus history was decided. Austrian armies were shifted south to defend Hapsburg Croatia, while Lascelles was able to escape unharried to Regensburg, and the Cougnonistes to Budweis. The German front, which had been so bitterly fought for so long, descended into an almost sinister silence – at least until the beginning of the *Kleinkrieg*.

The situation in Paris was almost comically similar to that in Vienna. In both cities, the great enemy had been defeated, but an older, more traditional one had reared its ugly head. General Boulanger wanted to lead the scraped-together Revolutionary armies personally against the British and Royal French, but Jean de Lisieux dissuaded him. He would be needed here, he claimed mysteriously. Lisieux did, however, ensure Boulanger arranged matters so that most of the troops going to the Chouan-held

---

[223] The 'Danubian Principalities' is a common contemporary name for the Romanian states of Wallachia and Moldavia.

lands would be made up of Sans-Culotte volunteers.

The Spanish were also a worry. Spain had been one of the first monarchist powers to declare war after the phlogistication of Louis XVI, and had been the first port of call for the Dauphin when he fled the country. Yet the Spanish prosecution of the war had been unenthusiastic. King Philip VI had always tried to steer the country through a path of peace since the disastrous Second Platinean War, focusing on colonial reorganisation to prevent a second breakaway like the UPSA and reforming finances in the Peninsula. His chief minister, the able Conde de Floridablanca, had favoured such policies even before Philip became King. Together they had prevented Jacobin Revolutionary ideas from gaining much purchase in Spain, even though the country had itself had several popular rebellions against the unpopular Charles III in recent history. Floridablanca's propaganda emphasised the Revolution's deistic-atheistic and French-supremacist principles, successfully inflaming popular (though not necessarily noble) opposition. After all, the rebellions against Charles III had partly been sparked by him being too close to French ideas.

Therefore, in the five years since the start of the war, the Spanish armies had not advanced a great deal. Under the competent but overly cautious General Fernando de Cuesta,[224] Spain occupied those regions of French territory to which it had a historic claim, such as Rousillon (French Catalonia) and Labourd (a heavily Basque part of Aquitaine). Andorra was also annexed. The Spanish were sometimes welcomed as liberators, particularly in those lands which had been Spanish prior to the Franco-Spanish wars of the seventeenth century, but were more often sullenly opposed by the locals. Revolutionary sentiment in the southwest of France was only moderate, but the Spanish troops did not behave particularly well and it was obvious to everyone that Spain was there for *pragmatique* reasons rather than some sort of altruistic restoration of their fellow Bourbon monarchy.[225] A march by Spanish troops to Paris was inconceivable, not necessarily because of the state of the Spanish Army (which was still undergoing

---

[224] An ATL 'brother' of Gregorio García de Cuesta.
[225] *'Pragmatisme'* is a term used in TTL equivalent to OTL's *Realpolitick*.

reorganisation after the lessons of the Second Platinean War) but because the Cortes refused to release the funding. No-one forgot that the French Revolution had ultimately been sparked by the expenditure of a century of war emptying the French treasury. Spain's economy was already shaky enough after the loss of a third of the New World empire without such risky military adventures.

The Spanish offensive did pick up after Hoche moved into Spanish Parma in October 1797 as part of his Italian campaign. Outrage at news of French atrocities was enough to spur Floridablanca into recommending a new offensive, if only for the sake of appearances. Cuesta therefore advanced into Gascony, laying siege to Bordeaux in an operation supported by amphibious descents by the Spanish Navy – the Revolution's lack of much naval force meant that the Spanish could operate almost with impunity. However, the siege was broken in July 1798 when a small French force under Custine, the victor of Toulon, was augmented by local militiamen and managed to defeat Cuesta's army, which was already suffering from disease. The Spanish retreated into Labourd, with the French pursuing, but a shock victory was won over Custine at the Battle of Bayonne when an outnumbered portion of the Spanish army defeated the French. The Spanish were led by a young major of Irish descent, Joaquín Blake y Joyes, who would go on to have an interesting career…

French attempts to drive the Spanish back any further failed, as the French armies facing the Spanish were simply too few with the demands of the Italian, German, and then Vendean fronts. However, the bloody nose at Bordeaux meant that Spanish policy reverted to a cautious consolidation of their historical claims. The final showdown on that front would have to wait until the fate of the Chouannerie was decided…

Chapter 40: The Double Revolution

From: "The Seigneur Offensive" by Philip Rathbone (Collins and Wilston of Albany, 1972)—

Jean-Baptiste Robespierre had been paranoid about the prospect of a British invasion of western France for many months before the Seigneur Offensive was actually launched. Although Robespierre had pushed hard for the prosecution of war against Austria, as the very successes of the Poséidon and Rubicon offensives led French armies ever deeper into Germany and Italy, he began to fear the possibility of an underdefended France falling to attack from the west.

Other historians, more pro-Administration, have argued that Robespierre's fear was not for the Republic but for his own position. Robespierre had masterminded the Terror for several years, and seemed unable to learn that it was impossible to kill all the enemies of the state (i.e., himself; Louis XIV would have approved), because every *chirurgeon*ing or phlogistication only served to turn more people's hearts against him. Enthusiasm for the Republic itself still ran high in France, but Robespierre was becoming an ever more isolated figure. His power was only the shadow of the tiger.[226] While he might be able to intimidate the masses, there remained men in France powerful enough to oppose him, men whose power lay in different arenas, who could not be

---

[226] The phrase 'the emperor's new clothes' dates from a Hans Christian Andersen story published in 1837, long after the POD so therefore does not exist in TTL. The phrase 'the shadow of the tiger', meaning the same thing, comes from an animal story by Georges Gallet, a sort of French analogue of Rudyard Kipling who lived in Kérala. In this story a crafty civet-cat intimidated a nest of snakes by simulating the shadow of a tiger, before one of the snakes saw through the illusion and ate him.

cowed through the emasculated National Legislative Assembly. To keep those men on side, Robespierre had to continue the idea that French was perpetually under threat and that any word raised against his Terror was tantamount to collaboration. To that end, as Leroux, Ney and Hoche effectively removed the immediate threat from Austria, Robespierre's propagandists talked up the threat from Spain. Some historians have even suggested that Robespierre deliberately permitted the Spanish to remain in possession of French land (until Bordeaux was attacked) in order to use that as part of his propaganda.

But the real threat to the Republic now came not from Spain, but from Britain – Britain and Royal French exiles joining up with the Chouan rebels in Brittany and the Vendée. Villeneuve had weakened the allied force, but not fatally so. Following his defeat, the British took the Republican-held fortress of Quiberon and marched into Brittany with their Royal French allies in the lead. The British commander, Frederick George the Prince of Wales, understood his own limitations as a battlefield general, but on the other hand was skilled as portraying the invasion as a liberation. He kept his men under control, ensuring the provosts made sure that they paid for everything they requisitioned from the locals, and hanged a couple of looters as an example. The Prince also sought out Catholic troops in his army and arranged them into small elite forces which he used when securing potentially sensitive sites, such as churches. Frederick was aware that the Chouannerie was partly ultra-Catholic in character, and knew that he had to ensure no accusations of Protestant atrocities were made. Technically, there should have been no Catholics in his army due to the Test Acts, but in practice there were always ways around these. In any case, the British opinion of Catholics was slowly improving as more accurate reports of Wesley's successes in Ireland began to leak out. This did, however, alienate some of the Huguenots who had joined the British Army, who saw it as a disgusting suck-up to the same forces who had led to their ancestors fleeing the country a hundred years before. Brittany and the Vendée still had one of the largest Huguenot populations in France – perhaps why the Catholic majority was so fervent, with an opposition to press against – and many Huguenot-descended British officers hotly wrote home to the papers concerning the Chouans' treatment of French Protestants.

Of course, this meant little in the face of the big picture. Everyone knew that the alliance was uneasy. England, and then Britain, had fought Bourbon France almost continuously for a hundred years, and had a long history of conflict stretching back before that. The alliance rested on the Royal French seeing the British as the lesser of two evils, and Britain putting one foot wrong could change their minds, reducing the war to another of the futile Anglo-French conflicts that had set the world alight so many times. Prince Frederick was willing to do anything to prevent that.

In Paris, Robespierre ordered the immediate creation of new armies to 'throw the English and the impure traitors back into the sea'. In a meeting with the two other Consuls, Boulanger opened his mouth to protest, only to find Lisieux's foot pressing down on his beneath the table. Lisieux quickly spoke up and said that of course it would be done.

Boulanger said nothing at the time, but after reading the operational plans that Lisieux drew up, he confronted his fellow Consul at the tavern which the 'Boulangerie' used as their usual meeting place. While Jean-Pierre Blanchard argued with Robert Surcouf about the possibility of flying balloons off the deck of a ship, Boulanger met Lisieux in an upper room. The exact content of the conversation is not known. Michel Chanson, Boulanger's onetime adjutant, later claimed that the General confided in him the words that were spoken, though there is no way verify this allegation. According to Chanson, the conversation ran...

BOULANGER. Jean, my friend, are you mad?[227] I have read your orders. They are a recipe for slaughter, nothing less!

LISIEUX. You are right, of course. We could try to prevent Jean-Baptiste's insane plans this time. We have succeeded before. But how long will it be before our constructive criticism becomes

---

[227] Boulanger is using *tu* rather than *vous* in the original French when he says 'you', reflecting his increasingly close political relationship with Lisieux over the past few years.

a sign that we are irredeemably 'impure' and 'treacherous' and we are looking at the inside of a phlogistication chamber?

BOULANGER. Jean – you cannot be saying this.

LISIEUX. Perhaps we may even share the same phlogistication chamber.

BOULANGER. You know that…that it is…it cannot be said!

LISIEUX. Precisely, old friend. It cannot be said. Friend Robespierre had spies everywhere. Is this the Republic we all sought to build when we pulled down the old regime? Is this liberty?

BOULANGER. I – I cannot say.

LISIEUX. You have commanded vast armies in the face of cannonballs flying about your head, yet you fear to say it. Such is the hold his Terror has on all of us. We must break it, for the sake of France. If Jean-Baptiste continues in his destructive regime, men will begin to think of him and the Republic as one. Then when he falls – for he must, before he reduces himself to the last man in France, everyone else executed as 'impure' – the Republic will fall with him. We cannot allow that.

BOULANGER. *(Long pause)* No. We cannot…what do you intend to gain by this madness?

LISIEUX. You will note that the new armies are drawn largely from the remaining Sans-Culotte militias.

BOULANGER. Those not yet part of your Gardes Nationales, of course…ah. You seek to…?

LISIEUX. Quite so. A new era is about to dawn, Pierre. We do not belong in the shadows.

It is not the place of the author to speak of the plausibility of this account. In any case, Boulanger approved Lisieux's plans, and new armies were formed up, drawn almost entirely from the Sans-Culottes and with inexperienced generals in command. They marched out of Paris in May 1799 and divided into two main forces, led by Paul Vignon and Jacques Pallière. Vignon's northern army assembled at Le Mans and then marched westward into Brittany, while Pallière's southern force was sent on to Poitiers and then wheeled to enter the Vendée.

By the time the two Republican armies attacked, at the end of

June, the British were well established. The remaining Republican holdouts at Lannion and Cherbourg were taken by British amphibious descents, securing control over all Brittany. A force moved into the Vendée under Sir Thomas Græme – though the politically aware Prince Frederick made sure to give it a Catholic and French vanguard – and cleared out the remaining Revolutionary strongholds that the Chouans had been unable to take, lacking artillery. All of the province of Brittany, and the western half of Poitou (which consisted of the Vendée) were now under Allied control. The Dauphin went to Nantes and was hailed as Louis XVII. He was blessed by the Bishop of Nantes (who had escaped the purge of the Second Estate) in his Cathedral, one step short of a full coronation. The two redeemed regions now had almost no supporters of the Revolution, as those who had backed it had fled eastward when the Chouannerie threw out the Republican occupiers.

Against this background, the two Republican forces attacked. Vignon's army met the main Anglo-French force, with Prince Frederick and Louis XVII present, near Laval. The Republicans were outnumbered and inexperienced, and were slaughtered by the Royalists and their British allies. Tellingly, the Republicans had also lacked any of the Cugnot toys that had been so useful against Austria. This was not because they did not exist. But Boulanger and Lisieux controlled their supply through the Boulangerie, and had ensured that none would be supplied. They wouldn't want that large group of Sans-Culottes to *win*, after all…

The southern battle, at Cholet, was less decisive. Græme met Pallière with a force only two-thirds as large, and part of that made up of Royal French, less reliable without their King there to steady them. The fact that it was Frenchman fighting Frenchman was never far away from the minds of either side. Nonetheless, Lisieux and Boulanger had not failed at deliberately engineering failure there, either. Though Græme did not actually destroy Pallière's army as thoroughly as Vignon's at Laval, Riflemen skirmishers attached to the 69th (South Lincolnshire) Foot did manage to kill Pallière himself. With little of a trained officer corps in command, the army simply disintegrated. The contrast with the orderly withdrawal of Leroux's army from Vienna after his death is telling. Boulanger had ensured that the best of the Republic's army had gone into Germany. According to Lisieux's plan, he now deliberately sent its worst against the British.

Pallière's army scattered over the countryside, some fleeing to Anjou and Aunice provinces. *La maraude* only served to turn more undecided locals to the Royalist cause. In truth, though, a bigger surge of support was the two victories themselves, trumpeted to the skies by British and Royalist propaganda. The Republic, seemingly invincible for so long, now appeared anything but.

Which was, of course, exactly what Lisieux had desired…

From: "The Double Revolution" by Daniel Dutourd (Université de Nantes Press, 1964)—

When the news of the defeats at Cholet and Laval reached it, Paris began buzzing with discontent. Fatally, this word came on the back of the news of the defeat at Vienna, when the government desperately needed a victory to restore morale. The Revolution was imperilled once again, and a scapegoat was needed, someone to be burned in *L'Épurateur*'s flame of liberty. Robespierre had had no trouble finding them in the past. Now, having left a trail of corpses longer than that of any king, he was struck down by his own success: with no credible political opponents left, only one man could be responsible for the defeats.

Traitor. Impure…

Paris had seen several uprisings in recent years, this one no less confused than those that had preceded it. Chroniclers report that, despite the purges after Hébert's death, part of the uprising was Royalist and Catholic in character, spurred on by the Royal successes in the Vendée. More of it, though, was made up of Republicans who sought to overthrow Robespierre and elect a new leader – for at this point most of them still thought of elections as a realistic prospect in a Jacobin state.

Both risings were held back by Lisieux's loyal Garde Nationale. Lisieux advised Robespierre that it would be best if he remained in a secure area until the rebellion was put down. Robespierre argued, saying that he would not be seen to be hiding from his enemies.

Lisieux…*insisted*. And Boulanger 'happened' to recommend the old Château de Versailles, now long since looted-out and used for storage of ammunition and troops' rations. Robespierre, belatedly realising that power had shifted and he was being forced, attempted to call upon the Sans-Culottes, over whom he had always held supreme authority. His great political act had been to skilfully slip into the shoes of Le Diamant, a man who would almost certainly have found him repugnant if they had ever met, and control Le Diamant's powerful supporters. Now, though, those supporters had been sent away: the competent to Germany, the incompetent to the west. Robespierre found himself without allies. He submitted.

The morning of July 31st, 1799 (Abricot Thermidor of the year 5) dawned with the news – not whispered, but shouted from the rooftops and trumpeted in the state-controlled newspapers – that Jean-Baptiste Robespierre was dead. He had hanged himself while hiding in Versailles, the editorials (controlled by Lisieux) said. The implication was clear, that Robespierre had begun to see himself as the very thing he had sought to destroy. A suicide note supposedly found on his body showed that he had literally signed his own death warrant, declaring himself an Enemy of the People, before summarily carrying out his own execution.

The vast majority of commentators, then and now, believe that Robespierre was murdered by Lisieux's men and the death disguised as a suicide. Some modern revisionist historians have suggested that Robespierre's suicide might in fact have been genuine – there had long been rumours that he kept a signed copy of his own death warrant about his person in case he ever found an impure thought entering his mind. Depression stemming from the realisation he had lost power might have pushed him over the edge. Whether Lisieux's hand truly slew him, though, it is certain that Lisieux had *planned* to do so, and whether Robespierre pre-empted him is ultimately unimportant.

Almost from the first day of the new regime, proclamations filled the air like cannonballs on one of Boulanger's battlefields. Lisieux had already been the Republic's main writer of pamphlets and propagandists, and now he turned them out for his own ends.

The 'erring' period of Robespierre was over, it said. The corrupt Consulate was dissolved and the National Legislative Assembly would convene after fresh elections to confirm a new constitution. Until that time, that constitution would take temporary effect. Who, exactly, had drawn up this constitution and when was never quite stated.

In any case, the constitution of the 'Apricot Revolution', as it was termed, reorganised the Republic considerably. Instead of a three-person Consulate, it saw a single ruler given the deliberately lowly-sounding title of 'Administrateur'. The Republic was then divided into *départements* according to a system that had been drawn up by Jacques-Guillaume Thouret. Thouret, a Norman, was a great Rationalist who had been instrumental in the creation of the metric system. He was one of the few members of the National Legislative Assembly who had not been cowed by Robespierre. His new division of France ignored the existing provincial boundaries and, indeed, geography – he simply divided France into squares based on lines of latitude and longitude. These square *départements* were named after the Revolutionary calendar's days – Paris was assigned as Abricot, of course…—and would each be ruled by a Modérateur, a theoretically locally-elected official loosely equivalent to the Bourbon-era Intendants.[228]

The Thouret plan was an attempt to balance the local privileges of the *ancien régime*, whose loss had been part of the reason behind the Breton rising, with the strongly centralised structure of the existing Republic. The Rationalist squares spoke of Thouret's agreement with Lisieux's philosophy that Revolutionary ideals could not be softened by compromise. "If we let the status quo affect our principles," he wrote, "our principles will be worn down…but if we stand firm, we will sculpt the world until it is fit for the Revolutionary system." Some less well educated Revolutionaries apparently thought this was literal, and there were rumours that Lisieux planned, after the conquest of Britain, to cut up the island and use its parts to build up all the partial *départements* along the coasts to perfect squares. Lisieux's control

---

[228] Unbelievably, the perfectly square Thouret départements were proposed in OTL, though they were never adopted.

of propaganda was such that an impression soon emerged that there was nothing he could not do.

Lisieux's first act as Administrateur was to use his loyal Garde Nationale to complete the crackdown on the Paris rising, its usefulness to him now passed. He then appointed Boulanger as First Marshal of the Army, a new post which would give the former general enough independence to form a more coherent response to the British invasion. Lisieux picked out those competent but awkward members of the NLA and other politicians – usually Robespierre loyalists – and made them Modérateurs of *départements*. This was central to Lisieux's political philosophy. "The former regime," he wrote, speaking of Robespierre, "thought that the wheels of revolution must be lubricated by the oil of sacrifice. Such a view ignores the fact that the 'oil' is in fact made of destroyed wheels. If it had been allowed to continue, soon we would have a great deal of oil and no wheels to lubricate…the correct view must be that men are a resource, just like wheat or iron or coal,[229] and should not be wasted. It is a gross irresponsibility not to extract their usefulness, whatever the circumstances."

These relatively mild words ultimately presaged a terror in some ways worse than Robespierre's, but for now Lisieux remained focused on the British problem. In August, the main Anglo-French army invaded Normandy. Support for the Royalists was more lukewarm there, as Normandy had had no particular special status before the Revolution as Brittany had, but the majority of Normans saw which way the wind was blowing and supported the King. Lisieux demanded a response from Boulanger, knowing that many more Royal successes could tip the balance of the mood of Paris towards royalism. He, more than anyone, knew how fickle the mob could be, and how fragile his position was.

Boulanger was already worried that his friend was heading towards becoming another Robespierre, with such demands, but

---

[229] Lisieux's naming of coal as a resource reflects how steam engines are growing in importance across the slowly industrialising republic. Of course, the fact that he was strongly involved in Cugnot's operations means he is somewhat ahead of the rest of France in this respect.

agreed that something had to be done. He had assembled another army, one almost as capable as the ones operating in Germany, made up mostly of troops who should be going as reinforcements to Leroux and Hoche. Lacking an experienced command general, Boulanger went himself, in the face of Lisieux's protests.

As Lisieux built his power in Paris, Boulanger's army moved into Normandy, occupying Évreux and easily defeating a small Anglo-Royal French force that had been sent ahead. The bulk of the Allied army was in Caen, having taken the city from loyal Revolutionaries at the end of September. Boulanger fought another small, filmish [cinematic] action near the town of Lisieux, Jean de Lisieux's home town – with which the propagandists, not least Lisieux himself, had much fun. Rather than trying to hold the damaged Caen against siege, the Prince of Wales ordered that the British army decamp and meet Boulanger on the field of battle. The British had not fought Cugnot engines before. They would soon find out what it was like, to their cost. Sir Ralph Abercromby held to traditional strategy of holding high ground and letting the enemy approach over a flat plain, a killing field. Just as Mozart had learned a few months before, this was not the winning tactic it had been before.

According to Michel Chanson, Boulanger called Caen 'my second Lille', referring to the victory he had won there, the first victory of the Jacobin Wars, by his use of the Cugnot-wagons. Now he had access to far more advanced Cugnot engines: Cugnot, Surcouf and the others had been working feverishly, spurred on by unlimited funding and the fear of failure.

Boulanger had many of the old-style *fardier* wagons, essentially just steam-driven alternatives to the horse, which could tow guns into position and then unlimber to allow them to fire. But now he also had what Cugnot called his *char de tir*, gun-chariot. These were larger, more cumbersome Cugnot-wagons that, rather than simply towing an ordinary gun, were actually built around large pieces of artillery (six- to twenty-four-pounders) and consisted of a large flatbed on tall wheels. *Char*s with trained crews could fire their gun whilst moving, a truly revolutionary development – though dealing with the recoil remained a problem, as the *char*s had a tendency to flip over. Cugnot's experiments with rotating cannon had been disastrous; in order to take the recoil, the wheels had to be aligned with the axis of the gun, allowing the wagon to roll backwards. Thus, Boulanger's *char*s had only fixed-focus guns, but it was enough to make a crucial tactical difference.

It was the novelty, the unknown of the Republican weapons more than their objective effectiveness which intimidated the Allied forces. Abercromby remarked "Have the Jacobins placed mills on wheels?" The French bombardment was no greater than many the veteran British and Royal French troops had weathered before, but the fact that it came from moving cannon was unnerving to troops experienced in fighting conventional artillery. It also meant that the British artillery found it harder to reply to the guns. Abercromby ordered the cavalry to sweep in and take the *char*s, if they could. Boulanger was reliably informed of all this, as he had a Blanchard observation balloon floating over the battlefield and signalling to him by flags, giving him an intelligence advantage over his opponents.

The British and Royal French cavalry did succeed in destroying several of the *char*s, though they were hampered by the sheer size of them ("Like trying to sabre down sailors standing on the deck when you are on the pier below" recalled one cavalryman, a native of Portsmouth). More were immobilised by lucky shots from British galloper guns, one-pounder cannons that could be shifted around the battlefield even more rapidly by being hitched up to fast horses. The *char*s were fragile in places, in particular vulnerable to having their steam-boilers punctured by roundshot, which could potentially spray their crews with boiling water.

But Boulanger had anticipated this. Behind and among the *char*s rolled the *tortue*s, the same vehicles Lisieux had used to crush the uprising after Hébert's death. They were armoured carriages, somewhat inspired by those developed by the Bohemians during the Thirty Years' War, but were driven by steam engines. Inside were troops with muskets and rifles firing through slits, protected by the armour from anything but a direct hit by a cannonball. The *tortue*s were slow and cumbersome, of little use as a real weapon of war, but the Allied cavalry did not realise what they were until it was too late. Countless British and Royal French cavalrymen were volleyed down, the Republicans holding their fire until the last moment. Then, unable to reply to this unseen assault, the cavalry fled.

This started a panic through the Allied ranks. Men who would stolidly march against armies five times their size did not know how to react to these new terrors. Privates became newly nervous when they realised their sergeants and officers had no more idea of what was happening when they did.

The irony was that Boulanger's vehicles could certainly not have climbed the high ground that Abercromby held. Yet the cautious Scottish general ordered a fighting retreat, while he worked out how to defeat the Republicans' new war machines. Despite the anxiety in the ranks, the British and Royal French (the latter led by Colonel Grouchy, an exile ally of Louis XVII) made an orderly withdrawal from the ridge and retreated westward.

Boulanger could not believe his luck. His infantry, marching in columns behind the vehicles, quickly seized the ridge and then unlimbered their conventional artillery, those towed by horses capable of climbing the ridge. The Republicans now directed a withering fire against the Allies as they withdrew, killing dozens of men with each plunging cannonball. If Boulanger had had cavalry of his own, the retreat might have become a rout – but the Revolution still had trouble recruiting trained horsemen.

Nonetheless, the engagement might never have been so well known if one of the last cannonballs fired had not come down in the middle of the British command. Ironically, it was not the ball that killed the battle's most famous casualty; it struck the ground before his horse, toppling it over on top of him, and it was this which broke his neck. In the confusion of the retreat, few except General Abercromby and his aides were aware of the incident, but the Prince of Wales had just ignominiously died.

The incident would have shockwaves far greater than Boulanger's successful repulsion of the Allies from Normandy. In Britain, King George collapsed upon being informed of his favourite son's death, and fell into an illness from which he never recovered. This came at the worst possible time, as Britain simultaneously entered a constitutional crisis. The Marquess of Rockingham's government had shed support throughout the war, with the old marquess now holding only the slimmest majority in the Commons. Liberal and Radical Whigs who supported the Revolution found themselves strange bedfellows with reactionary Tories who opposed the alliance with Catholic France, but nonetheless much of the Commons was united in opposition regardless of reasons. The victories in France initially made this opposition waver, but they were swiftly followed by the defeat at Caen. Rockingham worked frantically to prevent his government losing its majority. Too frantically; he worked himself to death, at a time when George III was beginning to lose lucidity, consumed by the death of his son.

London held its breath. The British Constitution relied on a balance of power between monarch and Parliament, but now Parliament had lost its Prime Minister and the King was in no state to perform his functions. There was talk of appointing a regent, but the authorisation for such an act would require a coherent government, which did not exist – and could not exist until a King or Regent asked someone to form one. The British political system was trapped in a vicious circle. The crisis was such that the previous topic of debate, whether Richard Wesley's calls for Catholic emancipation in Ireland should be granted (opposed by the King, who saw it a violation of his coronation oath to defend the Protestant faith), was temporarily forgotten.

From the chaos, Charles James Fox emerged. Leader of the parliamentary Radical faction among the Whigs, and a strong supporter of Revolutionary ideals, he spoke in favour of Lisieux and said that the excesses of the Robespierre period were now over. "We have fought the tyranny of the Bourbons for decades," he said in a speech to the divided Parliament. "Now shall we side with them against the liberty that we have been so rightfully proud of for so long? I say no!"

Fox's radical wing would normally not have received much support, but he was one of the few great orators in Parliament after Rockingham's death, and a natural leader. Liberal Whigs who had defected from Rockingham saw him as the lesser of two evils, and though Tories despised him, their desire to end the war was such that they temporarily supported him. The Whigs struggled to find a credible candidate for prime minister to oppose Fox, but could not. Richard Burke was too young and too Liberal, though he fiercely opposed the French Revolution as his father had. The Chancellor of the Exchequer, Thomas Townshend, was politically suited but lacked charisma, having failed to come out of Rockingham's shadow. There was even talk about rallying around Frederick Grenville, the ambassador who had escaped from the Republican French mob (his American colleague Thomas Jefferson not being so fortunate) and was now an MP, as a leader. But though Grenville had both charisma and a burning desire to oppose the Republic, he could not match Fox's oratory or ready political skill. Parliament remained paralysed, as news of further victories by Boulanger poured in.

The deadlock was broken on November 9th, coming on the same day as the news that Boulanger's lightning advance into Brittany had been halted by the combined British and Royal French forces near Mayenne. Boulanger, like Leroux in Germany, had outrun his supply lines and his army had become too dispersed. For example, he no longer had access to observation balloons, their transports being too large and cumbersome to move at his army's marching speed. The Royal French had scored a propaganda victory by managing to capture several of Boulanger's steam engines, denting their image of unknowable invincibility. The Jacobin French columns had also for the first time come up against well-drilled British infantry under Colonel Sir John Moore. British Riflemen picked off French officers as they tried to rally their men, and the machine-like volleying of the redcoats – twice as fast as any continental army, thanks to the British Army budgeting for them to train with real cartridges – had ground down the columns until even their well-trained soldiers turned and fled. It was far from a rout, but Boulanger was forced to retreat. The ultimate outcome of the war remained to be decided. On that day, George III finally slipped from life. His last words, spoken in a fever, were reported to be "I am and always will be a Virginian, and let no man speak ill of that."

Meanwhile, down in Saint-Hilaire, the legend of Leo Bone was being quietly made, presently overshadowed by greater events, but that does not enter into this tale.

Upon George III's death, Prince Henry William, despite the reservations of large parts of British society, became King Henry IX. He was crowned in Westminster Abbey on Christmas Day 1799, as the war in France ground to a halt and the armies retreated to their winter quarters. It seemed symbolic that a new century would begin with Henry IX's reign, for novelty abounded in the young, unexpected king's ideas.

Henry had always been aligned with Charles James Fox's Radicals, and it was no surprise that he asked Fox to form a government on January 14th 1800. Fox achieved a narrow majority in the Commons, part of his support coming from reactionary Tories who wanted to see the war ended at any cost and 'court party' MPs in the pocket of whoever sat upon the throne. Fox naturally always struggled to get legislation past the Lords, however. Fox formed his "New Cabinet" and immediately sent out peace feelers to Lisieux's new Administration.

The positions of the two states bore certain parallels. Both thought they were in a weaker position than they were, but would not admit it. Lisieux was certain that if Boulanger had not achieved total victory now, he never would, not without the unavailable armies stuck in Germany and Italy, while the British could easily reinforce across the Channel. He also knew that the republics in Italy, Swabia and Switzerland were creations of Robespierre and might not support his new regime. The British, on the other hand, thought that they had only barely held on against Boulanger's new machines of war, and it would take years of study in peacetime to figure out means of taking on the Revolutionary technology and tactics. "If the Jacobins throw us back into the sea, who is to say that Boulanger cannot conjure up a bridge of steam and send his troops into England?" wrote the Marquess of Stafford, a leading Tory thinker. He jested somewhat, but was in other ways remarkably prophetic. "We need time to understand that these new marvels are not magical but simply the product of man's ingenuity…time which we will not have unless this war is brought to a close."

Therefore, when Fox's government approached Lisieux's, the Peace of Caen was signed only weeks later, on 4th March 1800. The shock of the abrupt end of the war resounded in the British media, but much less so in France. Lisieux had already taken control of the press and was forming it into the legendary propaganda machine it would become. The French papers said that Boulanger had thrown the English into the sea, and that the rebel areas would remain under special military administration until they were purified enough to be integrated back into the Republic. Until that time, the French people were forbidden to travel into those regions, lest they become 'infected' by impure ideas. Lisieux borrowed heavily from Robespierre's language, but all of this was simply to conceal the fact that the areas were still held by rebels. As part of the peace treaty, Lisieux agreed to allow a rump Royal France consisting of Brittany and the Vendée, but no more. Louis XVII, appalled at the British betrayal under Fox, was forced to consent to this. He returned to Nantes and formed his capital there.

No-one thought the Peace of Mayenne (as it was called) would last for long. For both sides, it was a time for rebuilding. Fox might be naïve enough to think the Republic could be courted, but the majority of commentators knew the war would begin again one day.

For now, though, Britain returned to its domestic affairs and resumed putting down the last vestiges of the USE rebellion in Ireland, while the Republic turned its attention to Spain. This was the so-called Double Revolution, Lisieux coming to power in France and Henry IX and Fox in Britain. In North America, though, it is sometimes known as the Treble Revolution. American fervour for the war had died away slowly as Jefferson's death had faded into memory, and Lisieux was now wise enough to publicly apologise for the incident, associating it with Robespierre's dead regime. Some parts of the Empire, notably Carolina, disliked the alliance with Royal France as they presently coveted expansion into the remaining French colonies in America, which as yet remained loyal to the King. So, in July 1799, when a new general election was called, James Monroe's Constitutionalist Party won a majority of seats in the Continental Parliament, unseating Lord Hamilton's Patriots.

The Lord Deputy, the Duke of Grafton, formally asked Monroe to form a government and Monroe became America's third Lord President. He was the first not to to be a peer, refusing the offer of a title and preferring to focus on the Commons – like William Pitt, he believed that that was where power had shifted in this age. The Constitutionalists immediately formally ended the war with France, which had technically continued past the British peace due to Albert Gallatin, the American representative there, lacking the powers to sign the treaty. This was a problem which Monroe rectified with the upgrade of Gallatin's status to Lord Representative; later, he replaced Gallatin with a political ally, James Madison. Gallatin returned to New York to continue his work with maintaining peace and cooperation with the Howden, while Madison almost became treated as an absentee member of Fox's cabinet, his own radical-leaning sympathies lying well with the new British government's.

So four nations – Great Britain, Ireland, North America and France – had now been placed on wildly different courses. This did not mean, of course, that those courses would never again collide…

Chapter 41: The Space-Filling Empire

Capt. Christopher Nuttall: As we move away from Europe for a moment, a brief note should be made that most African names have been altered to their OTL spellings to avoid confusion, though often different and less French-influenced transliterations are the norm in this timeline. *(Pause)* I apologise for the absence of Drs Pylos and Lombardi, but I fear they had a somewhat heated argument over the nature of Societist doctrine *(indistinctly)* where did I put those bandages?

> *"If you rise from defeat, licking your wounds, and resolve that you should have the victory next time—first you must understand why you lost"*

– Michael Olesogun, Prime Minister of Guinea (1942-1946)

From: "A History of West Africa" by Lancelot Grieves (1964, Mancunium House Publishing)–

Prior to the Africa Bubble scandal of 1782, Guinea[230] was a largely unknown land to most Europeans. Many powers – England and then Britain, France, the Netherlands, Portugal and Denmark – had maintained trading posts along the coastline since the sixteenth and seventeenth centuries, but there was little penetration into the interior. Those trading posts dealt in African commodities such as ivory, gold – and slaves. Slavery was, in fact, the major motor of Eruopean trade with Guinea throughout most of the eighteenth century. A 'triangular trade' was practiced, with manufactured goods going from Europe to Africa, slaves

---

[230] The term Guinea is here used in a vague sense to mean all of Sub-Saharan West Africa, as it often was in the period in OTL.

from Africa to American colonies, and raw materials going from America to Europe. This status quo was not actively challenged until the second half of the eighteenth century.

Opposition to African slavery began as early as 1727, when the Quaker Church of Great Britain (the Society of Friends) made it doctrine to oppose the practice. The Quakers in America took somewhat longer to cleave to this, perhaps because slavery was all around them and vital for the economy of many areas of the colonies. The movement was nonetheless given a big boost when William Penn, the founder of Pennsylvania, had a change of heart and freed his slaves, thereafter supporting abolitionism. Court cases in the 1760s and 70s over American slaves brought to Britain were reviewed in the House of Lords, and it was judged that the abolition of (white) slavery made in 1101 by the Normans continued to apply. Slavery itself was therefore resolved to be illegal in Britain, and any slaves brought into the country legally automatically became freemen, although this was not necessarily *de facto* enforced. The slave *trade* was, however, violently defended by established business interests in the face of opposition by a growing abolitionist movement. The trade had made the fortunes of many *nouveau riche* families no less than the rise of industry, and was at the back of the first economic boom in Liverpool and other ports on the west coast of Britain. Those who had benefited from it would not give it up without a fight.

Elsewhere in Europe, opposition to slavery was initially slow to arise. The biggest move in the arena outside Britain was in Denmark, when King Christian VII abolished the slave trade as part of his moves to withdraw Danish trade from Africa in order to focus on building power in the Baltic. By this point, the trade was becoming less profitable in any case, so Christian's appeal to abolitionist sentiment was largely a calculated political move – but the fact that such a move was seen as holding any weight, even to a minority of the court, was an indication of how the subject was spreading through the intellectual classes in Europe. France and Portugal were the nations most hostile to the idea of abolishing slavery, both because their colonies depended heavily on the slave trade and because the French intellectual scene was dominated by pro-slavery thinkers such as Voltaire. Linnaean Racism, nowhere more enthusiastically embraced than by French thinkers even before the Revolution, also got in the way: it was easy to justify slavery on the grounds that Africans were incapable of success without white guidance. Of course, such theories were usually thought up by armchair philosophers who had not travelled to Africa itself to discover found that slaves were bought by European traders from quite sophisticated native states...

The first nation in the world to abolish slavery was the proto-United Provinces of South America, in 1784. Though even the country's name had not been thought of that point, the initially unofficial move was a ploy to gain wider support and an attempt to unite the people of the former Viceroyalty of Rio de la Plata behind the rebel government. Negro slaves were promised their freedom if they fought for the rebels. It fitted neatly into the general ideology of abolishing the *casta* system that powered the rebellion. Though after the war the promises were not always entirely lived up to (if slavery in name was banned, indentured servitude often remained) it was nonetheless an important exemplar for other countries.

The northern Confederations of the Empire of North America, and the colonies that had preceded them, drifted away from slavery throughout the late eighteenth and early nineteenth century. The General Assembly of New England passed a law calling for the gradual abolition of slavery in 1789, with the result that none would be born into slavery after that date within the Confederal boundaries (although the living slaves were unaffected). Pennsylvania, initially more hostile to the idea, was gradually won over by the actions of the Pennsylvania Abolition Society, backed by the influential natural philosopher and writer Benjamin Franklin. In 1795 the Pennsylvanian Confederal Assembly narrowly passed a law which included manumission similar to New England's, but – of huge significance for the course of American history – also banned the transport of new slaves into Pennsylvania. This meant it was almost impossible to import slaves into New York or New England from the southern Confederations, except by ship. New York itself still had long memories of the Negro Uprising of

1741 (which Prince Frederick had used in propaganda to attack Governor Cosby), but surrounded by "free" Confederations and with a growing abolitionist movement of its own, relented. The New York Assembly's law, passed in 1803, was a watered-down version of the other confederations' laws and did not apply to unincorporated territories or the Howden protectorate. However, it set another important precedent.

All of this background serves to explain why the African slave trade was slowing down throughout the second half of the eighteenth century. America and the West Indies also, by now, had enough of a black population to hypothetically sustain a future pool of slaves, largely making new imports uneconomical for the slaveholders. The triangular trade was impaired by this bottleneck, and Britain's Royal Africa Company was beset by economic difficulty, though the company itself had formally abandoned the slave trade after losing its monopoly in 1731. The last Director, David Andrews – who was later tried and sentenced to life imprisonment by the House of Lords – attempted to conceal the extent of the Company's debts, with the result that the Bubble wiped thousands of pounds off the New Jonathan's Stock Exchange when it broke in 1782. It was not, in fact, an economic bubble in the usual sense, but was so named because it reminded many commentators of the South Sea Bubble fifty years before. That meltdown had paralysed the British government and led to the creation of the (still unofficial) office of Prime Minister. This one would be no less influential.

The Prime Minister, the Marquess of Rockingham, was forced to resign over the scandal (though he would later return upon the collapse of Portland's government in the face of the threat of Robespierre's France). The new government, led by the Duke of Portland but masterminded by Edmund Burke, immediately distanced itself from the failures of the previous Ministry and decided to reform the Company considerably.

The Royal Africa Company had had an unhappy history thus far. Quite apart from being an organisation founded to trade inhumanely in human lives, it had been set up by James, the Duke of York in the seventeenth century – the same man who had later become the definition of evil to many non-Jacobite Britons as King James II. The Company had already survived several minor collapses and reinstatements throughout the eighteenth century, suffering from the loss of its slave monopoly and then refocusing on the gold dust and ivory trade. It had also been officially renamed so many times that any number of the names were in common circulation, and considered interchangeable – the Royal Africa Company, the African Company, the Guinea Company, the Negroland Company, and many more.

The Company's organisation was in a sad state, and the Portland Ministry decided that the best way to rejuvenate it would be to bring in talent from its far more successful sister organisation, the British East India Company. Despite facing hard competition from its French rival, the BEIC's trade had brought great wealth to Britain, while the RAC was struggling even to keep itself afloat.

Thus, the new Board of Directors set up for the RAC was made up partly of men brought over from the BEIC. The two most prominent – and famous – of these were Arthur Filling and Thomas Space, two junior EIC directors who could not have been more different. Filling was a dour Scotsman who had joined the Company's military and served in the Indian wars, losing an eye during the war with the last Nawab of Bengal, Siraj-ud-Daulah. He also had a keen acumen for business, and had found his way to his current position partly through careful investments with a small fortune he had taken during the sack of Calcutta. Space, on the other hand, was an idealistic Englishman from a privileged background, who had joined the Company mainly in order to visit exotic climes and learn about new peoples and languages. He was a strong opponent of slavery, being a member of Frederick Wilberforce's Committee for the Abolition of the Slave Trade, and importantly through that membership was on speaking terms with several of the most prominent among Britain's West African community. These included Olaudah Equiano, an escaped slave who had become a respected writer. There was thus Anglo-African participation in the Company's philosophy from the start, interest having been sparked among the several thousand 'Black Poor' inhabitants of London.

The challenge facing Filling and Space, as well as the other directors, was vast. The Company had singularly failed to find a new profitable trade niche since the loss of its slavery monopoly, and it was competing with both independent British traders and other European outposts along the West African coast – the French and the Portuguese, the Danes and the Dutch, though the Danish outposts were gradually turned over to the Dutch thanks to Christian VII's policies. After initially despairing of the difficulty of their task, Space claimed to have had a vision come to him in his sleep, along with a message: *look to the east.*

The implication was clear – after all, the Prime Minister had brought them in to make the RAC more like the BEIC. And the BEIC's current success was based on a more interventionist strategy, pushing influence deep into the hinterland while accepting natives into positions within the Company. The BEIC had not been much more than a trading company while it was limited to outposts on the fringes of the Mughal Empire, but now it was so much more. Could the RAC copy that success? There was only one way to find out.

The partnership of Filling and Space meant that the dual philosophy of the New Company was both profit-driven and yet possessed a moral aspect. After all, slavery was commonly practiced in the African states themselves, usually taking the form of enslaving war captives. "Once upon our time, our ancestors did the same," Space wrote in a letter to Filling. "Your grandfather many times removed may have captured and enslaved mine…" a reference to the fact that Space was from Northumberland, and that the Scots had practiced slave raids into English territory (and vice versa) during the eleventh and twelfth centuries. "Yet I can now be assured of even travelling to Edinburgh itself with no fear of being clapped in irons and forced to work the fields…do not our fellow human beings who happen to have been born in a distant land not deserve that same assurance?"

With that in mind, the New Company's directors cooperated with a contemporary group, the African Association,[231] made up

---

[231] An organisation of this name was founded in 1788 in OTL, but in TTL the name has been used a little earlier.

of natural philosophers and dedicated to the exploration of the West African interior. The Association included such luminaries as Joseph Banks, who had become famous publishing works on the fauna and flora of Canada, Newfoundland and the new western territories of the North American Empire[232]; John Ledyard, a New Englander who had joined the Association after failing to convince the British Government to finance a rival fur-trading company to oppose the Russians' efforts in Alyeska; and Daniel Houghton, a veteran and the group's leader, who was determined to find the exact location of the fabled Malinese city of Timbucktoo. It was obvious to Filling that such men could be of use to a Company searching for a new area in which to trade. Banks could identify economically important plants and animals using Linnaean techniques, Ledyard could figure out how to market them, and Houghton could help explore the interior. In return, having Company-subsidised access to a new land was an enheartening prospect to them.

The Company also soon became caught up with the Colonisation Movement, a loose alliance of societies operating both in Britain and America, dedicated to re-settling black freemen in West Africa. The Movement's diverse motives ranged from the belief that blacks could never live a normal life surrounded by white society, the idea that blacks who had been raised in such a society could go on to 'civilise' the natives, and the notion that moving former slaves back across the Atlantic was a restitution for the horrors of the slave trade in the past. The Company was approached by Equiano, one of the few Africans actually involved in the Movement's activities, with the idea of providing transport. This solved a problem Filling had noticed. His great idea was to change the *direction* of the triangular trade. Instead of raw materials going from America to Britain, they could go from Africa to Britain (once the Company located such materials that would be economically valuable). British goods could still be shipped profitably to America, as Britain

---

[232] OTL of course Banks accompanied Cook to Australia and gave his name to, among other things, *banksia*. Banks' work here is a bit less eye-catching so he's not a Sir (yet).

had begun to industrialise but America, hampered by the vast distances between its cities, had lagged behind. The problem was that he needed some commodity to go from America to Africa to complete the triangle. Freed slaves paying their way to found new colonies filled that gap, as well as providing a pleasing symmetry for more idealistic individuals such as Thomas Space.

The Company had earned enough in its first five years' worth of operations to sell off its outdated fleet – some of which were badly constructed former slaveships – and purchase new ships, often from the new dockyards in New England. The new fleet was more like the BEIC's East Indiamen, larger, more sturdy and with at least a desultory load of defensive armament. Like the BEIC, the RAC did not so much have merely a trading fleet as a full navy, suited to Filling and Space's ambitions.

The RAC sent numerous expeditions into the African hinterland, many of which did not return or returned with casualties, but an improved picture of the still half-legendary land was gradually built up. Filling knew how valuable the BEIC found those men who had a clear and concise knowledge of Indian affairs, and was trying to build up a similar cadre for Guinea.

The hinterland of what Europeans called the Gold Coast was ruled by the Ashanti Empire, a powerful and increasingly centralising confederation. Ashanti was ruled from the city-state of Kumasi by the *Ashantehene*, or King of all Ashanti. Thomas Space, upon visiting the area himself and recording his thoughts, compared the system of government to that of England under the Anglo-Saxons: the King enjoyed considerable power, but was elected by a council of the powerful rather than automatically inheriting his post. The Ashanti used a crude form of bicameral legislature (or advisory board), with most of the power held by a gerontocracy of the oldest and most powerful chiefs, but this was balanced by a second body, the *Nmerante*, made up of younger men. The King's authority was symbolised by his throne, a golden stool said to have descended from the heavens to the founder of Ashanti, Osei Tutu I, and was partly religious in character.[233] The

---

[233] In OTL, this sparked the infamous War of the Golden Stool in 1900 when a British Governor demanded the right to sit on it.

Ashanti religion, which focused heavily on various taboos, infused government to the point where it could be called a theocracy. The current King at the time of the Company's penetration was Otumfuo Nana Osei Kwame Panyin, who was seen as a stabilising influence after years of jockeying between the Oyoko Abohyen (his own) and the Beretuo dynasties. The Ashanti were the hereditary enemies of the Fanti Confederacy, another powerful state which already traded with Britain and the Netherlands. This was of interest to Filling, who knew from his BEIC history that divisions and power struggles between native kindgoms were open doors to have the boot-tip of British influence wedged into them so that trade concessions could be prised from them.

Further eastward, the area known as the Slave Coast was better known to the RAC, due to the fact that its local states had extensive slave-trade contacts with the Europeans there. Settlements by Britain and the Netherlands were joined by the small outpost of Whydah, which had been a Prussian venture ceded to the Saxons after the Third War of Supremacy. The Saxons, with no interest in African trade, had let it lapse, and the Company unilaterally seized the settlement, despite protests from the Dutch (who had had the same idea). Whydah had formerly been part of the Kingdom of Savi, which had been conquered by the Kingdom of Dahomey in 1727. Dahomey in turn, despite being one of the most powerful and warlike states in the region, had been conquered and vassalised in 1730 by the cavalry-using Yoruba empire of Oyo. The Dahomeans had lost the war despite their Ahosu (King) Agadja having invested heavily in European firearms. Now, though, the country was chafing under being forced to pay tribute to Oyo, and it was obvious that breaking free was on the mind of the current King, Kpengla. Kpengla was interested in buying more modern flintlock muskets for his troops, recognising that Agadja's failure had been partly due to having bought obsolete, unreliable matchlocks from the Danes. Filling could see another opportunity there – or two.

The Dahomean army included an elite corps of female warriors known as the 'Amazons' to Europeans, who made a connection with the Greek myth of that name. The victory over Savi was

393

considered to have been partly due to the shock deployment of the Amazons. The idea was exotic enough that, when the Company's agents published articles about it in the *Register*, British intellectual interest in Guinea was sparked and soon Africophiles even threatened to equal the orientalists fascinated by India and China.

Like Ashanti, Dahomey also had an elective monarchy, though the King had to prove his descent from their legendary founder. But the Dahomean voodoo religion required annual human sacrifices, and this pushed Space into describing the people as savages. It also explained why the Dahomeans were so enthusiastic about selling even their own people into the slave trade, given that their culture meant they placed a low value on human life (or more accurately saw this world as only the surface of a much more fundamental one, and that life or death was not a particularly important distinction). Of course, this did not stop the enterprising Filling investing heavily in trade missions to the Dahomean capital, Abomey. Beyond, on the other side of Oyo city itself was Benin,[234] barely yet breached by European traders but an important market in palm oil. The Company's interest was sparked.

Further west, Britain's acquisition of the French posts in Senegal after the Third War of Supremacy now paid dividends. Senegal had an existing colonial apparatus compared to the British one in Calcutta, with half-bloods (*Métis*, in French), filling many administrative positions and contributing largely to the area's culture. The former French colony was centred around Fort St. Louis and the island of Gorée, both of which were considered part of the government of the capital Dakar. Gorée had previously been English, as well as Dutch, so while the French had held the area for about eighty years prior to losing it, in many way the change in ownership had been accepted with a shrug by the locals. However, it is unlikely that Britain would have been so successful in the transfer of power if she had not appointed John Graves

---

[234] Confusingly, in OTL Dahomey (after ceasing to be a French colony) changed its name to Benin after independence, while the original Benin is now part of Nigeria.

Simcoe (later knighted) as Governor of the conquered territory after a period of mismanagement and corruption throughout the 1760s. Simcoe was a veteran of the Second Platinean War, who had observed the Platineans raising a regiment of freed black slaves and had even had his life saved by one such soldier. He thus had more enlightened views about what black Africans could achieve than many Britons or Americans.

Upon taking command in Dakar, Simcoe was quick to take action against corruption and root out several organisations still trading illegally with the French. Until the late 1780s, though, his grand designs could not be matched by reality, as he had few resources to work with. While Simcoe despised slavery, he recognised that Senegal's economy was dependent on it and that taking direct action against it, with no thought for the consequences, might do more harm than good.

This changed when the new Royal Africa Company moved in to Dakar, which had been included in its revised charter. Simcoe was innately suspicious of all merchants and speculators, but the fact that the RAC did not deal in slaves made a favourable impression. Arthur Filling discussed with him his plans for running British possessions in Guinea in a more BEIC-like manner. Simcoe, who had only served in America prior to this, was unaware of the details of this, and Filling spoke at length on the subject. It was the idea of sepoy regiments that stuck in Simcoe's head, more even than Space's plan to try to broaden Senegalese trade to the point where the slave trade might be wound down. This was the germ of what would become the Company's African equivalent of sepoys, native troopers trained and equipped in the British fashion—intended to exert the Company's will on, and in alliance with, native states. Although they were first raised by Simcoe in Senegal, the term for them that eventually stuck was 'Jagun', from the Yoruba word for a soldier, *ologunomo ogunjagunjagun*. This can perhaps be attributed to the fact that it sounds similar to *jäger* or 'hunter', the name used by various German armies for an elite skirmisher, and that the Company employed some German veterans from Hanover, Hesse and Brunswick to help train its native soldiers.

Simcoe soon needed many such troops, because Equiano and Space approached him with the idea of founding a black freedman colony in the region, to the south of Senegal proper. Simcoe agreed with the idea, partly because he thought such an example might eventually lead to a decline in slavery elsewhere in the region. Coastal land around St George's Bay was purchased by the Company from the Kingdom of Koya, a local power that had had extensive diplomatic contacts with Britain and the French and recognised, from the changing of hands of Senegal, that Britain was now gaining supremacy in the region. Koya signed over the little-settled land in exchange for British help in a war against their neighbours, the Susu. Company troops, consisting largely of hired Hessian and Scottish mercenaries paired with Simcoe's first cohort of native soldiers, assisted the Koya and forced a Susu defeat in a war which ended in 1793. Koya then vassalised Susu and thus gained overall from the deal, at least in the short term.

The new colony was supported by the Colonisation Movement, and was named Freedonia, with the inhabitants being known as Freedes and the adjective being Freedish.[235] The capital, overlooking St George's Bay, was called Liberty.[236] The colonists who arrived in that first decade were a very diverse crew, from many places and many classes. Some were educated, such as Equiano, who became the first Lieutenant-Governor of the colony and set a precedent that they would not be ruled by a white man appointed by London. There were many 'Black Poor', as the blacks of London who had become stranded there after being press-ganged into the Royal Navy were called, and a few of them brought white English wives with them. Many freed blacks from the northern Confederations of North America, and the West Indies, came also. This vast range of colonists meant that mutual communication was often difficult, and a simplified creole version of English known as 'Freedic' or the 'Tongue of Liberty' became the common language.

---

[235] While this may sound questionable, these were actually terms considered for the USA in OTL by the Founding Fathers, and given that Sierra Leone was originally called the Province of Freedom...

[236] Built on the site of OTL Freetown.

Freedonia was at first under serious risk of attack from native powers – Koya and Susu were only two among many – and bandits, including slavers. Because of this, Equiano raised militia regiments from the colonists, sharing resources with Simcoe's jaguns, and began a tradition of close cooperation between the Freedes and the Company. Filling had envisaged a BEIC-like bureaucracy consisting of blacks who spoke English and understood British methods of government; the Freedes were a pool of just such people, and ones who passed on their ideas to genuine natives as the colony grew.

Yet all of what the Company achieved would have been impossible, or at least very difficult, without the work performed by James Edward Smith. Smith was a natural philosopher and Linnaean, who ignored Linnaeus' racial theories and worked on what Linnaeus himself had seen as the far more important work, his classification of animals and plants. Originally Linnaeus' intention had been to find economically important plants that could be grown back in Europe. In this he had never succeeded much himself, but his successors such as Smith eventually did so. In this he was assisted by Alexander von Humboldt, a Dutch natural scientist of Prussian birth.[237] Humboldt originally approached the British in 1800 after failing to sell his new idea to the Dutch. While based in Africa, he had travelled to Dutch Suriname three years before and then made an expedition down into Meridian Peru. Humboldt's writings are now keenly studied by those who can see, in his incidental descriptions of the country and its people, the seeds of resentment and rebellion against the regime in Córdoba, which had taken power away from conservative Lima and ended its *casta* system.

But Humboldt himself was mainly interested in the fauna and flora of the region, and in particular the cinchona tree – the source of quinine or 'Jesuit's bark', a remedy for malaria that had been known of since the seventeenth century, yet had not been

---

[237] Due to Prussia being reduced to a rump in TTL, Humboldt went to the Netherlands instead to get his university education, and then joined the Dutch East India Company in order to study new animals and plants in exotic climes.

widely adopted. "It almost goes without saying," he wrote, "that among Protestant physicians, hatred of the Jesuits and religious intolerance lie at the bottom of the long conflict over the good or harm effected by Peruvian Bark." Perhaps this, or simply the fact that it was such an ambitious plan, led to the Dutch VOC rejecting his thoughts on how to change this. The RAC, however, had the equally visionary Smith, who listened to Humboldt's idea and then recommended it to Filling and Space.

It was certainly a bold idea. Humboldt advocated the planting of new plantations of cinchona trees in West Africa, thus providing a ready supply of quinine to combat the endemic local malaria, which had so far killed many whites who settled and traded there – along with some of the re-settled blacks.[238] The prevalent theory that black resistance to malaria was intrinsic and not due simply to growing up in the region turned out to be wrong, which was serious, as part of the Company's economic policy (rely on educated British black colonists as administrators) rested on it.

After some hesitation, Filling invested in the idea. A fleet of Company ships travelled to Peru in 1805 – just in time to avoid a certain period of unpleasantness – and returned bearing transplanted trees, seeds and also a great deal of the dried bark itself. It returned at a crucial time, as the Company's chief scout Daniel Houghton was dying of the disease. His dramatic cure by the bark, witnessed by the Ahosu of Dahomey (who he had been visiting at the time) served to convince the local Africans of quinine's efficacy more easily than might otherwise have been expected.

The plantations were not initially a great success, the local climate being unsuited for them. Smith and Humboldt used Linnaean principles to deduce the right climate, building variedly-heated sheds and air-pumped phlogisticateurs to vary the air pressure before considering which test plants survived. The Company continued to import quinine from Peru for years afterwards before eventually becoming self-sufficient after obtaining more suitable lands for plantations. Furthermore, malaria was far from the only

---

[238] OTL, a British expedition in 1860 led by Clements Markham did the same for Ceylon/Sri Lanka, which is now a big producer of quinine.

deadly disease plaguing the region. Yet nonetheless, Humboldt's cinchona plantations ultimately served to work a remarkable transformation on Guinea...

Chapter 42: Jiyendo

From : "IMPERIUM ORIENTALE: The Rise of the Russo-Lithuanian Pacific Company" by Brivibas Goštautas (Royal Livonian Press, 1956)—

An oft-stated apparent 'historical paradox' is that many of the strokes that led to Russian dominance in the East were made at a time when Russia herself was convulsed by civil war. In fact this simply illustrates that – even before the formal founding of the RLPC – the Pacific expansion was as remote and separated from St Petersburg as the British and French East India Companies were from London and Paris. Just as French East India remained loyal to the Dauphin even at a time when there was no Royal France, the Russians and Lithuanians in the Far East continued with their operations without even *knowing* about the Russian Civil War until late 1798. This was probably just as well, as the First Fleet included a number of politically suspect Leib Guards who Peter III had deliberately exiled, suspecting them of supporting Catherine. Had news of the Civil War reached Okhotsk earlier, it is likely that the 'Japanese venture' would have torn itself apart. As it was, by the time any potential Potemkinites were aware of the situation further west, things were too hectic for any disunion to arise…

Let us recall that in early 1795, the mercurial Lithuanian expedition leader Moritz Benyovsky, impatient with Pavel Lebedev-Lastoschkin's progress in expanding the Okhotsk colony, decided to unilaterally launch an expedition to Edzo in order to establish trade relations with the Matsumae Han who ruled there. However, being unfamiliar with the waters, Benyovsky's ships were blown off course in a storm and they landed in the north of the island, in the area still inhabited by the indigenous

Aynyu people. Benyovsky was adamant that the expedition sail again as soon as possible, but was beset by two problems: firstly, both his ships had been damaged by striking rocks off the coast and were taking on water, their pumps not capable of keeping the level steady for a long voyage; and secondly, they still had no clue where they were or how to get to Matsumae-town. At this point, Benyovsky's second-in-command, Jonas Raudauskas, suggested that it might be best to return to Okhotsk for repairs and make a later attempt, as that was the port that the ships had the best chance of being able to find, and within the range that their leaking hulls permitted. Benyovsky vetoed this: according to his logbook, because he thought it would still be too far for the pumps to keep the ships afloat. In practice, almost all historians believe he rejected it simply because he was unwilling to swallow his pride and return to Lebedev with his tail between his legs.

Instead, Benyovsky ordered a landfall at the nearest natural harbour that could be found, and that the ships be beached for repairs. This was perhaps overly ambitious, particularly for the young and still fairly inexperienced Lithuanian navy, but the beaching operation was accomplished satisfactorily. However, Benyovsky's carpenter, Antanas Vaitkus, claimed that the trees visible from the harbour were unsuitable for plankage. Benyovsky threw a fit and threatened to have Vaitkus hanged from the yardarm, but at that point was interrupted by Raudauskas informing him that the Aynyu natives had been sighted, watching the beached ships curiously from a distance.

Benyovsky was never one to miss an opportunity like this. Most captains would have assumed that any native activity was likely to be hostile, and prepared to defend their ships. Instead, he immediately ordered that both ships' crews be scoured for any speakers of the Aynyu language. Two were found; a Nivkh and a Russian out of Yakutsk who had previously dealt with the Nivkhs.[239] Benyovsky sent them, along with his captain of

---

[239] The Nivkhs are the native people of Sakhalin, who before this point acted as intermediaries between the Russians, Japanese, Chinese and Aynyu (what little contact there was).

marines, Ulrich von Münchhausen,[240] to treat with the Aynyu.

The natives turned out to be surprisingly hospitable. Although conversation was slow and halting at first, Benyovsky himself learned the language quickly[241] and a relationship was soon established. The Aynyu contacted their chieftains and, in exchange for part of Benyovsky's trade goods, agreed to find the appropriate timber Vaitkus required and bring it to the Lithuanians. Of course, Benyovsky's trade goods had been intended for the Japanese, not tribal peoples like the Aynyu. European naval explorers who expected to encounter the latter commonly brought things like jewellery, fine steel blades and so forth. Benyovsky had planned to trade with the Japanese, considered an advanced and civilised people about which one fact in Russia was particularly known, via the Dutch: the Japanese had banned firearms back in the days of firelock muskets. Benyovsky had thought that they might change their mind when they saw the latest rifled products out of European gunsmiths. In the end, though, he mostly ended up trading them to Aynyu hunters…or at least they *claimed* to be hunters.

Of course, Benyovsky was not stupid. He realised that trading weapons to a people surrounding his stricken ships was not necessarily the best idea in the world. To that end, he tasked Münchhausen – who was quite an accomplished spy and tracker – to tail those Aynyu buying the most rifles and find out if they were planning an attack on the Lithuanian ships. What Münchhausen found, though, was even more extraordinary: the Aynyu were indeed planning an attack, but on someone else entirely.

It was not until one of Lebedev's ships, the *Zhemchug*, finally found the beached Lithuanians six months later (still with no sign of the promised timber from the Aynyu) that Benyovsky learned

---

[240] Anglophones may not realise it, but Baron (Karl Friedrich Hieronymus) von Münchhausen was a real person, a German who was page to Anthony Ulrich, Regent of Russia, and then joined the Russian Army and served in the wars against the Ottoman Empire. In TTL he has had a similar career, but also fought in the War of the Polish Partition and married a Lithuanian. His son Ulrich (named after his old master) has joined the Lithuanian navy as a marine; OTL he did not have children.

[241] As he did Malagasy in OTL when he came to Madagascar.

the name of the place where his ships had landed – *Shiretoko Hanto…*

The Aynyu rebellion of 1797 was an event difficult to predict.[242] Tension had certainly been rising for a long time, with the Matsumae Han slowly changing trade rules over time to favour Japanese interests over the Aynyu, and occasionally engaging in land displacement and resettlement. The Daimyo of Matsumae had begun to interpret his Shogunal grant for trade with the Aynyu as a license to rule over them. But the catalyst for this particular revolt could have been anything. In this case, it was an accusation that the Japanese had attempted to deliberately poison Aynyu chieftains at a trade meeting. Whether this claim had any accuracy to it was irrelevant: it was enough to unite many disparate Aynyu tribes under a charismatic leader, who called himself Aynoyna, after the first man in the Aynyu religious tradition.

It is likely that, without Benyovsky and Lebedev, the rebellion would have gone the same way as that of Shakushain a century earlier: the Aynyu might have scored some early victories, but as soon as they inflicted a serious defeat on the Matsumae, it would be enough to make the Shogunate concerned enough to send forces to restore order there. The Matsumae enjoyed many special privileges, such as being exempt from the *sankin kotai*,[243] precisely because they were seen as no real threat to the Tokugawa.

This time, however, things were different. Some of the Aynyu – not many, but enough – were armed with European firearms. It was sufficient to result in the complete rolling-back of all Matsumae settlements north of the Ishikari plain. By 1799, the mood in Matsumae-town was panicked. The Daimyo of Matsumae decided to send a call for help to Edo, only to be assassinated by one of his lieutenants, who feared a purge like the one after the Shakushain Revolt – when, for a generation

---

[242] OTL there was a more minor rebellion in 1789 – this, on the other hand, is as big as the 17th-century Shakushain's Revolt.

[243] A system by which the Shogun essentially took members of the various Hans' *daimyo* hostage in Edo, to guard against potential betrayal and factionalism.

afterwards, the Tokugawa had imposed their own men on the Matsumae, throwing out all existing Matsumae ministers and generals. The Han descended into chaos, with only vague reports of the situation reaching Niphon.[244]

By 1800, things had stabilised, apparently. The new Daimyo, Matsumae Hidoshi – barely more than a boy – sent a representative to the newly rebuilt Shogunal palace in Edo, who reported that the situation was under control and the Aynyu had been defeated once again. Hidoshi apologised that he could not come himself at the present, as tradition demanded, as matters were still too volatile at home. Emperor Tenmei[245] and the Shogun, Tokugawa Iemochi,[246] were relieved to hear the news, as the country was still recovering from a succession of natural disasters that had hit in 1772, including a great fire in Edo, destructive typhoons, volcanoes and earthquakes. Authorising a military expedition against the Aynyu would have made already strained finances creak alarmingly. Later chroniclers of Yapontsi affairs would record this as a warning or prophecy to both Court and Bakufu. If so, it was not heeded. Matsumae had always looked after itself, and no-one thought to send an envoy to check that the representative was telling the truth.

In reality, the Aynyu had won the revolt – at least in the short term. It was likely that their dominance would not have lasted long, as their temporary, artificial unity began to break up as differing tribal interests re-asserted themselves. But Benyovsky had had another of what Lebedev described sourly as 'his great ideas, of which he has fifty in a day, perhaps three of which will not result in us being killed by the end of that day'. From his talks with the Aynyu, and later some Japanese as he visited the lands conquered by the Aynyu, Benyovsky had built up a slowly improving picture

---

[244] Niphon (not Nippon) is an archaic name for Honshu.

[245] In TTL Emperor Emperor Go-Momozono had a son, who became Emperor Tenmei, and married his daughter to a royal from a distant branch of the family (who in OTL became Emperor Kokaku). Tenmei's name means 'dawn' and reflects a hope for a bright future after the disasters of the 1770s. A forlorn hope.

[246] Not the later OTL Tokugawa by that name, but an earlier use of the name.

of Japanese society – stratified and built strongly on tradition and history. He knew that, no matter how optimistic Lebedev might be, there was no way that the Shogun would permit Russian and Lithuanian trade through Edzo. It was simply against the rules.

That, of course, assumed that the Shogun *knew* about that trade...

The strategy Benyovsky adopted was similar to those sometimes used in Germany, Mughal India, the Ottoman Empire, and even his native Polish-Lithuanian Commonwealth before its dissolution. If the system was just that stratified, the way to deal with it was not to try and change it, but just to play it. The fact that most foreign trade was forbidden under the Tokugawa was irrelevant if the Shogunate didn't *realise* it was foreign trade.

Therefore, the Russo-Lithuanian forces co-opted the dead Matsumae Daimyo's third son, Hidoshi, who had been dismissed from the succession in most Japanese's minds as his elder brothers fought in the burning house of the Aynyu revolt. Münchhausen was made the boy's bodyguard and filled him with tall tales of Europe, Russia and the adventures of himself and his father. It was obvious to the Shogun in Edo that such a young Daimyo must have a regent of some kind, but he never dreamed that it might be a round-eyed barbarian.

The Russians and Lithuanians, the latter now with repaired ships, descended upon Matsumae town in August 1799, just as the Aynyu had drawn off most of the Matsumae's remaining army. Once upon a time, two hundred years before, Japan had had one of the largest and most powerful navies in the world, but under the Tokugawa *sakoku* system of isolationism, the very construction of oceangoing ships was forbidden. With no ships and no cannon – also banned – the Matsumae were effectively defenceless against the descent.

Led by Peter's suspect Leib Guards, the Russo-Lithuanian forces took the city and broke into the castle, using European cannon taken from the Lithuanian ships to batter down the mediaeval walls. After a brief struggle which culminated in the deaths of the two elder Matsumae brothers, the town were secured. Benyovsky's wild gamble had worked, to Lebedev's not-so-private amazement. Of course, things were helped by the fact that the Matsumae's influential family surgeon, Sugimura Goro, had fallen from grace during the dead brothers' power struggle and was willing to help Hidoshi and the Russians establish themselves in return for regaining his former prominence. It was primarily Sugimura who helped the Russians and Lithuanians first insinuate their way into Japanese society – a fact which means Yapontsi nationalists ever since have equated his name with Judas.

By 1801, then, when news of the now-complete Civil War was just breaking in Okhotsk, Benyovsky and Lebedev had finally established a position. Under the guise of internal Japanese trade quietly continuing with a Han that had always been a little... edgy, a little *odd*—and so it was not entirely a surprise to find some unusual new goods included there—Europeans other than the Dutch had finally broken into Tokugawa's closed market. *Sakoku* had been, unknowingly, breached.

Things were therefore looking up for the venturers, at least for the present. But back in Okhotsk, people were getting careless. As soon as Emperor Paul heard of the successes, he sent more men and more supplies to expand the colony and the trade. The correct response, perhaps, but it meant a lot more trade going through the Amur region...a region whose precise status had been left carefully undefined for a long time, and a very good reason.

Trade with Japan had proved a surprisingly easy nut to crack, though few men would have had the daring to accomplish it. China...China was a different story...

Chapter 43: Hounded by the Afghans

*"I forget the throne of Delhi when I remember the mountain tops of
my Afghan land. If I must choose between the world and you, I shall
not hesitate to claim your barren deserts as my own."*

– Ahmad Shah Durrani

From: "A History of Northern India" by Philippe Desaix (1954)-

The eighteenth century was a turbulent time for warfare and
politics across the globe, to the extent that some have theorised
that worldwide crises might have been precipitated by unusual
shifts in climate or the coronal energy from the sun. But such
speculation lies beyond the scope of the conventional historian's
work. Suffice to say that Europe was far from alone in seeing
turmoil and rapid changes in that era, though in Europe the
chaos of the eighteenth century soon faded into memory beside
the viciousness of the early nineteenth.

Persia suffered a series of civil wars throughout the century. The
long-standing Safavid dynasty was brought down by a weak Shah,
Soltan Hossein, and invasions by rebellious Ghilzai Afghans out
of Kandahar. The Ghilzais, led by Mir Mahmud Hotaki, killed
Soltan Hossein's brother, the Persian governor of Kandahar, and
then attacked Persia proper in 1722. The Safavid response was
muted, hampered by the fact that Soltan Hossein's corrupt court
did not see fit to inform him of the invasion until the capital,
Isfahan, was already under siege. The Afghans starved the city out,
deposed Soltan Hossein and forced him to crown Mir Mahmud
as Shah of Persia.

However, the Persian armies did not recognise the legitimacy
of the coronation or Mir Mahmud's authority, and remained
hostile to the Afghans. Soltain Hossein's son, Tahmasp, fled to the

Qajar tribe of the north and established a government-in-exile in Tabriz. He declared himself Shah and was recognised by the Ottoman Sultan, Ahmed III, and the Emperor of all the Russias, Peter the Great. The Ottomans and the Russians were both cheerfully using Persia's difficulties to expand their own influence in disputed regions such as Mesopotamia and the Caucasus; however, both Constantinople and St Petersburg feared the other gaining too much influence over Persia as a whole, and so both backed Tahmasp as the rightful ruler.

Meanwhile, the Persian general Nadir Shah Afshar pretended to submit to the Afghan ruler of occupied Mashhad, Malek Mahmud, but then escaped and began building up his own army. Mashhad was a holy city and one of great symbolic importance to the Persian nation, so the Afghan occupation was more important than the city's strategic value alone. Tahmasp II and the Qajar leader, Fath Ali Khan, asked Nadir Shah to join them. He agreed and soon halted the Afghan advance, then began to drive Mir Mahmud's men back. He discovered that Fath Ali Khan was in treacherous contact with Malek Mahmud and revealed this to Tahmasp, who executed Fath Ali Khan and made Nadir chief of his army instead. He took the title 'Tahmasp Qoli' (servant of Tahmasp) and began increasing his personal power through his military command. His success in retaking Mashhad in 1726 made him a legendary figure, a Persian Alexander as many would later call him.

Nadir decided not to directly attack occupied Isfahan, but instead invaded Herat, which was controlled by the Abdali tribe of Afghans. He defeated them and many joined his army, adding valuable cavalry strength. The Abdalis assisted Nadir Shah in two epic victories against the new Ghilzai leader, Ashraf, who then fled and abandoned the city of Isfahan to the Persians in 1729. After Tahmasp made his triumphal entry into the city, Nadir then pursued Ashraf back into Khorasan. Ashraf was eventually murdered by some of his own soldiers.

The Ottomans' gains during this Persian civil war were largely undone by Nadir's campaign against them in 1730, though he was hampered by a rebellion by the Abdalis—who briefly seized

Isfahan and consumed Nadir's time in subduing them. The Ottoman general Topaz Osman Pasha also foiled Nadir's plans to attack Baghdad, one of his few defeats. However, Nadir was now sufficiently powerful that he was able to force Tahmasp to abdicate in favour of his baby son Abbas III, to whom Nadir became regent. In all but name, he had become Shah himself.

Nadir's reign had considerable consequences for Persia itself, both in his attempted reforms and in his unashamedly barbaric attitude towards subduing any internal opposition – he idolised Tamerlane and his infamous practices. Nadi's reign would end, perhaps inevitably, in his assassination in 1747. Persia descended into a second civil war, a three-way conflict between the Qajars, Nadir's nephew Adil Shah and a new Zand dynasty founded by Karim Khan. In the end, the Zands won, but by this time, much of Nadir's territorial gains had been undone.[247]

But, in the long run, Nadir's reign was perhaps even more influential for Afghanistan and the north of India than it was for Persia itself. As part of his campaign against the Ghilzais, he conquered Kandahar in 1737 and founded a new city near it, named Nadirabad after himself – aping the Alexandrian legend once more. As part of this conquest, he freed numerous prisoners of the Ghilzais, important hostages from the ruling lines of the other Afghan tribes. Among these was Ahmad Khan Abdali and his brother Zulfikar Khan Abdali, sons of the Abdali chief. Nadir took a liking to Ahmad Khan, calling him '*Dur-i-Durrani*' ("Pearl of Pearls") and making him head of his Abdali cavalry.

Ahmad Khan then participated in Nadir Shah's invasion of the Mughal Empire. That once-powerful state had declined since the days of Aurangzeb, and its current ruler, Mohammed Shah, was unable to prevent encroachments by the growing Maratha Empire from the south. Nadir continued his conquest of Afghanistan, taking Kabul and Ghazni, then – using the pretext of pursuing enemy Afghans over the border – conquered Lahore and crossed the Indus. With assistance from the Abdalis,

---

[247] Up till this point this is all OTL. In TTL the Zands won, or rather *stayed dominant* rather than briefly holding power and then being defeated by the Qajars.

he defeated the Mughals at the Battle of Karnal in 1739. Mohammed Shah bought off Nadir's army with almost his entire treasury; the Persians withdrew, but took with them the Peacock Throne, symbol of the Mughal Emperors, and the Koh-i-Noor and Darya-ye Noor diamonds, along with much other booty. Such was the loot, in fact, that Nadir was able to suspend taxation in Persia for three years upon his triumphal return, increasing his popularity with the Persian people.

Upon Nadir's assassination in 1747, Ahmad Khan accused Adil Shah of having a hand in his uncle's murder. He withdrew his Abdali forces from the Persian army, fighting their way through Adil Shah's forces all the way back to Kandahar. The Abdali chiefs then called a *Loya Jirga* to choose a new leader; after nine days' worth of indecisive squabbling – in which Ahmad Khan himself remained silent – Sabir Shah Abdali, a respected holy man, spoke up and declared that, despite his youth, Ahmad Khan was the only one he saw with the qualities to take up the burden of rule. The chiefs agreed and Ahmad Khan Abdali became Ahmad Shah Durrani, changing the name of the Abdali tribe to the Durranis in honour of Nadir's nickname for him.

Under Ahmad Shah's rule, the newly-minted Durrani tribe immediately began consolidating their power over all Afghanistan. Ghazni was taken from the Ghilzais and Kabul from its own ruler. As he did not recognise any of the claimants to the throne of Persia as legitimate, Ahmad Shah therefore did not limit his campaigns to Afghanistan, taking Herat and Mashhad in 1750-51. But the main force of his will was directed not at Persia, but at India. Exceeding his hero Nadir's brief, Alexandrian push into the subcontinent, Ahmad Shah was able to achieve lasting success against the still-divided Mughals. After three separate invasions of the Punjab, the Mughal Emperor, Ahmad Shah Bahadur, was forced to concede all of the Sindh and Kashmir—and most of the Punjab itself—to Ahmad Shah.

Ahmad Shah was occupied for some years as the rebellious Sikhs of the Punjab rose up against his forces, ejecting them from Lahore briefly before Ahmad Shah returned with the bulk of the army to reconquer the city. In 1756, he attacked the Mughals once again and besieged Delhi, overthrowing Ahmad Shah Bahadur and installing a puppet emperor, Alamgir II. He married his second son Nadir to Alamgir's daughter[248] to cement his control, and Nadir mostly remained in Delhi while his father continued to campaign with his elder son Timur.

Ahmad Shah and Timur returned to Afghanistan in 1757, pausing on the way back to sack the Sikh holy city of Amritsar and defile its Golden Temple, increasing the bitterness between Sikh and Afghan. Ahmad Shah did not remain in Afghanistan for long; the Indian situation soon began to fall apart, as the vigorous Maratha Empire continued to attack the cowed Mughals and drove the Afghans out of the Punjab. Ahmad Shah returned and led his army to a crushing, epic victory at the Third Battle of Panipat in 1761, which saw the Marathas smashed so utterly that their empire broke apart into a loose, disunited confederacy. This bought time for the Mughals to reform and regroup; Ahmad Shah assisted his son Nadir in seizing control of the once-great empire on the death of Alamgir. Nadir's son Ibrahim Shah, out of Alamgir's daughter, would have a legitimacy to rule the empire afterwards.

The Durranis controlled northern India, and the Marathas were too disunited to pose a serious threat again, but the Sikhs continued to stubbornly rebel every year or two, forcing Ahmad Shah to continuously return to India to put down their rebellions. The constant travel weakened his health and he died of cancer in 1773. Upon his death, his first son Timur brought most of the Durrani army back to Afghanistan and called a *Loya Jirga* which elected him new leader, while Nadir remained in Delhi and successfully put down an attempted rebellion led by the brilliant Mughal general Mirza Najaf Khan. After Nadir held on, Mirza Najaf retreated to Oudh, whose Nawab was married to his sister, and focused on reforming the Oudhi army. In doing so,

---

[248] A significant difference to OTL where it was his first son, Timur. Though the *names* of Ahmad Shah's sons are the same as OTL, in *character* they are different to OTL, being born after the POD of this timeline. Timur was a bit of a Richard Cromwell-like figure to his father's Oliver in OTL.

he extensively studied the infantry tactics and technology of the British East India Company, which held Bengal and made Oudh a protectorate.[249]

After a hesitation that could have turned into yet another civil war, the sons of Ahmad Shah Durrani came to an agreement to divide their father's empire. Both agreed that the sheer size of the Durrani legacy was too large and needed too much attention for any one man to rule, as their father's fate had shown. Timur took the Afghan territories – which were presently too threatened by a newly resurgent Zand Persia for him to worry about India anyway – and Nadir, of course, continued to rule from Delhi. Sindh and Rajputana went to Nadir, Kashmir to Timur. Neither could agree about the Punjab; in any case, the situation was taken out of their hands when the Sikhs rebelled once more in 1781 and neither Nadir nor Timur could spare the forces to put down the rebellion. An independent Sikh Confederacy sandwiched between the two halves of the Durrani Empire was thus quietly allowed to remain for the present, so long as it did not attempt to expand.

The Durranis of Afghanistan lost some lands to the Zands, including Mashhad and Nishapur, but successfully retained Herat. However, Timur did subdue Kafiristan, an area which proved to be at least as troublesome as the Sikhs had been. Timur's son Ahmad Shah (II) went on to conquer the northern part of Baluchistan.

But in India, the Durranis of Delhi (often known as the Neo-Mughals or Neo-Moguls to European writers) began to reform and centralise the old empire, assisted by the fact that most of the Empire's enemies were too busy fighting each other to threaten Nadir's throne. His reign was focused on strengthening the power of centralised imperial institutions, knowing that new threats would soon arise.

And this was the situation in northern India that now felt the distant impact of the War of the Ferengi Alliance in the south. For the combined forces of Britain, Royal France and Haidarabad marched upon Tippoo Sultan's Mysore…

---

[249] Oudh is the contemporary English spelling of Awadh.

Chapter 44: I Really Love Your Tiger Light

"Tippoo Sultan…a perfect exemplar for demonstrating the fact that any atrocity is excusable by intellectual society, if it be hidden beneath a veneer of progressive thought."

– George Spencer-Churchill

From: "India in the Age of Revolution" by Dr Anders Ohlmarks (English translation)–

The scene in Mysore was set for a confrontation. The Tippoo Sultan, aided and abetted by a Republican French mission led by René Leclerc, saw an opportunity in Travancore. The old king had died and was succeeded by his young son Balarama Varma. The Tippoo claimed the succession was illegitimate and invaded, ignoring the French East India Company's treaty with the Kingdom of Travancore. On October 15th 1799 the Mysorean army, headed by the Tippoo's new Cugnot-wagons (carrying his famed rockets) crossed over from Dindigool – which the Tippoo had conquered during one of the Mysore-Haidarabad Wars of the 1770s – and into Travancore.

Travancore was a small state, which had no real chance of defeating Mysore in the long run, but nonetheless had a capable army made up mostly of Hindoos of the Nayar martial caste. Unfortunately for the Travancoreans, the state was in such turmoil at the time that this army suffered from the lack of an effective chain of command, and thus did not delay the Mysorean onslaught as much as it might have done. Balarama Varma might be young, but he had already learned the ruthlessness any ruler in chaotic Kerala needed to control his fractious, divided subjects. Almost as soon as he had succeeded to the throne, he had his father's old Dalawa,[250] Raja Kesavadas, assassinated. He then elevated his corrupt favourite, Jayanthan Sankaran Nampoothiri, to the position of Dalawa. Nampoothiri soon proved to be an unpopular minister, ordering the *tahsildar*s[251] to exact excessive levels of taxes, most of which went into his own pocket. By extension, Balarama Varma himself became seen as ineffective and despotic in the eyes of the Travancorean people.

Thus there was plenty of division for Tippoo Sultan to exploit. Two powerful relatives of the murdered Raja Kesavadas, Chempakaraman Kumaran Pillai and Erayiman Pillai, had a grudge against both Balarama Varma and Nampoothiri. In addition to this, one of Nampoothiri's own *tahsildar*, Velu Thampi, went rogue and fancied himself as a better Dalawa than his master. Travancore was already struggling with these internal problems even before the Mysoreans crossed the border.

The conquest of Travancore was thus brief. The panicky Balarama Varma sent his entire Nayar army out of the capital Trivandrum.[252] They were to to meet the Mysoreans at Colachel, site of a famous Travancorean victory over the Dutch East India Company in the 1740s—which had kept European influence out of Kerala for another two generations. This time, though, the Travancoreans were routed. The Tippoo's army, swelled by levies from the lands acquired in the Mysore-Haidarabad wars, was large enough to defeat the Travancoreans by conventional combat alone. However, the screaming Mysorean rocket barrages, fired from carriages that moved without horses and belched clouds of steam, were enough to put the fear of God (or Allah) into even the most hardened Nayars. The remnants of the army, led by Krishna Pillai, withdrew to Nagercoil in the south, which had been bypassed by the Mysorean invasion, and fortified their position.

---

[250] Dalawa is the Keralan form of the title Dewan (Divan), which signifies 'taxmaster' in the original Persian/Mughal…however, in the Indian imperial successor states of this era, it had taken on a greater significance, meaning something more like prime minister.

[251] District (*tahsil*) tax collectors.

[252] Traditional English spelling of the city nowadays more commonly named as Thiruvananthapuram.

Meanwhile, the rebel *tahsildar* Velu Thampi had attacked undefended Trivandrum, sufficiently intimidating Balarama Varma into forcing him to order the execution of Nampoothiri. Velu Thampi then became the new Dalawa, but did not have long to savour his position. The Mysoreans attacked Trivandrum on December 3rd 1799, and the undefended city was swiftly surrendered by Velu Thampi, always quick to look after number one. Tippoo Sultan, who led his army personally, had Balarama Varma beheaded by a portable *chirurgien* that had been brought on campaign by René Leclerc. "It is gratifying to see the instrument of liberty dispose of tyrants so far from home," Leclerc wrote in his diary, apparently without irony.

Although the Tippoo did not trust Velu Thampi, he left him as regional governor of Travancore, which was now directly annexed to Mysore as a province. The Tippoo's ideas were indeed revolutionary; usually even the European trading companies tried to work within the established Mughal system, subverting rather than overturning it. But with one stroke, Tippoo Sultan abolished the long-standing Kingdom of Travancore, just as he had done to Cochin in 1789.

With the capture of Trivandrum, the emissaries from the FEIC there – around fifty French factors led by Henri de La Tour d'Auvergne[253] – were turned over by Velu Thampi to the Tippoo. Leclerc, still smarting from his humiliation at Rochambeau's hands, insisted that the FEIC men should be immediately *chirurgien*ed as traitors. Instead, the Tippoo left them unharmed at first, but brought them back to Mysore and had them paraded triumphantly through the streets of Mysore city. The factors were then interrogated and some were indeed executed, mostly by being thrown to the Tippoo's menagerie of tigers rather than by the *chirurgien*, a practice which Leclerc thought barbaric.

---

[253] Third son of Godefroy Charles Henri de La Tour d'Auvergne, the 6th Duke of Bouillon. As the Duke died in the early stages of the Revolution and the Revolutionaries have killed his two elder sons, Henri is now the Duke, although neither he nor anyone else nearby knows this. He went east to seek his fortune after his father squandered a large part of the ancestral Bouillon fortune on entertainments for his mistress, thus following a similar career path to Britain's John Pitt.

The aristocratic d'Auvergne, to Leclerc's outrage, was allowed to survive. After gleaning all he could from the defiant Company men, the Tippoo had them thrown in the dungeons of his fortress at Seringapatam, where several more died of ill-treatment.

Southern India now held its breath. The Tippoo, knowing that the FEIC could expect no help from home, had gambled with his audacious move. He hoped either to force Rochambeau to back down, or else to trigger a war which Mysore would win. The FEIC had plenty of firepower and sepoys in its Carnatic heartland, but Mysore's expansion since the 1750s had eclipsed this, and the Tippoo's enthusiasm for adopting European weapons had more than erased the technological disparity. He waited to see which way Rochambeau would jump, while readying his army for a second invasion if it came to war.

What did emerge was nothing that the Tippoo could have predicted. More emissaries than Leclerc had come from Europe, and not all of them served Republican France. Louis XVII realised that he had to ensure the loyalty of all his colonies lest they be subverted by Jacobins – which would be all the excuse Britain needed to move in and grab them for herself. A joint British and Royal French mission had thus been sent to Madras at about the same time as Leclerc and *L'Épurateur*. This mission, consisting of the three ships of the line *Toulon*, *Fougueux* and HMS *Majestic*, arrived at Madras barely a month after Leclerc was sent away, and later called in at Calcutta. They brought news of the formal alliance between Britain and the Bourbons (at this point, the situation was still confused enough that many thought the alliance really had been engineered by Captain Leo Bone).

Sir John Pitt, the Governor-General of British India, was in a quandary. His instincts told him that now was the time to hit the (Royal) French colonies and factories with everything he had, taking advantage of their weakness, isolation, and the Mysorean aggression. "The enemy of my enemy is my friend" had always been the modus operandi in India, both among the European trading companies and the native country powers.

On the other hand...ever since Dupleix, the FEIC had long been forced by necessity to fight on its own, with little support from an introverted Versailles disinterested in knowing where the money paying for its balls and banquets was coming from. The Tippoo's subversion of the pattern of native alliances had undone some of the FEIC's fighting strength, but not all. Even an isolated FEIC was not entirely helpless before a treacherous BEIC strike. Pitt knew he could only get away with such a bald defiance of orders if he delivered an indubitable triumph, and that was far from certain.

The Royal French would be an ally, then, but a decidedly subordinate one. Here was a chance for Britain to overturn the pattern of French dominance in southern India, not by outright conflict but by the same manipulation both had used for generations to work within the decaying Mughal imperial system.

The "Pitt-Rochambeau Accord" is often cited (inaccurately) as the name of the general Anglo-Royal French alliance, demonstrating how significant it was. The meeting of the old French veteran and the young, vigorous Englishman at Cuddalore produced a general agreement. The British and French would cooperate against Mysore, with the resulting booty being divvied up between them. Haidarabad also entered the war, albeit unenthusiastically, based on the promise of the return of Mysorean-conquered territories such as Carnool and Guntoor. The Nizam of Haidarabad's main contribution to the war effort was from his celebrated heavy artillery, 'the Nizam's beautiful daughters'.

When the Tippoo heard the news, he had the first three messengers thrown to his tigers, convinced they could only be enemy agents spreading amateurish fear-mongering. It was not until the British portion of the 'Ferengi Alliance' moved into Carnool that he realised the reports had been true. Meanwhile, French sepoys led by Rochambeau's deputy, Colonel Julien de Champard, attacked Baba Maha. This was another region which had only been recently conquered by Mysore during the late wars. The French at first enjoyed remarkable success against the cursory levels of Mysorean troops stationed there, but the Tippoo then readied his main army and shifted east into the country, meeting the French at Jalarpet. Once more the Tippoo's blazing rockets worked their terrifying magic, backed up by his cavalry and sharpshooting riflemen, and the French retreated – though they were not routed.

A secondary, southern French army led by Jean-Paul du Tourd was more successful. Du Tourd's force crossed from Tinnevelly into southern Travancore and attacked Nagercoil, defeating the besieging Mysorean army and allowing the remnants of the Travancorean army, led by Krishna Pillai, to escape. After securing their supply trains – armies in India were dependent on oxen above all else – the French and their new Travancorean allies then moved north in June and July of 1800. The Tippoo had left only a small force garrisoning Trivandrum, not expecting such a turnaround, and Trivandrum fell once again in August 1800. Velu Thampi attempted to flee but was cut down by a mob before any soldiers could reach him. Du Tourd and Krishna Pillai installed Chempakaraman Kumaran Pillai, a relative of the executed Raja Kesavedas, as Dalawa. The throne, however, remained empty – no-one from the former royal line had survived but distant cousins, and this prove an increasingly knotty problem.

The Royal French had engaged the Tippoo and neatly undone his provocative invasion – thus fulfilling their defensive pact with Travancore and increasing their popularity in southern India. It was the British, however, who delivered the real hammer blow. After reclaiming Carnool and Guntoor for the Nizam – Carnool went back to Haidarabad proper, while Guntoor was rejoined to the Circars that were Haidarabadi in name but administered by the BEIC – the British and Haidarabadi army moved into northern Mysore itself. Following the conquest of Kolar, the British met their first serious challenge with a Mysorean army led by Yaar Mohammed at Bangalore in August. Although the Tippoo had the majority of his kingdom's forces with himself facing the French, Mysore was large enough to field enough troops to at least stand on the defensive against multiple enemies at once. The battle at Bangalore at first went badly for the British, with the Tippoo's rockets wreaking as much havoc on the experienced veterans of the BEIC as they did on anyone else.

What saved the day was that the Mysorean army included

portions of unreliable infantry recruited from Malabar, which had only been conquered by Mysore a few years ago, and these broke when the British tried a desperate cavalry charge led by Major Henry Paget. This small victory sufficiently rallied the morale of the British army in the face of the screaming rockets, and the loud booms of the Nizam's artillery replying served to strengthen the hearts of both regular and sepoy troopers. Brilliantly executing a moving square in the face of the rocket bombardment – their commanders correctly calculating that the inaccurate rockets would be less effective against the tightly-packed square formation than conventional artillery was – the 77th Highlanders led the attack on the Mysorean lines. The Mysorean army crumbled in the face of the assault, Yaar Mohammed withdrew with his remaining troops, and Bangalore fell to the BEIC.

Recognising that the British were now a more direct threat to his centre of power than the Royal French, the Tippoo decided to cut his losses and retreat to Mysore city. His hope was to withstand a siege at his fortress city of Seringapatam, while the strange bedfellows of the Ferengi Alliance quarrelled with each other and their alignment crumbled. Furthermore, a long siege could weaken the besiegers as much as it did the besieged, and Seringapatam was well equipped to withstand even the strongest assault.

However, the Tippoo had reckoned without the British and French having access to the Nizam's beautiful daughters. The Mysorean army remained strong enough to turn north and engage the British at Charmapatna in September, forcing them back briefly, as Champard's northern French army pushed westward in the face of retreating Mysorean opposition.

By the 14th of November 1800, the stage was set; the Mysoreans had abandoned the field, save for occasional raids, in favour of digging in at Seringapatam. The French successfully took Mysore city almost unopposed, while the British opened up the siege of Seringapatam. Rockets and rifles from the walls cut bloodily into the British ranks, but those were swelled when they were joined by more Royal French troops out of the Carnatic on 13th January. The Tippoo attempted to lure the allies into a trap, leaking information through spies that part of Seringapatam's walls was weak and required rebuilding. In fact a second, stronger wall had already been built behind the visible wall, and the killing field between the two had been mined with gunpowder and more rockets, which would bounce around in the confined space and burn any Forlorn Hope to a crisp. A bloody nose, the Tippoo hoped, might weaken the Allies enough to force a retreat, or at least leave them more vulnerable to a sally from the gates.

After more than a month's worth of bitter siege warfare, the Allies took the bait and battered down the weak outer wall with the guns of Haidarabad. The attack, which would be a joint Anglo-French operation, was staged on 21st January 1801. The Tippoo waited near his trap, desiring to light the long fuse himself.

The attack went in at night, silently, with no preceding artillery barrage to give it away. The first Forlorn Hope was made up of the Scots from the 78th, the second by French soldiers of the FEIC. The space between the walls rapidly filled up with confused soldiers and sepoys, throwing burning carcasses around to light up the area, uncertain when confronted by the second wall before them. The Tippoo lit the fuse…and nothing happened.

Historians have mused on the question as to whether the Tippoo ever knew that he had been betrayed by his minister Mir Sadiq, who had made a deal with the French in exchange for a powerful position in postwar Mysore. Mir Sadiq had sabotaged the trap by secretly having an underground channel dug from Seringapatam's moat into the dead space between the walls, soaking the gunpowder and fuses with water. Only a few rockets went off, triggered by the burning carcasses rather than the Tippoo. Though slowed down by the second wall, the British and French brought it down with sappers and then clambered over a second breach. After that, it was hand-to-hand urban fighting with all the bitter struggle that evokes in any era.

Tippoo Sultan went down with a rifle in one hand and a sabre in the other, finally killed by French sepoy Ali Sayyid with a pistol after slaying many of his foes. His heroic last stand was immortalised in the poem *Le Tigre* by Besson, and was generally praised even by his enemies, who were more used to Indian rulers fleeing and switching sides in the noxious and uncertain political climate of the time. His general Yaar Mohammed, consumed by guilt at his failure to protect his sovereign, fled north and eventually entered the court of the Durrani Mughal Emperor, incidentally bringing news of both the fall of Mysore and new European innovations to the north of India. Mir Sadiq was indeed rewarded with the chief ministry of (a much reduced) Kingdom of Mysore, and the French restored the former Hindoo Wodeyar dynasty to the throne – whose members the Tippoo had kept unharmed, though imprisoned, to avoid antagonising his own Hindoo populace. Leclerc, facing capture by the Royalists, turned his pistol on himself rather be humiliated by Rochambeau again.

What to do with the rest of the Mysorean empire, as Tippoo had predicted, antagonised the temporary Franco-British alliance following the victory. The French were unquestionably in the weaker position in India for the first time in fifty years, but were not so weak that they could be ignored or forced into a humiliating position. The situation was perhaps helped by the death of Rochambeau of natural causes in March 1801, not long after hearing of the victory at Seringapatam. As no new Governor-General could be appointed due to the hectic situation back in Europe, Champard took the position by default. He was assisted by Du Tourd and by Henri d'Auvergne, who had been freed from the Tippoo's dungeons with his remaining men – weakened but alive. Champard was a vigorous negotiator capable of keeping up with Britain's Pitt, and between them the two hashed out a treaty which was, if not truly equitable, at least stopped the two old enemies from decaying back into open warfare.

Based on this treaty, France's sphere of influence now took in Baba Mahal, Dindigool, Cochin and Travancore. As the latter two kingdoms had no royal claimants left, they were formally annexed to the dominions of the Nawab of Arcot, who by this point was merely a French client. D'Auvergne was appointed resident in both Cochin and Travancore, while Du Tourd was made resident of Mysore. Britain, in addition to having effective control over Guntoor as noted before, was awarded Coorg, Malabar and Mangalore. Parts of Malabar were taken over by the Dutch East

India Company operating out of Calicut as Mysorean power collapsed, and this was not seriously contested by the British. The idea behind Pitt's strategy was to concede French control of southern India, but ultimately block off their direct overland access to the north of India, allowing its untapped treasures to be the property of the BEIC alone.

One immediate impact from the War of the Ferengi Alliance was a new perception in Indian thought, that the French were pro-Hindoo and the British were pro-Muslim. This was derived from the fact that the French had restored the Wodeyars, while the British worked closely with Haidarabad. Although little based in fact, it proved increasingly influential, and ultimately undermined the carefully confessionally neutral position that the two Companies had spent so long trying to protect (unlike their Portuguese counterpart with its active missionary activity). This went on to have interesting consequences with respect to European relations with the two major warring powers of northern India, the Durrani Neo-Mughal Empire and the Maratha Confederacy...

Chapter 45: Silver and Fire

From: "That Brief Interlude: Novamund[254] between the wars" by Felipe de Herrera (English translation)—

When several former Spanish colonies won their independence in 1785 (not to become the United Provinces of South America until the Convention of Córdoba five years later), most experienced commentators considered their situation to be unstable. The Spanish defeat had caused as many problems for Córdoba as it had for Madrid. The postwar United Provinces did not merely include those colonies which had risen in rebellion against Spain in the first place – the Plate, Chile and Upper Peru – but also occupied Lower Peru, whose population was mostly strongly loyalist in character. Lima in particular, having been the capital of the Viceroyalty of Peru, resented being effectively turned into a frontier backwater by the upstart Córdoba. The United Provinces helped maintain order by their alliances with the successful Indian states which had risen from the earlier phase of the rebellion: Tupac Amaru II's Tahuantinsuyo, ruled from Cusco, and Tomas Katari's Aymara, ruled from Chuqiyapu (La Paz). Three uprisings in Lima, mostly led by the Peninsular elite, were crushed between 1785 and 1805 by Meridian and Indian soldiers, only increasing the local resentment every time, of course.

The United Provinces itself developed as a conservative republic on Dutch lines, quite naturally as the Constitution drawn up at the Convention of Córdoba had been partly inspired by the previous revolt of the Dutch United Provinces from Spain in the sixteenth and seventeenth centuries. In place of a Stadtholder, the

---

[254] A term used by some in TTL to mean 'the Americas' to avoid the problem of 'American' being used as the demonym specifically of the ENA. It derives from 'New World' in Latin.

Meridian Constitution created the office of a President-General. Like the Dutch Stadtholder, the Meridian President-General was initially elected for life, but the UPSA had a more democratic means of election which was not limited to a few powerful long-standing families.[255] This was arguably half because the UPSA was frontier country rather than a European state and more used to such 'ramshackle' means of governance, and some have suggested that democratic ideology arose more from this everyday practice rather than idealism. Also, in the colonial period the would-be United Provinces had been politically dominated by Peninsulares, those born in Spain, and thus the new nativist, Criollo-dominated regime installed by the revolution frowned upon recruiting from the former important families – though of course they could not afford to disenfranchise them altogether.

In any case many Peninsulare families fled the United Provinces of their own accord, particularly those whose businesses or political contacts were strongly tied to Spain and the Spanish Crown. Among them was Ambrosio O'Higgins, an Irish exile who had remained loyal to Spain in his capacity as commanding general of the force fighting against the Mapuche Indians in southern Chile. When his lieutenants approached him in 1783 and declared that the army would return to Santiago to fight against the Spaniards, whether O'Higgins wanted it or not, he swiftly made his escape. O'Higgins hid out in Valdivia for the remainder of the war, and then took ship under an assumed name after the Peace of London. He rejoined the Spanish Imperial Service in Monterey (capital of the Captaincy-General of California) and served in various capacities before being reassigned as field-marshal of the

---

[255] Under the initial Meridian constitution, the President-General is elected by the Cortes Nacionales, whose members were in turn elected by local constituencies. The suffrage is relatively broad for the time, about the same as in the Empire of North America – the most important rebel issue was that Criollos would have the same rights as Peninsulares, with the old limpieza table abolished. However, even wealthy blacks and full-blooded Indians tend to be denied the vote by default, at least at the moment, though this is not actually enshrined in law. For mixed-race people it typically depends on their exact circumstances, the province they live in and how big a bribe they can afford.

army of New Granada in 1792. O'Higgins' background was in military engineering, which he combined with his experience fighting the Mapuche in unconventional combat, recognising that European-style warfare was of limited use in New Granada's difficult terrain. To O'Higgins, only one enemy was possible, of course – the United Provinces who had set back his career and humiliated him by forcing him to hide in Valdivia for two years.

Based on these assumptions, he remodelled the army and militia of New Granada. Although many of the more traditionalist officers under his command were aghast at O'Higgins' unconventional style, the Viceroy of New Granada, Antonio Caballero y Góngora, approved. Caballero had become Viceroy himself for his service in the 1780s when New Granada, like the Plate, had threatened to rise up in rebellion. The rebels, calling themselves Comuneros after the sixteenth-century Spanish people's revolt, had been motivated by less dramatic circumstances than the Platineans – primarily it was a revolt by Criollos in response to increased taxation – but it had nonetheless threatened to result in the loss of *all* the Spanish colonies in South America. Caballero had successfully defused the situation with diplomacy, in a tried-and-tested method that had been used by many leaders throughout history to put down such mass revolts, such as the English Kings Richard II and Henry VIII. He persuaded the Audiencia to agree to all the rebels' demands, waited for them to disperse and return to their homes, and then simply repudiated the agreement. Such a strategy worked because the Comuneros were by now too dispersed and confused to rise again effectively, and the loyalist forces were able to capture and execute the rebel ringleaders.

For this success, Caballero had eventually been elevated to Viceroy. He now suspected the United Provinces of fanning the remaining embers of Comunero sympathy in New Granada. The United Provinces had yet to develop formalised political parties, but there was a *de facto* divison in the Cortes Nacionales between those who believed that the UPSA had reached its natural borders – perhaps even exceeded them – and that they should focus in building a new national identity and developing the country, lest it fragment from being too diverse and unconnected; and those who, on the contrary, thought that the United Provinces' liberty should be spread to all the Spanish-speaking peoples of the Americas, and perhaps even beyond. This spread of liberty would, naturally, be accomplished by the conquest and annexation of the remaining 'unfree' lands into the UPSA. The two unofficial groupings would eventually be the genesis of the Partido Amarillo and the Partido Colorado (the Yellow and Red Parties) respectively.

For now, the division between the future parties was held in abeyance by the President-General, Simón Riquelme de la Barrera Goycochea. Riquelme was a Chilean, descended from a family that had moved to Chile in the sixteenth century, and thus was arguably a perfect candidate to balance Meridian interests – the political culture at the time was dominated by Platineans, making a Chilean a neutral arbiter, and his provable ancestry meant that he suited the nativist sensibilities of the post-revolutionary United Provinces.[256] But Riquelme was in his seventies, and his death in 1794 – the year of the French Revolution – prompted a dramatic reshuffling of interests.

A new election in the Cortes Nacionales to appoint a new President-General provoked a more vicious and partisan contest than before: previously the Spanish had been a sufficient bogeyman to force all Meridian politicians to work together regardless of their disagreements. This was no longer the case. In the end, the Cortes narrowly declared for Miguel de Azcuénaga, a young hero of the never-ending battles with the Mapuche like Ambrosio O'Higgins before him. Unlike O'Higgins, Azcuénaga was a fervent Meridian patriot, but he was politically cautious and did not support expansionism, for two reasons. Firstly, his experiences with the Mapuche and the Llano had persuaded him that the United Provinces needed to put their own house in order before adopting a foreign policy of any kind, never mind some hare-brained war of liberation to the north. Secondly, he argued that the United Provinces was presently in a very good

---

[256] OTL, Riquelme's daughter Isabella gave birth to Ambrosio O'Higgins' illegitimate son Bernardo, but in TTL they have never met, as Ambrosio O'Higgins did not take quite the same path in the Spanish Imperial Service.

position with respect to foreign relations. The UPSA enjoyed full free trade rights with both the Portuguese Empire and the British American possessions, and this trade – particularly the renewed interest in Peruvian quinine provoked by Britain's expansion into Guinea – supported an economic boom.

In his inaugural speech, Azcuénaga dismissed those who would throw away such a potential golden age for more resentful far-flung territories. "Have any of those deputies [who favour expansion] even visited Lima?" he asked rhetorically in a 1796 speech. "Imagine two, three, ten more Limas, scattered across northern provinces which suck in men and money like a drain, spitting out only trouble in return. That is what they would have – assuming of course we did not lose, stabbed in the back by restless natives, our fair ports bombarded once more, our precious and hard-won independence lost. We would throw away our liberty and consign our children to lick the Spanish bootheel once again. Madness. Nothing less." But he was increasingly a voice in the wilderness. As more news of the French Revolution filtered down with the trade from Europe, Azcuénaga's enemies grew restless. Even Azcuénaga's supporters trumpeted the birth of liberty in one politically stagnant Catholic nation, with the obvious hope that Spain would soon follow. Some of the reactionaries had schemes in mind just as crazy as their expansionist counterparts, imagining a huge commonwealth of Spanish-speaking republics in which Spain herself would be equal to the UPSA or what was presently the loyalist colonies. Of course, one day such a dream would no longer seem so implausible, though its final form none could have foreseen.

The United Provinces also had a relatively large French-speaking population, originating from the troops of the Duc de Noailles from the Second Platinean War who had deserted in favour of building a better life in the UPSA. Among them was the Duc de Noailles' own son Jean-Louis-Paul-François Denoailles, who became a fervent believer in Platinean liberty. He gave up his own noble title – the dukedom passing to his younger brother Antoine in France, who would meet the phlogisticateur in 1799. Although initially serving as a soldier in the *Fuerzas Armadas de los Provincias Unidas* (the Meridian army), he swiftly turned back to his first love – chemistry – and worked alongside Joseph Priestley when he fled to the UPSA in 1796, condemned at home for supporting the French Revolution. Between them, they both put the UPSA on the map of science by making discoveries comparable with those of Davy in Britain. (Republican France did not make many chemical discoveries in the 1790s, partly due to Lisieux's focus on those sciences that at the time seemed most useful in war, partly because they kept executing their existing chemists of noble blood). Priestley and Denoailles also developed immense personal fortunes from Priestley's invention of carbonated water – the secret remained safe for twenty years, at the end of which the the Priestley Aereated Water Company had a secure position as the largest supplier. Noailles' son Henri (Enrique) hit upon the idea of adding quinine to make a health tonic. This sold millions of bottles both in South America itself, and in the British, Dutch and Portuguese possessions in Africa and India. The quinine dependence of those lands also meant that the UPSA remained the sole supplier of this product even after the secret of carbonated water got out.

More importantly from a political point of view, there was Jean-Charles Pichegru, who had started out as a captain in the Duc de Noailles' army. Like Noailles' son, he had joined the *Fuerzas Armadas* after defecting, but unlike Noailles' son he decided to stay there. He rose through the ranks until by 1798 he was the commanding general against the Mapuche, like Azcuénaga before him. Pichegru, like many of the French in the UPSA, supported the French Revolution and by extension argued for military action to spread liberty further around the world, just as France was doing in the Germanies and Italy. Pichegru's similar age and background to Azcuénaga gave him a certain authority, undermining Azcuénaga's position when Pichegru opposed the conclusions Azcuénaga had drawn from the same service against the Indians. Pichegru became a deputy in 1799 without leaving the army. In the Cortes he supported Juan José Castelli, possibly the greatest orator in the Cortes and leader of the nascent radical revolutionary expansionist party—usually called the *Partido*

Solidaridad (Party of Solidarity, solidarity with France and other Revolutionary governments). Castelli argued that now was the time to strike, while the forces of reaction were on the back foot all over the world.

1801 came and the United Provinces held a general election. The French Revolution had caught the imagination of the population, both the liberal intellectuals drawn from Criollo and Peninsulare backgrounds, and the poor from what used to be the lower *casta*s. Even those who could not vote directly often influenced those who could, a village headman sometimes casting a vote for all his citizens. The electorate returned a Cortes dominated by pro-revolutionary and expansionist deputies, many of whom looked to the *Partido Solidaridad* for leadership. However, this was insufficient to reach the position that Castelli wanted. By the original Constitution of Córdobn, only the President-General had the power to declare war, and Presidents-General were elected for life. Azcuénaga was still a young man and there was no way to legally impeach him (though such a provision would eventually be added to the Constitution by an amendment).

The assassination of Azcuénaga in February 1802 has been debated ever since its occurrence, hardly less hotly now than then. Many people believe that Azcuénaga was assassinated on Castelli's orders in order to force a new presidential election. On the other hand, the official explanation is not implausible, either – that Azcuénaga was shot by a Spanish loyalist from Lima. It could either have been a random attack or a deliberate attempt by the loyalist movements to put the expansionists in power – they, too, wanted war and the chance for the UPSA to collapse that Azcuénaga had warned of.

If this was the case, it worked. The Meridian population was outraged by the audacity of the attack, and a new crackdown was launched in Peru. After a month of official mourning, a new presidential election was called. Castelli stood against Juan Andrés, a reactionary deputy who was also a Jesuit.[257] Andrés

---

[257] OTL Andrés was a compiler of European literature who settled in Naples after the Jesuits were expelled from Spain. TTL, he is more interested in collecting native American Indian mythology and folk tales, and

received more votes than the political situation a few months ago might have suggested, both due to some public sympathy with Azcuénaga's views after his assassination and due to the remaining general respect for the Jesuits among the people of the UPSA, especially the lower classes. However, Castelli nonetheless won the contest by a significant margin, and was sworn in by the Archbishop of Córdoba[258] on 16th April 1802. He immediately began placing his own men into positions of power – Pichegru was made Marshal-General of the *Fuerzas Armadas* – and preparing the country for a war of liberation.

Meanwhile, in New Granada, Ambrosio O'Higgins had been made Viceroy in 1797 after the retirement of Caballero, and had received the title Marquis of Caracas from the Spanish Crown. He died in 1801, but his son Bernardo[259] was a colonel in the army and commanded some of the respect of his father. The younger O'Higgins was as certain as his father that it was only a matter of time before there was open war between the United Provinces and the Spanish Empire. All that was needed was a trigger to ignite the tension.

A trigger that would come, though neither side would realise it for a while, in 1804…

---

moved to the UPSA instead, eventually going into politics.

[258] A note on religion in the UPSA. The UPSA is avowedly Catholic, but the Papacy is in the pocket of Spain and thus the Pope refuses to appoint or recognise the local bishops. For that reason, the UPSA has developed a *de facto* national catholic church not unlike Henry VIII's Anglo-Catholic regime in sixteenth-century England, which recognises the Pope's authority in theory but then ignores him in practice. Jansenism has a significant and growing following in Meridian religious thinking.

[259] His father picked the same name for his son, but this is not OTL's Bernardo O'Higgins. TTL's version was born by a legitimate marriage to a Peninsulare lady of Caracas.

Chapter 46: The Unsinkable Lusitania

"With the example of the Portuguese phoenix before us, it is small wonder that the gentlemen in question hold such theories; but we should be careful not to confuse human activity with natural processes, as the two run on decidedly different physical laws."

– Frederick Paley, in a lecture attacking Catastrophism at the Royal Society (1825)

From: "A History of Portugal" by Giuseppe Scappaticci, Royal Palermo Press (1942, English translation 1951)—

In many ways, the Great Earthquake of 1755 was the central event in Portuguese history. The earthquake came at a decisive moment, disastrously so in many ways. Among speculative romantics [alternate historians] hailing from that country, musing on the possibility of the earthquake never happening is by far the most common scenario for tales, no matter what our determinist geologists might say about the unlikelihood of such a notion. But this is forgiveable. The earthquake was one of the greatest in European history, reaching far beyond Portugal – where it did by far the most damage – to be felt as far away as Finland, to topple buildings in western Ireland. To a Europe that was catching its breath in the dark valley between the War of the Austrian Succession and the War of the Diplomatic Revolution, this natural disaster was unexpected and catastrophic.[260] Many pondered the possibility of it being a punishment from God for human activities, an idea that appeared (in a less coherent fashion)

---

[260] A British historian would probably call these the Second and Third Wars of Supremacy. Recall that the War of the Diplomatic Revolution is the alternate (curtailed) Seven Years' War.

among Enlightenment thinkers' circles as readily as it did those of priests and peasants.

Regardless of the cause, the earthquake devastated Portugal. King Joseph I and the royal family were fortunate enough to have been taking mass outside Lisbon when the earthquake struck, but witnessed the devastation that killed hundreds of thousands of people and destroyed countless artworks, libraries and examples of fine architecture. The quake did not spare Portugal's other cities, though Lisbon was perhaps the hardest hit. Portuguese history itself was going up in smoke before the King's eyes, and his own royal Ribeira Palace joined the list of buildings destroyed. It was a chaotic scene that could have destroyed a nation, particularly considering Spain was becoming more hostile over the unsatisfactory outcome to the Guaraní War in South America. This would eventually lead to the First Platinean War just a few years later, illustrating how desperate Portugal's situation could have been.

Fortuitously, Joseph I's Prime Minister, Sebastião José de Carvalho e Melo[261] rose to the challenge of dealing with the earthquake: while many panicked or despaired, not least the royal family, he simply spoke his famous quote: "What to do now? Bury the dead and feed the living." He organised rescue efforts and the construction of tent cities to house refugees, while also sending survey teams around the country to learn what the signs immediately preceding the earthquake had been. Troops from the Portuguese Army were called in to feed the people and keep the peace, publicly hanging looters so the rest got the message quickly. It was essential that such an event never be allowed to happen again: earthquakes might not be preventable as such, but their damage could be limited. Carvalho took a personal hand in the reconstruction of Lisbon, laying out buildings structured to better resist seismic shock, and wider streets than in the old city, the *mottos*. "One day they will seem small," he said, presciently given the coming age of Cugnot steam wagons.

Carvalho had long opposed the entrenched powers of the Portuguese nobility, considering them reactionary, out-of-touch

---

[261] Recall that he never becomes the Marquis of Pombal in TTL.

and ineffective. His masterful handling of the earthquake boosted his own popularity with the Portuguese people, as well as that of the King, and he used the opportunity to secure his hold on power. In 1758 a plot by the powerful Távora and Aveiro families against the King – possibly concocted by Carvalho himself, though scholars are divided – gave him the excuse to execute most of their members and annex their lands to the Crown. As well as eliminating his enemies, the Portuguese treasury needed every peso it could get. Carvalho's rebuilding plans were grand and well-reasoned, but expensive.

The Prime Minister effectively ran the country, successfully leading the damaged country through the First Platinean War, until Joseph I's death in 1769.[262] At this point, the crown passed to his eldest daughter, now Maria I, as queen regnant and co-monarch with her uncle and husband Peter III. One of Maria's first acts was to remove Carvalho from his post and banish him from the country to Brazil, having singularly opposed his policies throughout his premiership.[263] Of course, Carvalho soon crossed into what was then the Spanish Viceroyalty of Peru[264] and eventually joined political forces with his old sparring partner and fellow exile, the former Prime Minister of Spain the Marquis of Ensenada.

Although the two influential political thinkers died before the Second Platinean War, their writings and their making Buenos Aires a hotbed of radical thinking doubtless helped inspire the Platinean Revolution and the creation of the United Provinces of South America. That could be considered revenge on Ensenada's

---

[262] Ten years earlier than OTL; as he died of the aftereffects of a wound from an old, failed assassination attempt, he could have died at any time from the stress of the earthquake, the rebuilding efforts and the Távora plot.

[263] Such as ejecting the Jesuits from Portugal and abolishing slavery in Portuguese India. OTL, ten years later, Maria just put Carvalho (Pombal) under house arrest; TTL she's younger and more inexperienced, with different advisors, and sends him further away.

[264] TTL the Spanish never created a Viceroyalty of Rio de la Plata, one reason why the people in the region are so resentful, and it's all still part of the Viceroyalty of Peru up until the Second Platinean War.

part over Spain, but for Carvalho it was a last laugh – for no matter how power-seeking he was, he remained a Portuguese patriot who wanted the best for his country. Under Maria and Peter, Portugal's economy had slumped due to their appointments of incompetent favourites as ministers, and the recovery from the earthquake damage had stalled. But the creation of the UPSA, and Portugal's role as an undeclared ally during the war, meant that free trade was now opened up between the Portuguese colonies and the UPSA, just as it was between the UPSA and Britain. The Spanish-imposed trade monopoly in the Americas was crumbling rapidly. Brazil was now able to trade openly with the government in Córdoba, and the colony's economy boomed. In addition, many Portuguese dispossessed by the earthquake damage (many were still living in temporary accommodations fifteen years later) took the opportunity to emigrate to Brazil, seeking their fortunes as news of new opportunities filtered across the Atlantic. Not all of those stories were true, and not all emigrants found restitution – but enough did to encourage yet more.

Portugal was rocked by the news of Peter III's death in 1786 in a hunting "accident", in which he was shot down in front of the Queen. Accusations of foul play were never proven, although a plot backed by the spiritual successors of Carvalho in the Portuguese court was suspected. In any case, the King's death before her eyes sent the Queen into a manic depression from which she never recovered.[265] After a few months of deadlocked crisis in the Portuguese court, the Queen was declared unfit to rule and her son, Peter, Prince of Brazil[266] acceded to the throne at the age of 25 as King Peter IV. The former Queen retired to a convent until her death in 1795.

In the first few months of Peter's reign, a sour saying began circulating in reactionary circles: "Are we certain that he is his father's son, and not Carvalho's?" Peter was a dynamic ruler who

---

[265] Maria was known as Maria the Mad in OTL and suffered the same syndrome some years later, in 1799. Some historians claim it was porphyria instead.

[266] Maria's children are different to OTL. The eldest, born in 1761, is Prince Peter (Pedro).

brought an air of hands-on determination to the Portuguese monarchy that it had not had for many years. He kept on the (by now aged) Prime Minister Martinho de Melo e Castro, one of his mother's more reasonable choices for the job. Melo died two years later, but Peter's freer hand gave him time to implement some of his more ambitious policies, which had been shot down by Queen Maria's more reactionary court. Melo had grand ideas for Brazil as the jewel of the Portuguese Empire, using the new influx of colonists to develop and further colonise the land, building trade links with the new UPSA and blocking the Spanish out of most of South America. Peter granted him a green light for these policies if Melo would give him his support – by now quite strong in the court – for radical domestic upheavals.

After Melo's death in 1788, Peter appointed his like-minded son Jaime as Viceroy of Brazil, continuing the development of the colony's relations with the UPSA.[267] He worked with the Captain-General of the frontier province of Rio Grande do Sul, Jorge de Sepúlveda, who had been exiled from Joseph I's court for fighting a duel with the British ambassador years before. Sepúlveda knew the situation on the ground better than Melo the younger and was able to help turn the Viceroy's dreams into reality; in return, Melo backed Sepúlveda's policy of firmly enforcing the vaguely defined Brazilian/Meridian border and driving out any Indians who straddled the border – as well as increasing direct control over the border regions, this meant that trade between the UPSA and Brazil was more tightly controlled, and customs and taxation raised more funds for the treasury.

Peter then appointed the Duke of Cadaval, Nuno Caetano

---

[267] Of course the in-timeline author cannot note this, but Jaime de Melo el Castro's enlightened policies also help dampen independence sentiment in Brazil at the time, although this is already different to OTL due to the fact that the great independence of the 1780s happened right next door, in Rio de la Plata, rather than up in North America – i.e. both the good and bad parts of the revolution are on display to the Brazilian people, rather than just rumours and propaganda. There had already been numerous rebellions in Brazil, but they were typically focused only on a particular region rather than seeking to unite all the Portuguese colonial outposts that gradually became one country.

Álvares Pereira de Melo, as Prime Minister of Portugal. Although a reasonably capable politician and astute at manipulating the court, in terms of ideas and policies Cadaval was a nonentity – which was exactly what Peter wanted. Murmured accusations of Bourbon-style absolutism came from the more reactionary elements of the court (those that had survived Carvalho's purges) as Peter centralised power and laid forth his policies. Melo and his son could have Brazil: it was the rest of the Portuguese colonial empire Peter was interested in.

Plenty of colonial enthusiasts in Portugal had torn their hair out after the earthquake and the damage it had cost, complaining that Portugal would spend the next hundred years trying to repair the damage, and missing countless opportunities for colonisation and trade to the east and south. The country had already suffered from one hiatus in its colonial programme, during the neglect of the personal union with Spain in the seventeenth century. A second could kill the empire, which was already struggling (along with its traditional rival, the Dutch) to keep up with the emerging powers of Britain and France. In particular, the Portuguese East India Company's trading operations in India were being threatened by the constantly changing situation there, not least because of the actions of the increasingly bullish British and French East India Companies. Both now seemed more interested in gaining a monopoly through force than in trade itself.

But Peter argued that those pessimists had it the wrong way around. The damage to Lisbon and the other cities was indeed something that could take generations to rebuild and millions to finance. The response to that should *not* be to neglect the empire and focus on that rebuilding, but to the turn the empire into more of a cash generator and let the reconstruction handle itself. Furthermore, more developed colonies – as with Brazil – would let dispossessed people emigrate as colonists, relieving the housing pressures at home. Many people were sceptical of the young, vigorous king's forceful dream, and a plot led by the Duchess of Lafões to have Peter assassinated, and return the mad Maria to the throne, was uncovered in 1789. Once more the taunt about Peter being Carvalho's spiritual son went around, as the conspirators were mostly executed and had their lands seized by the crown. Power continued to centralise, but Peter took a leaf out of Christian VII of Denmark's book and revived the Portuguese Cortes as a way of playing off the commoners against the nobles and the Church. This move is probably what saved his kingdom from much revolutionary sentiment in the late 1790s, an impressive achievement considering the fact that many people still lacked proper housing and recovery from the earthquake was still slow.

Peter appointed new viceroys and governors to the Portuguese colonies in Africa and India. Perhaps the most prominent of these was João Parreiras da Silva, called 'the Portugee Pitt' by English admirers, who was appointed governor of Goa and Viceroy of Portuguese India. Elsewhere too Peter's investment in the navy, the East India Company, and in colonial development yielded results. The Portuguese were fortunate in that they made considerable financial gains off the back of other nations' expansion – the British stabilising Guinea and the Dutch in the Cape meant that the Portuguese possessions at Bissau, Angola and Mozambique had new trade opportunities opened up to them. But Parreiras did not sit idle and wait for wealth to come to him – he went out and sought it.

The Portuguese in India had made much capital (political and literal) off their good relations with the Maratha Empire for the last century or so. Goanese soldiers and especially artillery were loaned to Indian princes in their own battles, and the Portuguese East India Company continued to dominate the trade of western India, their only serious rival the Dutch in Calicut. However, matters were changing. The decisive defeat of the Marathas by the Afghan Durranis at the Third Battle of Panipat in 1761 shattered the Maratha Empire into a looser Confederacy plagued with infighting. Furthermore, British and French incursions into the interior of India – culminating in the joint intervention into Mysore in 1801 – threatened to shake the Portuguese near-monopoly on trade in the region. Both Britain and France had large numbers of both European and sepoy troops on the ground, and the Portuguese could not back up their negotiating position without the same. Peter increased recruitment for the Army and introduced the policy of bringing Brazilian-recruited troops out of the country and deploying them into other theatres – probably inspired by the British use of American troops abroad in the War of the British Succession and thereafter.

Parreiras received the army he needed to enforce his will, and by 1794 the Portuguese were on firmer ground in India. The Marathas were disintegrating, Berar having become a British protectorate while the House of Scindia fought a bitter war for leadership over the remnants with the House of Holkar.[268] At this point Parreiras pulled off a diplomatic coup. The Peshwas, theoretically the leaders of the Empire, had been reduced to ruling the land of Konkan from their capital at Poona, not far from British (and once-Portuguese) Bombay. Furthermore, their power had been further reduced by a series of coups and assassinations from Ragunathrao, brother of the Peshwa killed at Panipat and perpetual regent (and attempted assassin) towards his ruling nephews.

By the 1790s, the young Madhavarao Narayan, son of one of those nephews, was Peshwa, but all his matters of state were handled by his able chief minister, Nana Fadnavis. Respected by the leaders of the European trading companies, Fadnavis was the sole reason for the survival of the Peshwa's domain in the face of pressure from all sides. His assassination in 1795 – coincidentally on the same day as Louis XV's execution in Paris, and probably committed by former Ragunathrao supporters – triggered open warfare. Madhavarao struggled to hold on to his throne as a pretender, while Raosaheb (claiming to be the son of Ragunathrao) arose in the east. With backing from the Nizam of Haidarabad, he marched on Poona. Madhavarao's control over his army started to disintegrate without the authority of Fadnavis, and he abandoned the city, fleeding to Raigad near British Bombay. It was obviously his hope to appeal for help from the British, but the British Governor-General of Bombay was not the most capable of men and could not have helped him

---

[268] The Scindias ruled Gwalior and Ujjain, while the Holkars ruled Indore and Malwa. The other Maratha states have their own ruling dynasties.

even if he was. In recent years, as military intervention became more important, Bombay had decidedly slipped down the ranks of importance among British Indian cities, for all the effort that had been put into acquriring it from the Portuguese in the first place a hundred and fifty years earlier. The Governor-General of Calcutta was already de facto ruler of all British India, a fact that would be formalised a few years later, and John Pitt was too busy with the events leading up to the War of the Ferengi Alliance to intervene in this dispute on the other side of the country.

However, Parreiras offered his services instead. The Portuguese continued to be viewed with more suspicion than the British and French in India thanks to their efforts with the Inquisition in earlier years, but the desperate Madhavarao was willing to take anything he could get. Knowing perfectly well what he was letting himself in for, he accepted.

The pretender Raosaheb, having sacked Poona, retreated from the city in the face of the Portuguese and Goanese army. A cautious and realistic general, he decided that the best way to defeat such a force was to starve it out. To that end, he ordered his own army to retreat to the fortress city of Gawhilghoor to the east, while maintaining a scorched-earth policy to try and deny the Portuguese provender. However, in the process he lost a large part of his own army, mercenaries who deserted once the chance of plunder was lost in the face of a siege.

Raosaheb's strategy was sensible enough. Gawhilghoor was a legendary fortress in that part of India, thought to be impenetrable. Situated in the mountains north of the Deccan Plateau, it was known as the Fortress of the Skies and was defended both by strong walls and a ravine forming a natural defence between the walls. By this point Raosaheb's army had shrunk to only around four thousand, but even that many men could hold the fortress against a much larger army.

It was difficult to bring the Goanese guns up the mountain to blow a breach in the walls, and they failed to make much impression once they were there. After a failed frontal assault against the main gate which suffered heavy casualties, Parreiras adopted a different approach. A second frontal attack was implemented by sepoys as a diversion, while his Portuguese soldiers stood by with ladders to attempt an escalade of the walls near the gatehouse. The daring plan was supported by *Cazadores* (Riflemen) stationed higher on a mountain ledge, who could accurately shoot down those enemy soldiers on the walls who planned to throw back the ladders and fight the escalading troops. In the event most records of the battle suggest it was the *Cazadores* who turned the tide, as otherwise Raosaheb's men would have been able to defeat the escalade. With the accurate rifle bullets raining down from above, though, the Marathas retreated and the Portuguese were able to capture the gatehouse, opening the door to their main army. The rebels were defeated, and Raosaheb brought back to Poona for a public execution.

The brief Peshwa's War served to place Portugal in a firm position of influence over the Peshwa's domains in Konkan, vassalising Madhavarao. Working on the British model, Parreiras appointed a 'resident' at Pune whose real job was to inform the Peshwa what foreign policy he should set if he knew what was good for him. Ironically enough this involved shutting out British Bombay to some trade, just under the level of provocation that would get the British angry enough to intervene. Although Peter IV pursued the renewal of the old Anglo-Portuguese Alliance in American and African waters, India – as always – was another question.

Similar Portuguese interventions took place elsewhere, with renewed tinkering in spheres of influence that had previously been tacitly ceded to the Dutch: Portuguese ambassadors were sent to the anti-Dutch Kingdom of Kandy that ruled the interior of Ceylon, and (with less success, due to the tight Dutch system of control) several Javanese states. These were mostly due to Parreiras' influence: due to his famous victory at Gawhilghoor in 1796, he received greater favours, a vice-countship and more powers from the King. He sought to establish a single policy for all Portuguese colonial and imperial activity in the Indian Ocean, which he saw as his rightful domain.

Possibly Parreiras' greatest achievement was his alliance with Zand Persia. The Zand dynasty had proved to be relatively non-belligerent by Persian standards, but wars persisted in coming their way. In particular, a near-continuous battle with the Durranis of Khorasan had persisted ever since Ahmad Shah Durrani's death, in which by the 1790s the Persians were starting to gain the upper hand. The Persians were also concerned about the Ottomans, for three reasons: as a source of direct aggression; in that their activities in the Crimea might drag Russia into intervention (particularly given Persia had taken the opportunity of the Russian Civil War to annex all of Azerbaijan); and the fact that Ottoman, and Ottoman-backed Omani, trade was usurping traditionally Persian-influenced lands in East Africa. Zanzibar, the great trading city whose name was Persian for 'land of the blacks', had become first Portuguese and then Omani (since 1698). The Zands were better informed about European philosophies than most Persian dynasties, obvious given their interest in the French Revolution (whereas the Ottomans dismissed it as 'a Christian affair') and so it is perhaps not surprising that Shah-Advocate Ali Zand Shah[269] is known to have quoted 'if you would seek peace, prepare for war'…

Historically Portuguse-Persian relations had been fairly hostile, but the more moderate Zands could recognise the value of an alliance. The Zand leadership was tolerant enough to allow a few trade posts full of Catholics on the Persian coast – though the Persian people sometimes disagreed, persecuting their own Assyrian Christians in response – and, in exchange for this opening of trade, the Portuguese trained elements of the Persian army in European warfare, though other elements were kept traditional: the Zands were hedging their bets.

The full import of the Portuguese-Persian alliance, of course, would not come into play until the start of the Time of Troubles, after the early stages of the Jacobin Wars…

---

[269] Recall that the Zands call their Shahs 'Advocate of the People' instead.

Chapter 47: Finisterre

"While we waited at the bottom of the world, someone turned it upside down..."

- Jean-François de Galaup, comte de La Pérouse (private journal)

From: "Exploration and Discovery in the late 18th Century" (English translation) by Francois Laforce, Nouvelle Université de Nantes, 1961—

We have already covered the first two voyages of La Pérouse. The first, led by his flagship *d'Estaing* and accompanied by four frigates and a supply ship, was an arguably successful mapping mission that dramatically expanded French knowledge of the Pacific region, at a time when British investment in South Sea exploration had reached a low ebb. The second part of the mission, to establish new trade contacts, was less successful. Both Qing China and Japan were in highly isolationist moods and refused any attempts to expand trade.

Corea, under the ageing King Hyojang,[270] was more open to trade than it had been in the past, but was more interested in an exchange of ideas than the bread-and-butter trade which was what the emptying French treasury of the 1780s desperately needed. Nonetheless, La Pérouse allowed his two chief natural philosophers, the astronomer Laplace and the natural historian Lamarck, as well as the other scientific gentlemen among his crew,

---

[270] This is not the same Hyojang as OTL, once again just a shared name. OTL's Hyojang was King Yeongjo's firstborn son, who died young in 1728 – and also in TTL, because this is too early for 'butterflies'. This Hyojang is Yeongjo's third son, named in honour of the first. The second son, Prince Sado, was disqualified and forced to commit suicide due to being a mentally unstable murderer (in both OTL and TTL).

to trade ideas with the Coreans. La Pérouse's account of Corea was of great interest in Europe, which had been out of touch with the country since King Yeongjo cracked down on Catholic missionaries in the 1750s. The European reading audience discovered that Hyojang, on his accession in 1770, had reversed this decision and tolerated Catholicism. This was thought partly to be due to Hyojang's favouring the Silhak Movement, a Neo-Confucian school of thought which sought reforms to the corrupt Corean system of government of the eighteenth century.

The leader of the current 'Third Wave' of the Silhak Movement was Jeong Yak-yong, who had written a manifesto (the *Mongmin Shimsu*) whilst under house arrest by Yeongjo for his Catholic beliefs and his controversial reform ideas. Jeong's ideas are comparable with those taking shape at the same time in Zand Persia, that the state must be headed by a King, but that the rights of common people must be inalienable, and they must be given a voice in the running of the state. He also favoured a utilitarian approach to philosophy and technology, and poured scorn on the Corean status quo which saw more interest in obscure poetry and etymology than things which would actually be of use to Corea lifting itself out of its subordinate position to China – unlike most Corean political thinkers, Jeong did not believe this subordination was an inevitability of history and geography.[271] Hyojang released Jeong from prison and used him as an advisor; he, and other prominent Silhak thinkers such as Pak Je-ga – who criticised the Chinese-style system of examination for civil service posts, arguing that this supposedly meritocratic approach had become corrupt and led to incompetents in positions of power – clashed with more traditional Confucians in open debates at court. The Silhak, although in the minority, won several political victories from the fact that their opponents had grown comfortable and complacent from having no opposition under Yeongjo's authoritarian rule.

Like Zand ideas, Silhak writings were transmitted back to Europe (in this case via La Pérouse) and may have had some influence on the French Revolution, English Reformism, and

---

[271] The Silhak Movement also existed in OTL.

other European radical movements of the period, much as the French Revolution influenced Persia in turn. The Coreans also acquired some European military technology from the French, primarily innovations artillery, which in the eastern school of warfare was still held to be paramount. Although the Corean infantry would suffer from using outdated muskets for some years to come, this artillery knowledge nonetheless represented a significant advantage over other armies in the region – the Chinese having failed in their attempts to acquire superior European artillery from both the Swedes and the Russians. Additionally, Jeong's position of power, together with his former career masterminding the construction of fortresses for the Corean government (before converting to Catholicism and developing radical political ideas) meant that Hyojang embarked upon a campaign of fortress-building along the border with China and elsewhere. This was partly in key with the Silhak idea that Corea should be able to stand up to China one day, rather than forever being a vassal, and partly because Hyojang wanted a series of royal strongpoints that could be held against rebellious nobles who objected to Silhak action against their corruption, and granting more power to their peasants. However, the nobles and traditional Confucians retained enough power at court to successfully shoot down a Silhak plan to collectivise farming on a village basis. The won some other victories, but the Silhak were more successful than most had predicted, and Jeong's blend of Catholicism with Neo-Confucianism (inherited from the seventeenth-century missionary to China Matteo Ricci) became Corea's most influential, if not most popular, religion/ideology.

Corea was, of course, only one of the places that La Pérouse visited on his first voyage. His ships explored the South Sea Islands, the Galapogos Islands (whose fauna Lamarck would use to argue for his ideas of spontaneous evolution), and the long-forgotten Dutch discovery of New Zealand, which the French renamed Autiaraux after the name given to it by its Mauré natives. La Pérouse's supplying of some Mauré tribes with muskets in return for supplies dramatically upset the balance of power in Autiaraux for many years to come.

After exploring the unexpectedly fertile south coast of New Holland (as it was then called), the fleet returned to France in 1793. Despite the deepening economic crisis, La Pérouse and his scientific allies were so popular and influential that they received enough ships and funds to return to New Holland (or La Pérouse's Land as it was officially renamed) and plant a colony. Possibly Louis XVI believed that such a colony would make a good prestige project to help re-inspire public faith in his government, replacing the losses in the wars in America. That proved to be inaccurate, but by the time the French Revolution broke out, the large fleet was already rounding the Cape of Good Hope.

The next six years have been celebrated in countless, mostly French-penned, novels and films. La Pérouse returned to the site he had named Albi after his hometown[272] and established a full-blown colony on the site of their former temporary camp. He was accompanied by his scientific men – Lamarck and Laplace now joined by others such as Jacques-Julien Houtou de Labillardière, a botanist, and C.F Beautemps-Beaupré, a hydrographical engineer who mapped the approaches to Albi bay, and many others, in such detail that the colony suffered fewer accidents in that regard than any other colony in unknown lands in history. Lamarck was impatient to learn more about the fauna of the new continent (and Labillardière, of course, thought the same about the flora) and advocated that La Pérouse plant other outposts so that their hinterlands could be explored in detail, with the outposts as bases for resupply. La Pérouse was extremely doubtful about whether this was a good idea, only about eight months after Albi was established but, on the other hand, his success in this country had been and would be partly due to what worth the natural philosophers could extract from it. He beat Lamarck's ambitious ideas down to one further outpost colony, which Beautemps-Beaupré was asked to site. The engineer, after surveying several bays along the coast north of Albi, chose one whose country – and afterwards the city placed there – was named Béron after the native name.[273]

---

[272] On the site of OTL Sydney.

[273] This is the site of OTL Melbourne, in OTL not founded until many

The colony cities, Albi and smaller Béron, came into existence with relatively large populations, not least because Louis XVI had taken a leaf out of Britain's book and given La Pérouse all the most politically awkward people he could find as colonists. This meant that the colonist population was somewhat sullen and resentful, but La Pérouse was helped by the fact that the rather barren terrain behind the colonies, filled with natives (whom the French rather inaccurately called *indiens*[274]) who were not unreasonably resentful at all these mysterious white strangers appearing on their land. This meant the colonists had to stick together, no matter how awkward their divisions were, or die.

They nearly died anyway. Lamarck had overestimated the farming potential of New Gascony[275] and the colonies proved unable to feed themselves. Trade with the Indiens proved unhelpful due to a wider difference in values than even that between Europeans and the Mauré, and also because the natives simply had little to trade. Only around Béron was a lasting relationship achieved with the local Ouarandjeré people, although European diseases worked their toll even with that agreement.

To prevent starvation, La Pérouse decided to return to Autiaraux and trade with the Mauré for staple crops, and perhaps farming advice in these climes (although the climates of La Pérouse's Land and Autiaraux proved different enough for this not to be of much use). At the same time, he sent his second-in-command, Captain Philippe Durand of the *Émeraude*, to try the same mission with the Dutch East India Company and the South Sea islands. Durand was arguably more successful in terms of obtaining food and local crop seeds with which to improve the colony's supply situation, but La Pérouse's voyage was, inevitably, more colourful.

Less than ten years since he had first visited Autiaraux, he

years later. Béron is a French version of Birrarung, which is the OTL English transliteration of the name for the place by the native Wurundjeri tribe (spelled Ouarandjeré by the French here).
[274] The Aborigines were called Indians for a while by the British colonists in OTL as well.
[275] His name for the whole fertile south coast of Australia. Essentially New South Wales.

returned to find that the Mauré *iwi* (tribe) he had traded with, the Egnaté Raucaoua,[276] had been busy. They were part of a tribal confederacy or *ouaca*[277] with three other tribes, called the Tainui, and had taken the opportunity afforded by La Pérouse's gifts to embark on an expansionist phase. The Tainui had managed to defeat the *iwi*s of Tetaitocquerau,[278] demolishing their *pa* fortresses after winning key open battles thanks to La Pérouse's muskets. The Tainui control of Tetaitocquerau was particularly significant because, according to Mauré legend, it was where their race first arrived in the islands in a fleet from Polynesia, and possessed a certain symbolic importance. Both because of this, and simply because of the Tainui absorbing the *iwi*s there, the inland Egnaté Touaritaux formed an alliance with the Egné Touaux of the eastern coast to resist the Tainui aggression.[279] By autumn 1795, when La Pérouse arrived, the Tainui offensive had largely petered out anyway, as they had run out of gunpowder for their muskets.

La Pérouse's return was welcomed by the Tainui, who had seen the advantages of trading with him before, and were willing to do so again – but this time with a little more experience and cunning. The Tainui's chief negotiator, Huiwai, offered as much supplies and expertise to La Pérouse as the Tainui could spare – if La Pérouse gave them not just more ammunition and weapons, but also the secret of how gunpowder was made. La Pérouse hesitated, knowing that the long-term impact of this would be great. He was persuaded to give in not simply by necessity but also by Lamarck, who noted that this would be a useful example to study of how important such weapons were in deciding the balance between peoples, and how this fitted into Linnaean Racialism. La Pérouse was unmoved by this cold and cynical maneouvre, but Lamarck

---

[276] The Ngāti Raukawa in English transliteration.

[277] *Waka* in English transliteration. It literally means 'canoe', reflecting the fact that the Maori confederacies basically originated as cooperative ventures to colonise new lands via canoe.

[278] Te Tai-tokerau in English transliteration; the Northland region of New Zealand.

[279] Ngāti Tūwharetoa and Ngai Tuhoe respectively in English transliteration.

had a powerful position and so he agreed to appease the man. In the coming years, the Tainui would resume their offensive, failing to conquer the Touaritaux-Touaux alliance, but successfully achieving domination over the Taranacquie[280] peoples of the south.

This meant that the Tainui-led 'empire of the musket' now extended over almost half of the northern island of Autiaraux known as Eahcinomawe.[281] The other half consisted of the Touaritaux-Touaux alliance and the nonaligned *iwi*s, most of whom began to side with the Touaritaux-Touaux. The latter managed to gain the secret of gunpowder from the Tainui by espionage around 1803, shifting the balance again. However the Tainui still had the advantage of having most of the muskets themselves, Maori metallurgy still being rudimentary and not up to making new guns. The main reason why the Tainui did not expand further was that their leadership had trouble holding down the resentful new peoples they had added to their domain, and guns made little difference to that, a point which Lamarck noted in his log. The new discoveries took a longer time to filter down to the southern isle named Tavay Pocnammoo, which had a far smaller population and was dominated by the Quai Taioux.[282] Generally speaking, the stage was set for the two major power groups to divide Eahcinomawe between them; what would happen next was anyone's guess.

La Pérouse's (and Durand's) assistance helped the colonies survive 1795 and 1796. It was at this point that the frigate *Richelieu*, attached to La Pérouse's force, encountered its British counterpart, HMS *Lively*, while on a voyage of exploration around the barren north of La Pérouse's Land and New Guinea. The British opened fire without warning, fortunately at long range. The *Richelieu*'s captain, Paul de Rossel, decided to flee as his men were unprepared and he had let fighting drills lapse due to the fleet's exile at the end of the world. The *Lively* gave chase,

---

[280] Taranaki in English transliteration.

[281] This was a name given to North Island by the French in OTL; its provenance is unclear, as is that cited for the South Island later.

[282] Kāi Tahu.

but a lucky shot from one of the *Richelieu*'s stern guns brought down her foremast, and the *Richelieu* was able to hide before the *Lively* could catch sight of them again in a sheltered New Guinea bay that de Rossel had recently mapped. A disappointed Captain Cooke[283] returned to Calcutta with a confused sighting of a French ship far from all regular shipping lanes.

Meanwhile de Rossel reported back to La Pérouse at Albi. La Pérouse held a meeting of his officers and the colonial leaders, along with the important natural philosophers. It was obvious that Britain and France had come to war in the time while La Pérouse's men had been cut off down in the south. La Pérouse was in a quandary: he could not learn exactly what was happening without sending a ship where it was vulnerable to being intercepted. He could send enough of his fleet to give any British attacker pause, but that would leave the colony underdefended. In the end he decided to send just one ship, the *Émeraude* under Captain Durand. The *Émeraude* never reached Madras, its intended destination. It is generally thought that the ship must have run aground in the Dutch East Indies, or been caught in a tropical storm, as no British records suggest it was ever intercepted by a Royal Navy vessel. In any case, this is considered one of the great 'what ifs' of speculative romantics, as Durand was perhaps the most fervent royalist and believer in absolutism among La Pérouse's crew. If he had reached Madras and participated in the Pitt-Rochambeau accord, it is likely that the colony in La Pérouse's Land would have looked towards Royal France. But it was not to be…

After the loss of the *Émeraude*, which of course he could not guess until two years had passed without word, La Pérouse insisted on waiting for definite confirmation the Anglo-French war was over before leaving. This came quite early, in March 1800, when the news was passed on by a Dutch merchantman that the *Richelieu* encountered near Java. La Pérouse left most of his fleet to guard the colony, but took the *D'Estaing* and three frigates home to France. Lamarck and Laplace came also, both having

---

[283] No, not that one, although it is an irony. This is John Cooke, or his analogue, who in OTL was killed at Trafalgar.

made several copies of their notes for each ship, ensuring that at least one reached France.

In the event, all four ships reached France in early November 1800. Again, history might have been different if they had landed in Nantes, which according to the official government line was a 'special administrations area' but was, in fact, the capital of Royal France. But La Pérouse landed in Bordeaux, held by the Republicans, and he and his men reported to Paris. They had heard confused rumours of the Revolution, mostly welcomed by La Pérouse's left-leaning crew of idealists and philosophers. The wilder stories been dismissed as Royalist or British propaganda. They rapidly learned this was not the case when they reached Paris, and found – by the order of Jean de Lisieux, the Administrateur – the old streets being torn up one house at a time and replaced with wide boulevards in Lisieux's favoured Utilitarian style. La Pérouse caused a stir, as no-one had openly declared a title of nobility for years. He was arrested and a court almost sent him to the phlogisticateur after a five-minute trial, but Lamarck spoke up for him and he was released. Lamarck in particular became a celebrity as his writings about the fauna of La Pérouse's Land were incorporated into Lisieux's own developing theories of racial supremacy. Lamarck's idea that the harsh environment of La Pérouse's Land had bred the large number of dangerous (poisonous, venomous, etc.) animals and plants there, an early example of theorised environmental breeding,[284] was used by Lisieux to advocate a harsh training regime for French soldiers (and as an excuse to crack down domestically).

La Pérouse was forced to renounce his title, but we shall continue to call him that, as history does. Lisieux was undecided on what to do with the colony. What France needed was trade and money, just as she had twenty years before under the King. La Pérouse's Land could not supply that, and Autiaraux was not profitable enough for the commodities that would make money. France needed India, which she had lost to the Royalists, or the East Indies, which were Dutch. It was the latter which persuaded Surcouf, one of Lisieux's inner circle, to suggest a new plan.

---

[284] Environmental breeding = natural selection.

Surcouf had become bored of his project to weaponise Cugnot's steam engine on ships following the peace with Britain, and wanted to return to his privateering days. Although France was still at war with Spain and the Spanish fleet at this point, the specific situation meant that France could afford to spare some frigates for such a venture. Surcouf's idea was to raid Dutch shipping from the East Indies under a neutral flag, or 'pulling an Englishman', as he called it (in reference to Francis Drake and the Spanish). If the Dutch protested, what could they do? Even with the Flemish alliance, the Stadtholder would be a fool to tangle with Revolutionary France in war, especially since his own position looked ever more precarious. Lisieux ordered his agents to stoke the fires of revolution in the Netherlands and Flanders as a distraction, then approved the plan. Surcouf, the natural philosophers, and a shaken La Pérouse returned to the fleet, expanded by seven new frigates and three ships of the line, and the fleet set off for La Pérouse's Land to begin their new commerce raiding mission. They arrived in Albi in February 1802 to learn that the colony had suffered an Indien attack, but had successfully beaten the natives back.

Immediately after returning, La Pérouse took a sloop on a trading mission to the Mauré and never came back. What happened was never proven, but it is considered highly likely that he and his men, mostly the more Royalist in sympathy among the crew, sold their services to the Mauré in exchange for protection and a hiding place from the Republicans. La Pérouse had been profoundly affected by ravaged Paris and the terror of the phlogisticateur. He wanted nothing more to do with Republican France. The fact that the Tainui did not make much headway against the eastern alliance, but both planted new colonies in Tavay Pocnammoo using improved canoes with European designs, suggesting that La Pérouse's men had split up and sought refuge with *both* nascent Mauré powers…

Chapter 48: Old Delicious and the Awkward Squad

1. The Great Cleansing
2. The War of Lightning
3. To Hold the Heart

– chapter headings in A.V. de la Costa's seminal *The Pyrenean War* (1924), quoted below:

April of 1800, it can be argued, was perhaps one of the most significant months of the Jacobin Wars – and this is a title hotly competed for. March had seen peace between Britain and Republican France, with a rump Royal France in Brittany and the Vendée being tolerated (for the moment) by the new regime of 'Administrateur' Jean de Lisieux, whom the British satirical press immediately nicknamed Old Delicious. Lisieux was certainly unamused by this portrayal, although the authenticity of his alleged diary in which he makes chilling remarks on the subject has never been proven. However, his mention of the English Germanic Republic, in which authorities would one day phlogisticate these violators of his human rights, has led most scholars to believe that the document is a forgery...unless Lisieux was uncharacteristically prophetic.

April saw what can, possibly, be termed the first cabinet meetings of Lisieux's regime. In truth, though no-one in Republican France would dare make the comparison, they were more in the spirit of an absolute monarch consulting with advisors before making his own unilateral decision. What checks remained on Lisieux's power remained not with any official elected body, but with the 'Boulangerie', the informal group of innovative thinkers who directed French military policy, and were increasingly taking over control of civil policy as well. Thouret, who masterminded Lisieux's scheme to cut up France into perfectly square départements each run by a (supposedly) elected Modérateur, swiftly became an integral part of the Boulangerie, and it was by this means that his Rationalist views became official policy.

Although Jacobin thinkers in Paris had long since been pumping out new ideas about metric measuring systems for length, distance and time, it was not until now that they were actually enforced. Draconian laws were enacted which punished people simply for saying the old names of the days of the week – which was often unavoidable even by the most strong-minded revolutionary, just out of habit. It was all part of Lisieux's general idea that the people must be treated harshly if the spirit of revolution was to remain pure – if compromise was attempted, that could only pollute the spirit and necessitate a second, bloodier corrective revolution. Lisieux believed in the value of human life, at least under his own definition, and claimed never to permit legal punishments that would impair a felon's ability to work afterwards. He believed that, if Robespierre had been allowed to continue with his endless purges of the 'impure', eventually France would have been an empty hexagon of untended land with one man at its centre – Robespierre – finally driving a knife into his own throat as he concluded that not even he lived up to his own ideals of purity. Lisieux, on the other hand, advocated the notion that revolutionary purity could be gained and lost – he rejected the former "original sin" approach, as it was nicknamed by some. Of course, in order to create true revolutionary purity in the impure, methods somewhat…drastic were often required.

Initially, though, Lisieux's focus was needfully on tackling France's immediate political and military situation rather than his own far-reaching vision for what the Republic would become. Boulanger's brilliant campaign in Normandy in 1799 had ended what could have been a Royalist counter-revolution. The Republicans had been unable to throw the Royalists into the sea, but the peace with Britain was nonetheless a chance that could not be missed. Lisieux was loathe to tolerate the claimant King sitting on Brittany and the Vendée, but recognised that for the moment there was no alternative. If he were to go back on his word and invade once a new army was assembled, then the fragile Fox government in Britain would fall and be replaced by more warmongerers who would simply start the conflict again. No; he was convinced the correct approach was to allow the Fox government to settle in place, to attempt to drive a wedge between London and Nantes (the de facto capital of Royal France), and to undermine Royal French interests around the world with every option one step short of war. Not only was Royal France's mere existence an affront to the Revolution – and the man who believed he personified it – but it lent credibility to the Royalist governors-general of French America and French India. Although Republicans had mostly failed to convince those lands to go over to the Republican line even when there had been no Royal France as such, the existence of Royal France certainly made that task much harder.

However, now the Royal Navy was no longer hostile, there was no overwhelming seafaring force to swipe nine out of every ten oceangoing Republican ships with emissaries out of the seas. Paris could now begin openly sending ships to stir up trouble for the Royalists in their colonies. Lisieux immediately began this project with what few ships remained after Villeneuve's Pyrrhic attacks on the 'Seigneur' fleets. Villeneuve himself was a difficult figure for Lisieux to deal with. The Royal French had traded him back in a prisoner exchange after the peace, and Republican opinion of the man was mixed. He had certainly fought bravely enough, but it was a hotly-debated question whether the British ships he had sunk had sufficiently reduced the Anglo-Royal French invasion fleet to justify losing virtually the whole remaining Republican fleet in the process. Lisieux's private opinion was no, but recognising the man's tarnished hero status, he sent him on a supposedly 'flag-flying' mission around the world. This set off in August 1800 after the shipyards had turned out some replacement ships of the line, built according to the new 'Rational' measurement system (not without ensuing problems) and incorporating new technologies. The Republicans also purchased some frigates from the Russians and the Danes, who sold off parts of the Swedish fleet that had come into their hands after the end of the Great Baltic War.

Lisieux was more willing to engage with 'reactionary states' than Robespierre had been, less afraid of being 'contaminated' by the contact. "Their fall is assured, so why should they not be permitted to grease the downward steps themselves?" he wrote.

In truth, of course, Villeneuve's 'flag-flying' mission carried weapons, pamphlets and professional terrorists to be let loose on the Royalist regimes in the French colonies. His fleet's first stop was the West Indies, and of that incident much more can be read elsewhere.

It is perhaps surprising that Villeneuve was ever allowed to return by the Royalists, but even at that early stage, one cannot underestimate the influence of one man who had been favourably impressed by Villeneuve, in the enduringly British manner of respect for an enemy – the inimitable Leo Bone…

From: "The Man With Three Names—A Life and Times of Napoleone Buonaparte" (Dr Henri Pelletier, University of Nantes Press, 1962)—

For Commodore Leo Bone, the aftermath of the Battle of Quiberon looked bleak. After having successfully drawn off the superior enemy ship *Jacobin*, the two had fought near the Isle of Yeu. Though the *Lewisborough* successfully sank the foe with her carronades, she had taken enough damage that her pumps were unable to prevent the water rising in her well – her own doom was only a matter of time. With a heavy heart, and a fateful indecision over whether to throw the guns overboard for more speed – he decided against it – Bone set sail for the nearest land. By this point this was the Vendean coast. Bone trusted to luck and God that he and his men would get out of this alive. And if there were any rumours that the God 'Old Boney' prayed to preferred his worshippers to speak in Latin and work rosary beads, his men did not think less of him on that account. Thus was the charisma that this remarkable man held over his mostly English sailors, men from a nation whose hatred of Catholicism was sometimes portrayed as an integral part of the national identity.

The *Lewisborough*, very low in the water by this time, was successfully and professionally beached near the town of Saint-Hilaire-de-Riez in the south of the Vendée. Bone's carpenter and bosun looked at the damage to the stern and shook their heads. If the ship could be repaired it could only be done in a proper shipyard, Portsmouth or Chatham. Furthermore, some of Bone's sailors had previously sailed on 'the horrible old *Lorient*', a captured ship from a previous war whose repairs had never quite been enough to make her operate at full capacity again. Even with full repairs, the *Lewisborough* might not be herself again. Morale was low.

Bone's heart sank, but he did not allow his face to show his dismay. Instead he rallied and roused his men, praising them for bringing the ship in safely. They were tired and miserable after this anticlimax to their battle, but Bone managed to keep them lively. He had a plan, a wild and dangerous plan – the kind of plan that he and his friend Horatio Nelson did best. It was a plan that could not only lead to their survival, but perhaps avoid the catastrophe they were facing. Bone knew that rescue was possible sooner or later, but without a functional ship, he could end up on half-pay for years – especially since the Republican naval threat was obviously dying out there in Quiberon even as he stood there. His men would be even worse off, suddenly ashore with no trade to work. Again like Nelson, he knew the importance of working the media to his advantage, and decided that the only way to escape such an obscure fate was to achieve some sort of filmish [cinematic] victory that would attract the attention of the *Gazette*. Given that he was a naval captain and his ship had just been hulled, it could be argued that this was perhaps a rather ambitious plan. But for Bone, it was hardly out of the ordinary.

The *Lewisborough*'s crew, under Bone's directions, removed most of the guns from the ship by means of pulleys, singing *The Sozzled Seaman*.[285] With the last '*way, hay, up she rises*', Bone was no longer in quite such an impossible situation. The *Lewisborough* had been a sixty-five gun ship, which meant Bone now had the

---

[285] The sea shanty *The Drunken Sailor* dates from long after the POD, and this version is not quite the same, but it's not unlikely that a similar one would develop. The same factors were there – the original, Irish tune, brought there by Irish sailors, and the suitability of the rhythm to the task of hoisting sails or yanking on ropes.

equivalent of a sizeable artillery brigade under his command, including carronades and howitzers. His men were unaccustomed to land warfare, of course, but could at least keep up a rapid rate of fire if they had a position to hold. It was a daring, almost insane plan, but Bone was quite certain that he had a destiny to fulfil, and it would not abandon him to die ignominiously in such an engagement. In this he was hardly unique – such men can, perhaps, be found three to a street – but his men believed in it too, and that made all the difference.

Bone's first act was to bring his crew to Saint-Hilaire itself, led by his Marine company under Major Rupert FitzRoy[286] to discourage any opportunists who thought this strange artillery column looked vulnerable. The red-coated Marines bore American rifles and hard expressions: though this part of the Vendée had slipped into anarchy, no-one bothered Leo Bone's men. Saint-Hilaire was sufficiently distant from the heart of the counter-revolution that while the local Royalists had defeated and overthrown their Republican rulers, the countryside retained some Republican sympathisers and these continued to strike as partisans or bandits. Saint-Hilaire was a town under virtual siege when Bone arrived. With the Royalist mayor killed by Republicans, and his unofficial successor a nonentity, there was a power vacuum – a vacuum which Leo Bone was only too happy to fill.

He called himself 'Napoléon Bonaparte', in the French style, and was thankful that he had learned French at Westminster School, even if he pronounced it atrociously. Before the people of Saint-Hilaire knew what was happening, Bone had virtually taken over the town, billeting his troops there and already preparing for drills. Some equipment and ammunition had been left on the beach, Bone lacking the men to carry it all, and he somehow dragooned the natives into assisting. By the third day, it was hard

---

[286] Third son of the Duke of Grafton, the Lord Deputy for North America. ITTL he went into the Marines rather than the regular British Army partly because his American childhood friends regaled him with stories of the heroic Lawrence Washington (later Lord Fredericksburg) during the Second War of Supremacy.

to remember that Saint-Hilaire had not always been the personal fiefdom of Leo Bone, or Napoléon Bonaparte. Either way, he had come a long way from the Napoleone Buonaparte, son of a minor Corsican noble, that he had been born as…

Lest the people of Saint-Hilaire think him some boorish warlord, mere days later Bone proved his right to act in such a way. He went out 'hunting' with FitzRoy's men. FitzRoy was an avid foxhunter, a sport which Bone himself had never felt an attraction for, and proved his eye when he shot seven Republican partisans dead at long range in the middle of supposed cover. That was only the start of it. The small-scale war against the local Jacobin sympathisers continued for three weeks: the final confrontation saw the rebels hole up in the inn of the nearby village of Le Fenouiller, an eminently defendable position against infantry assault. Recognising this, Bone simply revealed his artillery and pounded the place to dust. Although upsetting some of the locals with this act of absent vandalism, generally speaking the people of Saint-Hilaire, indeed the whole southern Vendée, praised his name for acting against the Republicans.

Bone's first victory against regular Republican troops, rather than partisans, came in August 1799. General Pallière's army had been crushed, but not actually destroyed, by General Græme at Cholet. Some of the remnants of the leaderless army fled into Anjou, while others came into the southern Vendée, feeding themselves by the customary practice of *la maraude*. Recognising how unpopular this made them with the locals, Bone saw another opportunity to act. By this point he had recruited something of a small army from the local folk, using his Marines as a hard core for training purposes. He took many men who wanted to fight the Republicans for Louis XVII, but were afraid of leaving their homes to fight elsewhere, and possibly leave their families vulnerable to attack. Bone built a locally-based army that fought for local concerns, albeit in the name of the new King.

After some early skirmishes, the ex-Pallière remnant – their leader's name by this point is not recorded – were pinned down west of La Roche-sur-Yon by Bone's forces. Having trapped the disorganised Republicans between two inferior forces, but ones which could stand their ground, Bone then once again unleashed his artillery. His sailors had been training hard, and by now they fought as well as any landsman in the role. The Republicans' column attack tactics made them easy targets for artillery, even more so when they formed square – and Bone managed to scrape together enough crude cavalry from local sources to force them into that formation for defence. The enemy army, now barely worthy of the name, was virtually annihilated. And the legend of Leo Bone grew...

By now, Bone was in touch with important locals, men who could send his reports back to England to be published in the *Gazette*, so that all would know of his exploits. It was a self-publicising tactic that had worked well for Julius Caesar millennia before, and it would work just as well for Leo Bone. Indeed, the popular adventures of the son were one reason why his father, the MP Charles Bone, was given a cabinet position (Paymaster of the Forces) by the Fox government at home.

In the latter stages of the war, Bone brought his new army north on the Dauphin's request. While Boulanger conquered in Normandy, 'General Bonaparte' held Angers against one of Boulanger's armies, using a convent for cover (and incidentally capitalising on the fury that the Republicans attacking such a site roused in the pious Vendeans). He made sure that this incident too was publicised, in the nascent Royal French papers as well as their British counterparts.

When the war finally came to an end, the Dauphin sent for Bone and ennobled him, creating the *Vicomté d'Angers*. (The British satirical press inevitably dubbed him 'Lord Angry' to go with his existing nickname of Old Boney). Bone's ramshackle army was officially made a new Royalist regiment, the *Régiment du Vendée du Sud*.

Once more, Bone's career trajectory paralleled that of his old friend Horatio Nelson, and indeed, once peace was signed with the new Lisieux regime, the two met in a café in Nantes to discuss their futures. Nelson spoke baldly of the lack of prospects in the postwar Royal Navy, of ships laid up, crews disbanded, officers stuck ashore on half-pay for years. Bone had similar thoughts.

They were both men of ambition, for though they loved the sea, they loved power even more. Both recognised that power was no longer to be found in the Royal Navy. Though Nelson had his *Mirabilis* still, and his rank, all that awaited him was a stuffy desk job with a guaranteed pension – a prize which some men would kill for, but which was anathema to this strange and mercurial officer. Bone told his friend of his own intentions, to resign his commission in order to pursue a military and political career in this new Royal France. He believed that the Royalists would eventually take back all of France, and thus becoming a big fish in a little pond at this point would pay high dividends later. Nelson considered this, before departing for his new Mediterranean command, thoughtful ramblings filling his diaries all the way to Malta…

From: "The Pyrenean War" by A.V. de la Costa (1924)—

…Lisieux's problem was not his control over France, which was rapidly becoming absolute, but control over France's satellite states. Currently in existence were Ney's Swabian Germanic Republic, Marat's Swiss Republic (which did not fit neatly into one of Lisieux's racial categories) and Hoche's Italian Latin Republic. In addition to this, the late General Leroux's subordinate, Fabien Lascelles, had seized control of much of Leroux's army and now claimed a Bavarian Germanic Republic ruled from Regensburg. Those who had opposed Lascelles, led by Phillipe St-Julien (and called the Cougnonistes after their first leader) were holed up in the Bohemian city of Budweis, but had made no attempt to set up a Bohemian republic. They struggled hard enough just to survive and fight off local militia attacks, Austria being unable to spare any regular troops for this theatre thanks to the Ottoman invasion of Dalmatia.

Most of these 'republics' were simply military dictatorships, whose role and policy would be determined solely by the man in charge. Lascelles, of course, was a fanatical Robespierre supporter and immediately dismissed Lisieux's regime as illegitimate, deviationist and 'crypto-Royalist'. He then claimed his own supposed Bavarian Germanic Republic was the only remaining example of true Jacobin revolutionary republicanism. To prove it, he immediately embarked on a Terror of purges quite equal to anything his hero Robespierre had ever done. This would, of course, have quite infamous consequences, but that is outside the scope of this work.

Meanwhile, Ney – after some consideration – accepted Lisieux's legitimacy. He had appointed himself First Consul of his Republic, and his second-in-command General Nicolas Ranier as the Second. However, Ney made a local sympathiser, Christoph Friedrich von Schiller, the Third Consul.[287] Schiller, a man of the liberal Enlightenment both politically and artistically, had enjoyed patronage under the previous Duke, Karl II Ludwig. On his succession, however, Karl's son had dismissed him from court, and now Schiller seized the opportunity to return to a position of power. Ney also created a copied National Legislative Assembly of local Badenese, Württembergers and others: in reality it had little power, but its existence helped smooth and placate local opinion – an example much quoted by the later school of Grevillite Reactivist thought.

Hoche, on the other hand, rejected Lisieux utterly; not on principle as Lascelles did, but because he saw this as his moment to achieve his own personal fiefdom, fully independent from France. Although more of a megalomaniac than Ney, he also created new institutions in Italy, trying to centralise powers and to create an identity out of formerly disparate states. This would have important consequences for the Italian Peninsula later on.

Lisieux hesitated over what to do with these truculent republics. His Robespierriste leanings told him that conflicting Revolutionary messages must be purged to leave only the true one. On the other hand, he was loath to spill the blood of fellow Republicans, while reactionaries prospered from the dispute. While agonising over the question with the Boulangerie, it was partly decided for him. On hearing of Robespierre's death, the Swiss rose up and overthrew Marat. It is said that the Consul of

---

[287] An ATL 'brother' of OTL's Friedrich Schiller, more of a political figure than OTL.

the Republic was assassinated out of the blue as he was walking down the Aarstrasse of Bern with an armed guard, though some have claimed it was a pure accident. Two men in a nearby house threw a tin bath out of the upper window, which hit Marat a sharp blow on the head and plunged him into a coma from which he never awoke. Regardless of whether this had been an intentional strike or not, the ensuing Swiss rising was certainly well coordinated, with Republican troops being divided, isolated and hammered by Swiss irregulars. Confusion prevailed in the aftermath, though – the French had executed so many important men of the old Confederation, and the rebel leaders had no real coherent vision for a Switzerland after the French. The united front swiftly fractured.

This was, of course, a disaster for Lisieux – holding Switzerland was vital to the French position in Germany. Therefore, he grudgingly accepted Boulanger's advice to engage with Hoche. By the Treaty of Savoy, France, Swabia and Italy divided Switzerland between them roughly on linguistic lines (thanks to Lisieux's racial policies). Hoche still refused to acknowledge Lisieux, but sent in his troops, and Lisieux bought his services for future operations with supplies and ammunition, treating him as a mercenary. The more loyal Ney was ordered to continue offensive operations against minor German states from his power base in Swabia. Although Ney was concerned about overstretch, as he struggled to administer German-speaking Switzerland as well as his existing lands, he obeyed. Franco-Swabian troops wheeled around the neutral Palatinate – Lisieux unwilling to venture war with Charles Theodore of Flanders – and overran much of Ansbach and Würzburger Mainz, before being halted by a joint Hessian-Würzburger army at Erbuch. Ney was forced to retreat from all Würzburger lands and signed the Treaty of Stuttgart in November 1801, which set down firm boundaries for the Swabian Republic. One consequence of this affair was that the Hessians and Würzburgers, along with Nassau, formed a united front in the ensuing chaos of the Mediatisation—in which they opposed the Dutch-Flemish and the Saxons and broadly supported the Hapsburgs.

With the situation stabilised in the Germanies, priority number one for France now became Spain. Aside from Royal France, the only foreign troops still standing on French soil were Spanish. Although General Custine had ejected the Spanish General Cuesta (two similar names which have confused generations of schoolboys) from Bordeaux in 1799, the French army in the south had been too poorly supplied, too low-priority, to beat the Spanish back any further. What reinforcements had been earmarked for that army had instead gone to attack the British and Royal French in the west as that front opened up. But now that theatre too was quiet, and the full might of Republican France could be turned on the Spanish.

Lisieux let Boulanger mastermind the attacks, with some political provisos: Firstly, that what Sans-Culottes regiments remained in France (more were with Lascelles in Bavaria) should form the core of the attacks and be at the forefront. Secondly that new regiments from Sans-Culotte demographic backgrounds should be raised, by deliberate skewing of the conscription process if necessary. Boulanger was too used to Lisieux by now to ask why. The Marshal defined his plan as having three broad stages: to cleanse the Spanish from France herself; to use the War of Lightning strategy once more in an invasion; and to hold Madrid, bringing Spain to terms. Both Boulanger and Lisieux were privately sceptical about the possibility of a Spanish Latin Republic, but Spain must be brought under some sort of control or influence if France was to prosper. Boulanger said that each of his three points required one year's campaign season.

Lisieux gave him everything he asked for. All the Republic's best innovations, the Cugnot *fardier* steam tractors, the *char*s and the *tortues*, balloons and vast conscript armies, were focused in the south, at Bordeaux and Montpellier. Both cities had been taken by the Spanish, only for them to be ejected in turn. Yet the Spanish held on doggedly to the south of France throughout the campaign season of 1799. This only changed when Boulanger launched his offensive, in 1800.

Cuesta's armies suffered three major defeats, at the Siege of Toulouse, the Battle of Pau and the Battle of Carcassonne (the latter actually fought quite a long distance away from the town of Carcassonne). The Spanish, like the British before them, struggled to counter the French's revolutionary new war machines and tactics, and their morale was not high. The war aims of the conflict had always been vague – initially some sort of hotblooded revenge for the King's execution and anti-Catholic policies, thrown into confusion by the establishment of Royal France and its open negotiations with the Republicans; then shifting to an attempt to annex historically Spanish lands, confused and discredited as Cuesta tried to hold onto lands far beyond those with any realistic claim.

There was no secret that King Philip VI was ill, though whether from a simple fever or syphilis depended on which faction at court you asked. His capable prime minister, the conde de Floridablanca, had died just two years before, and been succeeded by Francisco Saavedra de Sangronis—who had fought in the Second Platinean War[288] and been finance minister for some years, as well as serving as governor of several of the American possessions in turn. But Saavedra, though a worthy successor to Floridablanca, had only been in the job for two years, and only for six months before the King began to fall ill. His position at court looked ever shakier, and he was opposed by the Prince of Asturias, Charles, who had support from Saavedra's political enemy, Miguel Pedro Alcántara Abarca de Bolea, the Count of Aranda.[289] The situation was such that the Spanish government was paralysed and unable to respond as Boulanger and his lieutenants coolly rolled up Cuesta's army in the autumn of 1800.

What would follow would determine the fates, not merely of France and Spain, but ultimately of the whole world...

---

[288] OTL he fought in the American Revolutionary War.

[289] Unlike OTL, Pedro Pablo Alcántara Abarca de Bolea had a son.

MAP OF EUROPE IN 1800

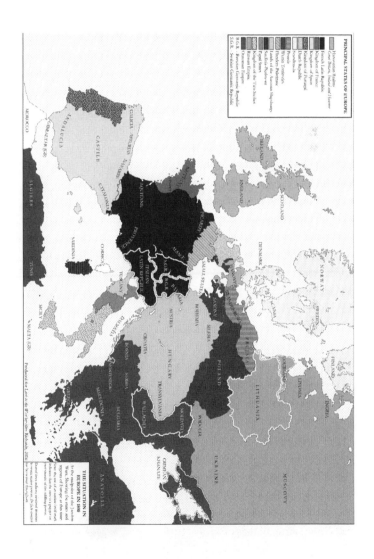

Chapter 49: La Disparition de l'Espagne

Tall ships and tall Dons,
Three times three,
What brought they from the conquered land
To the New World over the Sea?
Five crowns and five kings
and one hope for the free.

– Johannes Reuel Tollkühn, *Der Untergang von Spanien*, 1941

From: "The Pyrenean War" by A.V. de la Costa (1924)—

The campaign season of 1800 saw French forces push the Spanish armies back almost to the pre-war border, although the only place the French actually crossed the border was at the far eastern end, taking Llançà in Catalonia. Although one of Boulanger's armies attempted to force the pass of Col d'Ares, the Spanish successfully repulsed the attack. While the armies of Generals Cuesta and Blake were pressed back against the Pyrenees, the Spanish entrenched themselves in defensive positions over the winter and prepared to fight off a French mass attack. Although the Spanish government remained paralysed due to Philip VI's illness, there remained a general determination to keep hold of the formerly French Navarre, and troop deployments reflected this goal.

The campaign of 1800 provided important lessons for the French side. Boulanger had lost most of his most skilled generals in the previous few years' worth of fighting: Leroux had been slain before Vienna, Hoche had gone rogue, Ney was busy pacifying Swabia, Vignon and Pallière had been killed during the response to the Seigneur offensive. Analysing the war against Spain now exposed those commanders who deserved promotion, and Boulanger, as

Marshal of the Republican Army, enacted such promotions and weeded out the less capable generals. In accordance with Lisieux's "No (wasteful) killing" policy, less competent but loyal generals were usually relegated to garrison duty, although some of them ended up in more dangerous areas such as French-Switzerland or Swabia.

Some of the men Boulanger promoted are household names even to those ignorant of history: Claude Drouet, Etienne Devilliers, Olivier Bourcier. Some were from formerly aristocratic backgrounds, Lisieux being more amenable to accepting them than Robespierre had been, while others were commoners like Boulanger himself. While the Spanish dug in over the winter of 1800, Boulanger was, typically, planning a yet more ambitious offensive. It was at this time that Hoche began publishing self-aggrandising accounts of his own battles, easy considering his rule over northern Italian university cities with their endless supply of printing presses. Lisieux quickly banned such accounts in France, but Boulanger was able to obtain a copy illegally and spent some time studying them, reading between the biased lines to extract useful information. He travelled up and down the whole Franco-Spanish border, studying the problem his men had to face, and also read the accounts of the Bourbon generals from the campaign of a century earlier, during the First War of Supremacy.

In January 1801, Boulanger returned to Paris to discuss the forthcoming campaign with Lisieux and the Boulangerie. He learned of the interest that the return of La Pérouse had sparked, and how Lisieux was writing propaganda day and night to incorporate Lamarck's ideas of environmental breeding into Linnaean Racism. He was disappointed to learn that Vice-Admiral Surcouf was committed to privateering against the Dutch, but also discovered that Surcouf had promoted one of his subordinates, Fabien Lepelley, to counter-admiral and had turned over control of the Cugnot ship project to him. Lepelley was just as enthusiastic as Surcouf for the new innovations, which suited Boulanger fine…

It was some time before Lisieux could spare a few hours to talk over the campaign. Michel Chanson, Boulanger's adjutant, records that Boulanger spoke of Lisieux looking tired and having visibly aged. The Administrateur now cloistered himself in his room for hours at a time, continuously writing pamphlets and propaganda. He barely went out to look at the Republic he ruled, instead using his pen and ink to scratch at the paper as though gradually wearing down reality until it resembled what he believed it *should* look like.

Boulanger put forward his military conclusions to Lisieux and the Boulangerie, as well as a few members of the now largely symbolic National Legislative Assembly. He said that trying to force the Pyrenean passes would be unlikely to succeed. The Spanish were well entrenched, the passes were defended, and the terrain was difficult. Lisieux asked for the alternative, and Boulanger replied with Lisieux's own maxim that to hold the heart – the capital – of a nation is to hold the whole nation. It did not matter *how* that heart was approached, only that it was held, and then everything else would collapse.

The Marshal outlined another strategy, pointing out the fact that the French held Llançà. Troops could be slowly moved down there to support the attack, he added. It did not matter that the Spanish held the Pyrenees if Madrid was conquered.

Georges Besoin, a member of the NLA, objected that to try and conquer Spain while Spanish forces still occupied French soil was the heart of foolhardiness. Lisieux did not uphold his point, recognising Boulanger's argument that anything else Spain did would be irrelevant if Madrid was held. But Lisieux did argue that the Spanish were not fools, and that they would surely be shifting their own troops to drive the French out of Llançà. Boulanger agreed: his agents confirmed that the Spanish had moved an army under General Fernando Ballesteros to take back Llançà in the spring, an army that outnumbered the French occupiers three to one.

But that was all part of Boulanger's strategy.

Drawing frantically on a blackboard, Boulanger explained that he would assemble the bulk of his army in Leucate, then bring in a fleet from Toulon to transport them down to Spain. They would land in the Catalan town of Roses, on the southern side of the Cap de Creus, and thus trap Ballesteros' army between two French forces, crushing it.

Quite understandably, Besoin was sceptical. "And what precisely is the Spanish Mediterranean Fleet, which thanks to d'Estaing's treachery is several times the size of our own, doing in all this?" he asked sarcastically.

Boulanger smiled, and replied: "Lying in port, of course, for it shall be a windless day."

Lisieux was the first to realise what Boulanger meant. Seeing an immediate application for one of his pet projects, he almost immediately approved the offensive, with one proviso. Boulanger wanted to make only desultory attacks against Cuesta and Blake's armies in the Pyrenees, just sufficient to stop the Spanish shifting those troops away. Lisieux wanted a stronger attack, commanded by General Philippe Eustache and made up largely of Sans-Culotte levies. Eustache was himself of suspected loyalty, being a Jacobin fire-breather much like Lascelles in Bavaria, and a vocal supporter of Robespierre. But unlike Robespierre himself, Lisieux would not simply have him plucked from his command and phlogisticated. Every man that France had must be used to further her cause, though the means might vary...

The two offensives were termed Assaut-du-Sud and Tire-Bouchon (Southern Onslaught and Corkscrew) ; Lisieux's military policies tended to increase paperwork and counter-espionage, hence the explosion of the use of code names. Assaut-du-Sud was launched under Eustache in March, taking back Tarbe and Montrejou before stalling. Eustache himself was killed by a Spanish counterattack from Lourdes, led by the vigorous Irish exile Joaquin Blake, who successfully took back Tarbes shortly afterwards and threatened Pau. However, this only worked to the advantage of Boulanger's broader strategy. The Spanish government, led erratically by Saavedra, was convinced that the French hammer blows would come in the west, and while they left Ballesteros' army to threaten Llançà, it was not reinforced. At the same time, the French moved down sufficient forces overland until the French army in Llançà almost equalled Ballesteros', and it was placed under the command of Drouet.

In May, Ballesteros assaulted Llançà and pushed Drouet out, who then shifted his army to the west. Ballesteros pursued, leaving his army somewhat strung out behind him. On the 16th-19th, the calm days that they had been awaiting, Counter-Admiral Lepelley's men struck. The nascent Chappe semaphore towers (q.v.) alerted the fleet of the weather even as it was detected by stations elsewhere in France, allowing them time to prepare.

Just as Boulanger had planned, Surcouf and Cugnot's 'little toys' pulled out of their port at Toulon and steamed southwards to Leucate, where Devilliers and Bourcier were waiting with the bulk of the army (including Cugnot *fardiers* and other innovations). The French fleet was impressive in its novelty and in its numbers. The transports tended to be merchant craft or converted warships pulled by steam tugs, their useless masts torn out to provide more deck space. Surrounding them were Cugnot's steam-galleys, some equipped with paddlewheels, others with screws – the argument over which method was more powerful had become heated enough down at the manufactory in Toulon to result in several *yeux noirs*. Also accompanying the French fleet were a number of conventional galleys, some dating from the pre-Revolutionary fleet, others purchased from the Kingdom of Denmark after the conclusion of the Great Baltic War. French use of galleys had lapsed during Robespierre's consulship thanks to the abolition of slavery, but Lisieux's policies provided plenty of political prisoners to replace the former galley-slaves. Why simply execute such mentally suspect men, when their bodies could still serve their country…?

The French fleet was large enough to discourage casual attacks, but it was nonetheless met by a force of six startled Spanish galleys out of Cadaqués on the 18th. Although outnumbered, the Spanish were not struggling with the problems of new technology and inexperience as the French were, and managed to sink eight French ships and damage three others before succumbing to the French steam-galleys' powerful bow chasers. Fortunately for the French, the Spanish galleys were prevented from drawing close enough to the converted transports to damage them and drown any troops – all the French losses were of their own galleys, steam or conventional.

Lepelley dispatched one transport and escorts, under Bourcier, to take Cadaqués after the defeat of the enemy galleys. Bourcier stormed the town and captured the two Spanish frigates and brig that had been stationed there, helpless without wind. However, there was also an eighth galley, which made a desperate and quixotic attack on the French transport's steam tug, the *Palmipède*.[290] The galley's bow chaser fired a badly-timed shot as the *Palmipède* rose up on a crashing wave as the tide came in, meaning the cannonball only struck a glancing blow off the *Palmipède*'s screw, she being one of the screw-based steamers in the mixed fleet. To everyone's astonishment, as they learned after the battle, the damaged screw actually performed better than it had before the attack – by chance, the cannonball had created something similar in shape to a modern propeller. Once demonstrated to Cugnot and Jouffroy in Toulon, this spelt the end for an intriguing 'what-if' of history, the romantic-looking but inefficient paddlewheel-based steamship. Screws immediately became dominant.[291]

Meanwhile, the major force under Devilliers descended upon Roses and, as Boulanger had planned, Ballesteros' army was crushed between the two French forces and forced to surrender. Immediately afterwards, Drouet attacked southward into Catalonia, using the *Guerre d'éclair* strategy pioneered by Boulanger and Leroux. Barcelona fell in August, the Spanish garrison there being surprised by the unexpected assault – Drouet had successfully outrun the news in pre-Optel Spain. All of Catalonia was in French hands by September, and Lisieux declared the annexation of the country to France – having been persuaded of the Catalans' supposed French descent on linguistic grounds.

---

[290] Named after an earlier French attempt at a steamboat by Claude de Jouffroy. Jouffroy himself was imprisoned during Robespierre's tenure, but was then released by Lisieux and at this time is working with Cugnot in Toulon.

[291] A similar (but less violent) incident happened in OTL in 1837 to a steamship built by Francis Pettit Smith, who therefore accidentally discovered a superior form of propeller. By happening so early in TTL, this short-circuits some developments in propulsion technology and en-sures—for better or for worse—that paddlewheels die out early on.

Madrid heard of the fall of Barcelona at about this time, but this was also the time when matters came to a head in Spain's governmental crisis. Philip VI died on September 3rd, but by this point he had been driven insane by his disease, and his last words were a screaming declaration to disinherit his first son, Charles, Prince of Asturias. The King had become convinced that he had been poisoned by Charles' favourite, the Duke of Aranda, and demanded Aranda's execution before mercifully succumbing. The Kingdom was thus plunged into a constitutional crisis: Saavedra quickly issued declarations in the King's name claiming the legality of Philip's last order, while Aranda and the horrified Charles responded with legal judgements claiming the King had been insane and thus his orders should not be carried out. Saavedra quickly made an alliance with the Infante Philip, Philip's second son, and ordered that he be crowned King of the Spains in order to ensure a strong, united government in order to repel the French.

A virtual civil war erupted in Madrid between the Felipistas and Carlistas, sourly remembered by the Spanish writer Félix Ximinez as 'pausing in a burning house to fight over who shall rescue the silver'. The royal palace, built forty years before to replace one that had burned down, was promptly subjected to the indignity of history repeating itself. The loss of such a potent royal symbol undermined the credibility of the winner in the dispute, no matter who it was. In the end, by the end of November, the Felipistas and Saavedra had triumphed—while Aranda and the Carlistas, including Charles himself, fled to the northwest, where he still enjoyed the most popularity. The Carlista army, commanded by General Javier Castaños, went with him. José de Palafox, then a young lieutenant, was also a part of the Carlista force…

By the time Saavedra had seized power and Philip had been crowned as Philip VII, the French had overran all of Aragon and forced three more Spanish armies to surrender. Belatedly, Madrid ordered the withdrawal of Cuesta and Blake from the south of France, bringing their armies back over the Pyrenees, piecemeal, to protect Castile. However, Devilliers successfully led a force west from Catalonia that managed to seize three of the major mountain passes, while Boulanger coordinated an attack by the remnants of Eustache's Sans-Culottes to press the retreating army of Blake back against the mountains. A large Spanish Army was thus pounded to pieces a little at a time, the mountains meaning that it could not concentrate its forces against the French. Once more, the Republic's Gribeauval artillery and the steam *fardiers* that pulled it served the Administrateur's cause well. Cuesta's army survived, but the bombastic Cuesta was by this point convinced that the 'traitorous' Carlistas were more of a threat than the French, ignored orders from Madrid and moved west to attack Asturias.

Thus it was that Spain was chronically underdefended in the campaign season of 1802. By this point Boulanger had moved almost the entire French army into Aragon. The French forces now swept westward along a broad front, with a single central spearhead aimed at Madrid. Although Spain retained some good generals fighting for Philip VII and Saavedra, she lacked the manpower to resist France's giant conscript armies. There were moments of glory for Spain, such as the Felipista general Bernardo de Gálvez's[292] epic victory at Granada, driving back a French force under Drouet that drastically outnumbered his own. But no matter how many songworthy individual actions the Spanish warriors accomplished, the march of the French columns westward was like an unstoppable tide. Madrid, damaged by years of civil war, was indefensible. Philip VII and Saavedra abandoned it for Córdoba, then Seville, and finally Cadiz as the French closed in towards the end of 1802. At the same time, Charles, Aranda and Castaños managed to defeat Cuesta, with the only real winner being the French. Navarre was finally swallowed up once more by the Republican armies, a fact that was celebrated with parades in Paris. Lisieux sensed the mood of euphoria and shifted his plans into high gear...

The scale of the Spanish defeat provoked alarm in many circles. The King of Naples and Sicily, Charles VIII and VI, was

---

[292] In TTL neither his father nor he became Viceroy of New Spain, and his career has mainly focused on European conflicts, except a brief foray into Peru during the Second Platinean War.

descended from Charles III of Spain and the struggles of his fellow Bourbons created further interest in the two Kingdoms. The Neapolitan navy and even army was currently being reformed by a British ex-Admiral with an axe to grind, a man named Horatio Nelson. British political circles mumbled confusedly over the impact of the French victory, the Foxites cheering on the forces of radicalism as they overthrew another fossilised absolutist state, some Tories joining them due to the defeat of an old British enemy, while the moderate Burkeans reacted with alarm at the spread of the Revolution.

But perhaps the most significant response was in Lisbon. The Portuguese court was understandably alarmed at the rapid downfall of Spain and the thought that they could be next. Portugal and Republican France were not at war, but this had not stopped the French advance through Germany cutting across many neutral states and often unilaterally executing their royal families. Although Portugal was no German statelet, and her army had undergone considerable reforms since the lessons of the First Platinean War with Spain, the prospect of a war with the whole might of France – and perhaps a co-opted Spain – was enough to make another Lisbon earthquake seem trivial by comparison.

But, of course, Portugal had King Peter IV, who did not let himself be daunted by such minor issues as the impending destruction of his country. He called his ministers and the Cortes, including his chief minister the Duke of Cadaval, to a meeting in January 1803 in order to discuss their response to the French invasion of Spain. There were several views expressed, including those who argued that the best response was to pursue a policy of highly visible neutrality and sign treaties with France, as Flanders had. Peter scoffed at that, calling those who held that view 'tortoises', who thought they were safe if they hid from the world inside their shells. No, the only solution was a pre-emptive attack.

The King's ministers gaped at this, a piece of madness that seemed equal to anything his mother Maria had ever come out with. But Peter explained the method behind his shock pronouncement. If France co-opted Spain, they would have the same advantages that Spain always had in their wars with Portugal. But right now Spain was weak and reeling, struggling to respond. Now was the time for Portugal to occupy all the strongpoints first, and then hold them against any French attack, creating buffer zones against future attack.

Most of the King's ministers still thought this was quite absurd, but a refinement to the plan by Cadaval convinced most of them. The Portuguese foreign ministry approached Charles, who was still hiding out in Asturias, and offered to recognise him as King of Spain if he would consent to giving Portugal free rein in Spain. After some agonising, Charles agreed. After the Portuguese envoy left, he turned to Aranda and started enthusiastically declaring his ideas for how they would retake Madrid with Portuguese help and drive out the French. Aranda shook his head sadly and said that it was impossible – Portugal would be crushed as easily as Spain had been, he said. No, Charles had done the right thing, undermined his brother, gained some legitimacy, but there was no victory to be had here. The only option was to flee the country, then return when the situation was different. The French had other enemies. They might withdraw their troops to the other end of Europe, and *then* it would be time to return in glory, just as King Sebastian of Portugal would according to the old legend.

Charles was doubtful of this, but his mind was changed in March 1803 when the French finally took Cadiz and Philip VII surrendered to them. To the surprise of some commentators, the French did not immediately execute Philip VII. Lisieux and Boulanger had already agreed that a Spanish Latin Republic was not likely at present, and would have to wait until later. Spain did not have many centralised institutions – remove the monarchy and it would fragment. It would no longer be the case that to hold the capital was to hold the nation.

The revolution could wait, then.

The peace was not, in fact, all that punishing—at least on paper. France annexed all of the Basque lands, Catalonia, and a wide strip of territory in between, resulting in definitive French domination of the Pyrenees. Andorra was also abolished and annexed to France. France took Minorca from Spain and turned it into a naval base for its new steam fleet. However, the deepest strictures of the peace were not formalised in writing. Philip VII was virtually reduced to a French puppet, Saavedra quietly met with a 'Carlist assassin' in the night, and it was French 'advisors' who really set Spanish policy.

In April, just after Saavedra's assassination, Philip VII issued death warrants on all the other infantes of Spain, a clumsy French policy aimed at ensuring there were no other claimants. The other four – Philip VI had produced six sons but no daughters – were already turning towards Charles after Philip VII's humiliation, but now the Infantes Antonio, Ferdinand, John and Gabriel hastily high-tailed it for Asturias. By now, Charles recognised the truth of the Duke of Aranda's argument, as French and Felipist armies formed up to invade the Carlist-held lands. With a heavy heart, he gave the order to leave the country.

Charles had nine ships of the Spanish Navy loyal to him waiting in Corunna. Portugal gave him several more in return for his blessing for their annexation of Galicia – not a policy he would have countenanced in any situation less desperate, of course. Sickened by the Portuguese taking advantage of his weak position, he later bitterly remarked 'I am surprised Pedro did not ask for Tordesillas to be moved so that our rightful lands now extend from ten degrees west of Madrid to ten degrees east!'

It is the nine Spanish ships that are remembered, though. On them, they carried the last hope for a free Spain, the five Infantes, including the man who claimed to be King Charles IV of Spain. But each and every one of those five Infantes would one day be a King in his own right. For the fleet of Spain fled westwards from the ruin of their nation, westwards along the path that Columbus had traced more than three hundred years before, into the lands of the Indies…

Chapter 50: A Vision of the World

The South Seas—the last unexplored frontier. This, then, will be the voyage of His Majesty's Ship Enterprize. Our three-year mission: to explore strange new lands, to seek out new peoples and new kingdoms…to tread, bravely, where no Englishman, where no American, has set foot."

– Captain the Honourable George North, private journal

From: "A History of the Imperial Navy" by Sir Augustus Vanburen (1940)—

Many men have tried to claim a conclusive date for the foundation of the Imperial Navy. Few save the credulous and the schoolboy will attempt to claim that the Imperial Navy truly came into being only on the day when it was legally founded, in the fires of war of the Thirsty Thirties. Indeed, how could such an organisation have moved smoothly into action if it had not been acting independently for years before, waiting only for officialdom to catch up with reality (as is so often the case?)

No, the true date of the Imperial Navy's genesis must lie by definition earlier. Some have given it, perhaps with some justification, as 1796, the year that the American Preventive Cutter Service was founded. They argue that this was the first truly American manifestation of the British naval service – certainly the first with 'American' in the name – and thus qualifies as the spiritual ancestor of the Imperial Navy. However, this assumption fails on two counts. The Preventive Cutter Service, though officially an Imperial[293] organisation, was in practice the

---

[293] 'Imperial' in this sense has a similar meaning to 'federal' in the OTL USA, i.e. a national organisation defined and controlled by the central government. The counterpart is 'Confederal', referring to issues con-

responsibility of Confederal or even provincial authorities, and lacked any single unified military command. Its officers were not considered part of the Royal Navy, and with good reason: they were as to trained fighting sailors as militiamen were to regulars on land. This was not usually a problem, as the PCS' main role was to deter smugglers and illegal transporters,[294] but it certainly illustrates that the PCS cannot credibly be claimed to be a precursor to the Imperial Navy. Besides, ex-RN ships under American command had been stationed in provincial ports ever since the 1760s, though under not even a *theoretical* unified command, and the PCS simply represented a refinement of this.

It may be that we cannot, in fact, simply point to a single date at which the IN came into existence, but one highly iconic moment was certainly the launch of HMS *Enterprize* (later retroactively altered to HIMS). Some scholars have scoffed at the populist sentiment surrounding the 'myth' of the *Enterprize*, but to do so is to miss the point. We are not Rationalists and this is not a Rational world. It matters little that a thousand tiny changes in law and alterations in naval policy contributed far more to the foundation of the IN than did one ship. It is what people remember that defines our past, and by extension, our future.

Enterprize's own history is certainly worth examining. The first HMS *Enterprize* was a captured French craft, and thence descends the name, as do so many with a rich, incongruously British, history. *L'Entreprise*, a sixth-rate jackass frigate, was taken from her French captain by HMS *Tryton* in 1705, during the First War of Supremacy. Renamed HMS *Enterprize*, she survived for only two years under the command of Captain Paul before being wrecked off the English coast. But the Royal Navy, in its fickle way, remembered the name. In 1709, a newly constructed British frigate, a fifth-rate, was given the name *Enterprize*. And a legend began.

---

trolled by the governments of the Five Confederations.
[294] Illegal transporters = people who smuggle transported British convicts into the Empire, which has been illegal since the 1780s. Paid for by corrupt British justices of the peace who pocket the money from the Crown set aside for paying for the convicts' official transport to one of the authorised penal colonies.

Three more *Enterprize*s followed, each with its own log of adventures as thick as that of any Royal Navy ship. One was a captured Spanish craft, while the other two were British-built. The fifth HMS *Enterprize* was one of the *Rifleman* class of 28-gun sixth-rate frigates[295] and fought in the Second Platinean War under Captain Humphry Pellew, a Cornishman. This *Enterprize* fought in the Battle of Trafalgar in 1783 and acquitted herself well, to the extent that the *Gazette* decided to focus on Pellew's crew's heroism rather than dwelling on the overall embarrassing tactical defeat for the Royal Navy. After minor repairs at the Gosport Shipyard[296] in Virginia, *Enterprize* was then reassigned for escort convoy duty for the transports carrying American troops down to fight in the Plate. Pellew chafed at this inglorious duty, and was glad in late 1784 when he was released for freelance commerce raiding. In the latter stages of the Second Platinean War, it is considered that Pellew and his crew wrought sufficient havoc on the Franco-Spanish attempts to reinforce their troops by convoy that they may have shortened the war by months. For better or for worse.

But Pellew's *Enterprize* is of course best known for the First Battle of Falkland's Islands (known at the time as the *Islas Malvinas* in the proto-UPSA). In February 1785, months before the war's end, a Franco-Spanish force commanded by Admiral Pierre André de Suffren de Saint Tropez successfully trapped Pellew near the leeward shores of the islands. Refusing all calls to surrender, Pellew and his crew fought on, outnumbered, against two French ships of the line, a Spanish frigate and a Spanish ship of the line. In the end the *Enterprize* was sunk, but not before she took down both the Spanish frigate and the French flagship by an astonishingly foolhardy boarding action. Before being captured by the French marines, Pellew managed to shoot Suffren himself at long range with a rifled pistol, killing one of France's most gifted

---

[295] OTL this class, or its close analogue, was named for the *Enterprize* herself. Butterflies have resulted in the names reshuffling. *Rifleman* here is a reference to the Americans' famed skill with the rifled musket.

[296] In OTL this was later renamed the Norfolk Naval Shipyard. It was established in 1767 in both timelines.

admirals. Many speculative romantics of the French persuasion have mused on how things would have turned out differently later if Royal France had possessed a man of his calibre rather than the dithering d'Estaing.

A new *Enterprize* was not launched for a number of years. Perhaps the Royal Navy thought that the name was unlucky after the vessel's destruction, or perhaps that Pellew's gallant last stand was too legendary to live up to. In any case, the name disappeared from the Royal Navy lists for over a decade, not resurfacing even in the frantic shipbuilding period of 1785-1794 as the RN struggled to recover from its shock defeats in the Second Platinean War.

In truth, the circumstances of the French Revolution and the loss of much of the former French fleet to the Dauphin meant that Britain and the RN had little to fear, navally, from the French Latin Republic – in the short term at least. However, shipbuilding continued right up to the signing of the Treaty of Caen with Republican France after the Seigneur campaign. At this point, the new Fox ministry cancelled many of the shipbuilding contracts, alienating elements within the Royal Navy but saving considerable funds for a populist campaign of cutting taxes and reducing the national debt. This, however, opened up a vacuum in the Royal Navy's distribution.

Over the course of the eighteenth century, it had become apparent to the Lords of the Admiralty that the Royal Navy had to become a truly global force. Traditionally, the RN's role was to dominate the English Channel and, to a lesser extent, the Atlantic coastal waters of France, Spain, and the British Isles themselves. This would be a safeguard against invasion by the continental powers with their huge armies, as it had been since before 1588. However, as the century wore on, it soon became evident that naval warfare was just as important in other theatres of the world, and the Wars of Supremacy necessitated a greater Royal Navy presence elsewhere. Furthermore, William Pitt's policies of merely holding back France in Europe – by paying the Austrians and Prussians to do it for the British and Hanoverians – was based on the idea of seeking to win longer-term colonial victories over the French and the Spanish. In India of course this was ultimately unsuccessful,[297] because the battles were mostly fought on land rather than sea, and the French presence there was largely self-sustaining. However, in North America a powerful British naval presence was necessary to prevent French raids and to protect the valuable colonies in the West Indies, as well as to take French and Spanish islands there from their owners.

Given the economic value of the West Indies, it is unsurprising that the first British naval force to be explicitly stationed somewhere other than Britain herself was the West Indian Squadron, based in Jamaica. The Squadron's duties were multiple: to combat piracy, to defend the British plantations, to ward off Spanish attempts to prevent British trade with their own colonies, and, in the event of war, to transport redcoats to the Spanish- and French-held islands in order to take them away.

The Treaty of Amsterdam, which ended the Third War of Supremacy in 1759, saw those same valuable islands (such as Guadaloupe) returned to France after having been British-occupied during the war. Yet this was not such an unpopular diplomatic decision as had King William IV's to return Louisbourg at the end of the Second War of Supremacy (which was one of the catalysts for the War of the British Succession). Everyone understood that, ultimately, it mattered little if France possessed those sugar plantations, if Britain's Navy could cut her off from them whenever it pleased. The Royal French Navy, though respectable, had no significant bases outside Europe and lacked the Royal Navy's long-range power-projection capabilities.

The West Indian Squadron was boosted by the creation of the American Squadron in 1780, a response to Franco-Spanish activity near the American Atlantic seaboard at a time when most of the Royal Navy was engaged in the South Atlantic or guarding against invasion at home. The American Squadron was based at Williamsburg, the capital of Virginia, and soon royal charters were granted to open up subsidiary bases and shipyards in Boston and Charleston. Lewisborough in New Scotland was also converted into a base.[298] Most importantly, American

---

[297] Though not in OTL.

[298] The former Louisbourg. In TTL there is no Halifax yet, as the French

481

shipyards were in 1789 granted the right to build new warships for the RN as well as merchantmen. The Royal Navy even placed a permanent admiralty post in each base comparable to the big British base at Malta, capable of giving new (American) recruits officer training and setting lieutenancy examinations.

Ultimately, the purpose of this plan was to support the Royal Navy's painful rebirth in the wake of the defeats of the Second Platinean War. Letting the Americans look after themselves meant that the RN could focus on its primary objective of defending Britain. With the advent of the Jacobin Wars, this policy was altered somewhat. American shipbuilding was increased, with the intention of withdrawing fleet elements from the West Indian and American Squadrons and adjoining them to the Mediterranean Squadron and the Channel Fleet. This dated from a time when it was considered likely that the whole French Royal Navy would turn its colours and join the Revolutionaries. Due to the time it took for orders to cross the Atlantic, the plan was obsoleted almost by the time the Americans were reading it, but like all plans in such a crusty and conservative organisation as the RN of the time, it soon had a momentum all of its own. Thus it was that, despite the fact that no ships were in fact removed from the American and West Indian fleets, and peace was signed in 1800, the American shipyards were still going at full capacity as late as 1805. The Royal Navy would eventually come to be thankful for this, but at present it was largely a piece of politics on the part of the ruling Constitutionalist Party, which favoured a more independent American foreign policy and saw – with more perspicacity than usual – that the name American Squadron might one day signify command as well as geography.

However, this meant that at present, the Americans had more ships than they knew what to do with. Fortuitously, this came at the same time as a deepening crisis. In 1799, another 'Jenkin's Ear'-like incident startled newspapers in London and

---

abandoned any attempt to put bases in Nova Scotia (New Scotland) as the Americans have put more effort into holding and colonising it relative to OTL. A town named Bolingbroke will be founded near the site of OTL Halifax later on.

especially Fredericksburg, despite the ongoing war with the Republic. Though theoretically allies in that conflict, or at least cobelligerents, Britain and Spain were nonetheless clashing in the Oregon Country in the north-west of North America, south of the Russian outposts in Alyeska.[299] A small colony of British adventurers led by John Goodman had colonised Noochaland[300] in order to set up a new fur trade. Fur was the primary source of Russian interest in Alyeska, and Noochaland was just as rich in that regard. Goodman's men traded with the native Noochanoolth and Salish Indians, mainly for food and supplies in exchange for the usual European manufactured trade goods.

Goodman's furs were mainly sold on via the Pacific islands, in which he had a number of connections. He had previously traded at the court of King Kamehameha of Kohala, who was seeking to unite the Gavajski Islands under his rule at the time.[301] Kamehameha essentially served as an intermediary for Goodman's trade goods to be passed on to the other islands, and ultimately to Europeans (via the Dutch and Portuguese in the East Indies and the Spanish in the Philippines). This helped finance Kamehameha's own wars of unification, leading to the creation of a single Kingdom of Gavaji by 1804, and also sparked renewed interest in the central to north Pacific among several states. Not all of those states were European: down in Autiaraux, some among the feuding Mauré began to look back at the islands from which they had long ago travelled, and pondered…

But Goodman's activities also alerted the Spanish. The Viceroy

---

[299] Increased Russian government interest in the country's far eastern possessions in general, due to the activities of Lebedev and Benyovsky, means that the small Alyeskan (Alaskan) outposts are considerably larger and more developed by this point than OTL.

[300] TTL's name for Vancouver Island. Note that the Noochanoolth are only one of several tribes there, but they were the first one to be met by Europeans (in this case Goodman) and so the whole place gets named for them.

[301] Gavaji and Gavajski are the terms equivalent to Hawaii and Hawaiian in TTL, for reasons which will become clear. Note than in OTL at this point the islands were often known as the Sandwich Islands, but this was a name given to them by Captain Cook, who did not live to make his voyages of discovery in TTL.

of New Spain, Martín de Gálvez, was alarmed by British interest in a territory which was claimed by Spain according to the old treaties, even if it had never been colonised. He sent a mission north commanded by Admiral Juan Esteban Rodriguez. Rodriguez arrested Goodman and occupied his colony. The Spanish authorities had always had problems distinguishing between official British actions and those of individual British citizens, unsurprising considering the fact that the British government unofficially sanctioned a lot of privateers and secret missions against Spanish rule in Novamund. Thus, even as the Republican French fought both countries, a crisis grew in North America.

The Rockingham Ministry of the time was unwilling to act too strongly against Spain at a time when both countries were aligned against the Republicans. Thus it ultimately fell to the Americans to stake their own claim to the region. Britain had records of Sir Francis Drake possibly exploring the same lands earlier in the 16th century, having named it New Albion, but a ship needed to be sent to examine the territory in order to plausibly confirm this. Diplomats acting on behalf of the Duke of Grafton and James Monroe eventually secured Goodman's release, negotiating directly with Martínez. This diplomatic traffic between Fredericksburg and the City of Mexico was a sign of things to come, with London and Madrid being only peripherally involved. Goodman was released, but the Spanish remained in occupation of Noochaland and warned that British interference would not be tolerated. In response, the Americans – with the tacit assent of London – launched the mission of HMS *Enterprize*.

This sixth *Enterprize* was an American-built ship, from the same Gosport Shipyard in Virginia which had repaired her predecessor. Her construction incorporated many new innovations which might not have been approved by the more conservative Royal Navy establishment back in Britain. A fifth-rate, 36-gun frigate, she incorporated four of the new short-range carronades as well as a new design of bow-chaser with a rifled barrel. This had been developed by the American gunsmith James Murray-Pulteney, a relative of Patrick Ferguson of the breech-loading rifle. She carried a crew of 247 men under the command of Captain the Honourable George North. The Captain was the second son of the late Lord North, the former Lord Deputy of North America. George North had mostly grown up in Fredericksburg and thought of himself as a Virginian, and the rest of his crew was also largely American, although like any Royal Navy crew it had its share of eclectically recruited personnel. We know from the detailed records surrounding the voyage that the *Enterprize* carried a Malay, a Chinese, three Guineans, two black freedmen from Pennsylvania, thirty-nine Britons, three Frenchmen, two Spaniards, five Indians of the American variety and two of the Asian. The penultimate group was perhaps the most significant. Among the five Indians was John Vann, the son of the influential Cherokee leader James Vann, who was himself a cousin of the current Cherokee Emperor Moytoy IV Attaculla and essentially the Emperor's chief minister.[302] The elder Vann, who like many Cherokee leaders had part-European ancestry, wanted his son to see more of the world and to learn about naval practice. Also, just as the Americans had a secret motive for wanting to learn more about the Oregon Country, so did Vann and the Emperor of the Cherokee…

The *Enterprize* left Virginia in April 1801. She carried aboard her the naturalist Andrew Sibthorpe, a rival of Erasmus Darwin II who had achieved fame for his exploration of the flora and fauna of the Great Lakes a few years before. Sibthorpe was determined to find even more extraordinary creatures and plants to present to

---

[302] Recall in TTL that the British attempt to set up a single Cherokee Emperor and unify the tribes (in order to use them more effectively against the French and Spanish, and so treaties signed with a single leader are honoured) has been markedly more successful, due to colonial governments not changing policy so often. However, this is rather more London's definition of success than Charleston's, as the Carolinians at this time would have preferred a more disunited group of Indians that they could easily push aside in order to settle their lands. As it is, the fact that the Cherokee are much more united in TTL gives even the most fiery filibusterer pause—though the Carolinians had already obtained much of the Cherokee's *traditional* lands, the new native Empire has taken over many more from other tribes conquered as a result of their participation in the Anglo-Spanish wars.

the Royal Society.

Captain North proposed a leisurely course that would allow the *Enterprize* to 'fly the flag' for America in various ports – contrary to regulations, along with the White Ensign of the RN she flew the Jack and George of the Empire. To that end, the *Enterprize* sailed pointedly through the Spanish parts of the West Indies, pausing in British Havana in order to take on supplies. Sibthorpe, a noted Linnaean, wrote much-debated musings on how the new Carolinian colonists of Cuba were treating both the black slaves and the established Spanish hierarchy there, and how this fitted into Racialist philosophy, if at all. These were the days when the Carolinians were learning that they could not truly seek to dominate Cuba unless they cut deals with the old Spanish nobility, something which would eventually have profound effects on Carolinian views of confessional affairs and international relations.

The *Enterprize* crossed the Atlantic to briefly call in on the trade posts of the newly reinvigorated Royal Africa Company. Sibthorpe met Joseph Banks there and discussed the prospect of a truly universal system of classification. The ship then moved on, spent a week in the friendly port of Buenos Aires in the UPSA, and finally rounded the Horn through the Straits of Magellan. It was only on the return voyage, contrary to what many textbooks state, that the ship landed on Tierra del Fuego and Sibthorpe wrote about the natives—another of his works which would be hotly studied in later years.

Finally, the *Enterprize* sailed north through the Pacific. The hostile policies of the Spanish Empire meant that she could not call in at those ports enroute, but that was no great hardship for a vessel commanded by Nantucket whalers who knew these waters like the back of their hand. The *Enterprize* called in at Lahaina, the capital of what would become the Kingdom of Gavaji. Here Captain North met Goodman, who had made his way there after finally being released by the Spanish. Goodman was notably and vocally disappointed by North's refusal to give a definitive answer on whether Britain would stake a claim to the region and restore him to his colony. It is for that reason, many historians believe, that Goodman and his compatriots (not all of whom were British) gave up on attempting to gain British or American backing for their trade project, and instead turned their attention to other sponsors...

Interlude #7: A Touch of Chauvinism

Captain Christopher Nuttall: Now that you two have rejoined us, perhaps we may move on to other matters.

Dr Bruno Lombardi (somewhat indistinctly): Eb, bir. We have the shpecial rebort to considber…

Dr Theodoros Pylos: It is simply an illustration of how relatively minor alterations to our own timeline may –

Dr Bruno Lombardi:—in fact truly result in bajor rebercussions a few years down de line…dough I disagree wid my colleague's obinion of de so-called 'butterfly ebbect'…

Dr Theodoros Pylos: Be quiet, or I'll break your nose again.

Captain Christopher Nuttall (pointedly): Gentlemen…

Dr Theodoros Pylos: Very well. Let us consider the life of one General Anthony St. Leger…

From: "A History of Doncaster" by Dr Stephen Utterthwaite (1963)—

Anthony St. Leger was an Irishman, born in County Kildare in 1731 to an old family of Anglo-Norman extraction. As the fourth son and freed from responsibilities of being heir to the family lands, or being expected to enter the Church, he chose to join the Army after his education at Eton School and Peterhouse College, Cambridge. Towards the end of his Cambridge tenure, in 1752, St. Leger witnessed a parade through the streets of the university city by some of the American troops who had recently been instrumental in restoring King Frederick to his rightful place on the throne of Great Britain.

The parade was led by Sir William Pepperrell, Bt., a man of Massachussetts who had commanded the successful siege of Lewisborough (then Louisbourg, a French fortress) in the American theatre of the Second War of Supremacy. It was this victory that had invested Frederick with the tide of public feeling he needed to launch his bid for power, as the exiled prince had capitalised on American outrage when King William handed the fortress back to France at the Peace of Aix-la-Chappelle. Pepperrell had then fought in Ireland against the Jacobites, and was by 1752 one of the King's most trusted confidantes.

Pepperrell's teenage son, also called William,[303] was a colour ensign in the informal regiment, which would eventually become the 51st (Massachussetts) Foot.[304] As they paraded down Trumpington Street, Pepperrell the Younger tripped on a cobblestone and dropped the King's Colour he had been carrying. The embarrassment at such a potent image to the King's enemies, given Frederick's questionably legitimate taking of the throne, could have been tremendous. It is not hard to consider how the story could have spread and become a rallying cry for Williamites and Jacobites alike.

But the falling flag was snatched from the air by one of the countless students lining the street, a certain Anthony St. Leger, and quickly handed back to Ensign Pepperrell as he recovered. With a nod of thanks at a crisis averted, the ensign began a friendship that would change history...

---

[303] OTL Pepperrell did not marry or have any children. That he did in TTL can be considered a butterfly of Prince Frederick's activities in America upsetting the OTL political and economic tides.

[304] Called 'Pepperrell's Regiment', this existed in OTL in the Seven Years' War; here it has been formed a little earlier. Like the other American regiment, Shirley's 50th, in OTL it lost many men in the Seven Years' War and was disbanded afterwards, somewhat upsetting the Americans. In TTL the prestige of homegrown regiments is such (and with a shorter war) that the two regiments survived, but are eventually renamed after the regions in which they were raised (Massachussetts and New Hampshire) in line with the county system used in the rest of the British Army.

After the parade, St. Leger met with young William Pepperrell in the Eagle and Child pub on Bene't Street, the ensign buying him a drink in thanks.[305] This meeting developed into a wider conversation, with some of the older and more experienced officers in the regiment joining in – whether American-, Irish- or British-born, they had all fought in America. They filled St. Leger's head with tales of the extraordinary things to be seen in the New World, and while he had already been considering the Army as a career, this sealed his decision.

St. Leger signed up to the 51st a year later, not long before the regiment was due to be shipped back to America. The failure to ratify the Treaty of Aix-la-Chappelle had resulted in icy relations between London and Paris, and the Diplomatic Revolution with Austria was looming on the horizon. Everyone knew that another war was only a matter of time, and Anthony St. Leger did not want to miss it. He entered the regiment as an Ensign, but immediately bought himself a promotion to lieutenant with his share of the St. Leger land rents. By this point William Pepperrell the younger had also risen to that rank, and the two of them served under Captain Timothy Bush, a man of Connecticut and commander of the Light Company.[306]

The 51st fought in the Third War of Supremacy in America, taking considerable losses: Bush was killed in the Battle of Fort Niagara in 1759[307] and St. Leger was promoted to replace him. Pepperrell the younger was also promoted, commanding the Second Company. The war came to an end in that year with the capture of Quebec and the Treaty of Amsterdam, but peace did not endure for long. When the First Platinean War broke out in 1763, St. Leger and the rest of the 51st were sent to assist the Georgian militiamen and British regulars in the conquest of Florida. By

---

[305] This pub can still be visited, though today it is known as the Eagle. It opened as the Eagle and Child in 1667.

[306] An ancestor of the OTL American Bush political dynasty, who in TTL joined the army raised by Frederick to prosecute his return to Britain.

[307] In OTL Pepperrell's Regiment had mostly been killed or captured by the French in a separate battle at this point; in TTL, of course, the pattern of warfare is somewhat shifted.

this point St. Leger had married Caroline Phipps, the daughter of Sir Spencer Phipps, William Shirley's lieutenant-governor in Massachussetts—and she was with child. The campaign itself went fairly smoothly, but yellow fever and malaria cut swathes through the army, and though St. Leger himself survived, his pregnant wife fell victim to the fever and died in 1764.

Distraught and possessed with an inchoate fury at the world and everything in it, St. Leger threw himself into his work with a fey vigour. When he learned that the 51st were to remain in Florida on occupation duty, he transferred out of the regiment to the first one he knew would be sent to a war theatre: the 33rd Regiment of Foot (1st West Riding of Yorkshire Regiment).[308] The 33rd was a bit of an enigma: having fought hard and won a battle honour on the field at Dettingen, the battle where King George II had been killed and Prince William had found himself William IV, it was suspected of Williamite sympathies by some. On the other hand, it was too well-organised and professional for King Frederick to think about disbanding it lightly: it was known as 'the Pattern' among army reformers for its men's discipline, a model regiment for the others to copy. These two features, political unreliability and battlefield strength, were doubtless the major factors that resulted in the 33rd being sent to fight on the Portuguese front in 1765.

St. Leger arrived too late to participate in the unsuccessful Siege of Ciudad Rodrigo, but fought at Badajoz the year later. Although that siege was also a failure for the Anglo-Portuguese forces, he distinguished himsel—slaying seven Spanish cavalrymen from atop a heap of his dead privates, firing off their loaded muskets one at a time, before finally clubbing the last man to death with the butt of an unloaded musket. It was this act of mindless violence that seemed to bring St. Leger back to himself and burn away a little of his fey battle-madness. He fought more sobrely the year later in Galicia, being promoted to Major and third-in-command

---

[308] The regiment was not *officially* linked to the West Riding until the 1780s, but the writer is being a little anachronistic. In any case, the 33rd recruited mainly from the region long before this was officially recognised.

of the 33rd, which had been reduced by battlefield casualties.

At the end of the war, a still saddened but thoughtful St. Leger returned to England with the 33rd. He could not bring himself to ever look upon America again, associating it with the bittersweet loss of his wife, and had no desire to go back to Ireland. Instead, he settled down in the 33rd's own home territory, the West Riding of Yorkshire, and eventually bought the Park Hill Estate at Firbeck, near Rotherham. There, he retired from the Army and spent his half-pay on his new hobby, horse-breeding. Having mostly lost his appetite for blood after Badajoz, he found this a new obsession to throw himself into to recover from the pain of his wife's death. Despite not starting from particularly strong financial territory, by 1770 or so St. Leger was renowned for breeding some of the fastest three-year-old colts in the riding, the county – perhaps even the country.

St. Leger was fortunate in retrospect that in the 1770s the Kingdom of Great Britain's Prime Minister, Charles Watson-Wentworth, 2nd Marquess of Rockingham, was himself a son of the southern West Riding—his family owning the Wentworth Woodhouse estate not far from St. Leger's house. Whenever he tore himself away from the Westminster political scene, Rockingham would return to his northern home, and was interested in horse racing. Yorkshire lacked its own major sweepstakes, but St. Leger was nonetheless making money travelling the country in order to show off his colts. He became known as the "Irish Magician", with satirists in the Yorkshire newspapers presenting him as a fay capable of enchanting his horses with fairy powers.

Lord Rockingham met St. Leger in 1772 and persuaded him to stand for Parliament as a Patriot Whig. St. Leger's money and popularity meant that he easily topped the vote and was elected MP for Pontefract in the 1774 general election. St. Leger supported the policies of the Rockinghamite government and was also an advocate of granting greater powers to the Empire of North America. He was one of several British parliamentarians to participate in the direct negotiations that followed the 'Troubled Sixties', but unlike the majority was a moderate rather than a radical. St. Leger was instrumental in convincing the Parliament of Great Britain that the New Englanders would accept a single unitary confderacy; most MPs had thought this was not an option after the failure of such a venture under James II a century before.

However, St. Leger was arguably even more influential for Parliament when he was outside it. In 1776 he, Rockingham, and several other Yorkshiremen of influence met in the upper room of the Red Lion pub in Doncaster and proposed a new Yorkshire racing stakes to be based in the town, for three-year-old colts. Named the Rockingham Stakes[309] after the man who financed it, the race attracted a great deal of interest from all over the country, and eventually even farther afield. One of St. Leger's own horses predictably won the first Stakes, but soon he was facing stiff competition from breeders from every part of Great Britain, along with Ireland, France, and beyond. In 1782 he was surprised to be visited by Colonel Sir William Pepperrell the Younger, his former colleague in the 51st. Pepperrell, whose father had died in the 1760s, was now head of the regiment and offered St. Leger the lieutenant-colonelcy.

Although Pepperrell had brought a horse of his own to enter, by the 1780s the initial spark of interest in the race had waned, and St. Leger was becoming bored. He had finally married again in 1779, to Emily Lennox, the daughter of the Duke of Richmond. The Duke shared much with St. Leger, being a former Colonel of the 33rd, a Rockinghamite in Parliament, and supporting the parliamentary rights of the American Imperials. Although Emily gave St. Leger an heir, Charles St. Leger, and cemented the alliance between the families, St. Leger never truly loved her and was unable to let go of his longing for Caroline Phipps. He therefore experienced tension in his home life. For this reason, he jumped at Pepperrell's offer.

When the Second Platinean War broke out, the 51st was shipped to the Plate and fought under General Sir George

---

[309] In OTL it was simply called the St. Leger; they wanted to name it after Rockingham, but he refused, saying that although he had funded it, it was St. Leger's idea. In TTL Rockingham is still Prime Minister at this point (in OTL he was in opposition) so *not* calling it after him is not really an option, prestige-wise.

Washington, later 1st Baron Washington. St. Leger distinguished himself once more, winning himself a knighthood, and, unlike some of the British officers of his age stationed there, had not fought in the Plate on the wrong side a generation earlier. For that reason, he was often chosen as a representative to the Platinean revolutionaries. Both on the battlefield and in Buenos Aires, he learned that the Platineans were also interested in horse breeding, at least as much as the Americans: like the Americans, they possessed a country with grassy plains on which cavalry was king and the natives were restless. Thus, it is perhaps inevitable that when the war ended, Sir Anthony St. Leger returned to Britain with a number of new horses and a cometary trail of intrigued proto-Meridians in tow.

The new bloodlines from South America breathed new life into the Rockingham Stakes, even though Lord Rockingham himself had since fallen from grace thanks to the Africa Bubble scandal, and the amounts staked on the races rose dramatically as the rich and powerful entered their own colts. St. Leger was made a baronet in 1786, in recognition of how his work had made the Doncastrian economy boom and put both the town and the West Riding on the map.

St. Leger died in 1789, but what he left behind would change the world. For among those rich and powerful were, of course, many politicians: Rockingham's name and interest drew in even more than would have come simply for the Stakes themselves. This only intensified when the aged Rockingham was called back to be Prime Minister once more in 1796, and it was in the 1790s that the fear of invasion ran high once more among the British people. Even though Revolutionary France had lost most of her fleet, the fear remained: men worried that the fleets of the Netherlands or Spain could fall into French hands if those nations were defeated by French armies on land. The latter prophecy came true, at least in part, after Rockingham's death and peace had been made under Charles James Fox. Though the peace remained, few doubted it would last forever, and the idea of the Spanish fleet bringing the hardened French Republican hordes to British shores was not an idea that bore thinking about.

Thus, slowly, quietly, the Government – not Fox himself, who saw Lisieux's France through rose-tinted spectacles, but the moderate Whigs and occasional hardline Tories who provided his majority – began to invest in a new Army depot in the southern part of the North of England, near the geographic centre of the country. On paper, at least, it was simply an Army depot. In reality, it had rather more buildings than a mere military base would require, rather more investment, more defences for a place in the middle of the country.

There was a reason for all of this, of course. No matter what Fox thought, a French invasion was a real possibility, one day sooner or later. And if the French landed, they might well succeed in taking London. If they took London, then Parliament and the King would need a secure place to decamp to while they continued to prosecute the war effort. A place far from the coast, so that in the nightmare scenario of the French ruling the seas, they could not land troops directly. Not a major city, but one with excellent transport links for communicating with the armies. A place which plenty of MPs knew well enough from their excursions north for the sweepstakes.

Thus, in the first decade of the nineteenth century, the village of Finningley, a few miles from Doncaster and just over the border with Nottinghamshire, played host to the construction of Fort Rockingham, named for the former Prime Minister. A fort designed not merely for recruitment and supply, but to serve – in time of the nation's greatest peril – as an alternative seat of government... [310]

---

[310] In the OTL Napoleonic Wars, there was a similar facility built at Weedon in Northamptonshire. The more northerly location essentially reflects the paranoia of British parliamentarians about the unknown capabilities of French wonder weapons and whether they could overrun the South of England faster than they think. Well, that and the title of this interlude.

Epilogue: End of the Beginning

22/08/2019. Temporary headquarters of TimeLine L Preliminary Exploration Team, location classified. Captain Christopher G. Nuttall, seconded from British SAS, commanding officer.

Addressed to Director Stephen Rogers of the Thande Institute for Crosstime Exploration, Cambridge, United Kingdom.

Director Rogers:

I hope that our initial coverage of 'TimeLine L' was of interest to you. I realise that it may be frustrating to consider events so far removed in the past when it is the situation here and now that the Institute will wish to hear of. I have expressed similar thoughts myself to Dr Pylos, Dr Lombardi and their colleagues, but they assure me that it is only in the context of this knowledge that we will be able to truly appreciate the underlying forces which have driven this world to the strange situation in which we now find it.

For now at least things remain more or less recognisable as we leave you on the turn of the nineteenth century. But, my research team assures me, the seeds for what will come have already been sown. Just as we must look back centuries to see the ultimate causes of events in our own timeline like the World Wars, it seems that the beginnings of Societism and Diversitarianism stem from a time when history still seems not that far removed from our own.

I hope you will accept my recommendation that we continue our coverage of this timeline's background before moving to the contact phase. It is absolutely imperative that we do not put a foot wrong in making contact, as I'm sure you appreciate. Nor indeed should we countenance leaving this timeline altogether, as some have suggested. The opportunities here for the Institute are enormous.

Inform Dr Pataki that we are observing all necessary precautions as it is, but if he really wishes to send us another shipment of radiation treatment tablets through the Portal then he is more than welcome. We are all fairly well versed at this point in the local version of what English has become, so there is no need for the new enhanced translator app Lieutenant McConnell referred to in his message.

Thank you, sir, and we all hope to see our families again sooner or later. But the story of the world we find ourselves in is far from over.

CAPTAIN C. G. NUTTALL
22nd AUGUST 2019
LONDON, KINGDOM OF ENGLAND
'TIMELINE L'

TO BE CONTINUED
in
**LOOK TO THE WEST
VOLUME II
"UNCHARTED TERRITORY"**

APPENDIX A: LISTS OF RULERS

List of monarchs of the Kingdom of Great Britain (House of Hanover)

1714-1727: George I
1727-1743: George II
1743-1749: William IV
1749-1760: Frederick I
1760-1799: George III
1799-18??: Henry IX

List of Prime Ministers of the Kingdom of Great Britain

1721-1742: Robert Walpole, 1st Earl of Orford (Whig)
1742-1743: Spencer Compton, 1st Earl of Wilmington (Whig) - *real power rested in John Cartetet, Secretary of State for the Northern Department*
1743-1751: Henry Pelham (Whig) - *shared power with his brother, Thomas Pelham-Holles, 1st Duke of Newcastle-upon-Tyne*
1751-1758: William Pulteney, 1st Earl of Bath (Patriot Whig)
1758-1766: William Pitt (Patriot Whig)
1766-1782: Charles Watson-Wentworth, 2nd Marquess of Rockingham (Patriot Whig/Liberal Whig) - *First term*
1782-1796: William Cavendish-Bentinck, 3rd Duke of Portland (Liberal Whig) - *real power rested in Edmund Burke, Secretary of State for Foreign Affairs*
1796-1799: Charles Watson-Wentworth, 2nd Marquess of Rockingham (Liberal Whig) - *Second term*
December 1799 there was no Prime Minister due to the constitutional crisis at the time.
1800-18??: Charles James Fox (Radical/Reform)

List of Lords Deputy of the Empire of North America

1728-1751: Prince Frederick, Duke of Cornwall *(the future Emperor Frederick; retroactively backdated from the sinecure office of 'Lord Deputy for the Colonies')*
1751-1764: Thomas Fairfax, 6th Lord Fairfax of Cameron
1764-1790: William North, 2nd Earl of Guilford
1790-18??: Augustus FitzRoy, 3rd Duke of Grafton

List of Lords President of the Empire of North America

1788-1795: George Augustine Washington, 1st Viscount Washington (crossbencher)
1795-1799: Alexander Hamilton, 1st Baron Hamilton (Patriot)
1799-18??: James Monroe (Constitutionalist)

List of Kings of France

1715-1776: Louis XV
1776-1795: Louis XVI† *(OTL's Dauphin Louis-Ferdinand; executed)*
1795-18??: Louis XVII *(approximately OTL's Louis XVI; currently recognised only as King of the remnant 'Royal France')*

List of Kings of Spain

1724 (restoration) - 1746: Philip V
1746-1761: Ferdinand VI
1761-1788: Charles III
1788-18??: Philip VI; *ongoing disputed succession*

List of Kings of Portugal

1706-1750: John V
1750-1769: Joseph I
1769-1786: Maria I and Peter III *(co-monarchs)*
1787-1787: Maria I *(ruling alone in name only due to insanity for most of the year)*
1787-18??: Peter IV

List of Holy Roman Emperors

House of Hapsburg
1711-1740: Charles VI
House of Wittelsbach
1742-1745: Charles VII Albert *(with Maria Theresa as Archduchess of Austria)*
House of Hapsburg-Lorraine
1745-1773: Francis I *(with Maria Theresa as Archduchess of Austria)*
1773-1798: Ferdinand IV
1798-1830: Francis II (*Archduke of Austria, unelected claimant Holy Roman Emperor)*

List of Electors of Brandenburg and Kings in Prussia

1713-1740: Frederick William I
1740-1759: Frederick II† *(not called 'the Great'; died in battle)*
1759-1797: Frederick William II
1797-18??: Frederick III

List of Electors of Saxony

1694-1733: Frederick Augustus I *(also King Augustus II of Poland, called Augustus the Strong; Protestant)*
1733-1765: Frederick Augustus II *(also King Augustus III of Poland, called Augustus the Fat; converted to Catholicism)*
1765-1776: Frederick Christian I
1776-1797: Frederick Christian II
1797-18??: John George V

APPENDIX B: CHRONOLOGY OF "LOOK TO THE WEST", 1688-1800

This simplified date-event format Chronology serves to provide a convenient reference for readers wishing to recall the precise date of an event. In order to contextualise the broader history of this timeline, it begins before the Point of Divergence in 1727 with the convenient date of 1688, which (at least from a British perspective) set the upheavals of the 'Long Eighteenth Century' (1688-1815) into motion.

Please note that as it is impossible to write about events across the world simultaneously in a narrative format, the Chronology below includes some events which are not discussed in the main narrative of Volume I: in particular ongoings in China which will not appear until Volume II. You have been warned...

Part 1: Before the Point of Divergence (1688-1726)

1688-1697: The War of the Grand Alliance, aka the 'Zeroth War of Supremacy' or King William's War, in which a coalition of powers fight France to a standstill and forms the framing for the Glorious Revolution.

1688:

The First Glorious Revolution, in which the unpopular Catholic King James II of England and VII of Scotland is ejected from the country and replaced with William of Orange and his wife Mary, James' daughter.

On the other side of the world, much the same thing happens in the Kingdom of Ayutthaya, as King Narai (seen as a French puppet) is overthrown and trade with Europeans - except the Dutch through the port of Mergui - is banned.

1689:

William and Mary crowned as co-monarchs with the assent of Parliament. Parliament passes "An Act Declaring the Rights and Liberties of the Subject and Settling the Succession of the Crown", which sets down the British Bill of Rights and forms the basis of the British Constitution. Among other things, the Constitution severely limits the rights of Catholics, forbidding them the throne, the vote and public office.

1689-91:

The Williamite War in Ireland, which results in the French and James II being ejected from Ireland, and the country brought under effective British control. The siege of Limerick ends the war, with the 'Flight of the Wild Geese' as many Irish nobles flee to Spain or France. The Treaty of Limerick guarantees Catholic rights, but is rejected by the Protestant-dominated Irish Parliament and Anti-Catholic laws are implemented, to much resentment among the Irish populace.

1694:

Death of Queen Mary. All English judges wear black in mourning, beginning a tradition of judicial garb. William rules as sole monarch.

***1701-1714**: The First War of Supremacy, also known as the War of the Spanish Succession or Queen Anne's War. England/Great Britain, the Netherlands, Austria, Denmark, Portugal, Savoy, Portugal and the Aragonese **vs.** France, Bavaria, Hungarian rebels and the Castilians. The war is indecisive, with post-Hapsburg Spain receiving a Bourbon monarch but not entering personal union with France as Louis XIV had hoped. Territorial changes include: Britain receives Gibraltar and Minorca from Spain; Austria receives Naples, Sardinia, Milan and the Spanish Netherlands (the future Flanders); Savoy receives Sicily; British colonies in North America receive French Acadia and France gives up claim to Newfoundland and Rupert's Land.*

1701:

By the Act of Settlement, Parliament makes the heir to the throne after the childless Anne Electress Sophia of Hanover, although she predeceases Queen Anne and so her son will becomes George I.

1702:

Death of William III of England after his horse stumbled over a molehill and he broke his collarbone, which became infected. Jacobites raise their glasses to 'the little gentleman in black velvet'. James II's second daughter Anne becomes Queen Regnant. End of the personal union between the Dutch Republic and England/Scotland/Ireland, as Willem Friso (no close relation to William III) becomes claimant Stadtholder William IV of the Netherlands. However not all the Dutch provinces recognise this, and so the Netherlands is Stadtholder-less until 1747.

1707:

The Act of Union is passed, which unifies England and Scotland as the Kingdom of Great Britain. The Act abolishes the Scottish Parliament and Royal Scots Navy, and amalgamates them into their English counterparts.

Birth of Carolus Linnaeus in Sweden.

1709:

Attempted Jacobite rebellion under claimant James III Stuart is defeated by Sir George Byng. Future rebellions will instead be managed by James' son Charles Edward Stuart (Bonnie Prince Charlie).

1713:

Charles VI, Holy Roman Emperor and Archduke of Austria, has no male heir. He issues a Pragmatic Sanction recognising his daughter, Maria Theresa, as heir, and makes all the powers of Europe agree to it. However, it will transpire that quite a lot of them had their fingers crossed behind their backs.

1714:

Death of Queen Anne; George I, Elector of Hanover, becomes King of Great Britain and Ireland. As he does not speak English and lacks interest in British affairs, Parliament gains more real power during his reign.

In Virginia, the "First Wave of Germanna", as German Protestant religious refugees from the Rhineland and the Palatinate settle there.

1715:

Death of Louis XIV; his great-grandson Louis, one of the few to survive a series of deaths in the French royal family in the late 17th century, becomes King Louis XV at the age of five, with Philippe, Duc d'Orléans as regent. A Jacobite Rebellion in Scotland, led by the Earl of Mar, is crushed by Marshal Wade. More minor outbreaks in Cornwall and Northern England are also subdued.

1717:

"Second Wave of Germanna" as more German refugees settle in Virginia.

1718:

The Puckle Gun, an early cyclogun predecessor, is invented by James Puckle. Though technically impressive the technology is not viable at the time, though it will later be cited as the beginnings of such weapons.

1720:

The South Sea Bubble. Excessive speculation in the South Sea

Company causes an economic meltdown in the City of London. Parliament holds an inquiry and several prominent members of the current Whig government are forced to step down, leaving most of the power in the hands of Robert Walpole, the Paymaster of the Forces.

1721:

Robert Walpole becomes the first Prime Minister of Britain, i.e. the first minister to dominate a government, although the term Prime Minister is considered vulgar and derisive for years afterward. His official titles are First Lord of the Treasury, Chancellor of the Exchequer and Leader of the House of Commons, all united in one.

1722:

Williamsburgh, Virginia, becomes the first city in Britain's North American colonies as it receives a royal charter.

Part 2: The Exile (1727-1749)

1727:

Death of King George I of Great Britain. His son becomes George II of Great Britain. Much like his father, he does not get on with his eldest son, Frederick. At George's coronation (POINT OF DIVERGENCE FROM OUR TIMELINE) the King stumbles and falls and Frederick laughs at his father's public humiliation. This caps a series of violent disagreements between the two, with the result that George II disinherits Frederick, making his younger brother William the Prince of Wales, and sends Frederick into exile to the North American colonies, giving him the sinecure of Lord Deputy of the Colonies. In Virginia (which has not yet heard the news of Frederick's fall from grace), the new town of Fredericksburg, named in his honour, begins construction.

1728:

Prince Frederick arives in Virginia (the "Third Wave of Germanna"). He decides to settle in the town named in his honour (Fredericksburg), at the quite modest house later known as Little St James'.

1729:

Treaty of Seville forbids British ships from trading with Spanish colonies in the Americas - it is however frequently violated. Spanish ships commonly stop British ones for inspection.

1730:

Virginian House of Burgesses passes the Tobacco Inspection Act, which improves the quality of Virginian tobacco overall and places it in high demand in Europe. The scheme is the brainchild of William Gooch, the Royal Lieutenant-Governor (and de facto governor) of Virginia. Prince Frederick, a political ally of Gooch, invests heavily in tobacco plantations and uses the profits to build his still quite meagre funds.

With the assistance of British envoys, the Cherokee people of America politically unify under the leadership of the Chief of Tellico, who becomes Emperor Moytoy II.

1731:

A particularly brutal inspection by the Spanish of the British ship *Rebecca* in the Caribbean; the British captain, William Jenkins, has his ear cut off.

1732:

A scandal almost breaks as Prince Frederick is found to have made Mildred Gregory (twice-widowed sister of the Virginian planter Augustine Washington) pregnant. It would ruin his chances of regaining the kingship if news broke out, so Frederick reluctantly agrees to marry her, and to restore the Washingtons' lost lands and titles in England if he becomes King, in order to keep Augustine quiet. The son will go on to become King George III.

In Sweden, Carolus Linnaeus travels to Lapland for his study of the local flora and fauna.

In Britain, the future Lord North is born. Due to Prince Frederick's disgrace, he is named William rather than Frederick as in OTL.

1733:

Prince George Augustine of Cornwall, the future George III, is born. He is nicknamed George FitzFrederick by Williamites who do not recognise his father's marriage as legitimate.

In China, Hongli the Prince Bao, tipped to succeed his father the Yongzheng Emperor, dies when he drowns in a river.

1733-1738: *The First War of the Polish Succession. France, Spain and Savoy vs. Russia, Austria and Saxony over whether the elected King of Poland-Lithuania should be Stanisław Leszczyński or Frederick Augustus II, Elector of Saxony (respectively). George II of Britain wants to enter the war, but Walpole refuses, and the infuriated King is only able to assist Austria via his position of Elector of Hanover. Walpole recovers some popularity with the British people thanks to his decision to stay out of the war. Although the French-led side wins, the Saxon becomes King Augustus III of Poland at the compromise peace settlement. Austria receives Tuscany and Palma but* *transfers Naples and Sicily to Don Carlos, the former Duke of Parma and future King Charles III of Spain. This is the beginning of the end for the Polish-Lithuanian Commonwealth, which decays under Augustus III's indifferent rule.*

1734:

Frederick tours the American colonies, while Mildred remains behind and gives birth to Princess Mildred, the future Queen of Denmark. He forms a political alliance with the Lieutenant-Governor of Pennsylvania, Patrick Gordon, and then becomes involved in New York politics, backing the "Morrisite" opposition party against the tyrannical Lieutenant-Governor William Cosby, a fierce Georgian loyalist. He also visits New England and writes about the questionable loyalties of the French-descended people in British Nova Scotia.

In Britain, Robert Walpole's majority is reduced after he attempts to introduce an unpopular customs and excise tax. A new opposition party, the Patriot Boys, is formed. They support Prince Frederick and are led by skilled political orators such as William Pulteney, William Pitt and George Grenville.

1735:

Prince Frederick returns home to Virginia briefly, then tours the Carolinas before finally returning to Fredericksburg at the end of the year.

Linnaeus publishes his seminal work 'Systema Naturae' in the Netherlands. This is a controversial work, as it argues for a purely empirical system of classification, with no regard for the Great Chain of Being.

1738:

When Robert Jenkins exhibits his pickled ear in a jar in the House of Commons, British outrage is such that even Robert Walpole gives in and declares war on Spain - the War of Jenkins' Ear, which bleeds into the War of the Austrian Succession.

1740-1748: *The Second War of Supremacy, AKA the War of the Austrian Succession. After Charles VI of Austria's death, the powers of Europe conveniently forget they agreed to the Pragmatic Sanction, and war is declared. Maria Theresa's accession is really just a* casus belli, *however - in truth the war is mainly about Prussia's desire to take*

Silesia from Austria. Prussia, France, Spain, Bavaria, Naples and Sicily, and Sweden vs. Austria, Britain, Hanover, the Netherlands, Saxony, Sardinia and Russia. The war sees Maria Theresa appeal for assistance to her Hungarian subjects and receive important levies – a contrast to the Hungarian rebellion against Joseph I in the First War of Supremacy – and the powers of Europe astonished by the performance of the Prussian army under Frederick II. The Prussians use powerful new drills and tactics, and deploy an entirely professional army, not using unreliable (but cheaper) mercenaries. This leads to Maria Theresa, and others, copying the Prussians to some extent.

1741:

British general election reduces Robert Walpole's majority, especially in the rotten boroughs.

Admiral Edward Vernon, whose captain of Marines is Major Lawrence Washington (Augustine's elder son), is embarrassingly defeated in an attempted descent on the Spanish city of Cartagena-des-Indes in New Granada. This overshadows his earlier victory over the Spanish at Porto Bello in Darien.

Frederick II of Prussia wins an important victory at Mollwitz, bringing France and Sweden into the war on his side.

Governor George Clarke of New York puts down a slave revolt. He is the ancestor of future Supremacist Party leader Matthew Clarke.

1742:

Robert Walpole, his government having lost numerous constituencies in the 1741 General Election, resigns as Prime Minister and accepts a seat in the House of Lords as 1st Earl of Orford. He is succeeded by Spencer Compton, 1st Earl of Wilmington, but real power rests with the Secretary of State for the Northern Department, John Carteret.

Admiral Vernon takes Guantanamo from Spain, but is eventually repulsed by Cuban irregulars.

The Battle of Bloody Fields sees the repulsion of a Spanish attack on Georgia by the local militias. However, Georgian/Carolinian attempts to take Spanish Flordia are equally inconclusive.

A poorly coordinated Franco-Saxon-Bavarian army under Marshal de Broglie nonetheless manages to take most of Bohemia from Austria.

Heinrich Mühlenberg immigrates to America from the Germanies, founding a political dynasty and the Lutheran Church in America. He anglicises his name to 'Henry Mullenburgh'.

1743:

Sweden knocked out of the war by Russia, which annexes parts of Finland; however Russia also leaves the war soon afterwards. Austria, backed by Hungarian levies, ejects the French and their allies from Bohemia. Britain enters the European war, blockading the Neapolitan fleet in port, while King George II goes to Hanover and raises an army, which he leads into battle personally (though his son William, Prince of Wales and Duke of Cumberland, acts as general).

The Anglo-Hanoverians meet the French, led by the Duc de Noailles, at Dettingen. Despite Noailles' superior generalship, George's forces win the battle, but George himself is killed.

Wilmington dies and is replaced by Henry Pelham as Prime Minister. Pelham shares power with his brother Thomas, the Duke of Newcastle.

Death of Crown Prince Frederik of Denmark in a riding accident, thus making his younger brother Christian the heir apparent to King Christian VI.

1744:

In Oman, patriotic forces drive the Persians from the country and it becomes fully independent under the elected Imam Ahmed ibn Sayyid as-Sayyid. In TTL there is no Qais branch of the family and he is peacefully succeeded by his son Sayyid in time: Oman remains united.

Platinum is discovered in New Granada by Antonio de Ulloa y de Torre-Girault and Jorge Juan.

1745:

Prince William, now William IV, is defeated by Marshal Saxe at Fontenoy. He returns to Britain and puts down the Jacobite Rebellion in Scotland led by Bonnie Prince Charlie.

In North America New England forces, including Prince Frederick, take the fortress of Louisbourg from France.

Death of King Christian VI of Denmark; his second son

succeeds him as Christian VII, and enacts a radical reform programme. Christian VII reverses his father's introduction of adscription (essentially serfdom), restores the Danish Diet to play off the commoners against the nobility, and sells off Denmark's overseas colonies to finance a new military buildup in the Baltic.

Dutch inventor Pieter van Musschenbroek invents the Leyden Jar, the first primitive means for storing electric charge.

1746:

French forces in India under La Bourdonnais take Madras from the British East India Company.

1747:

French invasion of Austrian Netherlands leads to internal dissent in the Dutch Republic. A new settlement is established whereby the stadtholder of the provinces of Friesland and Gronigen becomes Stadtholder William IV, ending the Stadtholder-less period, and the office is also made hereditary, paving the way for a shift from oligarchic republic to monarchy.

British general election returns a shaky majority for the Pelhamites in the 10th Parliament of Great Britain.

In India, Dupleix attacks British-held Cuddalore, but is repulsed by an army under the British-allied Nawab of the Carnatic, Anwarooddin Mohammed Khan.

1748:

Treaty of Aix-la-Chappelle. Maria Theresa retains her titles, but Austria loses Silesia to Prussia and various territories in Italy to Parma and Sardinia. France returns the Austrian Netherlands to Austria, a highly unpopular move among the French people. King William IV of Britain agrees to return Louisbourg to France in return for Madras. However, this is equally unpopular with the Americans. Prince Frederick seizes his chance and, backed by American supporters who sign a Declaration of Right, claims the throne. The War of the British Succession begins.

Spain and Portugal enter negotiations aimed at refining the outdated zones of control in the Americas defined by the old Treaty of Torsedillas.

1749:

January - Hearing of Frederick's claim, William invokes the

Treason Act 1702 and imprisons some of Frederick's most prominent Patriot supporters. This clumsy response makes William less popular with the English people in general.

April - Williamite fleet, under the command of Admiral John Byng, sets sail for America;

Bonnie Prince Charlie leads a Jacobite fleet to Limerick in Ireland and starts a rising there against the absentee William. Fourth Jacobite Rebellion, including a minor rising in Scotland led by Lord Cosmo Gordon, which is rapidly crushed. Ireland, however, rages on.

August - Cunning plan by Frederick leads to William being assassinated at range on the deck of Byng's flagship by American riflemen. Frederick smooths things over and the war fizzles out. Byng's fleet winters in America, having turned to Frederick.

In India, Dupleix supports Chanda Sahib in his attempt to overthrow Anwarooddin Mohammed Khan, the Nawab of the Carnatic (and latterly his son Mohammed Ali).

Part 3: King Frederick (1750-1760)

1750:

March - Byng's fleet, with Frederick and American troops, sets sail for the British Isles.

May - Death of King John V of Portugal. His son becomes King Joseph I of Portugal. He takes an interest in the stalled colonial negotiations with Spain, and real progress begins to be made.

June - Frederick, after hearing about the Irish rising, diverts the fleet to Cork and lands there, seizing towns from Jacobite forces, though Lawrence Washington initially fails to take Limerick.

July - Spain and Portugal sign the Treaty of Madrid, setting down new colonial borders in the Americas based on the 46th meridian. The key provision is that Portugal will exchange Sacramento for the Spanish Jesuit 'Seven Missions'.

September - Battle of Kilkenny. Frederick's forces win the day. Charles Edward Stuart dead, no serious Jacobite claimants left after James Francis Edward Stuart's death. End of Jacobitism in the British Isles.

November - Triumphal entry of Frederick and American forces into London. Frederick marches into Parliament and dissolves it. He calls a general election, set for February.

December - Frederick's coronation. For the first time this form of the royal title is used… *Frederick the First, by the Grace of God King of Great Britain, France and Ireland, **Emperor of North America**, Defender of the Faith, etc.*

1751:

February - British general election vanquishes the Pelhamite Whigs and returns a handy majority for the Patriots. William Pulteney becomes Prime Minister; William Pitt Secretary of State for the Southern Department; George Grenville for the Northern Department. 11th Parliament passes important acts such as the

Act of Suppression (building roads in Scotland and Ireland to help put down further revolts), the Act of Succession (confirming Frederick as King but recognising William as William IV 'until his untimely death') and the Colonial Act, establishing the Empire of North America and some early institutions.

Peerages awarded to American supporters of Frederick, including Lawrence Washington becoming Marquess of Fredericksburg.

European powers reluctantly recognise Frederick's government. Frederick cancels William's signature on the Treaty of Aix-la-Chappelle. France keeps Madras in protest, and many British soldiers die from tropical disease and neglect while in French captivity in Madras, including the unknown (in TTL) Robert Clive.

The proxy war continues in the Carnatic. Britain fails to take Arcot, and Chanda Sahib wins the civil war, becoming the new Nawab of the Carnatic. Henceforth French influence in the region is paramount and Britain rarely exerts much influence south of the Circars.

1753:

King Frederick of Great Britain makes his first and only visit to Hanover.

Alarmed by French attempts to form alliances with the Indians of the Ohio Country, Iroquois leader King Hendrick approaches the Governor of New York, the Duke of Portland, for more Anglo-American assistance in repulsing French influence. Portland agrees and the Anglo-Iroquois alliance is cemented further.

The French build forts in Virginian-claimed Vandalia, at Fort Presque Isle and Fort Duquesne. Governor Dinwiddie of Virginia, after meeting with Portland and the Lord Deputy, sends troops to eject the French from the Ohio Country.

1754:

Lawrence Washington, despite his new lands, titles and House of Lords seat in Britain, chooses to return to America. This will set a precedent for later American nobles. The young George Washington remains in Britain and is tutored alongside George, Prince of Wales.

Dinwiddie's Virginian militiamen fail to take the French forts at Presque Isle and Duquesne. Because of this, the Virginian House of Burgesses passes reforms to improve the standard of militia military training, despite the ever-persistent fear of a standing army in British-derived nations.

The Pulteney government in Britain signs a treaty with Prussia, known as '*Les Deux Frédérics*' in France. This essentially amounts to the British abandoning their commitment to help Austria if Prussia attacks Silesia, in exchange for the Prussians agreeing to defend Hanover in the event of another German war. Austria and Britain have drifted apart since disagreements over accepting the Treaty of Aix-la-Chappelle.

Carolus Linnaeus visits London and meets the young Joseph Priestley, who persuades him to publish his controversial theories about human evolution.

In South America, the Seven Jesuit Missions agree to move from the now Portuguese territory, but their Guarani Indian friends object. A short war between combined Portuguese and Spanish forces and the Guaranis, which results in the defeat of the Guaranis but causes bad blood between the Portuguese and Spanish.

In China, the Yongzheng Emperor dies and is succeeded by his son Hongshi the Prince Zhong, who becomes the Daguo Emperor. Daguo's reign is marked for a programme of building defensive fortifications, 'the Second Great Wall', against the Dzungars, and for the invasion of Burma.

In the Holy Roman Empire, the *Konventionsthaler* (Convention Dollar) is created, a standard based on the Austrian dollar to which most of the currencies of the other German states are pegged to.

1755:

July - Corsican rebels finally eject their Genoese colonial occupiers from the island, declaring an independent Republic (technically a kingdom, but with the throne occupied symbolically by the Virgin Mary). It is noteworthy for being considered the first state in which women customarily had the vote.

November - the Great Lisbon Earthquake wreaks havoc in Portugal, and indeed across Europe, but is particularly devastating in the city for which it is named. Countless buildings destroyed and people made homeless. José de Carvalho e Melo, the Chief Minister, organises the recovery effort.

1756-1759: The Third War of Supremacy, also known as the War of the Diplomatic Revolution. Britain, Prussia, Ireland, Hanover, Brunswick, Hesse-Kassell and the Empire of North America vs. France, Russia, Austria, Sweden, Naples and Sicily, and Sardinia. Eventual defeat for the British coalition in Europe with the dismemberment of Prussia, though Prussian army tactics continue to educate the world. Total British victory in North America. Minor French victory in India.

1756:

May - The British East India Company in Bengal has built up a huge army with which to try and retake the lost cities from the French in the Carnatic. However, this army's existence has made their ally, Siraj-Ud-Daulah the Nawab of Bengal, nervous...

July - In India, Afghan leader Ahmad Shah Abdali conquers Delhi and marries his younger son Nadir to the daughter of his puppet Mughal Emperor Alamgir II.

August - Austria signs a formal alliance with France at Versailles - the 'Diplomatic Revolution', ending a century of Franco-Austrian enmity. In response, Britain declares war on France and Prussia invades Saxony. Start of the Third War of Supremacy.

October - After a lightning campaign by King Frederick II of Prussia, Saxony surrenders to the Prussians.

November - Pulteney announces a Cabinet reshuffle. George Grenville becomes Chancellor the Exchequer and Henry Fox takes over as Secretary of State for the Northern Department. Frederick II of Prussia, having secured Saxony, launches an invasion of Bohemia.

December - Death of Queen Mildred of Great Britain. King Frederick sinks into a depression from which he will never quite recover.

1757:

February - Prince George of Wales disappears. He secretly takes up a commission in America under the name Ralph Robinson, fighting alongside George Washington. French and allied Huron and Algonquin forces under Montcalm invade New York. After failing to be reinforced, the American Fort Frederick William surrenders to the French. However, the Algonquins, having different definitions of the rules of war, then perpetrate a looting and massacre on the British and American forces. This outrage increases the resolve of the American people to win the war, and more regiments and militias are raised.

May - Frederick II of Prussia retreats from Prague after an indecisive engagement with Austrian forces, deciding he does not have the troop numbers to hold the city.

French naval forces in the Mediterranean defeat British Admiral Edward Boscawen and take Minorca, which is later returned to Spain. Boscawen escapes court-martial but is effectively exiled to a West Indian command.

June - Siraj-Ud-Daulah, the Nawab of Bengal, betrays his British allies and takes Fort William at Calcutta in a surprise attack. British East India Company officers are trapped in the 'Black Hole of Calcutta', a tiny prison in which many die. Outrage among the Company and at home leads to an all-out attack on the Nawab's forces with the Company's new army, with the result that it is not deployed against the French.

September - Britain attempts a descent on the Isle d'Aix, as part of a strategy of tying up French troops with temporary landings on the French coast. The operation is an embarrassing and expensive failure, as shallow waters make it impossible to reinforce the British troops. Pitt refuses to authorise any more such operations. The French East India Company takes Fort St David at Cuddalore, decisively ending British power in the Carnatic.

November - Frederick II of Prussia wins a brilliant victory against a numerically superior Austro-French army at the Battle of Rossbach.

December - The outnumbered Prussians under Frederick II win a second victory against Austria at the Battle of Leuthen.

1758:

February - Britain occupies French colonies in West Africa, including Dakar.

June - Death of William Pulteney. King Frederick asks William Pitt to form a government. Henry Fox becomes Secretary of State for the Southern Department.

July - A Russian army under Pyotr Saltykov defeats the Prussians under von Wedel at the Battle of Paltzig. In Portugal, King Joseph I survives an assassination attempt, but the wound will trouble him for the rest of his life.

August - In Portugal, a plot by the Távora and Aveiro families against the King is discovered, giving Chief Minister Carvalho an excuse to execute many of their key members and make the rest flee into exile. Their lands are annexed to the Portuguese crown.

September - The British East India Company defeats the Nawab of Bengal's forces in a decisive campaign. The Nawab is killed during the final battle.

October - In a battle with Austria at Hochkirch, the Prussians are defeated and most of their artillery corps fall into enemy hands. The tide of war has begun to turn against King Frederick II.

1759:

The Annus Mirabilis, the Wonderful Year of Victories, in America.

May - The British East India Company takes Calcutta. The EIC seizes direct control over Bengal and parcels it out among a half-dozen puppet princes. End of the Nawabate.

July - Alaungpaya, Burmese King of Ava of the Konbaung Dynasty, conquers and annexes Pegu.

August - Frederick II of Prussia defeated by the Russians and Austrians at Kunersdorf, so decisively that he no longer cares for his own life and goes into battle himself, dying heroically after slaying many enemies.

The Hanoverians, neglected by Britain, are defeated at Minden by the French under the Marquis de Contades. However, the French invasion of Hanover stalls soon afterwards as their supply chains become overextended.

September - James Wolfe defeats Montcalm at Quebec, ending French control of Canada. "Ralph Robinson" is wounded and discovered to be Prince George in disguise. The unknown-in-TTL James Cook is killed in the battle. Wolfe is wounded but survives and is eventually made military governor of Canada. With the death of Frederick II and the war turning against the Prussians, a newly confident Saxony re-enters the war and attacks Prussia.

October - King Frederick I of Great Britain begins to sicken from a lung infection.

November - A Prussian army is annihilated by the Austrians under Daun, at Maxen. King Frederick William II of Prussia is a minor, and his uncle Prince Henry is regent. Henry believes the war is lost and sues for peace, knowing it will be harsh.

1760:

January - Treaty of Amsterdam, ending the Third War of Supremacy. This dismembers Prussia, returning Silesia to Austria and giving Cottbus, Liegnitz and the western possessions to Saxony. France fails to receive the Austrian Netherlands, again angering the French people. Britain/America receive the Ohio Country, Senegal and New France/Quebec from France, but the French retain Louisiana. Britain recognises French control of the Carnatic.

February - Death of Frederick I of Great Britain. Rapproachment with his son Prince George, soon to be George III, on his deathbed.

March - King Alaungpaya of Ava (in Burma) dies and is succeeded by his son Naungdawgyi. However, the Konbaung dynasty's rule is now disputed by General Myat Htun, who wants to restore the former Toungoo dynasty.

April – Under the terms of the Treaty of Aalborg, the Danish crown sells Greenland and Iceland to Britain. Both are in legal limbo for some years, with Greenland eventually becoming part of the ENA and Iceland its own small kingdom in personal union with Britain.

June - Treaty of Cedar Shoals between the Cherokee Empire and the Carolinian colonists. This is the official end to the Indian wars of the 1760s, which resulted in the virtual destruction of the Creek and Chickasaw nations, and formally divides their former lands between the Carolinians and their Cherokee allies.

Part 4: Frontier George (1761-1778)

1761:

January - Third Battle of Panipat in India as Ahmad Shah Abdali's Muslim Afghans fight the Hindu Maratha Empire. The battle is a crushing victory for the Afghans, with the Marathas shattering into a loose confederacy that then begins a slow decline.

February - Seeking to pull France out of her war debts, King Louis XV appoints Étienne de Silhouette as Comptroller-General of Finances. Silhouette largely fails in his attempts to tax the rich, but does succeed in ensuring that French East India Company profits largely go into the royal treasury.

April - Death of King Ferdinand VI of Spain. He is succeeded by his son, who becomes King Charles III. Charles had formerly ruled in Naples and brings with him his chief minister, Bernardo Tanucci - though for the present he reappoints the Marquis of Ensenada as chief minister of Spain.

November - In the Viceroyalty of New Spain, Jacinto Canek leads the Mayans into rebellion. The revolt is swiftly crushed by the Spanish, but memories of it persist for a long time.

1762:

March - Death of Empress Elizabeth of Russia. She is succeeded by her nephew, who becomes Emperor Peter III.

April - Matters in Burma come to a head, as Myat Htun's Toungoo forces besiege Ava. The British East India Company offers assistance to the ruling Konbaung dynasty's King Naungdawgyi in exchange for greater trading privileges. Naungdawgyi accepts.

1763-1767: The First Platinean War. Spain fights Portugal; Britain enters the war on the Portuguese side. Little territorial change, but the Spanish failure to defend the Rio de la Plata from an Anglo-American invasion - while the Platineans defeat the Anglo-Americans by besieging them with their own militias and forcing them to retreat - contributes considerably to the growth of nationalism in

South America.

1763:

A Spanish invasion of Portugal fails, partly due to the Portuguese using scorched earth tactics and burning crops in order to starve the Spanish armies operating in Portugal.

The Konbaung forces in Burma, with BEIC assistance, eject Myat Htun's Toungoo forces from Ava. Myat Htun instead goes north, seeking Chinese help in gaining the throne.

1764:

March - British and American troops, including the 51st and 52nd, invade Florida from what will become the Province of Georgia.

April - Lord Fairfax retires as Lord Deputy of North America. He is succeeded by Lord William North, the Earl of Guilford.

May - Second Spanish invasion of Portugal begins. This will also be repulsed, this time partly due to a British expeditionary force assisting the Portuguese.

June - Many German refugees fleeing religious persecution are settling in Russia, thanks to the Germanophile policies of Emperor Peter III. Among them are a Herr and Frau Kautzman, who settle in the Caucasus near Stavropol.

August - Anglo-Portuguese armies defeat the Spanish at Corunna and conquer Galicia.

1765:

May - British expeditionary force under Admiral Marriott Arbuthnot lands in Rio de la Plata.

June - Arbuthnot's forces occupy Buenos Aires. In Saxony, Elector Frederick Augustus II, who is also King Augustus III of Poland, dies. He is succeeded by his son Frederick Christian I in Saxony, but the Poles reject him and their *szlachta* attempt to elect a new king. However, the Sejm is deadlocked.

July - Spanish armies in South America conquer the last of the Rio Grand de Sul (OTL Uruguay) from Portugal.

August - Anglo-Portuguese siege of Ciudad Rodrigo begins. In Lorraine, Duke Stanisław Leszczyński dies and his territories revert to the crown of France.

September - Spanish break the siege of Ciudad Rodrigo,

forcing the British and Portuguese to retreat.

October - Start of the Crisis of 1765. The American national consciousness has grown considerably due to the recent and ongoing wars. The various liberal political clubs in the major American cities, with the help of Lord North, call a new Albany Congress and elect a North Commission, which travels to London in order to petition the British Government for greater self-rule for the Empire of North America. The Committee is led by Ben Franklin.

November - Birth of Nurul Huq, the future 'Father of Bengal', in a small village near Calcutta.

Antonio de Ulloa y de Torre-Girault, managing the quicksilver mines in Peru, is scapegoated by the Viceroy and is eventually reassigned to become governor of California.

1766:

April - Spanish attempt to retake Galicia from the Portuguese, but after some initial gains are defeated by the British near Santiago de Compostela and are repulsed again.

June - Arbuthnot's army in the Plate suffers its first major defeat, a considerable embarrassment to Britain, in a face-up battle with the Platinean militias as the British attempt to take the city of Rosario.

July - Emboldened Portuguese and British armies besiege Badajoz. Start of the Polish Civil War as the Sejm is unable to agree on a compromise candidate for king from among the Polish *szlachta* itself. In Britain, William Pitt dies, receiving a state funeral (while his heir John Pitt receives staggering debts). King George III asks Charles Watson-Wentworth, the Marquess of Rockingham, to form a new Patriot-Whig government.

August - Realising Spanish help is not forthcoming, the people of the Plate organise their own militias and begin attacking the British occupation forces, initially only in small groups. At this time, King Charles III of Spain is forced to flee into France due to food riots in Madrid; his troops soon put these down and he is able to return, but has suffered a considerable loss of face.

September - Even without much support from other Spanish armies, the fortress city of Badajoz weathers and defeats the

Anglo-Portuguese forces, who retreat to Elvas. In the Plate, the cautious Arbuthnot withdraws most of his troops to Buenos Aires. In Eastern Europe, Frederick William II of Prussia and Peter III of Russia sign a secret treaty aimed at the partition of Poland.

In China, the Daguo Emperor and his ministers agree to help Myat Htun return the Toungoo dynasty to the Avan throne.

October - A second Spanish invasion of Galicia wins a narrow, unconvincing victory, dislodging the Portuguese from most of the province but the Spanish armies being too badly gutted in the process to contemplate further offensive actions. Little movement on the Peninsular Front for the rest of the war.

November - The Americans finally succeed in their long siege of San Agustín, the capital and last redoubt of Spanish Florida. With its fall, the whole peninsula is now British/American-occupied. In Eastern Europe, negotiations begin between the Russo-Prussian alliance and Sweden to secure Swedish neutrality in the Polish war.

December – British/American-occupied Buenos Aires is besieged by Platinean militiamen.

1767-1771: The War of the Polish Partition. Russia and Prussia fight Austria, with some Poles and Lithuanians fighting on both sides as well as a confusion of private armies behind szlachta candidates for kingship. Russo-Prussian victory; the Commonwealth is divided at the Treaty of Stockholm, which gives Ruthenia to Russia, Krakow to Austria and Royal Prussia and southern Ducal Prussia to Prussia. The remainder of Poland is placed in personal union with Prussia, while Lithuania is separated and the Tsarevich of Russia, Paul, is made Grand Duke as Povilas I.

1767:

February - In the Plate, Arbuthnot orders his infamous retreat and abandons Buenos Aires to the Platineans, who raise the Burgundian cross flag in triumph.

March - The Treaty of Copenhagen ends the First Platinean War, signed on the 17th. Spain concedes Florida to the Empire of North America; all other borders *status quo ante bellum*.

April - Austria enters the Polish Civil War, producing a

Hapsburg candidate and occupying Krakow as a necessary first step to Warsaw.

May - Prussia and Russia declare war on Austria. Meanwhile, the Corsican Republic takes the island of Capraia from Genoa, which decides to give up its claim to Corsica and sell it to the French.

June - The Spanish chief minister, the Marquess of Ensenada, is exiled in disgrace to South America due to the lost war. He eventually goes to Buenos Aires and helps start up the radical Porteño school of political thought there. He is replaced with Richard Wall, a Hiberno-Spaniard.

July - In Russia, the Kautzmans' young son Heinrich is kidnapped in a Cossack raid. He will be raised by Yemelyan Pugachev, the Cossack leader.

August - The Hartford Tea Revolt in Connecticut, one of several taxation protests in America's "Troubled Sixties".

October - Parliament of Great Britain debates whether to grant further powers of self-government to the Empire of North America. Patriot-Whigs for; Tories against.

1768:

March - In America, the Georgian colonial government apparatus collapses after Savannah is sacked by the Chickasaw Indians. Georgia is reabsorbed into South Carolina, which will eventually itself reunify with North Carolina.

May - The French Army invades Corsica.

June - In Burma a Chinese army, coupled with Toungoo-aligned Burmese forces, marches on Konbaung-controlled Ava.

July - Pittsburgh Whisky Riots in Pennsylvania, part of the tax protests of the "Troubled Sixties".

1769:

May - The Spanish explorer Captain José de Unzaga discoveres the Hidden Gate (San Francisco Bay).

April - Death of King Joseph I of Portugal. He is succeeded by his daughter Maria as Queen Maria I, later known as Maria the Mad. She rules as co-monarch with her husband Peter (Pedro) III.

May - Queen Maria of Portugal dismisses the Chief Minister,

José de Carvalho e Melo, and replaces him with a stream of incompetent favourites. Carvalho goes into exile in Brazil, eventually moving to Buenos Aires to be with the Porteños.

June - The French army concludes the conquest of Corsica, though some Republican holdouts remain under the leadership of Filippo Antonio Pasquale de Paoli. Corsica will, however, be a poisoned apple for Bourbon France, as Corsican republican ideas will spread back to France via the French troops stationed there.

In Tahiti, a British mission led by Captain Henry Anson observes the transit of Venus.

August - Carlo Buonaparte, a Corsican Republican leader, flees to Britain with his family. He anglicises his name to Charles Bone and converts to Anglicanism so he may read a law degree at Cambridge.

September - The Chinese and Toungoo forces successfully eject the Konbaungs from Ava. King Naungdawgyi is killed in the siege of Ava-town. The Chinese break up Burma in order to better enforce their will: the Toungoo dynasty, in the form of King Mahadammayaza, is restored to a rump Avan state, with Myat Htun as eminence grise. Pegu, Lanna and Ayutthaya (the last two are Thai states) are freed from Avan control and become direct Chinese vassals. One of Naungdawgyi's brothers, Minhkaung Nawrahta, creates an independent state out of his viceroyalty of Tougou and plays off the Chinese against the British.

The King of Ayutthaya, Ekkathat, was killed while fighting in the war and is now succeeded by his brother Uthumphon, a monk who gives up that vocation to rule and proves competent.

November - Another brother of King Naungdawgyi, Hsinbyushin, takes what remains of the Konbaung forces south and west and invades and occupies Arakan, overthrowing the native rulers. A new state, Konbaung-Arakan, is formed and swiftly becomes an ally of the British.

1770:

July - Accession of King Hyojang of Corea. He reverses some of the policies of his predecessor Yeongjo, tolerating the practice of Catholicism and the Silhak Movement, led by Jeong Yak-yong, which combines Neo-Confucianism and Corean nationalism with some Christian ideas.

August - The electric eel is first reported in South America. In Britain, Henry Cavendish is able to duplicate the effects of the eel and the torpedo fish, another electric fish, using Leyden Jars inside a synthetic fish–demonstrating, controversially, that animal and synthetic electricity are the same.

September - King Uthumphon of Ayutthaya, taking advantage of political instability in Lanna, successfully unites it with Ayutthaya to form a single Thai state (known either as Ayutthaya or Siam).

Famine of 1770 in Bengal, worsened by the British East India Company's policies such as forcing farmers to grow opium poppies instead of food crops. The young Nurul Huq loses family members to starvation and develops a burning hatred of the British as a result.

October - Effective end of the War of the Polish Partition after defeat of the Austrian Army of Silesia by the Prussians and the retreat to Krakow on the eastern front. It will take months for the politicians to negotiate a treaty, however.

November - Death of Joseph François Dupleix, Governor-General of the French East India Company. He is succeeded by Jean-Baptiste Donatien de Vimeur, comte de Rochambeau. This is largely an attempt by Paris, invoking Silhouettiste policies, to place more central royal control over the FEIC - Rochambeau is the King's man.

1771:

January - Treaty of Stockholm ends the War of the Polish Partition. Austria, Prussia and Russia all annex some territory (Krakow, Royal and southern Ducal Prussia and Ruthenia respectively) while the rump Poland becomes a kingdom in personal union with Prussia, and the Grand Duchy of Lithuania is placed under the Russian Tsarevich Paul as Grand Duke Povilas.

March - After much wrangling, the North Commission publishes the 'North Plan' for the Empire of North America, popularly known as 'One Empire and Five Confederations'. This will be the basis for the American Constitution.

1772-1774: First Mysore-Haidarabad War between Mysorean

and FEIC forces on one side and Haidarabad and BEIC forces on the other. This particular war results in a minor Mysorean victory.

1772:

February - Emperor Peter III of Russia's wife Catherine makes a failed coup attempt involving the collusion of the Leib Guards. After securing his position and purging the Guards, Peter sends her into exile at Yekaterinburg.

March - Great Britain, Ireland and the Empire of North America switch over from the Julian to the Gregorian calendar. This causes some riots, partly because people believe days have actually been lost from their lives, but mostly because the governments cunningly put the switchover at a time where the days lost should have been holidays.

April - In Austria, the demands of the last two wars coupled to some unwise speculation lead to an economic crash. Austrian policy in the Germanies is weakened for a decade or so as the treasury struggles to recover, though Austrian interference in northern Italy continues apace.

August - Moritz Benyovsky, a Slovakian leader of one of the Polish patriotic brigades, flees the destruction of his force by the Prussians and ends up in Lithuania, where he joins the newly reformed Lithuanian Army.

September - Death of Louis XV of France, who dies a deeply unpopular man due to his habit of returning conquered provinces after wars and for failing to reform the French tax system. He is succeeded by his son the Dauphin, Louis-Ferdinand, as King Louis XVI.

November - France's King Louis XVI approves the revival of stalled research into Nicholas-Joseph Cugnot's steam-tractor technology.

1773:

March - With the death of Richard Wall, Charles III of Spain appoints his old Neapolitan chief minister, Bernardo Tanucci, as chief minister of Spain. The hardline anti-clericalist Tanucci swiftly proves unpopular, especially in Spain's colonial possessions.

April - John Pitt enlists in the BEIC as a cornet of cavalry.

May - Birth of Aleksandr Potemkin, allegedly the son of

Grigory Potemkin and Empress Catherine of Russia.

June - In Persia, Shah/Advocate Abol Fath Khan defeats the Qajars in Mazanderan. The Qajar leader, Agha Mohammed Khan, is killed in the battle. The future of Zand Persia is secured.

July - Death of Ahmad Shah Abdali, the great Afghan conqueror, from cancer exacerbated by constant travel in his campaigns. The Afghans call a *Loya Jirga* assembly which splits the Durrani Empire, the Afghan domains going to his first son Timur and the Indian ones to his second son Nadir, who becomes Emperor of the East Durrani or 'Neo-Mughal' Empire.

1774:

February - Carl Wilhelm Scheele, the Swedish apothecary and chemist, begins his research into lufts [gases]. This will eventually result in the discovery of elluftium [oxygen] and illuftium [nitrogen], as well as a gas known as 'scheelium' at the time which will one day be identified as murium [chlorine]. This is more or less as OTL, but in OTL Scheele's discoveries were never widely publicised.

April - Pavel Lebedev-Lastoschkin, out of Yakutsk, leads a Russian trade expedition to Edzo [Hokkaido], northernmost island of Japan. He is rebuffed by the local Matsumae Han, who indicate they have no authority from the Shogun to conclude such deals and that trade with Japan is only available via Nagasaki. This is unreasonably far away from the Russian ports, and a disappointed Lebedev returns to Yakutsk.

July - Charles Bone receives his doctorate in law from the University of Cambridge and he founds a law practice in London, specialising in defending Catholics from employers who abuse the Test Acts.

1775:

January - Birth of Ivan Potemkin.

May - John Acton, a Briton in service with the Tuscan navy, distinguishes himself in an action against Algerine pirates at Algiers itself, in cooperation with the French and Spanish. Soon afterwards, his fame leads him to to leave the Tuscans and go to Naples, where he is employed in reorganising the Neapolitans' own outdated naval forces.

1776:

March - After months of argument between their representatives, the New England colonies of the ENA are amalgamated into the Confederation of New England, with its capital at Boston. This is the first of the Five Confederations to be formally created.

April - Exiled Emperor of Daiviet Le Cung Tong appeals to the Daguo Emperor of China for help in regaining his throne; Daguo agrees.

July - Irish-born war veteran and MP Anthony St. Leger (together with the Prime Minister Lord Rockingham) sets up the St. Leger Stakes, a series of high-stakes horse races, in Doncaster. Rockingham's patronage soon provokes much interest in the races from the Westminster political establishment.

1777 :

Charles Bone's son Leo (Napoleone Buonaparte) enters the Royal Navy as a midshipman and serves on HMS *Ardent*.

1778-1781: Second Mysore-Haidarabad War between Mysorean and FEIC forces on one side and Haidarabad and BEIC forces on the other. Haidarabad takes back Mysore's gains in the last war, but the BEIC loses influence at the Nizam's court due to mishandling by the British resident there.

1778:

Carl Wilhelm Scheele discovers elluftium [oxygen].

The Qing Chinese army defeats the Nguyen Lords of Daiviet at Than Hoa, restoring Emperor Le Cung Tong to his position as a Chinese puppet ruling northern Daiviet (Tonkin) while the Nguyens are left with the south (Cochinchina).

The rules of cricket are codified by the Pall Mall Cricket Club.

Part 5: The Age of Revolution (1779-1799)

1779-1785: The Second Platinean War. Spain and (theoretically) France vs. Peruvian Indian rebels, Platinean and Chilean colonial rebels, Britain and America, and (unofficially) Portugal. Defeat of the Bourbons with the creation of what will become the UPSA, although Britain suffers some embarrassing naval defeats in the process.

1779:

José Gabriel Condorcanqui, taking the name Tupac Amaru II as Sapa Inca of the Tahuantinsuyo people, shoots the tyrannical Spanish Governor of Peru, Antonio de Arriaga, and begins the Great Andean Rebellion. The rest of the year sees an unsuccessful attempt by the colonial authorities to quell the revolt.

First deployment of the Ferguson breech-loading rifle by the British Army. Initially the rifle is not widely adopted due to its high cost and long production time, although it sees some use by frontier forces in the ENA. Breech-loaders will not be popularised until the 1820s. At the same time, the Austrian army first deploys the *Repetierwindbüchse* (repeating air rifle) designed by Bartholomäus Girandoni, which though not suitable for general adoption, sees considerable use by skirmishers.

1780:

Linnaeus' *Taxonomy of Man* is published posthumously, in which he argues that man is simply another of the primates. The book causes an uproar, but its impact on natural history and theology is somewhat overshadowed by the fact that the chapters dealing with the different races of men become the kernel of the ideology of Linnaean Racism.

The American Squadron is created by the Royal Navy, a kernel of the later Imperial Navy.

On Christmas Day, Tupac Amaru II takes Cusco from the Spanish colonial authorities and has himself formally coronated.

1781:

February - Forces of the Viceroyalty of Peru fail to retake Cusco from Tupac Amaru II's rebelling Indians.

May - In Upper Peru (OTL Bolivia) Tomas Katari, another Indian rebel leader, is defeated before La Paz and, pursued by Spanish regulars, retreats into Lower Peru. He combines his forces with Tupac Amaru II's, strengthening them.

June - In India, after many failed rebellions against the Durrani Afghans, the Sikhs finally win their independence.

August - In Lithuania, Grand Duke Povilas (the future Emperor Paul of Russia) institutes a new shipbuilding programme, known as the Patriotic Fleet as it embodies the idea of a Lithuania which has its own independent forces and is not merely a vassal of Russia.

1782:

January - Carl Wilhelm Scheele publishes, in Swedish, his work on gases. Because of Linnaeus' controversies resulting in many leading European thinkers learning Swedish to read his work in the original, Scheele's discoveries become more widely known.

March - King Louis XVI launches a French expedition to South America, although at the time of launch, it is still unclear which side he is supporting in the war there. The expedition is led by Admiral de Grasse and the Duc de Noailles.

April - The Africa Bubble scandal results in the resignation of the Marquess of Rockingham as Prime Minister of Great Britain. He is replaced by the Duke of Portland, but real power rests in the Secretary of State for Foreign Affairs, Edmund Burke. The ruling Patriot party shifts its ideological positioning slightly and becomes known as the Liberal Whigs.

May - Birth of Philip Hamilton (son of Alexander Hamilton) in New York City.

August – The Duc de Noailles' expedition reaches the Plate. The Spanish have told their colonists that the French are their allies, while the French believe that they are there to attack the Spaniards in their moment of weakness, due to figurative crossed wires at the French foreign ministry. The result is a bloody occupation of undefended Buenos Aires by Noailles' army, with the Platineans bitterly blaming the Spanish for the incident. This is amplified by Spanish propaganda praising (invented) victories by the French against Tupac Amaru II.

1783:

January - Beginning of the Southern Rebellion, as the Rio de la Plata and Chile both rise in revolt against the Spanish. The Platineans begin building up their old militias again around cadres of veterans of the First Platinean War, and attack the French - initially without much success, as Noailles' forces are numerous and well-equipped.

February - Britain and the ENA enter the war in support of the Platinean rebels, hoping for expanded trade rights with any postwar independent state.

March - Tupac Amaru II takes Lima from the Spanish, but has trouble holding the strongly pro-Spanish city down.

April - Midshipman Leo Bone passes his lieutenantcy examination in Gibraltar. The new lieutenant is reassigned to HMS *Raisonnable*, where he first meets Lieutenant Horatio Nelson.

May - Maximilian III Wittelsbach, Elector of Bavaria, dies without issue. The electorate passes to Charles Theodore Sulzbach, Elector Palatine. Charles Theodore concludes a deal with the Austrians to swap Bavaria for the Austrian Netherlands, which now become the Duchy of Flanders. Bavaria is integrated into Austria (not very popular with the Bavarians) while Charles Theodore retains the Palatinate as well as Flanders. Although the Prussians would like to declare war over this (as in OTL), they are too busy trying to hold down the latest Polish rebellion to respond.

July - Anglo-American fleet under Admiral Howe defeats de Grasse at the Battle of the River Plate. The British fleet lands an army of mostly American troops led by General George Augustine Washington, who joins up with the Platinean rebels in order to attack the French in Buenos Aires.

August – Prince Henry of Prussia, uncle to King Frederick William II, is killed by Polish partisans in an ambush during the ongoing Polish rebellion. The loss of Henry as a valuable advisor is a blow to the King, who adopts savage retributions against the Poles which only poisons internal relations further.

September - Franco-Spanish fleet assembles at Cadiz to escort fresh troops to South America. The fleet is ambushed by Admiral Augustus Keppel in the Battle of Trafalgar, which is a shock defeat for the Royal Navy. Keppel is court-martialled and resigns in disgrace. However, the RN has destroyed enough French and Spanish troopships that the expedition is called off.

1784-1786: Third Mysore-Haidarabad War between Mysorean and FEIC forces on one side and Haidarabad and BEIC forces on the other. Due to poor communications between the BEIC and Haidarabad, the Mysoreans win a significant victory with blatant French help. The Nizam ejects the French from the Northern Circars in response and puts the British in charge there. The BEIC fights off the French and the British-Haidarabad alliance is subsequently strengthened.

1784:

March - Having caught wind of reports that the Franco-Spanish intend to occupy Malta, the Royal Navy quickly makes its move first and turn the island into what will become an important British naval base. Controversy is sparked throughout Europe at this preemptive strike, even though the British allow the Knights of St John to carry on in a ceremonial role.

April - The Spanish retake Lima from Tupac Amaru II.

Prince Lee Boe of Palau visits the Netherlands and is an instant celebrity, leading to renewed European interest in the South Sea islanders.

May - Disintegration of Franco-Spanish common policy as Louis XV attempts to use the Royal Navy's defeats as an opportunity to invade England. The French armies have still not assembled by the end of the war.

The Hanoverian-British composer and astronomer William Herschel dies while taking part on an astronomical mission in the South Seas.

June - Start of the Canadian Rebellion (by Québecois) against Britain and America.

The rebels in Rio de la Plata announce the abolition of slavery.

July - A French fleet commanded by the Comte d'Estaing, Jean-Baptiste Charles Henri Hector, defeats the British in a dramatic but strategically largely meaningless victory at the naval Battle of Bermuda.

August - Anglo-American siege of New Orleans defeated by the colonial French.

1785:

February - Anglo-American-Platinean-Chilean combined forces take La Paz from the Spanish.

March - In Britain, Shrapnel and Philips develop the hail shot (known as case shot in OTL), a potent anti-infantry weapon that remains a British military secret for a generation.

Birth of Thorvald Nielsen, a legendary adventurer, in Trondheim.

May - After a complicated amphibious invasion from Florida, American (mainly Carolinian) troops take Havana in Cuba.

Michael Hiedler, third son of a Bavarian printer, moves to Lower Austria in order to seek his fortune by enlisting in the Austrian army.

July - Canadian Rebellion crushed by British and New England troops. This revolt will result in Britain ceasing its policy of appeasing Québecois interests, instead giving a green light to the New Englanders to settle the land. Many Québecois are forcibly ejected, or choose to leave, and eventually go to Louisiana, where they become known as Canajuns.

August - The Treaty of London is signed, ending the Second Platinean War. The settlement represents a severe defeat for Spain, which is forced to concede the independence of what will become the UPSA with the loss of a third of its colonial empire. The ENA retains Cuba, although its exact status remains up in the air for the moment. France loses little on paper, just the largely unpopulated hinterland of Louisiana, but has drained its treasury, and this will have severe consequences…

September - King Charles III of Spain is forced once again to flee to France as the mob rules the streets of Madrid. Bernardo Tanucci is killed in the violence. When Charles returns, with the help of French troops, he is forced to appoint the liberal reformer José Moñino y Redondo, conde de Floridablanca, as chief minister.

October - British chemist Joseph Priestley publishes *On the Nature of Phlogiston*, in which he attempts to reconcile the established phlogiston-based theory of combustion with Scheele's discovery of elluftium [oxygen].

November - Admiral Jean-François de Galaup, comte de La Pérouse sets out on a voyage of discovery financed by the King of France. The voyage included La Pérouse's new flagship, *D'Estaing*, followed by four frigates and a supply ship.

1786 **March** - John Pitt achieves a Colonelcy in the BEIC army.

May - Death of King Peter III of Portugal in a hunting 'accident'. He is shot down in front of Queen Maria, who is driven mad by the experience. Within a year, power passes to her son, who becomes Peter IV.

June - An attempt by the French East India Company to conquer the town of Masoolipatam, in the Northern Circars, is defeated by the British East India Company and Haidarabad. John Pitt fights heroically at the battle, is wounded, and achieves fame and fortune.

July - Death of King Uthumphon of Ayutthaya. He is succeeded by his son, Maha Ekatotaphak, who places much power in the hands of his minister Prachai Tangsopon (possibly his bastard half-brother). Prachai tames rebellious nobles, establishes the Kongthap Bok (Royal Army) and establishes more state control over trade.

August - Lieutenant Leo Bone is promoted to Master and Commander, and is given the almost obsolete 28-gun frigate *Coventry*. He is soon marked out as a man to watch by the Royal Navy as he transforms the ship and its crew into a lethal fighting machine with a mixture of discipline, charisma, and unorthodox tactical ideas.

December - La Pérouse's fleet reaches Easter Island and the Galapagos. Lamarck and Laplace, who accompanied the voyage, observe the wildlife of the Galapagos, eventually resulting in their landmark book for Linnaeanism, *Observations on the Fauna of the Iles Galapagos*.

1787:

Death of King Christian VII of Denmark. He is succeeded by his son, who becomes King Johannes II.

Discovery of the habitable regions of Antipodea by La Pérouse, who names the land New Gascony.

Death of the Daguo Emperor of China. He is succeeded by his third son Yongli, who becomes the Guangzhong Emperor.

1788:

March - George III returns to North America.

June - King Peter IV of Portugal appoints Jaime de Melo el Castro as Viceroy of Brazil. Melo becomes a reforming viceroy and is responsible for effectively creating a unitary Brazilian colonial entity, Brazil formerly having been a loose arrangement of separate colonies.

July - King George III, in his capacity as Emperor George I of North America, opens the first Continental Parliament.

August - Lithuanian Patriotic Fleet, carrying ambassador Moritz Benyovsky, visits the Empire of North America as part of its flying-the-flag world tour.

1789-1791: Fourth Mysore-Haidarabad War between Mysorean and FEIC forces on one side and Haidarabad and BEIC forces on the other. Both sides fight hard and competently in the last of the Mysore-Haidarabad Wars. In the end, Tippoo Sultan of Mysore emerges with a victory, having taken Carnool and Guntoor from Haidarabad.

1789:

March - The British Admiralty grants American shipyards the right to build ships of war for the Royal Navy.

April - Charles Darwin (not that one) discovers light-sensitive silver salts, the beginning of the science of asimcony (photography).

May - Under pressure from the French and Spanish, Pope Gregory XV issues the papal bull *Discidium* which condemns the separation of the UPSA from Spain. This drives many Meridians towards Jansenist Catholicism, as any Catholic clergyman in the UPSA who rejects the bull is effectively considered a Jansenist by default.

June - The Great Famine strikes France. A failure by the King's government to respond coherently, coupled with the fact that the nobles continue to eat well, stokes the resentment of the French people towards the *ancien régime*.

July - In Portugal, a plot by the Duchess of Lafões against Peter IV is uncovered; Peter's response is another round of executions and land confiscations, further cowing the Portuguese nobility *vis-à-vis* royal power.

Maverick Chinese general Yu Wangshan defeats an attempt by the exiled Burmese Konbaung dynasty, led by Avataya Min, to retake Ava from the Chinese-backed Tougou dynasty. The Guangzhong Emperor, fearing Yu's alignment with neo-Manchu political factions, exiles him to the eastern forts of the "New Great Wall".

The city state of Toungoo supported Avataya Min during the war, so its ruler Shin Aung is toppled by the Chinese and replaced by his more pliable (but unpopular) nephew Hkaung Shwe.

August - In North America, the Continental Parliament passes the Anti-Transportation Act, barring the forced transportation and settlement of British convicts in areas claimed by American colonies.

HMS *Raisonnable*, under the command of Captain Robert Brathwaite, visits Naples. Her first lieutenant, Horatio Nelson, meets Sir John Acton. Nelson is initially offended by Acton's career of fighting for the Mediterranean powers rather than his British homeland.

October - General Assembly of New England passes a law abolishing slavery by gradual manumission.

1790:

February - Convention of Córdoba officially establishes the United Provinces of South America.

March - John Pitt becomes Governor-General of the BEIC (based in Calcutta).

Charles Town, capital of the Confederation of Carolina, is officially renamed Charleston.

April - Peter IV of Portugal revives the Cortes, using the commoners as another stick to beat the nobility into line with.

May - China under the Guangzhong Emperor begins tightening trade restrictions with Europeans in Canton, irritating the various East India Companies.

June - The Continental Parliament of North America passes a bill instituting an American Special Commissioner to be sent to Britain and Consuls to be sent to France and Spain, essentially a backdoor project for exploring the possibility of independent American ambassadors.

1791:

April - Death of Grigory Potemkin, former lover of Empress Catherine of Russia.

May - British general election returns a majority for the ruling Portland Ministry, in which real power rests in Edmund Burke. The ruling party is known as the Liberal Whigs, while Charles James Fox's Radical Whigs also increase their vote share.

Imitating his idol the Kangxi Emperor, the Guangzhong Emperor of China has his wayward son and heir Baoyu stripped of his position and relegated to a lowly position in an attempt to teach him humility; however, Baoyu hangs himself, the Empress dies from a miscarriage upon hearing the news, and Guangzhong withdraws into seclusion with only two heirs, Baoli and Baoyi, left.

June - While making observations of sunspots, the Neapolitan astronomer Giuseppe Piazzi accidentally discovers paraerythric (infra-red) light. His discovery will remain controversial for years to come.

July - France is thrown into a panic due to rumours that a comet is due to strike the country.

At the height of a cursory Austro-Wallachian border war, cavalryman Michael Hiedler is slightly wounded, decorated, and given the noble title of Edler von Strones. He settles near the village of Strones, marries, and fathers two children.

August - Persecuted by an angry mob for his radical political sympathies, Joseph Priestley flees Britain for the United Provinces of South America, where he will set up a very profitable soda water business.

La Pérouse visits the Kingdom of Corea, performing a little trade with King Hyojang. This includes artillery.

September - HMS *Coventry* is paid off. Commander Leo

Bone, taking most of his crew with him, is made post and given command of the frigate HMS *Diamond*.

1792:

May - A joint Russo-Lithuanian mission, commanded by Moritz Benyovsky and Pavel Lebedev-Lastoschkin, sets off for Okhotsk from the Baltic the long way around, assisted by Dutch navigators.

June - Captain Horatio Nelson, commanding HMS *Habana*, visits Naples for the second time. Sir John Acton is now effectively the prime minister to King Charles VI and VIII, and Nelson reaches a rapproachment with him. He also meets the King's daughter, Princess Carlotta, for the first time. The nature of their relationship is subject to many rumours, but she begins to argue for Nelson's interests at court.

July - British scientist Henry Cavendish, disappointed in fading interest in electricity research in his home country, goes to the UPSA to join his acquaintance Joseph Priestley.

August - Death in exile of Empress Catherine of Russia, wife of Peter III.

1793:

February - La Pérouse and his crew return to France after their first epic exploration of La Pérouse's Land [Australia]. Hoping to gain popular support from a national project, King Louis XVI agrees to fund a colonial venture there.

May - Captain Leo Bone and the HMS *Diamond* become famous for a hard-fought action against Algerine pirates off Malta.

Chinese heir Baoli is becoming as wayward as his dead brother; on prime minister Zeng Xiang's advice, the Guangzhou Emperor sends him to Mongolia under General Tang Zhoushou to have his ways beaten out of him on the frontier.

June - Richard Wesley, who had fought in India for the BEIC against Burmese-Arakan and Mysore, returns home to Ireland as his father has died. He is now the Earl of Mornington.

July - The rejuvenated British Royal Africa Company, under Simcoe in Dakar, intervenes in the Koya-Susu War on the Koya side - in exchange for the Koyans ceding the Company key land, which becomes the site of the freed-slave black colony of Freedonia.

La Pérouse, with more ships and carrying the natural philosophers Lamarck and Laplace, sets off once more from France for La Pérouse's Land.

August - Death of Abol Fath Khan, Shah-Advocate of Persia, from an illness. He is succeeded by his younger brother, who becomes Shah-Advocate Ali Zand Shah.

Chinese General Tang Zhoushou is called to Xinjiang to take advantage of the collapse of the Dzungars by the Kazakhs attacking from the west. However, he dies of a stomach ulcer, and his army - including the prince Baoli - comes under the commander of Yu Wangshan.

September - French Revolutionary thinker Jacques Tisserant, known as Le Diamant for his incorruptibility, publishes *La Carte de la France*, his pictorial manifesto for a new moderate and egalitarian French state.

October - Former slave Olaudah Equiano is appointed Lieutenant-Governor of the Crown Colony of Freedonia by the Governor of Dakar. This sets a precedent for the freed-slave colony to always be headed by a black leader.

1794:

February - The French Sans-Culottes, led by Le Diamant, march on the Palais de Versailles to present their demands to the King. Le Diamant's charisma and general discontent mean that the palace guards refuse to fire on the crowd. Louis XVI gives in and agrees to recall the Estates-General. The French Revolution has begun.

March - The Imperial Mint, in Fredericksburg, mints the first golden Emperors. These coins, worth one British pound each, are intended to replace the Spanish dollar as the main currency of the Empire of North America.

In Oceania, La Pérouse's fleet arrives in La Pérouse's Land, in the region called New Gascony [OTL New South Wales/ Victoria], and founds the town of Albi, starting the colony.

April - Act of Settlement (in North America) sees New England give up its westward expansion claims in exchange for the right to settle Canada with no restrictions.

In Corea, after the successful trade experiment with La Pérouse's fleet, King Hyojang opens the port of Pusan for foreign trade - mainly that of the Dutch East India Company.

Birth of Frederick Paley, son of the philosopher and Christian apologist William Paley.

June - In the UPSA, Joseph Priestley and Henry Cavendish, together with many local Meridian scientists, found the Solar Society of Córdoba, a mirror to the old Lunar Society of Birmingham of their youth. The Solar Society will be a centre for collaborative scientific research and knowledge exchange in the UPSA.

July - The recalled French Estates-General conclude that their existing mediaeval system is inadequate, and create a National Constitutional Convention. The Third Estate renames itself the *Communes*.

August - Anglo-American agreement results in Michigan being turned into a penal colony, later known as Susan-Mary.

October - the Benyovsky-Lebedev Russo-Lithuanian mission sights Nagasaki from a distance, but does not land.

December - the French National Constitutional Convention publishes its constitution, abolishing the Estates-General and replacing them with a new National Legislative Assembly. The Kingdom of France and Navarre becomes the Kingdom of the French People of the Latin Race, a constitutional monarchy.

*1795-1796: The Flemish War. Name for the early phase of the Franco-Austrian front of the Jacobin Wars, when the battleground was primarily Flanders and northeastern France. Revolutionary France **vs.** Austria, French royalists, Piedmont-Sardinia, and German allies from the various states of the Holy Roman Empire. Result: stalemate.*

1795:

January - French Constitution comes into force. The Comte de Mirabeau becomes chief minister and struggles to implement it in the face of opposition from the nobles and the Church.

February - Benyovsky-Lebedev mission lands in Okhotsk.

The French astronomer Charles Messier discovers the seventh planet, which he initially names "Étoile du Diamant" (the Diamond Star) after Le Diamant. This name is not widely accepted and the planet eventually becomes known as Dionysus.

March - The Dauphin of France, Louis-Auguste, travels to Navarre in order to sort out the implications of the new constitution there. Thus he is not present in Paris when subsequent events occur.

Pennsylvania Confederal Assembly abolishes both slavery and the slave trade.

April - Death of the Comte de Mirabeau. France is plunged into a constitutional crisis. The moderates in the NLA favour Jacques Necker as new chief minister while the Jacobin radicals put forward Jean-Baptiste Robespierre.

May - King Louis XVI decides on Jacques Tisserant (Le Diamant) as a compromise candidate for chief minister. However, a miscommunication means that when Le Diamant is sent for, troops arrive to escort him and this is mistaken for Le Diamant being arrested. In the ensuing riot, Le Diamant is accidentally shot, and the radical Jacobins quickly play upon the popular outrage at this to launch the new violent phase of the French Revolution.

A few days later, with most of the French Army defecting to the Jacobins and Sans-Culottes, the Marshal of France Phillipe Henri, the Marquis de Ségur, takes loyal troops and fortifies the Bastille, intending to bring the King there to keep him safe from the mob, but it is too late for this. The Sans-Culottes arrest the royal family, and radical Jacobin troops led by Georges Hébert manage to take the Bastille from Ségur. Ségur is brutally beheaded by an unknown Revolutionary soldier who becomes the iconic image, L'Épurateur.

On the 15th, the King is executed after a show trial, by the new 'Rational' means of phlogistication in a gas chamber.

Coincidentally, on the same day in India, Nana Fadnavis, chief minister to Peshwa Madhavarao Narayan of the Maratha Confederacy, is assassinated. The loss of his administrative abilities means the young Madhavarao struggles to contain a rebellion led by the pretender Raosaheb.

July - The Parliament of Great Britain debates responses to the

French Revolution as it takes this new radical turn. The ruling Portland-Burke Ministry is strongly opposed to the Revolution, while the Radical Whigs under Fox favour it.

In the Pacific, Lebedev and Benyovsky set off for Edzo again, but are blown off course, are unable to find the Matsumae Han, and their ship is wrecked in the north of the island. They are attacked by the native Aynyu [Ainu], but Benyovsky makes a parley and is able to convince the Aynyu to trade supplies and protection so that the ship may be repaired for some of the European goods it carries. Including guns.

August - Execution by phlogistication of Marie-Antoinette, wife of the Dauphin of France (who has fled to Spain from Navarre). Austria declares war on Revolutionary France in support of the exiled Dauphin.

The French mob targets the British Ambassador and American Consul, Frederick Grenville and Thomas Jefferson respectively. Grenville is badly wounded but escapes; Jefferson is killed. This provokes outrage in London and Fredericksburg.

In India, Raosaheb's forces (backed by the Nizam of Haidarabad) run Madhavarao Narayan out of Pune and he flees to Raigad, where he seeks help from the Portuguese East India Company.

September - First Austrian troops cross into French territory from Flanders and Baden. Furious battles against Revolutionary levies begin almost immediately.

The Parliament of Great Britain votes to declare war on France (by 385 to 164), although this news will not reach the Mediterranean for a while.

On the 17th, Royalist Toulon is besieged by Revolutionary armies led by Adam Phillipe, the former Comte de Custine. The French fleet there is led by the indecisive Comte d'Estaing, who hesitates over whether to fight or cleave to the new regime. He sends some of his forces to Corsica in order to bring back more supplies to relieve the siege, but exposure to Revolutionary ideas means that a large part of this force mutinies. Leo Bone, whose crew is having shore leave in Corsica, learns of the events in Toulon.

October - Leo Bone goes to Toulon and successfully cons

Admiral d'Estaing into believing that the British have concluded a deal with the Dauphin to fight the Revolutionaries and restore the throne, so the Royalist French fleet must go to Corsica and join with the British. Bone had intended to pull off the largest and most bloodless prize-taking ever, but is suprised to learn that his lie has become the truth by the time the fleet reaches Corsica. This is due to the implementation of the 'Burke Strategy', Edmund Burke's plan to support French royalists and not snatch their colonies - arguing that the French Republic is too dangerous to allow to exist, even if it means allying with Britain's old enemy the Bourbons.

The Sans-Culotte levies of the French Revolutionary army are defeated by General Johannes Mozart and his Austro-German army at the Battle of Laon. Mozart's army occupies Maubeuge.

Colonel Ney swiftly rises to prominence as he commands a fighting retreat against a second Austro-German army in the Col de Sauverne, in Lorraine.

Death of Emperor Peter III of Russia. He is legally succeeded by his son, who steps down as Grand Duke Paul I of Lithuania to become Emperor Paul I of Russia. However, this is contested by the brothers Potemkin.

In India, Portuguese EIC forces under João Pareiras da Silva attack Raosaheb's forces with the intention of restoring Madhavarao to the Peshwa-ship.

In Oceania, La Pérouse visits the Mauré for the second time, learning that the muskets the French sold them before have dramatically changed the pattern of warfare there, catapulting the Tainui to dominance, while they are opposed by the Touaritaux-Touaux Alliance. In order to help feed the new colony, the French give the Tainui not merely guns but the secret of making them, in exchange for crops and seed.

November - Continental Parliament votes 46-9 in favour for an American declaration of war on France.

In France, Pierre Boulanger wins his famous victory against Johannes Mozart at the Battle of Lille, using the new Cugnot-wagon technology to his advantage. This results in the French retaking Maubeuge and halting the Austrian advance into France.

The French inventor Louis Chappe, helped by the fact that his brother is a member of the NLA, receives French government funding to develop a semaphore communications network.

In Russia, the Potemkinites assemble their army and march on Moscow.

First rumours of the United Society of Equals, a republican movement in Ireland that is theoretically secular and in practice dominated by Protestants, especially Presbyterians.

December - On advice by General Sir Fairfax Washington, Viscount Amherst (commander-in-chief of the British Army) recommends that new regiments be raised in America. The Parliament of Great Britain passes the American Regiments Act (1795), which grants Fredericksburg plenipotentiary powers to raise troops.

After a series of indecisive battles along the Flemish border, the Austrian and Revolutionary French armies dig in for the winter.

Paul crowned Emperor of All the Russias in St Petersburg. However, news reaches him that the Potemkinites under General Saltykov have taken Moscow. Start of the Russian Civil War.

1796-1800: The Russian Civil War, which eventually broadens into the Great Baltic War. Romanovian Russians, Lithuania, and Denmark vs. Potemkinite Russians and Sweden. Result: Romanovian victory in Russia; Sweden defeated and forced into personal union with Denmark. The Ottoman Empire and Persia take advantage of the chaos to re-extend their influence into areas contested by Russia, primarily the Caucasus and also Bessarabia and the Khanate of the Crimea.

1796:

January - the people of Liège rise up and overthrow their Prince-Bishop, installing a copycat republic based on disseminated French propaganda.

February - General Mozart leaves winter quarters to besiege Liège, a miserable affair on both sides.

March - Jean de Lisieux, a French Revolutionary leader, publishes *La Vapeur est Républicaine*, 'Steam is Republican', a pamphlet which enshrines steam power as ideologically correct.

Lisieux and Boulanger form a political alliance with Cugnot and other French engineers and radical warriors, such as Blanchard and Surcouf. This research cabal becomes known as *La Boulangerie*, 'the Bakery'.

Paris sees the start of Robespierre's Reign of Terror, after Royalists holed up in a church/powder store blow up Georges Hébert and his Guard Nationale. The Republican reprisal is swift, with men sent to the *chirurgien* or phlogisticateur for the most minor imagined crime against the People. Lisieux, using Cugnot's new *Tortue* 'Tortoise' armoured steam-wagon, crushes part of the revolt and becomes a hero of the Jacobin mob. Lisieux replaces Hébert as third Consul, resulting in Danton being overlooked - he soon goes to the phlogisticateur himself, along with other personal enemies of Robespierre.

Meanwhile, Britain deploys an expeditionary force to Flanders under the command of the Prince of Wales, Frederick George.

In India, the Portuguese General Pareiras defeats Raosaheb's forces in the epic Siege of Gawhilgoor. This breakthrough restores Madhavarao to the Peshwa-ship (in truth, now only ruling the land of Konkan) but Portuguese 'guidance', expressed through a resident in Pune, now truly controls that region.

April - General Boulanger's deputy Thibault Leroux leads an army to relieve the siege of Liège. Mozart's starving army forced back into Flanders, and ravages the Flemish countryside with its marauding. Charles Theodore of Flanders and his minister Emmanuel Grosch take note, and fear for the resentment provoked by the Imperial presence. They enter secret negotiations with Boulanger and with Statdholder William V of the Netherlands.

Robespierre reduces the suffrage of the French Republic to Sans-Culottes only, growing ever more paranoid about there being enemies everywhere. The powers of the National Legislative Assembly are undermined daily.

In North America, the American Preventive Cutter Service is created. This coastguard's main role is to prevent smuggling and piracy, in particular the illegal private transportation of convicts to America. The Continental Parliament also authorises the creation of the Commission for Continental Regiments, the first

American 'ministry', which operates out of Cornubia Palace in Fredericksburg.

On the 25th (Gregorian calendar) or 14th (Russian calendar), in Russia, the Potemkinites successfully take the city of Smolensk from the Romanovians in an important victory. Emperor Paul retreats into Lithuania.

May - Full gearing-up of the spring campaign in Flanders. Mozart's Austrians make a second, more half-hearted siege of Liège, but the main force attempts to push deeper into France. Mozart fights Boulanger again at Cambrai and wins a pyrrhic victory with considerable Austro-German losses.

Retreating army of Emperor Paul of Russia is attacked by a Potemkinite force under Suvorov near Vitebsk. Perhaps one-third of Paul's army is destroyed. It is assumed by many that a Potemkin victory in the Russian civil war is now assured.

In America, the Treaty of Sandusky ends the Ohio War. This scattered conflict had been going on since the end of the Third War of Supremacy, and results in the defeat of the Lenape, Huron and Ottawa Indians with the victory of Pennsylvania, New York and the Iroquois. The Lenape and Ottawa are virtually destroyed, but the Huron confederacy fragments into separate tribes, some of which go west to join the Lakota, some go south and are allowed to settle in French Louisiana, and one - the Tahontaenrat - joins the Iroquois, forming the Seven Nations.

Alain Carpentier, wastrel son of Louis XVI's physician Henri Carpentier (who had risen from common birth to riches) escapes Robespierre's reign of terror and arrives in Nantes, much to the displeasure of many aristocrats like the Duke of Berry.

June - Mozart orders a retreat and regroup of the Austro-German army, resupplying from Flanders. However, Charles Theodore makes a shock announcement that Flanders is seceding from the Empire, and is supported by William V's Dutch Republic. Cut off and low on supplies, there is little prospect of the Austrians being able to fight their way through (after failing to force a Flemish border fort or retake Liège), so Mozart orders the army to wheel southwards in order to retreat to Trier.

Meanwhile, in North America, HMS *Marlborough* under

Captain Paul Wilkinson and the naturalist Erasmus Darwin II perform the first survey of Michigan, which had been named as a potential penal colony.

In Sweden, the Hat party takes control of the Riksdag for the first time since the 1760s. The Hats fear a future war of the Swedish succession - King Charles XII has no children - and therefore vote to intervene in Russia on the Potemkinite side, to secure Potemkinite Russia as an ally in any future conflict.

July - The Flemings eject the British expeditionary force from Flanders due to their declaration of neutrality. This embarrassment, coupled with Edmund Burke's death, leads to the fall of the Portland Ministry. It is replaced by a new war government under the ageing Marquess of Rockingham, while the Radicals and Radical-leaning Whigs under Charles James Fox become the main voice of opposition.

Meanwhile, the Flemings and Dutch fight to eject the Bavarian army 'of occupation' from Flanders, where it had been waiting to reinforce the Austrians.

August - Bavarian army retreats into the Empire. The Netherlands and Flanders formally sign their alliance into being with the Maastricht Pact. Mozart's army reaches Trier, by now a shadow of its former self after having been harried by the French enroute.

The disgraced Mozart is recalled to Vienna and replaced with Dagobert Sigmund von Wurmser.

To the south, the Genoese people overthrow their old oligarchic Republic and declare a Ligurian Republic, which is swiftly occupied by French forces under the mercurial Lazare Hoche.

In Russia, an attack by General Sergei Saltykov on St Petersburg is defeated by Mikhail Kamenski, who destroys the Potemkinite siege train and forces a retreat. This breaks a chain of Potemkinite victories and shows the Romanovians are still in the game.

September - Austrian forces finally break through the Col de Sauverne with heavy losses and spill into Lorraine. Ney is nonetheless recognised for his valiant actions and is promoted to General.

The Ottoman Empire begins its quiet intervention in the

Russian Civil War, exerting influence over the formerly Russian-influenced lands of Bessarabia, the Crimean Khanate and Georgia. The Georgians reject the Ottoman demands and King George XII sends Prince Piotr Bagration to Russia, insisting that Russia honours its treaty agreements to defend Georgia.

October - The Netherlands is hit by a brief wave of Revolution, inspired by the French. Flemish troops, fresh from the campaign against the Bavarians, assist Stadtholder William V's own Dutch army in putting down attempted revolts in the Hague and Amsterdam. The Dutch Republic remains.

November - The French under Hoche win some minor victories in Savoy against Piedmont-Sardinia.

Secret treaty of alliance between the Kingdom of Sweden and Potemkinite Russia. The Swedes begin building up their forces in Finland.

1797:

January - The Chinese heir Baoli returns to Beijing as a hero worshipper of Yu Wangshan and a supporter of the neo-Manchu movement. The Guangzhong Emperor dithers over whether to instead name his second son Baoyi, less dynamic but also less dangerous in his views, as heir.

Pablo Sanchez is born in Cervera, Spain.

February – The Georgian Prince Bagration is attacked by bandits in the Caucasus, but rescued by Heinrich Kautzman, the 'Bald Impostor'. The Georgians and Cossacks form an agreement, with King George XII of Georgia agreeing to become an Ottoman vassal for the present, committing his army along with the Cossacks to help the Romanovians win the Civil War, so that a Romanov Russia can come in later and reverse the situation.

March - Death of Frederick William II of Prussia, after a long illness. His son succeeds him as Frederick William III. With initial risings in Warsaw and Lodz, Poland immediately rebels, taking advantage of the instability of the change of regime. The rebel armies are commanded by the experienced mercenary Kazimierz Pułaski. The Polish rebellion is discreetly assisted by Lithuanian arms, although the Lithuanians mostly remain loyal to Grand Duke Peter and have little enthusiasm for reforming the old Commonwealth.

Start of the Great Aynyu (Ainu) Rebellion in Edzo (Hokkaido) against the Japanese Matsumae Han, aided and abbetted by Benyovsky's Russians trading guns to the Aynyu.

April - the French launch their Poséidon Offensive, a three-pronged strike consisting of the left under Ney hitting the Ausrians in Lorraine, the centre under Boulanger and Leroux invading Switzerland, and the right under Hoche attacking Piedmont.

In Toulon harbour, Surcouf demonstrates the first steamship, a paddlewheel tug known as the *Vápeur-Remorqueur*.

The Swedish-Potemkinite alliance is publicly revealed in Russia. Swedish armies based in Finland invade Russia, seeking to encircle St Petersburg. The King of Sweden officially recognises Alexander Potemkin as Emperor of All Russias.

The Continental Parliament creates the office of a Special Commissioner to Britain, essentially an ambassador in all but name, who will represent America's interests in London. The first of these is Albert Gallatin.

May - French under Leroux occupy Geneva and Basel, driving deeper into Switzerland.

In response to the Swedish entry into the Russian Civil War, Denmark declares war on Sweden and the Potemkinites, and officially recognises Paul Romanov as Emperor of All Russias. The Russian Civil War has become the Great Baltic War.

The Prussians begin withdrawing their troops from Austria's pan-German war effort in order to put down the Polish revolt, weakening the Germans on both a physical and moral level.

The Royal Danish Navy sorties and wins its first victory of the war, defeating an inferior Swedish naval force at the Battle of Anholt. The Kattegat falls under Danish control, although the Swedes still hold Malmö with a second fleet.

Death of Elector Frederick Christian II of Saxony. Childless, he is succeeded by his brother, who becomes John George V.

June - Wurmser's army, consisting of combined Austrian, Saxon and Hessian troops, narrowly defeats Ney at the Battle of Saint-Dié.

Hoche begins his celebrated campaign against the Austrians and Sardinians in Piedmont. He divides his forces in order to meet two Austrian armies, the northern one at Omegna under József Alvinczi and the southern under Paul Davidovich.

The Royal Swedish Navy under Admiral Carl August Ehrensvärd blockades Klaipeda and attempts to burn the Lithuanian fleet in harbour. However, the Lithuanian commander, Admiral Vatsunyas Radziwiłł, sacrifices his galleys in order to punch a hole in the Swedish line and allow his sail fleet to escape.

The Polish rebels convene a Sejm and elect John George V of Saxony as King of Poland. John George accepts and declares war on Prussia, withdrawing Saxon troops from the pan-German Austrian war effort in order to accomplish this. Ironically, as the Prussian and Saxon troops do not know for which reason they have been recalled, they often bivouac with each other on the way back across Germany. This begins a domino effect of German states recalling their troops, fearful of their neighbours possessing functional armies, fatally weakening Germany in the face of French aggression.

July - Wurmser occupies Nancy, putting the Austrians in a position to threaten Paris. But there they halt, waiting for reinforcements that will not come.

Hoche's offensive move makes Alvinczi hesitate long enough to smash Davidovich with the full force of his recombined army.

Russo-Lithuanian Romanovian armies under General Barclay de Tolly defeat Swedish invaders at the Battle of Seinai.

August - Leroux defeats most of the Swiss militias and occupies Bern.

Romanovian forces win a victory over the Swedes at the Battle of Alytus.

Hoche's army meets Alvinczi's now-outnumbered forces at Milan, defeats the Austrians and forces them to retreat through the chaos of Switzerland. The Piedmontese royal family, stripped of Austrian support, flees Piedmont for Sardinia.

October - With the withdrawal of the Hapsburgs from much of northern Italy, Hoche attacks and occupies Spanish Parma. In response to news of French atrocities, Spain steps up the war against France.

Concerned about the French victory on the other two fronts, Emperor Ferdinand IV orders Wurmser to retreat from Nancy, conceding the Austrian victory there in order to reassemble his armies to contest French control of Switzerland and Piedmont in the 1797 campaigning season.

The Swedes are defeated by the Romanovians at Trakai. This expels them from the Vojvodship of Trakai, but leaves them in control of the Eldership of Samogita, along with Courland and Swedish Prussia.

November - Jean Marat forced to resign his consulship and is installed as sole consul of the new Swiss Republic, secured by Leroux. Marat is replaced as consul of France by Boulanger, an unconstitutional move which is not contested thanks to Robespierre's Terror.

December - France begins quietly withdrawing troops from Switzerland and transferring them primarily to the German front.

1798:

January - In a calculated act of spite, the French burn down the Habichtsburg, the ancestral Hapsburg castle in Switzerland.

March - Thanks to Robespierre's paranoia about a British invasion of the unprotected French coast, French raw recruits are marched up and down western France in training to create a visible presence. This plan, however, somewhat backfires as the boorish conscripts' activities inflame the local Vendean and Breton disenchantment with the Revolution...

The Austrians begin their spring offensives, primarily on the Swiss and Italian fronts. They are initially highly successful. In Italy, Archduke Ferdinand proves his generalship when, together with Wurmser, he surrounds Hoche and forces him to retreat.

But, contrary to Austrian expectations, the French's own "Rubicon" offensive focuses on the Lorraine front. Two armies under Leroux and Ney sweep around from north and south, for the first time utilising the 'War of Lightning' doctrine that reduces the need for a supply train by making the troops live off the land. This means they often outrun the news of their coming.

Kiev falls to the new Cossack/Georgian Romanovian army.

The Battle of the Erbe Strait between the Russian and Lithuanian fleets on one side and the Swedes on the other. The Russo-Lithuanians win a pyrrhic tactical victory that is strategically a far greater gain - both navies are devastated as fighting forces, but this leaves the Swedes unable to oppose the Danes.

April - Ney's army takes Karlsruhe, capital of Baden, and the Badenese Margrave's family are publicly executed on Robespierre's orders. The French win several key battles against Austrian and local Swabian forces, the flatter terrain now lending deadly effect to their Cugnot weapons.

Supported by amphibious descents by the Spanish Navy, General Cuesta's Spanish army in Gascony besieges Bordeaux.

Charles Messier is executed by phlogistication, one of many French scientists to meet this fate under Robespierre's terror.

May - Ney's army occupies Stuttgart, capital of Württemberg, but the Duke and his family have already fled.

Now ruling the waves of the Baltic, the Danes perform a descent on Swedish Pomerania and swiftly seize the province.

Voronezh surrenders to Kautzman's army.

L'Épurateur, a French second-rate ship of the line, arrives in Madras and Republican envoy René Leclerc orders Governor-General Rochambeau to cleave to Paris' line. Rochambeau rejects him, and a fuming Leclerc goes to Mysore in order to gain the help of Tippoo Sultan, an admirer of revolutionary ideals.

June - With the French advance having reached Franconia, Boulanger orders Ney's army to disperse in order to occupy the territory gained, while Leroux's continues on towards Regensburg.

Having defeated the Danish army in Norway, the Swedes besiege Christiania.

Death by drowning of Myeongjo, first son of King Hyojang of Corea and champion of conservatives. Foul play is probable.

July - A French army under Custine breaks the Siege of Bordeaux; Cuesta's Spaniards retreat southwards.

Fall of Ulm to the French. Emperor Ferdinand IV desperately reinstates General Mozart.

Fall of Kazan to Kautzman's army.

United Society of Equals (USE) rises to prominence in Ireland; they are contacted and supplied with weapons and pamphlets by Lisieux. These are transported using co-opted Breton fishermen to beat the British blockade; however, some of the pamphlets end up staying in Brittany, and inflame Breton opinion against the Republic (which there was largely only a rumour).

August - Battle of Burgau between Davidovich's Austrians and Leroux's French. The result is a punishing French victory, Davidovich's infantry almost totally destroyed by the rapidly shifting enfilading and plunging fire afforded by the French Cugnot artillery. Ferdinand IV finally acquiesces to Mozart's demand that everything be pulled back for a last-ditch defence of Vienna, abandoning Regensburg. The Emperor leaves for the latter city.

Surrounded by Austrians thanks to Archduke Ferdinand's gambit, Hoche retreats into the Terrafirma of Venice.

The Bohemian inventor Wenzel Linck miniaturises and improves the Girandoni's 'wind rifle', making a short-range repeater that can be more easily pumped up by one person for more rapid fire. The 'Linck gun' is particularly popular with Austria's elite skirmishers, the Grenzers.

Full-scale seaborne Danish invasion of Scania. The Swedish government hastily begins recalling armies in order to try and prevent the Danes from breaking out further.

A small Spanish force under Major Joaquín Blake y Joyes defeats part of Custine's French army at the Battle of Bayonne.

Guarded only by a token Potemkinite force, Vitebsk is retaken by the Romanovians.

September - Hoche's troops fall upon Venice the city and pillage it. End of the Venetian Republic, its territories annexed to Hoche's purported Italian Republic. The Venetian territories in Dalmatia immediately become a sore point between Vienna and Constantinople. In response to the 'Rape of Venice', the Venetian fleet under Admiral Grimani flees to the port of Bari in Naples, and after negotiating with King Charles VI and VIII, takes up service with the Neapolitan navy.

Kautzman's army moves into the Moscow region. Rumour

exaggerates this into the idea that he has actually sacked the city.

October - On the 9th, the Vendée and Brittany explode into royalist revolt - the Chouannerie - against the French Republic. Britain prepares to intervene on their side.

General Alvinczi attempts to fight a delaying action against Leroux west of Regensburg, but is defeated - though he saves most of his army, which retreats southward. Emperor Ferdinand IV gives a passionate but insane speech in the Reichstag about the coming destruction, in which he declares the end of the Empire, before falling over dead from a heart attack. As he does so, the French advance on Regensburg and take the city...

Archduke Ferdinand prepares to besiege Hoche in Venice, but is recalled thanks to the success of the French Rubicon offensive in Germany. Hoche pursues the Austrians but is held back at the well-defended Brenner Pass. He is now nonetheless the undisputed master of northern Italy.

The second Battle of Smolensk between the Romanovians and Potemkinites. After three hard, gruelling days of combat, the Potemkinites are on the brink of victory, when news of Kautzman's supposed sacking of Moscow spreads and Potemkin's mostly Muscovite left wing collapses. Though the bulk of the Potemkinite army withdraws in good order, Alexander Potemkin is captured by the Romanovians.

Great Ulster Scare. Ireland explodes into rebellion as the USE seize key points all over Ulster and Leinster. The British garrison in Belfast, a strongly USE-supporting town, goes down fighting.

November - After being rebuffed by Surcouf, Robespierre nominates the fey Admiral Villeneuve to lead an outnumbered Republican naval force against the Anglo-Royal French fleets massing in British ports.

The USE take Dublin, burning the assembled Irish parliament to death inside their own building. The British garrison in Dublin, which had been cut back considerably due to the troops assembling for an invasion of France, is defeated and massacred by the vengeful USE. First reports of the Great Ulster Scare reach London, but it is already too far-gone to contain easily.

Death of the cautious Sultan Abdulhamid II of the Ottoman

Empire. He is succeeded by his more maverick nephew, who becomes Sultan Murad V. He appoints Mehmed Ali Pasha as Grand Vizier and the two of them begin eyeing the debated former Venetian territories in Dalmatia...

1799:

January - Richard Wesley, Earl of Mornington, survived the Dublin attack because he was at home in Galway. He now assembles a Royalist army against the USE and is widely praised for managing to call Irish Catholics to his banner - indeed his army is majority Catholic.

Birth of future Great American War General Alf Stotts in Congaryton, South Province, Carolina.

February - Britain launches the Seigneur Offensive. Four fleets, one Royal French, all protecting troopships, leave the southern ports for Brittany and the Vendée. Villeneuve manages to intercept one of the British fleets under Admiral Duncan at the Battle of Wight, before it forms up with the others, and sinks or disables most of its troopships.

Villeneuve then throws everything that remains at the Royal French fleet within the formed-up British forces, with the intention of killing Louis XVII, but though he does manage to board the latter's flagship and kill Admiral d'Estaing, his attack is successfully deflected by Leo Bone, who draws one of Villeneuve's ships away. Bone's ship defeats the enemy days later off the coast of France, but is holed and has to be beached.

The victorious British and Royal French, having defeated Villeneuve, attack Quiberon. Louis XVII lands and declares himself King.

Having reached the end of their supply lines, Leroux's army's offensive towards Vienna slows, but inexorably continues.

March - Leroux's army besieges Vienna. The French succeed in destroying several Austrian forts and other defences, but lose some of their artillery to a Hungarian attack at night.

Last Potemkinite armies disintegrate.

Wesley holds back the USE armies at Rosscommon and Kilkenny. This encourages the British government not to slow their planned Seigneur Offensive against France, but instead to send Wesley only three regular regiments to support him. These arrive in Limerick towards the end of the month.

April - The Battle of Vienna. As the French begin breaking down the capital's walls, General Mozart leads an army out in a desperate gamble to attack them on the field of battle. The French engage him and are on the brink of victor, but the Austrians are saved by the 'Miracle on the Danube', when Archduke Ferdinand returns from Italy in the nick of time with Croat cavalry, who break up the undisciplined French conscript infantry. Leroux is killed and Mozart mortally wounded.

The French army retreats under Cougnon, but the latter is killed by the maniacal Lascelles, who takes most of the army and retreats into Bavaria, setting up a tyrannical 'Bavarian Germanic Republic'. The rest, the 'Cougnonistes', under St-Julien, go north into Bohemia and effectively set up their own fiefdom around Budweis.

Panic in Matsumae-town in Edzo thanks to the Aynyu successes. The Daimyo decides to beg help from Edo in order to put down the rebellion, but is assassinated by one of his lieutenants who fears a purge by the Shogun. Matsumae dissolves into civil war.

Grand Duke Carlo of Tuscany, in support of his fellow Hapsburgs, attacks Lazare Hoche in the rear while the latter is engaged along the Alps, and manages to liberate Lucca, Modena and Mantua.

May - Thanks to Lisieux's and Boulanger's plotting, two deliberately inexperienced French armies under Paul Vignon and Jacques Pallière are sent to drive back the British in the Vendée.

Ottoman Empire declares war on Austria, invading Austrian-held Bosnia and sending troops under Dalmat Melek Pasha to seize the former Venetian territories in Dalmatia.

Battle of Carlow between Wesley's Royalists and the USE. Wesley now has artillery to match the USE's, and wins a limited victory. The USE, under the French General O'Neill, retreats. This is the end of the USE's victory streak and raises enthusiasm for Wesley elsewhere.

With the Swedish armies besieging St Petersburg being stripped of forces for the home front, Romanovian generals Kamenski and

Kurakin begin to drive back the reduced enemy forces.

Emperor Paul re-enters Moscow, held by Kautzman. Paul agrees to some of Kautzman's demands for serf emancipation in order to secure his support. He exiles Ivan Potemkin and Sergei Saltykov to Yakutsk, and installs Alexander Potemkin as Duke of a restored independent Courland. End of the Russian Civil War.

June - The two French armies in the Vendée are decisively defeated by the British, although part of Pallière's army escapes to the south. It is later defeated by a local militia organised by the shipwrecked Leo Bone and his crew, pressed into service using his ship's guns as artillery. This launches Bone as a hero and celebrity in the Vendean imagination.

Richard Wesley's army takes Kildare.

On North America's Pacific coast, the fur-trading operation of the British adventurer John Goodman on the island of Noochaland [Vancouver Island] is stopped by a Spanish expedition out of New Spain, who place him under arrest. Goodman is eventually released, but the incident highlights the importance of claiming the Pacific seaboard to the Americans and Russians. Goodman eventually goes to Gavaji [Hawaii].

An attack by the Austrians on Lascelles' troops, encamped on the Enns near Admont, is bloodily repulsed, demonstrating that Lascelles can fight.

July - The Apricot Revolution in France. Robespierre has no-one else left to blame for the failure in the Vendée. Lisieux smoothly maneouvres him out of power - he either commits suicide or is murdered - and Lisieux becomes sole Administrator of France. Having purged everything he can of Robespierre loyalists, Lisieux orders Boulanger to now send the full force of the Republican army against the British.

An Irish Royalist army under George Wesley (Richard's younger brother) takes Wicklow. A USE army to the south panics, congregates on Wexford and then disintegrates or flees to France.

The Swedes have held the Scanian front against the Danes, but the Russo-Lithuanians have begun to roll up their armies in the Baltic lands.

General election in America returns a majority for the Constitutionalist Party. The Lord Deputy, the Duke of Grafton, asks Constitutionalist leader James Monroe to form a government as Lord President.

August - In Japan, Benyovsky's Russo-Lithuanian ships attack Matsumae-town, defeat the defenders and install their own puppet Daimyo.

Leo Bone's irregulars near Saint-Hilaire fight regular Republican troops for the first time, and win.

September - British forces take Caen in Normandy. Alain Carpentier, largely due to being in the right place at the right time, manages to become a hero by leading a successful cavalry charge against the Republican French, achieving grudging acceptance for himself and his drunkard son Joseph at the Royal French court. He is made Comte de Toulouse (a largely meaningless title for the moment) in recognition of this.

Last Swedish army in Livonia surrenders, leaving the Russians and Lithuanians in control of the Swedes' former Baltic possessions. The Swedish army in Finland repulses an attempted attack by Kurakin.

After getting into numerous fights at King's College over political and philosophical disagreements, Philip Hamilton is sent by his father to work for the Royal Africa Company.

Around this time, due to his strong Confucian beliefs, the Guangzhong Emperor of China starts leaning on the 'Hongmen' of Canton in an effort to discourage the foreign trade which he perceives as a weakness.

October - Battle of Caen. Boulanger, assisted by new Cugnot weapons, decisively defeats the British and Royal French. The Prince of Wales is killed in the battle, meaning Prince Henry William is now the heir apparent. The British are swept out of Normandy.

The Austrians draw up a new army under General Giuseppe Bolognesi to drive Lascelles' rogue French troops farther away from Vienna. Lascelles, outnumbered, retreats through the Waldviertel. His troops perform a particularly vicious *maraude* as a scorched-earth policy against Bolognesi's army, and in the process murder many civilians, including the family of Michael Hiedler. He was hunting at the time and escapes, but is driven catatonic by the experience.

Dublin besieged and retaken by Wesley's forces. New York rifleman James Roosevelt shoots down General O'Neill; he later decides to stay and settle in Ireland.

Swedish King Charles XIII assassinated by a madman. His death, leaving no heirs, plunges Sweden into a constitutional crisis that only exacerbates the war defeats.

Death of Dharma Raja, King of Travancore. He is succeeded by his son Balarama Varma, but the Tippoo of Mysore declares he is too young to rule and uses this as a casus belli to invade. This belligerent move is part of a plan by Leclerc to force Rochambeau to back down or lose the FEIC's trade interests in Kerala.

November - On hearing of his favourite son's death, King George III of Great Britain descends into madness and is dead by December. At the same time, the ageing Prime Minister Rockingham works himself to death. The country is plunged into a constitutional crisis.

Boulanger's advance is stopped at Mayenne by the British. The front stalemates as the armies settle into winter quarters.

Further south, Leo Bone defeats a Republican French army at Angers, later earning him the title Viscount d'Angers from Louis XVII.

The Danish Diet negotiates directly with the Swedish Riksdag to reach a peace settlement.

The Austrian army of Bolognesi defeats Lascelles on the Ischl, but Lascelles saves the majority of his army and retreats into Bavaria.

December - Henry William crowned King Henry IX of Great Britain.

Richard Wesley's armies finally take Belfast, last city held by the USE. The aftermath of the siege is bloody and rapine, the frustrated armies unleashed on the populace.

Peace between Denmark and Sweden. The treaty restores a personal union between the kingdoms, with Johannes II becoming John IV of Sweden. However, aside from losing the most Danish-loyal part of Scania and her Baltic possessions, Sweden's territorial integrity is respected. This ends the Great Baltic War, and leaves Denmark as the dominant naval power in the Baltic.

TO BE CONTINUED...

Sea Lion Press

Sea Lion Press is the world's first online publishing house dedicated to alternate history. To find out more, and to see our full catalogue, visit **sealionpress.co.uk**. Sign up for our mailing list at **sealionpress.co.uk/contact** to be informed of all future releases.

Made in the USA
Columbia, SC
22 July 2020

14494279R00338